FROM THE PAGES OF
SIX PLAYS BY HENRIK IBSEN

Home life ceases to be free and beautiful as soon as it is founded on borrowing and debt.   (from _A Doll's House_, page 217)

Our house has been nothing but a play-room. Here I have been your doll-wife, just as at home I used to be papa's doll-child. And the children, in their turn, have been my dolls. I thought it fun when you played with me, just as the children did when I played with them. That has been our marriage, Torvald.   (from _A Doll's House_, page 313)

I believe that before all else I am a human being, just as much as you are—or at least that I should try to become one.
              (from _A Doll's House_, page 315)

It is the very mark of the spirit of rebellion to crave for happiness in this life. What right have we human beings to happiness?
              (from _Ghosts_, page 356)

I almost think we are all of us ghosts, Pastor Manders. It is not only what we have inherited from our father and mother that "walks" in us. It is all sorts of dead ideas, and lifeless old beliefs, and so forth. They have no vitality, but they cling to us all the same, and we cannot shake them off. Whenever I take up a newspaper, I seem to see ghosts gliding between the lines. There must be ghosts all the country over, as thick as the sands of the sea. And then we are, one and all, so pitifully afraid of the light.   (from _Ghosts_, page 372)

I always think there's no harm in being a bit civil to folks that have seen better days.   (from _The Wild Duck_, page 429)

Always do that, wild ducks do. They shoot to the bottom as deep as they can get, sir—and bite themselves fast in the tangle and seaweed—and all the devil's own mess that grows down there. And they never come up again. (from *The Wild Duck*, page 476)

I think he regards me simply as a useful property. And then it doesn't cost much to keep me. I am not expensive.

(from *Hedda Gabler*, page 604)

Tell me now, Hedda—was there not love at the bottom of our friend-ship? On your side, did you not feel as though you might purge my stains away—if I made you my confessor? Was it not so?

(from *Hedda Gabler*, page 643)

One is not always mistress of one's thoughts.

(from *Hedda Gabler*, page 681)

I will never retire! I will never give way to anybody! Never of my own free will. Never in this world will I do *that*!

(from *The Master Builder*, page 716)

I must tell you—I have begun to be so afraid—so terribly afraid of the younger generation. (from *The Master Builder*, page 751)

It is the *small* losses in life that cut one to the heart—the loss of all that other people look upon as almost nothing.

(from *The Master Builder*, pages 798–799)

Six Plays by
HENRIK IBSEN

With an Introduction and Notes
by MARTIN PUCHNER

Consulting Editorial Director
GEORGE STADE

BARNES & NOBLE CLASSICS
NEW YORK

ℬ
BARNES & NOBLE CLASSICS
NEW YORK

The present texts are from the Charles Scribner's Sons edition of *The Works of Henrik Ibsen*, edited by William Archer and published in 1911.

Introduction, Notes, and For Further Reading Copyright © 2003 by Martin Puchner.

Note on Henrik Ibsen, The World of Henrik Ibsen, Inspired by Henrik Ibsen, and Comments & Questions Copyright © 2003 by Fine Creative Media, Inc.

Six Plays by Henrik Ibsen
ISBN 1-59308-061-1
LC Control Number 2003108032

Produced by:
Fine Creative Media, Inc.
322 Eighth Avenue
New York, NY 10001

President & Publisher: Michael J. Fine
Consulting Editorial Director: George Stade
Editor: Jeffrey Broesche
Editorial Research: Jason Baker
Vice-President Production: Stan Last
Senior Production Manager: Mark A. Jordan
Production Editor: Kerriebeth Mello

Printed in the United States of America
QM
1 3 5 7 9 10 8 6 4 2
FIRST PRINTING

HENRIK IBSEN

HENRIK JOHAN IBSEN WAS born on March 20, 1828, in a small Norwegian town. After his father, a merchant, lost his business, the family lived in poverty. In 1844 Henrik took his first job as an apothecary's apprentice. In 1850, hoping for a career in medicine, he moved to Christiania (present-day Oslo) to attend a preparatory school; to support himself, he wrote plays and edited a weekly journal of satire. That same year he published his first play, *Catiline*, under a pen name.

After failing the university entrance exams, Ibsen took a job as a stage director and playwright at the Norwegian Theater in Bergen, where he wrote plays based on history and folklore. In 1857 he joined the Norwegian Theater in Christiania as artistic director; by the time the theater went bankrupt in 1862, he had come into his own as a writer. With financial help from government and private sources, he left Norway to spend the next twenty-seven years living abroad, mainly in Italy and Germany. Ibsen's early period culminated in the poetic dramas *Brand* (1866) and *Peer Gynt* (1867).

By 1870 Ibsen was in his second creative period, writing plays that implicitly criticized the social realities of the day. Among his greatest works of this period are *A Doll's House* (1879), *Ghosts* (1881), *The Wild Duck* (1884), and *Hedda Gabler* (1890). Ibsen was especially good at portraying female characters. Both Nora Helmer of *A Doll's House* and the title character of *Hedda Gabler* have intrigued and outraged theatergoers and readers since the plays first appeared. *Ghosts*, with its attack on social conventions and obligations, and *The Wild Duck*, which explores the values and risks inherent in idealism, were likewise praised and denounced. Despite the criticism leveled at Ibsen's work, throughout the last decades of the century it gained widespread recognition and acclaim. Many of the plays Ibsen wrote in the last years of his life—including *The Master Builder* (1892), *Little Eyolf* (1894), and *When We Dead*

Awaken (1899)—were highly symbolic. *John Gabriel Borkman* (1896) continued the social realism of his earlier writing.

Ibsen was the founder of modern prose drama. In discarding old-fashioned plots and emphasizing instead the psychological and moral depths of his characters and their profound conflicts with society and its conventions, he revolutionized dramatic writing. One of our greatest playwrights, Henrik Ibsen died in Christiania on May 23, 1906.

CONTENTS

The World of HENRIK IBSEN

1828   Henrik Johan Ibsen is born on March 20 in Skien, a small town in southern Norway.

1835   Henrik's father is forced to abandon his business.

1844   Henrik becomes an apothecary's apprentice in Grimstad, a coastal hamlet 70 miles south of Skien. He studies at night for the university entrance exams and begins writing his first play, *Catiline*.

1849   Ibsen completes *Catiline*.

1850   He moves to Christiania (present-day Oslo) to attend the Heltberg School, which prepares students for university study. He edits *Andhrimner*, a satirical weekly journal, to cover his expenses, and befriends Norwegian writer Bjørnsterne Bjørnson. Ibsen publishes *Catiline* under the pseudonym Brynjolf Bjarme. His one-act play *The Warrior's Barrow* premieres at the Christiania Theater.

1851   After failing the university entrance exams, Ibsen is hired as stage director and playwright at the Norwegian Theater in Bergen; he is to create a new play each year. In his first creative period, he writes poetic dramas with themes relating to history and folklore, but his early plays are not well received. He studies the works of the French writer Augustine-Eugène Scribe, whose formula for the "well-made play" he would later reject. He reads Hermann Hettner's *Das moderne Drama*, a treatise for a new theater.

1853   *St. John's Night* premieres in Bergen.

1854   A revised rendition of *The Warrior's Barrow* premieres in Bergen.

1855   *Lady Inger of Østraat*, about the liberation of medieval Norway, premieres in Bergen.

1856   *The Feast at Solhaug* premieres in Bergen. Ibsen becomes engaged to Suzannah Thoresen.

1857   Ibsen is hired as artistic director of the Norwegian Theater in Christiania. The play *Olaf Liljekrans* opens.

1858   *The Vikings at Helgeland*, a historical drama, opens. Ibsen marries Suzannah Thoresen.

1859   Ibsen writes the poems "On the Heights" and "In the Gallery." His son, Sigurd, is born.

1860   Ibsen writes *Svanhild*, a draft of the later *Love's Comedy*.

1862   The Norwegian Theater in Christiania goes bankrupt. Ibsen receives a grant to collect folklore. He establishes himself as a writer with publication of *Love's Comedy*, a satire on marriage. He becomes a consultant at the Norwegian Theater at Christiania.

1863   The play *The Pretenders*, set in medieval Norway, and the poem "A Brother in Need" are published.

1864   *The Pretenders* premieres. With the support of a grant, Ibsen goes to Rome, where he will live for the next four years; he will live abroad until 1891, doing most of his writing in Italy and Germany, and returning to Norway only for short visits in 1874 and 1885.

1866   He achieves prominence with publication of *Brand*, a drama in rhyming couplets about a minister whose extreme religiosity strips him of human sympathy and warmth; it is a huge success in Norway. He is awarded a Norwegian government stipend for artists.

1867   *Peer Gynt*, another poetic drama, premieres; the title character is a self-centered yet lovable opportunist.

1868   Ibsen and his family move to Dresden, Germany, where they will live for the next seven years.

1869   Ibsen begins the second stage of his career, in which he writes realistic social plays and expands the setting of his plays beyond Norway. *The League of Youth*, a political satire, premieres.

1871   He publishes *Poems*, his only collection of verse.

1873   He completes *Emperor and Galilean*, a drama about the Roman emperor Julian the Apostate.

1874   Ibsen commissions Edvard Grieg to write the incidental music for a staging of *Peer Gynt*.

1875   Ibsen relocates to Munich, where he will live for three years.

1876   The production of *Peer Gynt* set to music by Grieg premieres.

1877   *Pillars of Society*, a satire on small-town politics, premieres in Copenhagen.

1878   Ibsen moves back to Rome, where for the next seven years he spends a majority of his time.

1879   Ibsen completes *A Doll's House*, a social drama about marriage. It premieres in Copenhagen, applauded by many theatergoers but criticized by others for its unhappy ending.

1881   He publishes *Ghosts*, which is about the undermining of moral idealism and which touches on the taboo subject of venereal disease; the London *Daily Telegraph* calls the play "a dirty act done publicly."

1882   *Ghosts* is staged in Chicago, in Norwegian. In the play *An Enemy of the People*, which opens in Christiania, Ibsen tells the story of an idealistic truth-teller rejected by those around him; it also receives negative reviews.

1884   Ibsen publishes the poetic and symbolic drama *The Wild Duck*.

1885   Ibsen moves back to Munich, where he will spend the next six years.

1886   He completes *Rosmersholm*, which explores the conflict between unrestricted freedom and conservative traditions.

1890   He completes *Hedda Gabler*, about an idealistic but destructive woman; Oscar Wilde attends the opening and feels "pity and terror, as though the play had been Greek." George Bernard Shaw praises Ibsen in a lecture, "The Quintessence of Ibsenism" (published 1891).

1891   Ibsen returns to Norway and settles in Christiania. *The Master Builder* is published.

1893   *The Master Builder* premieres in Berlin; it is the first play in Ibsen's final period, when symbolism features strongly in his dramas.

1894   Ibsen completes *Little Eyolf*, a play about parental responsibility. In London, Clement Scott establishes an anti-Ibsen league. Ibsen moves into an apartment on the corner of Arbiensgate and Drammensveien in Christiania, where he will reside until his death; there is now a museum on the site.

1896   Ibsen publishes *John Gabriel Borkmann*, a realistic drama about the explosive household of a wealthy man ruined by a prison term for embezzlement.

1899   The symbolic drama *When We Dead Awaken* is Ibsen's last work
        to be published during his lifetime.
1900   Ibsen suffers his first stroke.
1901   After a second stroke, he will be bedridden until his death.
1906   Ibsen dies in Christiania on May 23.

INTRODUCTION

Ibsen's reputation as Europe's first and most consequential modern dramatist was made by scandal. The publication and performance of each new play unleashed storms of protest, mixing shock with aggression and disgust with censorship. Theater critics and audiences in England, France, Germany, Italy, and Ibsen's native Norway denounced the latest provocation flowing from Ibsen's pen with almost predictable frequency. These detractors found themselves attacked no less vehemently by a small but vocal band of defenders, such as George Bernard Shaw and William Archer in England and Georg Brandes in Scandinavia. Ibsen was a playwright capable of polarizing Europe into friends and enemies, forcing them to show their true colors; you were either for Ibsen or against him. As the debate about Ibsen escalated, this alternative turned into a more fundamental one: You were either for or against modern drama itself.

Many admirers of Ibsen later bemoaned the notoriety of their hero. The scandals, they claimed, focused on minor and accidental aspects of his work and therefore distracted from the poetic beauty of his plays and their imaginative treatment of the dramatic form. These calm and measured appreciations are justified enough, but they disregard one crucial fact—namely, that it was through these scandals that Ibsen came to be regarded not just as a well-known playwright, but also as the originator of modern drama. In order to be modern it is not enough to write compelling or even great plays; your plays must stir up the audience, strike them with surprise, attack their complacency. Being modern means offending the audience, so much so that the enraged audience can be seen as the primordial scene from which modern drama emerged. There is no author in the pantheon of modern drama whose name is not associated with provocation: Shaw and Wilde were censored; the openings of plays by Jarry and Artaud led to riots; and Brecht turned the provocation of the audience into a whole theory of modern drama. As much as connoisseurs of Ibsen want us to look beyond the provocation, this provocation is the first thing we must consider because it set the pattern on which the whole tradition of modern drama was modeled. Ibsen was the school for scandal from which all modern dramatists had to graduate.

Ibsen's scandals, his claims to modernity, were primarily based on the content of his plays, the kinds of things they dared to depict and the names they dared to speak. The best fodder for outrage were, predictably enough, all things having to do with illicit sexual activities, most particularly the assorted sexually transmitted diseases, sometimes reminiscent of syphilis but at other times vague and not medically specific, that appeared in his most notorious plays, *A Doll's House* and *Ghosts*. Other plays launched assaults on the bourgeois home and the nuclear family, depicted feminist rebellion against patriarchal society, and denounced the established Church. If these subjects made Ibsen enemies, they also made him friends—in particular, Shaw, whose polemical pamphlet *The Quintessence of Ibsenism* (1891) celebrates Ibsen as rebel for leftist causes. What better place to unmask the lies of the nuclear family than through the bourgeois drawing-room drama, turned against itself? Ibsen openly professed various radical opinions outside his plays as well; at one point he wrote that the state should be abolished altogether. In Ibsen social radicalism and dramatic radicalism seemed to have come to a happy union.

On second thought, however, Ibsen's politics, just as his attitude toward dramatic forms, become more ambiguous. He had little but contempt for democracy, seeing in it the rule of the mediocre majority over the more advanced minority. He even went on record as admiring Russia for its lack of a parliament, the emblem of debasing majority rule. And while *A Doll's House* was championed as a quintessentially feminist text and Nora's final speech as a great feminist manifesto, Ibsen denied an allegiance to feminism as a movement on several occasions. What he shared with socialism and feminism was only their objects of critique—the bourgeois family and its morality—but he differed with most reformers and revolutionaries as to the alternatives. While they agitated on behalf of some new collective or group, all Ibsen cared for was the freedom of the individual. But, one might ask, where does this attack on the state and this advocacy of the individual leave society, the social world that mediates between these two?

The mediation or struggle between the individual and the group is the subject matter of Ibsen's plays; it is the proper subject matter of drama more generally. While lyric poetry is concerned with the individual voice and epic with the mythology or history of a tribe or nation, drama is situated between the two, depicting always more than one person and fewer than all, a limited set of human beings in social interaction. For Ibsen, this interaction is always violent, the place where the clash between individual and collective occurs. In keeping with this distinction, his lyrical plays, *Brand* (1866) and *Peer Gynt* (1867), place more emphasis on the individual: Brand and Gynt are larger-than-life figures whose story is their battle against society. Ibsen's later prose plays emphasize the failure of the individual— Hedda Gabler and the Master Builder die more tragically—but what they all share is this struggle against the collective, the society, the majority. The play that addresses this struggle most directly, if not most subtly, is *Enemy of the People* (1882), the first play Ibsen wrote after turning from the lyrical plays toward a more realistic prose style (this play found an early translator in Eleanor Marx, youngest daughter of Karl Marx). *Enemy of the People* exposes the "quicksand" of lies underneath the pillars of society or community (the Norwegian *samfunde* has both meanings); the deceptive and pompous business baron is saved in the end only through an improbable turn of events and through his cleansing confession. However redeemed this character might emerge from the play, his moralizing talk about society, community, and its pillars is utterly unmasked and exposed as hypocrisy.

Those who wanted to turn Ibsen into a spokesperson for their radical causes continued to be frustrated by his insistence on the individual—and also by his addiction to medals, honors, and titles. For some, this individualism was even a sign that he had not really broken with the ideology he sought to demolish, namely the morality of the bourgeoisie, based as it is on individual rights that obscure the existence of classes and exploitation. This sentiment is perhaps best summed up by Robert Brustein, who reports Bertolt Brecht's remark about Ibsen: "Very good—for [his] own time and [his] own class" (quoted in Brustein, *The Theatre of Revolt*, p. 42; see "For Further Reading"). Ibsen may have been an enemy of bourgeois morality, but he was not able to imagine a true alternative to the bourgeois world.

The scandals Ibsen caused were due not only to the content of his plays, but also to their form. Indeed, if Shaw was the champion of Ibsen's radical content, William Archer was the champion of his radical form, what he considered to be Ibsen's path-breaking realism. Archer's claim that Ibsen's realism was the beginning of what was then called New Drama is surprising on several counts. Realism arose first as a description of the contemporary novel in the 1840s and '50s. Authors such as Balzac, Dickens, and Eliot were writing novels that depicted, with unheard-of detail, common or even low subjects such as city slums, worlds that had previously not been deemed fit for serious literature. The modernist novel, however, does not begin with these English and French realists of the mid-century, but rather with the subsequent generation that critiqued them. Conrad, Gide, Joyce, and Woolf all established themselves through an explicit critique of realism. Why then greet realism in drama as the beginning of something altogether new, radical, and modern?

One reason must be sought in the sorry state of the European theaters from the mid-century to the 1870s and 1880s. While the novel was gaining immense popularity and attracted many of the most gifted writers, the theaters were flooded with so-called "well-made plays"— a translation from the French expression *pièce bien-fait*—dramas that obeyed a set of techniques and formulas combining fast-moving action and a limited number of types. The naive husband, the trusted friend, the plotting wife—these figures were arranged in plots driven by a repertoire of devices such as intercepted letters, unforeseen confrontations, sudden revelations, and poisonous cups passing from hand to hand to end up invariably on the wrong lips. These techniques were not new—indeed, they can be found everywhere, including in Greek tragedy—but by the middle of the nineteenth century they had long become an empty shell, a set of cookbook recipes that were used in play after play, leaving little room for anything else. These plays may have been well made, but at the price of having become utterly predictable and repetitive. The most well-known writers of such well-made plays, Victorien Sardou and Augustine-Eugène Scribe, can be credited with ingenuity in finding ever-new combinations of these devices, but they were imitated zealously throughout Europe by less capable writers and with less witty results. So strong was the hold of the well-made play on the theater that its rules became identified with the requirements of the theater as such. It was left to novelists, such as

Émile Zola, to demand a new drama that would be the equivalent of the realist or naturalist novel. But the machinery of the well-made play was so deeply engrained in the theater industry that producers, managers, critics, and audiences held on to these plays with determination. It was only belatedly and against their massive opposition that a realist drama and theater could finally emerge.

Ibsen's career reflects this state of the theater with astonishing precision. In his early twenties, after having escaped from a dreary apprenticeship with a pharmacist and after a few years as a student, he landed a job at the new and very improvised Norwegian Theater of Bergen. There and at his subsequent post at a theater in the capital, Christiania (now Oslo), Ibsen got to know the theater—and this means that he got to know the well-made play—inside out. Although officially a dramatic author, Ibsen fulfilled every function in the production process, from director and stage manager to acting coach; the only thing he did not do was to appear on stage himself. The mid-century was the time when Norway, which was culturally still under the strong influence of its longtime colonizer, Denmark, sought to establish its own national theater. Even the literary language of Norway, the language in which Ibsen wrote, resembled Danish much more than modern Norwegian, which is closer to Swedish. It was in response to this Danish colonialism that Ibsen and his generation tried to build a Norwegian theater, to signal that Norway had not only gained political independence, but cultural independence as well.

Independence, however, did not lead to the emergence of a new Norwegian drama right away. At the time when Ibsen occupied his post, the Norwegian theaters of Bergen and Christiania were putting on the same well-made plays presented by the Danish theaters—only with Norwegian actors. Even the plays Ibsen wrote during these times—they are now forgotten and almost never performed—show his dependence on the well-made plays of Scribe and his Scandinavian imitators, even though they also manifest an incipient desire to go beyond this narrowly confined form. Ibsen simply did not know how to invent a new dramatic language and form. The theater seemed to require the rules dictated by this tradition, no matter whether they were implemented in French, Danish, or Norwegian.

And so Ibsen made three related and radical decisions: to stop working in the theater, to leave Norway, and to stop writing for the stage altogether. After significant periods of time he would return to all of these earlier modes and places: He would begin writing for the theater again; he would take part in productions; and eventually, at the end of his life, he even returned to Norway. But for the time being, the break with all three—Norway, theater, and drama—was the decision that, we can say in hindsight, laid the foundation for his new drama.

Ibsen moved to Rome in 1864 and there wrote in rapid succession two texts that would make him famous and that some still consider his most compelling works: *Brand* and *Peer Gynt*. Ibsen had stopped writing for the stage, but this does not mean that he had abandoned the dramatic form. Both plays are centered on the protagonist after whom they are named. These two protagonists make it their purpose to defy the limitations imposed on them by the social world, Brand to preach what he calls an "all-or-nothing" religion that demands absolute sacrifice of everything earthly, and Peer Gynt to treat the world as his oyster without having to pay for it. That they both fail in the end, that they both die, does not mean that their quest, their rebellion against the reality principle, is futile or in vain. Rather, it shows their determination to go to the limit, to follow their path to the bitter end.

Ibsen called both *Brand* and *Peer Gynt* dramatic poems; they belong to the category of the poetic reading or closet drama, a drama not to be staged. The break with the stage was salutary because in these two plays the oppressive machinery of the well-made play is gone without a trace. Relieved of the actual or presumed limitations of the theater, these two plays move with ease from place to place, crowd to crowd, fantastic scene to fantastic scene. No devices or tricks are needed to get people on and off the stage at the right moments to assure near misses or perfectly timed confrontations. It is never clear when Brand and Gynt are making things up, arranging the world to fit their grandiose plans, and when they understand that they are up against realities they cannot change. On the actual stage, a director would have to decide each time what is real and what is not: Do the trolls Gynt encounters look ugly or pretty; are they real or figments of his imagination? Ibsen did not have to worry about any of this because he had decided to write these plays as reading or closet dramas. Only this condition guaranteed that he could write freely, without taking into account the alleged limitations of the theater that served to justify the strict rules of the well-made play.

That Ibsen would achieve his breakthrough by breaking with the theater is, like so much in his career, representative of modern drama at large. Many of its most important figures, including Mallarmé, Maeterlinck, Stein, Yeats, Brecht, Artaud, and Beckett, launched their reforms and revolutions of drama and theater against the theater by variously withdrawing from it and attacking it on principle. For them, as for Ibsen, what needed to be opposed was not this or that theatrical style, but the theater as such. Many of them ended up writing closet dramas, while others turned their opposition to the theater into stunning new theatrical styles that seemed to go against everything anyone had ever seen on the stage. It was only gradually, often after many decades, that these modernist plays found their place in the repertory of established theaters, and only after these theaters had utterly changed the way in which they understood performance.

Ibsen had not only fled the theater, he had also fled Norway. He would move back and forth between Italy and Germany until 1891, with very few visits back. This self-imposed exile indicates not only his extreme dissatisfaction with the state of the theater in Norway, but also his aspiration to be more than a Norwegian writer, to be a European writer as well. Indeed, his exile may have helped him achieve this goal, in particular his remarkable successes on the German stage. But one factor played an even greater role, namely that he was able to attract ardent supporters, such as Shaw and Archer. The latter did more than defend Ibsen against the unending attacks. Having partly grown up in Norway, Archer was bilingual and translated a majority of Ibsen's plays into English. Even when Ibsen had resumed writing for the theater and his plays received performances everywhere, his European triumph was due to the translation of his plays as much as to stage performances.

Archer's translations err on the side of the literal, and subsequent translators have made Ibsen easier to speak on the stage. But his translations were not only significant for what they did for Ibsen at the time—their role in what is called the Ibsen campaign—they are also successful renderings of Ibsen for the reader today. That they seem at times old-fashioned is an advantage, reminding us that Ibsen's plays are more than 120 years old and not written in a present-day colloquial style. This is more the case in the original, for Ibsen's Danish-influenced Norwegian is quite difficult to understand, even for Norwegians. Archer's translations avoid the trap of suggesting a false familiarity and force us to approach Ibsen's plays as the historical documents that they are. It is for this reason that we decided to use these translations for the present volume, returning this monumental translation work back to print.

The circulation of Ibsen's plays in Archer's translations and editions corresponds to another pattern of modern drama. Because modern drama continued to have a vexed relation to the theater industry, much of it reached the public in the form of print. Shaw spent a great deal of time editing his plays for their publication, adding lengthy prefaces and stage directions addressed to readers and not only to potential producers and actors. Oscar Wilde got Beardsley to create remarkable etchings for an elaborate deluxe edition of *Salomé*, which, like some of Shaw's plays, had been prevented from public performance because of censorship. Stein, Joyce, Yeats, Artaud, and many others likewise took great care to have their plays appear as literary texts because they either could not or did not want to have them put on stage. While in previous centuries contemporary playwrights were often excluded from the canon of printed literature, the history of modern drama since Ibsen is also the history of drama as reading matter.

It was only after the breakthrough with *Brand* and *Peer Gynt* that Ibsen dared to return to the theater, to write plays for the stage once more. The first plays that followed proved the necessity of his previous abstinence, for despite the years of writing closet dramas, this return to the theater also signified his return to Scribe and the well-made play. Even after Ibsen had broken with the theater industry, his mind somehow still seemed to align the demands of the stage with the demands of the well-made play. The resurgence of Scribe is particularly visible in Ibsen's most notorious play from this period, *A Doll's House. A Doll's House* has among other Scribean elements a fateful letter waiting in a mailbox to be opened, a family friend who suddenly declares his love to the wife, a desperate husband trying to save his good name, a helpless wife in the hands of a blackmailer, an act of selfless sacrifice poorly rewarded—all this is the stuff from which the well-made play is crafted. If Ibsen had managed to get rid of this bag of tricks when he withdrew from the stage, he felt the need to rely on it once more when he returned.

Scribe resurfaced, but he resurfaced with a difference. Ibsen's plays can be seen as so many attempts to rework and undo Scribe, to use his devices but to detach them from the empty machinery of his plots. The most obvious strategy for such an undoing can be found again in *A Doll's House*, which suddenly, at the end, interrupts the workings of the intrigue and blackmail plot with a turn that astonished almost all audiences and that turned *A Doll's House* into one of Ibsen's scandals. The play does not end with a reconciliation but with a speech by Nora in which she denounces her husband and the society that produced him (and her). After this speech, she turns around and leaves her husband and her children by smashing the door; "that door slammed by Nora shook Europe," one critic observed (Lucas, *The Drama of Ibsen and Strindberg*, p. 149). This speech and the act that followed it was unusual because it violated the well-made play, it violated the bourgeois sense of responsibility of a mother and wife, and it put words and thoughts in the mouth of a female character who, throughout most of the play, seemed incapable of them. In other words, it violated the dramatic form, the moral consensus, and the internal plausibility of the character. For Ibsen, however, these were not so much flaws as first attempts to establish some distance from the well-made play, to signal unmistakably that he was doing something entirely different from what the audience had come to expect from a play set in a bourgeois drawing room.

Some of Ibsen's other plays use (or abuse) Scribean devices more sparingly than *A Doll's House*, and they detach them even more thoroughly—and not just at the end—from their supporting structure. It is important to recognize, however, that the continued visibility of these older elements does not challenge Ibsen's claim to being a modern dramatist. On the contrary, it embeds him in a larger tradition of modernism that has often been described as a reworking of older forms. Henry James and Eugene O'Neill used elements of melodrama that are endlessly reworked, while Virginia Woolf and James Joyce took realist plots and estranged them through various experiments and strategies. The complete break with predecessors may be a defining feature of modern drama and modernist art, but only as a self-created myth. If you scratch the surface of many modernist texts you find older forms hidden underneath. Ibsen was no exception to this rule—indeed, he can be quoted as one of its primary examples.

Ibsen's return to the stage connected him to another aspect of modernism: a set of new and innovative techniques of staging, a veritable revolution in theater practice. If Ibsen's fame is unthinkable without the scandals surrounding the publication and performance of his plays, it is equally unthinkable without the help of directors throughout Europe. While some famous actors, such as Sir Henry Irving and Sarah Bernhardt, refused to play Ibsen, some of the most remarkable directors took to his plays and turned them into entirely novel theater experiences. The first path-breaking director to perform Ibsen was Duke Georg II of Saxe-Meiningen, who performed Ibsen's historical drama *The Pretenders* as early as 1875. The influence of the Meiningen players on a whole generation of modernist directors cannot be underestimated. Everyone from Antoine and Granville-Barker to Stanislavsky and Reinhardt regarded the Duke as the first real director, the originator of the modern director's theater.

Most of the Duke's innovations are common practice now, and so it is difficult to appreciate their impact on contemporaries. One innovation was the Meiningen players' use of crowd scenes, of which there were several in *The Pretenders*. Action was no longer organized around the speeches of the lead actors but occurred simultaneously on several levels. One practice that helped achieve these famous crowd scenes was a singular devotion to ensemble acting. The players formed a cohesive group, and even the most talented actors would sometimes play small supporting roles. Other now-familiar elements employed by the players include historically accurate scenery and costumes, and a critique of the painted, two-dimensional scenery and use instead of a three-dimensional set. The Meiningen players' 1875 production of *The Pretenders* in Berlin was one of their first productions outside their provincial hometown and can therefore be seen as an important step in their career. Soon more tours followed, taking them to London in 1881, to Moscow in 1890, where a young Stanislavsky was awed by them, and finally to a tour of no less than thirty-eight European cities. After *The Pretenders*, the players presented other plays by Ibsen, most notably *Ghosts* in a landmark performance in 1886.

Many later directors, among them Antoine and Stanislavsky, were in one way or another influenced by the Meiningen players. In 1887 Antoine founded the Théâtre Libre, which became the first naturalist theater, and produced Ibsen's most notorious play, *Ghosts*, playing Oswald himself. Once more, a central innovator of the stage had decided to turn to an Ibsen play, and one of the notorious ones at that, to stage a revolution in the theater. The most influential director to champion Ibsen, however, was Stanislavsky, whose method of acting has set the standard for psychological realism and detail until today (Stanislavsky's method became particularly influential in the United States, shaping such actors as Dustin Hoffman and Robert DeNiro). What the Duke of Saxe-Meiningen had done for crowd and costume, Stanislavsky did for the creation, or building, of individual characters, demanding a whole new approach to rehearsal through the study of minutia of gestures and movement, involving the body and memory of the actor. Antoine had starred as Oswald in his production of *Ghosts*, and Stanislavksy played Doctor Stockmann in his production of *Enemy of the People*, a role that made him famous and that he would refer to many times in his treatises on acting. During his work in the theater in Bergen and Christiania, Ibsen had often complained about the constraints imposed by actors trained exclusively to perform in well-made plays. Finally, his desire to turn away from the simplistically drawn stock characters of the well-made play and toward complex and torn individuals had found its belated implementation in the theater.

It speaks to the richness of Ibsen's oeuvre that these champions of realism were soon joined by young directors of a very different sort: those working in small, avant-garde theaters under the name of symbolism. Foremost among them was Lugné-Poe, whose Théâtre de L'Œuvre focused on a strange new breed of plays that seemed closer to poetry than to drama, including the mysterious plays of Maurice Maeterlinck and Oscar Wilde's decadent *Salomé*. This same Lugné-Poe chose to put on, as one of the earliest plays after establishing his theater, two plays by Ibsen: *Rosmersholm* in 1893 and *The Master Builder* in 1894. How could Ibsen's so-called realist plays end up in the company of the aristocratic, biblical, and utterly artificial plays of symbolism? For one, it showed that many of Ibsen's most ardent defenders, in particular Shaw and Archer, had focused more or less exclusively on his realist plays, such as *Pillars of Society*, *A Doll's House*, and *Enemy of the People*. What was excluded were not only his earlier plays—in particular, his "dramatic poems" *Brand* and *Peer Gynt*—but also his later plays, including *Rosmersholm*, *The Master Builder*, and *When We Dead Awaken*, which Ibsen subtitled "dramatic epilogue."

What drew these diverse directors to Ibsen was the fact that these plays offer an intricate mixture of realist and symbolist modes. In the theater the very distinction between what is a symbol and what is a mere stage prop or technical device is often difficult to make. In *Enemy of the People*, the poisonous baths can be seen as a device to expose the hypocrisy of the town that profits from them. It turns out, not surprisingly, that the town doesn't really care about the beneficial effects of the water, but only about profits, and is even ready to suppress the truth if need be. It's not only the baths; the entire society is poisoned and needs to be cured by the solitary scientist who alone is interested in forcing out the truth. The poisonous cure is more than a simple plot device; it gathers Ibsen's entire critique of society into one single form.

Of all of Ibsen's plays, *The Wild Duck* is the one that revolves most explicitly around this process by which a simple device or stage prop becomes an objective correlative, something that gathers a whole range of meanings. The play's title names this correlative, the wild duck, but the play cannot decide what it signifies. In fact, in the final showdown the characters disagree as to how the wild duck relates to the persons and events taking place. Is the wild duck the domesticated father of Hialmar, who is reduced to going hunting in the attic? Is it Hialmar, whose natural strength has been buried underneath his self-deception? Is it Hialmar's daughter, who owns the duck and who ends up shooting herself instead of shooting the duck, as she had been tempted to do? Devices become charged with meaning, but these meanings can be multiple.

From the putatively simple device, we can thus move to the device that becomes an objective correlative and then to the objective correlative that becomes multiply charged. This series culminates in what is commonly described as the symbol. Even the objective correlative has not only a function but also a meaning, or several related meanings, and this multiplicity is further increased in such super-correlatives as the wild duck. But even if the play cannot decide on the ultimate meaning of the wild duck—whereas in *Enemy of the People* the meaning of the poisoned baths is clear—there are at least several comprehensible, if mutually exclusive, possibilities to choose from. Such clear-cut choices are no longer possible when it comes to the symbol. The final and self-destructive ascent onto the newly built tower of the Master Builder Solness may signify many things—his attempt to recapture his youth, his desire to build a real home, simple hubris, his escape from the dilemmas that plague his life—but it cannot be neatly translated into any one of these. They are suggested and hinted at, they variously intermingle, fading in and out of the image, without coming to a stop. Ibsen here takes the technical device, the stage prop, the objective correlative and turns all of these related modes into something much less tangible, something that expresses without allowing for a neat translation. We simply have to absorb this image, or symbol, and let it resonate richly with the play as a whole.

More fundamental to Ibsen's technique than the tension between prop and symbol, realism and symbolism, is a second tension that leads into the heart of modernism. Ibsen is the playwright who dared more than any of his contemporary writers to do away with old proprieties, to invent new forms, to break with the past. At the same time, however, his plays are everywhere haunted by this past; even as they announce their desire to escape the past, it always returns—for example, in the form of the character's childhood and formative experiences. Ibsen's plays are psychological plays in that they proceed by analyzing characters, by taking them apart layer by layer until these characters' actions are fully explained.

The past, however, is never just a question of the individual; it reaches beyond the control of the single character into the past of the family through various lines of inheritance: financial inheritance, biological inheritance, psychological inheritance, moral inheritance. It was Charles Darwin who gave the nineteenth-century obsession with the past and inheritance its scientific form, but his theory is one example of a more widespread consequence or effect of modernity: the return of the past. Attempting to break with the past and consequently being haunted by it is the double gesture that defines Ibsen's work. The play that manifests this effect particularly well and that refers to it in its title is *Ghosts*. Even though it is Ibsen's most radical and provocative play, it is, at the same time, the play most saturated with the return of the past through the deployment of various obscure forms of inheritance, captured under the general theme of the ghost and haunting. As the characters have to find out, it is not up to them to escape the past and to start anew. However much they may try, the past is stronger than their ability to leave it behind.

The theme of the ghost is perhaps Ibsen's most lasting commentary on the paradox of modernism and its drama, which he helped inaugurate: Modern drama ends up being turned backward as much as forward, excavating layers and layers of the past as much as imagining some new and entirely different future. Being modern means more than just being current or up to date. It signals a break with history, the sense that the past is fundamentally different and has little to teach the present and the future. Ibsen's plays remind us of the difficulty of being modern, that we cannot have modernism without being haunted by that which modernism wants to leave behind—that modern drama is a drama of ghosts.

MARTIN PUCHNER is Assistant Professor of English and comparative literature at Columbia University. He is the author of *Stage Fright: Modernism, Anti-Theatricality, and Drama* (Johns Hopkins University Press, 2002) and has published in *New Literary History*, *Theatre Journal*, *Modern Drama*, *Criticism*, and *Theatre Research International*, among others. He has written an essay on Joe Orton for Scribner's Sons' *Encyclopedia of British Writers* and has contributed to a collection entitled *Avant-Garde: New Perspectives* (Rodopi, 2000), as well as to *A New History of German Literature* (Harvard University Press). His introduction to Lionel Abel's *Tragedy and Metatheater* is forthcoming from Holmes and Meier. He has edited two special issues, one with Alan Ackerman on Moderism and Anti-Theatricality (*Modern Drama* 44:3) and the other on Kafka and the Theater (*The Germanic Review*, spring 2003). He is currently working on a book-length project on the manifesto as well as on a collection of essays entitled *Theater on Trial*. He has given public lectures at numerous theaters in New York and has been interviewed in a variety of venues, including National Public Radio.

Six Plays by Henrik Ibsen

PEER GYNT

(1867)

INTRODUCTION

Written after his first success, *Brand* (1865), *Peer Gynt* (1867) is Ibsen's second "dramatic poem," the second play he wrote after having left Norway and the theater, after deciding to settle in Italy and to write no longer for the stage. This decision to break with the theater, with the perceived limitations imposed by the stage, had an enormously liberating effect. The Aristotelian unities of time, place, and action had become a suffocating set of mechanical rules limiting dramatic literature, and Ibsen realized that a new drama could be written only outside and against the theater. The reading public had different and less rigid expectations than theater producers and audiences, and the printed page lent itself well to fantastic and imaginative material such as the adventures of *Peer Gynt*, which Ibsen had borrowed from a Norwegian folktale. Ibsen's decision was unusual, but not unique. There existed a long tradition of reading or closet dramas, including Goethe's *Faust* and the Romantic closet dramas of Shelley and Byron, as well as the tradition of the dramatic monologue—a heterogeneous group of plays that have in common their refusal to be put on stage. It is in this tradition that Ibsen placed *Peer Gynt*, which became an important precursor for the veritable explosion of closet dramas at the turn of the century, with Strindberg's *A Dream Play* being probably the best-known example.

One consequence of Ibsen's liberation from the stage was that he could write a play that moved freely from the Norwegian mountains to Morocco, developing a plot closer to that of an epic or a novel, one that follows the travels and adventures of a single character across different locales, spanning his entire lifetime from teenage boy to old man. Such dramatic structures would become common for later playwrights such as Strindberg and Brecht, whose plays are therefore called episodic or epic drama. Ibsen not only constructs such an epic plot, he also places at its center a character who thrives on telling stories to embellish reality. Just as Peer Gynt's stories fashion reality to suit his imagination, so Ibsen uses a narrative or epic drama for a new and imaginative play.

A second consequence of Ibsen's choice to write a dramatic poem is even more important but also more surprising: In comparison to Ibsen's earlier and later plays, *Peer Gynt* is more, not less, saturated with theatricality. Peer Gynt himself is a liar, a character who creates his own version of reality, his own fantastic world in defiance of all common sense and realism. The most theatrical scene is the one with the trolls; reality and fantasy are so blurred that one simply doesn't know the difference between them anymore. The troll world itself functions by imposing a different character on reality, by masking and deceiving the senses; in fact, the trolls want to operate on Gynt's eye so that their temporary charade will become permanent, so that he will see the world their way forever. This is the moment, however, when Gynt runs, because he does not want to accept any fabrication of reality except his own. Just as he had refused the realism of his mother, who wants him to become a good citizen, so he refuses the permanent fantasy of the trolls and chooses his own path, tells his own lies, fashions himself as best as he can until he returns to Norway to die.

Even though *Peer Gynt* was not written for the theater, Ibsen's growing fame, as well as contemporary reforms in theater practice, made directors think about the challenge of putting it on the stage nevertheless. It received its first performance at Christiania in 1876, eleven years after its publication, although the next production didn't occur until ten years later, in Copenhagen (1886). The first production outside Scandinavia was in Paris by the leading symbolist director Aurelion-Marie Lugné-Poe (1896); it was reviewed favorably by George Bernard Shaw. A notable production took place in London (1911), with a female actor, Pax Robertson, playing Peer Gynt, even though a major London production did not take place until 1922 at the Old Vic.

It is important to recognize that these productions did not proceed without Ibsen's approval. Ibsen himself had started to envision *Peer Gynt* on the stage, but never as regular drama. Instead he had turned to the most prominent Scandinavian composer, Edvard Grieg, and convinced him to write a musical score to go along with a theatrical production; for this purpose, Ibsen was even ready to cut the play substantially. The need for music that Ibsen perceived, however, is also indicative of his continued distrust of the theater. It was not as regular theater that he could imagine *Peer Gynt*, but only as a tone picture, as something between theater and opera, the latter having always been more amenable to lyrical drama. *Peer Gynt*'s later success on the stage thus does not retroactively question the wisdom of Ibsen's retreat from the stage. Rather, it demonstrates how necessary it was for him to recreate the dramatic form, and also how long it took for the theater to eventually catch up with this, his most daring play.

—Martin Puchner

CHARACTERS

ÅSE, a peasant's widow.

PEER GYNT, her son.

TWO OLD WOMEN with corn-sacks. ASLAK, a smith. WEDDING
   GUESTS. A KITCHEN-MASTER, A FIDDLER, etc.

A MAN AND WIFE, newcomers to the district.

SOLVEIG and LITTLE HELGA, their daughters.

THE FARMER AT HEGSTAD.

INGRID, his daughter.

THE BRIDEGROOM and HIS PARENTS.

THREE SÆTER-GIRLS. A GREEN-CLAD WOMAN.

THE OLD MAN OF THE DOVRË.

A TROLL-COURTIER. SEVERAL OTHERS. TROLL-MAIDENS and
   TROLL-URCHINS. A COUPLE OF WITCHES. BROWNIES,
   NIXIES, GNOMES, etc.

AN UGLY BRAT. A VOICE IN THE DARKNESS. BIRD-CRIES.

KARI, a cottar's wife.

Master COTTON, Monsieur BALLON, Herren VON EBERKOPF and
   TRUMPETERSTRÅLE, gentlemen on their travels. A THIEF and
   A RECEIVER.

ANITRA, daughter of a Bedouin chief.

ARABS, FEMALE SLAVES, DANCING-GIRLS, ETC.

THE MEMNON-STATUE (singing). THE SPHINX AT GIZEH (muta
   persona).

PROFESSOR BEGRIFFENFELDT, Dr. phil., director of the madhouse
   at Cairo.

HUHU, a language-reformer from the coast of Malabar. HUSSEIN, an
   eastern Minister. A FELLAH, with a royal mummy.

SEVERAL MADMEN, with their KEEPERS.

A NORWEGIAN SKIPPER and HIS CREW. A STRANGE PASSENGER.

A PASTOR. A FUNERAL-PARTY. A PARISH-OFFICER. A BUTTON-
   MOULDER. A LEAN PERSON.

*(The action, which opens in the beginning of the present [that is the
nineteenth] century, and ends towards our own days [1867], takes place partly
in Gudbrandsdale, and on the mountains around it, partly on the coast of
Morocco, in the desert of Sahara, in a madhouse at Cairo, at sea, etc.)*

ACT FIRST

Scene First

A wooded hillside near ÅSE's farm. A river rushes down the slope. On the further side of it an old mill-shed. It is a hot day in summer.

PEER GYNT, *a strongly-built youth of twenty, comes down the pathway. His mother, ÅSE, a small, slightly-built woman, follows him, scolding angrily.*

ÅSE
  Peer, you're lying!
PEER [*Without stopping.*]
  No, I am not!
ÅSE
  Well then, swear that it is true!
PEER
  Swear? Why should I?
ÅSE
  See, you dare not!
  It's a lie from first to last.
PEER [*Stopping.*]
  It is true—each blessed word!
ÅSE [*Confronting him.*]
  Don't you blush before your mother?
  First you skulk among the mountains
  Monthlong in the busiest season,
  Stalking reindeer in the snows;
  Home you come then, torn and tattered,
  Gun amissing, likewise game;—
  And at last, with open eyes,
  Think to get me to believe
  All the wildest hunters'-lies!—

Well, where did you find the buck, then?

PEER

West near Gendin.

ÅSE [*Laughing scornfully.*]

Ah! Indeed.

PEER

Keen the blast towards me swept;
Hidden by an alder-clump,
He was scraping in the snow-crust
After lichen——

ÅSE [*As before.*]

Doubtless, yes!

PEER

Breathlessly I stood and listened,
Heard the crunching of his hoof,
Saw the branches of one antler.
Softly then among the boulders
I crept forward on my belly.
Crouched in the moraine I peered up;—
Such a buck, so sleek and fat,
You, I'm sure, have ne'er set eyes on.

ÅSE

No, of course not!

PEER

Bang! I fired.
Clean he dropped upon the hillside.
But the instant that he fell,
I sat firm astride his back,
Gripped him by the left ear tightly,
And had almost sunk my knife-blade
In his neck, behind his skull—
When, behold! the brute screamed wildly,
Sprang upon his feet like lightning,
With a back-cast of his head
From my fist made knife and sheath fly,
Pinned me tightly by the thigh,
Jammed his horns against my legs,
Clenched me like a pair of tongs;—

Then forthwith away he flew
Right along the Gendin-Edge!

ÅSE [*Involuntarily.*]

Jesus save us——!

PEER

Have you ever
Chanced to see the Gendin-Edge?
Nigh on four miles long it stretches
Sharp before you like a scythe.
Down o'er glaciers, landslips, screes,
Down the toppling grey moraines,
You can see, both right and left,
Straight into the tarns that slumber,
Black and sluggish, more than seven
Hundred fathoms deep below you.
Right along the Edge we two
Clove our passage through the air.
Never rode I such a colt!
Straight before us as we rushed
'Twas as though there glittered suns.
Brown-backed eagles that were sailing
In the wide and dizzy void
Half-way 'twixt us and the tarns,
Dropped behind, like motes in air.
On the shores crashed hurtling ice-floes,
But no echo reached my ears.
Only sprites of dizziness* sprang,
Dancing, round;——they sang, they swung,
Circle-wise, past sight and hearing!

ÅSE [*Dizzy.*]

Oh, God save me!

PEER

All at once,
At a desperate, break-neck spot,

---

*This is the poet's own explanation of this difficult passage. *Hvirvlens vætter*, he
writes, is equivalent to *Svimmelhedens ånder*—that is, spirits of dizziness or vertigo.
(Translator's note)

Rose a great cock-ptarmigan,
Flapping, cackling, terrified,
From the crack where he lay hidden
At the buck's feet on the Edge.
Then the buck shied half around,
Leapt sky-high, and down we plunged,
Both of us, into the depths!
[ÅSE *totters, and catches at the trunk of a tree.* PEER GYNT *continues:*]
Mountain walls behind us, black,
And below a void unfathomed!
First we clove through banks of mist,
Then we clove a flock of sea-gulls,
So that they, in mid-air startled,
Flew in all directions, screaming.
Downward rushed we, ever downward.
But beneath us something shimmered,
Whitish, like a reindeer's belly.—
Mother, 'twas our own reflection
In the glass-smooth mountain tarn,
Shooting up towards the surface
With the same wild rush of speed
Wherewith we were shooting downwards.

ÅSE   [*Gasping for breath.*]
Peer! God help me——! Quickly, tell——
PEER
Buck from over, buck from under,
In a moment clashed together,
Scattering foam-flecks all around.
There we lay then, floating, plashing,—
But at last we made our way
Somehow to the northern shore;
Swam the buck, I clung behind him;—
I ran homewards——
ÅSE
But the buck, dear?
PEER
He's there still, for aught I know;—

[*Snaps his fingers, turns on his heel, and adds:*]
Catch him, and you're welcome to him!

ÅSE

And your neck you haven't broken?
Haven't broken both your thighs?
And your backbone, too, is whole?
Oh, dear Lord—what thanks, what praise,
Should be thine who helped my boy!
There's a rent, though, in your breeches;
But it's scarce worth talking of
When one thinks what dreadful things
Might have come of such a leap——!
[*Stops suddenly, looks at him open-mouthed and wide-eyed; cannot find words for some time, but at last bursts out:*]
Oh, you devil's story-teller,
Cross of Christ, how you can lie!
All this screed you foist upon me,
I remember now, I knew it
When I was a girl of twenty.
Gudbrand Glesnë it befell,
Never you, you——

PEER

Me as well.
Such a thing can happen twice.

ÅSE   [*Exasperated.*]

Yes, a lie, turned topsy-turvy,
Can be prinked and tinselled out,
Decked in plumage new and fine,
Till none knows its lean old carcass.
That is just what you've been doing,
Vamping up things, wild and grand,
Garnishing with eagles' backs
And with all the other horrors,
Lying right and lying left,
Filling me with speechless dread,
Till at last I recognised not
What of old I'd heard and known!

PEER

> If another talked like that
> I'd half kill him for his pains.

ÅSE   [*Weeping.*]

> Oh, would God I lay a corpse;
> Would the black earth held me sleeping.
> Prayers and tears don't bite upon him.—
> Peer, you're lost, and ever will be!

PEER

> Darling, pretty little mother,
> You are right in every word;—
> Don't be cross, be happy——

ÅSE

> Silence!
> Could I, if I would, be happy,
> With a pig like you for son?
> Think how bitter I must find it,
> I, a poor defenceless widow,
> Ever to be put to shame!
> [*Weeping again.*]
> How much have we now remaining
> From your grandsire's days of glory?
> Where are now the sacks* of coin
> Left behind by Rasmus Gynt?
> Ah, your father lent them wings,—
> Lavished them abroad like sand,
> Buying land in every parish,
> Driving round in gilded chariots.
> Where is all the wealth he wasted
> At the famous winter-banquet,
> When each guest sent glass and bottle
> Shivering 'gainst the wall behind him?

PEER

> Where's the snow of yester-year?

ÅSE

> Silence, boy, before your mother!

---

*Literally, "bushels." (Translator's note)

See the farmhouse! Every second
Window-pane is stopped with clouts.
Hedges, fences, all are down,
Beasts exposed to wind and weather,
Fields and meadows lying fallow,
Every month a new distraint——

PEER

Come now, stop this old-wife's talk!
Many a time has luck seemed drooping,
And sprung up as high as ever!

ÅSE

Salt-strewn is the soil it grew from.
Lord, but you're a rare one, you,——
Just as pert and jaunty still,
Just as bold as when the Pastor,
Newly come from Copenhagen,
Bade you tell your Christian name,
And declared that such a headpiece
Many a Prince down there might envy;
Till the cob your father gave him,
With a sledge to boot, in thanks
For his pleasant, friendly talk.——
Ah, but things went bravely then!
Provost,* Captain, all the rest,
Dropped in daily, ate and drank,
Swilling, till they well-nigh burst.
But 'tis need that tests one's neighbour.
Lonely here it grew, and silent,
From the day that "Gold-bag Jon"†
Started with his pack, a pedlar.
[*Dries her eyes with her apron.*]
Ah, you're big and strong enough,

---

*An ecclesiastical dignitary—something equivalent to a rural dean. (Translator's note)

† *Jon med Skjæppen*—literally, "John with the Bushel"—a nickname given him in his days of prosperity, in allusion to his supposed bushels of money. (Translator's note)

You should be a staff and pillar
For your mother's frail old age,—
You should keep the farm-work going,
Guard the remnants of your gear;—
[*Crying again.*]
Oh, God help me, small's the profit
You have been to me, you scamp!
Lounging by the hearth at home,
Grubbing in the charcoal embers;
Or, round all the country, frightening
Girls away from merry-makings—
Shaming me in all directions,
Fighting with the worst rapscallions——

PEER   [*Turning away from her.*]

Let me be.

ÅSE   [*Following him.*]

Can you deny
That you were the foremost brawler
In the mighty battle royal
Fought the other day at Lundë,
When you raged like mongrels mad?
Who was it but you that broke
Blacksmith Aslak's arm for him,—
Or at any rate that wrenched one
Of his fingers out of joint?

PEER

Who has filled you with such prate?

ÅSE   [*Hotly.*]

Cottar Kari heard the yells!

PEER   [*Rubbing his elbow.*]

Maybe, but 'twas I that howled.

ÅSE

You?

PEER

Yes, mother,—*I* got beaten.

ÅSE

What d'you say?

PEER
> He's limber, he is.

ÅSE
> Who?

PEER
> Why Aslak, to be sure.

ÅSE
> Shame—and shame; I spit upon you!
> Such a worthless sot as that,
> Such a brawler, such a sodden
> Dram-sponge to have beaten you!
> [*Weeping again.*]
> Many a shame and slight I've suffered;
> But that this should come to pass
> Is the worst disgrace of all.
> What if he be ne'er so limber,
> Need you therefore be a weakling?

PEER
> Though I hammer or am hammered,—
> Still we must have lamentations.
> [*Laughing.*]
> Cheer up, mother——

ÅSE
> What? You're lying
> Now again?

PEER
> Yes, just this once.
> Come now, wipe your tears away;—
> [*Clenching his left hand.*]
> See,—with this same pair of tongs,
> Thus I held the smith bent double,
> While my sledge-hammer right fist——

ÅSE
> Oh, you brawler! You will bring me
> With your doings to the grave!

PEER
> No, you're worth a better fate;
> Better twenty thousand times!

> Little, ugly, dear old mother,
> You may safely trust my word,—
> All the parish shall exalt you;
> Only wait till I have done
> Something—something really grand.

ÅSE [*Contemptuously.*]

> You!

PEER

> Who knows what may befall one.

ÅSE

> Could you but find so much sense,
> One day, as to do the darning
> Of your breeches for yourself!

PEER [*Hotly.*]

> I will be a king, a kaiser!

ÅSE

> Oh, God comfort me, he's losing
> All the little wits he'd left!

PEER

> Yes, I will! Just give me time!

ÅSE

> Give you time, you'll be a prince,
> So the saying goes, I think!

PEER

> You shall see!

ÅSE

> Oh, hold your tongue
> You're as mad as mad can be.—
> Ah, and yet it's true enough,—
> Something might have come of you,
> Had you not been steeped for ever
> In your lies and trash and moonshine.
> Hegstad's girl was fond of you.
> Easily you could have won her
> Had you wooed her with a will——

PEER

> Could I?

ÅSE

> The old man's too feeble
> Not to give his child her way.
> He is stiff-necked in a fashion;
> But at last 'tis Ingrid rules;
> And where she leads, step by step
> Stumps the gaffer, grumbling, after.
> [*Begins to cry again.*]
> Ah, my Peer!—a golden girl—
> Land entailed on her! Just think,
> Had you set your mind upon it,
> You'd be now a bridegroom brave,—
> You that stand here grimed and tattered!

PEER   [*Briskly.*]

> Come, we'll go a-wooing then!

ÅSE

> Where?

PEER

> At Hegstad!

ÅSE

> Ah, poor boy;
> Hegstad way is barred to wooers!

PEER

> How is that?

ÅSE

> Ah, woe is me!
> Lost the moment, lost the luck——

PEER

> Speak!

ÅSE   [*Sobbing.*]

> While in the Wester-hills
> You in air were riding reindeer,
> Here Mads Moen's won the girl!

PEER

> What! That women's-bugbear! He——

ÅSE

> Ay, she's taking him for husband.

PEER

> Wait you here till I have harnessed
> Horse and waggon——
> [*Going.*]

ÅSE

> Spare your pains.
> They are to be wed to-morrow——

PEER

> Pooh; this evening I'll be there!

ÅSE

> Fie now! Would you crown our miseries
> With a load of all men's scorn?

PEER

> Never fear; 'twill all go well.
> [*Shouting and laughing at the same time.*]
> Mother, jump! We'll spare the waggon;
> 'Twould take time to fetch the mare up——
> [*Lifts her up in his arms.*]

ÅSE

> Put me down!

PEER

> No, in my arms
> I will bear you to the wedding!
> [*Wades out into the stream.*]

ÅSE

> Help! The Lord have mercy on us!
> Peer! We're drowning——

PEER

> I was born
> For a braver death——

ÅSE

> Ay, true;
> Sure enough you'll hang at last!
> [*Tugging at his hair.*]
> Oh, you brute!

PEER

> Keep quiet now;
> Here the bottom's slippery-slimy.

ÅSE

 Ass!

PEER

 That's right, don't spare your tongue;
 That does no one any harm.
 Now it's shelving up again——

ÅSE

 Don't you drop me!

PEER

 Heisan! Hop!
 Now we'll play at Peer and reindeer;——
 [*Curvetting.*]
 I'm the reindeer, you are Peer!

ÅSE

 Oh, I'm going clean distraught!

PEER

 See now——we have reached the shallows;——
 [*Wades ashore.*]
 Come, a kiss now, for the reindeer;
 Just to thank him for the ride——

ÅSE   [*Boxing his ears.*]

 This is how I thank him!

PEER

 Ow!
 That's a miserable fare!

ÅSE

 Put me down!

PEER

 First to the wedding.
 Be my spokesman. You're so clever;
 Talk to him, the old curmudgeon;
 Say Mads Moen's good for nothing——

ÅSE

 Put me down!

PEER

 And tell him then
 What a rare lad is Peer Gynt.

ÅSE

    Truly, you may swear to that!
    Fine's the character I'll give you.
    Through and through I'll show you up;
    All about your devil's pranks
    I will tell them straight and plain——

PEER

    Will you?

ÅSE   [*Kicking with rage.*]

    I won't stay my tongue
    Till the old man sets his dog
    At you, as you were a tramp!

PEER

    H'm; then I must go alone.

ÅSE

    Ay, but I'll come after you!

PEER

    Mother dear, you haven't strength——

ÅSE

    Strength? When I'm in such a rage,
    I could crush the rocks to powder!
    Hu! I'd make a meal of flints!
    Put me down!

PEER

    You'll promise then——

ÅSE

    Nothing! I'll to Hegstad with you!
    They shall know you, what you are!

PEER

    Then you'll even have to stay here.

ÅSE

    Never! To the feast I'm coming!

PEER

    That you shan't.

ÅSE

    What will you do?

PEER

    Perch you on the mill-house roof.

[*He puts her up on the roof.* ÅSE *screams.*]

ÅSE
　Lift me down!

PEER
　Yes, if you'll listen——

ÅSE
　Rubbish!

PEER
　Dearest mother, pray——

ÅSE　[*Throwing a sod of grass at him.*]
　Lift me down this moment, Peer!

PEER
　If I dared, be sure I would.
　[*Coming nearer.*]
　Now remember, sit quite still.
　Do not sprawl and kick about;
　Do not tug and tear the shingles,——
　Else 'twill be the worse for you;
　You might topple down.

ÅSE
　You beast.

PEER
　Do not kick!

ÅSE
　I'd have you blown,
　Like a changeling, into space!*

PEER
　Mother, fie!

ÅSE
　Bah!

PEER
　Rather give your
　Blessing on my undertaking.
　Will you? Eh?

*It is believed in some parts of Norway that "changelings" (elf-children left in the stead of those taken away by the fairies) can, by certain spells, be made to fly away up the chimney. (Translator's note)

ÅSE

I'll thrash you soundly,
Hulking fellow though you be!

PEER

Well, good-bye then, mother dear!
Patience; I'll be back ere long.
[*Is going, but turns, holds up his finger warningly, and says:*]
Careful now, don't kick and sprawl!
[*Goes.*]

ÅSE

Peer! God help me, now he's off;
Reindeer-rider! Liar! Hei!
Will you listen!——No, he's striding
O'er the meadow———!
[*Shrieks.*]
Help. I'm dizzy!

TWO OLD WOMEN, *with sacks on their backs, come down the path to the mill.*

FIRST WOMAN

Christ, who's screaming?

ÅSE

It is I!

SECOND WOMAN

Åse! Well, you are exalted!

ÅSE

This won't be the end of it;—
Soon, God help me, I'll be heaven-high.

FIRST WOMAN

Bless your passing!

ÅSE

Fetch a ladder;
I must be down! That devil Peer——

SECOND WOMAN

Peer! Your son?

ÅSE

Now you can say

You have seen how he behaves.

FIRST WOMAN

    We'll bear witness.

ÅSE

    Only help me;
    Straight to Hegstad will I hasten——

SECOND WOMAN

    Is he there?

FIRST WOMAN

    You'll be revenged, then;
    Aslak Smith will be there too.

ÅSE   [*Wringing her hands.*]

    Oh, God help me with my boy;
    They will kill him ere they're done!

FIRST WOMAN

    Oh, that lot has oft been talked of;
    Comfort you: what must be must be!

SECOND WOMAN

    She is utterly demented.
    [*Calls up the hill.*]
    Eivind, Anders! Hei! Come here!

A MAN'S VOICE

    What's amiss?

SECOND WOMAN

    Peer Gynt has perched his
    Mother on the mill-house roof!

Scene Second

A hillock, covered with bushes and heather. The high-road runs behind it; a fence between.

PEER GYNT *comes along a footpath, goes quickly up to the fence, stops, and looks out over the distant prospect.*

PEER

    Yonder lies Hegstad. Soon I'll have reached it.

[*Puts one leg over the fence; then hesitates.*]
Wonder if Ingrid's alone in the house now?
[*Shades his eyes with his hand, and looks out.*]
No; to the farm guests are swarming like midges.—
H'm, to turn back now perhaps would be wisest.
[*Draws back his leg.*]
Still they must titter behind your back,
And whisper so that it burns right through you.
[*Moves a few steps away from the fence, and begins absently plucking leaves.*]
Ah, if I'd only a good strong dram now.
Or if I could pass to and fro unseen.—
Or were I unknown.—Something proper and strong
Were the best thing of all, for the laughter don't bite then.
[*Looks around suddenly as though afraid; then hides among the bushes.
Some* WEDDING-GUESTS* *pass by, going downwards towards the farm.*]

A MAN   [*In conversation as they pass.*]
His father was drunken, his mother is weak.

A WOMAN.
Ay, then it's no wonder the lad's good for nought.
[*They pass on. Presently* PEER GYNT *comes forward, his face flushed
with shame. He peers after them.*]

PEER   [*Softly.*]
Was it me they were talking of?
[*With a forced shrug.*]
Oh, let them chatter?
After all, they can't sneer the life out of my body.
[*Casts himself down upon the heathery slope; lies for some time flat on his
back with his hands under his head, gazing up into the sky.*]
What a strange sort of cloud! It is just like a horse.
There's a man on it too—and a saddle—and bridle.—
And after it comes an old crone on a broomstick.
[*Laughs quietly to himself.*]
It is mother. She's scolding and screaming: You beast!
Hei you, Peer Gynt——

---

*Sendingsfolk—literally, "folks with presents." When the Norwegian peasants are
bidden to a wedding feast, they bring with them presents of eatables. (Translator's
note)

[*His eyes gradually close.*]
Ay, now she is frightened.——
Peer Gynt he rides first, and there follow him many.——
His steed it is gold-shod and crested with silver.
Himself he has gauntlets and sabre and scabbard.
His cloak it is long, and its lining is silken.
Full brave is the company riding behind him.
None of them, though, sits his charger so stoutly.
None of them glitters like him in the sunshine.——
Down by the fence stand the people in clusters,
Lifting their hats, and agape gazing upwards.
Women are curtseying. All the world knows him,
Kaiser Peer Gynt, and his thousands of henchmen.
Sixpenny pieces and glittering shillings
Over the roadway he scatters like pebbles.
Rich as a lord grows each man in the parish.
High o'er the ocean Peer Gynt goes a-riding.
Engelland's Prince on the seashore awaits him;
There too await him all Engelland's maidens.
Engelland's nobles and Engelland's Kaiser,
See him come riding and rise from their banquet.
Raising his crown, hear the Kaiser address him——

ASLAK THE SMITH   [*To some other young men, passing along the road.*]
Just look at Peer Gynt there, the drunken swine——!

PEER   [*Starting half up.*]
What, Kaiser——!

THE SMITH   [*Leaning against the fence and grinning.*]
Up with you, Peer, my lad!

PEER
What the devil? The smith! What do you want here?

THE SMITH   [*To the others.*]
He hasn't got over the Lundëspree yet.

PEER   [*Jumping up.*]
You'd better be off!

THE SMITH
I am going, yes.
But tell us, where have you dropped from, man?
You've been gone six weeks. Were you troll-taken, eh?

PEER

I have been doing strange deeds, Aslak Smith!

THE SMITH   [*Winking to the others.*]

Let us hear them, Peer!

PEER

They are nought to you.

THE SMITH   [*After a pause.*]

You're going to Hegstad?

PEER

No.

THE SMITH

Time was

They said that the girl there was fond of you.

PEER

You grimy crow———!

THE SMITH   [*Falling back a little.*]

Keep your temper, Peer.

Though Ingrid has jilted you, others are left;——

Think—son of Jon Gynt! Come on to the feast;

You'll find there both lambkins and well-seasoned widows———

PEER

To hell———

THE SMITH

You will surely find one that will have you.——

Good evening! I'll give your respects to the bride.——

[*They go off, laughing and whispering.*]

PEER   [*Looks after them a while, then makes a defiant motion and turns half round.*]

For my part, may Ingrid of Hegstad go marry

Whoever she pleases. It's all one to me.

[*Looks down at his clothes.*]

My breeches are torn. I am ragged and grim.——

If only I had something new to put on now.

[*Stamps on the ground.*]

If only I could, with a butcher-grip,

Tear out the scorn from their very vitals!

[*Looks round suddenly.*]

What was that? Who was it that tittered behind there?

H'm, I certainly thought—— No no, it was no one.—
I'll go home to mother.
[*Begins to go upwards, but stops again and listens towards Hegstad.*]
They're playing a dance!
[*Gazes and listens; moves downwards step by step, his eyes glisten; he rubs his hands down his thighs.*]
How the lasses do swarm! Six or eight to a man!
Oh, galloping death,—I must join in the frolic!—
But how about mother, perched up on the mill-house——
[*His eyes are drawn downwards again; he leaps and laughs.*]
Hei, how the Halling* flies over the green!
Ay, Guttorm, he can make his fiddle speak out!
It gurgles and booms like a foss† o'er a scaur.
And then all that glittering bevy of girls!—
Yes, galloping death, I must join in the frolic!
[*Leaps over the fence and goes down the road.*]

SCENE THIRD

The farm-place at Hegstad. In the background, the dwelling-house. A
THRONG OF GUESTS. *A lively dance in progress on the green.* THE
FIDDLER *sits on a table.* THE KITCHEN-MASTER‡ *is standing in
the doorway.* COOKMAIDS *are going to and fro between the different
buildings. Groups of* ELDERLY PEOPLE *sit here and there, talking.*

A WOMAN   [*Joins a group that is seated on some logs of wood.*]
     The bride? Oh yes, she is crying a bit;
     But that, you know, isn't worth heeding.
THE KITCHEN-MASTER   [*In another group.*]
     Now then, good folk, you must empty the barrel.
A MAN
     Thanks to you, friend; but you fill up too quick.
A LAD   [*To the* FIDDLER, *as he flies past, holding a* GIRL *by the hand.*]
     To it now, Guttorm, and don't spare the fiddle-strings!

*A somewhat violent peasant dance. (Translator's note)
†Foss (in the North of England "force")—a waterfall. (Translator's note)
‡A sort of master of ceremonies. (Translator's note)

THE GIRL

    Scrape till it echoes out over the meadows!

OTHER GIRLS   [*Standing in a ring round a lad who is dancing.*]

    That's a rare fling!

A GIRL

    He has legs that can lift him!

THE LAD   [*Dancing.*]

    The roof here is high,* and the walls wide asunder.

THE BRIDEGROOM   [*Comes whimpering up to his* FATHER, *who is standing talking with some other men, and twitches his jacket.*]

    Father, she will not; she is so proud!

HIS FATHER

    What won't she do?

THE BRIDEGROOM

    She has locked herself in.

HIS FATHER

    Well, you must manage to find the key.

THE BRIDEGROOM

    I don't know how.

HIS FATHER

    You're a nincompoop!

    [*Turns away to the others. The* BRIDEGROOM *drifts across the yard.*]

A LAD

    [*Comes from behind the house.*]

    Wait a bit, girls! Things'll soon be lively!

    Here comes Peer Gynt.

THE SMITH   [*Who has just come up.*]

    Who invited him?

THE KITCHEN-MASTER

    No one.

    [*Goes towards the house.*]

THE SMITH   [*To the girls.*]

    If he should speak to you, never take notice!

---

*To kick the rafters is considered a great feat in the Halling dance. The boy means that, in the open air, his leaps are not limited even by the rafters. (Translator's note)

A GIRL   [*To the others.*]
> No, we'll pretend that we don't even see him.

PEER GYNT   [*Comes in heated and full of animation, stops right in front of the group, and claps his hands.*]
> Which is the liveliest girl of the lot of you?

A GIRL   [*As he approaches her.*]
> I am not.

ANOTHER   [*Similarly.*]
> I am not.

A THIRD
> No; nor I either.

PEER   [*To a fourth.*]
> You come along, then, for want of a better.

THE GIRL
> Haven't got time.

PEER   [*To a fifth.*]
> Well then, you!

THE GIRL   [*Going.*]
> I'm for home.

PEER
> To-night? are you utterly out of your senses?*

THE SMITH   [*After a moment, in a low voice.*]
> See, Peer, she's taken a greybeard for partner.

PEER   [*Turns sharply to an elderly man.*]
> Where are the unbespoke girls?

THE MAN
> Find them out.
> [*Goes away from him.*]

PEER GYNT *has suddenly become subdued. He glances shyly and furtively at the group. All look at him, but no one speaks. He approaches other groups. Wherever he goes there is silence; when he moves away they look after him and smile.*

*A marriage party among the peasants will often last several days. (Translator's note)

PEER   [*To himself.*]
   Mocking looks; needle-keen whispers* and smiles.
   They grate like a sawblade under the file!
   [*He slinks along close to the fence.* SOLVEIG, *leading little* HELGA *by
   the hand, comes into the yard, along with her* PARENTS.]
A MAN   [*To another, close to* PEER GYNT.]
   Look, here are the new folk.
THE OTHER
   The ones from the west?
THE FIRST MAN
   Ay, the people from Hedal.
THE OTHER
   Ah yes, so they are.
PEER   [*Places himself in the path of the new-comers, points to* SOLVEIG,
   and asks the FATHER:]
   May I dance with your daughter?
THE FATHER   [*Quietly.*]
   You may so; but first
   We must go to the farm-house and greet the good people.
   [*They go in.*]
THE KITCHEN-MASTER   [*To* PEER GYNT, *offering him drink.*]
   Since you are here, you'd best take a pull at the liquor.
PEER   [*Looking fixedly after the new-comers.*]
   Thanks; I'm for dancing; I am not athirst.
   [*The* KITCHEN-MASTER *goes away from him.* PEER GYNT *gazes
   towards the house and laughs.*]
   How fair! Did ever you see the like!
   Looked down at her shoes and her snow-white apron—!
   And then she held on to her mother's skirt-folds,
   And carried a psalm-book wrapped up in a kerchief—!
   I must look at that girl.
   [*Going into the house.*]
A LAD   [*Coming out of the house, with several others.*]
   Are you off so soon, Peer,
   From the dance?
PEER
   No, no.

*Literally, "thoughts." (Translator's note)

THE LAD

> Then you're heading amiss!
>
> [*Takes hold of his shoulder to turn him round.*]

PEER

> Let me pass!

THE LAD

> I believe you're afraid of the smith.

PEER

> I afraid!

THE LAD

> You remember what happened at Lundë?
>
> [*They go off, laughing, to the dancing-green.*]

SOLVEIG

> [*In the doorway of the house.*]
>
> Are you not the lad that was wanting to dance?

PEER

> Of course it was me; don't you know me again?
>
> [*Takes her hand.*]
>
> Come, then!

SOLVEIG

> We mustn't go far, mother said.

PEER

> Mother said! Mother said! Were you born yesterday?*

SOLVEIG

> Now you're laughing———!

PEER

> Why sure, you are almost a child.
>
> Are you grown up?

SOLVEIG

> I read with the pastor last spring.†

PEER

> Tell me your name, lass, and then we'll talk easier.

SOLVEIG

> My name is Solveig. And what are you called?

---

*Literally, "last year." (Translator's note)

†"To read with the pastor," the preliminary to confirmation, is currently used as synonymous with "to be confirmed." (Translator's note)

PEER

Peer Gynt.

SOLVEIG   [*Withdrawing her hand.*]

Oh heaven!

PEER

Why, what is it now?

SOLVEIG

My garter is loose; I must tie it up tighter.

[*Goes away from him.*]

THE BRIDEGROOM   [*Pulling at his* MOTHER's *gown.*]

Mother, she will not——!

HIS MOTHER

She will not? What?

THE BRIDEGROOM

She won't, mother——

HIS MOTHER

What?

THE BRIDEGROOM

Unlock the door.

HIS FATHER   [*Angrily, below his breath.*]

Oh, you're only fit to be tied in a stall.

HIS MOTHER

Don't scold him. Poor dear, he'll be all right yet.

[*They move away.*]

A LAD   [*Coming with a whole crowd of others from the dancing-green.*]

Peer, have some brandy?

PEER

No.

THE LAD

Only a drain?

PEER   [*Looking darkly at him.*]

Got any?

THE LAD

Well, I won't say but I have.

[*Pulls out a pocket flask and drinks.*]

Ah! How it stings your throat!—Well?

PEER

Let me try it.

[*Drinks.*]

ANOTHER LAD

Now you must try mine as well, you know.

PEER

No!

THE LAD

Oh, what nonsense; now don't be a fool.

Take a pull, Peer!

PEER

Well then, give me a drop.

[*Drinks again.*]

A GIRL　　[*Half aloud.*]

Come, let's be going.

PEER

Afraid of me, wench?

A THIRD LAD

Who isn't afraid of you?

A FOURTH

At Lundë

You showed us clearly what tricks you could play.

PEER

I can do more than that, when I once get started.

THE FIRST LAD　　[*Whispering.*]

Now he's forging ahead!

SEVERAL OTHERS　　[*Forming a circle around him.*]

Tell away! Tell away!

What can you——?

PEER

To-morrow!

OTHERS

No, now, to-night!

A GIRL

Can you conjure, Peer?

PEER

I can call up the devil!

A MAN

My grandam could do that before I was born!

PEER

Liar! What *I* can do, that no one else can.

I one day conjured him into a nut.

It was worm-bored, you see!

SEVERAL   [*Laughing.*]

Ay, that's easily guessed!

PEER

He cursed, and he wept, and he wanted to bribe me

With all sorts of things——

ONE OF THE CROWD

But he had to go in?

PEER

Of course. I stopped up the hole with a peg.

Hei! If you'd heard him rumbling and grumbling!

A GIRL

Only think!

PEER

It was just like a bumble-bee buzzing.

THE GIRL

Have you got him still in the nut?

PEER

Why, no;

By this time that devil has flown on his way.

The grudge the smith bears me is all his doing.

A LAD

Indeed?

PEER

I went to the smithy, and begged

That he would crack that same nutshell for me.

He promised he would!——laid it down on his anvil;

But Aslak, you know, is so heavy of hand;——

For ever swinging that great sledge-hammer——

A VOICE FROM THE CROWD

Did he kill the foul fiend?

PEER

He laid on like a man.

But the devil showed fight, and tore off in a flame

Through the roof, and shattered the wall asunder.

SEVERAL VOICES
>And the smith———?

PEER
>Stood there with his hands all scorched.
>And from that day onwards, we've never been friends.
>[*General laughter.*]

SOME OF THE CROWD
>That yarn is a good one.

OTHERS
>About his best.

PEER
>Do you think I am making it up?

A MAN
>Oh no,
>That you're certainly not; for I've heard the most on't
>From my grandfather———

PEER
>Liar! It happened to me.

THE MAN
>Yes, like everything else.

PEER   [*With a fling.*]
>I can ride, I can,
>Clean through the air, on the bravest of steeds!
>Oh, many's the thing I can do, I tell you!
>[*Another roar of laughter.*]

ONE OF THE GROUP
>Peer, ride through the air a bit!

MANY
>Do, dear Peer Gynt———!

PEER
>You may spare you the trouble of begging so hard.
>I will ride like a hurricane over you all!
>Every man in the parish shall fall at my feet!

AN ELDERLY MAN
>Now he is clean off his head.

ANOTHER
>The dolt!

A THIRD

    Braggart!

A FOURTH

    Liar!

PEER   [*Threatening them.*]

    Ay, wait till you see!

A MAN   [*Half drunk.*]

    Ay, wait; you'll soon get your jacket dusted!

OTHERS

    Your back beaten tender! Your eyes painted blue!

    [*The crowd disperses, the elder men angry, the younger laughing and jeer-ing.*]

THE BRIDEGROOM   [*Close to* PEER GYNT.]

    Peer, is it true you can ride through the air?

PEER   [*Shortly.*]

    It's all true, Mads! You must know I'm a rare one!

THE BRIDEGROOM

    Then have you got the Invisible Cloak too?

PEER

    The Invisible Hat, do you mean? Yes, I have.

    [*Turns away from him.* SOLVEIG *crosses the yard, leading little* HELGA.]

PEER   [*Goes towards them; his face lights up.*]

    Solveig! Oh, it is well you have come!

    [*Takes hold of her wrist.*]

    Now will I swing you round fast and fine!

SOLVEIG

    Loose me!

PEER

    Wherefore?

SOLVEIG

    You are so wild.

PEER

    The reindeer is wild, too, when summer is dawning.

    Come then, lass; do not be wayward now!

SOLVEIG   [*Withdrawing her arm.*]

    Dare not.

PEER
> Wherefore?

SOLVEIG
> No, you've been drinking.
> [*Moves off with* HELGA.]

PEER
> Oh, if I had but my knife-blade driven
> Clean through the heart of them,—one and all!

THE BRIDEGROOM   [*Nudging him with his elbow.*]
> Peer, can't you help me to get at the bride?

PEER   [*Absently.*]
> The bride? Where is she?

THE BRIDEGROOM
> In the store-house.

PEER
> Ah.

THE BRIDEGROOM
> Oh, dear Peer Gynt, you must try at least!

PEER
> No, you must get on without my help.
> [*A thought strikes him; he says softly but sharply:*]
> Ingrid! The store-house!
> [*Goes up to* SOLVEIG.]
> Have you thought better on't?
> [SOLVEIG *tries to go; he blocks her path.*]
> You're ashamed to, because I've the look of a tramp.

SOLVEIG   [*Hastily.*]
> No, that you haven't; that's not true at all!

PEER
> Yes! And I've taken a drop as well;
> But that was to spite you, because you had hurt me.
> Come then!

SOLVEIG
> Even if I wished to, I daren't.

PEER
> Who are you frightened of?

SOLVEIG
> Father, most.

PEER

> Father? Ay, ay; he is one of the quiet ones!
> One of the godly, eh?—Answer, come!

SOLVEIG

> What shall I say?

PEER

> Is your father a psalm-singer?*
> And you and your mother as well, no doubt?
> Come, will you speak?

SOLVEIG

> Let me go in peace.

PEER

> No!
>
> [*In a low but sharp and threatening tone.*]
> I can turn myself into a troll!
> I'll come to your bedside at midnight to-night.
> If you should hear some one hissing and spitting,
> You mustn't imagine it's only the cat.
> It's me, lass! I'll drain out your blood in a cup,
> And your little sister, I'll eat her up;
> Ay, you must know I'm a were-wolf at night;—
> I'll bite you all over the loins and the back——
> [*Suddenly changes his tone, and entreats, as if in dread:*]
> Dance with me, lass!

SOLVEIG　　[*Looking darkly at him.*]

> You were ugly then.
> [*Goes into the house.*]

THE BRIDEGROOM　　[*Comes sidling up again.*]

> I'll give you an ox if you'll help me!

PEER

> Then come!
> [*They go out behind the house. At the same moment a crowd of men come forward from the dancing green; most of them are drunk. Noise and hubbub. SOLVEIG, HELGA, and their PARENTS appear among a number of elderly people in the doorway.*]

---

*Literally, "a reader." (Translator's note)

THE KITCHEN-MASTER [*To the* SMITH, *who is the foremost of the crowd.*]
    Keep peace now!

THE SMITH [*Pulling off his jacket.*]
    No, we must fight it out here.*
    Peer Gynt or I must be taught a lesson.†

SOME VOICES
    Ay, let them fight for it!

OTHERS
    No, only wrangle!

THE SMITH
    Fists must decide; for the case is past words.

SOLVEIG'S FATHER
    Control yourself, man!

HELGA
    Will they beat him, mother?

A LAD
    Let us rather taunt him with all his lies.

ANOTHER
    Kick him out of the company.

A THIRD
    Spit in his eyes.

A FOURTH [*To the* SMITH.]
    You're not backing out, smith?

THE SMITH [*Flinging away his jacket.*]
    The jade shall be slaughtered!

SOLVEIG'S MOTHER [*To* SOLVEIG.]
    There, you can see how that windbag is thought of.

ÅSE [*Coming up with a stick in her hand.*]
    Is that son of mine here? Now he's in for a drubbing!
    Oh! how heartily I will dang him!

THE SMITH [*Rolling up his shirt-sleeves.*]
    That switch is too light for a carcase like his.

SOME OF THE CROWD
    The smith will dang him!

---

*Literally, "Here shall judgment be called for." (Translator's note)

†Literally, "Must be bent to the hillside," made to bite the dust—but not in the sense of being killed. (Translator's note)

OTHERS
  Bang him!
THE SMITH   [*Spits on his hands and nods to* ÅSE.]
  Hang him!
ÅSE
  What? Hang my Peer? Ay, just try if you dare;—
  Åse and I,* we have teeth and claws!—
  Where is he?
  [*Calls across the yard.*]
  Peer!
THE BRIDEGROOM   [*Comes running up.*]
  Oh, God's death on the cross!
  Come father, come mother, and——
HIS FATHER
  What is the matter?
THE BRIDEGROOM
  Just fancy, Peer Gynt——!
ÅSE   [*Screams.*]
  Have you taken his life?
THE BRIDEGROOM
  No, but Peer Gynt——! Look, there on the hillside——!
THE CROWD
  With the bride.
ÅSE   [*Lets her stick sink.*]
  Oh, the beast!
THE SMITH   [*As if thunderstruck.*]
  Where the slope rises sheerest
  He's clambering upwards, by God, like a goat!
THE BRIDEGROOM   [*Crying.*]
  He's shouldered her, mother, as I might a pig!
ÅSE   [*Shaking her fist up at him.*]
  Would God you might fall, and——!
  [*Screams out in terror.*]
  Take care of your footing!
THE HEGSTAD FARMER   [*Comes in, bare-headed and white with rage.*]
  I'll have his life for this bride-rape yet!
ÅSE
  Oh no, God punish me if I let you!

---

*A peasant idiom. (Translator's note)

ACT SECOND

SCENE FIRST

A narrow path, high up in the mountains. Early morning.

PEER GYNT *comes hastily and sullenly along the path.* INGRID, *still wearing some of her bridal ornaments, is trying to hold him back.*

PEER
    Get you from me!
INGRID   [*Weeping.*]
    After this, Peer?
    Whither?
PEER
    Where you will for me.
INGRID   [*Wringing her hands.*]
    Oh, what falsehood!
PEER
    Useless railing
    Each alone must go his way.
INGRID
    Sin—and sin again unites us!
PEER
    Devil take all recollections!
    Devil take the tribe of women—
    All but one——!
INGRID
    Who is that one, pray?
PEER
    'Tis not you.
INGRID
    Who is it then?

PEER

> Go! Go thither whence you came!
> Off! To your father!

INGRID

> Dearest, sweetest——

PEER

> Peace!

INGRID

> You cannot mean it, surely,
> What you're saying?

PEER

> Can and do.

INGRID

> First to lure——and then forsake me!

PEER

> And what terms have you to offer?

INGRID

> Hegstad Farm, and more besides.

PEER

> Is your psalm-book in your kerchief?
> Where's the gold-mane on your shoulders?
> Do you glance adown your apron?
> Do you hold your mother's skirt-fold?
> Speak!

INGRID

> No, but——

PEER

> Went you to the Pastor*
> This last spring-tide?

INGRID

> No, but Peer——

PEER

> Is there shyness in your glances?
> When I beg, can you deny?

INGRID

> Heaven! I think his wits are going.

*See note p. 33. (Translator's note)

PEER
> Does your presence sanctify?*
> Speak!

INGRID
> No, but——

PEER
> What's all the rest then?
> [*Going.*]

INGRID   [*Blocking his way.*]
> Know you it will cost your neck
> Should you fail me?

PEER
> What do I care?

INGRID
> You may win both wealth and honour
> If you take me——

PEER
> Can't afford.

INGRID   [*Bursting into tears.*]
> Oh, you lured me——!

PEER
> You were willing.

INGRID
> I was desperate!

PEER
> Frantic I.

INGRID   [*Threatening.*]
> Dearly shall you pay for this!

PEER
> Dearest payment cheap I'll reckon.

INGRID
> Is your purpose set?

PEER
> Like flint.

---

*Blir der Helg når en dig ser?——literally, "Does it become a holy-day (or holy-tide) when one sees you?" (Translator's note)

INGRID

Good! we'll see, then, who's the winner!

[*Goes downwards.*]

PEER   [*Stands silent a moment, then cries:*]

Devil take all recollections!

Devil take the tribe of women!

INGRID   [*Turning her head, and calling mockingly upwards:*]

All but one!

PEER

Yes, all but one.

[*They go their several ways.*]

SCENE SECOND

Near a mountain tarn; the ground is soft and marshy round about. A
storm is gathering.

ÅSE *enters, calling and gazing around her despairingly, in every direction.*
SOLVEIG *has difficulty in keeping up with her.* SOLVEIG'S FATHER *and*
MOTHER, *with* HELGA, *are some way behind.*

ÅSE   [*Tossing about her arms, and tearing her hair.*]

All things are against me with wrathful might!

Heaven, and the waters, and the grisly mountains!

Fog-scuds from heaven roll down to bewilder him!

The treacherous waters are lurking to murder him!

The mountains would crush him with landslip and rift!—

And the people too! They're out after his life!

God knows they shan't have it! I can't bear to lose him!

Oh, the oaf! to think that the fiend should tempt him!

[*Turning to* SOLVEIG.]

Now isn't it clean unbelievable this?

He, that did nought but romance and tell lies;—

He, whose sole strength was the strength of his jaw;

He, that did never a stroke of true work;—

He——! Oh, a body could both cry and laugh!—

Oh, we clung closely in sorrow and need.

Ay, you must know that my husband, he drank,

Loafed round the parish to roister and prate,
Wasted and trampled our gear under foot.
And meanwhile at home there sat Peerkin and I—
The best we could do was to try to forget;
For ever I've found it so hard to bear up.
It's a terrible thing to look fate in the eyes;
And of course one is glad to be quit of one's cares,
And try all one can to hold thinking aloof.
Some take to brandy, and others to lies;
And we—why we took to fairy-tales
Of princes and trolls and of all sorts of beasts;
And of bride-rapes as well. Ah, but who could have dreamt
That those devil's yarns would have stuck in his head?
[*In a fresh access of terror*].
Hu! What a scream! It's the nixie or droug!*
Peer! Peer!—Up there on that hillock———!
[*She runs to the top of a little rise, and looks out over the tarn.* SOLVEIG'S
FATHER *and* MOTHER *come up.*]

ÅSE
Not a sign to be seen!

THE FATHER   [*Quietly.*]
It is worst for him!

ÅSE   [*Weeping.*]
Oh, my Peer! Oh, my own lost lamb!

THE FATHER   [*Nods mildly.*]
You may well say lost.

ÅSE
Oh no, don't talk like that!
He is so clever. There's no one like him.

THE FATHER
You foolish woman!

ÅSE
Oh ay; oh ay;
Foolish I am, but the boy's all right!

THE FATHER   [*Still softly and with mild eyes.*]
His heart is hardened, his soul is lost.

*A malevolent water-monster. (Translator's note)

ÅSE [*In terror.*]

    No, no, he can't be so hard, our Lord!

THE FATHER

    Do you think he can sigh for his debt of sin?

ÅSE [*Eagerly.*]

    No, but he can ride through the air on a buck, though!

THE MOTHER

    Christ, are you mad?

THE FATHER

    Why, what do you mean?

ÅSE

    Never a deed is too great for him.

    You shall see, if only he lives so long——

THE FATHER

    Best if you saw him on the gallows hanging.

ÅSE [*Shrieks.*]

    Oh, cross of Christ!

THE FATHER

    In the hangman's hands,

    It may be his heart would be turned to repentance.

ÅSE [*Bewildered.*]

    Oh, you'll soon talk me out of my senses!

    We must find him!

THE FATHER

    To rescue his soul.

ÅSE

    And his body!

    If he's stuck in the swamp, we must drag him out;

    If he's taken by trolls, we must ring the bells for him.

THE FATHER

    H'm!——Here's a sheep-path——

ÅSE

    The Lord will repay you

    Your guidance and help!

THE FATHER

    It's a Christian's duty.

ÅSE

    Then the others, fie! they are heathens all;

    There was never a one that would go with us——

THE FATHER
> They knew him too well.

ÅSE
> He was too good for them!
> [*Wrings her hands.*]
> And to think—and to think that his life is at stake!

THE FATHER
> Here are tracks of a man.

ÅSE
> Then it's here we must search!

THE FATHER
> We'll scatter around on this side of our sæter.*
> [*He and his wife go on ahead.*]

SOLVEIG   [*To* ÅSE.]
> Say on; tell me more.

ÅSE   [*Drying her eyes.*]
> Of my son, you mean?

SOLVEIG
> Yes;—
> Tell everything!

ÅSE   [*Smiles and tosses her head.*]
> Everything?—Soon you'd be tired!

SOLVEIG
> Sooner by far will you tire of the telling
> Than I of the hearing.

SCENE THIRD

> *Low, treeless heights, close under the mountain moorlands; peaks in the*
> *distance. The shadows are long; it is late in the day.*

PEER GYNT *comes running at full speed, and stops short on the hillside.*

PEER
> The parish is all at my heels in a pack!
> Every man of them armed or with gun or with club.

---

*Sæter—a châlet, or small mountain farm, where the cattle are sent to pasture
in the summer months. (Translator's note)

Foremost I hear the old Hegstad-churl howling.—
Now it's noised far and wide that Peer Gynt is abroad!
It is different, this, from a bout with a smith!
This is life! Every limb grows as strong as a bear's.
[*Strikes out with his arms and leaps in the air.*]
To crush, overturn, stem the rush of the foss!*
To strike! Wrench the fir-tree right up by the root!
This is life! This both hardens and lifts one high!
To hell then with all of the savourless lies!

THREE SÆTER GIRLS   [*Rush across the hillside, screaming and singing.*]
Trond of the Valfjeld! Bård and Kårë!
Troll-pack! To-night would you sleep in our arms?

PEER
To whom do you call?

THE GIRLS
To the trolls! to the trolls!

FIRST GIRL
Trond, come with kindness!

SECOND GIRL
Bård, come with force!

THIRD GIRL
The cots in the sæter are all standing empty!

FIRST GIRL
Force is kindness!

SECOND GIRL
And kindness is force!

THIRD GIRL
If lads are awanting, one plays with the trolls.

PEER
Why, where are the lads, then?

ALL THREE   [*With a horse-laugh.*]
They cannot come hither.

FIRST GIRL
Mine called me his sweetheart and called me his darling.
Now he has married a grey-headed widow.

*Foss (in the North of England "force")—a waterfall. (Translator's note)

SECOND GIRL

    Mine met a gipsy-wench north on the upland.

    Now they are tramping the country together.

THIRD GIRL

    Mine put an end to our bastard brat.

    Now his head's grinning aloft on a stake.

ALL THREE

    Trond of the Valfjeld! Bård and Kårë!

    Troll-pack! To-night would you sleep in our arms?

PEER   [*Stands, with a sudden leap, in the midst of them.*]

    I'm a three-headed troll, and the boy for three girls!

THE GIRLS

    Are you such a lad, eh?

PEER

    You shall judge for yourselves!

FIRST GIRL

    To the hut! To the hut!

SECOND GIRL

    We have mead!

PEER

    Let it flow!

THIRD GIRL

    No cot shall stand empty this Saturday night!

SECOND GIRL   [*Kissing him.*]

    He sparkles and glisters like white-heated iron.

THIRD GIRL   [*Doing likewise.*]

    Like a baby's eyes from the blackest tarn.

PEER   [*Dancing in the midst of them.*]

    Heavy of heart and wanton of mind.

    The eyes full of laughter, the throat of tears!

THE GIRLS   [*Making mocking gestures towards the mountain-tops, screaming and singing.*]

    Trond of the Valfjeld! Bård and Kårë!

    Troll-pack!—To-night who shall sleep in our arms?

    [*They dance away over the heights, with* PEER GYNT *in their midst.*]

SCENE FOURTH

Among the Rondë mountains. Sunset. Shining snow-peaks all around.

PEER GYNT *enters, dizzy and bewildered.*

PEER

    Tower over tower arises!
    Hei, what a glittering gate!
    Stand! Will you stand! It's drifting
    Further and further away!
    High on the vane the wind-cock
    Arches his wings for flight;——
    Blue spread the rifts and bluer,
    Locked is the fell and barred.——
    What are those trunks and tree-roots,
    That grow from the ridge's clefts?
    They are warriors heron-footed!
    Now they, too, are fading away.
    A shimmering like rainbow-streamers
    Goes shooting through eyes and brain.
    What is it, that far-off chiming?
    What's weighing my eyebrows down?
    Hu, how my forehead's throbbing—
    A tightening red-hot ring——!
    I cannot think who the devil
    Has bound it around my head!
    [*Sinks down.*]
    Flight o'er the Edge of Gendin—
    Stuff and accursed lies!
    Up o'er the steepest hill-wall
    With the bride,—and a whole day drunk;
    Hunted by hawks and falcons,
    Threatened by trolls and such,
    Sporting with crazy wenches:——
    Lies and accursed stuff!
    [*Gazes long upwards.*]
    Yonder sail two brown eagles.

Southward the wild geese fly.
And here I must splash and stumble
In quagmire and filth knee-deep!
[*Springs up.*]
I'll fly too! I will wash myself clean in
The bath of the keenest winds!
I'll fly high! I will plunge myself fair in
The glorious christening-font!
I will soar far over the sæter;
I will ride myself pure of soul;
I will forth o'er the salt sea waters,
And high over Engelland's prince!
Ay, gaze as ye may, young maidens;
My ride is for none of you;
You're wasting your time in waiting—!
Yet maybe I'll swoop down, too.—
What has come of the two brown eagles—?
They've vanished, the devil knows where!—
There's the peak of a gable rising;
It's soaring on every hand;
It's growing from out the ruins;—
See, the gateway is standing wide!
Ha-ha, yonder house, I know it;
It's grandfather's new-built farm!
Gone are the clouts from the windows;
The crazy old fence is gone.
The lights gleam from every casement;
There's a feast in the hall to-night.
There, that was the provost clinking
The back of his knife on his glass;—
There's the captain flinging his bottle,
And shivering the mirror to bits.—
Let them waste; let it all be squandered!
Peace, mother; what need we care!
'Tis the rich Jon Gynt gives the banquet;
Hurrah for the race of Gynt!
What's all this bustle and hubbub?
Why do they shout and bawl?

The captain is calling the son in;——
Oh, the provost would drink my health.
In then, Peer Gynt, to the judgment;
It rings forth in song and shout:
Peer Gynt, thou art come of great things,
And great things shall come of thee!
[*Leaps forward, but runs his head against a rock, falls, and remains stretched on the ground.*]

SCENE FIFTH

A hillside, wooded with great soughing trees. Stars are gleaming through the leaves; birds are singing in the tree-tops.

A GREEN-CLAD WOMAN *is crossing the hillside;* PEER GYNT *follows her, with all sorts of lover-like antics.*

THE GREEN-CLAD ONE   [*Stops and turns round.*]
    Is it true?
PEER   [*Drawing his finger across his throat.*]
    As true as my name is Peer;——
    As true as that you are a lovely woman!
    Will you have me? You'll see what a fine man I'll be;
    You shall neither tread the loom nor turn the spindle.
    You shall eat all you want, till you're ready to burst.
    I never will drag you about by the hair——
THE GREEN-CLAD ONE
    Nor beat me!
PEER
    No, can you think I would!
    We kings' sons never beat women and such.
THE GREEN-CLAD ONE
    You're a king's son.
PEER
    Yes.
THE GREEN-CLAD ONE
    I'm the Dovrë-King's daughter.

PEER

> Are you! See there, now, how well that fits in!

THE GREEN-CLAD ONE

> Deep in the Rondë has father his palace.

PEER

> My mother's is bigger, or much I'm mistaken.

THE GREEN-CLAD ONE

> Do you know my father? His name is King Brosë.

PEER

> Do you know my mother? Her name is Queen Åsë.

THE GREEN-CLAD ONE

> When my father is angry the mountains are riven.

PEER

> They reel when my mother by chance falls a-scolding.

THE GREEN-CLAD ONE

> My father can kick e'en the loftiest roof-tree.*

PEER

> My mother can ride through the rapidest river.

THE GREEN-CLAD ONE

> Have you other garments besides those rags?

PEER

> Ho, you should just see my Sunday clothes!

THE GREEN-CLAD ONE

> My week-day gown is of gold and silk.

PEER

> It looks to me liker tow and straws.

THE GREEN-CLAD ONE

> Ay, there is one thing you must remember:—
> This is the Rondë-folk's use and wont:
> All our possessions have two-fold form.
> When shall you come to my father's hall,
> It well may chance that you're on the point
> Of thinking you stand in a dismal moraine.

PEER

> Well now, with us its precisely the same.

---

*Kicking the rafters is a much-admired exploit in peasant dancing. See note, p. 30. (Translator's note)

Our gold will seem to you litter and trash!
And you'll think, mayhap, every glittering pane
Is nought but a bunch of old stockings and clouts.
THE GREEN-CLAD ONE
Black t seems white, and ugly seems fair.
PEER
Big it seems little, and dirty seems clean.
THE GREEN-CLAD ONE   [*Falling on his neck.*]
Ay, Peer, now I see that we fit, you and I!
PEER
Like the leg and the trouser, the hair and the comb.
THE GREEN-CLAD ONE   [*Calls away over the hillside.*]
Bridal-steed! Bridal-steed! Come, bridal-steed mine!
[*A gigantic pig comes running in with a rope's end for a bridle and an old sack for a saddle.* PEER GYNT *vaults on its back, and seats the* GREEN-CLAD ONE *in front of him.*]
PEER
Hark-away! Through the Rondë-gate gallop we in!
Gee-up, gee-up, my courser fine!
THE GREEN-CLAD ONE   [*Tenderly.*]
Ah, but lately I wandered and moped and pined—
One never can tell what may happen to one!
PEER   [*Thrashing the pig and trotting off.*]
You may know the great by their riding-gear.

Scene Sixth

The Royal Halt of the King of the Dovrë-Trolls. A great assembly of TROLL-COURTIERS, GNOMES, *and* BROWNIES. THE OLD MAN OF THE DOVRË *sits on the throne, crowned, and with his sceptre in his hand. His* CHILDREN *and* NEAREST RELATIONS *are ranged on both sides.* PEER GYNT *stands before him. Violent commotion in the hall.*

THE TROLL-COURTIERS
Slay him: a Christian-man's son has deluded
The Dovrë-King's loveliest maid!

A TROLL-IMP
>May I hack him on the fingers?

ANOTHER
>May I tug him by the hair?

A TROLL-MAIDEN
>Hu, hei, let me bite him in the haunches!

A TROLL-WITCH   [*With a ladle.*]
>Shall he be boiled into broth and bree?

ANOTHER TROLL-WITCH   [*With a chopper.*]
>Shall he roast on a spit or be browned in a stewpan?

THE OLD MAN OF THE DOVRË
>Ice to your blood, friends!
>[*Beckons his counsellors closer around him.*]
>Don't let us talk big.
>We've been drifting astern in these latter years;
>We can't tell what's going to stand or to fall,
>And there's no sense in turning recruits away.
>Besides the lad's body has scarce a blemish,
>And he's strongly-built too, if I see aright.
>It's true, he has only a single head;
>But my daughter, too, has no more than one.
>Three-headed trolls are gone clean out of fashion;
>One hardly sees even a two-header now,
>And even those heads are but so-so ones.
>[*To* PEER GYNT.]
>It's my daughter, then, you demand of me?

PEER
>Your daughter and the realm to her dowry, yes.

THE OLD MAN
>You shall have the half while I'm still alive,
>And the other half when I come to die.

PEER
>I'm content with that.

THE OLD MAN
>Ay, but stop, my lad;——
>You also have some undertakings to give.
>If you break even one, the whole pact's at an end,
>And you'll never get away from here living.

First of all you must swear that you'll never give heed
To aught that lies outside the Rondë-hills' bounds;
Day you must shun, and deeds, and each sunlit spot.

PEER
Only call me king, and that's easy to keep.

THE OLD MAN
And next—now for putting your wits to the test.
[*Draws himself up in his seat.*]

THE OLDEST TROLL-COURTIER [*To* PEER GYNT.]
Let us see if you have a wisdom-tooth
That can crack the Dovrë-King's riddle-nut!

THE OLD MAN
What difference is there 'twixt trolls and men?

PEER
No difference at all, as it seems to me.
Big trolls would roast you and small trolls would claw you;—
With us it were likewise, if only they dared.

THE OLD MAN
True enough; in that and in more we're alike.
Yet morning is morning, and even is even,
And there is a difference all the same.—
Now let me tell you wherein it lies:
Out yonder, under the shining vault,
Among men the saying goes: "Man, be thyself!"
At home here with us, 'mid the tribe of the trolls,
The saying goes: "Troll, to thyself be—enough!"

THE TROLL-COURTIER [*To* PEER GYNT.]
Can you fathom the depth?

PEER
It strikes me as misty.

THE OLD MAN
My son, that "Enough," that most potent and sundering
Word, must be graven upon your escutcheon.

PEER [*Scratching his head.*]
Well, but——

THE OLD MAN
It must, if you here would be master!

PEER

> Oh well, let it pass; after all, it's no worse——

THE OLD MAN

> And next you must learn to appreciate
> Our homely, everyday way of life.
> [*He beckons; two* TROLLS *with pigs'-heads, white night-caps, and so
> forth, bring in food and drink.*]
> The cow gives cakes and the bullock mead;
> Ask not if its taste be sour or sweet;
> The main matter is, and you mustn't forget it,
> It's all of it home-brewed.

PEER   [*Pushing the things away from him.*]

> The devil fly off with your home-brewed drinks
> I'll never get used to the ways of this land.

THE OLD MAN

> The bowl's given in, and it's fashioned of gold.
> Whoso own the gold bowl, him my daughter holds dear.

PEER   [*Pondering.*]

> It is written: Thou shalt bridle the natural man;——
> And I daresay the drink may in time seem less sour.
> So be it!
> [*Complies.*]

THE OLD MAN

> Ay, that was sagaciously said.
> You spit?

PEER

> One must trust to the force of habit.

THE OLD MAN

> And next you must throw off your Christian-man's garb;
> For this you must know to our Dovrë's renown:
> Here all things are mountain-made, nought's from the dale,
> Except the silk bow at the end of your tail.

PEER   [*Indignant.*]

> I haven't a tail!

THE OLD MAN

> Then of course you must get one.
> See my Sunday-tail, Chamberlain, fastened to him.

PEER

I'll be hanged if you do! Would you make me a fool?

THE OLD MAN

None comes courting my child with no tail at his rear.

PEER

Make a beast of a man!

THE OLD MAN

Nay, my son, you mistake;

I make you a mannerly wooer, no more.

A bright orange bow we'll allow you to wear,

And that passes here for the highest of honours.

PEER [Reflectively.]

It's true, as the saying goes: Man's but a mote.

And it's wisest to follow the fashion a bit.

Tie away!

THE OLD MAN

You're a tractable fellow, I see.

THE COURTIER

Just try with what grace you can waggle and whisk it!

PEER [Peevishly.]

Ha, would you force me to go still further?

Do you ask me to give up my Christian faith?

THE OLD MAN

No, that you are welcome to keep in peace.

Doctrine goes free; upon that there's no duty;

It's the outward cut one must tell a troll by.

If we're only at one in our manners and dress,

You may hold as your faith what to us is a horror.

PEER

Why, in spite of your many conditions, you are

A more reasonable chap than one might have expected.

THE OLD MAN

We troll-folk, my son, are less black than we're painted;*

That's another distinction between you and us.——

But the serious part of the meeting is over;

Now let us gladden our ears and our eyes.

*Literally, "Better than our reputation." (Translator's note)

Music-maid, forth! Set the Dovrë-harp sounding!
Dancing-maid, forth! Tread the Dovrë-hall's floor!
[*Music and a dance.*]

THE COURTIER
How like you it?

PEER
Like it? H'm——

THE OLD MAN
Speak without fear!
What see you?

PEER
Why something unspeakably grim:*
A bell-cow with her hoof on a gut-harp strumming.
A sow in socklets a-trip to the tune.

THE COURTIERS
Eat him!

THE OLD MAN
His sense is but human, remember!

TROLL-MAIDENS
Hu, tear away both his ears and his eyes!

THE GREEN-CLAD ONE   [*Weeping.*]
Hu-hu! And this we must hear and put up with,
When I and my sister make music and dance.

PEER
Oho, was it you? Well, a joke at the feast,
You must know, is never unkindly meant.

THE GREEN-CLAD ONE
Can you swear it was so?

PEER
Both the dance and the music
Were utterly charming, the cat claw me else.

THE OLD MAN
This same human nature's a singular thing;
It sticks to people so strangely long.

Ustyggelig stygt. Ustyggelig seems to be what Mr. Lewis Carroll calls a portmanteau word, compounded of *usigelig* ("unspeakable") and *styg* ("ugly"). The words
might be rendered "beyond grimness grim." (Translator's note)

If it gets a gash in the fight with us,
It heals up at once, though a scar may remain.
My son-in-law, now, is as pliant as any;
He's willingly thrown off his Christian-man's garb,
He's willingly drunk from our chalice of mead,
He's willingly fastened the tail to his back,—
So willing, in short, did we find him in all things,
I thought to myself the old Adam, for certain,
Had for good and all been kicked out of doors;
But lo! in two shakes he's atop again.
Ay ay, my son, we must treat you, I see,
To cure this pestilent human nature.

PEER

What will you do?

THE OLD MAN

In your left eye, first,
I'll scratch you a bit, till you see awry;
But all that you see will seem fine and brave.
And then I'll just cut your right window-pane out——

PEER

Are you drunk?

THE OLD MAN   [*Lays a number of sharp instruments on the table.*]

See, here are the glazier's tools.
Blinkers you'll wear, like a raging bull.
Then you'll recognise that your bride is lovely,—
And ne'er will your vision be troubled, as now,
With bell-cows harping and sows that dance.

PEER

This is madman's talk!

THE OLDEST COURTIER

It's the Dovrë-King speaking;
'Tis he that is wise, and 'tis you that are crazy!

THE OLD MAN

Just think how much worry and mortification
You'll thus escape from, year out, year in.
You must remember, your eyes are the fountain
Of the bitter and searing lye of tears.

PEER

> That's true; and it says in our sermon-book:
> If thine eye offend thee, then pluck it out.
> But tell me, when will my sight heal up
> Into human sight?

THE OLD MAN

> Nevermore, my friend.

PEER

> Indeed! In that case, I'll take my leave.

THE OLD MAN

> What would you without?

PEER

> I would go my way.

THE OLD MAN

> No, stop! It's easy to slip in here,
> But outward the Dovrë-King's gate opens not.

PEER

> You wouldn't detain me by force, I hope?

THE OLD MAN

> Come now, just listen to reason, Prince Peer!
> You have gifts for trolldom. He acts—does he not?—
> Even now in a passably troll-like fashion?
> And you'd fain be a troll?

PEER

> Yes, I would, sure enough.
> For a bride, and a well-managed kingdom to boot,
> I can put up with losing a good many things.
> But there is a limit to all things on earth.
> The tail I've accepted, it's perfectly true;
> But no doubt I can loose what the Chamberlain tied.
> My breeches I've dropped; they were old and patched;
> But no doubt I can button them on again.
> And lightly enough I can slip my cable
> From these your Dovrëfied ways of life.
> I am willing to swear that a cow is a maid;
> An oath one can always eat up again;—
> But to know that one never can free oneself,
> That one can't even die like a decent soul;

To live as a hill-troll for all one's days—
To feel that one never can beat a retreat,—
As the book has it, that's what your heart is set on;
But that is a thing I can never agree to.

THE OLD MAN

Now, sure as I live, I shall soon lose my temper;
And then I am not to be trifled with.
You pasty-faced loon! Do you know who I am?
First with my daughter you make too free——

PEER

There you lie in your throat!

THE OLD MAN

You must marry her.

PEER

Do you dare to accuse me——?

THE OLD MAN

What? Can you deny
That you lusted for her in heart and eye?

PEER   [*With a snort of contempt.*]

No more? Who the deuce cares a straw for that?

THE OLD MAN

It's ever the same with this humankind.
The spirit you're ready to own with your lips,
But in fact nothing counts that your fists cannot handle.
So you really think, then, that lust matters nought?
Wait; you shall soon have ocular proof of it——

PEER

You don't catch me with a bait of lies!

THE GREEN-CLAD ONE

My Peer, ere the year's out, your child will be born.

PEER

Open doors let me go!

THE OLD MAN

In a he-goat's skin,
You shall have the brat after you.

PEER   [*Mopping the sweat off his brow.*]

Would I could waken!

THE OLD MAN
>Shall we send him to the palace?

PEER
>You can send him to the parish!

THE OLD MAN
>Well well, Prince Peer; that's your own look-out.
>But one thing's certain, what's done is done;
>And your offspring, too, will be sure to grow;
>Such mongrels shoot up amazingly fast——

PEER
>Old man, don't act like a headstrong ox!
>Hear reason, maiden! Let's come to terms.
>You must know I'm neither a prince nor rich;——
>And whether you measure or whether you weigh me,
>Be sure you won't gain much by making me yours.
>[THE GREEN-CLAD ONE *is taken ill, and is carried out by* TROLL-MAIDS.]

THE OLD MAN   [*Looks at him for a while in high disdain; then says:*]
>Dash him to shards on the rock-walls, children!

THE TROLL-IMPS
>Oh dad, mayn't we play owl-and-eagle first!
>The wolf-game! Grey-mouse and glow-eyed cat!

THE OLD MAN
>Yes, but quick. I am worried and sleepy. Good-night!
>[*He goes.*]

PEER   [*Hunted by the* TROLL-IMPS.]
>Let me be, devil's imps!
>[*Tries to escape up the chimney.*]

THE IMPS
>Come brownies! Come nixies!
>Bite him behind!

PEER
>Ow!
>[*Tries to slip down the cellar trap-door.*]

THE IMPS
>Shut up all the crannies!

THE TROLL-COURTIER
>Now the small-fry are happy!

PEER   [*Struggling with a little* IMP *that has bit himself fast to his ear.*]
    Let go will you, beast!
THE COURTIER   [*Hitting him across the fingers.*]
    Gently, you scamp, with a scion of royalty!
PEER
    A rat-hole!——
    [*Runs to it.*]
THE IMPS
    Be quick, Brother Nixie, and block it!
PEER
    The old one was bad, but the youngsters are worse!
THE IMPS
    Slash him!
PEER
    Oh, would I were small as a mouse!
    [*Rushing around.*
THE IMPS   [*Swarming round him.*]
    Close the ring! Close the ring!
PEER   [*Weeping.*]
    Were I only a louse!
    [*He falls.*]
THE IMPS
    Now into his eyes!
PEER   [*Buried in a heap of* IMPS.]
    Mother, help me, I die!
    [*Church bells sound far away.*]
THE IMPS
    Bells in the mountain! The Black-Frock's cows!
    [THE TROLLS *take to flight, amid a confused uproar of yells and shrieks. The palace collapses; everything disappears.*]

SCENE SEVENTH

Pitch darkness.

PEER GYNT *is heard beating and slashing about him with a large bough.*

PEER
>   Answer! Who are you?

A VOICE IN THE DARKNESS
>   Myself.

PEER
>   Clear the way!

THE VOICE
>   Go roundabout, Peer! The hill's roomy enough.

PEER   [*Tries to force a passage at another place, but strikes against something.*]
>   Who are you?

THE VOICE
>   Myself. Can you say the same?

PEER
>   I can say what I will; and my sword can smite!
>   Mind yourself! Hu, hei, now the blow falls crushing!
>   King Saul slew hundreds; Peer Gynt slew thousands!
>   [*Cutting and slashing.*]
>   Who are you?

THE VOICE
>   Myself.

PEER
>   That stupid reply
>   You may spare; it doesn't clear up the matter.
>   What are you?

THE VOICE
>   The great Boyg.*

PEER
>   Ah, indeed!
>   The riddle was black; now I'd call it grey.
>   Clear the way then, Boyg!

THE VOICE
>   Go roundabout, Peer!

PEER
>   No, through!

---

*A mysteriously shaped great troll. Ibsen took Peer Gynt's encounter with the Boyg from the folktale "Peer Gynt and the Boyg."

[*Cuts and slashes.*]

There he fell!

[*Tries to advance, but strikes against something.*]

Ho ho, are there more here?

THE VOICE

The Boyg, Peer Gynt! the one and the only!

It's the Boyg that's unwounded, and the Boyg that was hurt,

Its the Boyg that is dead, and the Boyg that's alive.

PEER   [*Throws away the branch.*]

The weapon is troll-smeared;* but I have my fists!

[*Fights his way forward.*]

THE VOICE

Ay, trust to your fists, lad, trust to your body.

Hee-hee, Peer Gynt, so you'll reach the summit.

PEER   [*Falling back again.*]

Forward or back, and it's just as far;—

Out or in, and it's just as strait!

He is there! And there! And he's round the bend!

No sooner I'm out than I'm back in the ring.—

Name who you are! Let me see you! What are you?

THE VOICE

The Boyg.

PEER   [*Groping around.*]

Not dead, not living; all slimy; misty.

Not so much as a shape! It's as bad as to battle

In a cluster of snarling, half-wakened bears!

[*Screams.*]

Strike back at me, can't you!

THE VOICE

The Boyg isn't mad.

PEER

Strike!

THE VOICE

The Boyg strikes not.

PEER

Fight! You shall!

*Rendered harmless by magical anointing.

THE VOICE
>The great Boyg conquers, but does not fight.

PEER
>Were there only a nixie here that could prick me!
>Were there only as much as a year-old troll!
>Only something to fight with. But here there is nothing—
>Now he's snoring! Boyg!

THE VOICE
>What's your will?

PEER
>Use force!

THE VOICE
>The great Boyg conquers in all things without it.*

PEER   [*Biting his own arms and hands.*]
>Claws and ravening teeth in my flesh!
>I must feel the drip of my own warm blood.
>[*A sound is heard like the wing-strokes of great birds.*]

BIRD-CRIES
>Comes he now, Boyg?

THE VOICE
>Ay, step by step.

BIRD-CRIES
>All our sisters far off! Gather here to the tryst!

PEER
>If you'd save me now, lass, you must do it quick!
>Gaze not adown so, lowly and bending.—
>Your clasp-book! Hurl it straight into his eyes!

BIRD-CRIES
>He totters!

THE VOICE
>We have him.

BIRD-CRIES
>Sisters! Make haste!

PEER
>Too dear the purchase one pays for life

---

*Med lempe—literally, "by gentleness" or "easy-goingness." "Quiescence" is somewhere near the idea. (Translator's note)

In such a heart-wasting hour of strife.

[*Sinks down.*]

BIRD-CRIES

Boyg, there he's fallen! Seize him! Seize him!

[*A sound of bells and of psalm-singing is heard far away.*]

THE BOYG   [*Shrinks up to nothing, and says in a gasp:*]

He was too strong. There were women behind him.

SCENE EIGHTH

Sunrise. The mountain-side in front of ÅSE's *sæter.*
The door is shut; all is silent and deserted.

PEER GYNT *is lying asleep by the wall of the sæter.*

PEER   [*Wakens, and looks about him with dull and heavy eyes. He spits.*]

What wouldn't I give for a pickled herring!

[*Spits again, and at the same moment catches sight of* HELGA, *who appears carrying a basket of food.*]

Ha, child, are you there? What is it you want?

HELGA

It is Solveig——

PEER   [*Jumping up.*]

Where is she?

HELGA

Behind the sæter.

SOLVEIG   [*Unseen.*]

If you come nearer, I'll run away!

PEER   [*Stopping short.*]

Perhaps you're afraid I might take you in my arms?

SOLVEIG

For shame.

PEER

Do you know where I was last night?——

Like a horse-fly the Dovrë-King's daughter is after me.

SOLVEIG

Then it was well that the bells were set ringing.

PEER

Peer Gynt's not the lad they can lure astray.——
What do you say?

HELGA   [*Crying.*]

Oh, she's running away!
[*Running after her.*]
Wait!

PEER   [*Catches her by the arm.*]

Look here, what I have in my pocket.
A silver button, child! You shall have it,——
Only speak for me!

HELGA

Let me be; let me go!

PEER

There you have it.

HELGA

Let go; there's the basket of food.

PEER

God pity you if you don't——

HELGA

Uf, how you scare me!

PEER   [*Gently; letting her go.*]

No, I only meant: beg her not to forget me!
[HELGA *runs off.*]

ACT THIRD

SCENE FIRST

Deep in the pine-woods. Grey autumn weather. Snow is falling.

PEER GYNT stands in his shirt-sleeves, felling timber.

PEER   [Hewing at a large fir-tree with twisted branches.]
Oh ay, you are tough, you ancient churl;
But it's all in vain, for you'll soon be down.
[Hews at it again.]
I see well enough you've a chain-mail shirt,
But I'll hew it through, were it never so stout.——
Ay, ay, you're shaking your twisted arms;
You've reason enough for your spite and rage;
But none the less you must bend the knee——!
[Breaks off suddenly.]
Lies! 'Tis an old tree and nothing more.
Lies! It was never a steel-clad churl;
It's only a fir-tree with fissured bark.——
It is heavy labour this hewing timber;
But the devil and all when you hew and dream too.——
I'll have done with it all—with this dwelling in mist,
And, broad-awake, dreaming your senses away.——
You're an outlaw, lad! You are banned to the woods.
[Hews for a while rapidly.]
Ay, an outlaw, ay. You've no mother now
To spread your table and bring your food.
If you'd eat, my lad, you must help yourself,
Fetch your rations raw from the wood and stream,
Split your own fir-roots* and light your own fire,

*Tyri, resinous pine-wood which burns with a bright blaze. (Translator's note)

Bustle around, and arrange and prepare things.
Would you clothe yourself warmly you must stalk your deer;
Would you found you a house, you must quarry the stones;
Would you build up its walls, you must fell the logs,
And shoulder them all to the building-place.——
[*His axe sinks down; he gazes straight in front of him.*]
Brave shall the building be. Tower and vane
Shall rise from the roof-tree, high and fair.
And then I will carve, for the knob on the gable,
A mermaid, shaped like a fish from the navel.
Brass shall there be on the vane and the doorlocks.
Glass I must see and get hold of too.
Strangers, passing, shall ask amazed:
What is that glittering far on the hillside?
[*Laughs angrily.*]
Devil's own lies! There they come again.
You're an outlaw, lad!
[*Hewing vigorously.*]
A bark-thatched hovel
Is shelter enough both in rain and frost.
[*Looks up at the tree.*]
Now he stands wavering. There; only a kick,
And he topples and measures his length on the ground;——
The thick-swarming undergrowth shudders around him
[*Begins lopping the branches from the trunk; suddenly he listens, and
stands motionless with his axe in the air.*]
There's some one after me.——Ay, are you that sort,
Old Hegstad-churl; would you play me false?
[*Crouches behind the tree, and peeps over it.*]
A lad! One only. He seems afraid.
He peers all round him. What's that he hides
'Neath his jacket? A sickle. He stops and looks round,——
Now he lays his hand on a fence-rail flat.
What's this now? Why does he lean like that——?
Ugh, ugh! Why, he's chopped his finger off!
A whole finger off!——He bleeds like an ox.——
Now he takes to his heels with his fist in a clout.

[*Rises.*]
What a devil of a lad! An unmendable* finger!
Right off! And with no one compelling him to it!
Ho, now I remember! It's only thus
You can 'scape from having to serve the King.
That's it. They wanted to send him soldiering,
And of course the lad didn't want to go.——
But to chop off——? To sever for good and all——?
Ay, think of it—wish it done—will it to boot,—
But do it——! No, that's past my understanding!
[*Shakes his head a little; then goes on with his work.*]

SCENE SECOND

A room in ÅSE's house. Everything in disorder; boxes standing open; wearing apparel strewn around. A cat is lying on the bed.

ÅSE *and the* COTTAR'S WIFE *are hard at work packing things together and putting them straight.*

ÅSE   [*Running to one side.*]
    Kari, come here!
KARI
    What now?
ÅSE   [*On the other side.*]
    Come here——?
    Where is——? Where shall I find——? Tell me where——?
    What am I seeking? I'm out of my wits!
    Where is the key of the chest?
KARI
    In the key-hole.
ÅSE
    What is that rumbling?
KARI
    The last cart-load.

Umistelig—unlosable, indispensable, irreplaceable. (Translator's note)

They're driving to Hegstad.

ÅSE [*Weeping.*]

How glad I'd be
In the black chest myself to be driven away!
Oh, what must a mortal abide and live through!
God help me in mercy! The whole house is bare!
What the Hegstad-churl left now the Bailiff* has taken.
Not even the clothes on my back have they spared.
Fie! Shame on them all that have judged so hardly!
[*Seats herself on the edge of the bed.*]
Both the land and the farm-place are lost to our line;
The old man was hard, but the law was still harder;—
There was no one to help me, and none would show mercy;
Peer was away; not a soul to give counsel.

KARI

But here, in this house, you may dwell till you die.

ÅSE

Ay, the cat and I live on charity.

KARI

God help you, mother; your Peer's cost you dear.

ÅSE

Peer? Why, you're out of your senses, sure!
Ingrid came home none the worse in the end.
The right thing had been to hold Satan to reckoning;—
He was the sinner, ay, he and none other;
The ugly beast tempted my poor boy astray.

KARI

Had I not better send word to the parson?
Mayhap you're worse than you think you are.

ÅSE

To the parson? Truly I almost think so.
[*Starts up.*]
But, oh God, I can't! I'm the boy's own mother;
And help him I must; it's no more than my duty;

Lensmand, the lowest functionary in the Norwegian official scale—a sort of parish officer. (Translator's note)

I must do what I can when the rest forsake him.
They've left him his coat; I must patch it up.
I wish I dared snap up the fur-rug as well!
What's come of the hose?

KARI

They are there, 'mid that rubbish.

ÅSE

[*Rummaging about.*]
Why, what have we here? I declare it's an old
Casting-ladle, Kari! With this he would play
Button-moulder, would melt, and then shape, and then stamp
   them.
One day—there was company—in the boy came,
And begged of his father a lump of tin.
"Not tin," says Jon, "but King Christian's coin;
Silver; to show you're the son of Jon Gynt."
God pardon him, Jon; he was drunk, you see,
And then he cared neither for tin nor for gold.
Here are the hose. Oh, they're nothing but holes;
They want darning, Kari!

KARI

Indeed but they do.

ÅSE

When that is done, I must get to bed;
I feel so broken, and frail, and ill——
[*Joyfully.*]
Two woollen-shirts, Kari;—they've passed them by!

KARI

So they have indeed.

ÅSE

It's a bit of luck.
One of the two you may put aside;
Or rather, I think we'll e'en take them both;—
The one he has on is so worn and thin.

KARI

But oh, Mother Åse, I fear it's a sin.

ÅSE

> Maybe; but remember the priest holds out
> Pardon for this and our other sinnings.

SCENE THIRD

> *In front of a settler's newly built hut in the forest. A reindeer's horns over*
> *the door. The snow is lying deep around. It is dusk.*

PEER GYNT *is standing outside the door, fastening a large wooden bar to it.*

PEER   [*Laughing between whiles.*]

> Bars I must fix me; bars that can fasten
> The door against troll-folk, and men, and women.
> Bars I must fix me; bars that can shut out
> All the cantankerous little hobgoblins.——
> They come with the darkness, they knock and they rattle:
> Open, Peer Gynt, we're as nimble as thoughts are!
> 'Neath the bedstead we bustle, we rake in the ashes,
> Down the chimney we hustle like fiery-eyed dragons.
> Hee-hee! Peer Gynt; think you staples and planks
> Can shut out cantankerous hobgoblin-thoughts?
> [SOLVEIG *comes on snow-shoes over the heath; she has a shawl over her*
> *head, and a bundle in her hand.*]

SOLVEIG

> God prosper your labour. You must not reject me.
> You sent for me hither, and so you must take me.

PEER

> Solveig! It cannot be——! Ay, but it is!——
> And you're not afraid to come near to me!

SOLVEIG

> One message you sent me by little Helga;
> Others came after in storm and in stillness.
> All that your mother told bore me a message,
> That brought forth others when dreams sank upon me.
> Nights full of heaviness, blank, empty days,
> Brought me the message that now I must come.

It seemed as though life had been quenched down there;
I could nor laugh nor weep from the depths of my heart.
I knew not for sure how you might be minded;
I knew but for sure what I should do and must do.

PEER

But your father?

SOLVEIG

In all of God's wide earth
I have none I can call either father or mother.
I have loosed me from all of them.

PEER

Solveig, you fair one—
And to come to me?

SOLVEIG

Ay, to you alone;
You must be all to me, friend and consoler.
[*In tears.*]
The worst was leaving my little sister;—
But parting from father was worse, still worse;
And worst to leave her at whose breast I was borne;—
Oh no, God forgive me, the worst I must call
The sorrow of leaving them all, ay all!

PEER

And you know the doom that was passed in spring?
It forfeits my farm and my heritage.

SOLVEIG

Think you for heritage, goods, and gear,
I forsook the paths all my dear ones tread?

PEER

And know you the compact? Outside the forest
Whoever may meet me may seize me at will.

SOLVEIG

I ran upon snow-shoes; I asked my way on;
They said, "Whither go you?" I answered, "I go home."

PEER

Away, away then with nails and planks!
No need now for bars against hobgoblin-thoughts.
If you dare dwell with the hunter here,

I know the hut will be blessed from ill.
Solveig! Let me look at you! Not too near!
Only look at you! Oh, but you are bright and pure!
Let me lift you! Oh, but you are fine and light!
Let me carry you, Solveig, and I'll never be tired!
I will not soil you. With outstretched arms
I will hold you far out from me, lovely and warm one!
Oh, who would have thought I could draw you to me,—
Ah, but I have longed for you, daylong and nightlong.
Here you may see I've been hewing and building;—
It must down again, dear; it is ugly and mean——

SOLVEIG

Be it mean or brave,—here is all to my mind.
One so lightly draws breath in the teeth of the wind.
Down below it was airless; one felt as though choked;
That was partly what drove me in fear from the dale.
But here, with the fir-branches soughing o'er-head,—
What a stillness and song!—I am here in my home.

PEER

And know you that surely? For all your days?

SOLVEIG

The path I have trodden leads back nevermore.

PEER

You are mine then! In! In the room let me see you!
Go in! I must go to fetch fir-roots* for fuel.
Warm shall the fire be and bright shall it shine,
You shall sit softly and never be a-cold.
[*He opens the door;* SOLVEIG *goes in. He stands still for a while, then laughs aloud with joy and leaps into the air.*]

PEER

My king's daughter! Now I have found her and won her!
Hei! Now the palace shall rise, deeply founded!

He seizes his axe and moves away; at the same moment an OLD-LOOKING WOMAN, *in a tattered green gown, comes out from the wood; an* UGLY BRAT, *with an ale-flagon in his hand, limps after, holding on to her skirt.*

*"Tyri," resinous pine-wood which burns with a bright blase. (Translator's note)

THE WOMAN

 Good evening, Peer Lightfoot!

PEER

 What is it? Who's there?

THE WOMAN

 Old friends of yours, Peer Gynt! My home is near by.
 We are neighbours.

PEER

 Indeed! That is more than I know.

THE WOMAN

 Even as your hut was builded, mine built itself too.

PEER [*Going.*]

 I'm in haste——

THE WOMAN

 Yes, that you are always, my lad;
 But I'll trudge behind you and catch you at last.

PEER

 You're mistaken, good woman!

THE WOMAN

 I was so before;
 I was when you promised such mighty fine things.

PEER

 I promised——? What devil's own nonsense is this?

THE WOMAN

 You've forgotten the night when you drank with my sire?
 You've forgot——?

PEER

 I've forgot what I never have known.
 What's this that you prate of? When last did we meet?

THE WOMAN

 When last we met was when first we met.
 [*To* THE BRAT]
 Give your father a drink; he is thirsty, I'm sure.

PEER

 Father? You're drunk, woman! Do you call him——?

THE WOMAN

 I should think you might well know the pig by its skin!
 Why, where are your eyes? Can't you see that he's lame
 In his shank, just as you too are lame in your soul?

PEER

Would you have me believe——?

THE WOMAN

Would you wriggle away——?

PEER

This long-leggëd urchin——!

THE WOMAN

He's shot up apace.

PEER

Dare you, you troll-snout, father on me——?

THE WOMAN

Come now, Peer Gynt, you're as rude as an ox.

[*Weeping.*]

Is it my fault if no longer I'm fair,

As I was when you lured me on hillside and lea?

Last fall, in my labour, the Fiend held my back,

And so 'twas no wonder I came out a fright.

But if you would see me as fair as before,

You have only to turn yonder girl out of doors,

Drive her clean out of your sight and your mind;——

Do but this, dear my love, and I'll soon lose my snout!

PEER

Begone from me, troll-witch!

THE WOMAN

Ay, see if I do!

PEER

I'll split your skull open——!

THE WOMAN

Just try if you dare!

Ho-ho, Peer Gynt, I've no fear of blows!

Be sure I'll return every day of the year.

Through the door, set ajar, I'll peep in at you both.

When you're sitting with your girl on the fireside bench,——

When you're tender, Peer Gynt,——when you'd pet and caress
　her,——

I'll seat myself by you, and ask for my share.

She there and I——we will take you by turns.

Farewell, dear my lad, you can marry to-morrow.

PEER
>You nightmare of hell!

THE WOMAN
>By-the-bye, I forgot!
>You must rear your own youngster, you light-footed scamp!
>Little imp, will you go to your father?

THE BRAT   [*Spits at him.*]
>Faugh!
>I'll chop you with my hatchet; only wait, only wait!

THE WOMAN   [*Kisses* THE BRAT.]
>What a head he has got on his shoulders, the dear!
>You'll be dad's living image when once you're a man!

PEER   [*Stamping.*]
>Oh, would you were as far———!

THE WOMAN
>As we now are near?

PEER   [*Clenching his hands.*]
>And all this———!

THE WOMAN
>For nothing but thoughts and desires!
>It is hard on you, Peer!

PEER
>It is worst for another!—
>Solveig, my fairest, my purest gold!

THE WOMAN
>Oh ay, 'tis the guiltless must smart, said the devil:
>His mother boxed his ears when his father was drunk!
>[*She trudges off into the thicket with* THE BRAT, *who throws the flagon at* PEER GYNT.]

PEER   [*After a long silence.*]
>The Boyg said, "Go roundabout!"—so one must here.—
>There fell my fine palace, with crash and clatter
>There's a wall around her whom I stood so near,
>Of a sudden all's ugly—my joy has grown old.—
>Roundabout, lad! There's no way to be found.
>Right through all this, from where you stand to her.
>Right through? H'm, surely there should be one.
>There's a text on repentance, unless I mistake.

But what? What is it? I haven't the book,
I've forgotten it mostly, and here there is none
That can guide me aright in the pathless wood.——
Repentance? And maybe 'twould take whole years
Ere I fought my way through. 'Twere a meagre life, that.
To shatter what's radiant, and lovely, and pure,
And clinch it together in fragments and shards?
You can do it with a fiddle, but not with a bell.
Where you'd have the sward green, you must mind not to trample.
'Twas nought but a lie though, that witch-snout business!
Now all that foulness is well out of sight.——
Ay, out of sight maybe, but not out of mind.
Thoughts will sneak stealthily in at my heel.
Ingrid! And the three, they that danced on the heights!
Will they too want to join us? With vixenish spite
Will they claim to be folded, like her, to my breast,
To be tenderly lifted on outstretched arms?
Roundabout, lad; though my arms were as long
As the root of the fir, or the pine-tree's stem,——
I think even then I should hold her too near
To set her down pure and untarnished again.——
I must roundabout here, then, as best I may,
And see that it bring me nor gain nor loss.
One must put such things from one, and try to forget.——
[*Goes a few steps towards the hut, but stops again.*]
Go in after this? So befouled and disgraced?
Go in with that troll-rabble after me still?
Speak, yet be silent; confess, yet conceal——?
[*Throws away his axe.*]
It's a holy-day evening. For me to keep tryst,
Such as now I am, would be sacrilege.

SOLVEIG   [*In the doorway.*]
    Are you coming?
PEER   [*Half aloud.*]
    Roundabout!
SOLVEIG
    What?

PEER

  You must wait.

  It is dark, and I've got something heavy to fetch.

SOLVEIG

  Wait; I will help you; the burden we'll share.

PEER

  No, stay where you are! I must bear it alone.

SOLVEIG

  But don't go too far, dear!

PEER

  Be patient, my girl;

  Be my way long or short—you must wait.

SOLVEIG   [*Nodding to him as he goes.*]

  Yes, I'll wait.

  [PEER GYNT *goes down the wood-path.* SOLVEIG *remains standing in the open half-door.*]

Scene Fourth

  ÅSE's *room. Evening. The room is lighted by a wood fire on the open hearth. A cat is lying on a chair at the foot of the bed.*

ÅSE *lies in the bed, fumbling about restlessly with her hands on the coverlet.*

ÅSE

  Oh, Lord my God, isn't he coming?

  The time drags so drearily on.

  I have no one to send with a message;

  And I've much, oh so much, to say.

  I haven't a moment to lose now!

  So quickly! Who could have foreseen?

  Oh me, if I only were certain

  I'd not been too strict with him!

PEER GYNT   [*Enters.*]

  Good evening!

ÅSE

    The Lord give you gladness!
    You've come then, my boy, my dear!
    But how dare you show face in the valley?
    You know your life's forfeit here.

PEER

    Oh, life must e'en go as it may go;
    I felt that I must look in.

ÅSE

    Ay, now Kari is put to silence,
    And I can depart in peace!

PEER

    Depart? Why, what are you saying?
    Where is it you think to go?

ÅSE

    Alas, Peer, the end is nearing;
    I have but a short time left.

PEER   [*Writhing, and walking towards the back of the room.*]

    See there now! I'm fleeing from trouble;
    I thought at least here I'd be free——!
    Are your hands and your feet a-cold, then?

ÅSE

    Ay, Peer; all will soon be o'er. —
    When you see that my eyes are glazing,
    You must close them carefully.
    And then you must see to my coffin;
    And be sure it's a fine one, dear.
    Ah no, by-the-bye——

PEER

    Be quiet!
    There's time yet to think of that.

ÅSE

    Ay, ay.
    [*Looks restlessly round the room.*]
    Here you see the little
    They've left us! It's like them, just.

PEER   [*With a writhe.*]

    Again!

[*Harshly.*]

Well, I know it was my fault.

What's the use of reminding me?

ÅSE

You! No, that accursed liquor,

From that all the mischief came!

Dear my boy, you know you'd been drinking;

And then no one knows what he does;

And besides, you'd been riding the reindeer;

No wonder your head was turned!

PEER

Ay, ay; of that yarn enough now.

Enough of the whole affair.

All that's heavy we'll let stand over

Till after—some other day.

[*Sits on the edge of the bed.*]

Now, mother, we'll chat together;

But only of this and that,——

Forget what's awry and crooked,

And all that is sharp and sore.——

Why see now, the same old pussy!

So she is alive then, still?

ÅSE

She makes such a noise o' nights now;

You know what that bodes, my boy!

PEER   [*Changing the subject.*]

What news is there here in the parish?

ÅSE   [*Smiling.*]

There's somewhere about, they say,

A girl who would fain to the uplands——

PEER   [*Hastily.*]

Mads Moen, is he content?

ÅSE

They say that she hears and heeds not

The old people's prayers and tears.

You ought to look in and see them;——

You, Peer, might perhaps bring help——

PEER

    The smith, what's become of him now?

ÅSE

    Don't talk of that filthy smith.

    Her name I would rather tell you,

    The name of the girl, you know——

PEER

    Nay, now we will chat together,

    But only of this and that,——

    Forget what's awry and crooked,

    And all that is sharp and sore.

    Are you thirsty? I'll fetch you water.

    Can you stretch you? The bed is short.

    Let me see;——if I don't believe, now,

    It's the bed that I had when a boy!

    Do you mind, dear, how oft in the evenings

    You sat at my bedside here,

    And spread the fur coverlet o'er me,

    And sang many a lilt and lay?

ÅSE

    Ay, mind you? And then we played sledges,

    When your father was far abroad.

    The coverlet served for sledge-apron,

    And the floor for an ice-bound fiord.

PEER

    Ah, but the best of all, though,——

    Mother, you mind that too?

    The best was the fleet-foot horses——

ÅSE

    Ay, think you that I've forgot?——

    It was Kari's cat that we borrowed;

    It sat on the log-scooped chair——

PEER

    To the castle west of the moon, and

    The castle east of the sun,

    To Soria-Moria Castle

    The road ran both high and low.

    A stick that we found in the closet,

For a whip-shaft you made it serve.

ÅSE

Right proudly I perked on the box-seat——

PEER

Ay, ay; you threw loose the reins,
And kept turning round as we travelled,
And asked me if I was cold.
God bless you, ugly old mother,—
You were ever a kindly soul——!
What's hurting you now?

ÅSE

My back aches,
Because of the hard, bare boards.

PEER

Stretch yourself; I'll support you.
There now, you're lying soft.

ÅSE   [Uneasily.]

No, Peer, I'd be moving!

PEER

Moving?

ÅSE

Ay, moving; 'tis ever my wish.

PEER

Oh, nonsense! Spread o'er you the bed-fur.
Let me sit at your bedside here.
There; now we'll shorten the evening
With many a lild and lay.

ÅSE

Best bring from the closet the prayer-book:
I feel so uneasy of soul.

PEER

In Soria-Moria Castle
The King and the Prince give a feast.
On the sledge-cushions lie and rest you;
I'll drive you there over the heath——

ÅSE

But, Peer dear, am I invited?

PEER

> Ay, that we are, both of us.
>
> [*He throws a string round the back of the chair on which the cat is lying,
> takes up a stick, and seats himself at the foot of the bed.*]
>
> Gee-up! Will you stir yourself, Black-boy?
>
> Mother, you're not a-cold?
>
> Ay, ay; by the pace one knows it,
>
> When Granë begins to go!

ÅSE

> Why, Peer, what is it that's ringing——?

PEER

> The glittering sledge-bells, dear!

ÅSE

> Oh, mercy, how hollow it's rumbling.

PEER

> We're just driving over a fiord.

ÅSE

> I'm afraid! What is that I hear rushing
>
> And sighing so strange and wild?

PEER

> It's the sough of the pine-trees, mother,
>
> On the heath. Do you but sit still.

ÅSE

> There's a sparkling and gleaming afar now;
>
> Whence comes all that blaze of light.

PEER

> From the castle's windows and doorways.
>
> Don't you hear, they are dancing?

ÅSE

> Yes.

PEER

> Outside the door stands St. Peter,
>
> And prays you to enter in.

ÅSE

> Does he greet us?

PEER

> He does, with honour,
>
> And pours out the sweetest wine.

ÅSE

>Wine! Has he cakes as well, Peer?

PEER

>Cakes? Ay, a heaped-up dish.
>And the dean's wife* is getting ready
>Your coffee and your dessert.

ÅSE

>Lord, Lord! shall we two come together?

PEER

>As freely as ever you will.

ÅSE

>Oh, deary, Peer, what a frolic
>You're driving me to, poor soul!

PEER [*Cracking his whip.*]

>Gee-up; will you stir yourself, Black-boy!

ÅSE

>Peer, dear, you're driving right?

PEER [*Cracking his whip again.*]

>Ay, broad is the way.

ÅSE

>This journey,
>It makes me so weak and tired.

PEER

>There's the castle rising before us;
>The drive will be over soon.

ÅSE

>I will lie back and close my eyes then,
>And trust me to you, my boy!

PEER

>Come up with you, Granë, my trotter!
>In the castle the throng is great;
>They bustle and swarm to the gateway:
>Peer Gynt and his mother are here!
>What say you, Master Saint Peter?
>Shall mother not enter in?
>You may search a long time, I tell you,

Salig provstinde—literally, "the late Mrs. Provost." (Translator's note)

Ere you find such an honest old soul.
Myself I don't want to speak of;
I can turn at the castle gate.
If you'll treat me, I'll take it kindly;
If not, I'll go off just as pleased.
I have made up as many flim-flams
As the devil at the pulpit desk,
And called my old mother a hen, too,
Because she would cackle and crow.
But her you shall honour and reverence,
And make her at home indeed;
There comes not a soul to beat her
From the parishes nowadays.——
Ho-ho; here comes God the Father!
Saint Peter! you're in for it now!
[*In a deep voice.*]
"Have done with these jack-in-office airs, sir;
Mother Åse shall enter free!"
[*Laughs loudly, and turns towards his mother.*]
Ay, didn't I know what would happen?
Now they dance to another tune!
[*Uneasily.*]
Why, what makes your eyes so glassy?
Mother! Have you gone out of your wits——?
[*Goes to the head of the bed.*]
You mustn't lie there and stare so——!
Speak, mother; it's I, your boy!
[*Feels her forehead and hands cautiously; then throws the string on the chair, and says softly:*]
Ay, ay!——You can rest yourself, Granë;
For e'en now the journey's done.
[*Closes her eyes, and bends over her.*]
For all of your days I thank you,
For beatings and lullabys!
But see, you must thank me back, now——
[*Presses his cheek against her mouth.*]
There; that was the driver's fare.*

Tak for skyds—literally, "thanks for the drive."

THE COTTAR'S WIFE   [*Entering.*]

    What? Peer! Ah, then we are over

    The worse of the sorrow and need!

    Dear Lord, but she's sleeping soundly—

    Or can she be——?

PEER

    Hush; she is dead.

    [KARI *weeps beside the body;* PEER GYNT *walks up and down the room for some time; at last he stops beside the bed.*]

PEER

    See mother buried with honour.

    I must try to fare forth from here.

KARI

    Are you faring afar?

PEER

    To seaward.

KARI

    So far!

PEER

    Ay, and further still.

    [*He goes.*]

ACT FOURTH

SCENE FIRST

On the south-west coast of Morocco. A palm-grove. Under an awning, on ground covered with matting, a table spread for dinner. Further back in the grove hammocks are slung. In the offing lies a steam-yacht, flying the Norwegian and American colours. A jolly-boat drawn up on the beach. It is towards sunset.

PEER GYNT, *a handsome middle-aged gentleman, in an elegant travelling-dress, with a gold-rimmed double eyeglass hanging at his waistcoat, is doing the honours at the head of the table.* MR. COTTON,* MONSIEUR BALLON, HERR VON EBERKOPF, *and* HERR TRUMPETERSTRÅLE, *are seated at the table finishing dinner.*

PEER GYNT
    Drink, gentlemen! If man is made
    For pleasure, let him take his fill then.
    You know 'tis written: Lost is lost,
    And gone is gone———. What may I hand you?
TRUMPETERSTRÅLE.†
    As host you're princely, Brother Gynt!
PEER
    I share the honour with my cash,
    With cook and steward———
MR. COTTON
    Very well;‡
    Let's pledge a toast to all the four!

*In the original "Master Cotton." (Translator's note)
†This name is comic; it is Swedish for "trumpet blast."
‡In the original (early editions) "Werry well." (Translator's note)

MONSIEUR BALLON*

   Monsieur, you have a *gout*,[†] a *ton*,[‡]
   That nowadays is seldom met with
   Among men living *en garçon*,——[§]
   A certain—what's the word——?

VON EBERKOPF[||]

   A dash,
   A tinge of free soul-contemplation,
   And cosmopolitanisation,[#]
   An outlook through the cloudy rifts
   By narrow prejudice unhemmed,
   A stamp of high illumination,
   An *Ur-Natur*,** with lore of life,
   To crown the trilogy, united.
   Nicht wahr,[††] Monsieur, 'twas that you meant?

MONSIEUR BALLON

   Yes, very possible; not quite
   So loftily it sounds in French.

VON EBERKOPF

   Ei was[‡‡] That language is so stiff.——
   But the phenomenon's final cause
   If we would seek——

PEER

   It's found already.
   The reason is that I'm unmarried.
   Yes, gentlemen, completely clear
   The matter is. What should a man be?

---

*This name is comic; it is French for "balloon."
† Taste (French). All foreign words used in the translation appear in the original.
‡ Tone (French).
§Bachelor (French).
|| This name is comic; it is German for "boars head."
#This may not be a very lucid or even very precise rendering of *Verdensborger-domsforpagtning;* but this line, and indeed the whole speech, is pure burlesque; and the exact sense of nonsense is naturally elusive. (Translator's note)
**Original character (German).
††Isn't it (German).
‡‡Oh, well (German).

Himself, is my concise reply.
He should regard himself and his.
But can he, as a sumpter-mule*
For others' woe and others' weal?

VON EBERKOPF

But this same in-and-for-yourself-ness,
I'll answer for't, has cost you strife——

PEER

Ah yes, indeed; in former days;
But always I came off with honour.
Yet one time I ran very near
To being trapped against my will.
I was a brisk and handsome lad,
And she to whom my heart was given,
She was of royal family——

MONSIEUR BALLON

Of royal——?

PEER   [*Carelessly.*]

One of those old stocks,
you know the kind——

TRUMPETERSTRÅLE   [*Thumping the table.*]

Those noble-trolls.

PEER   [*Shrugging his shoulders.*]

Old fossil Highnesses who make it
Their pride to keep plebeian blots
Excluded from their line's escutcheon.

MR. COTTON

Then nothing came of the affair?

MONSIEUR BALLON

The family opposed the marriage?

PEER

Far from it!

MONSIEUR BALLON

Ah!

PEER   [*With forbearance.*]

You understand

*Literally, "pack-camel."

That certain circumstances made for
Their marrying us without delay.
But truth to tell, the whole affair
Was, first to last, distasteful to me.
I'm finical in certain ways,
And like to stand on my own feet.
And when my father-in-law came out
With delicately veiled demands
That I should change my name and station,
And undergo ennoblement,
With much else that was most distasteful,
Not to say quite inacceptable.—
Why then I gracefully withdrew,
Point-blank declined his ultimatum—
And so renounced my youthful bride.
[*Drums on the table with a devout air.*]
Yes, yes; there is a ruling Fate!
On that we mortals may rely;
And 'tis a comfortable knowledge.

MONSIEUR BALLON

And so the matter ended, eh?

PEER

Oh no, far otherwise I found it;
For busy-bodies mixed themselves,
With furious outcries, in the business.
The juniors of the clan were worst;
With seven of them I fought a duel.
That time I never shall forget,
Though I came through it all in safety.
It cost me blood; but that same blood
Attests the value of my person,
And points encouragingly towards
The wise control of Fate aforesaid.

VON EBERKOPF

Your outlook on the course of life
Exalts you to the rank of thinker.
Whilst the mere commonplace empiric
Sees separately the scattered scenes,

And to the last goes groping on,
You in one glance can focus all things.
One norm to all things you apply.
You point each random rule of life,
Till one and all diverge like rays
From one full-orbed philosophy.—
And you have never been to college?

PEER
I am, as I've already said,
Exclusively a self-taught man.
Methodically naught I've learned;
But I have thought and speculated,
And done much desultory reading.
I started somewhat late in life,
And then, you know, it's rather hard
To plough ahead through page on page,
And take in all of everything.
I've done my history piecemeal;
I never have had time for more.
And, as one needs in days of trial
Some certainty to place one's trust in,
I took religion intermittently.
That way it goes more smoothly down.
One should not read to swallow all,
But rather see what one has use for.

MR. COTTON
Ay, that is practical!

PEER   [*Lights a cigar.*]
Dear friends
Just think of my career in general.
In what case came I to the West?
A poor young fellow, empty-handed;
I had to battle sore for bread;
Trust me, I often found it hard.
But life, my friends, ah, life is dear,
And, as the phrase goes, death is bitter.
Well! Luck, you see, was kind to me;
Old Fate, too, was accommodating.

I prospered; and, by versatility,
I prospered better still and better.
In ten years' time I bore the name
Of Crœsus 'mongst the Charleston shippers.
My fame flew wide from port to port,
And fortune sailed on board my vessels——

MR. COTTON

What did you trade in?

PEER

I did most
In negro slaves for Carolina,
And idol-images for China.

MONSIEUR BALLON

Fi donc!*

TRUMPETERSTRÅLE

The devil, Uncle Gynt!

PEER

You think, no doubt, the business hovered
On the outer verge of the allowable?
Myself I felt the same thing keenly.
It struck me even as odious.
But, trust me, when you've once begun,
It's hard to break away again.
At any rate it's no light thing,
In such a vast trade-enterprise,
That keeps whole thousands in employ,
To break off wholly, once for all.
That "once for all" I can't abide,
But own, upon the other side,
That I have always felt respect
For what are known as consequences;
And that to overstep the bounds
Has ever somewhat daunted me.
Besides, I had begun to age.
Was getting on towards the fifties;—
My hair was slowly growing grizzled;

*Damn (French).

And, though my health was excellent,
Yet painfully the thought beset me:
Who knows how soon the hour may strike,
The jury verdict be delivered
That parts the sheep and goats asunder?
What could I do? To stop the trade
With China was impossible.
A plan I hit on——opened straightway
A new trade with the self-same land.
I shipped off idols every spring,
Each autumn sent forth missionaries,
Supplying them with all they needed,
As stockings, Bibles, rum, and rice——

MR. COTTON
Yes, at a profit?

PEER
Why, of course.
It prospered. Dauntlessly they toiled.
For every idol that was sold
They got a coolie well baptized,
So that the effect was neutralised.
The mission-field lay never fallow,
For still the idol-propaganda
The missionaries held in check.

MR. COTTON
Well, but the African commodities?

PEER
There, too, my ethics won the day.
I saw the traffic was a wrong one
For people of a certain age.
One may drop off before one dreams of it.
And then there were the thousand pitfalls
Laid by the philanthropic camp;
Besides, of course, the hostile cruisers,
And all the wind-and-weather risks.
All this together won the day.
I thought: Now, Peter, reef your sails!
See to it you amend your faults!

So in the South I bought some land,
And kept the last meat-importation,
Which chanced to be a superfine one.
They throve so, grew so fat and sleek,
That 'twas a joy to me, and them too.
Yes, without boasting, I may say
I acted as a father to them,—
And found my profit in so doing.
I built them schools, too, so that virtue
Might uniformly be maintained at
A certain general *niveau*,*
And kept strict watch that never its
Thermometer should sink below it.
Now, furthermore, from all this business
I've beat a definite retreat;—
I've sold the whole plantation, and
It's tale of live-stock, hide and hair.
At parting, too, I served around,
To big and little, gratis grog,
So men and women all got drunk,
And widows got their snuff as well.
So that is why I trust,—provided
The saying is not idle breath:
Whoso does not do ill, does good,—
My former errors are forgotten,
And I, much more than most, can hold
My misdeeds balanced by my virtues.

VON EBERKOPF   [*Clinking glasses with him.*]
How strengthening it is to hear
A principle thus acted out,
Freed from the night of theory,
Unshaken by the outward ferment!

PEER   [*Who has been drinking freely during the preceding passages.*]
We Northland men know how to carry
Our battle through! The key to the art
Of life's affairs is simply this:

*Level (French).

To keep one's ear close shut against
The ingress of one dangerous viper.

MR. COTTON

What sort of viper, pray, dear friend?

PEER

A little one that slyly wiles you
To tempt the irretrievable.
[*Drinking again.*]
The essence of the art of daring,
The art of bravery in act,
Is this: To stand with choice-free foot
Amid the treacherous snares of life,—
To know for sure that other days
Remain beyond the day of battle,—
To know that ever in the rear
A bridge for your retreat stands open.
This theory has borne me on,
Has given my whole career its colour;
And this same theory I inherit,
A race-gift, from my childhood's home.

MONSIEUR BALLON

You are Norwegian?

PEER

Yes, by birth;
But cosmopolitan in spirit.
For fortune such as I've enjoyed
I have to thank America.
My amply-furnished library
I owe to Germany's later schools.
From France, again, I get my waistcoats,
My manners, and my spice of wit,—
From England an industrious hand,
And keen sense for my own advantage.
The Jew has taught me how to wait.
Some taste for *dolce far niente**
I have received from Italy,—

*Sweet idleness (Italian).

And one time, in a perilous pass,
To eke the measure of my days,
I had recourse to Swedish steel.

TRUMPETERSTRÅLE   [*Lifting up his glass.*]
Ay, Swedish steel——?

VON EBERKOPF
The weapon's wielder
Demands our homage first of all!

[*They clink glasses and drink with him. The wine begins to go to his head.*]

MR. COTTON
All this is very good indeed;——
But, sir, I'm curious to know
What with your gold you think of doing.

PEER   [*Smiling.*]
H'm; doing? Eh?

ALL FOUR   [*Coming closer.*]
Yes, let us hear!

PEER
Well, first of all, I want to travel.
You see, that's why I shipped you four,
To keep me company, at Gibraltar.
I needed such a dancing-choir
Of friends around my gold-calf-altar——

VON EBERKOPF
Most witty!

MR. COTTON
Well, but no one hoists
His sails for nothing but the sailing.
Beyond all doubt, you have a goal;
And that is——?

PEER
To be Emperor.*

ALL FOUR
What?

---

*In the original *kejser*. We have elsewhere used the word "Kaiser," but in this scene, and in scenes 7 and 8 of this act, the ordinary English form seemed preferable. (Translator's note)

PEER   [*Nodding.*]
    Emperor!
THE FOUR
    Where?
PEER
    O'er all the world.
MONSIEUR BALLON
    But how, friend——?
PEER
    By the might of gold!
    That plan is not at all a new one;
    It's been the soul of my career.
    Even as a boy, I swept in dreams
    Far o'er the ocean on a cloud.
    I soared with train and golden scabbard,—
    And flopped down on all-fours again.
    But still my goal, my friends, stood fast.—
    There is a text, or else a saying,
    Somewhere, I don't remember where,
    That if you gained the whole wide world,
    But lost yourself, your gain were but
    A garland on a cloven skull.
    That is the text—or something like it;
    And that remark is sober truth.
VON EBERKOPF
    But what then is the Gyntish Self?
PEER
    The world behind my forehead's arch,
    In force of which I'm no one else
    Than I, no more than God's the Devil.
TRUMPETERSTRÅLE
    I understand now where you're aiming!
MONSIEUR BALLON
    Thinker sublime!
VON EBERKOPF
    Exalted poet!
PEER   [*More and more elevated.*]
    The Gyntish Self—it is the host

Of wishes, appetites, desires,——
The Gyntish Self, it is the sea
Of fancies, exigencies, claims,
All that, in short, makes my breast heave,
And whereby I, as I, exist.
But as our Lord requires the clay
To constitute him God o' the world,
So I, too, stand in need of gold,
If I as Emperor would figure.

MONSIEUR BALLON

You have the gold, though?

PEER

Not enough.
Ay, maybe for a nine-days' flourish,
As Emperor *à la** Lippe-Detmold.[†]
But I must be myself *en bloc*,[‡]
Must be the Gynt of all the planet,
Sir Gynt throughout, from top to bottom!

MONSIEUR BALLON   [*Enraptured.*]

Possess the earth's most exquisite beauty!

VON EBERKOPF

All century-old Johannisberger!

TRUMPETERSTRÅLE

And all the blades of Charles the Twelfth!

MR. COTTON

But first a profitable opening
For business——

PEER

That's already found;
Our anchoring here supplied me with it.
To night we set off, northward ho!
The papers I received on board
Have brought me tidings of importance——!
[*Rises with uplifted glass.*

---

*Comic misuse of the French expression for "in the manner of."
†Small German principality.
‡In one piece (French).

It seems that Fortune ceaselessly
Aids him who has the pluck to seize it——

THE GUESTS
Well? Tell us——!

PEER
Greece is in revolt.

ALL FOUR   [*Springing up.*]
What! Greece——?

PEER
The Greeks have risen in Hellas.

THE FOUR
Hurrah!

PEER
And Turkey's in a fix!
[*Empties his glass.*]

MONSIEUR BALLON
To Hellas! Glory's gate stands open!
I'll help them with the sword of France!

VON EBERKOPF
And I with war-whoops—from a distance.

MR. COTTON
And I as well—by taking contracts!

TRUMPETERSTRÅLE
Lead on! I'll find again in Bender
The world-renownëd spur-strap-buckles!*

MONSIEUR BALLON   [*Falling on* PEER GYNT's *neck.*]
Forgive me, friend, that I at first
Misjudged you quite!

VON EBERKOPF   [*Pressing his hands.*]
I, stupid hound,
Took you for next door to a scoundrel!

MR. COTTON
Too strong that; only for a fool——

---

*An allusion to the spurs with which Charles XII is said to have torn the caftan of the Turkish Vizier who announced to him that the Sultan had concluded a truce with Russia. The boots and spurs, it would appear, have been preserved, but with the buckles missing. (Translator's note)

TRUMPETERSTRÅLE [*Trying to kiss him.*]
 I, Uncle, for a specimen
 Of Yankee riff-raff's meanest spawn——!
 Forgive me——!
VON EBERKOPF
 We've been in the dark——
PEER
 What stuff is this?
VON EBERKOPF
 We now see gathered
 In glory all the Gyntish host
 Of wishes, appetites, and desires——!
MONSIEUR BALLON [*Admiringly.*]
 So this is being Monsieur Gynt!
VON EBERKOPF [*In the same tone.*]
 This I call being Gynt with honour!
PEER
 But tell me——?
MONSIEUR BALLON
 Don't you understand?
PEER
 May I be hanged if I begin to!
MONSIEUR BALLON
 What? Are you not upon your way
 To join the Greeks, with ship and money——?
PEER [*Contemptuously.*]
 No, many thanks! I side with strength,
 And lend my money to the Turks.
MONSIEUR BALLON
 Impossible!
VON EBERKOPF
 Witty, but a jest!
PEER [*After a short silence, leaning on a chair and assuming a dignified mien.*]
 Come, gentlemen, I think it best
 We part before the last remains
 Of friendship melt away like smoke.
 Who nothing owns will lightly risk it.

When in the world one scarce commands
The strip of earth one's shadow covers,
One's born to serve as food for powder.
But when a man stands safely landed,
As I do, then his stake is greater.
Go you to Hellas. I will put you
Ashore, and arm you gratis too.
The more you eke the flames of strife,
The better will it serve my purpose.
Strike home for freedom and for right!
Fight! storm! make hell hot for the Turks;——
And gloriously end your days
Upon the Janissaries lances.——
But I——excuse me——
[*Slaps his pocket.*]
I have cash,
And am myself, Sir Peter Gynt.
[*Puts up his sunshade, and goes into the grove, where the hammocks are partly visible.*]

TRUMPETERSTRÅLE
The swinish cur!

MONSIEUR BALLON
No taste for glory——!

MR. COTTON
Oh, glory's neither here nor there;
But think of the enormous profits
We'd reap if Greece should free herself.

MONSIEUR BALLON
I saw myself a conqueror,
By lovely Grecian maids encircled.

TRUMPETERSTRÅLE
Grasped in my Swedish hands, I saw
The great, heroic spur-strap-buckles!

VON EBERKOPF
I my gigantic Fatherland's
Culture saw spread o'er earth and sea——!

MR. COTTON
The worst's the loss in solid cash.

God dam! I scarce can keep from weeping!
I saw me owner of Olympus.
If to its fame the mountain answers,
There must be veins of copper in it,
That could be opened up again.
And furthermore, that stream Castalia,*
Which people talk so much about,
With fall on fall, at lowest reckoning,
Must mean a thousand horse-power good——

TRUMPETERSTRÅLE

Still I will go! My Swedish sword
Is worth far more than Yankee gold!

MR. COTTON

Perhaps; but, jammed into the ranks,
Amid the press we'd all be drowned;
And then where would the profit be?

MONSIEUR BALLON

Accurst! So near to fortune's summit,
And now stopped short beside its grave!

MR. COTTON   [Shakes his fist towards the yacht.]

That long black chest holds coffered up
The nabob's golden nigger-sweat——!

VON EBERKOPF

A royal notion! Quick! Away!
It's all up with his empire now!
Hurrah!

MONSIEUR BALLON

What would you?

VON EBERKOPF

Seize the power!
The crew can easily be bought.
On board then. I annex the yacht!

MR. COTTON

You—what——?

*Mr. Cotton seems to have confounded Olympus with Parnassus. (Translator's note)

VON EBERKOPF

    I grab the whole concern!

    [*Goes down to the jolly-boat.*]

MR. COTTON

    Why then self-interest commands me

    To grab my share.

    [*Goes after him.*]

TRUMPETERSTRÅLE

    What scoundrelism!

MONSIEUR BALLON

    A scurvy business—but—*enfin!**

    [*Follows the others.*]

TRUMPETERSTRÅLE

    I'll have to follow, I suppose,—

    But I protest to all the world——!†

    [*Follows.*]

Scene Second

Another part of the coast. Moonlight with drifting clouds. The yacht is seen far out, under full steam.

PEER GYNT *comes running along the beach; now pinching his arms, now gazing out to sea.*

PEER

    A nightmare!—Delusion!—I'll soon be awake!

    She's standing to sea! And at furious speed!—

    Mere delusion! I'm sleeping! I'm dizzy and drunk!

    [*Clenches his hands.*]

    It's not possible I should be going to die!

    [*Tearing his hair.*]

    A dream! I'm determined it shall be a dream!

---

*In the end (French).

†An allusion to the attitude of Sweden during the Danish War of 1863–64, with special reference to the diplomatic notes of the Minister for Foreign Affairs, Grev Manderström. He is also aimed at in the character of Hussein in the last scene of this act. (Translator's note)

Oh, horror! It's only too real, worse luck!

My brute-beasts of friends———! Do but hear me, oh Lord!

Since though art so wise and so righteous———!

Oh judge———!

[*With upstretched arms.*]

It is *I*, Peter Gynt! Oh, our Lord, give but heed!

Hold thy hand o'er me, Father; or else I must perish!

Make them back the machine! Make them lower the gig!

Stop the robbers! Make something go wrong with the rigging!

Hear me! Let other folks' business lie over!

The world can take care of itself for the time!——

I'm blessed if he hears me! He's deaf as his wont is!

Here's a nice thing! A God that is bankrupt of help!

[*Beckons upwards.*]

Hist; I've abandoned the nigger-plantation!

And missionaries I've exported to Asia!

Surely one good turn should be worth another!

Oh, help me on board———!

[*A jet of fire shoots into the air from the yacht, followed by thick clouds of smoke; a hollow report is heard.* PEER GYNT *utters a shriek, and sinks down on the sands. Gradually the smoke clears away; the ship has disappeared.*]

PEER   [*Softly, with a pale face.*]

That's the sword of wrath!

In a crack to the bottom, every soul, man and mouse!

Oh, for ever blest be the lucky chance———

[*With emotion.*]

A chance? No, no, it was more than a chance.

I was to be rescued and they to perish.

Oh, thanks and praise for that thou hast kept me,

Hast cared for me, spite of all my sins!——

[*Draws a deep breath.*]

What a marvellous feeling of safety and peace

It gives one to know oneself specially shielded!

But the desert! What about food and drink?

Oh, something I'm sure to find. He'll see to that.

There's no cause for alarm;——

[*Loud and insinuatingly.*]

He would never allow
A poor little sparrow like me to perish!
Be but lowly of spirit. And give him time.
Leave it all in the Lord's hands; and don't be cast down.——
[*With a start of terror.*]
Can that be a lion that growled in the reeds——?
[*His teeth chattering.*]
No, it wasn't a lion.
[*Mustering up courage.*]
A lion, forsooth!
Those beasts, they'll take care to keep out of the way.
They know it's no joke to fall foul of their betters.
They have instinct to guide them;——they feel, what's a fact,
That it's dangerous playing with elephants.——
But all the same——. I must find a tree.
There's a grove of acacias and palms over there;
If I once can climb up, I'll be sheltered and safe,——
Most of all if I knew but a psalm or two.
[*Clambers up.*]
Morning and evening are not alike;
That text has been oft enough weighed and pondered.
[*Seats himself comfortably.*]
How blissful to feel so uplifted in spirit!
To think nobly is more than to know oneself rich.
Only trust in Him. He knows well what share
Of the chalice of need I can bear to drain
He takes fatherly thought for my personal weal;——
[*Casts a glance over the sea, and whispers with a sigh:*]
But economical——no, that he isn't!

SCENE THIRD

> *Night. An encampment of Moroccan troops on the edge of the desert.*
> *Watch-fires, with* SOLDIERS *resting by them.*

A SLAVE   [*Enters, tearing his hair.*]
   Gone is the Emperor's milk-white charger!

ANOTHER SLAVE   [*Enters, rending his garments.*]
    The Emperor's sacred robes are stolen!
AN OFFICER   [*Enters.*]
    A hundred stripes upon the foot-soles
    For all who fail to catch the robber!
    [*The troopers mount their horses, and gallop away in every direction.*]

Scene Fourth

    Daybreak. The grove of acacias and palms.

PEER GYNT *in his tree with a broken branch in his hand, trying to beat off a swarm of monkeys.*

PEER
    Confound it! A most disagreeable night.
    [*Laying about him.*]
    Are you there again? This is most accursëd!
    Now they're throwing fruit. No, it's something else.
    A loathsome beast is your Barbary ape!
    The Scripture says: Thou shalt watch and fight.
    But I'm blest if I can; I am heavy and tired,
    [*Is again attacked; impatiently:*]
    I must put a stopper upon this nuisance!
    I must see and get hold of one of these scamps,
    Get him hung and skinned, and then dress myself up,
    As best I may, in his shaggy hide,
    That the others may take me for one of themselves.——
    What are we mortals? Motes, no more;
    And it's wisest to follow the fashion a bit.——
    Again a rabble! They throng and swarm.
    Off with you! Shoo! They go on as though crazy.
    If only I had a false tail to put on now,——
    Only something to make me a bit like a beast.——
    What now? There's a pattering over my head——!
    [*Looks up.*]
    It's the grandfather ape,——with his fists full of filth——!
    [*Huddles together apprehensively, and keeps still for a while. The ape makes*

a motion; PEER GYNT *begins coaxing and wheedling him, as he might
a dog.*]
Ay,—are you there, my good old Bus!
He's a good beast, he is! He will listen to reason!
He wouldn't throw;—I should think not, indeed!
It is me! Pip-pip! We are first-rate friends!
Ai-ai! Don't you hear, I can talk your language?
Bus and I, we are kinsfolk, you see;—
Bus shall have sugar to-morrow———! The beast!
The whole cargo on top of me! Ugh, how disgusting!—
Or perhaps it was food! 'Twas in taste—indefinable;
And taste's for the most part a matter of habit.
What thinker is it who somewhere says:
You must spit and trust to the force of habit?—
Now here come the small-fry!
[*Hits and slashes around him.*]
It's really too bad
That man, who by rights is the lord of creation,
Should find himself forced to———! O murder! murder!
The old one was bad, but the youngsters are worse!

SCENE FIFTH

*Early morning. A stony region, with a view out over the desert. On one
side a cleft in the hill, and a cave.*

A THIEF *and a* RECEIVER *hidden in the cleft, with the Emperor's horse and
robes. The horse, richly caparisoned, is tied to a stone. Horsemen are seen afar off.*

THE THIEF
    The tongues of the lances
    All flickering and flashing,—
    See, see!
THE RECEIVER
    Already my head seems
    To roll on the sand-plain!
    Woe, woe!

THE THIEF   [*Folds his arms over his breast.*]
>My father he thieved;
>So his son must be thieving.

THE RECEIVER
>My father received;
>Still his son is receiving.*

THE THIEF
>Thy lot shalt thou bear still;
>Thyself shalt thou be still.

THE RECEIVER   [*Listening.*]
>Steps in the brushwood!
>Flee, flee! But where?

THE THIEF
>The cavern is deep,
>And the Prophet great!
>[*They make off, leaving the booty behind them. The horsemen gradually disappear in the distance.*]

PEER GYNT   [*Enters, cutting a reed whistle.*]
>What a delectable morning-tide!——
>The dung-beetle's rolling his ball in the dust;
>The snail creeps out of his dwelling-house.
>The morning; ay, it has gold in its mouth.——
>It's a wonderful power, when you think of it,
>That Nature has given to the light of day.
>One feels so secure, and so much more courageous,——
>One would gladly, at need, take a bull by the horns.——
>What a stillness all round! Ah, the joys of Nature,——
>Strange enough I should never have prized them before.
>Why go and imprison oneself in a city,
>For no end but just to be bored by the mob.——
>Just look how the lizards are whisking about,
>Snapping, and thinking of nothing at all.
>What innocence ev'n in the life of the beasts!
>Each fulfils the Creator's behest unimpeachably,

---

*This is not to be taken as a burlesque instance of the poet's supposed preoccupation with questions of heredity, but simply as an allusion to the fact that, in the East, thieving and receiving are regular and hereditary professions. (Translator's note)

Preserving its own special stamp undefaced;
Is itself, is itself, both in sport and in strife,
Itself, as it was at his primal: Be!
[*Puts on his eye glasses.*]
A toad. In the middle of a sandstone block.
Petrifaction all around him. His head alone peering.
There he's sitting and gazing as though through a window
At the world, and is—to himself enough.——
[*Reflectively.*]
Enough? To himself——? Where is it that's written?
I've read it, in youth, in some so-called classic.
In the family prayer-book? Or Solomon's Proverbs?
Alas, I notice that, year by year,
My memory for dates and for places is fading.
[*Seats himself in the shade.*]
Here's a cool spot to rest and to stretch out one's feet.
Why, look, here are ferns growing—edible roots.
[*Eats a little.*]
'Twould be fitter food for an animal;—
But the text says: Bridle the natural man!
Furthermore it is written: The proud shall be humbled,
And whoso abaseth himself, exalted.
[*Uneasily.*]
Exalted? Yes, that's what will happen with me;——
No other result can so much as be thought of.
Fate will assist me away from this place,
And arrange matters so that I get a fresh start.
This is only a trial; deliverance will follow,—
If only the Lord let's me keep my health.
[*Dismisses his misgivings, lights a cigar, stretches himself, and gazes out over the desert.*]
What an enormous, limitless waste!—
Far in the distance an ostrich is striding.—
What can one fancy was really God's
Meaning in all of this voidness and deadness?
This desert, bereft of all sources of life;
This burnt-up cinder, that profits no one;
This patch of the world, that for ever lies fallow;
This corpse, that never, since earth's creation,

Has brought its Maker so much as thanks,—
Why was it created?—How spendthrift is Nature!—
Is that sea in the east there, that dazzling expanse
All gleaming? It can't be; 'tis but a mirage.
The sea's to the west; it lies piled up behind me,
Dammed out from the desert by a sloping ridge.
[*A thought flashes through his mind.*]
Dammed out? Then I could———? The ridge is narrow.
Dammed out? It wants but a gap, a canal,—
Like a flood of life would the waters rush
In through the channel, and fill the desert!*
Soon would the whole of yon red-hot grave
Spread forth, a breezy and rippling sea.
The oases would rise in the midst, like islands;
Atlas would tower in green cliffs on the north;
Sailing-ships would, like stray birds on the wing,
Skim to the south, on the caravans' track.
Life-giving breezes would scatter the choking
Vapours, and dew would distil from the clouds.
People would build themselves town on town,
And grass would grow green round the swaying palm-trees.
The southland, behind the Sahara's wall,
Would make a new seaboard for civilisation.
Steam would set Timbuctoo's factories spinning;
Bornu would be colonised apace;
The naturalist would pass safely through Habes
In his railway-car to the Upper Nile.
In the midst of my sea, on a fat oasis,
I will replant the Norwegian race;
The Dalesman's blood is next door to royal;
Arabic crossing will do the rest.
Skirting a bay, on a shelving strand,
I'll build the chief city, Peeropolis.
The world is decrepit! Now comes the turn
Of Gyntiana, my virgin land!
[*Springs up.*]

*This proposal was seriously mooted about ten years after the appearance of *Peer Gynt*. (Translator's note)

Had I but capital, soon 'twould be done.——
A gold key to open the gate of the sea!
A crusade against Death! The close-fisted old churl
Shall open the sack he lies brooding upon.
Men rave about freedom in every land;——
Like the ass in the ark, I will send forth a cry
O'er the world, and will baptize to liberty
The beautiful, thrall-bounden coasts that shall be.
I must on! To find capital, eastward or west!
My kingdom—well, half of it, say—for a horse!
[*The horse in the cleft neighs.*]
A horse! Ay, and robes!—Jewels too,—and a sword!
[*Goes closer.*]
It can't be! It is though——! But how? I have read,
I don't quite know where, that the will can move mountains;——
But how about moving a horse as well——?
Pooh! Here stands the horse, that's a matter of fact;——
For the rest, why, *ab esse ad posse*, et cetera.
[*Puts on the dress and looks down at it.*]
Sir Peter—a Turk, too, from top to toe!
Well, one never knows what may happen to one.——
Gee-up, now, Granë, my trusty steed!
[*Mounts the horse.*]
Gold-slipper stirrups beneath my feet!—
You may know the great by their riding-gear!
[*Gallops off into the desert.*]

Scene Sixth

The tent of an Arab chief, standing alone on an oasis.

PEER GYNT, *in his eastern dress, resting on cushions. He is drinking coffee, and smoking a long pipe.* ANITRA, *and a bevy of* GIRLS, *dancing and singing before him.*

CHORUS OF GIRLS

The Prophet is come!
The Prophet, the Lord, the All-Knowing One,

To us, to us is he come,
O'er the sand-ocean riding!
The Prophet, the Lord, the Unerring One,
To us, to us is he come,
O'er the sand-ocean sailing!
Wake the flute and the drum!
The Prophet, the Prophet is come!

ANITRA

His courser is white as the milk is
That streams in the rivers of Paradise.
Bend every knee! Bow every head!
His eyes are as bright-gleaming, mild-beaming stars.
Yet none earth-born endureth
The rays of those stars in their blinding splendour!
Through the desert he came.
Gold and pearl-drops sprang forth on his breast.
Where he rode there was light.
Behind him was darkness;
Behind him raged drought and the simoom.
He, the glorious one, came!
Through the desert he came,
Like a mortal apparelled.
Kaaba, Kaaba stands void;—
He himself hath proclaimed it!

THE CHORUS OF GIRLS

Wake the flute and the drum!
The Prophet, the Prophet is come!

[*They continue the dance, to soft music.*]

PEER

I have read it in print—and the saying is true—
That no one's a prophet in his native land.—
This position is very much more to my mind
Than my life over there 'mong the Charleston merchants.
There was something hollow in the whole affair,
Something foreign at the bottom, something dubious behind it;—
I was never at home in their company,
Nor felt myself really one of the guild.
What tempted me into that galley at all?

To grub and grub in the bins of trade—
As I think it all over, I can't understand it;—
It happened so; that's the whole affair.—
To be oneself on a basis of gold
Is no better than founding one's house on the sand.
For your watch, and your ring, and the rest of your trappings,
The good people fawn on you, grovelling to earth;
They lift their hats to your jewelled breast-pin;
But your ring and your breast-pin are not your Person.—*
A prophet; ay, that is a clearer position.
At least one knows on what footing one stands.
If you make a success, it's yourself that receives
The ovation, and not your pounds-sterling and shillings.
One is what one is, and no nonsense about it;
One owes nothing to chance or to accident,
And needs neither licence nor patent to lean on.—
A prophet; ay, that is the thing for me.
And I slipped so utterly unawares into it,—
Just by coming galloping over the desert,
And meeting these children of nature *en route*.
The Prophet had come to them; so much was clear.
It was really not my intent to deceive——;
There's a difference 'twixt lies and oracular answers;
And then I can always withdraw again.
I'm in no way bound; it's a simple matter—;
The whole thing is private, so to speak;
I can go as I came; there's my horse ready saddled;
I am master, in short, of the situation.

ANITRA   [*Approaching the tent-door.*]
   Prophet and Master!
PEER
   What would my slave?
ANITRA
   The Sons of the desert await at thy tent-door;
   They pray for the light of thy countenance——

*Or "ego." (Translator's note)

PEER

    Stop!
    Say in the distance I'd have them assemble;
    Say from the distance I hear all their prayers.
    Add that I suffer no menfolk in here
    Men, my child, are a worthless crew,—
    Inveterate rascals you well may call them!
    Anitra, you can't think how shamelessly
    They have swind—— I mean they have sinned, my child!—
    Well, enough now of that; you may dance for me, damsels!
    The Prophet would banish the memories that gall him.

THE GIRLS   [Dancing.]

    The Prophet is good! The Prophet is grieving
    For the ill that the sons of the dust have wrought!
    The Prophet is mild; to his mildness be praises;
    He opens to sinners his Paradise!

PEER   [His eyes following ANITRA during the dance.]

    Legs as nimble as drumsticks flitting.
    She's a dainty morsel indeed, that wench!
    It's true she has somewhat extravagant contours,—
    Not quite in accord with the norms of beauty.
    But what is beauty? A mere convention,—
    A coin made current by time and place.
    And just the extravagant seems most attractive
    When one of the normal has drunk one's fill.
    In the law-bound one misses all intoxication.
    Either plump to excess or excessively lean;
    Either parlously young or portentously old;—
    The medium is mawkish.—
    Her feet—they are not altogether clean;
    No more are her arms; in especial one of them.
    But that is at bottom no drawback at all.
    I should rather call it a qualification—
    Anitra, come listen!

ANITRA   [Approaching.]

    Thy handmaiden hears!

PEER

    You are tempting, my daughter! The Prophet is touched.

If you don't believe me, then hear the proof;—
I'll make you a Houri in Paradise!

ANITRA

Impossible, Lord!

PEER

What? You think I am jesting?
I'm in sober earnest, as true as I live!

ANITRA

But I haven't a soul.

PEER

Then of course you must get one!

ANITRA

How, Lord?

PEER

Just leave me alone for that;—
I shall look after your education.
No soul? Why, truly you're not over bright,
As the saying goes. I've observed it with pain.
But pooh! for a soul you can always find room.
Come here! let me measure your brain-pan, child.—
There is room, there is room, I was sure there was.
It's true you never will penetrate
Very deep; to a large soul you'll scarcely attain;—
But never you mind; it won't matter a bit;—
You'll have plenty to carry you through with credit——

ANITRA

The Prophet is gracious——

PEER

You hesitate? Speak!

ANITRA

But I'd rather——

PEER

Say on; don't waste time about it.

ANITRA

I don't care so much about having a soul;—
Give me rather——

PEER

What, child?

ANITRA   [*Pointing to his turban.*]
    That lovely opal!
PEER   [*Enchanted, handing her the jewel.*]
    Anitra! Anitra! true daughter of Eve!
    I feel thee magnetic; for I am a man,
    And, as a much-esteemed author has phrased it:
    "Das Ewig-Weibliche ziehet uns an!"*

SCENE SEVENTH

A moonlight night. The palm-grove outside ANITRA's *tent.*

PEER GYNT *is sitting beneath a tree, with an Arabian lute in his hands. His beard and hair are clipped; he looks considerably younger.*

PEER GYNT   [*Plays and sings.*]
    I double-locked my Paradise,
    And took its key with me.
    The north-wind bore me seaward ho!
    While lovely women all forlorn
    Wept on the ocean strand.
    Still southward, southward clove my keel
    The salt sea-currents through.
    Where palms were swaying proud and fair,
    A garland round the ocean-bight,
    I set my ship afire.
    I climbed aboard the desert ship,
    A ship on four stout legs.
    It foamed beneath the lashing whip;—
    Oh, catch me; I'm a flitting bird;—
    I'm twittering on a bough!
    Anitra, thou'rt the palm-tree's must;
    That know I now full well!
    Ay, even the Angora goat-milk cheese
    Is scarcely half such dainty fare,

*Peer is thinking of a line from Johann Wolfgang von Goethe's *Faust*: "Das Ewig-Weibliche zieht uns hinan," which means "The eternal feminine draws us upward." However, he misquotes with words that mean "The eternal feminine attracts us."

Anitra, ah, as thou!
[*He hangs the lute over his shoulder, and comes forward.*]
Stillness! Is the fair one listening?
Has she heard my little song?
Peeps she from behind the curtain,
Veil and so forth cast aside?——
Hush! A sound as though a cork
From a bottle burst amain!
Now once more! And yet again!
Love-sighs can it be? or songs?——
No, it is distinctly snoring.——
Dulcet strain! Anitra sleepeth!
Nightingale, thy warbling stay!
Every sort of woe betide thee,
If with gurgling trill thou darest——
But, as says the text: Let be!
Nightingale, thou art a singer;
Ah, even such an one am I.
He, like me, ensnares with music
Tender, shrinking little hearts.
Balmy night is made for music;
Music is our common sphere;
In the act of singing, we are
We, Peer Gynt and nightingale.
And the maiden's very sleeping
Is my passion's crowning bliss;——
For the lips protruded o'er the
Beaker yet untasted quite——
But she's coming, I declare!
After all, it's best she should.

ANITRA   [*From the tent.*]
Master, call'st thou in the night?

PEER
Yes indeed, the Prophet calls.
I was wakened by the cat
With a furious hunting-hubbub——

ANITRA
Ah, not hunting-noises, Master;
It was something much, much worse.

PEER

What, then, was't?

ANITRA

Oh, spare me!

PEER

Speak!

ANITRA

Oh, I blush to——

PEER   [*Approaching.*]

Was it, mayhap,

That which filled me so completely

When I let you have my opal?

ANITRA   [*Horrified.*]

Liken thee, O earth's great treasure,

To a horrible old cat!

PEER

Child, from passion's standpoint viewed,

May a tom-cat and a prophet

Come to very much the same.

ANITRA

Master, jest like honey floweth

From thy lips.

PEER

My little friend,

You, like other maidens, judge

Great men by their outsides only.

I am full of jest at bottom,

Most of all when we're alone.

I am forced by my position

To assume a solemn mask.

Duties of the day constrain me;

All the reckonings and worry

That I have with one and all,

Make me oft a cross-grained prophet;

But it's only from the tongue out.——

Fudge, avaunt! *En tête-à-tête**

*Intimate, face-to-face encounter (French).

I'm Peer—well, the man I am.
Hei, away now with the prophet;
Me, myself, you have me here!
[*Seats himself under a tree, and draws her to him.*]
Come, Anitra, we will rest us
Underneath the palm's green fan-shade!
I'll lie whispering, you'll lie smiling;
Afterwards our rôles exchange we;
Then shall your lips, fresh and balmy,
To my smiling, passion whisper!

ANITRA   [*Lies down at his feet.*]
All thy words are sweet as singing,
Though I understand but little.
Master, tell me, can thy daughter
Catch a soul by listening?

PEER
Soul, and spirit's light and knowledge,
All in good time you shall have them.
When in east, on rosy streamers
Golden types print: Here is day,—
Then, my child, I'll give you lessons;
You'll be well brought up, no fear.
But, 'mid night's delicious stillness,
It were stupid if I should,
With a threadbare wisdom's remnants,
Play the part of pedagogue.—
And the soul, moreover, is not,
Looked at properly, the main thing.
It's the heart that really matters.

ANITRA
Speak, O Master! When thou speakest,
I see gleams, as though of opals!

PEER
Wisdom in extremes is folly;
Coward blossoms into tyrant;
Truth, when carried to excess,
Ends in wisdom written backwards.
Ay, my daughter, I'm forsworn

As a dog if there are not
Folk with o'erfed souls on earth
Who shall scarce attain to clearness.
Once I met with such a fellow,
Of the flock the very flower;
And even he mistook his goal,
Losing sense in blatant sound.—
See the waste round this oasis.
Were I but to swing my turban,
I could force the ocean-flood
To fill up the whole concern.
But I were a blockhead, truly
Seas and lands to go creating.
Know you what it is to live?

ANITRA

Teach me!

PEER

It is to be wafted
Dry-shod down the stream of time,
Wholly, solely as oneself.
Only in full manhood can I
Be the man I am, dear child!
Aged eagle moults his plumage,
Aged fogey lags declining,
Aged dame has ne'er a tooth left,
Aged churl gets withered hands,—
One and all get withered souls.
Youth! Ah Youth! I mean to reign,
As a sultan, whole and fiery,—
Not on Gyntiana's shores,
Under trellised vines and palm-leaves,—
But enthronëd in the freshness
Of a woman's virgin thoughts.—
See you now, my little maiden,
Why I've graciously bewitched you, —
Why I have your heart selected,
And established, so to speak,
There my being's Caliphate?

All your longings shall be mine.
I'm an autocrat in passion!
You shall live for me alone.
I'll be he who shall enthrall
You like gold and precious stones.
Should we part, then life is over,—
That is, your life, *nota bene!**
Every inch and fibre of you,
Will-less, without yea or nay,
I must know filled full of me.
Midnight beauties of your tresses,
All that's lovely to be named,
Shall, like Babylonian gardens,
Tempt your Sultan to his tryst.
After all, I don't complain, then,
Of your empty forehead-vault.
With a soul, one's oft absorbed in
Contemplation of oneself.
Listen, while we're on the subject,—
If you like it, faith, you shall
Have a ring about your ankle:—
'Twill be best for both of us.
I will be your soul by proxy;
For the rest—why, *status quo.*
[ANITRA *snores.*]
What! She sleeps! Then has it glided
Bootless past her, all I've said?—
No; it marks my influence o'er her
That she floats away in dreams
On my love-talk as it flows.
[*Rises, and lays trinkets in her lap.*]
Here are jewels! Here are more!
Sleep, Anitra! Dream of Peer——.
Sleep! In sleeping, you the crown have
Placed upon your Emperor's brow!
Victory on his Person's basis
Has Peer Gynt this night achieved.

---

* Take note; literally, note well (Latin).

Scene Eighth

A caravan route. The oasis is seen far off in the background.

PEER GYNT *comes galloping across the desert on his white horse, with AN-ITRA before him on his saddle-bow.*

ANITRA
Let be, or I'll bite you!
PEER
You little rogue!
ANITRA
What would you?
PEER
What would I? Play hawk and dove!
Run away with you! Frolic and frisk a bit!
ANITRA
For shame! An old prophet like you!
PEER
Oh, stuff!
The prophet's not old at all, you goose!
Do you think all this is a sign of age?
ANITRA
Let me go! I want to go home!
PEER
Coquette!
What, home! To papa-in-law! That would be fine!
We madcap birds that have flown from the cage
Must never come into his sight again.
Besides, my child, in the self-same place
It's wisest never to stay too long;
For familiarity lessens respect;—
Most of all when one comes as a prophet or such.
One should show oneself glimpse-wise and pass like a dream.
Faith, 'twas time that the visit should come to an end.
They're unstable of soul, are these sons of the desert;—
Both incense and prayers dwindled off towards the end.
ANITRA
Yes, but are you a prophet?

PEER

Your Emperor I am!

[*Tries to kiss her.*]

Why just see now how coy the wee woodpecker is!

ANITRA

Give me that ring that you have on your finger.

PEER

Take, sweet Anitra, the whole of the trash!

ANITRA

Thy words are as songs! Oh, how dulcet their sound!

PEER

How blessëd to know oneself loved to this pitch!

I'll dismount! Like your slave, I will lead your palfrey!

[*Hands her his riding-whip, and dismounts.*]

There now, my rosebud, you exquisite flower!

Here I'll go trudging my way through the sand,

Till a sunstroke o'ertakes me and finishes me.

I'm young, Anitra; bear that in mind!

You mustn't be shocked at my escapades.

Frolics and high jinks are youth's sole criterion!

And so, if your intellect weren't so dense,

You would see at a glance, oh my fair oleander,—

Your lover is frolicsome—*ergo*, he's young!

ANITRA

Yes, you are young. Have you any more rings?

PEER

Am I not? There, grab! I can leap like a buck!

Were there vine-leaves around, I would garland my brow.

To be sure I am young! Hei, I'm going to dance!

[*Dances and sings.*]

I am a blissful game-cock!

Peck me, my little pullet!

Hop-sa-sa! Let me trip it;—

I am a blissful game-cock!

ANITRA

You are sweating, my prophet; I fear you will melt;

Hand me that heavy bag hung at your belt.

PEER

Tender solicitude! Bear the purse ever;—
Hearts that can love are content without gold!
[*Dances and sings again.*]
Young Peer Gynt is the maddest wag;—
He knows not what foot he shall stand upon.
Pooh, says Peer;—pooh, never mind!
Young Peer Gynt is the maddest wag!

ANITRA

What joy when the Prophet steps forth in the dance!

PEER

Oh, bother the Prophet!—Suppose we change clothes!
Heisa! Strip off!

ANITRA

Your caftan were too long,
Your girdle too wide, and your stockings too tight——

PEER

*Eh bien!**
[*Kneels down.*]
But vouchsafe me a vehement sorrow;—
To a heart full of love, it is sweet to suffer!
Listen; as soon as we're home at my castle——

ANITRA

In your Paradise;—have we far to ride?

PEER

Oh, a thousand miles or——

ANITRA

Too far!

PEER

Oh, listen;—
You shall have the soul that I promised you once——

ANITRA

Oh, thank you; I'll get on without the soul.
But you asked for a sorrow——

PEER [*Rising.*]

Ay, curse me, I did!

*Oh, well (French).

A keen one, but short,—to last two or three days.
ANITRA
    Anitra obeyeth the Prophet!—Farewell!
    [*Gives him a smart cut across the fingers, and dashes off; at a tearing gal-
    lop, back across the desert.*]
PEER   [*Stands for a long time thunderstruck.*]
    Well now, may I be———!

Scene Ninth

The same place, an hour later.

PEER GYNT *is stripping off his Turkish costume, soberly and thoughtfully, bit
by bit. Last of all, he takes his little travelling-cap out of his coat pocket, puts
it on, and stands once more in European dress.*

PEER   [*Throwing the turban far away from him.*]
    There lies the Turk, then, and here stand I!—
    These heathenish doings are no sort of good.
    It's lucky 'twas only a matter of clothes,
    And not, as the saying goes, bred in the bone.—
    What tempted me into that galley at all?
    It's best, in the long run, to live as a Christian,
    To put away peacock-like ostentation,
    To base all one's dealings on law and morality,
    To be ever oneself, and to earn at the last a
    Speech at one's grave-side, and wreaths on one's coffin.
    [*Walks a few steps.*]
    The hussy;—she was on the very verge
    Of turning my head clean topsy-turvy.
    May I be a troll if I understand
    What it was that dazed and bemused me so.
    Well; it's well that's done: had the joke been carried
    But one step on, I'd have looked absurd.—
    I have erred;———but at least it's a consolation
    That my error was due to the false situation.
    It wasn't my personal self that fell.
    'Twas in fact this prophetical way of life,

So utterly lacking the salt of activity,
That took its revenge in these qualms of bad taste.
It's a sorry business this prophetising!
One's office compels one to walk in a mist;
In playing the prophet, you throw up the game*
The moment you act like a rational being.†
In so far I've done what the occasion demanded,
In the mere fact of paying my court to that goose.
But, nevertheless——
[*Bursts out laughing.*]
H'm, to think of it now!
To try to make time stop by jigging and dancing,
And to cope with the current by capering and prancing!
To thrum on the lute-strings, to fondle and sigh,
And end, like a rooster,——by getting well plucked,
Such conduct is truly prophetic frenzy.——
Yes, plucked!——Phew! I'm plucked clean enough indeed.
Well, well, I've a trifle still left in reserve;
I've a little in America, a little in my pocket,
So I won't be quite driven to beg my bread.——
And at bottom this middle condition is best.
I'm no longer a slave to my coachman and horses;
I haven't to fret about postchaise or baggage;
I am master, in short, of the situation.——
What path should I choose? Many paths lie before me;
And a wise man is known from a fool by his choice.
My business life is a finished chapter;
My love-sports, too, are a cast-off garment.
I feel no desire to live back like a crab.
"Forward or back, and it's just as far;
Out or in, and it's just as strait,"——
So I seem to have read in some luminous‡ work.——
I'll try something new, then; ennoble my course;
Find a goal worth the labour and money it costs.

---

*Literally, "you're looed" or "euchred." (Translator's note)
†Literally, "behave as though sober and wakeful." (Translator's note).
‡Literally, *spiritual*." (Translator's note)

Shall I write my life without dissimulation,—
A book for guidance and imitation?
Or, stay——! I have plenty of time at command;—
What if, as a travelling scientist,
I should study past ages and time's voracity?
Ay, sure enough, that is the thing for me!
Legends I read e'en in childhood's days,
And since then I've kept up that branch of learning.—
I will follow the path of the human race!
Like a feather I'll float on the stream of history,
Make it all live again, as in a dream,—
See the heroes battling for truth and right,
As an onlooker only, in safety ensconced,—
See thinkers perish and martyrs bleed,
See empires founded and vanish away,—
See world-epochs grow from their trifling seeds;
In short, I will skim off the cream of history.—
I must try to get hold of a volume of Becker,
And travel as far as I can by chronology.—
It's true—my grounding's by no means thorough,
And history's wheels within wheels are deceptive;—
But pooh; the wilder the starting-point,
The result will oft be the more original.—
How exalting it is, now, to choose a goal,
And drive straight for it, like flint and steel!
[*With quiet emotion.*]
To break off all round one, on every side,
The bonds that bind one to home and friends,—
To blow into atoms one's hoarded wealth,—
To bid one's love and its joys good night,—
All simply to find the arcana of truth,—
[*Wiping a tear from his eye.*]
That is the test of the true man of science!—
I feel myself happy beyond all measure.
Now I have fathomed my destiny's riddle.
Now 'tis but persevering through thick and thin!
It's excusable, sure, if I hold up my head,
And feel my worth, as the man, Peer Gynt,

Also called Human-life's Emperor.——
I will own the sum-total of bygone days;
I'll nevermore tread in the paths of the living.
The present is not worth so much as a shoe-sole;
All faithless and marrowless the doings of men;
Their soul has no wings and their deeds no weight;——
[Shrugs his shoulders.]
And women,—ah, they are a worthless crew!
[Goes off.]

SCENE TENTH

A summer day. Far up in the North. A hut in the forest. The door, with a
large wooden bar, stands open. Reindeer-horns over it. A flock of goats by
the wall of the hut.

A MIDDLE-AGED WOMAN, fair-haired and comely, sits spinning outside
in the sunshine.

THE WOMAN   [Glances down the path and sings.]
Maybe both the winter and spring will pass by,
And the next summer too, and the whole of the year;——
But thou wilt come one day, that know I full well;
And I will await thee, as I promised of old.*
[Calls the goats, spins, and sings again.]
God strengthen thee, whereso thou goest in the world!
God gladden thee, if at his footstool thou stand!
Here will I await thee till thou comest again;
And if thou wait up yonder, then there we'll meet, my friend!

SCENE ELEVENTH

In Egypt. Daybreak. MEMNON's STATUE amid the sands.

PEER GYNT enters on foot, and looks around him for a while.

*Sidst—literally, "when last we met." (Translator's note)

PEER GYNT

Here I might fittingly start on my wanderings.——
So now, for a change, I've become an Egyptian;
But Egyptian on the basis of the Gyntish I.
To Assyria next I will bend my steps.
To begin right back at the world's creation
Would lead to nought but bewilderment.
I will go round about all the Bible history;
It's secular traces I'll always be coming on;
And to look, as the saying goes, into its seams,
Lies entirely outside both my plan and my powers.
[*Sits upon a stone.*]
Now I will rest me, and patiently wait
Till the statue has sung its habitual dawn-song.
When breakfast is over, I'll climb up the pyramid;
If I've time, I'll look through its interior afterwards.
Then I'll go round the head of the Red Sea by land;
Perhaps I may hit on King Potiphar's grave.*
Next I'll turn Asiatic. In Babylon I'll seek for
The far-renowned harlots and hanging gardens,——
That's to say, the chief traces of civilisation.
Then at one bound to the ramparts of Troy.
From Troy there's a fareway by sea direct
Across to the glorious ancient Athens;——
There on the spot will I, stone by stone,
Survey the Pass that Leonidas† guarded.
I will get up the works of the better philosophers,
Find the prison where Socrates suffered, a martyr——-;
Oh no, by-the-bye——there's a war there at present——-!
Well, my studies in Hellas must e'en be postponed.
[*Looks at his watch.*]
It's really too bad, such an age as it takes
For the sun to rise. I am pressed for time.
Well then, from Troy——it was there I left off——

---

*In the Bible, Genesis 39, Potiphar was the commander of the Pharaoh's guard; his wife tried to seduce Joseph.

†King of Sparta, who in 480 B.C. died defending the Thermopylae pass against the Persian army.

[*Rises and listens.*]
What is that strange sort of murmur that's rushing——?
[*Sunrise.*]
MEMNON'S STATUE   [*Sings.*]
From the demigod's ashes there soar, youth renewing,
Birds ever singing.
Zeus the Omniscient
Shaped them contending.
Owls of wisdom,
My birds, where do they slumber?
Thou must die if thou rede not
The song's enigma!
PEER
How strange now,—I really fancied there came
From the statue a sound. Music, this, of the Past.
I heard the stone-accents now rising, now sinking.——
I will register it, for the learned to ponder.
[*Notes in his pocket-book.*]
"The statue did sing. I heard the sound plainly,
But didn't quite follow the text of the song.
The whole thing, of course, was hallucination.——
Nothing else of importance observed to-day."
[*Proceeds on his way.*]

Scene Twelfth

Near the village of Gizeh. The great SPHINX *carved out of the rock. In
the distance the spires and minarets of Cairo.*

PEER GYNT *enters; he examines the* SPHINX *attentively, now through his
eyeglass, now through his hollowed hand.*

PEER GYNT
Now, where in the world have I met before
Something half forgotten that's like this hobgoblin?
For met it I have, in the north or the south.
Was it a person? And, if so, who?
That Memnon, it afterwards crossed my mind,
Was like the Old Man of the Dovrë, so called,

Just as he sat there, stiff and stark,
Planted on end on the stumps of pillars.——
But this most curious mongrel here,
This changeling, a lion and woman in one,——
Does he come to me, too, from a fairy-tale,
Or from a remembrance of something real?
From a fairy-tale? Ho, I remember the fellow!
Why, of course it's the Boyg, that I smote on the skull,——
That is, I dreamt it,——I lay in fever.——
[*Going closer.*]
The self-same eyes, and the self-same lips;——
Not quite so lumpish; a little more cunning;
But the same, for the rest, in all essentials.——
Ay, so that's it, Boyg; so you're like a lion
When one sees you from behind and meets you in the day-time!
Are you still good at riddling? Come, let us try.
Now we shall see if you answer as last time!
[*Calls out towards the* SPHINX.]
Hei, Boyg, who are you?

A VOICE   [*Behind the* SPHINX.]
Ach, Sphinx, wer bist du?

PEER
What! Echo answers in German! How strange!

THE VOICE
Wer bist du?

PEER
It speaks it quite fluently too!
That observation is new, and my own.
[*Notes in his book.*]
"Echo in German. Dialect, Berlin."
[BEGRIFFENFELDT *comes out from behind the* SPHINX.]

BEGRIFFENFELDT*
A man.

PEER
Oh, then it was he that was chattering.
[*Notes again.*]

*This name is comic; in German it literally means "comprehended field."

"Arrived in the sequel at other results."

BEGRIFFENFELDT   [*With all sorts of restless antics.*]

Excuse me, mein Herr———! Eine Lebensfrage———!*

What brings you to this place precisely to-day?

PEER

A visit. I'm greeting a friend of my youth.

BEGRIFFENFELDT

What? The Sphinx———?

PEER   [*Nods.*]

Yes, I knew him in days gone by.

BEGRIFFENFELDT

Famos!† And that after such a night!

My temples are hammering as though they would burst!

You know him, man! Answer! Say on! Can you tell

What he is?

PEER

What he is? Yes, that's easy enough.

He's himself.

BEGRIFFENFELDT   [*With a bound.*]

Ha, the riddle of life lightened forth

In a flash to my vision!—It's certain he is

Himself?

PEER

Yes, he says so, at any rate.

BEGRIFFENFELDT

Himself! Revolution! thine hour is at hand!

[*Takes off his hat.*]

Your name, pray, mein Herr?

PEER

I was christened Peer Gynt.

BEGRIFFENFELDT   [*In rapt admiration.*]

Peer Gynt! Allegoric! I might have foreseen it.—

Peer Gynt? That must clearly imply: The Unknown,—

The Comer whose coming was augured to me———

PEER

What, really? And now you are here to meet———?

---

*The whole sentence means "Excuse me, Sir—! A question of life and death."

†Extraordinary (German).

BEGRIFFENFELDT

Peer Gynt! Profound! Enigmatic! Incisive!

Each word, as it were, an abysmal lesson!

What are you?

PEER   [*Modestly.*]

I've always endeavoured to be

Myself. For the rest, here's my passport, you see.

BEGRIFFENFELDT

Again that mysterious word at the bottom.

[*Seizes him by the wrist.*]

To Cairo! The Interpreters' Kaiser is found!

PEER

Kaiser?

BEGRIFFENFELDT

Come on!

PEER

Am I really known——?

BEGRIFFENFELDT   [*Dragging him away.*]

The Interpreters' Kaiser—on the basis of Self!

SCENE THIRTEENTH

In Cairo. A large courtyard, surrounded by high walls and buildings. Barred windows; iron cages.

THREE KEEPERS *in the courtyard.* A FOURTH *comes in.*

THE NEWCOMER

Schafmann, say, where's the director gone?

A KEEPER

He drove out this morning some time before dawn.

THE FIRST

I think something must have occurred to annoy him;

For last night——

ANOTHER

Hush, be quiet; he's there at the door!

[BEGRIFFENFELDT *leads* PEER GYNT *in, locks the gate, and puts the key in his pocket.*]

PEER   [*To himself.*]
  Indeed an exceedingly gifted man;
  Almost all that he says is beyond comprehension.
  [*Looks around.*]
  So this is the Club of the Savants, eh?

BEGRIFFENFELDT
  Here you will find them, every man jack of them;——
  The group of Interpreters threescore and ten;*
  Of late it has grown by a hundred and sixty——
  [*Shouts to the* KEEPERS.]
  Mikkel, Schlingelberg, Schafmann, Fuchs,——
  Into the cages with you at once!

THE KEEPERS
  We!

BEGRIFFENFELDT
  Who else, pray? Get in, get in!
  When the world twirls around, we must twirl with it too.
  [*Forces them into a cage.*]
  He's arrived this morning, the mighty Peer;——
  The rest you can guess,——I need say no more.
  [*Locks the cage door, and throws the key into a well.*]

PEER
  But, my dear Herr Doctor and Director, pray——?

BEGRIFFENFELDT
  Neither one nor the other! I was before——
  Herr Peer, are you secret? I must ease my heart——

PEER   [*With increasing uneasiness.*]
  What is it?

BEGRIFFENFELDT
  Promise you will not tremble.

PEER
  I will do my best, but——

*This is understood to refer to the authors of the Greek version of the Old Testament, known as the Septuagint. We are unable to account for the hundred and sixty recruits to their company. (Translator's note)

BEGRIFFENFELDT   [*Draws him into a corner, and whispers.*]
    The Absolute Reason
    Departed this life at eleven last night.
PEER
    God help me——!
BEGRIFFENFELDT
    Why, yes, it's extremely deplorable.
    And as I'm placed, you see, it is doubly unpleasant;
    For this institution has passed up to now
    For what's called a madhouse.
PEER
    A madhouse, ha!
BEGRIFFENFELDT
    Not now, understand!
PEER   [*Softly, pale with fear.*]
    Now I see what the place is!
    And the man is mad;—and there's none that knows it!
    [*Tries to steal away.*]
BEGRIFFENFELDT   [*Following him.*]
    However, I hope you don't misunderstand me?
    When I said he was dead, I was talking stuff.
    He's beside himself. Started clean out of his skin,——
    Just like my compatriot Münchausen's fox.*
PEER
    Excuse me a moment——
BEGRIFFENFELDT   [*Holding him back.*]
    I meant like an eel;—
    It was not like a fox. A needle through his eye;—
    And he writhed on the wall——
PEER
    Where can rescue be found!
BEGRIFFENFELDT
    A snick round his neck, and whip! out of his skin!
PEER
    He's raving! He's utterly out of his wits!

*Karl Friedrich von Münchausen (1720–1797), known as Baron Liar for telling stories of improbable adventures; he claimed to have made a fox jump out of its skin.

BEGRIFFENFELDT

> Now it's patent, and can't be dissimulated,
> That this from-himself-going must have for result
> A complete revolution by sea and land.
> The persons one hitherto reckoned as mad,
> You see, became normal last night at eleven,
> Accordant with Reason in its newest phase.
> And more, if the matter be rightly regarded,
> It's patent that, at the aforementioned hour,
> The sane folks, so called, began forthwith to rave.

PEER

> You mentioned the hour, sir; my time is but scant——

BEGRIFFENFELDT

> Your time, did you say? There you jog my remembrance!
> [*Opens a door and calls out.*]
> Come forth all! The time that shall be is proclaimed!
> Reason is dead and gone; long live Peer Gynt!

PEER

> Now, my dear good fellow——!
> [*The* LUNATICS *come one by one, and at intervals, into the courtyard.*]

BEGRIFFENFELDT

> Good morning! Come forth,
> And hail the dawn of emancipation!
> Your Kaiser has come to you!

PEER

> Kaiser?

BEGRIFFENFELDT

> Of course!

PEER

> But the honour's so great, so entirely excessive——

BEGRIFFENFELDT

> Oh, do not let any false modesty sway you
> At an hour such as this.

PEER

> But at least give me time——
> No, indeed, I'm not fit; I'm completely dumbfounded!

BEGRIFFENFELDT

> A man who has fathomed the Sphinx's meaning,

A man who's himself!

PEER

Ay, but that's just the rub.
It's true that in everything I am myself;
But here the point is, if I follow your meaning,
To be, so to phrase it, outside oneself.

BEGRIFFENFELDT

Outside? No, there you are strangely mistaken!
It's here, sir, that one is oneself with a vengeance;
Oneself, and nothing whatever besides.
We go, full sail, as our very selves.
Each one shuts himself up in the barrel of self,
In the self-fermentation he dives to the bottom,—
With the self-bung he seals it hermetically,
And seasons the staves in the well of self.
No one has tears for the other's woes;
No one has mind for the other's ideas.
We're our very selves, both in thought and tone,
Ourselves to the spring-board's uttermost verge,—
And so, if a Kaiser's to fill the Throne,
It is clear that you are the very man.

PEER

O would that the devil——!

BEGRIFFENFELDT

Come, don't be cast down;
Almost all things in nature are new at the first.
"Oneself";—come, here you shall see an example;
I'll choose you at random the first man that comes——
[*To a gloomy figure.*]
Good-day, Huhu? Well, my boy, wandering round
For ever with misery's impress upon you?

HUHU*

Can I help it, when the people,

*Huhu is a language reformer. His ideas are a caricature of a movement to insti-
tutionalize colloquial Norwegian as the official language of Norway. At the time of
Ibsen, the official language was still heavily influenced by Danish. It was in this Danish-
influenced language, and not present-day Norwegian, that Ibsen himself wrote.

Race* by race, dies untranslated.†
[*To* PEER GYNT.]
You're a stranger; will you listen?
PEER   [*Bowing.*]
Oh, by all means!
HUHU
Lend your ear then.——
Eastward far, like brow-borne garlands,
Lie the Malabarish seaboards.
Hollanders and Portugueses
Compass all the land with culture.
There, moreover, swarms are dwelling
Of the pure-bred Malabaris.
These have muddled up the language,
They now lord it in the country.——
But in long-departed ages
There the orang-outang was the ruler.
He, the forest's lord and master,
Freely fought and snarled in freedom.
As the hand of nature shaped him,
Just so grinned he, just so gaped he.
He could shriek unreprehended;
He was ruler in his kingdom.——
Ah, but then the foreign yoke came,
Marred the forest-tongue primeval.
Twice two hundred years of darkness‡
Brooded o'er the race of monkeys;
And, you know, nights so protracted
Bring a people to a standstill.——
Mute are now the wood-notes primal;
Grunts and growls are heard no longer;——
If we'd utter our ideas,
It must be by means of language.

*Literally, "generation."
†Literally, "uninterpreted."
‡An allusion to the long period of stagnation in the history of Norway under the Danish rule—say, from 1400 to 1800. (Translator's note)

What constraint on all and sundry!
Hollanders and Portugueses,
Half-caste race and Malabaris,
All alike must suffer by it.——
I have tried to fight the battle
Of our real, primal wood-speech,——
Tried to bring to life its carcass,——
Proved the people's right of shrieking,——
Shrieked myself, and shown the need of
Shrieks in poems for the people.——
Scantly, though, my work is valued.——
Now I think you grasp my sorrow.
Thanks for lending me a hearing;——
Have you counsel, let me hear it!

PEER   [*Softly.*]

It is written: Best be howling
With the wolves that are about you.
[*Aloud.*]
Friend, if I remember rightly,
There are bushes in Morocco,
Where orang-outangs in plenty
Live with neither bard nor spokesman;——
Their speech sounded Malabarish;——
It was classical and pleasing.
Why don't you, like other worthies,
Emigrate to serve your country?

HUHU

Thanks for lending me a hearing;——
I will do as you advise me.
[*With a large gesture.*]
East! thou hast disowned thy singer!
West! thou hast orang-outangs still!
[*Goes.*]

BEGRIFFENFELDT

Well, was he himself? I should rather think so.
He's filled with his own affairs, simply and solely.
He's himself in all that comes out of him,——
Himself, just because he's beside himself.

Come here! Now I'll show you another one
Who's no less, since last evening, accordant with Reason.
[*To a* FELLAH,* *with a mummy on his back.*]
King Apis, how goes it, my mighty lord?

THE FELLAH   [*Wildly, to* PEER GYNT.]

Am I King Apis?

PEER   [*Getting behind the* DOCTOR.]

I'm sorry to say
I'm not quite at home in the situation;
But I certainly gather, to judge by your tone——

THE FELLAH

Now you too are lying.

BEGRIFFENFELDT

Your Highness should state
How the whole matter stands.

THE FELLAH

Yes, I'll tell him my tale.
[*Turns to* PEER GYNT.]
Do you see whom I bear on my shoulders?
His name was King Apis of old.
Now he goes by the title of mummy,
And withal he's completely dead.
All the pyramids yonder he builded,
And hewed out the mighty Sphinx,
And fought, as the Doctor puts it,
With the Turks, both to rechts and links.
And therefore the whole of Egypt
Exalted him as a god,
And set up his image in temples,
In the outward shape of a bull.——
But *I* am this very King Apis,
I see that as clear as day;
And if you don't understand it,
You shall understand it soon.
King Apis, you see, was out hunting,
And got off his horse awhile,

---

*Peasant (Arabic).

And withdrew himself unattended
To a part of my ancestor's land.
But the field that King Apis manured
Has nourished me with its corn;
And if further proofs are demanded,
Know, I have invisible horns.
Now, isn't it most accursëd
That no one will own my might!
By birth I am Apis of Egypt,
But a fellah in other men's sight.
Can you tell me what course to follow?—
Then counsel me honestly.—
The problem is how to make me
Resemble King Apis the Great.

PEER

Build pyramids then, your highness,
And carve out a greater Sphinx,
And fight, as the Doctor puts it,
With the Turks, both to rechts and links.

THE FELLAH

Ay, that is all mighty fine talking!
A fellah! A hungry louse!
I, who scarcely can keep my hovel
Clear even of rats and mice.
Quick, man,—think of something better,
That'll make me both great and safe,
And further, exactly like to
King Apis that's on my back!

PEER

What if your highness hanged you,
And then, in the lap of earth,
'Twixt the coffin's natural frontiers,
Kept still and completely dead.

THE FELLAH

I'll do it! My life for a halter!
To the gallows with hide and hair!—
At first there will be some difference,

But that time will smooth away.

[*Goes off and prepares to hang himself.*]

BEGRIFFENFELDT

Ther's a personality for you, Herr Peer,—

A man of method——

PEER

Yes, yes; I see——;

But he'll really hang himself! God grant us grace!

I'll be ill;—I can scarcely command my thoughts.

BEGRIFFENFELDT

A state of transition; it won't last long.

PEER

Transition? To what? With your leave—I must go——

BEGRIFFENFELDT   [*Holding him.*]

Are you crazy?

PEER

Not yet——. Crazy? Heaven forbid!

[*A commotion. The Minister* HUSSEIN* *forces his way through the crowd.*]

HUSSEIN

They tell me a Kaiser has come to-day.

[*To* PEER GYNT.]

It is you?

PEER   [*In desperation.*]

Yes, that is a settled thing!

HUSSEIN

Good.—Then no doubt there are notes to be answered?

PEER   [*Tearing his hair.*]

Come on! Right you are, sir;—the madder the better!

HUSSEIN

Will you do me the honour of taking a dip?

[*Bowing deeply.*]

I am a pen.

PEER   [*Bowing still deeper.*]

Why then I am quite clearly

A rubbishy piece of imperial parchment.

*See note p. 109. (Translator's note)

HUSSEIN

My story, my lord, is concisely this:

They take me for a pounce-box,* and I am a pen.

PEER

My story, Sir Pen, is, to put it briefly:

I'm a blank sheet of paper that no one will write on.

HUSSEIN

No man understands in the least what I'm good for;

They all want to use me for scattering sand with!

PEER

I was in a woman's keeping a silver-clasped book;—

It's one and the same misprint to be either mad or sane!

HUSSEIN

Just fancy, what an exhausting life.

To be a pen and never taste the edge of a knife!

PEER   [*With a high leap.*]

Just fancy, for a reindeer to leap from on high—

To fall and fall—and never feel the ground beneath your hoofs!

HUSSEIN

A knife! I am blunt;—quick, mend me and slit me!

The world will go to ruin if they don't mend my point for me!

PEER

A pity for the world which, like other self-made things,

Was reckoned by the Lord to be so excellently good.

BEGRIFFENFELDT

Here's a knife!

HUSSEIN   [*Seizing it.*]

Ah, how I shall lick up the ink now!

Oh, what rapture to cut oneself!

[*Cuts his throat.*]

BEGRIFFENFELDT   [*Stepping aside.*]

Pray do not sputter.

PEER   [*In increasing terror.*]

Hold him!

*The pounce-box (for strewing "pounce" or sand on undried ink) had not yet been quite superseded by blotting-paper. (Translator's note)

HUSSEIN

Ay, hold me! That is the word!

Hold! Hold the pen! On the desk with the paper——!

[*Falls.*]

I'm outworn. The postscript—remember it, pray:

He lived and he died as a fate-guided pen.*

PEER   [*Dizzily.*]

What shall I——! What am I? Thou mighty——hold fast!

I am all that thou wilt,—I'm a Turk, I'm a sinner——

A hill-troll——; but help;—there was something that burst——!

[*Shrieks.*]

I cannot just hit on thy name at the moment;—

Oh, come to my aid, thou—all madmen's protector!

[*Sinks down insensible.*]

BEGRIFFENFELDT   [*With a wreath of straw in his hand, gives a bound and sits astride of him.*]

Ha! See him in the mire enthronëd;—

Beside himself—— To crown him now!

[*Presses the wreath on* PEER GYNT's *head, and shouts:*]

Long life, long life to Self-hood's Kaiser!

SCHAFMANN   [*In the cage.*]

Es lebe hoch der grosse Peer!

*En påholden pen. Underskrive med påholden pen—to sign by touching a pen which is guided by another. (Translator's note)

ACT FIFTH

SCENE FIRST

On board a ship on the North Sea, off the Norwegian coast. Sunset.
Stormy weather.

PEER GYNT, *a vigorous old man, milk grizzled hair and beard, is standing*
aft on the poop. He is dressed half sailor-fashion, with a pea-jacket and long
boots. His clothing is rather the worse for wear; he himself is weather-beaten,
and has a somewhat harder expression. The CAPTAIN *is standing beside the*
steersman at the wheel. The crew are forward.

PEER GYNT   [*Leans with his arms on the bulwark, and gazes towards the*
    land.]
    Look at Hallingskarv* in his winter furs;——
    He's ruffling it, old one, in the evening glow.
    The Jokel, his brother, stands behind him askew;
    He's got his green ice-mantle still on his back.
    The Folgefånn, now, she is mighty fine,——
    Lying there like a maiden in spotless white.
    Don't you be madcaps, old boys that you are!
    Stand where you stand; you're but granite knobs.
THE CAPTAIN   [*Shouts forward.*]
    Two hands to the wheel, and the lantern aloft!
PEER
    It's blowing up stift——
THE CAPTAIN
    ——for a gale to-night.

*For Hallingskarv and, in the same speech, Jokel and Folgefånn, the translator
has provided the note "mountains and glaciers."

PEER

> Can one see the Rondë Hills from the sea?

THE CAPTAIN

> No, how should you? They lie at the back of the snowfields.

PEER

> Or Blåhö?*

THE CAPTAIN

> No; but from up in the rigging,
> You've a glimpse, in clear weather, of Galdhöpiggen.

PEER

> Where does Hårteig lie?

THE CAPTAIN   [*Pointing.*]

> About over there.

PEER

> I thought so.

THE CAPTAIN

> You know where you are, it appears.

PEER

> When I left the country, I sailed by here;
> And the dregs, says the proverb, hang in to the last.
> [*Spits, and gazes at the coast.*]
> In there, where the screes and the clefts lie blue,—
> Where the valleys, like trenches, gloom narrow and black,—
> And underneath, skirting the open fiords,—
> It's in places like these human beings abide.
> [*Looks at the* CAPTAIN.]
> They build far apart in this country.

THE CAPTAIN

> Ay;
> Few are the dwellings and far between.

PEER

> Shall we get in by day-break?

THE CAPTAIN

> Thereabouts;
> If we don't have too dirty a night altogether.

---

*For Blåhö and, in the following lines, Galdhöpiggen and Hårteig, the transla-
tor has provided the note "mountains and glaciers."

PEER

It grows thick in the west.

THE CAPTAIN

It does so.

PEER

Stop a bit!
You might put me in mind when we make up accounts—
I'm inclined, as the phrase goes, to do a good turn
To the crew——

THE CAPTAIN

I thank you.

PEER

It won't be much
I have dug for gold, and lost what I found;—
We are quite at loggerheads, Fate and I.
You know what I've got in safe keeping on board—
That's all I have left;—the rest's gone to the devil.

THE CAPTAIN

It's more than enough, though, to make you of weight
Among people at home here.

PEER

I've no relations.
There's no one awaiting the rich old curmudgeon.—
Well; that saves you, at least, any scenes on the pier!

THE CAPTAIN

Here comes the storm.

PEER

Well, remember then—
If any of your crew are in real need,
I won't look too closely after the money——

THE CAPTAIN

That's kind. They are most of them ill enough off;
They have all got their wives and their children at home.
With their wages alone they can scarce make ends meet;
But if they come home with some cash to the good,
It will be a return not forgot in a hurry.

PEER

What do you say? Have they wives and children?

Are they married?

THE CAPTAIN

Married? Ay, every man of them.

But the one that is worst off of all is the cook;

Black famine is ever at home in his house.

PEER

Married? They've folks that await them at home?

Folks to be glad when they come? Eh?

THE CAPTAIN

Of course,

In poor people's fashion.

PEER

And come they one evening,

What then?

THE CAPTAIN

Why, I daresay the goodwife will fetch

Something good for a treat——

PEER

And a light in the sconce?

THE CAPTAIN

Ay, ay, may be two; and a dram to their supper.

PEER

And there they sit snug! There's a fire on the hearth!

They've their children about them! The room's full of chatter;.

Not one hears another right out to an end,

For the joy that is on them——!

THE CAPTAIN

It's likely enough.

So it's really kind, as you promised just now,

To help eke things out.

PEER   [Thumping the bulwark.]

I'll be damned if I do!

Do you think I am mad? Would you have me fork out

For the sake of a parcel of other folks' brats?

I've slaved much too sorely in earning my cash.

There's nobody waiting for old Peer Gynt.

THE CAPTAIN

Well well; as you please then; your money's your own.

PEER

>Right! Mine it is, and no one else's.
>
>We'll reckon as soon as your anchor is down!
>
>Take my fare, in the cabin, from Panama here.
>
>Then brandy all round to the crew. Nothing more.
>
>If I give a doit more, slap my jaw for me, Captain.

THE CAPTAIN

>I owe you a quittance, and not a thrashing;—
>
>But excuse me, the wind's blowing up to a gale.
>
>[*He goes forward. It has fallen dark; lights are lit in the cabin. The sea increases. Fog and thick clouds.*]

PEER

>To have a whole bevy of youngsters at home;—
>
>Still to dwell in their minds as a coming delight;—
>
>To have others' thoughts follow you still on your path!—
>
>There's never a soul gives a thought to me.—
>
>Lights in the sconces! I'll put out those lights.
>
>I will hit upon something! I'll make them all drunk;—
>
>Not one of the devils shall go sober ashore.
>
>They shall all come home drunk to their children and wives!
>
>They shall curse; bang the table till it rings again,—
>
>They shall scare those that wait for them out of their wits!
>
>The goodwife shall scream and rush forth from the house,—
>
>Clutch her children along! All their joy gone to ruin!
>
>[*The ship gives a heavy lurch; he staggers and keeps his balance with difficulty.*]
>
>Why, that was a buffet and no mistake.
>
>The sea's hard at labour, as though it were paid for it;—
>
>It's still itself here on the coasts of the north;—
>
>A cross-sea, as wry and wrong-headed as ever——
>
>[*Listens.*]
>
>Why, what can those screams be?

THE LOOK-OUT   [*Forward.*]

>A wreck a-lee!

THE CAPTAIN   [*On the main deck, shouts.*]

>Starboard your helm! Bring her up to the wind!

THE MATE

>Are there men on the wreck?

THE LOOK-OUT

    I can just see three!

PEER

    Quick! lower the stern boat——

THE CAPTAIN

    She'd fill ere she floated.

    [*Goes forward.*]

PEER

    Who can think of that now?

    [*To some of the crew.*]

    If you're men, to the rescue!

    What the devil, if you should get a bit of a ducking!

THE BOATSWAIN

    It's out of the question in such a sea.

PEER

    They are screaming again! There's a lull in the wind.——

    Cook, will you risk it? Quick! I will pay——

THE COOK

    No, not if you offered me twenty pounds-sterling——

PEER

    You hounds! You chicken-hearts! Can you forget

    These are men that have goodwives and children at home?

    There they're sitting and waiting——

THE BOATSWAIN

    Well, patience is wholesome.

THE CAPTAIN

    Bear away from that sea!

THE MATE

    There the wreck capsized!

PEER

    All is silent of a sudden——!

THE BOATSWAIN

    Were they married, as you think,

    There are three new-baked widows even now in the world.

    [*The storm increases.* PEER GYNT *moves away aft.*]

PEER

    There is no faith left among men any more,——

    No Christianity,——well may they say it and write it;——

Their good deeds are few and their prayers are still fewer,
And they pay no respect to the Powers above them.——
In a storm like to-night's, he's a terror, the Lord is.
These beasts should be careful, and think, what's the truth,
That it's dangerous playing with elephants;——
And yet they must openly brave his displeasure!
I am no whit to blame; for the sacrifice
I can prove I stood ready, my money in hand.
But how does it profit me?——What says the proverb?
A conscience at ease is a pillow of down.
Oh ay, that is all very well on dry land,
But I'm blest if it matters a snuff on board ship,
When a decent man's out on the seas with such riff-raff.
At sea one can never be one's self;
One must go with the others from deck to keel;
If for boatswain and cook the hour of vengeance should strike,
I shall no doubt be swept to the deuce with the rest;——
One's personal welfare is clean set aside;——
One counts but as a sausage in slaughtering-time.——
My mistake is this: I have been too meek;
And I've had no thanks for it after all.
Were I younger, I think I would shift the saddle,
And try how it answered to lord it awhile.
There is time enough yet! They shall know in the parish
That Peer has come sailing aloft o'er the seas!
I'll get back the farmstead by fair means or foul;——
I will build it anew; it shall shine like a palace.
But none shall be suffered to enter the hall!
They shall stand at the gateway, all twirling their caps;——
They shall beg and beseech——that they freely may do;
But none gets so much as a farthing of mine.
If I've had to howl 'neath the lashes of fate,
Trust me to find folks I can lash in my turn——

THE STRANGE PASSENGER   [*Stands in the darkness at* PEER
　　GYNT's *side, and salutes him in friendly fashion.*]
　　Good evening!
PEER
　　Good evening! What——? Who are you?

THE PASSENGER

Your fellow-passenger, at your service.

PEER

Indeed? I thought I was the only one.

THE PASSENGER

A mistaken impression, which now is set right.

PEER

But it's singular that, for the first time to-night,

I should see you——

THE PASSENGER

I never come out in the day-time.

PEER

Perhaps you are ill? You're as white as a sheet——

THE PASSENGER

No, thank you—my health is uncommonly good.

PEER

What a raging storm!

THE PASSENGER

Ay, a blessëd one, man!

PEER

A blessëd one?

THE PASSENGER

Sea's running high as houses

Ah, one can feel one's mouth watering!

Just think of the wrecks that to-night will be shattered;—

And think, too, what corpses will drive ashore!

PEER

Lord save us!

THE PASSENGER

Have ever you seen a man strangled,

Or hanged,—or drowned?

PEER

This is going too far——!

THE PASSENGER

The corpses all laugh. But their laughter is forced;

And the most part are found to have bitten their tongues.

PEER

Hold off from me——!

THE PASSENGER
> Only one question, pray!
> If we, for example, should strike on a rock,
> And sink in the darkness——

PEER
> You think there is danger?

THE PASSENGER
> I really don't know what I ought to say.
> But suppose, now, I float and you go to the bottom——

PEER
> Oh, rubbish——

THE PASSENGER
> It's just a hypothesis.
> But when one is placed with one foot in the grave,
> One grows soft-hearted and open-handed——

PEER   [*Puts his hand in his pocket.*]
> Ho, money?

THE PASSENGER
> No, no; but perhaps you would kindly
> Make me a gift of your much-esteemed carcase——?

PEER
> This is too much!

THE PASSENGER
> No more than your body, you know!
> To help my researches in science——

PEER
> Begone!

THE PASSENGER
> But think, my dear sir——the advantage is yours!
> I'll have you laid open and brought to the light.
> What I specially seek is the centre of dreams,——
> And with critical care I'll look into your seams——

PEER
> Away with you!

THE PASSENGER
> Why, my dear sir——a drowned corpse——!

PEER
> Blasphemer! You're goading the rage of the storm!

I call it too bad! Here it's raining and blowing,
A terrible sea on, and all sorts of signs
Of something that's likely to shorten our days;—
And you carry on so as to make it come quicker!

THE PASSENGER

You're in no mood, I see, to negotiate further;
But time, you know, brings with it many a change——
[*Nods in a friendly fashion.*]
We'll meet when you're sinking, if not before;
Perhaps I may then find you more in the humour.
[*Goes into the cabin.*]

PEER

Unpleasant companions these scientists are!
With their freethinking ways——
[*To the* BOATSWAIN, *who is passing.*]
Hark, a word with you, friend!
That passenger? What crazy creature is he?

THE BOATSWAIN

I know of no passenger here but yourself.

PEER

No others? This thing's getting worse and worse.
[*To the* SHIP'S BOY, *who comes out of the cabin.*]
Who went down the companion just now?

THE BOY

The ship's dog, sir!
[*Passes on.*]

THE LOOK-OUT   [*Shouts.*]

Land close ahead!

PEER

Where's my box? Where's my trunk?
All the baggage on deck!

THE BOATSWAIN

We have more to attend to!

PEER

It was nonsense, captain! 'Twas only my joke;—
As sure as I'm here I will help the cook——

THE CAPTAIN

The jib's blown away!

THE MATE

    And there went the foresail!

THE BOATSWAIN   [*Shrieks from forward.*]

    Breakers under the bow!

THE CAPTAIN

    She will go to shivers!

    [*The ship strikes. Noise and confusion.*]

Scene Second

Close under the land, among sunken rocks and surf. The ship sinks. The jolly-boat, with two men in her, is seen for a moment through the scud. A sea strikes her; she fills and upsets. A shriek is heard; then all is silent for a while. Shortly afterwards the boat appears floating bottom upwards.

PEER GYNT *comes to the surface near the boat.*

PEER

    Help! Help! A boat! Help! I'll be drowned!

    Save me, oh Lord—as saith the text!

    [*Clutches hold of the boat's keel.*]

THE COOK   [*Comes up on the other side.*]

    Oh, Lord God—for my children's sake,

    Have mercy! Let me reach the land!

    [*Seizes hold of the keel.*]

PEER

    Let go!

THE COOK

    Let go!

PEER

    I'll strike!

THE COOK

    So'll I!

PEER

    I'll crush you down with kicks and blows!

    Let go your hold! She won't float two!

THE COOK

    I know it! Yield!

PEER

    Yield you!

THE COOK

    Oh yes!

    [*They fight; one of the* COOK's *hands is disabled; he clings on with the other.*]

PEER

    Off with that hand!

THE COOK

    Oh, kind sir—spare!

    Think of my little ones at home!

PEER

    I need my life far more than you,

    For I am lone and childless still.

THE COOK

    Let go! You've lived, and I am young!

PEER

    Quick; haste you; sink;—you drag us down.

THE COOK

    Have mercy! Yield in heaven's name!

    There's none to miss and mourn for you—

    [*His hands slips; he screams:*]

    I'm drowning!

PEER   [*Seizing him.*]

    By this wisp of hair

    I'll hold you; say your Lord's Prayer, quick!

THE COOK

    I can't remember; all turns black——

PEER

    Come, the essentials in a word——!

THE COOK

    Give us this day——!

PEER

    Skip that part, Cook;

    You'll get all you need, safe enough.

THE COOK
> Give us this day——
PEER
> The same old song!
> 'Tis plain you were a cook in life——
> [*The* COOK *slips from his grasp.*]
THE COOK　[*Sinking.*]
> Give us this day our——
> [*Disappears.*]
PEER
> Amen, lad!
> To the last gasp you were yourself.——
> [*Draws himself up on to the bottom of the boat.*]
> So long as there is life there's hope——
THE STRANGE PASSENGER　[*Catches hold of the boat.*]
> Good morning!
PEER
> Hoy!
THE PASSENGER
> I heard you shout.——
> It's pleasant finding you again.
> Well? So my prophecy came true!
PEER
> Let go! Let go! 'Twill scarce float one!
THE PASSENGER
> I'm striking out with my left leg.
> I'll float, if only with their tips
> My fingers rest upon this ledge.
> But apropos: your body——
PEER
> Hush!
THE PASSENGER
> The rest, of course, is done for, clean——
PEER
> No more!
THE PASSENGER
> Exactly as you please.
> [*Silence.*]

PEER
>Well?

THE PASSENGER
>I am silent.

PEER
>Satan's tricks!——
>What now?

THE PASSENGER
>I'm waiting.

PEER   [*Tearing his hair.*]
>I'll go mad!——
>What are you?

THE PASSENGER   [*Nods.*]
>Friendly.

PEER
>What else! Speak!

THE PASSENGER
>What think you? Do you know none other
>That's like me?

PEER
>Do I know the devil——?

THE PASSENGER   [*In a low voice.*]
>Is it his way to light a lantern
>For life's night-pilgrimage through fear?

PEER
>Ah, come! When once the thing's cleared up,
>You'd seem a messenger of light?

THE PASSENGER
>Friend,——have you once in each half-year
>Felt all the earnestness of dread?*

PEER
>Why, one's afraid when danger threatens;——
>But all your words have double meanings.†

Angst—literally, "dread" or "terror"—probably means here something like "conviction of sin." The influence of the Danish theologian Sören Kierkegård may be traced in this passage. (Translator's note)

†Literally, "Are set on screws." (Translator's note)

THE PASSENGER

> Ay, have you gained but once in life
> The victory that is given in dread?

PEER   [*Looks at him.*]

> Came you to ope for me a door,
> 'Twas stupid not to come before.
> What sort of sense is there in choosing
> Your time when seas gape to devour one?

THE PASSENGER

> Were, then, the victory more likely
> Beside your hearthstone, snug and quiet?

PEER

> Perhaps not; but your talk was quizzical.
> How could you fancy it awakening?

THE PASSENGER

> Where I come from, there smiles are prized
> As highly as pathetic style.

PEER

> All has its time; what fits the taxman,*
> So says the text, would damn the bishop.

THE PASSENGER

> The host whose dust inurned has slumbered
> Treads not on week-days the cothurnus.

PEER

> Avaunt thee, bugbear! Man, begone!
> I will not die! I must ashore!

THE PASSENGER

> Oh, as for that, be reassured;—
> One dies not midmost of Act Five.
> [*Glides away.*]

PEER

> Ah, there he let it out at last;—
> He was a sorry moralist.

***Tolder,* the biblical "publican." (Translator's note)

SCENE THIRD

Churchyard in a high-lying mountain parish.

A funeral is going on. By the grave, the PRIEST *and a gathering of people. The last verse of the psalm is being sung.* PEER GYNT *passes by on the road.*

PEER   [*At the gate.*]
　　Here's a countryman going the way of all flesh.
　　God be thanked that it isn't me.
　　[*Enters the churchyard.*]
THE PRIEST   [*Speaking beside the grave.*]
　　Now, when the soul has gone to meet its doom,
　　And here the dust lies, like an empty pod,—
　　Now, my dear friends, we'll speak a word or two
　　About this dead man's pilgrimage on earth.
　　He was not wealthy, neither was he wise,
　　His voice was weak, his bearing was unmanly,
　　He spoke his mind abashed and faltering,
　　He scarce was master at his own fireside;
　　He sidled into church, as though appealing
　　For leave, like other men, to take his place.
　　It was from Gudbrandsdale, you know, he came.
　　When here he settled he was but a lad;—
　　And you remember how, to the very last,
　　He kept his right hand hidden in his pocket.
　　That right hand in the pocket was the feature
　　That chiefly stamped his image on the mind,—
　　And therewithal his writhing, his abashed
　　Shrinking from notice wheresoe'er he went.
　　But, though he still pursued a path aloof,
　　And ever seemed a stranger in our midst,
　　You all know what he strove so hard to hide,—
　　The hand he muffled had four fingers only.—
　　I well remember, many years ago,
　　One morning; there were sessions held at Lundë.
　　'Twas war-time, and the talk in every mouth
　　Turned on the country's sufferings and its fate.

I stood there watching. At the table sat
The Captain, 'twixt the Bailiff* and the sergeants;
Lad after lad was measured up and down,
Passed, and enrolled, and taken for a soldier.
The room was full, and from the green outside,
Where thronged the young folks, loud the laughter rang.
A name was called, and forth another stepped,
One pale as snow upon the glacier's edge.
They bade the youth advance; he reached the table;
We saw his right hand swaddled in a clout;—
He gasped, he swallowed, battling after words,—
But, though the Captain urged him, found no voice.
Ah yes, at last! Then with his cheek aflame,
His tongue now failing him, now stammering fast
He mumbled something of a scythe that slipped
By chance, and shore his finger to the skin.
Straightway a silence fell upon the room.
Men bandied meaning glances; they made mouths;
They stoned the boy with looks of silent scorn.
He felt the hail-storm, but he saw it not.
Then up the Captain stood, the grey old man;
He spat, and pointed forth, and thundered "Go!"
And the lad went. On both sides men fell back,
Till through their midst he had to run the gauntlet.
He reached the door; from there he took to flight;—
Up, up he went,—through wood and over hillside,
Up through the stone-screes, rough, precipitous.
He had his home up there among the mountains.—
It was some six months later he came here,
With mother, and betrothed, and little child.
He leased some ground upon the high hill-side,
There where the waste lands trend away towards Lomb.
He married the first moment that he could;
He built a house; he broke the stubborn soil;
He throve, as many a cultivated patch

Lensmand, the lowest functionary in the Norwegian official scale—a sort of parish officer. (Translator's note)

Bore witness, bravely clad in waving gold.
At church he kept his right hand in his pocket,—
But sure I am at home his fingers nine
Toiled every whit as hard as others' ten.—
One spring the torrent washed it all away.
Their lives were spared. Ruined and stripped of all,
He set to work to make another clearing;
And, ere the autumn, smoke again arose
From a new, better-sheltered, mountain farm-house.
Sheltered? From torrent—not from avalanche;
Two years, and all beneath the snow lay buried.
But still the avalanche could not daunt his spirit.
He dug, and raked, and carted—cleared the ground—
And the next winter, ere the snow-blasts came,
A third time was his little homestead reared.
Three sons he had, three bright and stirring boys;
They must to school, and school was far away;—
And they must clamber, where the hill-track failed,
By narrow ledges past the headlong scree.
What did he do? The eldest had to manage
As best he might, and, where the path was worst,
His father bound a rope round him to stay him;—
The others on his back and arms he bore.
Thus he toiled, year by year, till they were men.
Now might he well have looked for some return.
In the New World, three prosperous gentlemen
Their school-going and their father have forgotten.
He was short-sighted. Out beyond the circle
Of those most near to him he nothing saw.
To him seemed meaningless as cymbals' tinkling
Those words that to the heart should ring like steel.
His race, his fatherland, all things high and shining,
Stood ever, to his vision, veiled in mist.
But he was humble, humble, was this man;
And since that sessions-day his doom oppressed him,
As surely as his cheeks were flushed with shame,
And his four fingers hidden in his pocket—
Offender 'gainst his country's laws? Ay, true!

But there is one thing that the law outshineth
Sure as the snow-white tent of Glittertind*
Has clouds, like higher rows of peaks, above it.
No patriot was he. Both for church and state
A fruitless tree. But there, on the upland ridge,
In the small circle where he saw his calling,
There he was great, because he was himself.
His inborn note rang true unto the end.
His days were as a lute with muted strings.
And therefore, peace be with thee, silent warrior,
That fought the peasants little fight, and fell!
It is not ours to search the heart and reins;—
That is no task for dust, but for its ruler;—
Yet dare I freely, firmly, speak my hope:
He scarce stands crippled now before his God!
[*The gathering disperses.* PEER GYNT *remains behind, alone.*]

PEER

Now that is what I call Christianity!
Nothing to seize on one's mind unpleasantly.—
And the topic—immovably being oneself,—
That the pastor's homily turned upon,—
Is full, in its essence, of edification.
[*Looks down upon the grave.*]
Was it he, I wonder, that hacked through his knuckle
That day I was out hewing logs in the forest?
Who knows? If I weren't standing here with my staff
By the side of the grave of this kinsman in spirit,
I could almost believe it was I that slept,
And heard in a vision my panegyric.—
It's a seemly and Christianlike custom indeed
This casting a so-called memorial glance
In charity over the life that is ended.
I shouldn't at all mind accepting my verdict
At the hands of this excellent parish priest.
Ah well, I dare say I have some time left

*A mountain in the Jotunheim. The name means "glittering peak." (Translator's note)

Ere the gravedigger comes to invite me to stay with him;—
And as Scripture has it: What's best is best,—
And: Enough for the day is the evil thereof,—*
and further: Discount not thy funeral.—
Ah, the Church, after all, is the true consoler.
I've hitherto scarcely appreciated it;—
But now I feel clearly how blessëd it is
To be well assured upon sound authority:
Even as thou sowest thou shalt one day reap.—
One must be oneself; for oneself and one's own
One must do one's best, both in great and in small things.
If the luck goes against you, at least you've the honour
Of a life carried through in accordance with principle.—
Now homewards! Though narrow and steep the path,
Though fate to the end may be never so biting—
Still old Peer Gynt will pursue his own way,
And remain what he is: poor, but virtuous ever.
[*Goes out.*]

SCENE FOURTH

> *A hill-side seamed by the dry bed of a torrent. A ruined mill-house beside the stream. The ground is torn up, and the whole place waste. Further up the hill, a large farm-house.*

An auction is going on in front of the farm-house. There is a great gathering of people, who are drinking, with much noise. PEER GYNT *is sitting on a rubbish-heap beside the mill.*

PEER

Forward and back, and it's just as far;
Out and in, and it's just as strait.—
Time wears away and the river gnaws on.
Go roundabout, the Boyg said;—and here one must.

*Den tid den sorg—literally, "That time that sorrow" or "care."

A MAN DRESSED IN MOURNING
>Now there is only rubbish left over.
>[*Catches sight of* PEER GYNT.]
>Are there strangers here too? God be with you, good friend!

PEER
>Well met! You have lively times here to-day.
>Is't a christening junket or wedding feast?

THE MAN IN MOURNING
>I'd rather call it a house-warming treat;—
>The bride is laid in a wormy bed.

PEER
>And the worms are squabbling for rags and clouts.

THE MAN IN MOURNING
>That's the end of the ditty; it's over and done.

PEER
>All the ditties end just alike;
>And they're all old together; I knew 'em as a boy.

A LAD OF TWENTY   [*With a casting-ladle.*]
>Just look what a rare thing I've been buying!
>In this Peer Gynt cast his silver buttons.

ANOTHER
>Look at mine, though! The money-bag* bought for a halfpenny.

A THIRD
>No more, eh? Twopence for the pedlar's pack!

PEER
>Peer Gynt? Who was he?

THE MAN IN MOURNING
>All I know is this:
>He was kinsman to Death and to Aslak the Smith.

A MAN IN GREY
>You're forgetting me, man! Are you mad or drunk?

THE MAN IN MOURNING
>You forget that at Hegstad was a storehouse door.

THE MAN IN GREY
>Ay, true; but we know you were never dainty.

---

*Literally, "the bushel." See note p. 15. (Translator's note)

THE MAN IN MOURNING

    If only she doesn't give Death the slip——

THE MAN IN GREY

    Come, kinsman! A dram, for our kinship's sake!

THE MAN IN MOURNING

    To the deuce with your kinship! You're maundering in
    drink——

THE MAN IN GREY

    Oh, rubbish; blood's never so thin as all that;
    One cannot but feel one's akin to Peer Gynt.
    [*Goes off with him.*]

PEER   [*To himself.*]

    One meets with acquaintances.

A LAD   [*Calls after the* MAN IN MOURNING.]

    Mother that's dead
    Will be after you, Aslak, if you wet your whistle.

PEER   [*Rises.*]

    The husbandman's saying seems scarce to hold here:
    The deeper one harrows the better it smells.

A LAD   [*With a bear's skin.*]*

    Look, the cat of the Dovrë! Well, only his fell,
    It was he chased the trolls out on Christmas Eve.

ANOTHER   [*With a reindeer skull.*]

    Here is the wonderful reindeer that bore,
    At Gendin, Peer Gynt over edge and scree.

A THIRD   [*With a hammer, calls out to the* MAN IN MOURNING.]

    Hei, Aslak, this sledge-hammer, say, do you know it?
    Was it this that you used when the devil clove the wall?

A FOURTH   [*Empty-handed.*]

    Mads Moen, here's the invisible cloak
    Peer Gynt and Ingrid flew off through the air with.

PEER

    Brandy here, boys! I feel I'm grown old;——
    I must put up to auction my rubbish and lumber!

A LAD

    What have you to sell, then?

---

*Reference to the folk tale of *Peer Gynt*, in which a white bear scares the trolls.

PEER

    A palace I have;—

    It lies in the Rondë; it's solidly built.

THE LAD

    A button is bid!

PEER

    You must run to a dram.

    'Twere a sin and a shame to bid anything less.

ANOTHER

    He's a jolly old boy this!

    [*The bystanders crowd around him.*]

PEER   [*Shouts.*]

    Granë, my steed;

    Who bids?

ONE OF THE CROWD

    Where's he running?

PEER

    Why, far in the west!

    Near the sunset, my lads! Ah, that courser can fly

    As fast, ay, as fast as Peer Gynt could lie.

VOICES

    What more have you got?

PEER

    I've both rubbish and gold!

    I bought it with ruin; I'll sell it at a loss.

A LAD

    Put it up!

PEER

    A dream of a silver-clasped book!

    That you can have for an old hook and eye.

THE LAD

    To the devil with dreams!

PEER

    Here's my Kaiserdom!

    I throw it in the midst of you; scramble for it!

THE LAD

    Is the crown given in?

PEER

    Of the loveliest straw.

    It will fit whoever first puts it on.

    Hei, there is more yet! An addled egg!

    A madman's grey hair! And the Prophet's beard!

    All these shall be his that will show on the hillside

    A post that has writ on it: Here lies your path!

THE BAILIFF   [*Who has come up.*]

    You're carrying on, my good man, so that almost

    I think that your path will lead straight to the lock-up.

PEER   [*Hat in hand.*]

    Quite likely. But, tell me, who was Peer Gynt?

THE BAILIFF

    Oh, nonsense——

PEER

    Your pardon! Most humbly I beg——!

THE BAILIFF

    Oh, he's said to have been an abominable liar——*

PEER

    A liar——?

THE BAILIFF

    Yes—all that was strong and great

    He made believe always that he had done it.

    But, excuse me, friend—I have other duties——

    [*Goes.*]

PEER

    And where is he now, this remarkable man?

AN ELDERLY MAN

    He fared over seas to a foreign land;

    It went ill with him there, as one well might foresee;—

    It's many a year now since he was hanged.

PEER

    Hanged! Ay, ay! Why, I thought as much;

    Our lamented Peer Gynt was himself to the last.

    [*Bows.*]

    Good-bye,—and best thanks for to-day's merry meeting.

    [*Goes a few steps, but stops again.*]

**Digter: means also "poet." (Translator's note)

You joyous youngsters, you comely lasses,—
Shall I pay my shot with a traveller's tale?

SEVERAL VOICES

Yes; do you know any?

PEER

Nothing more easy.—
[*He comes nearer; a look of strangeness comes over him.*]
I was gold-digging once in San Francisco.
There were mountebanks swarming all over the town.
One with his toes could perform on the fiddle;
Another could dance a Spanish halling* on his knees;
A third, I was told, kept on making verses
While his brain-pan was having a hole bored right through it.
To the mountebank-meeting came also the devil;—
Thought he'd try his luck with the rest of them.
His talent was this: in a manner convincing,
He was able to grunt like a flesh-and-blood pig.
He was not recognised, yet his manners attracted.
The house was well filled; expectation ran high.
He stepped forth in a cloak with an ample cape to it;
Man mus sich drappiren, as the Germans say.
But under the mantle—what none suspected—
He'd managed to smuggle a real live pig.
And now he opened the representation;
The devil he pinched, and the pig gave voice.
The whole thing purported to be a fantasia
On the porcine existence, both free and in bonds;
And all ended up with a slaughter-house squeal—
Whereupon the performer bowed low and retired—
The critics discussed and appraised the affair;
The tone of the whole was attacked and defended.
Some fancied the vocal expression too thin,
While some thought the death-shriek too carefully studied;
But all were agreed as to one thing: *qua* grunt,
The performance was grossly exaggerated.—
Now that, you see, came of the devil's stupidity

---

*A somewhat violent peasant dance. (Translator's note)

In not taking the measure of his public first.
[*He bows and goes off. A puzzled silence comes over the crowd.*]

Scene Fifth

Whitsun Eve.——In the depths of the forest. To the back, in a clearing, is a hut with a pair of reindeer horns over the porch-gable.

PEER GYNT *is creeping among the undergrowth, gathering wild onions.*

PEER

Well, this is one standpoint. Where is the next?
One should try all things and choose the best.
Well, I have done so,—beginning from Cæsar,
And downwards as far as to Nebuchadnezzar.
So I've had, after all, to go through Bible history;—
The old boy has come back to his mother again.
After all it is written: Of the earth art thou come.—
The main thing in life is to fill one's belly.
Fill it with onions? That's not much good;—
I must take to cunning, and set out snares.
There's water in the beck here; I shan't suffer thirst;
And I count as the first 'mong the beasts after all.
When my time comes to die—as most likely it will,—
I shall crawl in under a wind-fallen tree;
Like the bear, I will heap up a leaf-mound above me,
And I'll scratch in big print on the bark of the tree:
Here rests Peer Gynt, that decent soul
Kaiser o'er all of the other beasts.—
Kaiser?
[*Laughs inwardly.*]
Why, you old soothsayer's-dupe!
No Kaiser are you; you are nought but an onion.
I'm going to peel you now, my good Peer!
You won't escape either by begging or howling.
[*Takes an onion and strips off one coat after another.*]
There lies the outermost layer, all torn;
That's the shipwrecked man on the jolly-boat's keel.

Here's the passenger layer, scanty and thin;—
And yet in its taste there's a tang of Peer Gynt.
Next underneath is the gold-digger ego;
The juice is all gone—if it ever had any.
This coarse-grained layer with the hardened skin
Is the peltry hunter by Hudson's Bay.
The next one looks like a crown;—oh, thanks!
We'll throw it away without more ado.
Here's the archæologist, short but sturdy,
And here is the Prophet, juicy and fresh.
He stinks, as the Scripture has it, of lies,
Enough to bring the water to an honest man's eyes.
This layer that rolls itself softly together
Is the gentleman, living in ease and good cheer.
The next one seems sick. There are black streaks upon it;—
Black symbolises both parsons and niggers.
[*Pulls off several layers at once.*]
What an enormous number of swathings!
Is not the kernel soon coming to light?
[*Pulls the whole onion to pieces.*]
I'm blest if it is! To the innermost centre,
It's nothing but swathings—each smaller and smaller.—
Nature is witty!
[*Throws the fragments away.*]
The devil take brooding!
If one goes about thinking, one's apt to stumble.
Well, *I* can at any rate laugh at that danger;—
For here on all fours I am firmly planted.
[*Scratches his head.*]
A queer enough business, the whole concern!
Life, as they say, plays with cards up its sleeve;*
But when one snatches at them, they've disappeared,
And one grips something else,—or else nothing at all.
[*He has come near to the hut; he catches sight of it and starts.*]

---

*This and the following line, literally translated, run thus: "Life, as it's called, has a fox behind its ear. But when one grasps at him, Reynard takes to his heels." "To have a fox behind the ear" is a proverbial expression for insincerity, double-dealing. (Translator's note)

This hut? On the heath——! Ha!

[*Rubs his eyes.*]

It seems exactly

As though I had known this same building before.——

The reindeer-horns jutting above the gable!——

A mermaid, shaped like a fish from the navel!——

Lies! there's no mermaid! But nails—and planks,——

Bars too, to shut out hobgoblin thoughts—

SOLVEIG   [*Singing in the hut.*]

Now all is ready for Whitsun Eve.

Dearest boy of mine, far away,

Comest thou soon?

Is thy burden heavy,

Take time, take time;——

I will await thee;

I promised of old.*

PEER   [*Rises, quiet and deadly pale.*]

One that's remembered,—and one that's forgot.

One that has squandered,—and one that has saved.——

Oh, earnest!—and never can the game be played o'er!

Oh, dread!†—here was my Kaiserdom!

[*Hurries off along the wood path.*]

SCENE SIXTH

Night. A heath, with fir-trees. A forest fire has been raging; charred tree-trunks are seen stretching for miles. White mists here and there clinging to the earth.

PEER GYNT *comes running over the heath.*

PEER

Ashes, fog-scuds, dust wind-driven,——

Here's enough for building with!

Stench and rottenness within it;

*Sidst—literally, "when last we met." (Translator's note)

†See note p. 164. (Translator's note)

All a whited sepulchre.
Figments, dreams, and still born knowledge
Lay the pyramid's foundation;
O'er them shall the work mount upwards,
With its step on step of falsehood.
Earnest shunned, repentance dreaded,
Flaunt at the apex like a scutcheon,
Fill the trump of judgment with their:
"Petrus Gyntus Cæsar fecit!"
[*Listens.*]
What is this, like children's weeping?
Weeping, but half-way to song.—
Thread-balls* at my feet are rolling!—
[*Kicking at them.*]
Off with you! You block my path!

THE THREAD-BALLS   [*On the ground.*]
We are thoughts;
Thou shouldst have thought us;—
Feet to run on
Thou shouldst have given us!

PEER   [*Going round about.*]
I have given life to one;—
'Twas a bungled, crook-legged thing!

THE THREAD-BALLS
We should have soared up
Like clangorous voices,—
And here we must trundle
As grey-yarn thread-balls.

PEER   [*Stumbling.*]
Thread-clue! you accursed scamp!
Would you trip your father's heels?
[*Flees.*]

WITHERED LEAVES   [*Flying before the wind.*]
We are a watchword;
Thou shouldst have proclaimed us!
See how thy dozing

*Trolls were thought to reside in thread balls.

Has wofully riddled us.
The worm has gnawed us
In every crevice;
We have never twined us
Like wreaths round fruitage.

PEER

Not in vain your birth, however;—
Lie but still and serve as manure.

A SIGHING IN THE AIR

We are songs;
Thou shouldst have sung us!—
A thousand times over
Hast thou cowed us and smothered us.
Down in thy heart's pit
We have lain and waited;—
We were never called forth.
Thy gorge we poison!

PEER

Poison thee, thou foolish stave!
Had I time for verse and stuff?
[*Attempts a short cut.*] '

DEWDROPS   [*Dripping from the branches.*]

We are tears
Unshed for ever.
Ice-spears, sharp-wounding,
We could have melted.
Now the barb rankles
In the shaggy bosom;—
The wound is closed over;
Our power is ended.

PEER

Thanks;—I wept in Rondë-cloisters,—
None the less my tail-part smarted!

BROKEN STRAWS

We are deeds;
Thou shouldst have achieved us!
Doubt, the throttler,

Has crippled and riven us.
On the Day of Judgment
We'll come a-flock,
And tell the story,—
Then woe to you!

PEER

Rascal-tricks! How dare you debit
What is negative against me?
[*Hastens away.*]

ÅSE'S VOICE   [*Far away.*]

Fie, what a post-boy!
Hu, you've upset me
Here in the slush, boy!
Sadly it's smirched me.—
You've driven me the wrong way.
Peer, where's the castle?
The Fiend has misled you
With the switch from the cupboard.

PEER

Better haste away, poor fellow!
With the devil's sins upon you,
Soon you'll faint upon the hillside;—
Hard enough to bear one's own sins.
[*Runs off.*]

SCENE SEVENTH

Another part of the heath.

PEER GYNT   [*Sings.*]

A sexton! A sexton! where are you, hounds?
A song from braying precentor-mouths;
Around your hat-brim a mourning band;—
My dead are many; I must follow their biers!

THE BUTTON-MOULDER, *with a box of tools and a large casting-ladle,*
comes from a side path.

THE BUTTON-MOULDER

Well met, old gaffer!

PEER

Good evening, friend!

THE BUTTON-MOULDER

The man's in a hurry. Why, where is he going?

PEER

To a grave-feast.

THE BUTTON-MOULDER

Indeed? My sight's not very good;—

Excuse me,—your name doesn't chance to be Peer?

PEER

Peer Gynt, as the saying is.

THE BUTTON-MOULDER

That I call luck!

It's precisely Peer Gynt I am sent for to-night.

PEER

You're sent for? What do you want?

THE BUTTON-MOULDER

Why, see here;

I mould buttons; and you must go into my ladle.

PEER

What to do there?

THE BUTTON-MOULDER

To be melted up.

PEER

To be melted?

THE BUTTON-MOULDER

Here it is, empty and scoured.

Your grave is dug ready, your coffin bespoke.

The worms in your body will live at their ease;—

But I have orders, without delay,

On Master's behalf to fetch in your soul.

PEER

It can't be! Like this, without any warning——!

THE BUTTON-MOULDER

It's an old tradition at burials and births

To appoint in secret the day of the feast,

With no warning at all to the guest of honour.

PEER

Ay, ay, that's true. All my brain's awhirl.
You are————?

THE BUTTON-MOULDER

Why, I told you—a button-moulder.

PEER

I see! A pet child has many nicknames.
So that's it, Peer; it is there you're to harbour,
But these, my good man, are most unfair proceedings!
I'm sure I deserve better treatment than this;—
I'm not nearly so bad as perhaps you think,—
Indeed I've done more or less good in the world;—
At worst you may call me a sort of a bungler,—
But certainly not an exceptional sinner.

THE BUTTON-MOULDER

Why that is precisely the rub, my man;
You're no sinner at all in the higher sense;
That's why you're excused all the torture-pangs,
And, like others, land in the casting-ladle.

PEER

Give it what name you please—call it ladle or pool;*
Spruce ale and swipes, they are both of them beer.
Avaunt from me, Satan!

THE BUTTON-MOULDER

You can't be so rude
As to take my foot for a horse's hoof?

PEER

On horse's hoof or on fox's claws†—
Be off; and be careful what you're about!

THE BUTTON-MOULDER

My friend, you're making a great mistake.
We're both in a hurry, and so, to save time,
I'll explain the reason of the whole affair.
You are, with your own lips you told me so,

Pöl, otherwise *Svovlpöl*—the sulphur pool of hell. (Translator's note)
†See note p. 177. (Translator's note)

No sinner on the so called heroic scale,——
Scarce middling even——

PEER

Ah, now you're beginning
To talk common sense——

THE BUTTON-MOULDER

Just have patience a bit——
But to call you a good man were going too far.——

PEER

Well, you know I have never laid claim to that.

THE BUTTON-MOULDER

You're nor one thing nor t'other then, only so-so.
A sinner of really grandiose style
Is nowadays not to be met on the highways.
It wants much more than merely to wallow in mire;
For both vigour and earnestness go to a sin.

PEER

Ay, it's very true that remark of yours;
One has to lay on, like the old Berserkers.

THE BUTTON-MOULDER

You, friend, on the other hand, took your sin lightly.

PEER

Only outwardly, friend, like a splash of mud.

THE BUTTON-MOULDER

Ah, we'll soon be at one now. The sulphur pool
Is no place for you, who but plashed in the mire.

PEER

And in consequence, friend, I may go as I came?

THE BUTTON-MOULDER

No, in consequence, friend, I must melt you up.

PEER

What tricks are these that you've hit upon
At home here, while I've been in foreign parts?

THE BUTTON-MOULDER

The custom's as old as the Snake's creation;
It's designed to prevent loss of good material.
You've worked at the craft—you must know that often
A casting turns out, to speak plainly, mere dross;

The buttons, for instance, have sometimes no loop to them.
What did you do then?

PEER

Flung the rubbish away.

THE BUTTON-MOULDER

Ah, yes; Jon Gynt was well known for a waster,
So long as he'd aught left in wallet or purse.
But Master, you see, he is thrifty, he is;
And that is why he's so well-to-do.
He flings nothing away as entirely worthless
That can be made use of as raw material.
Now, you were designed for a shining button
On the vest of the world; but your loop gave way;
So into the waste-box you needs must go,
And then, as they phrase it, be merged in the mass.

PEER

You're surely not meaning to melt me up,
With Dick, Tom, and Hal,* into something new?

THE BUTTON-MOULDER

That's just what I do mean, and nothing else.
We've done it already to plenty of folks.
At Kongsberg† they do just the same with coin
That's been current so long that its impress is lost.

PEER

But this is the wretchedest miserliness!
My dear good friend, let me get off free;—
A loopless button, a worn out farthing,—
What is that to a man in your Master's position?

THE BUTTON-MOULDER

Oh, so long as, and seeing, the spirit is in you,
You always have value as so much metal.

PEER

No, I say! No! With both teeth and claws
I'll fight against this! Sooner anything else!

*Literally, "With Peter and Paul."
†The Royal Mint is at Kongsberg, a town in southern Norway.

THE BUTTON-MOULDER

But what else? Come now, be reasonable.
You know you're not airy enough for heaven——

PEER

I'm not hard to content; I don't aim so high;—
But I won't be deprived of one doit of my Self.
Have me judged by the law in the old-fashioned way!
For a certain time place me with Him of the Hoof;—
Say a hundred years, come the worst to the worst;
That, now, is a thing that one surely can bear;
They say that the torment is moral no more,
So it can't be so pyramid-like after all.
It is, as 'tis written, a mere transition;
And as the fox said: One waits; there comes
An hour of deliverance; one lives in seclusion,
And hopes in the meantime for happier days.—
But this other notion—to have to be merged,
Like a mote, in the carcass of some outsider,—
This casting-ladle business, this Gynt-cessation,—
It stirs up my innermost soul in revolt!

THE BUTTON-MOULDER

Bless me, my dear Peer, there is surely no need
To get so wrought up about trifles like this.
Yourself you never have been at all;—
Then what does it matter, your dying right out?

PEER

Have *I* not been——? I could almost laugh!
Peer Gynt, then, has been something else, I suppose!
No, Button-moulder, you judge in the dark.
If you could but look into my very reins,
You'd find only Peer there, and Peer all through,—
Nothing else in the world, no, nor anything more.

THE BUTTON-MOULDER

It's impossible. Here I have got my orders.
Look, here it is written: Peer Gynt shalt thou summon.
He has set at defiance his life's design;
Clap him into the ladle with other spoilt goods.

PEER

    What nonsense! They must mean some other person.

    Is it really Peer? It's not Rasmus, or Jon?

THE BUTTON-MOULDER

    It is many a day since I melted them.

    So come quietly now, and don't waste my time.

PEER

    I'll be damned if I do! Ay, 'twould be a fine thing

    If it turned out to-morrow some one else was meant.

    You'd better take care what you're at, my good man!

    Think of the onus you're taking upon you————

THE BUTTON-MOULDER

    I have it in writing————

PEER

    At least give me time.

THE BUTTON-MOULDER

    What good would that do you?

PEER

    I'll use it to prove

    That I've been myself all the days of my life:

    And that's the question that's in dispute.

THE BUTTON-MOULDER

    You'll prove it? And how?

PEER

    Why, by vouchers and witnesses.

THE BUTTON-MOULDER

    I'm sadly afraid Master will not accept them.

PEER

    Impossible! However, enough for the day*——!

    My dear man, allow me a loan of myself;

    I'll be back again shortly. One is born only once,

    And one's self, as created, one fain would stick to.

    Come, are we agreed?

THE BUTTON-MOULDER

    Very well then, so be it.

    But remember, we meet at the next cross-roads.

    [PEER GYNT *runs off.*]

*Den tid den sorg—literally, "That time that sorrow" or "care." (Translator's note)

SCENE EIGHTH

A further point on the heath.

PEER   [*Running hard.*]
    Time is money, as the Scripture says.
    If I only knew where the cross-roads are;—
    They may be near and they may be far.
    The earth burns beneath me like red-hot iron.
    A witness! A witness! Oh, where shall I find one?
    It's almost unthinkable here in the forest.
    The world is a bungle! A wretched arrangement,
    When a right must be proved that is patent as day!

An OLD MAN, *bent with age, with a staff in his hand and a bag on his back, is trudging in front of him.*

THE OLD MAN   [*Stops.*]
    Dear, kind sir—a trifle to a houseless soul!
PEER
    Excuse me; I've got no small change in my pocket——
OLD MAN
    Prince Peer! Oh, to think we should meet again——!
PEER
    Who are you?
THE OLD MAN
    You forget the Old Man in the Rondë?
PEER
    Why, you're never——?
THE OLD MAN
    The King of the Dovrë, my boy!
PEER
    The Dovrë-King? Really? The Dovrë-King?
    Speak!
THE OLD MAN
    Oh, I've come terribly down in the world——!
PEER
    Ruined?
THE OLD MAN
    Ay, plundered of every stiver

Here am I tramping it, starved as a wolf.

PEER

Hurrah! Such a witness doesn't grow on the trees.

THE OLD MAN

My Lord Prince, too, has grizzled a bit since we met.

PEER

My dear father-in-law, the years gnaw and wear one.——
Well well, a truce to all private affairs,——
And pray, above all things, no family jars.
I was then a sad madcap——

THE OLD MAN

Oh yes; oh yes;——
His Highness was young; and what won't one do then?
But his Highness was wise in rejecting his bride.
He saved himself thereby both worry and shame
For since then she's utterly gone to the bad——

PEER

Indeed!

THE OLD MAN

She has led a deplorable life;*
And, just think,——she and Trond are now living together.

PEER

Which Trond?

THE OLD MAN

Of the Valfjeld.

PEER

It's he? Aha;
It was he I cut out with the sæter-girls.

THE OLD MAN

But my grandson has shot up both stout and tall,
And has flourishing children all over the land——

PEER

Now, my dear man, spare us this flow of words;——
I've something quite different troubling my mind.——
I've got into rather a ticklish position,

Hun gik nu for koldt vand og lud—literally, "to live on cold water and lye"—to
live wretchedly and be badly treated.

And am greatly in need of a witness or voucher;——
That's how you could help me best, father-in-law,
And I'll find you a trifle to drink my health.

THE OLD MAN

You don't say so; can I be of use to his Highness?
You'll give me a character, then, in return?

PEER

Most gladly. I'm somewhat hard pressed for cash,
And must cut down expenses in every direction.
Now hear what's the matter. No doubt you remember
That night when I came to the Rondë a-wooing——

THE OLD MAN

Why, of course, my Lord Prince!

PEER

Oh, no more of the Prince!
But no matter. You wanted, by sheer brute force,
To bias my sight, with a slit in the lens,
And to change me about from Peer Gynt to a troll.
What did *I* do then? I stood out against it,——
Swore I would stand on no feet but my own;
Love, power, and glory at once I renounced,
And all for the sake of remaining myself.
Now this fact, you see, you must swear to in Court——

THE OLD MAN

No, I'm blest if I can.

PEER

Why, what nonsense is this?

THE OLD MAN

You surely don't want to compel me to lie?
You pulled on the troll-breeches, don't you remember,
And tasted the mead——

PEER

Ay, you lured me seductively;——
But I flatly declined the decisive test,
And that is the thing you must judge your man by.
It's the end of the ditty that all depends on.

THE OLD MAN

But it ended, Peer, just in the opposite way.

PEER

What rubbish is this?

THE OLD MAN

When you left the Rondë,

You inscribed my motto upon your escutcheon.*

PEER

What motto?

THE OLD MAN

The potent and sundering word.

PEER

The word?

THE OLD MAN

That which severs the whole race of men

From the troll-folk: Troll! To thyself be enough!

PEER   [*Recoils a step.*]

Enough!

THE OLD MAN

And with every nerve in your body,

You've been living up to it ever since.

PEER

What, I? Peer Gynt?

THE OLD MAN   [*Weeps.*]

It's ungrateful of you!

You've lived as a troll, but have still kept it secret.

The word I taught you has shown you the way

To swing yourself up as a man of substance;—

And now you must needs come and turn up your nose

At me and the word you've to thank for it all.

PEER

Enough! A hill-troll! An egoist!

This must be all rubbish; that's perfectly certain.

THE OLD MAN   [*Pulls out a bundle of old newspapers.*]

I daresay you think we don't take in the papers?

Wait; here I'll show you in red and black†

How the "Bloksberg Post" eulogises you;

---

*Literally, "Wrote my motto behind your ear." (Translator's note)
†Clearly the troll-substitute for "in black and white." (Translator's note)

And the "Heklefjeld Journal" has done the same
Ever since the winter you left the country.—
Do you care to read them? You're welcome Peer.
Here's an article, look you, signed "Stallion-hoof."
And here too is one: "On Troll-Nationalism."
The writer points out and lays stress on the truth
That horns and a tail are of little importance,
So long as one has but a strip of the hide.
"Our enough," he concludes, "gives the hallmark of trolldom
To man,"—and proceeds to cite you as an instance.

PEER

A hill-troll? I?

THE OLD MAN

Yes, that's perfectly clear.

PEER

Might as well have stayed quietly where I was?
Might have stayed in the Rondë in comfort and peace?
Saved my trouble and toil and no end of shoe-leather?
Peer Gynt—a troll? Why, it's rubbish! It's stuff!
Good-bye! There's a halfpenny to buy you tobacco.

THE OLD MAN

Nay, my good Prince Peer!

PEER

Let me go! You're mad,
Or else doting. Off to the hospital with you!

THE OLD MAN

Oh, that is exactly what I'm in search of.
But, as I told you, my grandson's offspring
Have become overwhelmingly strong in the land,
And they say that I only exist in books.
The saw says: One's kin are unkindest of all;
I've found to my cost that that saying is true.
It's cruel to count as mere figment and fable——

PEER

My dear man, there are others who share the same fate.

THE OLD MAN

And ourselves we've no Mutual Aid Society,

No alms-box or Penny Savings Bank;——
In the Rondë, of course, they'd be out of place.

PEER

No, that curs'd: To thyself be enough was the word there!

THE OLD MAN

Oh, come now, the Prince can't complain of the word.
And if he could manage by hook or by crook——

PEER

My man, you have got on the wrong scent entirely;
I'm myself, as the saying goes, fairly cleaned out*——

THE OLD MAN

You surely can't mean it? His Highness a beggar?

PEER

Completely. His Highness's ego's in pawn.
And it's all your fault, you accursëd trolls!
That's what comes of keeping bad company.

THE OLD MAN

So there came my hope toppling down from its perch again!
Good-bye! I had best struggle on to the town——

PEER

What would you do there?

THE OLD MAN

I will go to the theatre.
The papers are clamouring for national talents——

PEER

Good luck on your journey; and greet them from me.
If I can but get free, I will go the same way.
A farce I will write them, a mad and profound one;
It's name shall be: "Sic transit gloria mundi."

[*He runs off along the road; the* OLD MAN *shouts after him.*]

*Literally, "on a naked hill." (Translator's note)

Scene Ninth

[*At a cross-road.*]

PEER GYNT
Now comes the pinch, Peer, as never before!
This Dovrish Enough has passed judgment upon you.
The vessel's a wreck; one must float with the spars.
All else; but to go to the scrap-heap—no, no!
THE BUTTON-MOULDER   [*At the cross-road.*]
Well now, Peer Gynt, have you found your voucher?
PEER
Is this, then, the cross-road? Well, that is short work!
THE BUTTON-MOULDER
I can see on your face, as it were on a signboard,
The gist of the paper before I have read it.
PEER
I got tired of the hunt;—one might lose one's way——
THE BUTTON-MOULDER
Yes; and what does it lead to, after all?
PEER
True enough; in the wood, and by night as well——
THE BUTTON-MOULDER
There's an old mail, though, trudging. Shall we call him here?
PEER
No, let him go. He is drunk, my dear fellow!
THE BUTTON-MOULDER
But perhaps he might——
PEER
Hush; no—let him alone!
THE BUTTON-MOULDER
Well, shall we begin then?
PEER
One question—just one:
What is it, at bottom, this "being oneself"?
THE BUTTON-MOULDER
A singular question, most odd in the mouth
Of a man who but now——

PEER

Come, a straightforward answer.

THE BUTTON-MOULDER

To be oneself is: to slay oneself.

But on you that answer is doubtless lost;

And therefore we'll say: to stand forth everywhere

With Master's intention displayed like a sign-board.

PEER

But suppose a man never has come to know

What Master meant with him?

THE BUTTON-MOULDER

He must divine it.

PEER

But how oft are divinings beside the mark,—

Then one's carried "ad undas"* in middle career.

THE BUTTON-MOULDER

That is certain. Peer Gynt; in default of divining

The cloven-hoofed gentleman finds his best hook.

PEER

This matter's excessively complicated.—

See here! I no longer plead being myself;—

It might not be easy to get it proven.

That part of my case I must look on as lost.

But just now, as I wandered alone o'er the heath,

I felt my conscience-shoe pinching me;

I said to myself: After all, you're a sinner——

THE BUTTON-MOULDER

You seem bent on beginning all over again——

PEER

No, very far from it; a great one I mean;

Not only in deeds, but in words and desires.

I've lived a most damnable life abroad——

THE BUTTON-MOULDER

Perhaps; I must ask you to show me the schedule!

---

*To the waves (Latin); here the phrase means getting shipwrecked or lost.

PEER

> Well well, give me time; I will find out a parson,
> Confess with all speed, and then bring you his voucher.

THE BUTTON-MOULDER

> Ay, if you can bring me that, then it is clear
> You may yet escape from the casting-ladle.
> But Peer, I'd my orders——

PEER

> The paper is old;
> It dates no doubt from a long past period;—
> At one time I lived with disgusting slackness,
> Went playing the prophet, and trusted in Fate.
> Well, may I try?

THE BUTTON-MOULDER

> But——!

PEER

> My dear, good man,
> I'm sure you can't have so much to do.
> Here, in this district, the air is so bracing,
> It adds an ell to the people's ages.
> Recollect what the Justedal parson wrote:
> "It's seldom that any one dies in this valley."

THE BUTTON-MOULDER

> To the next cross-roads then; but not a step further.

PEER

> A priest I must catch, if it be with the tongs.
> [*He starts running.*]

SCENE TENTH

A heather-clad hillside with a path following the windings of the ridge.

PEER

> This may come in useful in many ways,
> Said Esben as he picked up a magpie's wing.
> Who could have thought one's account of sins
> Would come to one's aid on the last night of all?

Well, whether or no, it's a ticklish business;
A move from the frying-pan* into the fire;—
But then there's a proverb of well-tried validity
Which says that as long as there's life there is hope.

A LEAN PERSON *in a priest's cassock, kilted-up high, and with a birding-net over his shoulder, comes hurrying along the ridge.*

PEER

Who goes there? A priest with a fowling-net!
Hei, hop! I'm the spoilt child of fortune indeed!
Good evening, Herr Pastor! the path is bad——

THE LEAN ONE

Ah yes; but what wouldn't one do for a soul?

PEER

Aha! then there's some one bound heavenwards?

THE LEAN ONE

No;
I hope he is taking a different road.

PEER

May I walk with Herr Pastor a bit of the way?

THE LEAN ONE

With pleasure; I'm partial to company.

PEER

I should like to consult you——

THE LEAN ONE

Heraus!† Go ahead!

PEER

You see here before you a good sort of man.
The laws of the state I have strictly observed,
Have made no acquaintance with fetters or bolts;—
But it happens at times that one misses one's footing
And stumbles——

THE LEAN ONE

Ah yes; that occurs to the best of us.

PEER

Now these trifles you see——

---

*Literally, "the ashes." (Translator's note)
†Out! (German).

THE LEAN ONE

    Only trifles?

PEER

    Yes;

    From sinning *en gros* I have ever refrained.

THE LEAN ONE

    Oh then, my dear fellow, pray leave me in peace;—

    I'm not the person you seem to think me.—

    You look at my fingers? What see you in them?

PEER

    A nail-system somewhat extremely developed.

THE LEAN ONE

    And now? You are casting a glance at my feet?

PEER   [*Pointing.*]

    That's a natural hoof?

THE LEAN ONE

    So I flatter myself.

PEER   [*Raises his hat.*]

    I'd have taken my oath you were simply a parson;

    And I find I've the honour——. Well, best is best;—

    When the hall door stands wide,—shun the kitchen way;

    When the king's to be met with,—avoid the lackey.

THE LEAN ONE

    Your hand! You appear to be free from prejudice.

    Say on then, my friend; in what way can I serve you?

    Now you mustn't ask me for wealth or power;

    I couldn't supply them although I should hang for it.

    You can't think how slack the whole business is;—

    Transactions have dwindled most pitiably.

    Nothing doing in souls; only now and again

    A stray one——

PEER

    The race has improved so remarkably?

THE LEAN ONE

    No, just the reverse; it's sunk shamefully low;—

    The majority end in a casting-ladle.

PEER

Ah yes——I have heard that ladle mentioned;

In fact, 'twas the cause of my coming to you.

THE LEAN ONE

Speak out!

PEER

If it were not too much to ask,

I should like——

THE LEAN ONE

A harbour of refuge? eh?

PEER

You've guessed my petition before I have asked.

You tell me the business is going awry;

So I daresay you will not be over-particular.

THE LEAN ONE

But, my dear——

PEER

My demands are in no way excessive.

I shouldn't insist on a salary;

But treatment as friendly as things will permit.

THE LEAN ONE

A fire in your room?

PEER

Not too much fire;——and chiefly

The power of departing in safety and peace,——

The right, as the phrase goes, of freely withdrawing

Should an opening offer for happier days.

THE LEAN ONE

My dear friend, I vow I'm sincerely distressed;

But you cannot imagine how many petitions

Of similar purport good people send in,

When they're quitting the scene of their earthly activity.

PEER

But now that I think of my past career,

I feel I've an absolute claim to admission——

THE LEAN ONE

'Twas but trifles, you said——

PEER

In a certain sense;
But, now I remember, I've trafficked in slaves——

THE LEAN ONE

There are men that have trafficked in wills and souls,
But who bungled it so that they failed to get in.

PEER

I've shipped Bramah-figures in plenty to China.

THE LEAN ONE

Mere wish-wash again! Why, we laugh at such things.
There are people that ship off far gruesomer figures
In sermons, in art, and in literature,
Yet have to stay out in the cold——

PEER

Ah, but then,
Do you know——I once went and set up as a prophet!

THE LEAN ONE

In foreign parts? Humbug! Why most people's *Sehen
Ins Blaue** ends in the casting-ladle.
If you've no more than that to rely upon,
With the best of good will, I can't possibly house you.

PEER

But hear this: In a shipwreck——I clung to a boat's keel,——
And it's written: A drowning man grasps at a straw,——
Furthermore it is written: You're nearest yourself,——
So I half-way divested a cook of his life.

THE LEAN ONE

It were all one to me if a kitchen-maid
You had half-way divested of something else.
What sort of stuff is this half-way jargon,
Saving your presence? Who, think you, would care
To throw away dearly-bought fuel, in times
Like these, on such spiritless rubbish as this?
There now, don't be enraged; 'twas your sins that I scoffed at;
And excuse my speaking my mind so bluntly.——

---

*Literally, seeing into the blue (German); an adaptation of the idiom for "going into the blue," which means having no goal or purpose.

Come, my dearest friend, banish this stuff from your head,*
And get used to the thought of the casting-ladle.
What would you gain if I lodged you and boarded you?
Consider; I know you're a sensible man.
Well, you'd keep your memory; that's so far true;—
But the retrospect o'er recollection's domain
Would be, both for heart and for intellect,
What the Swedes call "Mighty poor sport"† indeed.
You have nothing either to howl or to smile about;
No cause for rejoicing nor yet for despair;
Nothing to make you feel hot or cold;
Only a sort of a something to fret over.

PEER

It is written: It's never so easy to know
Where the shoe is tight that one isn't wearing.

THE LEAN ONE

Very true; I have—praise be to so-and-so!—
No occasion for more than a single odd shoe.
But it's lucky we happened to speak of shoes;
It reminds me that I must be hurrying on;—
I'm after a roast that I hope will prove fat;
So I really mustn't stand gossiping here.—

PEER

And may one inquire, then, what sort of sin-diet
The man has been fattened on?

THE LEAN ONE

I understand
He has been himself both by night and by day,
And that, after all, is the principal point.

PEER

Himself? Then do such folks belong to your parish?

THE LEAN ONE

That depends; the door, at least, stands ajar for them.
Remember, in two ways a man can be
Himself—there's a right and wrong side to the jacket.

*Literally, "knock out that tooth." (Translator's note)
†*Bra litet rolig.*

You know they have lately discovered in Paris
A way to take portraits by help of the sun.
One can either produce a straightforward picture,
Or else what is known as a negative one.
In the latter the lights and the shades are reversed,
And they're apt to seem ugly to commonplace eyes;
But for all that the likeness is latent in them,
And all you require is to bring it out.
If, then, a soul shall have pictured itself
In the course of its life by the negative method,
The plate is not therefore entirely cashiered,—
But without more ado they consign it to me.
For ulterior treatment I take it in hand,
And by suitable methods effect its development.
I steam it, I dip it, I burn it, I scour it,
With sulphur and other ingredients like that,
Till the image appears which the plate was designed for,—
That, namely, which people call positive.
But for one who, like you, has smudged himself out,
Neither sulphur nor potash avails in the least.

PEER

I see; one must come to you black as a raven
To turn out a white ptarmigan? Pray what's the name
Inscribed 'neath the negative counterfeit
That you're now to transfer to the positive side?

THE LEAN ONE

The name's Peter Gynt.

PEER

Peter Gynt? Indeed?
Is Herr Gynt himself?

THE LEAN ONE

Yes, he vows he is.

PEER

Well, he's one to be trusted, that same Herr Peter.

THE LEAN ONE

You know him, perhaps?

PEER

Oh yes, after a fashion;—

One knows all sorts of people.

THE LEAN ONE

I'm pressed for time;
Where saw you him last?

PEER

It was down at the Cape.

THE LEAN ONE

Di Buona Speranza?*

PEER

Just so; but he sails
Very shortly again, if I'm not mistaken.

THE LEAN ONE

I must hurry off then without delay.
I only hope I may catch him in time!
That Cape of Good Hope——I could never abide it;——
It's ruined by missionaries from Stavanger.
[*He rushes off southwards.*]

PEER

The stupid hound! There he takes to his heels
With his tongue lolling out. He'll be finely sold.
It delights me to humbug an ass like that.
He to give himself airs, and to lord it forsooth!
He's a mighty lot, truly, to swagger about!
He'll scarcely grow fat at his present trade;——
He'll soon drop from his perch with his whole apparatus.——
H'm, I'm not over-safe in the saddle either;
I'm expelled, one may say, from self-owning nobility.[†]
[*A shooting star is seen; he nods after it.*]
Greet all friends from Peer Gynt, Brother Starry-Flash!
To flash forth, to go out, and be naught at a gulp——
[*Pulls himself together as though in terror, and goes deeper in among the mists; stillness for awhile; then he cries:*]
Is there no one, no one in all the whirl,——

*Di Buona Speranza: Cape of Good Hope.

†"*Selvejer-Adlen.*" *Selvejer* (literally, "self-owner") means a freeholder, as opposed to a *husmand* or tenant. There is of course a play upon words in the original. (Translator's note)

In the void no one, and no one in heaven——!

[*He comes forward again further down, throws his hat upon the ground, and tears at his hair. By degrees a stillness comes over him.*]

So unspeakably poor, then, a soul can go
Back to nothingness, into the grey of the mist.
Thou beautiful earth, be not angry with me
That I trampled thy grasses to no avail.
Thou beautiful sun, thou hast squandered away
Thy glory of light in an empty hut.
There was no one within it to hearten and warm;——
The owner, they tell me, was never at home.
Beautiful sun and beautiful earth,
You were foolish to bear and give light to my mother.
The spirit is niggard and nature lavish;
And dearly one pays for one's birth with one's life.——
I will clamber up high, to the dizziest peak;
I will look once more on the rising sun,
Gaze till I'm tired o'er the promised land;
Then try to get snowdrifts piled up over me.
They can write above them: "Here No One lies buried";
And afterwards,——then——! Let things go as they can.

CHURCH-GOERS   [*Singing on the forest path.*]

Oh, morning thrice blest,
When the tongues of God's kingdom
Struck the earth like to flaming steel!
From the earth to his dwelling
Now the heirs' song ascendeth
In the tongue of the kingdom of God.

PEER   [*Crouches as in terror.*]

Never look there! there all's desert and waste.——
I fear I was dead long before I died.

[*Tries to slink in among the bushes, but comes upon the cross-roads.*]

THE BUTTON-MOULDER

Good morning, Peer Gynt! Where's the list of your sins?

PEER

Do you think that I haven't been whistling and shouting
As hard as I could?

THE BUTTON-MOULDER
>And met no one at all?

PEER
>Not a soul but a tramping photographer.

THE BUTTON-MOULDER
>Well, the respite is over.

PEER
>Ay, everything's over.
>The owl smells the daylight. Just list to the hooting!

THE BUTTON-MOULDER
>It's the matin-bell ringing——

PEER   [*Pointing.*]
>What's that shining yonder?

THE BUTTON-MOULDER
>Only light from a hut.

PEER
>And that wailing sound——?

THE BUTTON-MOULDER
>But a woman singing.

PEER
>Ay, there—there I'll find
>The list of my sins——

THE BUTTON-MOULDER   [*Seizing him.*]
>Set your house in order!
>[*They have come out of the underwood, and are standing near the hut. Day is dawning.*]

PEER
>Set my house in order? It's there! Away!
>Get you gone! Though your ladle were huge as a coffin,
>It were too small, I tell you, for me and my sins.

THE BUTTON-MOULDER
>Well, to the third cross-road, Peer; but then——
>[*Turns aside and goes.*]

PEER   [*Approaches the hut.*]
>Forward and back, and it's just as far.
>Out and in, and it's just as strait.
>[*Stops.*]
>No!—like a wild, an unending lament,

Is the thought: to come back, to go in, to go home.

[*Takes a few steps on, but stops again.*]

Round about, said the Boyg!

[*Hears singing in the hut.*]

Ah no; this time at least

Right through, though the path may be never so strait!

[*He runs towards the hut; at the same moment* SOLVEIG *appears in the doorway, dressed for church, with a psalm-book wrapped in a kerchief, and a staff in her hand. She stands there erect and mild.*]

PEER   [*Flings himself down on the threshold.*]

Hast thou doom for a sinner, then speak it forth!

SOLVEIG

He is here! He is here! Oh, to God be the praise!

[*Stretches out her arms as though groping for him.*]

PEER

Cry out all my sins and my trespasses!

SOLVEIG

In nought hast thou sinned, oh my own only boy.

[*Gropes for him again, and finds him.*]

THE BUTTON-MOULDER   [*Behind the house.*]

The sin-list, Peer Gynt?

PEER

Cry aloud my crime!

SOLVEIG   [*Sits down beside him.*]

Thou hast made all my life as a beautiful song.

Blessëd be thou that at last thou hast come!

Blessëd, thrice blessëd our Whitsun-morn meeting!

PEER

Then I am lost!

SOLVEIG

There is one that rules all things.

PEER   [*Laughs.*]

Lost! Unless thou canst answer riddles.

SOLVEIG

Tell me them.

PEER

Tell them! Come on! To be sure!

Canst thou tell where Peer Gynt has been since we parted?

SOLVEIG

Been?

PEER

With his destiny's seal on his brow;

Been, as in God's thought he first sprang forth!

Canst thou tell me? If not, I must get me home,——

Go down to the mist-shrouded regions.

SOLVEIG   [*Smiling.*]

Oh, that riddle is easy.

PEER

Then tell what thou knowest!

Where was I, as myself, as the whole man, the true man?

Where was I, with God's sigil upon my brow?

SOLVEIG

In my faith, in my hope, and in my love.*

PEER   [*Starts back.*]

What sayest thou——? Peace! These are juggling words.

Thou art mother thyself to the man that's there.

SOLVEIG

Ay, that I am; but who is his father?

Surely he that forgives at the mother's prayer.

PEER   [*A light shines in his face; he cries:*]

My mother; my wife; oh, thou innocent woman!——

In thy love—oh, there hide me, hide me!

[*Clings to her and hides his face in her lap. A long silence. The sun rises.*]

SOLVEIG   [*Sings softly.*]

Sleep thou, dearest boy of mine!

I will cradle thee, I will watch thee——

The boy has been sitting on his mother's lap.

They two have been playing all the life-day long.

The boy has been resting at his mother's breast

All the life-day long. God's blessing on my joy.

The boy has been lying close in to my heart,

All the life-day long. He is weary now.

---

*I min Tro, i mit Håb og i min Kjærlighed. We have entirely sacrificed the metre of the line, feeling it impossible to mar its simplicity by any padding. *Kjærlighed* also means "charity," in the biblical sense. (Translator's note)

Sleep thou, dearest boy of mine!
I will cradle thee, I will watch thee.

THE BUTTON-MOULDER'S VOICE　[*Behind the house.*]

At the last cross-road we will meet again, Peer;
And then we'll see whether——; I say no more.

SOLVEIG　[*Sings louder in the full daylight.*]

I will cradle thee, I will watch thee;
Sleep and dream thou, dear my boy!

A DOLL'S HOUSE

(1879)

INTRODUCTION

A DOLL'S HOUSE (1879; *Et dukkehjem*) did not make Ibsen famous, but it did make him notorious. Immediately after its publication, it was staged in Copenhagen, Stockholm, Christiania, and Bergen, and very soon outside Scandinavia as well—for example, in Munich and other German cities (1880), Vienna (1881), Milwaukee (1882), and Louisville, Kentucky (1883). It also was a publishing success, mandating immediate reprints and translations into many languages, including English and German in the 1880s, Swedish (1880), Finnish (1880), Polish (1882), Russian (1883), Italian (1894), Dutch (1887), Serbo-Croatian (1891), Spanish (1894), Portuguese (1894), Hungarian (1894), and Catalan (1903).

The immediate and lasting success of *A Doll's House* established Ibsen's reputation as an enemy of bourgeois morality, as a subversive playwright whose primary goal was to unmask the hypocrisies of bourgeois society. William Archer, Ibsen's most accomplished and influential translator and promoter, published some of Ibsen's notes that seem to confirm this impression: "A woman cannot be herself in the society of the present day, which is an exclusively masculine society, with laws framed by men and with a judicial system that judges feminine conduct from a masculine point of view" (*William Archer on Ibsen*, p. 206; see "For Further Reading"). Ibsen really seemed out to accuse this society and everyone in it of collaboration, writing what George Bernard Shaw gleefully called a "propagandistic play" (*The Quintessence of Ibsenism*, p. 40).

Given the extreme reactions, both positive and negative, to *A Doll's House*, it is surprising to note that for the most part it is a rather traditional play based on a blackmail plot. It is only at the end that things take a sudden and startling turn. Instead of concluding with reconciliation, forgiveness, and reestablishment of familial order, the play has Nora force her husband into a discussion that quickly turns into what contemporaries saw as a feminist declaration of independence—and she leaves. This abrupt change was too much for many contemporaries. A German producer promptly came up with a symptomatic solution: to have the play conclude with a reconciliation. In fact, he coaxed Ibsen into writing that travestied ending himself; it was the best Ibsen could do since there was little chance for him to take legal action.

However, *A Doll's House* shocks the audience not bluntly but subtly. Ibsen embedded the traditional plot and its abrupt ending in an intricate network of images, props, and parallel constructions. A homely Christmas tree, for example, is contrasted with an excessive tarantella dance. Nora's triumphant escape is colored by the difficult life of her friend Mrs. Linden, whose unhappy marriage has ended with her husband's death but who finds herself now even more at a loss about what to do. Doctor Rank, the trusted friend of the family, maintains an ambiguous position as well, for he is in love with Nora, who toys with him even as she keeps him at a distance. Theatrically speaking, then, *A Doll's House* does not so much offer clear-cut solutions as it outlines problems.

For a playwright obsessed with the question of the home and the house, the metaphor of the doll's house signifies more than just the infantilization of Nora by her husband. It is part of Ibsen's repeated attempt to think rigorously about the bourgeois home, to expose all that is false and infantile about it. Why must the home be a place that is shielded from the world outside? Why must it constitute a separate and female sphere? It is this larger social institution of the home that Ibsen attacks in play after play and that takes the form of a plea: If we want to stop living in doll's houses, we have to start growing up.

—Martin Puchner

CHARACTERS

TORVALD HELMER.
NORA, his wife.
DOCTOR RANK.
MRS. LINDEN.*
NILS KROGSTAD.
THE HELMERS' THREE CHILDREN.
ANNA,[†] their nurse.
A MAID-SERVANT (ELLEN).
A PORTER.

The action passes in Helmer's house (a flat) in Christiania.

*In the original "Fru Linde." (Translator's note)
†In the original "Anne-Marie." (Translator's note)

ACT FIRST

*A room comfortably and tastefully, but not expensively, furnished. In the
back, on the right, a door leads to the hall; on the left another door
leads to HELMER's study. Between the two doors a pianoforte. In the
middle of the left wall a door, and nearer the front a window. Near the
window a round table with arm-chairs and a small sofa. In the right
wall, somewhat to the back, a door, and against the same wall, further
forward, a porcelain stove; in front of it a couple of arm-chairs and a
rocking-chair. Between the stove and the side-door a small table.
Engravings on the walls. A what-not with china and bric-à-brac. A small
bookcase filled with handsomely bound books. Carpet. A fire in the stove.
It is a winter day.*

*A bell rings in the hall outside. Presently the outer door of the flat is heard to
open. Then NORA enters, humming gaily. She is in outdoor dress, and carries
several parcels, which she lays on the right-hand table. She leaves the door into
the hall open, and a PORTER is seen outside, carrying a Christmas-tree and
a basket, which he gives to the MAID-SERVANT who has opened the door.*

NORA
> Hide the Christmas-tree carefully, Ellen; the children must on no
> account see it before this evening, when it's lighted up.
> [*To the* PORTER, *taking out her purse.*]
> How much?

PORTER
> Fifty öre.

NORA
> There is a crown. No, keep the change.
> [*The* PORTER *thanks her and goes.* NORA *shuts the door. She contin-
> ues smiling in quiet glee as she takes off her outdoor things. Taking from
> her pocket a bag of macaroons, she eats one or two. Then she goes on tip-
> toe to her husband's door and listens.*]

NORA

Yes; he is at home.

[*She begins humming again, crossing to the table on the right.*]

HELMER   [*In his room.*]

Is that my lark twittering there?

NORA   [*Busy opening some of her parcels.*]

Yes, it is.

HELMER

Is it the squirrel frisking around?

NORA

Yes!

HELMER

When did the squirrel get home?

NORA

Just this minute.

[*Hides the bag of macaroons in her pocket and wipes her mouth.*]

Come here, Torvald, and see what I've been buying.

HELMER

Don't interrupt me.

[*A little later he opens the door and looks in, pen in hand.*]

Buying, did you say? What! All that? Has my little spendthrift
been making the money fly again?

NORA

Why, Torvald, surely we can afford to launch out a little now. It's
the first Christmas we haven't had to pinch.

HELMER

Come come; we can't afford to squander money.

NORA

Oh yes, Torvald, do let us squander a little, now—just the least
little bit! You know you'll soon be earning heaps of money.

HELMER

Yes, from New Year's Day. But there's a whole quarter before my
first salary is due.

NORA

Never mind; we can borrow in the meantime.

HELMER

Nora!

[*He goes up to her and takes her playfully by the ear.*]

Still my little featherbrain! Supposing I borrowed a thousand crowns to-day, and you made ducks and drakes of them during Christmas week, and then on New Year's Eve a tile blew off the roof and knocked my brains out——

NORA   [*Laying her hand on his mouth.*]

Hush! How can you talk so horridly?

HELMER

But supposing it were to happen—what then?

NORA

If anything so dreadful happened, it would be all the same to me whether I was in debt or not.

HELMER

But what about the creditors?

NORA

They! Who cares for them? They're only strangers.

HELMER

Nora, Nora! What a woman you are! But seriously, Nora, you know my principles on these points. No debts! No borrowing! Home life ceases to be free and beautiful as soon as it is founded on borrowing and debt. We two have held out bravely till now, and we are not going to give in at the last.

NORA   [*Going to the fireplace.*]

Very well—as you please, Torvald.

HELMER   [*Following her.*]

Come come; my little lark mustn't droop her wings like that. What? Is my squirrel in the sulks?

[*Takes out his purse.*]

Nora, what do you think I have here?

NORA   [*Turning round quickly.*]

Money!

HELMER

There!

[*Gives her some notes.*]

Of course I know all sorts of things are wanted at Christmas.

NORA   [*Counting.*]

Ten, twenty, thirty, forty. Oh, thank you, thank you, Torvald! This will go a long way.

HELMER

I should hope so.

NORA

Yes, indeed; a long way! But come here, and let me show you all I've been buying. And so cheap! Look, here's a new suit for Ivar, and a little sword. Here are a horse and a trumpet for Bob. And here are a doll and a cradle for Emmy. They're only common; but they're good enough for her to pull to pieces. And dress-stuffs and kerchiefs for the servants. I ought to have got something better for old Anna.

HELMER

And what's in that other parcel?

NORA   [Crying out.]

No, Torvald, you're not to see that until this evening!

HELMER

Oh! Ah! But now tell me, you little spendthrift, have you thought of anything for yourself?

NORA

For myself! Oh, I don't want anything.

HELMER

Nonsense! Just tell me something sensible you would like to have.

NORA

No, really I don't know of anything—— Well, listen, Torvald——

HELMER

Well?

NORA   [Playing with his coat-buttons, without looking him in the face.]

If you really want to give me something, you might, you know— you might——

HELMER

Well? Out with it!

NORA   [Quickly.]

You might give me money, Torvald. Only just what you think you can spare; then I can buy something with it later on.

HELMER

But, Nora——

NORA

Oh, please do, dear Torvald, please do! I should hang the money in lovely gilt paper on the Christmas-tree. Wouldn't that be fun?

HELMER

What do they call the birds that are always making the money fly?

NORA

Yes, I know——spendthrifts,* of course. But please do as I ask you, Torvald. Then I shall have time to think what I want most. Isn't that very sensible, now?

HELMER   [*Smiling.*]

Certainly; that is to say, if you really kept the money I gave you, and really spent it on something for yourself. But it all goes in housekeeping, and for all manner of useless things, and then I have to pay up again.

NORA

But, Torvald——

HELMER

Can you deny it, Nora dear?

[*He puts his arm round her.*]

It's a sweet little lark, but it gets through a lot of money. No one would believe how much it costs a man to keep such a little bird as you.

NORA

For shame! How can you say so? Why, I save as much as ever I can.

HELMER   [*Laughing.*]

Very true——as much as you can——but that's precisely nothing.

NORA   [*Hums and smiles with covert glee.*]

H'm! If you only knew, Torvald, what expenses we larks and squirrels have.

HELMER

You're a strange little being! Just like your father——always on the look-out for all the money you can lay your hands on; but the moment you have it, it seems to slip through your fingers; you

---

*Spillefugl——literally, "playbird," meaning a gambler. (Translator's note)

never know what becomes of it. Well, one must take you as you are. It's in the blood. Yes, Nora, that sort of thing is hereditary.

NORA

I wish I had inherited many of papa's qualities.

HELMER

And I don't wish you anything but just what you are—my own, sweet little song-bird. But I say—it strikes me you look so— so—what shall I call it?—so suspicious to-day——

NORA

Do I?

HELMER

You do, indeed. Look me full in the face.

NORA   [Looking at him.]

Well?

HELMER   [Threatening with his finger.]

Hasn't the little sweet-tooth been playing pranks to-day?

NORA

No; how can you think such a thing!

HELMER

Didn't she just look in at the confectioner's?

NORA

No, Torvald; really——

HELMER

Not to sip a little jelly?

NORA

No; certainly not.

HELMER

Hasn't she even nibbled a macaroon or two?

NORA

No, Torvald, indeed, indeed!

HELMER

Well, well, well; of course I'm only joking.

NORA   [Goes to the table on the right.]

I shouldn't think of doing what you disapprove of.

HELMER

No, I'm sure of that; and, besides, you've given me your word——
[Going towards her.]

Well, keep your little Christmas secrets to yourself, Nora
darling. The Christmas-tree will bring them all to light, I daresay.

NORA

Have you remembered to invite Doctor Rank?

HELMER

No. But it's not necessary; he'll come as a matter of course.
Besides, I shall ask him when he looks in to-day. I've ordered
some capital wine. Nora, you can't think how I look forward to
this evening.

NORA

And I too. How the children will enjoy themselves, Torvald!

HELMER

Ah, it's glorious to feel that one has an assured position and
ample means. Isn't it delightful to think of?

NORA

Oh, it's wonderful!

HELMER

Do you remember last Christmas? For three whole weeks
beforehand you shut yourself up every evening till long past
midnight to make flowers for the Christmas-tree, and all sorts of
other marvels that were to have astonished us. I was never so
bored in my life.

NORA

I didn't bore myself at all.

HELMER   [*Smiling.*]

But it came to little enough in the end, Nora.

NORA

Oh, are you going to tease me about that again? How could I
help the cat getting in and pulling it all to pieces?

HELMER

To be sure you couldn't, my poor little Nora. You did your best
to give us all pleasure, and that's the main point. But, all the
same, it's a good thing the hard times are over.

NORA

Oh, isn't it wonderful?

HELMER

Now I needn't sit here boring myself all alone; and you needn't
tire your blessed eyes and your delicate little fingers———

NORA   [*Clapping her hands.*]

> No, I needn't, need I, Torvald? Oh, how wonderful it is to think
> of?
> [*Takes his arm.*]
> And now I'll tell you how I think we ought to manage, Torvald.
> As soon as Christmas is over——
> [*The hall-door bell rings.*]
> Oh, there's a ring!
> [*Arranging the room.*]
> That's somebody come to call. How tiresome!

HELMER

> I'm "not at home" to callers; remember that.

ELLEN   [*In the doorway.*]

> A lady to see you, ma'am.

NORA

> Show her in.

ELLEN   [*To* HELMER.]

> And the doctor has just come, sir.

HELMER

> Has he gone into my study?

ELLEN

> Yes, sir.
> [HELMER *goes into his study.* ELLEN *ushers in* MRS. LINDEN, *in
> travelling costume, and goes out, closing the door.*]

MRS. LINDEN   [*Embarrassed and hesitating.*]

> How do you do, Nora?

NORA   [*Doubtfully.*]

> How do you do?

MRS. LINDEN

> I see you don't recognise me.

NORA

> No, I don't think——oh yes!——I believe——
> [*Suddenly brightening.*]
> What, Christina! Is it really you?

MRS. LINDEN

> Yes; really I!

NORA

> Christina! And to think I didn't know you! But how could I——

[*More softly.*]

How changed you are, Christina!

MRS. LINDEN

Yes, no doubt. In nine or ten years———

NORA

Is it really so long since we met? Yes, so it is. Oh, the last eight years have been a happy time, I can tell you. And now you have come to town? All that long journey in mid-winter! How brave of you!

MRS. LINDEN

I arrived by this morning's steamer.

NORA

To have a merry Christmas, of course. Oh, how delightful! Yes, we will have a merry Christmas. Do take your things off. Aren't you frozen?

[*Helping her.*]

There; now we'll sit cosily by the fire. No, you take the armchair; I shall sit in this rocking-chair.

[*Seizes her hands.*]

Yes, now I can see the dear old face again. It was only at the first glance——— But you're a little paler, Christina—and perhaps a little thinner.

MRS. LINDEN

And much, much older, Nora.

NORA

Yes, perhaps a little older—not much—ever so little.

[*She suddenly checks herself; seriously.*]

Oh, what a thoughtless wretch I am! Here I sit chattering on, and——— Dear, dear Christina, can you forgive me!

MRS. LINDEN

What do you mean, Nora?

NORA   [*Softly.*]

Poor Christina! I forgot: you are a widow.

MRS. LINDEN

Yes; my husband died three years ago.

NORA

I know, I know; I saw it in the papers. Oh, believe me, Christina,

I did mean to write to you; but I kept putting it off, and something always came in the way.

MRS. LINDEN

I can quite understand that, Nora dear.

NORA

No, Christina; it was horrid of me. Oh, you poor darling! how much you must have gone through!—And he left you nothing?

MRS. LINDEN

Nothing.

NORA

And no children?

MRS. LINDEN

None.

NORA

Nothing, nothing at all?

MRS. LINDEN

Not even a sorrow or a longing to dwell upon.

NORA   [Looking at her incredulously.]

My dear Christina, how is that possible?

MRS. LINDEN   [Smiling sadly and stroking her hair.]

Oh, it happens so sometimes, Nora.

NORA

So utterly alone! How dreadful that must be! I have three of the loveliest children. I can't show them to you just now; they're out with their nurse. But now you must tell me everything.

MRS. LINDEN

No, no; I want you to tell me——

NORA

No, you must begin; I won't be egotistical to-day. To-day I'll think only of you. Oh! but I must tell you one thing—perhaps you've heard of our great stroke of fortune?

MRS. LINDEN

No. What is it?

NORA

Only think! my husband has been made manager of the Joint Stock Bank.

MRS. LINDEN

Your husband! Oh, how fortunate!

NORA

Yes; isn't it? A lawyer's position is so uncertain, you see, especially when he won't touch any business that's the least bit— shady, as of course Torvald never would; and there I quite agree with him. Oh! you can imagine how glad we are. He is to enter on his new position at the New Year, and then he'll have a large salary, and percentages. In future we shall be able to live quite differently—just as we please, in fact. Oh, Christina, I feel so lighthearted and happy! It's delightful to have lots of money, and no need to worry about things, isn't it?

MRS. LINDEN

Yes; at any rate it must be delightful to have what you need.

NORA

No, not only what you need, but heaps of money—heaps!

MRS. LINDEN   [*Smiling.*]

Nora, Nora, haven't you learnt reason yet? In our schooldays you were a shocking little spendthrift.

NORA   [*Quietly smiling.*]

Yes; that's what Torvald says I am still.

[*Holding up her forefinger.*]

But "Nora, Nora" is not so silly as you all think. Oh! I haven't had the chance to be much of a spendthrift. We have both had to work.

MRS. LINDEN

You too?

NORA

Yes, light fancy work: crochet, and embroidery, and things of that sort;

[*Carelessly.*]

and other work too. You know, of course, that Torvald left the Government service when we were married. He had little chance of promotion, and of course he required to make more money. But in the first year after our marriage he overworked himself terribly. He had to undertake all sorts of extra work, you know, and to slave early and late. He couldn't stand it, and fell dangerously ill. Then the doctors declared he must go to the South.

MRS. LINDEN

You spent a whole year in Italy, didn't you?

NORA

Yes, we did. It wasn't easy to manage, I can tell you. It was just
after Ivar's birth. But of course we had to go. Oh, it was a
wonderful, delicious journey! And it saved Torvald's life. But it
cost a frightful lot of money, Christina.

MRS. LINDEN

So I should think.

NORA

Twelve hundred dollars! Four thousand eight hundred crowns!*
Isn't that a lot of money?

MRS. LINDEN

How lucky you had the money to spend.

NORA

We got it from father, you must know.

MRS. LINDEN

Ah, I see. He died just about that time, didn't he?

NORA

Yes, Christina, just then. And only think! I couldn't go and nurse
him! I was expecting little Ivar's birth daily; and then I had my
poor sick Torvald to attend to. Dear, kind old father! I never saw
him again, Christina. Oh! that's the hardest thing I have had to
bear since my marriage.

MRS. LINDEN

I know how fond you were of him. But then you went to Italy?

NORA

Yes; you see, we had the money, and the doctors said we must
lose no time. We started a month later.

MRS. LINDEN

And your husband came back completely cured.

NORA

Sound as a bell.

MRS. LINDEN

But——the doctor?

---

*The dollar was the old unit of currency in Norway. The crown was substituted
for it shortly before the date of this play. (Translator's note)

NORA

What do you mean?

MRS. LINDEN

I thought as I came in your servant announced the doctor——

NORA

Oh, yes; Doctor Rank. But he doesn't come professionally. He is our best friend, and never lets a day pass without looking in. No, Torvald hasn't had an hour's illness since that time. And the children are so healthy and well, and so am I.

[*Jumps up and claps her hands.*]

Oh, Christina, Christina, what a wonderful thing it is to live and to be happy!—Oh, but it's really too horrid of me! Here am I talking about nothing but my own concerns.

[*Seats herself upon a footstool close to* CHRISTINA, *and lays her arms on her friend's lap.*]

Oh, don't be angry with me! Now tell me, is it really true that you didn't love your husband? What made you marry him, then?

MRS. LINDEN

My mother was still alive, you see, bedridden and helpless; and then I had my two younger brothers to think of. I didn't think it would be right for me to refuse him.

NORA

Perhaps it wouldn't have been. I suppose he was rich then?

MRS. LINDEN

Very well off, I believe. But his business was uncertain. It fell to pieces at his death, and there was nothing left.

NORA

And then——?

MRS. LINDEN

Then I had to fight my way by keeping a shop, a little school, anything I could turn my hand to. The last three years have been one long struggle for me. But now it is over, Nora. My poor mother no longer needs me; she is at rest. And the boys are in business, and can look after themselves.

NORA

How free your life must feel!

MRS. LINDEN

No, Nora; only inexpressibly empty. No one to live for!

[*Stands up restlessly.*]

That's why I could not bear to stay any longer in that out-of-the way corner. Here it must be easier to find something to take one up—to occupy one's thoughts. If I could only get some settled employment—some office work.

NORA

But, Christina, that's such drudgery, and you look worn out already. It would be ever so much better for you to go to some watering-place and rest.

MRS. LINDEN   [*Going to the window.*]

I have no father to give me the money, Nora.

NORA   [*Rising.*]

Oh, don't be vexed with me.

MRS. LINDEN   [*Going to her.*]

My dear Nora, don't you be vexed with me. The worst of a position like mine is that it makes one so bitter. You have no one to work for, yet you have to be always on the strain. You must live; and so you become selfish. When I heard of the happy change in your fortunes—can you believe it?—I was glad for my own sake more than for yours.

NORA

How do you mean? Ah, I see! You think Torvald can perhaps do something for you.

MRS. LINDEN

Yes; I thought so.

NORA

And so he shall, Christina. Just you leave it all to me. I shall lead up to it beautifully!—I shall think of some delightful plan to put him in a good humour! Oh, I should so love to help you.

MRS. LINDEN

How good of you, Nora, to stand by me so warmly! Doubly good in you, who know so little of the troubles and burdens of life.

NORA

I? I know so little of——?

MRS. LINDEN   [*Smiling.*]

Oh, well—a little fancy-work, and so forth.—You're a child, Nora.

NORA   [*Tosses her head and paces the room.*]

Oh, come, you mustn't be so patronising!

MRS. LINDEN

No?

NORA

You're like the rest. You all think I'm fit for nothing really serious——

MRS. LINDEN

Well, well——

NORA

You think I've had no troubles in this weary world.

MRS. LINDEN

My dear Nora, you've just told me all your troubles.

NORA

Pooh—those trifles!

[*Softly.*]

I haven't told you the great thing.

MRS. LINDEN

The great thing? What do you mean?

NORA

I know you look down upon me, Christina; but you have no right to. You are proud of having worked so hard and so long for your mother.

MRS. LINDEN

I am sure I don't look down upon any one; but it's true I am both proud and glad when I remember that I was able to keep my mother's last days free from care.

NORA

And you're proud to think of what you have done for your brothers, too.

MRS. LINDEN

Have I not the right to be?

NORA

Yes indeed. But now let me tell you, Christina—I, too, have something to be proud and glad of.

MRS. LINDEN

I don't doubt it. But what do you mean?

NORA

Hush! Not so loud. Only think, if Torvald were to hear! He mustn't—not for worlds! No one must know about it, Christina—no one but you.

MRS LINDEN

Why, what can it be?

NORA

Come over here.

[*Draws her down beside her on the sofa.*]

Yes, Christina—I, too, have something to be proud and glad of. I saved Torvald's life.

MRS. LINDEN

Saved his life? How?

NORA

I told you about our going to Italy. Torvald would have died but for that.

MRS. LINDEN

Well—and your father gave you the money.

NORA   [*Smiling.*]

Yes, so Torvald and every one believes; but——

MRS. LINDEN

But——?

NORA

Papa didn't give us one penny. It was *I* that found the money.

MRS. LINDEN

You? All that money?

NORA

Twelve hundred dollars. Four thousand eight hundred crowns. What do you say to that?

MRS. LINDEN

My dear Nora, how did you manage it? Did you win it in the lottery?

NORA   [*Contemptuously.*]

In the lottery? Pooh! Any one could have done that!

MRS. LINDEN

Then wherever did you get it from?

NORA   [*Hums and smiles mysteriously.*]

H'm; tra-la-la-la.

MRS. LINDEN

Of course you couldn't borrow it.

NORA

No? Why not?

MRS. LINDEN

Why, a wife can't borrow without her husband's consent.

NORA   [*Tossing her head.*]

Oh! when the wife has some idea of business, and knows how to set about things——

MRS. LINDEN

But, Nora, I don't understand——

NORA

Well, you needn't. I never said I borrowed the money. There are many ways I may have got it.

[*Throws herself back on the sofa.*]

I may have got it from some admirer. When one is so—attractive as I am——

MRS. LINDEN

You're too silly, Nora.

NORA

Now I'm sure you're dying of curiosity, Christina——

MRS. LINDEN

Listen to me, Nora dear: haven't you been a little rash?

NORA   [*Sitting upright again.*]

Is it rash to save one's husband's life?

MRS. LINDEN

I think it was rash of you, without his knowledge——

NORA

But it would have been fatal for him to know! Can't you understand that? He wasn't even to suspect how ill he was. The doctors came to me privately and told me his life was in danger—that nothing could save him but a winter in the South. Do you think I didn't try diplomacy first? I told him how I longed to have a trip abroad, like other young wives; I wept and prayed; I said he ought to think of my condition, and not to thwart me; and then I hinted that he could borrow the money. But then, Christina, he got almost angry. He said I was frivolous, and that it was his duty as a husband not to yield to my whims

and fancies—so he called them. Very well, thought I, but saved
you must be; and then I found the way to do it.

MRS. LINDEN

And did your husband never learn from your father that the
money was not from him?

NORA

No; never. Papa died at that very time. I meant to have told him
all about it, and begged him to say nothing. But he was so ill—
unhappily, it wasn't necessary.

MRS. LINDEN

And you have never confessed to your husband?

NORA

Good heavens! What can you be thinking of? Tell him, when he
has such a loathing of debt! And besides—how painful and
humiliating it would be for Torvald, with his manly self-respect,
to know that he owed anything to me! It would utterly upset the
relation between us; our beautiful, happy home would never
again be what it is.

MRS. LINDEN

Will you never tell him?

NORA   [Thoughtfully, half smiling.]

Yes, some time perhaps—many, many years hence, when I'm—
not so pretty. You mustn't laugh at me! Of course I mean when
Torvald is not so much in love with me as he is now; when it
doesn't amuse him any longer to see me dancing about, and
dressing up and acting. Then it might be well to have something
in reserve.

[Breaking off.]

Nonsense! nonsense! That time will never come. Now, what do
you say to my grand secret, Christina? Am I fit for nothing now?
You may believe it has cost me a lot of anxiety. It has been no
joke to meet my engagements punctually. You must know,
Christina, that in business there are things called instalments, and
quarterly interest, that are terribly hard to provide for. So I've
had to pinch a little here and there, wherever I could. I couldn't
save much out of the housekeeping, for of course Torvald had to
live well. And I couldn't let the children go about badly dressed;
all I got for them, I spent on them, the blessed darlings!

MRS. LINDEN

Poor Nora! So it had to come out of your own pocket-money.

NORA

Yes, of course. After all, the whole thing was my doing. When Torvald gave me money for clothes, and so on, I never spent more than half of it; I always bought the simplest and cheapest things. It's a mercy that everything suits me so well—Torvald never had any suspicions. But it was often very hard, Christina dear. For it's nice to be beautifully dressed—now, isn't it?

MRS. LINDEN

Indeed it is.

NORA

Well, and besides that, I made money in other ways. Last winter I was so lucky—I got a heap of copying to do. I shut myself up every evening and wrote far into the night. Oh, sometimes I was so tired, so tired. And yet it was splendid to work in that way and earn money. I almost felt as if I was a man.

MRS. LINDEN

Then how much have you been able to pay off?

NORA

Well, I can't precisely say. It's difficult to keep that sort of business clear. I only know that I've paid everything I could scrape together. Sometimes I really didn't know where to turn. [*Smiles.*]

Then I used to sit here and pretend that a rich old gentleman was in love with me——

MRS. LINDEN

What! What gentleman?

NORA

Oh, nobody!—that he was dead now, and that when his will was opened, there stood in large letters: "Pay over at once everything of which I die possessed to that charming person, Mrs. Nora Helmer."

MRS. LINDEN

But, my dear Nora—what gentleman do you mean?

NORA

Oh dear, can't you understand? There wasn't any old gentleman: it was only what I used to dream and dream when I was at my wits' end for money. But it doesn't matter now—the tiresome old creature may stay where he is for me. I care nothing for him or his will; for now my troubles are over.

[*Springing up.*]

Oh, Christina, how glorious it is to think of! Free from all anxiety! Free, quite free. To be able to play and romp about with the children; to have things tasteful and pretty in the house, exactly as Torvald likes it! And then the spring will soon be here, with the great blue sky. Perhaps then we shall have a little holiday. Perhaps I shall see the sea again. Oh, what a wonderful thing it is to live and to be happy!

[*The hall door bell rings.*]

MRS. LINDEN   [*Rising.*]

There's a ring. Perhaps I had better go.

NORA

No; do stay. No one will come here. It's sure to be some one for Torvald.

ELLEN   [*In the doorway.*]

If you please, ma'am, there's a gentleman to speak to Mr. Helmer.

NORA

Who is the gentleman?

KROGSTAD   [*In the doorway.*]

It is I, Mrs. Helmer.

[MRS. LINDEN *starts and turns away to the window.*]

NORA   [*Goes a step towards him, anxiously, speaking low.*]

You? What is it? What do you want with my husband?

KROGSTAD

Bank business—in a way. I hold a small post in the Joint Stock Bank, and your husband is to be our new chief, I hear.

NORA

Then it is——?

KROGSTAD

Only tiresome business, Mrs. Helmer; nothing more.

NORA

Then will you please go to his study.

[KROGSTAD *goes. She bows indifferently while she closes the door into the hall. Then she goes to the stove and looks to the fire.*]

MRS. LINDEN
    Nora—who was that man?

NORA
    A Mr. Krogstad—a lawyer.

MRS. LINDEN
    Then it was really he?

NORA
    Do you know him?

MRS. LINDEN
    I used to know him—many years ago. He was in a lawyer's office
    in our town.

NORA
    Yes, so he was.

MRS. LINDEN
    How he has changed!

NORA
    I believe his marriage was unhappy.

MRS. LINDEN
    And he is a widower now?

NORA
    With a lot of children. There! Now it will burn up.
    [*She closes the stove, and pushes the rocking-chair a little aside.*]

MRS. LINDEN
    His business is not of the most creditable, they say?

NORA
    Isn't it? I daresay not. I don't know. But don't let us think of
    business—it's so tiresome.

DR. RANK *comes out of* HELMER's *room.*

RANK   [*Still in the doorway.*]
    No, no; I'm in your way. I shall go and have a chat with your
    wife.
    [*Shuts the door and sees* MRS. LINDEN.]
    Oh, I beg your pardon. I'm in the way here too.

NORA
    No, not in the least.
    [*Introduces them.*]
    Doctor Rank—Mrs. Linden.

RANK

Oh, indeed; I've often heard Mrs. Linden's name; I think I passed you on the stairs as I came up.

MRS. LINDEN

Yes; I go so very slowly. Stairs try me so much.

RANK

Ah——you are not very strong?

MRS. LINDEN

Only overworked.

RANK

Nothing more? Then no doubt you've come to town to find rest in a round of dissipation?

MRS. LINDEN

I have come to look for employment.

RANK

Is that an approved remedy for overwork?

MRS. LINDEN

One must live, Doctor Rank.

RANK

Yes, that seems to be the general opinion.

NORA

Come, Doctor Rank——you want to live yourself.

RANK

To be sure I do. However wretched I may be, I want to drag on as long as possible. All my patients, too, have the same mania. And it's the same with people whose complaint is moral. At this very moment Helmer is talking to just such a moral incurable——

MRS. LINDEN　[*Softly.*]

Ah!

NORA

Whom do you mean?

RANK

Oh, a fellow named Krogstad, a man you know nothing about—corrupt to the very core of his character. But even he began by announcing, as a matter of vast importance, that he must live.

NORA

Indeed? And what did he want with Torvald?

RANK

I haven't an idea; I only gathered that it was some bank business.

NORA

I didn't know that Krog—that this Mr. Krogstad had anything to do with the Bank?

RANK

Yes. He has got some sort of place there.

[*To* MRS. LINDEN.]

I don't know whether, in your part of the country, you have people who go grubbing and sniffing around in search of moral rottenness—and then, when they have found a "case," don't rest till they have got their man into some good position, where they can keep a watch upon him. Men with a clean bill of health they leave out in the cold.

MRS. LINDEN

Well, I suppose the—delicate characters require most care.

RANK   [*Shrugs his shoulders.*]

There we have it! It's that notion that makes society a hospital.

[NORA, *deep in her own thoughts, breaks into half-stifled laughter and claps her hands.*]

RANK

Why do you laugh at that? Have you any idea what "society" is?

NORA

What do I care for your tiresome society? I was laughing at something else—something excessively amusing. Tell me, Doctor Rank, are all the employees at the Bank dependent on Torvald now?

RANK

Is that what strikes you as excessively amusing?

NORA   [*Smiles and hums.*]

Never mind, never mind!

[*Walks about the room.*]

Yes, it is funny to think that we—that Torvald has such power over so many people.

[*Takes the bag from her pocket.*]

Doctor Rank, will you have a macaroon?

RANK

What!—macaroons! I thought they were contraband here.

NORA

Yes; but Christina brought me these.

MRS. LINDEN

What! I———?

NORA

Oh, well! Don't be frightened. You couldn't possibly know that Torvald had forbidden them. The fact is, he's afraid of me spoiling my teeth. But, oh bother, just for once!—That's for you, Doctor Rank!

[*Puts a macaroon into his mouth.*]

And you too, Christina. And I'll have one while we're about it— only a tiny one, or at most two.

[*Walks about again.*]

Oh dear, I am happy! There's only one thing in the world I really want.

RANK

Well; what's that?

NORA

There's something I should so like to say—in Torvald's hearing.

RANK

Then why don't you say it?

NORA

Because I daren't, it's so ugly.

MRS. LINDEN

Ugly.

RANK

In that case you'd better not. But to us you might———What is it you would so like to say in Helmer's hearing?

NORA

I should so love to say "Damn it all!"*

RANK

Are you out of your mind?

MRS. LINDEN

Good gracious, Nora———!

---

*Död og pine—literally, "death and torture," but by usage a comparatively mild oath. (Translator's note)

RANK

Say it——there he is!

NORA   [*Hides the macaroons.*]

Hush——sh——sh.

HELMER *comes out of his room, hat in hand, with his overcoat on his arm.*

NORA   [*Going to him.*]

Well, Torvald dear, have you got rid of him?

HELMER

Yes; he has just gone.

NORA

Let me introduce you——this is Christina, who has come to town——

HELMER

Christina? Pardon me, I don't know——

NORA

Mrs. Linden, Torvald dear——Christina Linden.

HELMER   [*To* MRS. LINDEN.]

Indeed! A school-friend of my wife's, no doubt?

MRS. LINDEN

Yes; we knew each other as girls.

NORA

And only think! she has taken this long journey on purpose to speak to you.

HELMER

To speak to me!

MRS. LINDEN

Well, not quite——

NORA

You see, Christina is tremendously clever at office-work, and she's so anxious to work under a first-rate man of business in order to learn still more——

HELMER   [*To* MRS. LINDEN.]

Very sensible indeed.

NORA

And when she heard you were appointed manager——it was telegraphed, you know——she started off at once, and——

Torvald, dear, for my sake, you must do something for Christina.
Now can't you?

HELMER

It's not impossible. I presume Mrs. Linden is a widow?

MRS. LINDEN

Yes.

HELMER

And you have already had some experience of business?

MRS. LINDEN

A good deal.

HELMER

Well, then, it's very likely I may be able to find a place for you.

NORA   [Clapping her hands.]

There now! There now!

HELMER

You have come at a fortunate moment, Mrs. Linden.

MRS. LINDEN

Oh, how can I thank you———?

HELMER   [Smiling.]

There is no occasion.

[Puts on his overcoat.]

But for the present you must excuse me———

RANK

Wait; I am going with you.

[Fetches his fur coat from the hall and warms it at the fire.]

NORA

Don't be long, Torvald dear.

HELMER

Only an hour; not more.

NORA

Are you going too, Christina?

MRS. LINDEN   [Putting on her walking things.]

Yes; I must set about looking for lodgings.

HELMER

Then perhaps we can go together?

NORA   [Helping her.]

What a pity we haven't a spare room for you; but it's
impossible———

MRS. LINDEN

> I shouldn't think of troubling you. Good-bye, dear Nora, and
> thank you for all your kindness.

NORA

> Good-bye for the present. Of course you'll come back this
> evening. And you, too, Doctor Rank. What! If you're well
> enough? Of course you'll be well enough. Only wrap up warmly.
> [*They go out, talking, into the hall. Outside on the stairs are heard chil-
> dren's voices.*]
> There they are! There they are!
> [*She runs to the outer door and opens it. The nurse, ANNA, enters the hall
> with the children.*]
> Come in! Come in!
> [*Stoops down and kisses the children.*]
> Oh, my sweet darlings! Do you see them, Christina? Aren't they
> lovely?

RANK

> Don't let us stand here chattering in the draught.

HELMER

> Come, Mrs. Linden; only mothers can stand such a temperature.
> [*DR. RANK, HELMER, and MRS. LINDEN go down the stairs;
> ANNA enters the room with the children; NORA also, shutting the door.*]

NORA

> How fresh and bright you look! And what red cheeks you've got!
> Like apples and roses.
> [*The children chatter to her during what follows.*]
> Have you had great fun? That's splendid! Oh, really! You've been
> giving Emmy and Bob a ride on your sledge!—both at once, only
> think! Why, you're quite a man, Ivar. Oh, give her to me a little,
> Anna. My sweet little dolly!
> [*Takes the smallest from the nurse and dances with her.*]
> Yes, yes; mother will dance with Bob too. What! Did you have a
> game of snowballs? Oh, I wish I'd been there. No; leave them,
> Anna; I'll take their things off. Oh, yes, let me do it; it's such
> fun. Go to the nursery; you look frozen. You'll find some hot
> coffee on the stove.
> [*The NURSE goes into the room on the left. NORA takes off the chil-*

dren's things and throws them down anywhere, while the children talk all together.]

Really! A big dog ran after you? But he didn't bite you? No; dogs don't bite dear little dolly children. Don't peep into those parcels, Ivar. What is it? Wouldn't you like to know? Take care— it'll bite! What? Shall we have a game? What shall we play at? Hide-and-seek? Yes, let's play hide-and-seek. Bob shall hide first. Am I to? Yes, let me hide first.

[*She and the children play, with laughter and shouting, in the room and the adjacent one to the right. At last* NORA *hides under the table; the children come rushing in, look for her, but cannot find her, hear her half-choked laughter, rush to the table, lift up the cover and see her. Loud shouts. She creeps out, as though to frighten them. Fresh shouts. Meanwhile there has been a knock at the door leading into the hall. No one has heard it. Now the door is half opened and* KROGSTAD *appears. He waits a little; the game is renewed.*]

KROGSTAD

I beg your pardon, Mrs. Helmer——

NORA   [*With a suppressed cry, turns round and half jumps up.*]

Ah! What do you want?

KROGSTAD

Excuse me; the outer door was ajar—somebody must have forgotten to shut it——

NORA   [*Standing up.*]

My husband is not at home, Mr. Krogstad.

KROGSTAD

I know it.

NORA

Then what do you want here?

KROGSTAD

To say a few words to you.

NORA

To me?

[*To the children, softly.*]

Go in to Anna. What? No, the strange man won't hurt mamma. When he's gone we'll go on playing.

[*She leads the children into the left-hand room, and shuts the door behind them. Uneasy, in suspense.*]

It is to me you wish to speak?

KROGSTAD

Yes, to you.

NORA

To-day? But it's not the first yet——

KROGSTAD

No, to-day is Christmas Eve. It will depend upon yourself
whether you have a merry Christmas.

NORA

What do you want? I'm not ready to-day——

KROGSTAD

Never mind that just now. I have come about another matter. You
have a minute to spare?

NORA

Oh, yes, I suppose so; although——

KROGSTAD

Good. I was sitting in the restaurant opposite, and I saw your
husband go down the street——

NORA

Well?

KROGSTAD

——with a lady.

NORA

What then?

KROGSTAD

May I ask if the lady was a Mrs. Linden?

NORA

Yes.

KROGSTAD

Who has just come to town?

NORA

Yes. To-day.

KROGSTAD

I believe she is an intimate friend of yours.

NORA

Certainly. But I don't understand——

KROGSTAD

I used to know her too.

NORA

I know you did.

KROGSTAD

Ah! You know all about it. I thought as much. Now, frankly, is Mrs. Linden to have a place in the Bank?

NORA

How dare you catechise me in this way, Mr. Krogstad—you, a subordinate of my husband's? But since you ask, you shall know. Yes, Mrs. Linden is to be employed. And it is I who recommended her, Mr. Krogstad. Now you know.

KROGSTAD

Then my guess was right.

NORA   [Walking up and down.]

You see one has a wee bit of influence, after all. It doesn't follow because one's only a woman—— When people are in a subordinate position, Mr. Krogstad, they ought really to be careful how they offend anybody who—h'm——

KROGSTAD

——who has influence?

NORA

Exactly.

KROGSTAD   [Taking another tone.]

Mrs. Helmer, will you have the kindness to employ your influence on my behalf?

NORA

What? How do you mean?

KROGSTAD

Will you be so good as to see that I retain my subordinate position in the Bank?

NORA

What do you mean? Who wants to take it from you?

KROGSTAD

Oh, you needn't pretend ignorance. I can very well understand that it cannot be pleasant for your friend to meet me; and I can also understand now for whose sake I am to be hounded out.

NORA

But I assure you——

KROGSTAD

>Come come now, once for all: there is time yet, and I advise you to use your influence to prevent it.

NORA

>But, Mr. Krogstad, I have no influence—absolutely none.

KROGSTAD

>None? I thought you said a moment ago——

NORA

>Of course not in that sense. I! How can you imagine that I should have any such influence over my husband?

KROGSTAD

>Oh, I know your husband from our college days. I don't think he is any more inflexible than other husbands.

NORA

>If you talk disrespectfully of my husband, I must request you to leave the house.

KROGSTAD

>You are bold, madam.

NORA

>I am afraid of you no longer. When New Year's Day is over, I shall soon be out of the whole business.

KROGSTAD   [*Controlling himself.*]

>Listen to me, Mrs. Helmer. If need be, I shall fight as though for my life to keep my little place in the Bank.

NORA

>Yes, so it seems.

KROGSTAD

>It's not only for the salary: that is what I care least about. It's something else—— Well, I had better make a clean breast of it. Of course you know, like every one else, that some years ago I— got into trouble.

NORA

>I think I've heard something of the sort.

KROGSTAD

>The matter never came into court; but from that moment all paths were barred to me. Then I took up the business you know about. I had to turn my hand to something; and I don't think I've been one of the worst. But now I must get clear of it all. My

sons are growing up; for their sake I must try to recover my character as well as I can. This place in the Bank was the first step; and now your husband wants to kick me off the ladder, back into the mire.

NORA

But I assure you, Mr. Krogstad, I haven't the least power to help you.

KROGSTAD

That is because you have not the will; but I can compel you.

NORA

You won't tell my husband that I owe you money?

KROGSTAD

H'm; suppose I were to?

NORA

It would be shameful of you.

[*With tears in her voice.*]

The secret that is my joy and my pride—that he should learn it in such an ugly, coarse way—and from you. It would involve me in all sorts of unpleasantness——

KROGSTAD

Only unpleasantness.

NORA   [*Hotly.*]

But just do it. It's you that will come off worst, for then my husband will see what a bad man you are, and then you certainly won't keep your place.

KROGSTAD

I asked whether it was only domestic unpleasantness you feared?

NORA

If my husband gets to know about it, he will of course pay you off at once, and then we shall have nothing more to do with you.

KROGSTAD   [*Coming a pace nearer.*]

Listen, Mrs. Helmer: either your memory is defective, or you don't know much about business. I must make the position a little clearer to you.

NORA

How so?

KROGSTAD

When your husband was ill, you came to me to borrow twelve hundred dollars.

NORA

I knew of nobody else.

KROGSTAD

I promised to find you the money——

NORA

And you did find it.

KROGSTAD

I promised to find you the money, on certain conditions. You were so much taken up at the time about your husband's illness, and so eager to have the wherewithal for your journey, that you probably did not give much thought to the details. Allow me to remind you of them. I promised to find you the amount in exchange for a note of hand, which I drew up.

NORA

Yes, and I signed it.

KROGSTAD

Quite right. But then I added a few lines, making your father security for the debt. Your father was to sign this.

NORA

Was to——? He did sign it!

KROGSTAD

I had left the date blank. That is to say, your father was himself to date his signature. Do you recollect that?

NORA

Yes, I believe——

KROGSTAD

Then I gave you the paper to send to your father, by post. Is not that so?

NORA

Yes.

KROGSTAD

And of course you did so at once; for within five or six days you brought me back the document with your father's signature; and I handed you the money.

NORA

Well? Have I not made my payments punctually?

KROGSTAD

Fairly—yes. But to return to the point: You were in great trouble at the time, Mrs. Helmer.

NORA

I was indeed!

KROGSTAD

Your father was very ill, I believe?

NORA

He was on his death-bed.

KROGSTAD

And died soon after?

NORA

Yes.

KROGSTAD

Tell me, Mrs. Helmer: do you happen to recollect the day of his death? The day of the month, I mean?

NORA

Father died on the 29th of September.

KROGSTAD

Quite correct. I have made inquiries. And here comes in the remarkable point—

[*Produces a paper*]

which I cannot explain.

NORA

What remarkable point? I don't know——

KROGSTAD

The remarkable point, madam, that your father signed this paper three days after his death!

NORA

What! I don't understand——

KROGSTAD

Your father died on the 29th of September. But look here: he has dated his signature October 2nd! Is not that remarkable, Mrs. Helmer?

[NORA *is silent.*]

Can you explain it?

[NORA *continues silent.*]

It is noteworthy, too, that the words "October 2nd" and the year are not in your father's handwriting, but in one which I believe I know. Well, this may be explained; your father may have forgotten to date his signature, and somebody may have added the date at random, before the fact of your father's death was known. There is nothing wrong in that. Everything depends on the signature. Of course it is genuine, Mrs. Helmer? It was really your father himself who wrote his name here?

NORA   [*After a short silence, throws her head back and looks defiantly at him.*]

No, it was not. *I* wrote father's name.

KROGSTAD

Ah!——Are you aware, madam, that that is a dangerous admission?

NORA

How so? You will soon get your money.

KROGSTAD

May I ask you one more question? Why did you not send the paper to your father?

NORA

It was impossible. Father was ill. If I had asked him for his signature, I should have had to tell him why I wanted the money; but he was so ill I really could not tell him that my husband's life was in danger. It was impossible.

KROGSTAD

Then it would have been better to have given up your tour.

NORA

No, I couldn't do that; my husband's life depended on that journey. I couldn't give it up.

KROGSTAD

And did it never occur to you that you were playing me false?

NORA

That was nothing to me. I didn't care in the least about you. I couldn't endure you for all the cruel difficulties you made, although you knew how ill my husband was.

KROGSTAD

Mrs. Helmer, you evidently do not realise what you have been guilty of. But I can assure you it was nothing more and nothing worse that made me an outcast from society.

NORA

> You! You want me to believe that you did a brave thing to save
> your wife's life?

KROGSTAD

> The law takes no account of motives.

NORA

> Then it must be a very bad law.

KROGSTAD

> Bad or not, if I produce this document in court, you will be
> condemned according to law.

NORA

> I don't believe that. Do you mean to tell me that a daughter has
> no right to spare her dying father trouble and anxiety?—that a
> wife has no right to save her husband's life? I don't know much
> about the law, but I'm sure you'll find, somewhere or another,
> that that is allowed. And you don't know that—you, a lawyer!
> You must be a bad one, Mr. Krogstad.

KROGSTAD

> Possibly. But business—such business as ours—I do understand.
> You believe that? Very well; now do as you please. But this I may
> tell you, that if I am flung into the gutter a second time, you
> shall keep me company.
>
> [*Bows and goes out through hall.*]

NORA   [*Stands a while thinking, then tosses her head.*]

> Oh nonsense! He wants to frighten me. I'm not so foolish as that.
> [*Begins folding the children's clothes. Pauses.*]
> But——? No, it's impossible! Why, I did it for love!

CHILDREN   [*At the door, left.*]

> Mamma, the strange man has gone now.

NORA

> Yes, yes, I know. But don't tell any one about the strange man.
> Do you hear? Not even papa!

CHILDREN

> No, mamma; and now will you play with us again?

NORA

> No, no; not now.

CHILDREN

> Oh, do, mamma; you know you promised.

NORA

Yes, but I can't just now. Run to the nursery; I have so much to do. Run along, run along, and be good, my darlings!

[*She pushes them gently into the inner room, and closes the door behind them. Sits on the sofa, embroiders a few stitches, but soon pauses.*]

No!

[*Throws down the work, rises, goes to the hall door and calls out.*]

Ellen, bring in the Christmas-tree!

[*Goes to table, left, and opens the drawer; again pauses.*]

No, it's quite impossible!

ELLEN   [*With Christmas-tree.*] Where shall I stand it, ma'am?

NORA

There, in the middle of the room.

ELLEN

Shall I bring in anything else?

NORA

No, thank you, I have all I want.

[ELLEN, *having put down the tree, goes out.*]

NORA   [*Busy dressing the tree.*]

There must be a candle here—and flowers there.—That horrible man! Nonsense, nonsense! there's nothing to be afraid of. The Christmas-tree shall be beautiful. I'll do everything to please you, Torvald; I'll sing and dance, and——

Enter HELMER *by the hall door, with a bundle of documents.*

NORA

Oh. You're back already?

HELMER

Yes. Has anybody been here?

NORA

Here? No.

HELMER

That's odd. I saw Krogstad come out of the house.

NORA

Did you? Oh, yes, by-the-bye, he was here for a minute.

HELMER

Nora, I can see by your manner that he has been begging you to put in a good word for him.

NORA

Yes.

HELMER

And you were to do it as if of your own accord? You were to say nothing to me of his having been here. Didn't he suggest that too?

NORA

Yes, Torvald; but——

HELMER

Nora, Nora! And you could condescend to that! To speak to such a man, to make him a promise! And then to tell me an untruth about it!

NORA

An untruth!

HELMER

Didn't you say that nobody had been here?

[*Threatens with his finger.*]

My little bird must never do that again! A song-bird must sing clear and true; no false notes.

[*Puts his arm round her.*]

That's so, isn't it? Yes, I was sure of it.

[*Lets her go.*]

And now we'll say no more about it.

[*Sits down before the fire.*]

Oh, how cosy and quiet it is here!

[*Glances into his documents.*]

NORA   [*Busy with the tree, after a short silence.*]

Torvald!

HELMER

Yes.

NORA

I'm looking forward so much to the Stenborgs' fancy ball the day after to-morrow.

HELMER

And I'm on tenterhooks to see what surprise you have in store for me.

NORA

Oh, it's too tiresome!

HELMER

What is?

NORA

I can't think of anything good. Everything seems so foolish and meaningless.

HELMER

Has little Nora made that discovery?

NORA   [*Behind his chair, with her arms on the back.*]

Are you very busy, Torvald?

HELMER

Well——

NORA

What papers are those?

HELMER

Bank business.

NORA

Already!

HELMER

I have got the retiring manager to let me make some necessary changes in the staff and the organization. I can do this during Christmas week. I want to have everything straight by the New Year.

NORA

Then that's why that poor Krogstad——

HELMER

H'm.

NORA   [*Still leaning over the chair-back and slowly stroking his hair.*]

If you hadn't been so very busy, I should have asked you a great, great favour, Torvald.

HELMER

What can it be? Out with it.

NORA

Nobody has such perfect taste as you; and I should so love to look well at the fancy ball. Torvald, dear, couldn't you take me in hand, and settle what I'm to be, and arrange my costume for me?

HELMER

Aha! So my wilful little woman is at a loss, and making signals of distress.

NORA

Yes, please, Torvald. I can't get on without your help.

HELMER

Well, well, I'll think it over, and we'll soon hit upon something.

NORA

Oh, how good that is of you!

[*Goes to the tree again; pause.*]

How well the red flowers show.—Tell me, was it anything so very dreadful this Krogstad got into trouble about?

HELMER

Forgery, that's all. Don't you know what that means?

NORA

Mayn't he have been driven to it by need?

HELMER

Yes; or, like so many others, he may have done it in pure heedlessness. I am not so hard-hearted as to condemn a man absolutely for a single fault.

NORA

No, surely not, Torvald!

HELMER

Many a man can retrieve his character, if he owns his crime and takes the punishment.

NORA

Punishment——?

HELMER

But Krogstad didn't do that. He evaded the law by means of tricks and subterfuges; and that is what has morally ruined him.

NORA

Do you think that——?

HELMER

Just think how a man with a thing of that sort on his conscience must be always lying and canting and shamming. Think of the mask he must wear even towards those who stand nearest him— towards his own wife and children. The effect on the children— that's the most terrible part of it, Nora.

NORA

Why?

HELMER

Because in such an atmosphere of lies home life is poisoned and contaminated in every fibre. Every breath the children draw contains some germ of evil.

NORA   [*Closer behind him.*]

Are you sure of that?

HELMER

As a lawyer, my dear, I have seen it often enough. Nearly all cases of early corruption may be traced to lying mothers.

NORA

Why—mothers?

HELMER

It generally comes from the mother's side; but of course the father's influence may act in the same way. Every lawyer knows it too well. And here has this Krogstad been poisoning his own children for years past by a life of lies and hypocrisy—that is why I call him morally ruined.

[*Holds out both hands to her.*]

So my sweet little Nora must promise not to plead his cause. Shake hands upon it. Come, come, what's this? Give me your hand. That's right. Then it's a bargain. I assure you it would have been impossible for me to work with him. It gives me a positive sense of physical discomfort to come in contact with such people.

[*NORA draws her hand away, and moves to the other side of the Christmas-tree.*]

NORA

How warm it is here. And I have so much to do.

HELMER   [*Rises and gathers up his papers.*]

Yes, and I must try to get some of these papers looked through before dinner. And I shall think over your costume too. Perhaps I may even find something to hang in gilt paper on the Christmas-tree.

[*Lays his hand on her head.*]

My precious little song-bird!

[*He goes into his room and shuts the door.*]

NORA   [*Softly, after a pause.*]

It can't be. It's impossible. It must be impossible!

ANNA   [*At the door, left.*]

The little ones are begging so prettily to come to mamma.

NORA

No, no, no; don't let them come to me! Keep them with you,
Anna.

ANNA

Very well, ma'am.

[*Shuts the door.*]

NORA   [*Pale with terror.*]

Corrupt my children!— Poison my home!

[*Short pause. She throws back her head.*]

It's not true! It can never, never be true!

ACT SECOND

The same room. In the corner, beside the piano, stands the Christmas-tree, stripped, and with the candles burnt out. NORA's *outdoor things lie on the sofa.*

NORA, *alone, is walking about restlessly. At last she stops by the sofa, and takes up her cloak.*

NORA   [*Dropping the cloak.*]
    There's somebody coming!
    [*Goes to the hall door and listens.*]
    Nobody; of course nobody will come to-day, Christmas-day; nor to-morrow either. But perhaps——
    [*Opens the door and looks out.*]
    —No, nothing in the letter box; quite empty.
    [*Comes forward.*]
    Stuff and nonsense! Of course he won't really do anything. Such a thing couldn't happen. It's impossible! Why, I have three little children.

ANNA *enters from the left, with a large cardboard box.*

ANNA
    I've found the box with the fancy dress at last.
NORA
    Thanks; put it down on the table.
ANNA   [*Does so.*]
    But I'm afraid it's very much out of order.
NORA
    Oh, I wish I could tear it into a hundred thousand pieces!
ANNA
    Oh, no. It can easily be put to rights—just a little patience.
NORA
    I shall go and get Mrs. Linden to help me.

ANNA

Going out again? In such weather as this! You'll catch cold, ma'am, and be ill.

NORA

Worse things might happen.——What are the children doing?

ANNA

They're playing with their Christmas presents, poor little dears; but——

NORA

Do they often ask for me?

ANNA

You see they've been so used to having their mamma with them.

NORA

Yes; but, Anna, I can't have them so much with me in future.

ANNA

Well, little children get used to anything.

NORA

Do you think they do? Do you believe they would forget their mother if she went quite away?

ANNA

Gracious me! Quite away?

NORA

Tell me, Anna——I've so often wondered about it——how could you bring yourself to give your child up to strangers?

ANNA

I had to when I came to nurse my little Miss Nora.

NORA

But how could you make up your mind to it?

ANNA

When I had the chance of such a good place? A poor girl who's been in trouble must take what comes. That wicked man did nothing for me.

NORA

But your daughter must have forgotten you.

ANNA

Oh, no, ma'am, that she hasn't. She wrote to me both when she was confirmed and when she was married.

NORA   [*Embracing her.*]

> Dear old Anna—you were a good mother to me when I was little.

ANNA

> My poor little Nora had no mother but me.

NORA

> And if my little ones had nobody else, I'm sure you would——— Nonsense, nonsense!
>
> [*Opens the box.*]
>
> Go in to the children. Now I must——— You'll see how lovely I shall be to-morrow.

ANNA

> I'm sure there will be no one at the ball so lovely as my Miss Nora.
>
> [*She goes into the room on the left.*]

NORA   [*Takes the costume out of the box, but soon throws it down again.*]

> Oh, if I dared go out. If only nobody would come. If only nothing would happen here in the meantime. Rubbish; nobody is coming. Only not to think. What a delicious muff! Beautiful gloves, beautiful gloves! To forget—to forget! One, two, three, four, five, six———
>
> [*With a scream.*]
>
> Ah, there they come.
>
> [*Goes towards the door, then stands irresolute.*]

MRS. LINDEN *enters from the hall, where she has taken off her things.*

NORA

> Oh, it's you, Christina. There's nobody else there? I'm so glad you have come.

MRS. LINDEN

> I hear you called at my lodgings.

NORA

> Yes, I was just passing. There's something you must help me with. Let us sit here on the sofa—so. To-morrow evening there's to be a fancy ball at Consul Stenborg's overhead, and Torvald wants me to appear as a Neapolitan fisher-girl, and dance the tarantella; I learned it at Capri.

MRS. LINDEN

I see—quite a performance.

NORA

Yes, Torvald wishes it. Look, this is the costume; Torvald had it made for me in Italy. But now it's all so torn, I don't know——

MRS. LINDEN

Oh, we shall soon set that to rights. It's only the trimming that has come loose here and there. Have you a needle and thread? Ah, here's the very thing.

NORA

Oh, how kind of you.

MRS. LINDEN [*Sewing.*]

So you're to be in costume to-morrow, Nora? I'll tell you what— I shall come in for a moment to see you in all your glory. But I've quite forgotten to thank you for the pleasant evening yesterday.

NORA [*Rises and walks across the room.*]

Oh, yesterday, it didn't seem so pleasant as usual.—You should have come to town a little sooner, Christina.—Torvald has certainly the art of making home bright and beautiful.

MRS. LINDEN

You too, I should think, or you wouldn't be your father's daughter. But tell me—is Doctor Rank always so depressed as he was last evening?

NORA

No, yesterday it was particularly noticeable. You see, he suffers from a dreadful illness. He has spinal consumption, poor fellow. They say his father was a horrible man, who kept mistresses and all sorts of things—so the son has been sickly from his childhood, you understand.

MRS. LINDEN [*Lets her sewing fall into her lap.*]

Why, my darling Nora, how do you come to know such things?

NORA [*Moving about the room.*]

Oh, when one has three children, one sometimes has visits from women who are half—half doctors—and they talk of one thing and another.

MRS. LINDEN [*Goes on sewing; a short pause.*]

Does Doctor Rank come here every day?

NORA

Every day of his life. He has been Torvald's most intimate friend
from boyhood, and he's a good friend of mine too. Doctor Rank
is quite one of the family.

MRS. LINDEN

But tell me—is he quite sincere? I mean, isn't he rather given to
flattering people?

NORA

No, quite the contrary. Why should you think so?

MRS. LINDEN

When you introduced us yesterday he said he had often heard my
name; but I noticed afterwards that your husband had no notion
who I was. How could Doctor Rank——?

NORA

He was quite right, Christina. You see, Torvald loves me so
indescribably, he wants to have me all to himself, as he says. When
we were first married he was almost jealous if I even mentioned any
of my old friends at home; so naturally I gave up doing it. But I often
talk of the old times to Doctor Rank, for he likes to hear about them.

MRS. LINDEN

Listen to me, Nora! You are still a child in many ways. I am older
than you, and have had more experience. I'll tell you something?
You ought to get clear of all this with Dr. Rank.

NORA

Get clear of what?

MRS. LINDEN

The whole affair, I should say. You were talking yesterday of a
rich admirer who was to find you money— —

NORA

Yes, one who never existed, worse luck. What then?

MRS. LINDEN

Has Doctor Rank money?

NORA

Yes, he has.

MRS. LINDEN

And nobody to provide for?

NORA

Nobody. But——?

MRS. LINDEN

And he comes here every day?

NORA

Yes, I told you so.

MRS. LINDEN

I should have thought he would have had better taste.

NORA

I don't understand you a bit.

MRS. LINDEN

Don't pretend, Nora. Do you suppose I can't guess who lent you the twelve hundred dollars?

NORA

Are you out of your senses? How can you think such a thing? A friend who comes here every day! Why, the position would be unbearable!

MRS. LINDEN

Then it really is not he?

NORA

No, I assure you. It never for a moment occurred to me——— Besides, at that time he had nothing to lend; he came into his property afterwards.

MRS. LINDEN

Well, I believe that was lucky for you, Nora dear.

NORA

No, really, it would never have struck me to ask Dr. Rank——— And yet, I'm certain that if I did———

MRS. LINDEN

But of course you never would.

NORA

Of course not. It's inconceivable that it should ever be necessary. But I'm quite sure that if I spoke to Doctor Rank———

MRS. LINDEN

Behind your husband's back?

NORA

I must get clear of the other thing; that's behind his back too. I must get clear of that.

MRS. LINDEN

Yes, yes, I told you so yesterday; but———

NORA   [*Walking up and down.*]
    A man can manage these things much better than a woman.
MRS. LINDEN
    One's own husband, yes.
NORA
    Nonsense.
    [*Stands still.*]
    When everything is paid, one gets back the paper.
MRS. LINDEN
    Of course.
NORA
    And can tear it into a hundred thousand pieces, and burn it up,
    the nasty, filthy thing!
MRS. LINDEN   [*Looks at her fixedly, lays down her work, and rises
    slowly.*]
    Nora, you are hiding something from me.
NORA
    Can you see it in my face?
MRS. LINDEN
    Something has happened since yesterday morning. Nora, what is
    it?
NORA   [*Going towards her.*]
    Christina——!
    [*Listens.*]
    Hush! There's Torvald coming home. Do you mind going into
    the nursery for the present? Torvald can't bear to see
    dressmaking going on. Get Anna to help you.
MRS. LINDEN   [*Gathers some of the things together.*]
    Very well; but I shan't go away until you have told me all about
    it.
    [*She goes out to the left, as* HELMER *enters from the hall.*]
NORA   [*Runs to meet him.*]
    Oh, how I've been longing for you to come, Torvald dear!
HELMER
    Was that the dressmaker——?
NORA
    No, Christina. She's helping me with my costume. You'll see
    how nice I shall look.

HELMER

Yes, wasn't that a happy thought of mine?

NORA

Splendid! But isn't it good of me, too, to have given in to you about the tarantella?*

HELMER [Takes her under the chin.]

Good of you! To give in to your own husband? Well well, you little madcap, I know you don't mean it. But I won't disturb you. I daresay you want to be "trying on."

NORA

And you are going to work, I suppose?

HELMER

Yes.

[Shows her a bundle of papers.]

Look here. I've just come from the Bank——

[Goes towards his room.]

NORA

Torvald.

HELMER [Stopping.]

Yes?

NORA

If your little squirrel were to beg you for something so prettily——

HELMER

Well?

NORA

Would you do it?

HELMER

I must know first what it is.

NORA

The squirrel would skip about and play all sorts of tricks if you would only be nice and kind.

HELMER

Come, then, out with it.

NORA

Your lark would twitter from morning till night——

*Originally a southern Italian folk dance, named after a poisonous spider.

HELMER

Oh, that she does in any case.

NORA

I'll be an elf and dance in the moonlight for you, Torvald.

HELMER

Nora—you can't mean what you were hinting at this morning?

NORA   [*Coming nearer.*]

Yes, Torvald, I beg and implore you!

HELMER

Have you really the courage to begin that again?

NORA

Yes, yes; for my sake, you must let Krogstad keep his place in the Bank.

HELMER

My dear Nora, it's his place I intend for Mrs. Linden.

NORA

Yes, that's so good of you. But instead of Krogstad, you could dismiss some other clerk.

HELMER

Why, this is incredible obstinacy! Because you have thoughtlessly promised to put in a word for him, I am to———!

NORA

It's not that, Torvald. It's for your own sake. This man writes for the most scurrilous newspapers; you said so yourself. He can do you no end of harm. I'm so terribly afraid of him———

HELMER

Ah, I understand; it's old recollections that are frightening you.

NORA

What do you mean?

HELMER

Of course you're thinking of your father.

NORA

Yes—yes, of course. Only think of the shameful slanders wicked people used to write about father. I believe they would have got him dismissed if you hadn't been sent to look into the thing, and been kind to him, and helped him.

HELMER

My little Nora, between your father and me there is all the

difference in the world. Your father was not altogether
unimpeachable. I am; and I hope to remain so.

NORA

Oh, no one knows what wicked men may hit upon. We could
live so quietly and happily now, in our cosy, peaceful home, you
and I and the children, Torvald! That's why I beg and implore
you——

HELMER

And it is just by pleading his cause that you make it impossible
for me to keep him. It's already known at the Bank that I intend
to dismiss Krogstad. If it were now reported that the new
manager let himself be turned round his wife's little finger——

NORA

What then?

HELMER

Oh, nothing, so long as a wilful woman can have her way——! I
am to make myself a laughing-stock to the whole staff, and set
people saying that I am open to all sorts of outside influence?
Take my word for it, I should soon feel the consequences. And
besides—there is one thing that makes Krogstad impossible for
me to work with——

NORA

What thing?

HELMER

I could perhaps have overlooked his moral failings at a
pinch——

NORA

Yes, couldn't you, Torvald?

HELMER

And I hear he is good at his work. But the fact is, he was a
college chum of mine—there was one of those rash friendships
between us that one so often repents of later. I may as well
confess it at once—he calls me by my Christian name; and he is
tactless enough to do it even when others are present. He
delights in putting on airs of familiarity—Torvald here, Torvald
there! I assure you it's most painful to me. He would make my
position at the Bank perfectly unendurable.

NORA

Torvald, surely you're not serious?

HELMER

No? Why not?

NORA

That's such a petty reason.

HELMER

What! Petty! Do you consider me petty!

NORA

No, on the contrary, Torvald dear; and that's just why——

HELMER

Never mind; you call my motives petty; then I must be petty too. Petty! Very well!—Now we'll put an end to this, once for all. [*Goes to the door into the hall and calls.*] Ellen!

NORA

What do you want?

HELMER   [*Searching among his papers.*]

To settle the thing. [*ELLEN enters.*] Here; take this letter; give it to a messenger. See that he takes it at once. The address is on it. Here's the money.

ELLEN

Very well, sir. [*Goes with the letter.*]

HELMER   [*Putting his papers together.*]

There, Madam Obstinacy.

NORA   [*Breathless.*]

Torvald—what was in the letter?

HELMER

Krogstad's dismissal.

NORA

Call it back again, Torvald! There's still time. Oh, Torvald, call it back again! For my sake, for your own, for the children's sake! Do you hear, Torvald? Do it! You don't know what that letter may bring upon us all.

HELMER

Too late.

NORA

Yes, too late.

HELMER

My dear Nora, I forgive your anxiety, though it's anything but
flattering to me. Why should you suppose that *I* would be afraid
of a wretched scribbler's spite? But I forgive you all the same, for
it's a proof of your great love for me.

[*Takes her in his arms.*]

That's as it should be, my own dear Nora. Let what will happen—when it comes to the pinch, I shall have strength and
courage enough. You shall see: my shoulders are broad enough to
bear the whole burden.

NORA   [*Terror-struck.*]

What do you mean by that?

HELMER

The whole burden, I say——

NORA   [*With decision.*]

That you shall never, never do!

HELMER

Very well; then we'll share it, Nora, as man and wife. That is
how it should be.

[*Petting her.*]

Are you satisfied now? Come, come, come, don't look like a
scared dove. It's all nothing—foolish fancies.—Now you ought
to play the tarantella through and practise with the tambourine. I
shall sit in my inner room and shut both doors, so that I shall
hear nothing. You can make as much noise as you please.

[*Turns round in doorway.*]

And when Rank comes, just tell him where I'm to be found.

[*He nods to her, and goes with his papers into his room, closing the door.*]

NORA   [*Bewildered with terror, stands as though rooted to the ground, and
whispers.*]

He would do it. Yes, he would do it. He would do it, in spite of
all the world.—No, never that, never, never! Anything rather
than that! Oh, for some way of escape! What shall I do——!

[*Hall bell rings.*]

Doctor Rank——!—Anything, anything, rather than——!

[NORA *draws her hands over her face, pulls herself together, goes to the door and opens it.* RANK *stands outside hanging up his fur coat. During what follows it begins to grow dark.*]

NORA

Good afternoon, Doctor Rank. I knew you by your ring. But you mustn't go to Torvald now. I believe he's busy.

RANK

And you?

[*Enters and closes the door.*]

NORA

Oh, you know very well, I have always time for you.

RANK

Thank you. I shall avail myself of your kindness as long as I can.

NORA

What do you mean? As long as you can?

RANK

Yes. Does that frighten you?

NORA

I think it's an odd expression. Do you expect anything to happen?

RANK

Something I have long been prepared for; but I didn't think it would come so soon.

NORA   [*Catching at his arm.*]

What have you discovered? Doctor Rank, you must tell me!

RANK   [*Sitting down by the stove.*]

I am running down hill. There's no help for it.

NORA   [*Draws a long breath of relief.*]

It's you——?

RANK

Who else should it be?——Why lie to one's self? I am the most wretched of all my patients, Mrs. Helmer. In these last days I have been auditing my life-account——bankrupt! Perhaps before a month is over, I shall lie rotting in the churchyard.

NORA

Oh! What an ugly way to talk.

RANK

The thing itself is so confoundedly ugly, you see. But the worst of it is, so many other ugly things have to be gone through first.

There is only one last investigation to be made, and when that is over I shall know pretty certainly when the break-up will begin. There's one thing I want to say to you: Helmer's delicate nature shrinks so from all that is horrible: I will not have him in my sick-room——

NORA

But, Doctor Rank——

RANK

I won't have him, I say—not on any account! I shall lock my door against him.—As soon as I am quite certain of the worst, I shall send you my visiting-card with a black cross on it; and then you will know that the final horror has begun.

NORA

Why, you're perfectly unreasonable to-day; and I did so want you to be in a really good humour.

RANK

With death staring me in the face?—And to suffer thus for another's sin! Where's the justice of it? And in one way or another you can trace in every family some such inexorable retribution——

NORA [Stopping her ears.]

Nonsense, nonsense! Now cheer up!

RANK

Well, after all, the whole thing's only worth laughing at. My poor innocent spine must do penance for my father's wild oats.

NORA [At table, left.]

I suppose he was too fond of asparagus and Strasbourg pâté, wasn't he?

RANK

Yes; and truffles.

NORA

Yes, truffles, to be sure. And oysters, I believe?

RANK

Yes, oysters; oysters, of course.

NORA

And then all the port and champagne! It's sad that all these good things should attack the spine.

RANK

Especially when the luckless spine attacked never had any good of them.

NORA

Ah, yes, that's the worst of it.

RANK   [*Looks at her searchingly.*]

H'm——

NORA   [*A moment later.*]

Why did you smile?

RANK

No; it was you that laughed.

NORA

No; it was you that smiled, Dr. Rank.

RANK   [*Standing up.*]

I see you're deeper than I thought.

NORA

I'm in such a crazy mood to-day.

RANK

So it seems.

NORA   [*With her hands on his shoulders.*]

Dear, dear Doctor Rank, death shall not take you away from Torvald and me.

RANK

Oh, you'll easily get over the loss. The absent are soon forgotten.

NORA   [*Looks at him anxiously.*]

Do you think so?

RANK

People make fresh ties, and then——

NORA

Who make fresh ties?

RANK

You and Helmer will, when I am gone. You yourself are taking time by the forelock, it seems to me. What was that Mrs. Linden doing here yesterday?

NORA

Oh!——you're surely not jealous of poor Christina?

RANK

    Yes, I am. She will be my successor in this house. When I am out of the way, this woman will perhaps——

NORA

    Hush! Not so loud! She's in there.

RANK

    To-day as well? You see!

NORA

    Only to put my costume in order—dear me, how unreasonable you are!

    [*Sits on sofa.*]

    Now do be good, Doctor Rank! To-morrow you shall see how beautifully I shall dance; and then you may fancy that I'm doing it all to please you—and of course Torvald as well.

    [*Takes various things out of box.*]

    Doctor Rank, sit down here, and I'll show you something.

RANK   [*Sitting.*]

    What is it?

NORA

    Look here. Look!

RANK

    Silk stockings.

NORA

    Flesh-coloured. Aren't they lovely? It's so dark here now; but to-morrow—— No, no, no; you must only look at the feet. Oh, well, I suppose you may look at the rest too.

RANK

    H'm——

NORA

    What are you looking so critical about? Do you think they won't fit me?

RANK

    I can't possibly give any competent opinion on that point.

NORA   [*Looking at him a moment.*]

    For shame!

    [*Hits him lightly on the ear with the stockings.*]

    Take that.

    [*Rolls them up again.*]

RANK

    And what other wonders am I to see?

NORA

    You sha'n't see anything more; for you don't behave nicely.

    [*She hums a little and searches among the things.*]

RANK   [*After a short silence.*]

    When I sit here gossiping with you, I can't imagine—I simply cannot conceive—what would have become of me if I had never entered this house.

NORA   [*Smiling.*]

    Yes, I think you do feel at home with us.

RANK   [*More softly—looking straight before him.*]

    And now to have to leave it all——

NORA

    Nonsense. You sha'n't leave us.

RANK   [*In the same tone.*]

    And not to be able to leave behind the slightest token of gratitude; scarcely even a passing regret—nothing but an empty place, that can be filled by the first comer.

NORA

    And if I were to ask you for——? No——

RANK

    For what?

NORA

    For a great proof of your friendship.

RANK

    Yes—yes?

NORA

    I mean—for a very, very great service——

RANK

    Would you really, for once, make me so happy?

NORA

    Oh, you don't know what it is.

RANK

    Then tell me.

NORA

    No, I really can't, Doctor Rank. It's far, far too much—not only a service, but help and advice besides——

RANK

So much the better. I can't think what you can mean. But go on.
Don't you trust me?

NORA

As I trust no one else. I know you are my best and truest friend.
So I will tell you. Well then, Doctor Rank, there is something
you must help me to prevent. You know how deeply, how
wonderfully Torvald loves me; he wouldn't hesitate a moment
to give his very life for my sake.

RANK   [*Bending towards her.*]

Nora—do you think he is the only one who——?

NORA   [*With a slight start.*]

Who——?

RANK

Who would gladly give his life for you?

NORA   [*Sadly.*]

Oh!

RANK

I have sworn that you shall know it before I—go. I shall never
find a better opportunity.—Yes, Nora, now I have told you; and
now you know that you can trust me as you can no one else.

NORA   [*Standing up; simply and calmly.*]

Let me pass, please.

RANK   [*Makes way for her, but remains sitting.*]

Nora——

NORA   [*In the doorway.*]

Ellen, bring the lamp.

[*Crosses to the stove.*]

Oh dear, Doctor Rank, that was too bad of you.

RANK   [*Rising.*]

That I have loved you as deeply as—any one else? Was that too
bad of me?

NORA

No, but that you should have told me so. It was so
unnecessary——

RANK

What do you mean? Did you know——?

[*ELLEN enters with the lamp; sets it on the table and goes out again.*]

RANK

Nora——Mrs. Helmer——I ask you, did you know?

NORA

Oh, how can I tell what I knew or didn't know? I really can't say—— How could you be so clumsy, Doctor Rank? It was all so nice!

RANK

Well, at any rate, you know now that I am at your service, body and soul. And now, go on.

NORA   [*Looking at him.*]

Go on—now?

RANK

I beg you to tell me what you want.

NORA

I can tell you nothing now.

RANK

Yes, yes! You mustn't punish me in that way. Let me do for you whatever a man can.

NORA

You can do nothing for me now.——Besides, I really want no help. You shall see it was only my fancy. Yes, it must be so. Of course! [*Sits in the rocking-chair, looks at him and smiles.*] You are a nice person, Doctor Rank! Aren't you ashamed of yourself, now that the lamp is on the table?

RANK

No; not exactly. But perhaps I ought to go—for ever.

NORA

No, indeed you mustn't. Of course you must come and go as you've always done. You know very well that Torvald can't do without you.

RANK

Yes, but you?

NORA

Oh, you know I always like to have you here.

RANK

That is just what led me astray. You are a riddle to me. It has often seemed to me as if you liked being with me almost as much as being with Helmer.

NORA

Yes; don't you see? There are people one loves, and others one likes to talk to.

RANK

Yes—there's something in that.

NORA

When I was a girl, of course I loved papa best. But it always delighted me to steal into the servants' room. In the first place they never lectured me, and in the second it was such fun to hear them talk.

RANK

Ah, I see; then it's their place I have taken?

NORA   [*Jumps up and hurries towards him.*]

Oh, my dear Doctor Rank, I don't mean that. But you understand, with Torvald it's the same as with papa——

ELLEN *enters from the hall.*

ELLEN

Please, ma'am——

[*Whispers to* NORA, *and gives her a card.*]

NORA   [*Glancing at card.*]

Ah!

[*Puts it in her pocket.*]

RANK

Anything wrong?

NORA

No, no, not in the least. It's only—it's my new costume——

RANK

Your costume! Why, it's there.

NORA

Oh, that one, yes. But this is another that—I have ordered it—Torvald mustn't know——

RANK

Aha! So that's the great secret.

NORA

Yes, of course. Please go to him; he's in the inner room. Do keep him while I——

RANK

Don't be alarmed; he sha'n't escape.

[*Goes into* HELMER's *room.*]

NORA   [*To* ELLEN.]

Is he waiting in the kitchen?

ELLEN

Yes, he came up the back stair——

NORA

Didn't you tell him I was engaged?

ELLEN

Yes, but it was no use.

NORA

He won't go away?

ELLEN

No, ma'am, not until he has spoken to you.

NORA

Then let him come in; but quietly. And, Ellen—say nothing about it; it's a surprise for my husband.

ELLEN

Oh, yes, ma'am, I understand.

[*She goes out.*]

NORA

It is coming! The dreadful thing is coming, after all. No, no, no, it can never be; it shall not!

[*She goes to* HELMER's *door and slips the bolt.* ELLEN *opens the hall door for* KROGSTAD, *and shuts it after him. He wears a travelling-coat, high boots, and a fur cap.*]

NORA   [*Goes towards him.*]

Speak softly; my husband is at home.

KROGSTAD

All right. That's nothing to me.

NORA

What do you want?

KROGSTAD

A little information.

NORA

Be quick, then. What is it?

KROGSTAD

You know I have got my dismissal.

NORA

I couldn't prevent it, Mr. Krogstad. I fought for you to the last, but it was of no use.

KROGSTAD

Does your husband care for you so little? He knows what I can bring upon you, and yet he dares——

NORA

How could you think I should tell him?

KROGSTAD

Well, as a matter of fact, I didn't think it. It wasn't like my friend Torvald Helmer to show so much courage——

NORA

Mr. Krogstad, be good enough to speak respectfully of my husband.

KROGSTAD

Certainly, with all due respect. But since you are so anxious to keep the matter secret, I suppose you are a little clearer than yesterday as to what you have done.

NORA

Clearer than you could ever make me.

KROGSTAD

Yes, such a bad lawyer as I——

NORA

What is it you want?

KROGSTAD

Only to see how you are getting on, Mrs. Helmer. I've been thinking about you all day. Even a mere money-lender, a gutter-journalist, a——in short, a creature like me——has a little bit of what people call feeling.

NORA

Then show it; think of my little children.

KROGSTAD

Did you and your husband think of mine? But enough of that. I only wanted to tell you that you needn't take this matter too seriously. I shall not lodge any information, for the present.

NORA

No, surely not. I knew you wouldn't.

KROGSTAD

The whole thing can be settled quite amicably. Nobody need
know. It can remain among us three.

NORA

My husband must never know.

KROGSTAD

How can you prevent it? Can you pay off the balance?

NORA

No, not at once.

KROGSTAD

Or have you any means of raising the money in the next few
days?

NORA

None—that I will make use of.

KROGSTAD

And if you had, it would not help you now. If you offered me
ever so much money down, you should not get back your I.O.U.

NORA

Tell me what you want to do with it.

KROGSTAD

I only want to keep it—to have it in my possession. No outsider
shall hear anything of it. So, if you have any desperate scheme in
your head——

NORA

What if I have?

KROGSTAD

If you should think of leaving your husband and children——

NORA

What if I do?

KROGSTAD

Or if you should think of—something worse——

NORA

How do you know that?

KROGSTAD

Put all that out of your head.

NORA

How did you know what I had in my mind?

KROGSTAD

Most of us think of that at first. I thought of it, too; but I hadn't the courage——

NORA　[*Tonelessly.*]

Nor I.

KROGSTAD　[*Relieved.*]

No, one hasn't. You haven't the courage either, have you?

NORA

I haven't, I haven't.

KROGSTAD

Besides, it would be very foolish.——Just one domestic storm, and it's all over. I have a letter in my pocket for your husband——

NORA

Telling him everything?

KROGSTAD

Sparing you as much as possible.

NORA　[*Quickly.*]

He must never read that letter. Tear it up. I will manage to get the money somehow——

KROGSTAD

Pardon me, Mrs. Helmer, but I believe I told you——

NORA

Oh, I'm not talking about the money I owe you. Tell me how much you demand from my husband—I will get it.

KROGSTAD

I demand no money from your husband.

NORA

What do you demand then?

KROGSTAD

I will tell you. I want to regain my footing in the world. I want to rise; and your husband shall help me to do it. For the last eighteen months my record has been spotless; I have been in bitter need all the time; but I was content to fight my way up, step by step. Now, I've been thrust down again, and I will not be satisfied with merely being reinstated as a matter of grace. I want to rise, I tell you. I must get into the Bank again, in a higher position than before. Your husband shall create a place on purpose for me——

NORA

He will never do that!

KROGSTAD

He will do it; I know him—he won't dare to show fight! And when he and I are together there, you shall soon see! Before a year is out I shall be the manager's right hand. It won't be Torvald Helmer, but Nils Krogstad, that manages the Joint Stock Bank.

NORA

That shall never be.

KROGSTAD

Perhaps you will——?

NORA

Now I have the courage for it.

KROGSTAD

Oh, you don't frighten me! A sensitive, petted creature like you——

NORA

You shall see, you shall see!

KROGSTAD

Under the ice, perhaps? Down into the cold, black water? And next spring to come up again, ugly, hairless, unrecognisable——

NORA

You can't terrify me.

KROGSTAD

Nor you me. People don't do that sort of thing, Mrs. Helmer. And, after all, what would be the use of it? I have your husband in my pocket, all the same.

NORA

Afterwards? When I am no longer——?

KROGSTAD

You forget, your reputation remains in my hands!

[NORA *stands speechless and looks at him.*]

Well, now you are prepared Do nothing foolish. As soon as Helmer has received my letter, I shall expect to hear from him. And remember that it is your husband himself who has forced me back again into such paths. That I will never forgive him. Good-bye, Mrs. Helmer.

[*Goes out through the hall.* NORA *hurries to the door, opens it a little, and listens.*]

NORA

He's going. He's not putting the letter into the box. No, no, it would be impossible!

[*Opens the door further and further.*]

What's that. He's standing still; not going down stairs. Has he changed his mind? Is he——?

[*A letter falls into the box.* KROGSTAD's *footsteps are heard gradually receding down the stair.* NORA *utters a suppressed shriek, and rushes forward towards the sofa-table; pause.*] In the letter-box!

[*Slips shrinkingly up to the hall door.*]

There it lies.——Torvald, Torvald—now we are lost!

MRS. LINDEN *enters from the left with the costume.*

MRS. LINDEN

There, I think it's all right now. Shall we just try it on?

NORA   [*Hoarsely and softly.*]

Christina, come here.

MRS. LINDEN   [*Throws down the dress on the sofa.*]

What's the matter? You look quite distracted.

NORA

Come here. Do you see that letter? There, see—through the glass of the letter-box.

MRS. LINDEN

Yes, yes, I see it.

NORA

That letter is from Krogstad——

MRS. LINDEN

Nora—it was Krogstad who lent you the money?

NORA

Yes; and now Torvald will know everything.

MRS. LINDEN

Believe me, Nora, it's the best thing for both of you.

NORA

You don't know all yet. I have forged a name——

MRS. LINDEN

Good heavens!

NORA

Now, listen to me, Christina; you shall bear me witness——

MRS. LINDEN

How "witness"? What am I to——?

NORA

If I should go out of my mind—it might easily happen——

MRS. LINDEN

Nora!

NORA

Or if anything else should happen to me—so that I couldn't be here——!

MRS. LINDEN

Nora, Nora, you're quite beside yourself!

NORA

In case any one wanted to take it all upon himself—the whole blame—you understand——

MRS. LINDEN

Yes, yes; but how can you think——?

NORA

You shall bear witness that it's not true, Christina. I'm not out of my mind at all; I know quite well what I'm saying; and I tell you nobody else knew anything about it; I did the whole thing, I myself. Remember that.

MRS. LINDEN

I shall remember. But I don't understand what you mean——

NORA

Oh, how should you? It's the miracle coming to pass.

MRS. LINDEN

The miracle?

NORA

Yes, the miracle. But it's so terrible, Christina; it mustn't happen for all the world.

MRS. LINDEN

I shall go straight to Krogstad and talk to him.

NORA

Don't; he'll do you some harm.

MRS. LINDEN

Once he would have done anything for me.

NORA

He?

MRS. LINDEN

Where does he live?

NORA

Oh, how can I tell———? Yes———

[*Feels in her pocket.*]

Here's his card. But the letter, the letter———!

HELMER   [*Knocking outside.*]

Nora!

NORA   [*Shrieks in terror.*]

Oh, what is it? What do you want?

HELMER

Well, well, don't be frightened. We're not coming in; you've bolted the door. Are you trying on your dress?

NORA

Yes, yes, I'm trying it on. It suits me so well, Torvald.

MRS. LINDEN   [*Who has read the card.*]

Why, he lives close by here.

NORA

Yes, but it's no use now. We are lost. The letter is there in the box.

MRS. LINDEN

And your husband has the key?

NORA

Always.

MRS. LINDEN

Krogstad must demand his letter back, unread. He must find some pretext———

NORA

But this is the very time when Torvald generally———

MRS. LINDEN

Prevent him. Keep him occupied. I shall come back as quickly as I can.

[*She goes out hastily by the hall door.*]

NORA   [*Opens HELMER's door and peeps in.*]

Torvald!

HELMER

Well, may one come into one's own room again at last? Come,
Rank, we'll have a look——

[*In the doorway.*]

But how's this?

NORA

What, Torvald dear?

HELMER

Rank led me to expect a grand transformation.

RANK   [*In the doorway.*]

So I understood. I suppose I was mistaken.

NORA

No, no one shall see me in my glory till to-morrow evening.

HELMER

Why, Nora dear, you look so tired. Have you been practising too
hard?

NORA

No, I haven't practised at all yet.

HELMER

But you'll have to——

NORA

Oh yes, I must, I must! But, Torvald, I can't get on at all without
your help. I've forgotten everything.

HELMER

Oh, we shall soon freshen it up again.

NORA

Yes, do help me, Torvald. You must promise me—— Oh, I'm so
nervous about it. Before so many people—— This evening you
must give yourself up entirely to me. You mustn't do a stroke of
work; you mustn't even touch a pen. Do promise, Torvald dear!

HELMER

I promise. All this evening I shall be your slave. Little helpless
thing——! But, by-the-bye, I must just——

[*Going to hall door.*]

NORA

What do you want there?

HELMER

Only to see if there are any letters.

NORA

No, no, don't do that, Torvald.

HELMER

Why not?

NORA

Torvald, I beg you not to. There are none there.

HELMER

Let me just see.

[*Is going.*]

[NORA, *at the piano, plays the first bars of the tarantella.*]

HELMER   [*At the door, stops.*]

Aha!

NORA

I can't dance to-morrow if I don't rehearse with you first.

HELMER   [*Going to her.*]

Are you really so nervous, dear Nora?

NORA

Yes, dreadfully! Let me rehearse at once. We have time before dinner. Oh, do sit down and play for me, Torvald dear; direct me and put me right, as you used to do.

HELMER

With all the pleasure in life, since you wish it.

[*Sits at piano.*]

[NORA *snatches the tambourine out of the box, and hurriedly drapes herself in a long parti-coloured shawl; then, with a bound, stands in the middle of the floor.*]

NORA

Now play for me! Now I'll dance!

[HELMER *plays and* NORA *dances.* RANK *stands at the piano behind* HELMER *and looks on.*]

HELMER   [*Playing.*]

Slower! Slower!

NORA

Can't do it slower!

HELMER

Not so violently, Nora.

NORA

I must! I must!

HELMER   [*Stops.*]

   No, no, Nora—that will never do.

NORA   [*Laughs and swings her tambourine.*]

   Didn't I tell you so!

RANK

   Let me play for her.

HELMER   [*Rising.*]

   Yes, do—then I can direct her better.

   [RANK *sits down to the piano and plays;* NORA *dances more and more wildly.* HELMER *stands by the stove and addresses frequent corrections to her; she seems not to hear. Her hair breaks loose, and falls over her shoulders. She does not notice it, but goes on dancing.* MRS. LINDEN *enters and stands spellbound in the doorway.*]

MRS. LINDEN

   Ah——!

NORA

   [*Dancing.*]

   We're having such fun here Christina!

HELMER

   Why, Nora dear, you're dancing as if it were a matter of life and death.

NORA

   So it is.

HELMER

   Rank, stop! This is the merest madness. Stop, I say!

   [RANK *stops playing, and* NORA *comes to a sudden standstill.*]

HELMER   [*Going towards her.*]

   I couldn't have believed it. You've positively forgotten all I taught you.

NORA   [*Throws the tambourine away.*]

   You see for yourself.

HELMER

   You really do want teaching.

NORA

   Yes, you see how much I need it. You must practise with me up to the last moment. Will you promise me, Torvald?

HELMER

   Certainly, certainly.

NORA

Neither to-day nor to-morrow must you think of anything but me. You mustn't open a single letter—mustn't look at the letter-box.

HELMER

Ah, you're still afraid of that man——

NORA

Oh yes, yes, I am.

HELMER

Nora, I can see it in your face—there's a letter from him in the box.

NORA

I don't know, I believe so. But you're not to read anything now; nothing ugly must come between us until all is over.

RANK   [*Softly, to* HELMER.]

You mustn't contradict her.

HELMER   [*Putting his arm around her.*]

The child shall have her own way. But to-morrow night, when the dance is over——

NORA

Then you shall be free.

ELLEN *appears in the doorway, right.*

ELLEN

Dinner is on the table, ma'am.

NORA

We'll have some champagne, Ellen.

ELLEN

Yes, ma'am.
[*Goes out.*]

HELMER

Dear me! Quite a banquet.

NORA

Yes, and we'll keep it up till morning.
[*Calling out.*]
And macaroons, Ellen—plenty—just this once.

HELMER   [*Seizing her hand.*]

Come, come, don't let us have this wild excitement! Be my own little lark again.

NORA

Oh yes, I will. But now go into the dining-room; and you too, Doctor Rank. Christina, you must help me to do up my hair.

RANK   [*Softly, as they go.*]

There's nothing in the wind? Nothing——I mean——?

HELMER

Oh no, nothing of the kind. It's merely this babyish anxiety I was telling you about.

[*They go out to the right.*]

NORA

Well?

MRS. LINDEN

He's gone out of town.

NORA

I saw it in your face.

MRS. LINDEN

He comes back to-morrow evening. I left a note for him.

NORA

You shouldn't have done that. Things must take their course. After all, there's something glorious in waiting for the miracle.

MRS. LINDEN

What is it you're waiting for?

NORA

Oh, you can't understand. Go to them in the dining-room; I shall come in a moment.

[MRS. LINDEN *goes into the dining-room.* NORA *stands for a moment as though collecting her thoughts; then looks at her watch.*]

NORA

Five. Seven hours till midnight. Then twenty-four hours till the next midnight. Then the tarantella will be over. Twenty-four and seven? Thirty-one hours to live.

HELMER *appears at the door, right.*

HELMER

What has become of my little lark?

NORA   [*Runs to him with open arms.*]

Here she is!

ACT THIRD

The same room. The table, with the chairs around it, in the middle. A lighted lamp on the table. The door to the hall stands open. Dance music is heard from the floor above.

MRS. LINDEN *sits by the table and absently turns the pages of a book. She tries to read, but seems unable to fix her attention; she frequently listens and looks anxiously towards the hall door.*

MRS. LINDEN   [*Looks at her watch.*]
   Not here yet; and the time is nearly up. If only he hasn't——
   [*Listens again.*]
   Ah, there he is.
   [*She goes into the hall and cautiously opens the outer door; soft footsteps are heard on the stairs; she whispers.*]
   Come in; there is no one here.
KROGSTAD   [*In the doorway.*]
   I found a note from you at my house. What does it mean?
MRS. LINDEN
   I must speak to you.
KROGSTAD
   Indeed? And in this house?
MRS. LINDEN
   I could not see you at my rooms. They have no separate en-
   trance. Come in; we are quite alone. The servants are asleep, and
   the Helmers are at the ball upstairs.
KROGSTAD   [*Coming into the room.*]
   Ah! So the Helmers are dancing this evening? Really?
MRS. LINDEN
   Yes. Why not?
KROGSTAD
   Quite right. Why not?

MRS. LINDEN

And now let us talk a little.

KROGSTAD

Have we two anything to say to each other?

MRS. LINDEN

A great deal.

KROGSTAD

I should not have thought so.

MRS. LINDEN

Because you have never really understood me.

KROGSTAD

What was there to understand? The most natural thing in the
world—a heartless woman throws a man over when a better
match offers.

MRS. LINDEN

Do you really think me so heartless? Do you think I broke with
you lightly?

KROGSTAD

Did you not?

MRS. LINDEN

Do you really think so?

KROGSTAD

If not, why did you write me that letter?

MRS. LINDEN

Was it not best? Since I had to break with you, was it not right
that I should try to put an end to all that you felt for me?

KROGSTAD   [*Clenching his hands together.*]

So that was it? And all this—for the sake of money!

MRS. LINDEN

You ought not to forget that I had a helpless mother and two
little brothers. We could not wait for you, Nils, as your
prospects then stood.

KROGSTAD

Perhaps not; but you had no right to cast me off for the sake of
others, whoever the others might be.

MRS. LINDEN

I don't know. I have often asked myself whether I had the right.

KROGSTAD   [*More softly.*]

When I had lost you, I seemed to have no firm ground left under my feet. Look at me now. I am a shipwrecked man clinging to a spar.

MRS. LINDEN

Rescue may be at hand.

KROGSTAD

It was at hand; but then you came and stood in the way.

MRS. LINDEN

Without my knowledge, Nils. I did not know till to-day that it was you I was to replace in the Bank.

KROGSTAD

Well, I take your word for it. But now that you do know, do you mean to give way?

MRS. LINDEN

No, for that would not help you in the least.

KROGSTAD

Oh, help, help——! I should do it whether or no.

MRS. LINDEN

I have learnt prudence. Life and bitter necessity have schooled me.

KROGSTAD

And life has taught me not to trust fine speeches.

MRS. LINDEN

Then life has taught you a very sensible thing. But deeds you will trust?

KROGSTAD

What do you mean?

MRS. LINDEN

You said you were a shipwrecked man, clinging to a spar.

KROGSTAD

I have good reason to say so.

MRS. LINDEN

I too am shipwrecked, and clinging to a spar. I have no one to mourn for, no one to care for.

KROGSTAD

You made your own choice.

MRS. LINDEN

No choice was left me.

KROGSTAD

Well, what then?

MRS. LINDEN

Nils, how if we two shipwrecked people could join hands?

KROGSTAD

What!

MRS. LINDEN

Two on a raft have a better chance than if each clings to a separate spar.

KROGSTAD

Christina!

MRS. LINDEN

What do you think brought me to town?

KROGSTAD

Had you any thought of me?

MRS. LINDEN

I must have work or I can't bear to live. All my life, as long as I can remember, I have worked; work has been my one great joy. Now I stand quite alone in the world, aimless and forlorn. There is no happiness in working for one's self. Nils, give me somebody and something to work for.

KROGSTAD

I cannot believe in all this. It is simply a woman's romantic craving for self-sacrifice.

MRS. LINDEN

Have you ever found me romantic?

KROGSTAD

Would you really——? Tell me: do you know all my past?

MRS. LINDEN

Yes.

KROGSTAD

And do you know what people say of me?

MRS. LINDEN

Did you not say just now that with me you could have been another man?

KROGSTAD

    I am sure of it.

MRS. LINDEN

    Is it too late?

KROGSTAD

    Christina, do you know what you are doing? Yes, you do; I see it in your face. Have you the courage then———?

MRS. LINDEN

    I need some one to be a mother to, and your children need a mother. You need me, and I—I need you. Nils, I believe in your better self. With you I fear nothing.

KROGSTAD   [*Seizing her hands.*]

    Thank you—thank you, Christina. Now I shall make others see me as you do.—Ah, I forgot———

MRS. LINDEN   [*Listening.*]

    Hush! The tarantella! Go! go!

KROGSTAD

    Why? What is it?

MRS. LINDEN

    Don't you hear the dancing overhead? As soon as that is over they will be here.

KROGSTAD

    Oh yes, I shall go. Nothing will come of this, after all. Of course, you don't know the step I have taken against the Helmers.

MRS. LINDEN

    Yes, Nils, I do know.

KROGSTAD

    And yet you have the courage to———?

MRS. LINDEN

    I know to what lengths despair can drive a man.

KROGSTAD

    Oh, if I could only undo it!

MRS. LINDEN

    You could. Your letter is still in the box.

KROGSTAD

    Are you sure?

MRS. LINDEN

    Yes; but———

KROGSTAD   [*Looking to her searchingly.*]

Is that what it all means? You want to save your friend at any price. Say it out—is that your idea?

MRS. LINDEN

Nils, a woman who has once sold herself for the sake of others, does not do so again.

KROGSTAD

I shall demand my letter back again.

MRS. LINDEN

No, no.

KROGSTAD

Yes, of course. I shall wait till Helmer comes; I shall tell him to give it back to me—that it's only about my dismissal—that I don't want it read——

MRS. LINDEN

No, Nils, you must not recall the letter.

KROGSTAD

But tell me, wasn't that just why you got me to come here?

MRS. LINDEN

Yes, in my first alarm. But a day has passed since then, and in that day I have seen incredible things in this house. Helmer must know everything; there must be an end to this unhappy secret. These two must come to a full understanding. They must have done with all these shifts and subterfuges.

KROGSTAD

Very well, if you like to risk it. But one thing I can do, and at once——

MRS. LINDEN   [*Listening.*]

Make haste! Go, go! The dance is over; we're not safe another moment.

KROGSTAD

I shall wait for you in the street.

MRS. LINDEN

Yes, do; you must see me home.

KROGSTAD

I never was so happy in all my life!

[KROGSTAD *goes out by the outer door. The door between the room and the hall remains open.*]

MRS. LINDEN   [*Arranging the room and getting her outdoor things to-gether.*]

What a change! What a change! To have some one to work for, to live for; a home to make happy! Well, it shall not be my fault if I fail.—I wish they would come.—

[*Listens.*]

Ah, here they are! I must get my things on.

[*Takes bonnet and cloak. HELMER's and NORA's voices are heard outside, a key is turned in the lock, and HELMER drags NORA almost by force into the hall. She wears the Italian costume with a large black shawl over it. He is in evening dress and wears a black domino, open.*]

NORA   [*Struggling with him in the doorway.*]

No, no, no! I won't go in! I want to go upstairs again; I don't want to leave so early!

HELMER

But, my dearest girl——!

NORA

Oh, please, please, Torvald, I beseech you—only one hour more!

HELMER

Not one minute more, Nora dear; you know what we agreed. Come, come in; you're catching cold here.

[*He leads her gently into the room in spite of her resistance.*]

MRS. LINDEN

Good-evening.

NORA

Christina!

HELMER

What, Mrs. Linden! You here so late?

MRS. LINDEN

Yes, I ought to apologise. I did so want to see Nora in her costume.

NORA

Have you been sitting here waiting for me?

MRS. LINDEN

Yes; unfortunately I came too late. You had gone upstairs already, and I felt I couldn't go away without seeing you.

HELMER   [*Taking* NORA's *shawl off.*]

Well then, just look at her! I assure you she's worth it. Isn't she lovely, Mrs. Linden?

MRS. LINDEN

Yes, I must say——

HELMER

Isn't she exquisite? Every one said so. But she's dreadfully obstinate, dear little creature. What's to be done with her? Just think, I had almost to force her away.

NORA

Oh, Torvald, you'll be sorry some day that you didn't let me stay, if only for one half-hour more.

HELMER

There! You hear her, Mrs. Linden? She dances her tarantella with wild applause, and well she deserved it, I must say——though there was, perhaps, a little too much nature in her rendering of the idea——more than was, strictly speaking, artistic. But never mind—— the point is, she made a great success, a tremendous success. Was I to let her remain after that——to weaken the impression? Not if I know it. I took my sweet little Capri girl——my capricious little Capri girl, I might say——under my arm; a rapid turn round the room, a curtsey to all sides, and——as they say in novels——the lovely apparition vanished! An exit should always be effective, Mrs. Linden; but I can't get Nora to see it. By Jove! it's warm here. [*Throws his domino on a chair and opens the door to his room.*] What! No light there? Oh, of course. Excuse me—— [*Goes in and lights candles.*]

NORA   [*Whispers breathlessly.*]

Well?

MRS. LINDEN   [*Softly.*]

I've spoken to him.

NORA

And——?

MRS. LINDEN

Nora——you must tell your husband everything——

NORA   [*Tonelessly.*]

I knew it!

MRS. LINDEN

You have nothing to fear from Krogstad; but you must speak out.

NORA

I shall not speak?

MRS. LINDEN

Then the letter will.

NORA

Thank you, Christina. Now I know what I have to do. Hush———!

HELMER   [*Coming back.*]

Well, Mrs. Linden, have you admired her?

MRS. LINDEN

Yes; and now I must say good-night.

HELMER

What, already? Does this knitting belong to you?

MRS. LINDEN   [*Takes it.*]

Yes, thanks; I was nearly forgetting it.

HELMER

Then you do knit?

MRS. LINDEN

Yes.

HELMER

Do you know, you ought to embroider instead?

MRS. LINDEN

Indeed! Why?

HELMER

Because it's so much prettier. Look now! You hold the
embroidery in the left hand, so, and then work the needle with
the right hand, in a long, graceful curve—don't you?

MRS. LINDEN

Yes, I suppose so.

HELMER

But knitting is always ugly. Just look—your arms close to your sides,
and the needles going up and down—there's something Chinese
about it.— They really gave us splendid champagne to-night.

MRS. LINDEN

Well, good-night, Nora, and don't be obstinate any more.

HELMER

Well said, Mrs. Linden!

MRS. LINDEN

Good-night, Mr. Helmer.

HELMER   [*Accompanying her to the door.*]

Good-night, good-night; I hope you'll get safely home. I should he glad to—but you have such a short way to go. Good-night, good-night.

[*She goes;* HELMER *shuts the door after her and comes forward again.*]

At last we've got rid of her: she's a terrible bore.

NORA

Aren't you very tired, Torvald?

HELMER

No, not in the least.

NORA

Nor sleepy?

HELMER

Not a bit. I feel particularly lively. But you? You do look tired and sleepy.

NORA

Yes, very tired. I shall soon sleep now.

HELMER

There, you see. I was right after all not to let you stay longer.

NORA

Oh, everything you do is right.

HELMER   [*Kissing her forehead.*]

Now my lark is speaking like a reasonable being. Did you notice how jolly Rank was this evening?

NORA

Indeed? Was he? I had no chance of speaking to him.

HELMER

Nor I, much; but I haven't seen him in such good spirits for a long time.

[*Looks at* NORA *a little, then comes nearer her.*]

It's splendid to be back in our own home, to be quite alone together! —Oh, you enchanting creature!

NORA

Don't look at me in that way, Torvald.

HELMER

I am not to look at my dearest treasure?—at all the loveliness that is mine, mine only, wholly and entirely mine?

NORA   [*Goes to the other side of the table.*]

You mustn't say these things to me this evening.

HELMER   [*Following.*]

I see you have the tarantella still in your blood—and that makes you all the more enticing. Listen! the other people are going now.

[*More softly.*]

Nora—soon the whole house will be still.

NORA

Yes, I hope so.

HELMER

Yes, don't you, Nora darling? When we are among strangers, do you know why I speak so little to you, and keep so far away, and only steal a glance at you now and then—do you know why I do it? Because I am fancying that we love each other in secret, that I am secretly betrothed to you, and that no one dreams that there is anything between us.

NORA

Yes, yes, yes. I know all your thoughts are with me.

HELMER

And then, when the time comes to go, and I put the shawl about your smooth, soft shoulders, and this glorious neck of yours, I imagine you are my bride, that our marriage is just over, that I am bringing you for the first time to my home—that I am alone with you for the first time—quite alone with you, in your trembling loveliness! All this evening I have been longing for you, and you only. When I watched you swaying and whirling in the tarantella—my blood boiled—I could endure it no longer; and that's why I made you come home with me so early——

NORA

Go now, Torvald! Go away from me. I won't have all this.

HELMER

What do you mean? Ah, I see you're teasing me, little Nora! Won't—won't! Am I not your husband——?

[*A knock at the outer door.*]

NORA   [*Starts.*]

Did you hear——?

HELMER   [*Going towards the hall.*]

    Who's there?

RANK   [*Outside.*]

    It is I; may I come in for a moment?

HELMER   [*In a low tone, annoyed.*]

    Oh! what can he want just now?

    [*Aloud.*]

    Wait a moment.

    [*Opens door.*]

    Come, it's nice of you to look in.

RANK

    I thought I heard your voice, and that put it into my head.

    [*Looks round.*]

    Ah, this dear old place! How cosy you two are here!

HELMER

    You seemed to find it pleasant enough upstairs, too.

RANK

    Exceedingly. Why not? Why shouldn't one take one's share of
    everything in this world? All one can, at least, and as long as one
    can. The wine was splendid——

HELMER

    Especially the champagne.

RANK

    Did you notice it? It's incredible the quantity I contrived to get
    down.

NORA

    Torvald drank plenty of champagne, too.

RANK

    Did he?

NORA

    Yes, and it always puts him in such spirits.

RANK

    Well, why shouldn't one have a jolly evening after a well-spent
    day?

HELMER

    Well-spent! Well, I haven't much to boast of in that respect.

RANK   [*Slapping him on the shoulder.*]

    But I have, don't you see?

NORA

I suppose you have been engaged in a scientific investigation, Doctor Rank?

RANK

Quite right.

HELMER

Bless me! Little Nora talking about scientific investigations!

NORA

Am I to congratulate you on the result?

RANK

By all means.

NORA

It was good then?

RANK

The best possible, both for doctor and patient—certainty.

NORA   [Quickly and searchingly.]

Certainty?

RANK

Absolute certainty. Wasn't I right to enjoy myself after that?

NORA

Yes, quite right, Doctor Rank.

HELMER

And so say I, provided you don't have to pay for it to-morrow.

RANK

Well, in this life nothing is to be had for nothing.

NORA

Doctor Rank—I'm sure you are very fond of masquerades?

RANK

Yes, when there are plenty of amusing disguises——

NORA

Tell me, what shall we two be at our next masquerade?

HELMER

Little featherbrain! Thinking of your next already!

RANK

We two? I'll tell you. You must go as a good fairy.

HELMER

Ah, but what costume would indicate that?

RANK

She has simply to wear her everyday dress.

HELMER

Capital! But don't you know what you will be yourself?

RANK

Yes, my dear friend, I am perfectly clear upon that point.

HELMER

Well?

RANK

At the next masquerade I shall be invisible.

HELMER

What a comical idea!

RANK

There's a big black hat—haven't you heard of the invisible hat? It comes down all over you, and then no one can see you.

HELMER   [*With a suppressed smile.*]

No, you're right there.

RANK

But I'm quite forgetting what I came for. Helmer, give me a cigar—one of the dark Havanas.

HELMER

With the greatest pleasure.

[*Hands cigar-case.*]

RANK   [*Takes one and cuts the end off.*]

Thank you.

NORA   [*Striking a wax match.*]

Let me give you a light.

RANK

A thousand thanks.

[*She holds the match. He lights his cigar at it.*]

RANK

And now, good-bye!

HELMER

Good-bye, good-bye, my dear fellow.

NORA

Sleep well, Doctor Rank.

RANK

Thanks for the wish.

NORA

Wish me the same.

RANK

You? Very well, since you ask me—Sleep well. And thanks for the light.

[*He nods to them both and goes out.*]

HELMER   [*In an undertone.*]

He's been drinking a good deal.

NORA   [*Absently.*]

I daresay.

[HELMER *takes his bunch of keys from his pocket and goes into the hall.*]

Torvald, what are you doing there?

HELMER

I must empty the letter-box; it's quite full; there will be no room for the newspapers to-morrow morning.

NORA

Are you going to work to-night?

HELMER

You know very well I am not.—Why, how is this? Some one has been at the lock.

NORA

The lock——?

HELMER

I'm sure of it. What does it mean? I can't think that the servants——? Here's a broken hair-pin. Nora, it's one of yours.

NORA   [*Quickly.*]

It must have been the children——

HELMER

Then you must break them of such tricks.— There! At last I've got it open.

[*Takes contents out and calls into the kitchen.*]

Ellen!—Ellen, just put the hall door lamp out.

[*He returns with letters in his hand, and shuts the inner door.*]

HELMER

Just see how they've accumulated.

[*Turning them over.*]

Why, what's this?

NORA   [*At the window.*]

The letter! Oh no, no, Torvald!

HELMER

Two visiting-cards—from Rank.

NORA

From Doctor Rank?

HELMER   [*Looking at them.*]

Doctor Rank. They were on the top. He must just have put them in.

NORA

Is there anything on them?

HELMER

There's a black cross over the name. Look at it. What an unpleasant idea! It looks just as if he were announcing his own death.

NORA

So he is.

HELMER

What! Do you know anything? Has he told you anything?

NORA

Yes. These cards mean that he has taken his last leave of us. He is going to shut himself up and die.

HELMER

Poor fellow! Of course I knew we couldn't hope to keep him long. But so soon——! And to go and creep into his lair like a wounded animal——

NORA

When we must go, it is best to go silently. Don't you think so, Torvald?

HELMER   [*Walking up and down.*]

He had so grown into our lives, I can't realise that he is gone. He and his sufferings and his loneliness formed a sort of cloudy background to the sunshine of our happiness.—Well, perhaps it's best as it is—at any rate for him.

[*Stands still.*]

And perhaps for us too, Nora. Now we two are thrown entirely upon each other.

[*Takes her in his arms.*]

My darling wife! I feel as if I could never hold you close enough.

Do you know, Nora, I often wish some danger might threaten
you, that I might risk body and soul, and everything, everything,
for your dear sake.

NORA   [*Tears herself from him and says firmly:*]

Now you shall read your letters, Torvald.

HELMER

No, no; not to-night. I want to be with you, my sweet wife.

NORA

With the thought of your dying friend——?

HELMER

You are right. This has shaken us both. Unloveliness has come
between us—thoughts of death and decay. We must seek to cast
them off. Till then—we will remain apart.

NORA   [*Her arms round his neck.*]

Torvald! Good-night! good-night!

HELMER   [*Kissing her forehead.*]

Good-night, my little song-bird. Sleep well, Nora. Now I shall go
and read my letters.

[*He goes with the letters in his hand into his room and shuts the door.*]

NORA   [*With wild eyes, gropes about her, seizes* HELMER's *domino,
throws it round her, and whispers quickly, hoarsely, and brokenly.*]

Never to see him again. Never, never, never.

[*Throws her shawl over her head.*]

Never to see the children again. Never, never.—Oh that black,
icy water! Oh that bottomless——! If it were only over! Now
he has it; he's reading it. Oh, no, no, no, not yet. Torvald, good-
bye——! Good-bye, my little ones——!

[*She is rushing out by the hall; at the same moment* HELMER *flings his
door open, and stands there with an open letter in his hand.*]

HELMER

Nora!

NORA   [*Shrieks.*]

Ah——!

HELMER

What is this? Do you know what is in this letter?

NORA

Yes, I know. Let me go! Let me pass!

HELMER   [*Holds her back.*]

Where do you want to go?

NORA   [*Tries to break away from him.*]

You shall not save me, Torvald.

HELMER   [*Falling back.*]

True! Is what he writes true? No, no, it is impossible that this can be true.

NORA

It is true. I have loved you beyond all else in the world.

HELMER

Pshaw—no silly evasions!

NORA   [*A step nearer him.*]

Torvald——!

HELMER

Wretched woman—what have you done!

NORA

Let me go—you shall not save me! You shall not take my guilt upon yourself!

HELMER

I don't want any melodramatic airs.

[*Locks the outer door.*]

Here you shall stay and give an account of yourself. Do you understand what you have done? Answer! Do you understand it?

NORA   [*Looks at him fixedly, and says with a stiffening expression.*]

Yes; now I begin fully to understand it.

HELMER   [*Walking up and down.*]

Oh! what an awful awakening! During all these eight years—she who was my pride and my joy—a hypocrite, a liar—worse, worse—a criminal. Oh, the unfathomable hideousness of it all! Ugh! Ugh!

[NORA *says nothing, and continues to look fixedly at him.*]

HELMER

I ought to have known how it would be. I ought to have foreseen it. All your father's want of principle—be silent!—all your father's want of principle you have inherited—no religion, no morality, no sense of duty. How I am punished for screening him! I did it for your sake; and you reward me like this.

NORA

Yes—like this.

HELMER

You have destroyed my whole happiness. You have ruined my future. Oh, it's frightful to think of! I am in the power of a scoundrel; he can do whatever he pleases with me, demand whatever he chooses; he can domineer over me as much as he likes, and I must submit. And all this disaster and ruin is brought upon me by an unprincipled woman!

NORA

When I am out of the world, you will be free.

HELMER

Oh, no fine phrases. Your father, too, was always ready with them. What good would it do me, if you were "out of the world," as you say? No good whatever! He can publish the story all the same; I might even he suspected of collusion. People will think I was at the bottom of it all and egged you on. And for all this I have you to thank—you whom I have done nothing but pet and spoil during our whole married life. Do you understand now what you have done to me?

NORA   [With cold calmness.]

Yes.

HELMER

The thing is so incredible, I can't grasp it. But we must come to an understanding. Take that shawl off. Take it off, I say! I must try to pacify him in one way or another—the matter must be hushed up, cost what it may.—As for you and me, we must make no outward change in our way of life—no outward change, you understand. Of course, you will continue to live here. But the children cannot be left in your care. I dare not trust them to you.— Oh, to have to say this to one I have loved so tenderly—whom I still——! But that must be a thing of the past. Henceforward there can be no question of happiness, but merely of saving the ruins, the shreds, the show——

[A ring; HELMER starts.]

What's that? So late! Can it be the worst? Can he——? Hide yourself, Nora; say you are ill.

[NORA stands motionless. HELMER goes to the door and opens it.]

ELLEN   [*Half dressed, in the hall.*]
>Here is a letter for you, ma'am.

HELMER
>Give it to me.
>[*Seizes the letter and shuts the door.*]
>Yes, from him. You shall not have it. I shall read it.

NORA
>Read it!

HELMER   [*By the lamp.*]
>I have hardly the courage to. We may both be lost, both you and
>I. Ah! I must know.
>[*Hastily tears the letter open; reads a few lines, looks at an enclosure; with
>a cry of joy.*]
>Nora!
>[NORA *looks inquiringly at him.*]

HELMER
>Nora!—Oh! I must read it again.—Yes, yes, it is so. I am saved!
>Nora, I am saved!

NORA
>And I?

HELMER
>You too, of course; we are both saved, both of us. Look here—
>he sends you back your promissory note. He writes that he
>regrets and apologises that a happy turn in his life—— Oh, what
>matter what he writes. We are saved, Nora! No one can harm
>you. Oh, Nora, Nora——; but first to get rid of this hateful
>thing. I'll just see——
>[*Glances at the I.O.U.*]
>No, I will not look at it; the whole thing shall be nothing but a
>dream to me.
>[*Tears the I.O.U. and both letters in pieces. Throws them into the fire and
>watches them burn.*]
>There! it's gone!—He said that ever since Christmas Eve——
>Oh, Nora, they must have been three terrible days for you!

NORA
>I have fought a hard fight for the last three days.

HELMER
>And in your agony you saw no other outlet but—— No; we

won't think of that horror. We will only rejoice and repeat—it's over, all over! Don't you hear, Nora? You don't seem able to grasp it. Yes, it's over. What is this set look on your face? Oh, my poor Nora, I understand: you cannot believe that I have forgiven you. But I have, Nora; I swear it. I have forgiven everything. I know that what you did was all for love of me.

NORA

That is true.

HELMER

You loved me as a wife should love her husband. It was only the means that, in your inexperience, you misjudged. But do you think I love you the less because you cannot do without guidance? No, no. Only lean on me; I will counsel you, and guide you. I should be no true man if this very womanly helplessness did not make you doubly dear in my eyes. You mustn't dwell upon the hard things I said in my first moment of terror, when the world seemed to be tumbling about my ears. I have forgiven you, Nora—I swear I have forgiven you.

NORA

I thank you for your forgiveness.

[*Goes out, to the right.*]

HELMER

No, stay——!

[*Looking through the doorway.*]

What are you going to do?

NORA [*Inside.*]

To take off my masquerade dress.

HELMER [*In the doorway.*]

Yes, do, dear. Try to calm down, and recover your balance, my scared little song-bird. You may rest secure. I have broad wings to shield you.

[*Walking up and down near the door.*]

Oh, how lovely—how cosy our home is, Nora! Here you are safe; here I can shelter you like a hunted dove whom I have saved from the claws of the hawk. I shall soon bring your poor beating heart to rest; believe me, Nora, very soon. To-morrow all this will seem quite different—everything will be as before. I shall not need to tell you again that I forgive you; you will feel for yourself that it is true. How could you think I could find it in my heart to drive you away, or even so much as to reproach you? Oh, you don't know a true man's heart, Nora. There is something indescribably sweet and soothing to a man in having forgiven his wife——honestly forgiven her, from the bottom of his heart. She becomes his property in a double sense. She is as though born again; she has become, so to speak, at once his wife and his child. That is what you shall henceforth be to me, my bewildered, helpless darling. Don't be troubled about anything, Nora; only open your heart to me, and I will be both will and conscience to you.

[NORA *enters in everyday dress.*]

Why, what's this? Not gone to bed? You have changed your dress?

NORA

Yes, Torvald; now I have changed my dress.

HELMER

But why now, so late——?

NORA

I shall not sleep to-night.

HELMER

But, Nora dear——

NORA   [*Looking at her watch.*]

It's not so late yet. Sit down, Torvald; you and I have much to say to each other.

[*She sits at one side of the table.*]

HELMER

Nora—what does this mean? Your cold, set face——

NORA

Sit down. It will take some time. I have much to talk over with you.

[HELMER *sits at the other side of the table.*]

HELMER

You alarm me, Nora. I don't understand you.

NORA

No, that is just it. You don't understand me; and I have never understood you—till to-night. No, don't interrupt. Only listen to what I say.——We must come to a final settlement, Torvald.

HELMER

How do you mean?

NORA   [*After a short silence.*]

Does not one thing strike you as we sit here?

HELMER

What should strike me?

NORA

We have been married eight years. Does it not strike you that this is the first time we two, you and I, man and wife, have talked together seriously?

HELMER

Seriously! What do you call seriously?

NORA

During eight whole years, and more—ever since the day we first met—we have never exchanged one serious word about serious things.

HELMER

Was I always to trouble you with the cares you could not help me to bear?

NORA

I am not talking of cares. I say that we have never yet set ourselves seriously to get to the bottom of anything.

HELMER

Why, my dearest Nora, what have you to do with serious things?

NORA

There we have it! You have never understood me.—I have had great injustice done me, Torvald; first by father, and then by you.

HELMER

What! By your father and me?—By us, who have loved you more than all the world?

NORA   [*Shaking her head.*]

You have never loved me. You only thought it amusing to be in love with me.

HELMER

Why, Nora, what a thing to say!

NORA

Yes, it is so, Torvald. While I was at home with father, he used to tell me all his opinions, and I held the same opinions. If I had others I said nothing about them, because he wouldn't have liked

it. He used to call me his doll-child, and played with me as I
played with my dolls. Then I came to live in your house——

HELMER

What an expression to use about our marriage!

NORA   [*Undisturbed.*]

I mean I passed from father's hands into yours. You arranged
everything according to your taste; and I got the same tastes as
you; or I pretended to——I don't know which——both ways,
perhaps; sometimes one and sometimes the other. When I look
back on it now, I seem to have been living here like a beggar,
from hand to mouth. I lived by performing tricks for you,
Torvald. But you would have it so. You and father have done me a
great wrong. It is your fault that my life has come to nothing.

HELMER

Why, Nora, how unreasonable and ungrateful you are! Have you
not been happy here?

NORA

No, never. I thought I was; but I never was.

HELMER

Not——not happy!

NORA

No; only merry. And you have always been so kind to me. But
our house has been nothing but a play-room. Here I have been
your doll-wife, just as at home I used to be papa's doll-child. And
the children, in their turn, have been my dolls. I thought it fun
when you played with me, just as the children did when I played
with them. That has been our marriage, Torvald.

HELMER

There is some truth in what you say, exaggerated and
overstrained though it be. But henceforth it shall be different.
Play-time is over; now comes the time for education.

NORA

Whose education? Mine, or the children's?

HELMER

Both, my dear Nora.

NORA

Oh, Torvald, you are not the man to teach me to be a fit wife for
you.

HELMER

And you can say that?

NORA

And I——how have I prepared myself to educate the children?

HELMER

Nora!

NORA

Did you not say yourself, a few minutes ago, you dared not trust them to me?

HELMER

In the excitement of the moment! Why should you dwell upon that?

NORA

No——you were perfectly right. That problem is beyond me. There is another to be solved first——I must try to educate myself. You are not the man to help me in that. I must set about it alone. And that is why I am leaving you.

HELMER   [*Jumping up.*]

What——do you mean to say——?

NORA

I must stand quite alone if I am ever to know myself and my surroundings; so I cannot stay with you.

HELMER

Nora! Nora!

NORA

I am going at once. I daresay Christina will take me in for to-night——

HELMER

You are mad! I shall not allow it! I forbid it!

NORA

It is of no use your forbidding me anything now. I shall take with me what belongs to me. From you I will accept nothing, either now or afterwards.

HELMER

What madness this is!

NORA

To-morrow I shall go home——I mean to what was my home. It will be easier for me to find some opening there.

HELMER

Oh, in your blind inexperience——

NORA

I must try to gain experience, Torvald.

HELMER

To forsake your home, your husband, and your children! And you don't consider what the world will say.

NORA

I can pay no heed to that. I only know that I must do it.

HELMER

This is monstrous! Can you forsake your holiest duties in this way?

NORA

What do you consider my holiest duties?

HELMER

Do I need to tell you that? Your duties to your husband and your children.

NORA

I have other duties equally sacred.

HELMER

Impossible! What duties do you mean?

NORA

My duties towards myself.

HELMER

Before all else you are a wife and a mother.

NORA

That I no longer believe. I believe that before all else I am a human being, just as much as you are—or at least that I should try to become one. I know that most people agree with you, Torvald, and that they say so in books. But henceforth I can't be satisfied with what most people say, and what is in books. I must think things out for myself, and try to get clear about them.

HELMER

Are you not clear about your place in your own home? Have you not an infallible guide in questions like these? Have you not religion?

NORA

Oh, Torvald, I don't really know what religion is.

HELMER

What do you mean?

NORA

I know nothing but what Pastor Hansen told me when I was confirmed. He explained that religion was this and that. When I get away from all this and stand alone, I will look into that matter too. I will see whether what he taught me is right, or, at any rate, whether it is right for me.

HELMER

Oh, this is unheard of! And from so young a woman! But if religion cannot keep you right, let me appeal to your conscience—for I suppose you have some moral feeling? Or, answer me: perhaps you have none?

NORA

Well, Torvald, it's not easy to say. I really don't know—I am all at sea about these things. I only know that I think quite differently from you about them. I hear, too, that the laws are different from what I thought; but I can't believe that they can be right. It appears that a woman has no right to spare her dying father, or to save her husband's life! I don't believe that.

HELMER

You talk like a child. You don't understand the society in which you live.

NORA

No, I do not. But now I shall try to learn. I must make up my mind which is right—society or I.

HELMER

Nora, you are ill; you are feverish; I almost think you are out of your senses.

NORA

I have never felt so much clearness and certainty as to-night.

HELMER

You are clear and certain enough to forsake husband and children?

NORA

Yes, I am.

HELMER

Then there is only one explanation possible.

NORA

What is that?

HELMER

You no longer love me.

NORA

No; that is just it.

HELMER

Nora!——Can you say so!

NORA

Oh, I'm so sorry, Torvald; for you've always been so kind to me. But I can't help it. I do not love you any longer.

HELMER   [*Mastering himself with difficulty.*]

Are you clear and certain on this point too?

NORA

Yes, quite. That is why I will not stay here any longer.

HELMER

And can you also make clear to me how I have forfeited your love?

NORA

Yes, I can. It was this evening, when the miracle did not happen; for then I saw you were not the man I had imagined.

HELMER

Explain yourself more clearly; I don't understand.

NORA

I have waited so patiently all these eight years; for of course I saw clearly enough that miracles don't happen every day. When this crushing blow threatened me, I said to myself so confidently, "Now comes the miracle!" When Krogstad's letter lay in the box, it never for a moment occurred to me that you would think of submitting to that man's conditions. I was convinced that you would say to him, "Make it known to all the world"; and that then——

HELMER

Well? When I had given my own wife's name up to disgrace and shame——?

NORA

Then I firmly believed that you would come forward, take everything upon yourself, and say, "I am the guilty one."

HELMER

Nora——!

NORA

You mean I would never have accepted such a sacrifice? No,

certainly not. But what would my assertions have been worth in opposition to yours?——That was the miracle that I hoped for and dreaded. And it was to hinder that that I wanted to die.

HELMER

I would gladly work for you day and night, Nora—bear sorrow and want for your sake. But no man sacrifices his honour, even for one he loves.

NORA

Millions of women have done so.

HELMER

Oh, you think and talk like a silly child.

NORA

Very likely. But you neither think nor talk like the man I can share my life with. When your terror was over—not for what threatened me, but for yourself—when there was nothing more to fear—then it seemed to you as though nothing had happened. I was your lark again, your doll, just as before—whom you would take twice as much care of in future, because she was so weak and fragile.

[*Stands up.*]

Torvald—in that moment it burst upon me that I had been living here these eight years with a strange man, and had borne him three children.——Oh, I can't bear to think of it! I could tear myself to pieces!

HELMER   [*Sadly.*]

I see it, I see it; an abyss has opened between us.——But, Nora, can it never be filled up?

NORA

As I now am, I am no wife for you.

HELMER

I have strength to become another man.

NORA

Perhaps—when your doll is taken away from you.

HELMER

To part—to part from you! No, Nora, no; I can't grasp the thought.

NORA   [*Going into room on the right.*]

The more reason for the thing to happen.

[*She comes back with out-door things and a small travelling-bag, which she places on a chair.*]

HELMER

Nora, Nora, not now! Wait till to-morrow.

NORA   [*Pulling on cloak.*]

I can't spend the night in a strange man's house.

HELMER

But can we not live here, as brother and sister———?

NORA   [*Fastening her hat.*]

You know very well that wouldn't last long.

[*Puts on the shawl.*]

Good-bye, Torvald. No, I won't go to the children. I know they are in better hands than mine. As I now am, I can be nothing to them.

HELMER

But some time, Nora—some time———?

NORA

How can I tell? I have no idea what will become of me.

HELMER

But you are my wife, now and always!

NORA

Listen, Torvald—when a wife leaves her husband's house, as I am doing, I have heard that in the eyes of the law he is free from all duties towards her. At any rate, I release you from all duties. You must not feel yourself bound, any more than I shall. There must be perfect freedom on both sides. There, I give you back your ring. Give me mine.

HELMER

That too?

NORA

That too.

HELMER

Here it is.

NORA

Very well. Now it is all over. I lay the keys here. The servants know about everything in the house—better than I do. To-morrow, when I have started, Christina will come to pack up the things I brought with me from home. I will have them sent after me.

HELMER

All over! all over! Nora, will you never think of me again?

NORA

Oh, I shall often think of you, and the children, and this house.

HELMER

May I write to you, Nora?

NORA

No—never. You must not.

HELMER

But I must send you——

NORA

Nothing, nothing.

HELMER

I must help you if you need it.

NORA

No, I say. I take nothing from strangers.

HELMER

Nora—can I never be more than a stranger to you?

NORA   [*Taking her travelling-bag.*]

Oh, Torvald, then the miracle of miracles would have to happen——

HELMER

What is the miracle of miracles?

NORA

Both of us would have to change so that——Oh, Torvald, I no longer believe in miracles.

HELMER

But *I* will believe. Tell me! We must so change that——?

NORA

That communion between us shall be a marriage. Good-bye.

[*She goes out by the hall door.*]

HELMER   [*Sinks into a chair by the door with his face in his hands.*]

Nora! Nora!

[*He looks round and rises.*]

Empty. She is gone.

[*A hope springs up in him.*]

Ah! The miracle of miracles——?!

[*From below is heard the reverberation of a heavy door closing.*]

GHOSTS:
A FAMILY DRAMA
IN THREE ACTS

(1881)

INTRODUCTION

BESIDES *A DOLL'S HOUSE* (1879), the play immediately following it, *Ghosts* (1881; *Gengangere*), is the most notorious Ibsen ever wrote. This time, however, the scandal was not due to an abrupt, implausible, and unorthodox ending, but to a study of what happens when a female character does not leave the oppressive atmosphere of the patriarchal home. While Nora in *A Doll's House* deserts her home, Mrs. Alving stays; the scandal of a wife leaving her husband is avoided, but the result is worse. *Ghosts* is a play that diagnoses the price at which a family is salvaged.

While *A Doll's House* goes against the traditional expectation of a conciliatory end with a clean break, *Ghosts* is formally coherent, seeking not so much to break a traditional plot but to reimagine the oldest of all traditional forms: tragedy. Ibsen knew that tragedy could not be applied to the bourgeois world; it had to be radically reinvented. This is particularly the case with that most vexed of tragic categories: fate. The language in which Ibsen reinvented Greek fate was that of medical and moral inheritance. Not the Gods or the fates, but nature dictates the terms of human life.

Mrs. Alving keeps up appearances in order to save her son from knowing that his father is morally bankrupt; this is her struggle and her only desire. But in Ibsen's modern tragedy, the forces that shape character are larger than the will of any individual. The son grows up far from the internally broken home, protected from all knowledge, but the family history ends up repeating itself anyway, for he has "inherited" his father's failings. The son begins to show the same desire as his father, and more important, he is dying from a disease that is really nothing more than the outer sign for an inner corruption that cannot be stopped by anyone. And so the son drifts toward his bitter end, waiting for the final morphine shots to be given by his mother.

Ghosts uses some of the elements of Ibsen's other plays: a hypocritical minister; a shocking revelation about the past; the question of scandal and appearances; even a "cheap" suspense trick in the form of a new orphanage that lacks an insurance policy and burns down. All these elements, however, are merely the frame within which Ibsen tries to imagine a modern tragedy centered around Mrs. Alving, whose self-sacrificing attempts to shield her son from his inherited fate end up bringing about this fate all the more surely. The scandal surrounding this play may have had to do with its overt treatment of moral disease and inheritance, but it was also a reaction to this attempt to create a radically modern tragedy, for which the audience was little prepared and to which it responded with fear and loathing. *Ghosts* is a great modern tragedy and the model for a whole tradition of modern tragedy from Eugene O'Neill's *Long Day's Journey into Night* to the tragedies of Arthur Miller and Tennessee Williams.

Ghosts was first performed in Chicago in Norwegian, before it proceeded to shock audiences across Europe in Helingborg, Copenhagen, Stockholm, Christiania (all 1883), Augsburg (1886), Berlin (1887), Paris (1890), and London (1891), assisted by a host of translations into English, German, French, Russian (all before 1891), as well as Czech (1891), Polish (1891), Italian (1892), Catalan (1894), and Portuguese (1895). For theater historians, *Ghosts* is significant because it was the first Ibsen play directed by André Antoine, the promoter of naturalism on the stage. That Antoine would be drawn to this play is not surprising, since its central theme of inheritance resonates with the naturalist doctrine that the formation of character is determined by environment and inheritance, leaving little room for free will and self-creation. The past here becomes the environment by which these characters find themselves trapped and from which they cannot escape. Zola had bemoaned the lack of naturalist plays and theater practice. Antoine and Ibsen both laid the groundwork for naturalism to become a central movement for both dramatic literature and its presentation on the stage. Other notable directors followed suit—for example, Max Reinhardt, whose celebrated 1906 production was designed by one of the most famous expressionist painters, Edvard Munch.

—Martin Puchner

CHARACTERS

MRS. HELEN ALVING, widow of Captain Alving, late Chamberlain*
    to the King.
OSWALD ALVING, her son, a painter.
PASTOR MANDERS.
JACOB ENGSTRAND, a carpenter.
REGINA ENGSTRAND, Mrs. Alving's maid.

The action takes place at Mrs. Alving's country house, beside one of the large fjords in Western Norway.

*Chamberlain (*Kammerherre*) is a distinction conferred by the King on men of wealth and position, and is not hereditary. (Translator's note)

ACT FIRST

A spacious garden-room, with one door to the left, and two doors to the right. In the middle of the room a round table, with chairs about it. On the table lie books, periodicals, and newspapers. In the foreground to the left a window, and by it a small sofa, with a work-table in front of it. In the background, the room is continued into a somewhat narrower conservatory, the walls of which are formed by large panes of glass. In the right-hand wall of the conservatory is a door leading down into the garden. Through the glass wall a gloomy fjord-landscape is faintly visible, veiled by steady rain.

ENGSTRAND, *the carpenter, stands by the garden door. His left leg is somewhat bent; he has a clump of wood under the sole of his boot.* REGINA, *with an empty garden syringe in her hand, hinders him from advancing.*

REGINA   [*In a low voice.*]
   What do you want? Stop where you are. You're positively dripping.
ENGSTRAND
   It's the Lord's own rain, my girl.
REGINA
   It's the devil's rain, *I* say.
ENGSTRAND
   Lord, how you talk, Regina.
   [*Limps a step or two forward into the room.*]
   It's just this as I wanted to say——
REGINA
   Don't clatter so with that foot of yours, I tell you! The young master's asleep upstairs.
ENGSTRAND
   Asleep? In the middle of the day?

REGINA

It's no business of yours.

ENGSTRAND

I was out on the loose last night——

REGINA

I can quite believe that.

ENGSTRAND

Yes, we're weak vessels, we poor mortals, my girl——

REGINA

So it seems.

ENGSTRAND

——and temptations are manifold in this world, you see. But all
the same, I was hard at work, God knows, at half-past five this
morning.

REGINA

Very well; only be off now. I won't stop here and have
*rendezvous's** with you.

EGSTRAND

What do you say you won't have?

REGINA

I won't have any one find you here; so just you go about your
business.

ENGSTRAND   [*Advances a step or two.*]

Blest if I go before I've had a talk with you. This afternoon I shall
have finished my work at the school-house, and then I shall take
to-night's boat and be off home to the town.

REGINA   [*Mutters.*]

Pleasant journey to you!

ENGSTRAND

Thank you, my child. To-morrow the Orphanage is to be
opened, and then there'll be fine doings, no doubt, and plenty of
intoxicating drink going, you know. And nobody shall say of
Jacob Engstrand that he can't keep out of temptation's way.

REGINA

Oh!

---

*A *rendezvous* (French) is an intimate date. All foreign words used in the translation appear in the original.

ENGSTRAND

You see, there's to be heaps of grand folks here to-morrow.
Pastor Manders is expected from town, too.

REGINA

He's coming to-day.

ENGSTRAND

There, you see! And I should be cursedly sorry if he found out
anything against me, don't you understand?

REGINA

Oho! is that your game?

ENGSTRAND

Is what my game?

REGINA   [*Looking hard at him.*]

What are you going to fool Pastor Manders into doing, this time?

ENGSTRAND

Sh! sh! Are you crazy? Do *I* want to fool Pastor Manders? Oh no!
Pastor Manders has been far too good a friend to me for that.
But I just wanted to say, you know——that I mean to be off home
again to-night.

REGINA

The sooner the better, say I.

ENGSTRAND

Yes, but I want you with me, Regina.

REGINA   [*Open-mouthed.*]

You want me——? What are you talking about?

ENGSTRAND

I want you to come home with me, I say.

REGINA   [*Scornfully.*]

Never in this world shall you get me home with you.

ENGSTRAND

Oh, we'll see about that.

REGINA

Yes, you may be sure we'll see about it! Me, that have been
brought up by a lady like Mrs. Alving! Me, that am treated
almost as a daughter here! Is it me you want to go home with
you?——to a house like yours? For shame!

ENGSTRAND

> What the devil do you mean? Do you set yourself up against your father, you hussy?

REGINA   [*Mutters without looking at him.*]

> You've said often enough I was no concern of yours.

ENGSTRAND

> Pooh! Why should you bother about that——

REGINA

> Haven't you many a time sworn at me and called me a——? *Fi donc!**

ENGSTRAND

> Curse me, now, if ever I used such an ugly word.

REGINA

> Oh, I remember very well what word you used.

ENGSTRAND

> Well, but that was only when I was a bit on, don't you know? Temptations are manifold in this world, Regina.

REGINA

> Ugh!

ENGSTRAND

> And besides, it was when your mother was that aggravating—I had to find something to twit her with, my child. She was always setting up for a fine lady.
>
> [*Mimics.*]
>
> "Let me go, Engstrand; let me be. Remember I was three years in Chamberlain Alving's family at Rosenvold."
>
> [*Laughs.*]
>
> Mercy on us! She could never forget that the Captain was made a Chamberlain while she was in service here.

REGINA

> Poor mother! you very soon tormented her into her grave.

ENGSTRAND   [*With a twist of his shoulders.*]

> Oh, of course! I'm to have the blame for everything.

REGINA   [*Turns away; half aloud.*]

> Ugh——! And that leg too!

*Damn (French).

ENGSTRAND
>What do you say, my child?

REGINA
>*Pied de mouton.* *

ENGSTRAND
>Is that English, eh?

REGINA
>Yes.

ENGSTRAND
>Ay, ay; you've picked up some learning out here; and that may come in useful now, Regina.

REGINA   [*After a short silence.*]
>What do you want with me in town?

ENGSTRAND
>Can you ask what a father wants with his only child? Ain't I a lonely, forlorn widower?

REGINA
>Oh, don't try on any nonsense like that with me! Why do you want me?

ENGSTRAND
>Well, let me tell you, I've been thinking of setting up in a new line of business.

REGINA   [*Contemptuously.*]
>You've tried that often enough, and much good you've done with it.

ENGSTRAND
>Yes, but this time you shall see, Regina! Devil take me——

REGINA   [*Stamps.*]
>Stop your swearing!

ENGSTRAND
>Hush, hush; you're right enough there, my girl. What I wanted to say was just this—I've laid by a very tidy pile from this Orphanage job.

REGINA
>Have you? That's a good thing for you.

---

*Leg of lamb (French). *Mouton* (sheep) is also a derogatory expression for simplemindedness.

ENGSTRAND

What can a man spend his ha'pence on here in this country hole?

REGINA

Well, what then?

ENGSTRAND

Why, you see, I thought of putting the money into some paying speculation. I thought of a sort of a sailor's tavern——

REGINA

Pah!

ENGSTRAND

A regular high-class affair, of course; not any sort of pig-sty for common sailors. No! damn it! it would be for captains and mates, and——and——regular swells, you know.

REGINA

And I was to——?

ENGSTRAND

You were to help, to be sure. Only for the look of the thing, you understand. Devil a bit of hard work shall you have, my girl. You shall do exactly what you like.

REGINA

Oh, indeed!

ENGSTRAND

But there must be a petticoat in the house; that's as clear as daylight. For I want to have it a bit lively-like in the evenings, with singing and dancing, and so on. You must remember they're weary wanderers on the ocean of life.

[*Nearer.*]

Now don't be a fool and stand in your own light, Regina. What's to become of you out here? Your mistress has given you a lot of learning; but what good is that to you? You're to look after the children at the new Orphanage, I hear. Is that the sort of thing for you, eh? Are you so dead set on wearing your life out for a pack of dirty brats?

REGINA

No; if things go as I want them to—— Well there's no saying—— there's no saying.

ENGSTRAND

What do you mean by "there's no saying"?

REGINA

> Never you mind.——How much money have you saved?

ENGSTRAND

> What with one thing and another, a matter of seven or eight
> hundred crowns.

REGINA

> That's not so bad.

ENGSTRAND

> It's enough to make a start with, my girl.

REGINA

> Aren't you thinking of giving me any?

ENGSTRAND

> No, I'm blest if I am!

REGINA

> Not even of sending me a scrap of stuff for a new dress?

ENGSTRAND

> Come to town with me, my lass, and you'll soon get dresses
> enough.

REGINA

> Pooh! I can do that on my own account, if I want to.

ENGSTRAND

> No, a father's guiding hand is what you want, Regina. Now, I've
> got my eye on a capital house in Little Harbour Street. They
> don't want much ready-money; and it could be a sort of a
> Sailors' Home, you know.

REGINA

> But I will not live with you! I have nothing whatever to do with
> you. Be off!

ENGSTRAND

> You wouldn't stop long with me, my girl. No such luck! If you
> knew how to play your cards, such a fine figure of a girl as
> you've grown in the last year or two——

REGINA

> Well?

ENGSTRAND

> You'd soon get hold of some mate—or maybe even a
> captain——

REGINA

I won't marry any one of that sort. Sailors have no *savoir vivre*.*

ENGSTRAND

What's that they haven't got?

REGINA

I know what sailors are, I tell you. They're not the sort of people
to marry.

ENGSTRAND

Then never mind about marrying them. You can make it pay all
the same.

[*More confidentially.*]

He—the Englishman—the man with the yacht—he came down
with three hundred dollars, he did; and she wasn't a bit
handsomer than you.

REGINA [*Making for him.*]

Out you go!

ENGSTRAND [*Falling back.*]

Come, come! You're not going to hit me, I hope.

REGINA

Yes, if you begin talking about mother I shall hit you. Get away
with you, I say!

[*Drives him back towards the garden door.*]

And don't slam the doors. Young Mr. Alving——

ENGSTRAND

He's asleep; I know. You're mightily taken up about young Mr.
Alving——

[*More softly.*]

Oho! you don't mean to say it's him as——?

REGINA

Be off this minute! You're crazy, I tell you! No, not that way.
There comes Pastor Manders. Down the kitchen stairs with you.

ENGSTRAND [*Towards the right.*]

Yes, yes, I'm going. But just you talk to him as is coming there.
He's the man to tell you what a child owes its father. For I am
your father all the same, you know. I can prove it from the
church register.

*Knowing how to lead a pleasurable life (French).

[*He goes out through the second door to the right, which* REGINA *has opened, and closes again after him.* REGINA *glances hastily at herself in the mirror, dusts herself with her pocket handkerchief and settles her neck-tie; then she busies herself with the flowers.*]

PASTOR MANDERS, *wearing an overcoat, carrying an umbrella, and with a small travelling-bag on a strap over his shoulder, comes through the garden door into the conservatory.*

MANDERS
Good-morning, Miss Engstrand.

REGINA   [*Turning round, surprised and pleased.*]
No, really! Good-morning, Pastor Manders. Is the steamer in already?

MANDERS
It is just in.
[*Enters the sitting-room.*]
Terrible weather we have been having lately.

REGINA   [*Follows him.*]
It's such blessed weather for the country, sir.

MANDERS
No doubt; you are quite right. We townspeople give too little thought to that.
[*He begins to take off his overcoat.*]

REGINA
Oh, mayn't I help you?—There! Why, how wet it is! I'll just hang it up in the hall. And your umbrella, too—I'll open it and let it dry.
[*She goes out with the things through the second door on the right.* PASTOR MANDERS *takes off his travelling-bag and lays it and his hat on a chair. Meanwhile* REGINA *comes in again.*]

MANDERS
Ah, it's a comfort to get safe under cover. I hope everything is going on well here?

REGINA
Yes, thank you, sir.

MANDERS
You have your hands full, I suppose, in preparation for to-morrow?

REGINA

Yes, there's plenty to do, of course.

MANDERS

And Mrs. Alving is at home, I trust?

REGINA

Oh dear, yes. She's just upstairs, looking after the young master's chocolate.

MANDERS

Yes, by-the-bye—I heard down at the pier that Oswald had arrived.

REGINA

Yes, he came the day before yesterday. We didn't expect him before to-day.

MANDERS

Quite strong and well, I hope?

REGINA

Yes, thank you, quite; but dreadfully tired with the journey. He has made one rush right through from Paris—the whole way in one train, I believe. He's sleeping a little now, I think; so perhaps we'd better talk a little quietly.

MANDERS

Sh!—as quietly as you please.

REGINA   [*Arranging an arm-chair beside the table.*]

Now, do sit down, Pastor Manders, and make yourself comfortable.

[*He sits down; she places a footstool under his feet.*]

There! Are you comfortable now, sir?

MANDERS

Thanks, thanks, extremely so.

[*Looks at her.*]

Do you know, Miss Engstrand, I positively believe you have grown since I last saw you.

REGINA

Do you think so, sir? Mrs. Alving says I've filled out too.

MANDERS

Filled out? Well, perhaps a little; just enough.

[*Short pause.*]

REGINA

Shall I tell Mrs. Alving you are here?

MANDERS

Thanks, thanks, there is no hurry, my dear child. —By-the-bye, Regina, my good girl, tell me: how is your father getting on out here?

REGINA

Oh, thank you, sir, he's getting on well enough.

MANDERS

He called upon me last time he was in town.

REGINA

Did he, indeed? He's always so glad of a chance of talking to you, sir.

MANDERS

And you often look in upon him at his work, I daresay?

REGINA

I? Oh, of course, when I have time, I——

MANDERS

Your father is not a man of strong character, Miss Engstrand. He stands terribly in need of a guiding hand.

REGINA

Oh, yes; I daresay he does.

MANDERS

He requires some one near him whom he cares for, and whose judgment he respects. He frankly admitted as much when he last came to see me.

REGINA

Yes, he mentioned something of the sort to me. But I don't know whether Mrs. Alving can spare me; especially now that we've got the new Orphanage to attend to. And then I should be so sorry to leave Mrs. Alving; she has always been so kind to me.

MANDERS

But a daughter's duty, my good girl—— Of course, we should first have to get your mistress's consent.

REGINA

But I don't know whether it would be quite proper for me, at my age, to keep house for a single man.

MANDERS

What! My dear Miss Engstrand! When the man is your own father!

REGINA

Yes, that may be; but all the same—— Now, if it were in a thoroughly nice house, and with a real gentleman——

MANDERS

Why, my dear Regina——

REGINA

——one I could love and respect, and be a daughter to——

MANDERS

Yes, but my dear, good child——

REGINA

Then I should be glad to go to town. It's very lonely out here; you know yourself, sir, what it is to be alone in the world. And I can assure you I'm both quick and willing. Don't you know of any such place for me, sir?

MANDERS

I? No, certainly not.

REGINA

But, dear, dear sir, do remember me if——

MANDERS   [Rising.]

Yes, yes, certainly, Miss Engstrand.

REGINA

For if I——

MANDERS

Will you be so good as to tell your mistress I am here?

REGINA

I will, at once, sir.

[She goes out to the left.]

MANDERS   [Paces the room two or three times, stands a moment in the background with his hands behind his back, and looks out over the garden. Then he returns to the table, takes up a book, and looks at the title-page; starts, and looks at several books.]

Ha—indeed!

MRS. ALVING enters by the door on the left; she is followed by REGINA, who immediately goes out by the first door on the right.

MRS. ALVING   [*Holds out her hand.*]
  Welcome, my dear Pastor.

MANDERS
  How do you do, Mrs. Alving? Here I am as I promised.

MRS. ALVING
  Always punctual to the minute.

MANDERS
  You may believe it was not so easy for me to get away. With all
  the Boards and Committees I belong to——

MRS. ALVING
  That makes it all the kinder of you to come so early. Now we can
  get through our business before dinner. But where is your
  portmanteau?*

MANDERS   [*Quickly.*]
  I left it down at the inn. I shall sleep there to-night.

MRS. ALVING   [*Suppressing a smile.*]
  Are you really not to be persuaded, even now, to pass the night
  under my roof?

MANDERS
  No, no, Mrs. Alving; many thanks. I shall stay at the inn, as usual.
  It is so conveniently near the landing-stage.

MRS. ALVING
  Well, you must have your own way. But I really should have
  thought we two old people——

MANDERS
  Now you are making fun of me. Ah, you're naturally in great
  spirits to-day—what with to-morrow's festival and Oswald's
  return.

MRS. ALVING
  Yes; you can think what a delight it is to me! It's more than two
  years since he was home last. And now he has promised to stay
  with me all the winter.

MANDERS
  Has he really? That is very nice and dutiful of him. For I can well
  believe that life in Rome and Paris has very different attractions
  from any we can offer here.

*Suitcase (French).

MRS. ALVING

Ah, but here he has his mother, you see. My own darling boy—
he hasn't forgotten his old mother!

MANDERS

It would be grievous indeed, if absence and absorption in art and
that sort of thing were to blunt his natural feelings.

MRS. ALVING

Yes, you may well say so. But there's nothing of that sort to fear
with him. I'm quite curious to see whether you know him again.
He'll be down presently; he's upstairs just now, resting a little on
the sofa. But do sit down, my.dear Pastor.

MANDERS

Thank you. Are you quite at liberty——?

MRS. ALVING

Certainly.
[*She sits by the table.*]

MANDERS

Very well. Then let me show you——
[*He goes to the chair where his travelling-bag lies, takes out a packet of pa-
pers, sits down on the opposite side of the table, and tries to find a clear
space for the papers.*]
Now, to begin with, here is——
[*Breaking off.*]
Tell me, Mrs. Alving, how do these books come to be here?

MRS. ALVING

These books? They are books I am reading.

MANDERS

Do you read this sort of literature?

MRS. ALVING

Certainly I do.

MANDERS

Do you feel better or happier for such reading?

MRS. ALVING

I feel, so to speak, more secure.

MANDERS

That is strange. How do you mean?

MRS. ALVING

Well, I seem to find explanation and confirmation of all sorts of things I myself have been thinking. For that is the wonderful part of it, Pastor Manders—there is really nothing new in these books, nothing but what most people think and believe. Only most people either don't formulate it to themselves, or else keep quiet about it.

MANDERS

Great heavens! Do you really believe that most people——?

MRS. ALVING

I do, indeed.

MANDERS

But surely not in this country? Not here among us?

MRS. ALVING

Yes, certainly; here as elsewhere.

MANDERS

Well, I really must say——!

MRS. ALVING

For the rest, what do you object to in these books?

MANDERS

Object to in them? You surely do not suppose that I have nothing better to do than to study such publications as these?

MRS. ALVING

That is to say, you know nothing of what you are condemning?

MANDERS

I have read enough about these writings to disapprove of them.

MRS. ALVING

Yes; but your own judgment——

MANDERS

My dear Mrs. Alving, there are many occasions in life when one must rely upon others. Things are so ordered in this world; and it is well that they are. Otherwise, what would become of society?

MRS. ALVING

Well, well, I daresay you're right there.

MANDERS

Besides, I of course do not deny that there may be much that is attractive in such books. Nor can I blame you for wishing to keep up with the intellectual movements that are said to be going on

in the great world—where you have let your son pass so much
of his life. But——

MRS. ALVING

But?

MANDERS   [*Lowering his voice.*]

But one should not talk about it, Mrs. Alving. One is certainly
not bound to account to everybody for what one reads and
thinks within one's own four walls.

MRS. ALVING

Of course not; I quite agree with you.

MANDERS

Only think, now, how you are bound to consider the interests of
this Orphanage, which you decided on founding at a time
when—if I understand you rightly—you thought very differently
on spiritual matters.

MRS. ALVING

Oh, yes; I quite admit that. But it was about the Orphanage——

MANDERS

It was about the Orphanage we were to speak; yes. All I say is:
prudence, my dear lady! And now let us get to business.
[*Opens the packet, and takes out a number of papers.*]
Do you see these?

MRS. ALVING

The documents?

MANDERS

All—and in perfect order. I can tell you it was hard work to get
them in time. I had to put on strong pressure. The authorities are
almost morbidly scrupulous when there is any decisive step to be
taken. But here they are at last.
[*Looks through the bundle.*]
See! here is the formal deed of gift of the parcel of ground
known as Solvik in the Manor of Rosenvold, with all the newly
constructed buildings, schoolrooms, master's house, and chapel.
And here is the legal fiat for the endowment and for the Bye-
laws of the Institution. Will you look at them?
[*Reads.*]
"Bye-laws for the Children's Home to be known as 'Captain
Alving's Foundation.'"

MRS. ALVING   [*Looks long at the paper.*]
>So there it is.

MANDERS
>I have chosen the designation "Captain" rather than
>"Chamberlain." "Captain" looks less pretentious.

MRS. ALVING
>Oh, yes; just as you think best.

MANDERS
>And here you have the Bank Account of the capital lying at
>interest to cover the current expenses of the Orphanage.

MRS. ALVING
>Thank you; but please keep it——it will be more convenient.

MANDERS
>With pleasure. I think we will leave the money in the Bank for
>the present. The interest is certainly not what we could wish——
>four per cent, and six months' notice of withdrawal. If a good
>mortgage could be found later on——of course it must be a first
>mortgage and an unimpeachable security——then we could
>consider the matter.

MRS. ALVING
>Certainly, my dear Pastor Manders. You are the best judge in
>these things.

MANDERS
>I will keep my eyes open at any rate. ——But now there is one
>thing more which I have several times been intending to ask you.

MRS. ALVING
>And what is that?

MANDERS
>Shall the Orphanage buildings be insured or not?

MRS. ALVING
>Of course they must be insured.

MANDERS
>Well, wait a moment, Mrs. Alving. Let us look into the matter a
>little more closely.

MRS. ALVING
>I have everything insured; buildings and movables and stock and
>crops.

MANDERS

Of course you have——on your own estate. And so have I——of
course. But here, you see, it is quite another matter. The
Orphanage is to be consecrated, as it were, to a higher purpose.

MRS. ALVING

Yes, but that's no reason——

MANDERS

For my own part, I should certainly not see the smallest
impropriety in guarding against all contingencies——

MRS. ALVING

No, I should think not.

MANDERS

But what is the general feeling in the neighbourhood? You, of
course, know better than I.

MRS. ALVING

Well——the general feeling——

MANDERS

Is there any considerable number of people——really responsible
people——who might be scandalised?

MRS. ALVING

What do you mean by "really responsible people"?

MANDERS

Well, I mean people in such independent and influential
positions that one cannot help attaching some weight to their
opinions.

MRS. ALVING

There are several people of that sort here who would very likely
be shocked if——

MANDERS

There, you see! In town we have many such people. Think of all
my colleague's adherents! People would be only too ready to
interpret our action as a sign that neither you nor I had the right
faith in a Higher Providence.

MRS. ALVING

But for your own part, my dear Pastor, you can at least tell
yourself that——

MANDERS

Yes, I know——I know; my conscience would be quite easy, that is true enough. But nevertheless we should not escape grave misinterpretation; and that might very likely react unfavourably upon the Orphanage.

MRS. ALVING

Well, in that case——

MANDERS

Nor can I entirely lose sight of the difficult—I may even say painful—position in which *I* might perhaps be placed. In the leading circles of the town, people take a lively interest in this Orphanage. It is, of course, founded partly for the benefit of the town, as well; and it is to be hoped it will, to a considerable extent, result in lightening our Poor Rates. Now, as I have been your adviser, and have had the business arrangements in my hands, I cannot but fear that I may have to bear the brunt of fanaticism——

MRS. ALVING

Oh, you mustn't run the risk of that.

MANDERS

To say nothing of the attacks that would assuredly be made upon me in certain papers and periodicals, which——

MRS. ALVING

Enough, my dear Pastor Manders. That consideration is quite decisive.

MANDERS

Then you do not wish the Orphanage to be insured?

MRS. ALVING

No. We will let it alone.

MANDERS   [*Leaning back in his chair.*]

But if, now, a disaster were to happen? One can never tell—— Should you be able to make good the damage?

MRS. ALVING

No; I tell you plainly I should do nothing of the kind.

MANDERS

Then I must tell you, Mrs. Alving—we are taking no small responsibility upon ourselves.

MRS. ALVING

Do you think we can do otherwise?

MANDERS

No, that is just the point; we really cannot do otherwise. We ought not to expose ourselves to misinterpretation; and we have no right whatever to give offence to the weaker brethren.

MRS. ALVING

You, as a clergyman, certainly should not.

MANDERS

I really think, too, we may trust that such an institution has fortune on its side; in fact, that it stands under a special providence.

MRS. ALVING

Let us hope so, Pastor Manders.

MANDERS

Then we will let it take its chance?

MRS. ALVING

Yes, certainly.

MANDERS

Very well. So be it.

[*Makes a note.*]

Then—no insurance.

MRS. ALVING

It's odd that you should just happen to mention the matter to-day——

MANDERS

I have often thought of asking you about it——

MRS. ALVING

——for we very nearly had a fire down there yesterday.

MANDERS

You don't say so!

MRS. ALVING

Oh, it was a trifling matter. A heap of shavings had caught fire in the carpenter's workshop.

MANDERS

Where Engstrand works?

MRS. ALVING

Yes. They say he's often very careless with matches.

MANDERS

He has so much on his mind, that man—so many things to fight against. Thank God, he is now striving to lead a decent life, I hear.

MRS. ALVING

Indeed! Who says so?

MANDERS

He himself assures me of it. And he is certainly a capital workman.

MRS. ALVING

Oh, yes; so long as he's sober——

MANDERS

Ah, that melancholy weakness! But he is often driven to it by his injured leg, he says. Last time he was in town I was really touched by him. He came and thanked me so warmly for having got him work here, so that he might be near Regina.

MRS. ALVING

He doesn't see much of her.

MANDERS

Oh, yes; he has a talk with her every day. He told me so himself.

MRS. ALVING

Well, it may be so.

MANDERS

He feels so acutely that he needs some one to keep a firm hold on him when temptation comes. That is what I cannot help liking about Jacob Engstrand: he comes to you so helplessly, accusing himself and confessing his own weakness. The last time he was talking to me—— Believe me, Mrs. Alving, supposing it were a real necessity for him to have Regina home again——

MRS. ALVING   [*Rising hastily.*]

Regina!

MANDERS

——you must not set yourself against it.

MRS. ALVING

Indeed I shall set myself against it. And besides—Regina is to have a position in the Orphanage.

MANDERS

But, after all, remember he is her father——

MRS. ALVING

Oh, I know very well what sort of a father he has been to her. No! She shall never go to him with my goodwill.

MANDERS   [Rising.]

My dear lady, don't take the matter so warmly. You sadly misjudge poor Engstrand. You seem to be quite terrified——

MRS. ALVING   [More quietly.]

It makes no difference. I have taken Regina into my house, and there she shall stay.

[Listens.]

Hush, my dear Mr. Manders; say no more about it.

[Her face lights up with gladness.]

Listen! there is Oswald coming downstairs. Now we'll think of no one but him.

OSWALD ALVING, in a light overcoat, hat in hand, and smoking a large meerschaum, enters by the door on the left; he stops in the doorway.

OSWALD

Oh, I beg your pardon; I thought you were in the study.

[Comes forward.]

Good-morning, Pastor Manders.

MANDERS   [Staring.]

Ah——! How strange——!

MRS. ALVING

Well now, what do you think of him, Mr. Manders?

MANDERS

I——I——can it really be——?

OSWALD

Yes, it's really the Prodigal Son, sir.

MANDERS   [Protesting.]

My dear young friend——

OSWALD

Well, then, the Lost Sheep Found.

MRS. ALVING

Oswald is thinking of the time when you were so much opposed to his becoming a painter.

MANDERS

    To our human eyes many a step seems dubious, which afterwards proves——

    [*Wrings his hand.*]

    But first of all, welcome, welcome home! Do not think, my dear Oswald—I suppose I may call you by your Christian name?

OSWALD

    What else should you call me?

MANDERS

    Very good. What I wanted to say was this, my dear Oswald— you must not think that I utterly condemn the artist's calling. I have no doubt there are many who can keep their inner self unharmed in that profession, as in any other.

OSWALD

    Let us hope so.

MRS. ALVING   [*Beaming with delight.*]

    I know one who has kept both his inner and his outer self unharmed. Just look at him, Mr. Manders.

OSWALD   [*Moves restlessly about the room.*]

    Yes, yes, my dear mother; let's say no more about it.

MANDERS

    Why, certainly—that is undeniable. And you have begun to make a name for yourself already. The newspapers have often spoken of you, most favourably. Just lately, by-the-bye, I fancy I haven't seen your name quite so often.

OSWALD   [*Up in the conservatory.*]

    I haven't been able to paint so much lately.

MRS. ALVING

    Even a painter needs a little rest now and then.

MANDERS

    No doubt, no doubt. And meanwhile he can be preparing himself and mustering his forces for some great work.

OSWALD

    Yes.—Mother, will dinner soon be ready?

MRS. ALVING

    In less than half an hour. He has a capital appetite, thank God.

MANDERS

    And a taste for tobacco, too.

OSWALD

    I found my father's pipe in my room——

MANDERS

    Aha——then that accounts for it!

MRS. ALVING

    For what?

MANDERS

    When Oswald appeared there, in the doorway, with the pipe in his mouth, I could have sworn I saw his father, large as life.

OSWALD

    No, really?

MRS. ALVING

    Oh, how can you say so? Oswald takes after me.

MANDERS

    Yes, but there is an expression about the corners of the mouth—something about the lips—that reminds one exactly of Alving: at any rate, now that he is smoking.

MRS. ALVING

    Not in the least. Oswald has rather a clerical curve about his mouth, I think.

MANDERS

    Yes, yes; some of my colleagues have much the same expression.

MRS. ALVING

    But put your pipe away, my dear boy; I won't have smoking in here.

OSWALD   [*Does so.*]

    By all means. I only wanted to try it; for I once smoked it when I was a child.

MRS. ALVING

    You?

OSWALD

    Yes. I was quite small at the time. I recollect I came up to father's room one evening when he was in great spirits.

MRS. ALVING

    Oh, you can't recollect anything of those times.

OSWALD

    Yes, I recollect it distinctly. He took me on his knee, and gave me the pipe. "Smoke, boy," he said; "smoke away, boy!" And I smoked as hard as I could, until I felt I was growing quite pale, and the

perspiration stood in great drops on my forehead. Then he burst
out laughing heartily——

MANDERS

That was most extraordinary.

MRS. ALVING

My dear friend, it's only something Oswald has dreamt.

OSWALD

No, mother, I assure you I didn't dream it. For——don't you
remember this?——you came and carried me out into the nursery.
Then I was sick, and I saw that you were crying.——Did father
often play such practical jokes?

MANDERS

In his youth he overflowed with the joy of life——

OSWALD

And yet he managed to do so much in the world; so much that
was good and useful; although he died so early.

MANDERS

Yes, you have inherited the name of an energetic and admirable
man, my dear Oswald Alving. No doubt it will be an incentive to
you——

OSWALD

It ought to, indeed.

MANDERS

It was good of you to come home for the ceremony in his
honour.

OSWALD

I could do no less for my father.

MRS. ALVING

And I am to keep him so long! That is the best of all.

MANDERS

You are going to pass the winter at home, I hear.

OSWALD

My stay is indefinite, sir.——But, ah! it is good to be at home!

MRS. ALVING   [*Beaming.*]

Yes, isn't it, dear?

MANDERS   [*Looking sympathetically at him.*]

You went out into the world early, my dear Oswald.

OSWALD

I did. I sometimes wonder whether it wasn't too early.

MRS. ALVING

Oh, not at all. A healthy lad is all the better for it; especially when he's an only child. He oughtn't to hang on at home with his mother and father, and get spoilt.

MANDERS

That is a very disputable point, Mrs. Alving. A child's proper place is, and must be, the home of his father's.

OSWALD

There I quite agree with you, Pastor Manders.

MANDERS

Only look at your own son—there is no reason why we should not say it in his presence—what has the consequence been for him? He is six or seven and twenty, and has never had the opportunity of learning what a well-ordered home really is.

OSWALD

I beg your pardon, Pastor; there you're quite mistaken.

MANDERS

Indeed? I thought you had lived almost exclusively in artistic circles.

OSWALD

So I have.

MANDERS

And chiefly among the younger artists?

OSWALD

Yes, certainly.

MANDERS

But I thought few of those young fellows could afford to set up house and support a family.

OSWALD

There are many who cannot afford to marry, sir.

MANDERS

Yes, that is just what I say.

OSWALD

But they may have a home for all that. And several of them have, as a matter of fact; and very pleasant, well-ordered homes they are, too.

[MRS. ALVING *follows with breathless interest; nods, but says nothing.*]

MANDERS

But I'm not talking of bachelors' quarters. By a "home" I understand the home of a family, where a man lives with his wife and children.

OSWALD

Yes; or with his children and his children's mother.

MANDERS   [*Starts; clasps his hands.*]

But, good heavens——

OSWALD

Well?

MANDERS

Lives with——his children's mother!

OSWALD

Yes. Would you have him turn his children's mother out of doors?

MANDERS

Then it is illicit relations you are talking of! Irregular marriages, as people call them!

OSWALD

I have never noticed anything particularly irregular about the life these people lead.

MANDERS

But how is it possible that a——a young man or young woman with any decency of feeling can endure to live in that way?——in the eyes of all the world!

OSWALD

What are they to do? A poor young artist——a poor girl—— marriage costs a great deal. What are they to do?

MANDERS

What are they to do? Let me tell you, Mr. Alving, what they ought to do. They ought to exercise self-restraint from the first; that is what they ought to do.

OSWALD

That doctrine will scarcely go down with warm-blooded young people who love each other.

MRS. ALVING

No, scarcely!

MANDERS [*Continuing.*]

How can the authorities tolerate such things! Allow them to go
on in the light of day!

[*Confronting* MRS. ALVING.]

Had I not cause to be deeply concerned about your son? In
circles where open immorality prevails, and has even a sort of
recognised position———!

OSWALD

Let me tell you, sir, that I have been in the habit of spending
nearly all my Sundays in one or two such irregular homes———

MANDERS

Sunday of all days!

OSWALD

Isn't that the day to enjoy one's self? Well, never have I heard an
offensive word, and still less have I witnessed anything that could
be called immoral. No; do you know when and where I have
come across immorality in artistic circles?

MANDERS

No, thank heaven, I don't!

OSWALD

Well, then, allow me to inform you. I have met with it when one
or other of our pattern husbands and fathers has come to Paris to
have a look round on his own account, and has done the artists
the honour of visiting their humble haunts. They knew what was
what. These gentlemen could tell us all about places and things
we had never dreamt of.

MANDERS

What! Do you mean to say that respectable men from home here
would———?

OSWALD

Have you never heard these respectable men, when they got
home again, talking about the way in which immorality runs
rampant abroad?

MANDERS

Yes, no doubt———

MRS. ALVING

I have too.

OSWALD

Well, you may take their word for it. They know what they are
talking about!

[*Presses his hands to his head.*]

Oh! that that great, free, glorious life out there should be defiled
in such a way!

MRS. ALVING

You mustn't get excited, Oswald. It's not good for you.

OSWALD

Yes; you're quite right, mother. It's bad for me, I know. You see,
I'm wretchedly worn out. I shall go for a little turn before
dinner. Excuse me, Pastor: I know you can't take my point of
view; but I couldn't help speaking out.

[*He goes out by the second door to the right.*]

MRS. ALVING

My poor boy!

MANDERS

You may well say so. Then this is what he has come to!

[MRS. ALVING *looks at him silently.*]

MANDERS   [*Walking up and down.*]

He called himself the Prodigal Son. Alas! alas!

[MRS. ALVING *continues looking at him.*]

MANDERS

And what do you say to all this?

MRS. ALVING

I say that Oswald was right in every word.

MANDERS   [*Stands still.*]

Right? Right! In such principles?

MRS. ALVING

Here, in my loneliness, I have come to the same way of thinking,
Pastor Manders. But I have never dared to say anything. Well!
now my boy shall speak for me.

MANDERS

You are greatly to be pitied, Mrs. Alving. But now I must speak
seriously to you. And now it is no longer your business manager
and adviser, your own and your husband's early friend, who
stands before you. It is the priest—the priest who stood before
you in the moment of your life when you had gone farthest astray.

MRS. ALVING

And what has the priest to say to me?

MANDERS

I will first stir up your memory a little. The moment is well chosen. To-morrow will be the tenth anniversary of your husband's death. To-morrow the memorial in his honour will be unveiled. To-morrow I shall have to speak to the whole assembled multitude. But to-day I will speak to you alone.

MRS. ALVING

Very well, Pastor Manders. Speak.

MANDERS

Do you remember that after less than a year of married life you stood on the verge of an abyss? That you forsook your house and home? That you fled from your husband? Yes, Mrs. Alving—fled, fled, and refused to return to him, however much he begged and prayed you?

MRS. ALVING

Have you forgotten how infinitely miserable I was in that first year?

MANDERS

It is the very mark of the spirit of rebellion to crave for happiness in this life. What right have we human beings to happiness? We have simply to do our duty, Mrs. Alving! And your duty was to hold firmly to the man you had once chosen, and to whom you were bound by the holiest ties.

MRS. ALVING

You know very well what sort of life Alving was leading—what excesses he was guilty of.

MANDERS

I know very well what rumours there were about him; and I am the last to approve the life he led in his young days, if report did not wrong him. But a wife is not appointed to be her husband's judge. It was your duty to bear with humility the cross which a Higher Power had, in its wisdom, laid upon you. But instead of that you rebelliously throw away the cross, desert the backslider whom you should have supported, go and risk your good name and reputation, and—nearly succeed in ruining other people's reputation into the bargain.

MRS. ALVING

Other people's? One other person's, you mean.

MANDERS

It was incredibly reckless of you to seek refuge with me.

MRS. ALVING

With our clergyman? With our intimate friend?

MANDERS

Just on that account. Yes, you may thank God that I possessed the necessary firmness; that I succeeded in dissuading you from your wild designs; and that it was vouchsafed me to lead you back to the path of duty, and home to your lawful husband.

MRS. ALVING

Yes, Pastor Manders, that was certainly your work.

MANDERS

I was but a poor instrument in a Higher Hand. And what a blessing has it not proved to you, all the days of your life, that I induced you to resume the yoke of duty and obedience! Did not everything happen as I foretold? Did not Alving turn his back on his errors, as a man should? Did he not live with you from that time, lovingly and blamelessly, all his days? Did he not become a benefactor to the whole district? And did he not help you to rise to his own level, so that you, little by little, became his assistant in all his undertakings? And a capital assistant, too—oh, I know, Mrs. Alving, that praise is due to you.   But now I come to the next great error in your life.

MRS. ALVING

What do you mean?

MANDERS

Just as you once disowned a wife's duty, so you have since disowned a mother's.

MRS. ALVING

Ah——!

MANDERS

You have been all your life under the dominion of a pestilent spirit of self-will. The whole bias of your mind has been towards insubordination and lawlessness. You have never known how to endure any bond. Everything that has weighed upon you in life you have cast away without care or conscience, like a burden you

were free to throw off at will. It did not please you to be a wife
any longer, and you left your husband. You found it troublesome
to be a mother, and you sent your child forth among strangers.

MRS. ALVING

Yes, that is true. I did so.

MANDERS

And thus you have become a stranger to him.

MRS. ALVING

No! no! I am not.

MANDERS

Yes, you are; you must be. And in what state of mind has he
returned to you? Bethink yourself well, Mrs.Alving. You sinned
greatly against your husband;—that you recognise by raising
yonder memorial to him. Recognise now, also, how you have
sinned against your son—there may yet be time to lead him back
from the paths of error. Turn back yourself, and save what may
yet be saved in him. For

[*With uplifted forefinger*]

verily, Mrs. Alving, you are a guilt-laden mother!—This I have
thought it my duty to say to you.

[*Silence.*]

MRS. ALVING   [*Slowly and with self-control.*]

You have now spoken out, Pastor Manders; and to-morrow you
are to speak publicly in memory of my husband. I shall not speak
to-morrow. But now I will speak frankly to you, as you have
spoken to me.

MANDERS

To be sure; you will plead excuses for your conduct——

MRS. ALVING

No. I will only tell you a story.

MANDERS

Well——?

MRS. ALVING

All that you have just said about my husband and me, and our life
after you had brought me back to the path of duty—as you
called it—about all that you know nothing from personal observation. From that moment you, who had been our intimate
friend, never set foot in our house again.

MANDERS

You and your husband left the town immediately after.

MRS. ALVING

Yes; and in my husband's lifetime you never came to see us. It was business that forced you to visit me when you undertook the affairs of the Orphanage.

MANDERS   [*Softly and hesitatingly.*]

Helen——if that is meant as a reproach, I would beg you to bear in mind——

MRS. ALVING

——the regard you owed to your position, yes; and that I was a runaway wife. One can never be too cautious with such unprincipled creatures.

MANDERS

My dear——Mrs. Alving, you know that is an absurd exaggeration——

MRS. ALVING

Well well, suppose it is. My point is that your judgment as to my married life is founded upon nothing but common knowledge and report.

MANDERS

I admit that. What then?

MRS. ALVING

Well, then, Pastor Manders——I will tell you the truth. I have sworn to myself that one day you should know it——you alone!

MANDERS

What is the truth, then?

MRS. ALVING

The truth is that my husband died just as dissolute as he had lived all his days.

MANDERS   [*Feeling after a chair.*]

What do you say?

MRS. ALVING

After nineteen years of marriage, as dissolute——in his desires at any rate——as he was before you married us.

MANDERS

And those——those wild oats——those irregularities——those excesses, if you like——you call "a dissolute life"?

MRS. ALVING

Our doctor used the expression.

MANDERS

I do not understand you.

MRS. ALVING

You need not.

MANDERS

It almost makes me dizzy. Your whole married life, the seeming union of all these years, was nothing more than a hidden abyss!

MRS. ALVING

Neither more nor less. Now you know it.

MANDERS

This is——this is inconceivable to me. I cannot grasp it! I cannot realise it! But how was it possible to——? How could such a state of things be kept secret?

MRS. ALVING

That has been my ceaseless struggle, day after day. After Oswald's birth, I thought Alving seemed to be a little better. But it did not last long. And then I had to struggle twice as hard, fighting as though for life or death, so that nobody should know what sort of man my child's father was. And you know what power Alving had of winning people's hearts. Nobody seemed able to believe anything but good of him. He was one of those people whose life does not bite upon their reputation. But at last, Mr. Manders—for you must know the whole story—the most repulsive thing of all happened.

MANDERS

More repulsive than what you have told me!

MRS. ALVING

I had gone on bearing with him, although I knew very well the secrets of his life out of doors. But when he brought the scandal within our own walls——

MANDERS

Impossible! Here!

MRS. ALVING

Yes; here in our own home. It was there
[*Pointing towards the first door on the right*],
in the dining-room, that I first came to know of it. I was busy

with something in there, and the door was standing ajar. I heard
our housemaid come up from the garden, with water for those
flowers.

MANDERS

Well——?

MRS. ALVING

Soon after, I heard Alving come in too. I heard him say something
softly to her. And then I heard—

[*With a short laugh*]

—oh! it still sounds in my ears, so hateful and yet so ludicrous—
I heard my own servant-maid whisper, "Let me go, Mr. Alving!
Let me be!"

MANDERS

What unseemly levity on his part! But it cannot have been more
than levity, Mrs. Alving; believe me, it cannot.

MRS. ALVING

I soon knew what to believe. Mr. Alving had his way with the
girl; and that connection had consequences, Mr. Manders.

MANDERS [*As though petrified.*]

Such things in this house! in this house!

MRS. ALVING

I had borne a great deal in this house. To keep him at home in
the evenings, and at night, I had to make myself his boon companion in his secret orgies up in his room. There I have had to sit
alone with him, to clink glasses and drink with him, and to listen
to his ribald, silly talk. I have had to fight with him to get him
dragged to bed——

MANDERS [*Moved.*]

And you were able to bear all this!

MRS. ALVING

I had to bear it for my little boy's sake. But when the last insult
was added; when my own servant-maid——; then I swore to
myself: This shall come to an end! And so I took the reins into
my own hand—the whole control—over him and everything
else. For now I had a weapon against him, you see; he dared not
oppose me. It was then I sent Oswald away from home. He was
nearly seven years old, and was beginning to observe and ask
questions, as children do. That I could not bear. It seemed to me

the child must be poisoned by merely breathing the air of this polluted home. That was why I sent him away. And now you can see, too, why he was never allowed to set foot inside his home so long as his father lived. No one knows what that cost me.

MANDERS

You have indeed had a life of trial.

MRS. ALVING

I could never have borne it if I had not had my work. For I may truly say that I have worked! All the additions to the estate—all the improvements—all the labour-saving appliances, that Alving was so much praised for having introduced—do you suppose he had energy for anything of the sort?—he, who lay all day on the sofa, reading an old Court Guide! No; but I may tell you this too: when he had his better intervals, it was I who urged him on; it was I who had to drag the whole load when he relapsed into his evil ways, or sank into querulous wretchedness.

MANDERS

And it is to this man that you raise a memorial?

MRS. ALVING

There you see the power of an evil conscience.

MANDERS

Evil——? What do you mean?

MRS. ALVING

It always seemed to me impossible but that the truth must come out and be believed. So the Orphanage was to deaden all rumours and set every doubt at rest.

MANDERS

In that you have certainly not missed your aim, Mrs. Alving.

MRS. ALVING

And besides, I had one other reason. I was determined that Oswald, my own boy, should inherit nothing whatever from his father.

MANDERS

Then it is Alving's fortune that——?

MRS. ALVING

Yes. The sums I have spent upon the Orphanage, year by year, make up the amount—I have reckoned it up precisely—the amount which made Lieutenant Alving "a good match" in his day.

MANDERS

I don't understand——

MRS. ALVING

It was my purchase-money. I do not choose that that money should pass into Oswald's hands. My son shall have everything from me—everything.

OSWALD ALVING *enters through the second door to the right; he has taken off his hat and overcoat in the hall.*

MRS. ALVING   [*Going towards him.*]

Are you back again already? My dear, dear boy!

OSWALD

Yes. What can a fellow do out of doors in this eternal rain? But I hear dinner is ready. That's capital!

REGINA   [*With a parcel, from the dining-room.*]

A parcel has come for you, Mrs. Alving.

[*Hands it to her.*]

MRS. ALVING   [*With a glance at* MR. MANDERS.]

No doubt copies of the ode for to-morrow's ceremony.

MANDERS

H'm——

REGINA

And dinner is ready.

MRS. ALVING

Very well. We will come directly. I will just——

[*Begins to open the parcel.*]

REGINA   [*To* OSWALD.]

Would Mr. Alving like red or white wine?

OSWALD

Both, if you please.

REGINA

Bien. Very well, sir.

[*She goes into the dining-room.*]

OSWALD

I may as well help to uncork it.

[*He also goes into the dining room, the door of which swings half open behind him.*]

MRS. ALVING   [*Who has opened the parcel.*]

Yes, I thought so. Here is the Ceremonial Ode, Pastor Manders.

MANDERS   [*With folded hands.*]

With what countenance I am to deliver my discourse
to-morrow————!

MRS. ALVING

Oh, you will get through it somehow.

MANDERS   [*Softly, so as not to be heard in the dining-room.*]

Yes; it would not do to provoke scandal.

MRS. ALVING   [*Under her breath, but firmly.*]

No. But then this long, hateful comedy will be ended. From the
day after to-morrow, I shall act in every way as though he who is
dead had never lived in this house. There shall be no one here
but my boy and his mother.

[*From the dining-room comes the noise of a chair overturned, and at the
same moment is heard:*]

REGINA   [*Sharply, but in a whisper.*]

Oswald! take care! are you mad? Let me go!

MRS. ALVING   [*Starts in terror.*]

Ah————!

[*She stares wildly towards the half-open door. OSWALD is heard laughing and humming. A bottle is uncorked.*]

MANDERS   [*Agitated.*]

What can be the matter? What is it, Mrs. Alving?

MRS. ALVING   [*Hoarsely.*]

Ghosts! The couple from the conservatory—risen again!

MANDERS

Is it possible! Regina————? Is she————?

MRS. ALVING

Yes. Come. Not a word————!

[*She seizes PASTOR MANDERS by the arm, and walks unsteadily towards the dining-room.*]

ACT SECOND

The same room. The mist still lies heavy over the landscape.

MANDERS *and* MRS. ALVING *enter from the dining-room.*

MRS. ALVING   [*Still in the doorway.*]
Velbekomme,* Mr. Manders.
[*Turns back towards the dining-room.*]
Aren't you coming too, Oswald?

OSWALD   [*From within.*]
No, thank you. I think I shall go out a little.

MRS. ALVING
Yes, do. The weather seems a little brighter now.
[*She shuts the dining-room door, goes to the hall door, and calls:*]
Regina!

REGINA   [*Outside.*]
Yes, Mrs. Alving?

MRS. ALVING
Go down to the laundry, and help with the garlands.

REGINA
Yes, Mrs. Alving.
[MRS. ALVING *assures herself that* REGINA *goes; then shuts the door.*]

MANDERS
I suppose he cannot overhear us in there?

MRS. ALVING
Not when the door is shut. Besides, he's just going out.

*A phrase equivalent to the German *Prosit die Mahlzeit*—"May good digestion wait on appetite."

MANDERS

    I am still quite upset. I don't know how I could swallow a morsel of dinner.

MRS. ALVING   [*Controlling her nervousness, walks up and down.*]

    Nor I. But what is to be done now?

MANDERS

    Yes; what is to be done? I am really quite at a loss. I am so utterly without experience in matters of this sort.

MRS. ALVING

    I feel sure that, so far, no mischief has been done.

MANDERS

    No; heaven forbid! But it is an unseemly state of things, nevertheless.

MRS. ALVING

    It is only an idle fancy on Oswald's part; you may be sure of that.

MANDERS

    Well, as I say, I am not accustomed to affairs of the kind. But I should certainly think——

MRS. ALVING

    Out of the house she must go, and that immediately. That is as clear as daylight——

MANDERS

    Yes, of course she must.

MRS. ALVING

    But where to? It would not be right to——

MANDERS

    Where to? Home to her father, of course.

MRS. ALVING

    To whom did you say?

MANDERS

    To her—— But then, Engstrand is not——? Good God, Mrs. Alving, it's impossible! You must be mistaken after all.

MRS. ALVING

    Unfortunately there is no possibility of mistake. Johanna confessed everything to me; and Alving could not deny it. So there was nothing to be done but to get the matter hushed up.

MANDERS

    No, you could do nothing else.

MRS. ALVING

The girl left our service at once, and got a good sum of money
to hold her tongue for the time. The rest she managed for herself
when she got to town. She renewed her old acquaintance with
Engstrand, no doubt let him see that she had money in her
purse, and told him some tale about a foreigner who put in here
with a yacht that summer. So she and Engstrand got married in
hot haste. Why, you married them yourself.

MANDERS

But then how to account for———? I recollect distinctly
Engstrand coming to give notice of the marriage. He was quite
overwhelmed with contrition, and bitterly reproached himself
for the misbehaviour he and his sweetheart had been guilty of.

MRS. ALVING

Yes; of course he had to take the blame upon himself.

MANDERS

But such a piece of duplicity on his part! And towards me too! I
never could have believed it of Jacob Engstrand. I shall not fail to
take him seriously to task; he may be sure of that. —And then
the immorality of such a connection! For money———! How
much did the girl receive?

MRS. ALVING

Three hundred dollars.

MANDERS

Just think of it—for a miserable three hundred dollars, to go and
marry a fallen woman!

MRS. ALVING

Then what have you to say of me? I went and married a fallen
man.

MANDERS

Why—good heavens!—what are you talking about! A fallen
man!

MRS. ALVING

Do you think Alving was any purer when I went with him to the
altar than Johanna was when Engstrand married her?

MANDERS

Well, but there is a world of difference between the two
cases———

MRS. ALVING

Not so much difference after all—except in the price:—a miserable three hundred dollars and a whole fortune.

MANDERS

How can you compare such absolutely dissimilar cases? You had taken counsel with your own heart and with your natural advisers.

MRS. ALVING   [*Without looking at him.*]

I thought you understood where what you call my heart had strayed to at the time.

MANDERS   [*Distantly.*]

Had I understood anything of the kind, I should not have been a daily guest in your husband's house.

MRS. ALVING

At any rate, the fact remains that with myself I took no counsel whatever.

MANDERS

Well then, with your nearest relatives—as your duty bade you— with your mother and your two aunts.

MRS. ALVING

Yes, that is true. Those three cast up the account for me. Oh, it's marvellous how clearly they made out that it would be downright madness to refuse such an offer. If mother could only see me now, and know what all that grandeur has come to!

MANDERS

Nobody can be held responsible for the result. This, at least, remains clear: your marriage was in full accordance with law and order.

MRS. ALVING   [*At the window.*]

Oh, that perpetual law and order! I often think that is what does all the mischief in this world of ours.

MANDERS

Mrs. Alving, that is a sinful way of talking.

MRS. ALVING

Well, I can't help it; I must have done with all this constraint and insincerity. I can endure it no longer. I must work my way out to freedom.

MANDERS

What do you mean by that?

MRS. ALVING   [*Drumming on the window-frame.*]

I ought never to have concealed the facts of Alving's life. But at that time I dared not do anything else—I was afraid, partly on my own account. I was such a coward.

MANDERS

A coward?

MRS. ALVING

If people had come to know anything, they would have said— "Poor man! with a runaway wife, no wonder he kicks over the traces."

MANDERS

Such remarks might have been made with a certain show of right.

MRS. ALVING   [*Looking steadily at him.*]

If I were what I ought to be, I should go to Oswald and say, "Listen, my boy: your father led a vicious life——"

MANDERS

Merciful heavens——!

MRS. ALVING

——and then I should tell him all I have told you—every word of it.

MANDERS

You shock me unspeakably, Mrs. Alving.

MRS. ALVING

Yes; I know that. I know that very well. I myself am shocked at the idea.

[*Goes away from the window.*]

I am such a coward.

MANDERS

You call it "cowardice" to do your plain duty? Have you forgotten that a son ought to love and honour his father and mother?

MRS. ALVING

Do not let us talk in such general terms. Let us ask: Ought Oswald to love and honour Chamberlain Alving?

MANDERS

Is there no voice in your mother's heart that forbids you to destroy your son's ideals?

MRS. ALVING

But what about the truth?

MANDERS

But what about the ideals?

MRS. ALVING

Oh—ideals, ideals! If only I were not such a coward!

MANDERS

Do not despise ideals, Mrs. Alving; they will avenge themselves cruelly. Take Oswald's case: he, unfortunately, seems to have few enough ideals as it is; but I can see that his father stands before him as an ideal.

MRS. ALVING

Yes, that is true.

MANDERS

And this habit of mind you have yourself implanted and fostered by your letters.

MRS. ALVING

Yes; in my superstitious awe for duty and the proprieties, I lied to my boy, year after year. Oh, what a coward—what a coward I have been!

MANDERS

You have established a happy illusion in your son's heart, Mrs. Alving; and assuredly you ought not to undervalue it.

MRS. ALVING

H'm; who knows whether it is so happy after all——? But, at any rate, I will not have any tampering with Regina. He shall not go and wreck the poor girl's life.

MANDERS

No; good God—that would be terrible!

MRS. ALVING

If I knew he was in earnest, and that it would be for his happiness——

MANDERS

What? What then?

MRS. ALVING

But it couldn't be; for unfortunately Regina is not the right sort of woman.

MANDERS

Well, what then? What do you mean?

MRS. ALVING

If I weren't such a pitiful coward, I should say to him, "Marry her, or make what arrangement you please, only let us have nothing underhand about it."

MANDERS

Merciful heavens, would you let them marry! Anything so dreadful——! so unheard of——

MRS. ALVING

Do you really mean "unheard of"? Frankly, Pastor Manders, do you suppose that throughout the country there are not plenty of married couples as closely akin as they?

MANDERS

I don't in the least understand you.

MRS. ALVING

Oh yes, indeed you do.

MANDERS

Ah, you are thinking of the possibility that—— Alas! yes, family life is certainly not always so pure as it ought to be. But in such a case as you point to, one can never know—at least with any certainty. Here, on the other hand—that you, a mother, can think of letting your son——!

MRS. ALVING

But I cannot—I wouldn't for anything in the world; that is precisely what I am saying.

MANDERS

No, because you are a "coward," as you put it. But if you were not a "coward," then——? Good God! a connection so shocking!

MRS. ALVING

So far as that goes, they say we are all sprung from connections of that sort. And who is it that arranged the world so, Pastor Manders?

MANDERS.

Questions of that kind I must decline to discuss with you, Mrs.

Alving; you are far from being in the right frame of mind for
them. But that you dare to call your scruples "cowardly"——!

MRS. ALVING

Let me tell you what I mean. I am timid and faint-hearted
because of the ghosts that hang about me, and that I can never
quite shake off.

MANDERS

What do you say hangs about you?

MRS. ALVING

Ghosts! When I heard Regina and Oswald in there, it was as
though ghosts rose up before me. But I almost think we are all of
us ghosts, Pastor Manders. It is not only what we have inherited
from our father and mother that "walks" in us. It is all sorts of
dead ideas, and lifeless old beliefs, and so forth. They have no
vitality, but they cling to us all the same, and we cannot shake
them off. Whenever I take up a newspaper, I seem to see ghosts
gliding between the lines. There must be ghosts all the country
over, as thick as the sands of the sea. And then we are, one and
all, so pitifully afraid of the light.

MANDERS

Aha—here we have the fruits of your reading. And pretty fruits
they are, upon my word! Oh, those horrible, revolutionary,
freethinking books!

MRS. ALVING

You are mistaken, my dear Pastor. It was you yourself who set
me thinking; and I thank for it with all my heart.

MANDERS

I!

MRS. ALVING

Yes—when you forced me under the yoke of what you called
duty and obligation; when you lauded as right and proper what
my whole soul rebelled against as something loathsome. It was
then that I began to look into the seams of your doctrines. I
wanted only to pick at a single knot; but when I had got that
undone, the whole thing ravelled out. And then I understood that
it was all machine-sewn.

MANDERS   [Softly, with emotion.]

And was that the upshot of my life's hardest battle?

MRS. ALVING

Call it rather your most pitiful defeat.

MANDERS

It was my greatest victory, Helen—the victory over myself.

MRS. ALVING

It was a crime against us both.

MANDERS

When you went astray, and came to me crying, "Here I am; take me!" I commanded you, saying, "Woman, go home to your lawful husband." Was that a crime?

MRS. ALVING

Yes, I think so.

MANDERS

We two do not understand each other.

MRS. ALVING

Not now, at any rate.

MANDERS

Never—never in my most secret thoughts have I regarded you otherwise than as another's wife.

MRS. ALVING

Oh—indeed?

MANDERS

Helen——!

MRS. ALVING

People so easily forget their past selves.

MANDERS

I do not. I am what I always was.

MRS. ALVING   [*Changing the subject.*]

Well well well; don't let us talk of old times any longer. You are now over head and ears in Boards and Committees, and I am fighting my battle with ghosts, both within me and without.

MANDERS

Those without I shall help you to lay. After all the terrible things I have heard from you to-day, I cannot in conscience permit an unprotected girl to remain in your house.

MRS. ALVING

Don't you think the best plan would be to get her provided for?—I mean, by a good marriage.

MANDERS

No doubt. I think it would be desirable for her in every respect.
Regina is now at the age when—— Of course I don't know
much about these things, but——

MRS. ALVING

Regina matured very early.

MANDERS

Yes, I thought so. I have an impression that she was remarkably
well developed, physically, when I prepared her for
confirmation. But in the meantime, she ought to be at home,
under her father's eye—— Ah! but Engstrand is not—— That
he—that he—could so hide the truth from me!

[*A knock at the door into the hall.*]

MRS. ALVING

Who can this be? Come in!

ENGSTRAND   [*In his Sunday clothes, in the doorway.*]

I humbly beg your pardon, but——

MANDERS

Aha! H'm——

MRS. ALVING

Is that you, Engstrand?

ENGSTRAND

——there was none of the servants about, so I took the great
liberty of just knocking.

MRS. ALVING

Oh, very well. Come in. Do you want to speak to me?

ENGSTRAND   [*Comes in.*]

No, I'm obliged to you, ma'am; it was with his Reverence I
wanted to have a word or two.

MANDERS   [*Walking up and down the room.*]

Ah—indeed! You want to speak to me, do you?

ENGSTRAND

Yes, I'd like so terrible much to——

MANDERS   [*Stops in front of him.*]

Well; may I ask what you want?

ENGSTRAND

Well, it was just this, your Reverence: we've been paid off down
yonder—my grateful thanks to you, ma'am,—and now

everything's finished, I've been thinking it would be but right and proper if we, that have been working so honestly together all this time—well, I was thinking we ought to end up with a little prayer-meeting to-night.

MANDERS

A prayer-meeting? Down at the Orphanage?

ENGSTRAND

Oh, if your Reverence doesn't think it proper——

MANDERS

Oh yes, I do; but—h'm—

ENGSTRAND

I've been in the habit of offering up a little prayer in the evenings, myself——

MRS. ALVING

Have you?

ENGSTRAND

Yes, every now and then—just a little edification, in a manner of speaking. But I'm a poor, common man, and have little enough gift, God help me!—and so I thought, as the Reverend Mr. Manders happened to be here, I'd——

MANDERS

Well, you see, Engstrand, I have a question to put to you first. Are you in the right frame of mind for such a meeting? Do you feel your conscience clear and at ease?

ENGSTRAND

Oh, God help us, your Reverence! we'd better not talk about conscience.

MANDERS

Yes, that is just what we must talk about. What have you to answer?

ENGSTRAND

Why—a man's conscience—it can be bad enough now and then.

MANDERS

Ah, you admit that. Then perhaps you will make a clean breast of it, and tell me—the real truth about Regina?

MRS. ALVING   [*Quickly.*]

Mr. Manders!

MANDERS [*Reassuringly.*]

Please allow me——

ENGSTRAND

About Regina! Lord, what a turn you gave me!

[*Looks at* MRS. ALVING.]

There's nothing wrong about Regina, is there?

MANDERS

We will hope not. But I mean, what is the truth about you and
Regina? You pass for her father, eh!

ENGSTRAND [*Uncertain.*]

Well——h'm——your Reverence knows all about me and poor Johanna.

MANDERS

Come now, no more prevarication! Your wife told Mrs. Alving
the whole story before quitting her service.

ENGSTRAND

Well, then, may——! Now, did she really?

MANDERS

You see we know you now, Engstrand.

ENGSTRAND

And she swore and took her Bible oath——

MANDERS

Did she take her Bible oath?

ENGSTRAND

No; she only swore; but she did it that solemn-like.

MANDERS

And you have hidden the truth from me all these years? Hidden
it from me, who have trusted you without reserve, in everything.

ENGSTRAND

Well, I can't deny it.

MANDERS

Have I deserved this of you, Engstrand? Have I not always been
ready to help you in word and deed, so far as it lay in my power?
Answer me. Have I not?

ENGSTRAND

It would have been a poor look-out for me many a time but for
the Reverend Mr. Manders.

MANDERS

And this is how you reward me! You cause me to enter
falsehoods in the Church Register, and you withhold from me,
year after year, the explanations you owed alike to me and to the
truth. Your conduct has been wholly inexcusable, Engstrand; and
from this time forward I have done with you!

ENGSTRAND   [*With a sigh.*]

Yes! I suppose there's no help for it.

MANDERS

How can you possibly justify yourself?

ENGSTRAND

Who could ever have thought she'd have gone and made bad
worse by talking about it? Will your Reverence just fancy
yourself in the same trouble as poor Johanna——

MANDERS

I!

ENGSTRAND

Lord bless you, I don't mean just exactly the same. But I mean, if
your Reverence had anything to be ashamed of in the eyes of the
world, as the saying goes. We menfolk oughtn't to judge a poor
woman too hardly, your Reverence.

MANDERS

I am not doing so. It is you I am reproaching.

ENGSTRAND

Might I make so bold as to ask your Reverence a bit of a
question?

MANDERS

Yes, if you want to.

ENGSTRAND

Isn't it right and proper for a man to raise up the fallen?

MANDERS

Most certainly it is.

ENGSTRAND

And isn't a man bound to keep his sacred word?

MANDERS

Why, of course he is; but——

ENGSTRAND

When Johanna had got into trouble through that Englishman——

or it might have been an American or a Russian, as they call them—well, you see, she came down into the town. Poor thing, she'd sent me about my business once or twice before: for she couldn't bear the sight of anything as wasn't handsome; and I'd got this damaged leg of mine. Your Reverence recollects how I ventured up into a dancing saloon, where seafaring men was carrying on with drink and devilry, as the saying goes. And then, when I was for giving them a bit of an admonition to lead a new life——

MRS. ALVING   [At the window.]

H'm——

MANDERS

I know all about that, Engstrand; the ruffians threw you downstairs. You have told me of the affair already. Your infirmity is an honour to you.

ENGSTRAND

I'm not puffed up about it, your Reverence. But what I wanted to say was, that when she came and confessed all to me, with weeping and gnashing of teeth, I can tell your Reverence I was sore at heart to hear it.

MANDERS

Were you indeed, Engstrand? Well, go on.

ENGSTRAND

So I says to her, "The American, he's sailing about on the boundless sea. And as for you, Johanna," says I, "you've committed a grievous sin, and you're a fallen creature. But Jacob Engstrand," says I, "he's got two good legs to stand upon, he has——" You see, your Reverence, I was speaking figurative-like.

MANDERS

I understand quite well. Go on.

ENGSTRAND

Well, that was how I raised her up and made an honest woman of her, so as folks shouldn't get to know how as she'd gone astray with foreigners.

MANDERS

In all that you acted very well. Only I cannot approve of your stooping to take money——

ENGSTRAND

Money? I? Not a farthing!

MANDERS   [*Inquiringly to* MRS. ALVING.]

But——

ENGSTRAND

Oh, wait a minute!—now I recollect. Johanna did have a trifle of money. But I would have nothing to do with that. "No," says I, "that's mammon; that's the wages of sin. This dirty gold—or notes, or whatever it was—we'll just fling that back in the American's face," says I. But he was off and away, over the stormy sea, your Reverence.

MANDERS

Was he really, my good fellow?

ENGSTRAND

He was indeed, sir. So Johanna and I, we agreed that the money should go to the child's education; and so it did, and I can account for every blessed farthing of it.

MANDERS

Why, this alters the case considerably.

ENGSTRAND

That's just how it stands, your Reverence. And I make so bold as to say as I've been an honest father to Regina, so far as my poor strength went; for I'm but a weak vessel, worse luck!

MANDERS

Well, well, my good fellow——

ENGSTRAND

All the same, I bear myself witness as I've brought up the child, and lived kindly with poor Johanna, and ruled over my own house, as the Scripture has it. But it couldn't never enter my head to go to your Reverence and puff myself up and boast because even the likes of me had done some good in the world. No, sir; when anything of that sort happens to Jacob Engstrand, he holds his tongue about it. It don't happen so terrible often, I daresay. And when I do come to see your Reverence, I find a mortal deal that's wicked and weak to talk about. For I said it before, and I says it again—a man's conscience isn't always as clean as it might be.

MANDERS

Give me your hand, Jacob Engstrand.

ENGSTRAND

Oh, Lord! your Reverence——

MANDERS

Come, no nonsense

[*wrings his hand.*]

There we are!

ENGSTRAND

And if I might humbly beg your Reverence's pardon——

MANDERS

You? On the contrary, it is I who ought to beg your pardon——

ENGSTRAND

Lord, no, sir!

MANDERS

Yes, assuredly. And I do it with all my heart. Forgive me for misunderstanding you. I only wish I could give you some proof of my hearty regret, and of my good-will towards you——

ENGSTRAND

Would your Reverence do it?

MANDERS

With the greatest pleasure.

ENGSTRAND

Well then, here's the very chance. With the bit of money I've saved here, I was thinking I might set up a Sailors' Home down in the town.

MRS. ALVING

You?

ENGSTRAND

Yes; it might be a sort of Orphanage, too, in a manner of speaking. There's such a many temptations for seafaring folk ashore. But in this Home of mine, a man might feel like as he was under a father's eye, I was thinking.

MANDERS

What do you say to this, Mrs. Alving?

ENGSTRAND

It isn't much as I've got to start with, Lord help me! But if I could only find a helping hand, why——

MANDERS

Yes, yes; we will look into the matter more closely. I entirely approve of your plan. But now, go before me and make everything ready, and get the candles lighted, so as to give the place an air of festivity. And then we will pass an edifying hour together, my good fellow; for now I quite believe you are in the right frame of mind.

ENGSTRAND

Yes, I trust I am. And so I'll say good-bye, ma'am, and thank you kindly; and take good care of Regina for me—

[*Wipes a tear from his eye*]—

poor Johanna's child. Well, it's a queer thing, now; but it's just like as if she'd growd into the very apple of my eye. It is, indeed. [*He bows and goes out through the hall.*]

MANDERS

Well, what do you say of that man now, Mrs. Alving? That was a very different account of matters, was it not?

MRS. ALVING

Yes, it certainly was.

MANDERS

It only shows how excessively careful one ought to be in judging one's fellow creatures. But what a heartfelt joy it is to ascertain that one has been mistaken! Don't you think so?

MRS. ALVING

I think you are, and will always be, a great baby, Manders.

MANDERS

I?

MRS. ALVING   [*Laying her two hands upon his shoulders.*]

And I say that I have half a mind to put my arms round your neck, and kiss you.

MANDERS   [*Stepping hastily back.*]

No, no! God bless me! What an idea!

MRS. ALVING   [*With a smile.*]

Oh, you needn't be afraid of me.

MANDERS   [*By the table.*]

You have sometimes such an exaggerated way of expressing yourself. Now, let me just collect all the documents, and put them in my bag.

[*He does so.*]

There, that's all right. And now, good-bye for the present. Keep your eyes open when Oswald comes back. I shall look in again later.

[*He takes his hat and goes out through the hall door.*]

MRS. ALVING   [*Sighs, looks for a moment out of the window, sets the room in order a little, and is about to go into the dining-room, but stops at the door with a half-suppressed cry.*]

Oswald, are you still at table?

OSWALD   [*In the dining room.*]

I'm only finishing my cigar.

MRS. ALVING

I thought you had gone for a little walk.

OSWALD

In such weather as this?

[*A glass clinks.* MRS. ALVING *leaves the door open, and sits down with her knitting on the sofa by the window.*]

OSWALD

Wasn't that Pastor Manders that went out just now?

MRS. ALVING

Yes; he went down to the Orphanage.

OSWALD

H'm.

[*The glass and decanter clink again.*]

MRS. ALVING   [*With a troubled glance.*]

Dear Oswald, you should take care of that liqueur. It is strong.

OSWALD

It keeps out the damp.

MRS. ALVING

Wouldn't you rather come in here, to me?

OSWALD

I mayn't smoke in there.

MRS. ALVING

You know quite well you may smoke cigars.

OSWALD

Oh, all right then; I'll come in. Just a tiny drop more first.—— There!

[*He comes into the room with his cigar, and shuts the door after him. A short silence.*]

Where has the pastor gone to?

MRS. ALVING

I have just told you; he went down to the Orphanage.

OSWALD

Oh, yes; so you did.

MRS. ALVING

You shouldn't sit so long at table, Oswald.

OSWALD [*Holding his cigar behind him.*]

But I find it so pleasant, mother.

[*Strokes and caresses her.*]

Just think what it is for me to come home and sit at mother's own table, in mother's room, and eat mother's delicious dishes.

MRS. ALVING

My dear, dear boy!

OSWALD [*Somewhat impatiently, walks about and smokes.*]

And what else can I do with myself here? I can't set to work at anything.

MRS. ALVING

Why can't you?

OSWALD

In such weather as this? Without a single ray of sunshine the whole day?

[*Walks up the room.*]

Oh, not to be able to work——!

MRS. ALVING

Perhaps it was not quite wise of you to come home?

OSWALD

Oh, yes, mother; I had to.

MRS. ALVING

You know I would ten times rather forgo the joy of having you here, than let you——

OSWALD [*Stops beside the table.*]

Now just tell me, mother: does it really make you so very happy to have me home again?

MRS. ALVING

Does it make me happy!

OSWALD [*Crumpling up a newspaper.*]

I should have thought it must be pretty much the same to you whether I was in existence or not.

MRS. ALVING

Have you the heart to say that to your mother. Oswald?

OSWALD

But you've got on very well without me all this time.

MRS. ALVING

Yes; I have got on without you. That is true.

[*A silence. Twilight slowly begins to fall.* OSWALD *paces to and fro across the room. He has laid his cigar down.*]

OSWALD   [*Stops beside* MRS. ALVING.]

Mother, may I sit on the sofa beside you?

MRS. ALVING   [*Makes room for him.*]

Yes, do, my dear boy.

OSWALD   [*Sits down.*]

There is something I must tell you, mother.

MRS. ALVING   [*Anxiously.*]

Well?

OSWALD   [*Looks fixedly before him.*]

For I can't go on hiding it any longer.

MRS. ALVING

Hiding what? What is it?

OSWALD   [*As before.*]

I could never bring myself to write to you about it; and since I've come home——

MRS. ALVING   [*Seizes him by the arm.*]

Oswald, what is the matter?

OSWALD

Both yesterday and to-day I have tried to put the thoughts away from me—to cast them off; but it's no use.

MRS. ALVING   [*Rising.*]

Now you must tell me everything, Oswald!

OSWALD   [*Draws her down to the sofa again.*]

Sit still; and then I will try to tell you.—I complained of fatigue after my journey——

MRS. ALVING

Well? What then?

OSWALD

But it isn't that that is the matter with me; not any ordinary fatigue——

MRS. ALVING [*Tries to jump up.*]

    You are not ill, Oswald?

OSWALD [*Draws her down again.*]

    Sit still, mother. Do take it quietly. I'm not downright ill, either; not what is commonly called "ill."

    [*Clasps his hands above his head.*]

    Mother, my mind is broken down—ruined—I shall never be able to work again!

    [*With his hands before his face, he buries his head in her lap, and breaks into bitter sobbing.*]

MRS. ALVING [*White and trembling.*]

    Oswald! Look at me! No, no; it's not true.

OSWALD [*Looks up with despair in his eyes.*]

    Never to be able to work again! Never!—never! A living death! Mother, can you imagine anything so horrible?

MRS. ALVING

    My poor boy! How has this horrible thing come upon you?

OSWALD [*Sitting upright again.*]

    That's just what I cannot possibly grasp or understand. I have never led a dissipated life—never, in any respect. You mustn't believe that of me, mother! I've never done that.

MRS. ALVING

    I am sure you haven't, Oswald.

OSWALD

    And yet this has come upon me just the same—this awful misfortune!

MRS. ALVING

    Oh, but it will pass over, my dear, blessed boy. It's nothing but over-work. Trust me, I am right.

OSWALD [*Sadly.*]

    I thought so too, at first; but it isn't so.

MRS. ALVING

    Tell me everything, from beginning to end.

OSWALD

    Yes, I will.

MRS. ALVING

    When did you first notice it?

OSWALD

It was directly after I had been home last time, and had got back to Paris again. I began to feel the most violent pains in my head—chiefly in the back of my head, they seemed to come. It was as though a tight iron ring was being screwed round my neck and upwards.

MRS. ALVING

Well, and then?

OSWALD

At first I thought it was nothing but the ordinary headache I had been so plagued with while I was growing up——

MRS. ALVING

Yes, yes——

OSWALD

But it wasn't that. I soon found that out. I couldn't work any more. I wanted to begin upon a big new picture, but my powers seemed to fail me; all my strength was crippled; I could form no definite images; everything swam before me—whirling round and round. Oh, it was an awful state! At last I sent for a doctor—and from him I learned the truth.

MRS. ALVING

How do you mean?

OSWALD

He was one of the first doctors in Paris. I told him my symptoms; and then he set to work asking me a string of questions which I thought had nothing to do with the matter. I couldn't imagine what the man was after——

MRS. ALVING

Well?

OSWALD

At last he said: "There has been something worm-eaten in you from your birth." He used that very word—*vermoulu.*

MRS. ALVING   [*Breathlessly.*]

What did he mean by that?

OSWALD

I didn't understand either, and begged him to explain himself more clearly. And then the old cynic said—

[*Clenching his fist.*]

Oh——!

MRS. ALVING

What did he say?

OSWALD

He said, "The sins of the fathers are visited upon the children."

MRS. ALVING   [*Rising slowly.*]

The sins of the fathers——!

OSWALD

I very nearly struck him in the face——

MRS. ALVING   [*Walks away across the room.*]

The sins of the fathers——

OSWALD   [*Smiles sadly.*]

Yes; what do you think of that? Of course I assured him that such a
thing was out of the question. But do you think he gave in? No, he
stuck to it; and it was only when I produced your letters and
translated the passages relating to father——

MRS. ALVING

But then——?

OSWALD

Then of course he had to admit that he was on the wrong track;
and so I learned the truth—the incomprehensible truth! I ought
not to have taken part with my comrades in that light-hearted,
glorious life of theirs. It had been too much for my strength. So I
had brought it upon myself!

MRS. ALVING

Oswald! No, no; do not believe it!

OSWALD

No other explanation was possible, he said. That's the awful part
of it. Incurably ruined for life—by my own heedlessness! All that
I meant to have done in the world—I never dare think of it
again—I'm not able to think of it. Oh! if I could only live over
again, and undo all I have done!

[*He buries his face in the sofa.*]

MRS. ALVING   [*Wrings her hands and walks, in silent struggle, backwards
and forwards.*]

OSWALD   [*After a while, looks up and remains resting upon his elbow.*]

If it had only been something inherited—something one wasn't
responsible for! But this! To have thrown away so shamefully,

thoughtlessly, recklessly, one's own happiness, one's own health, everything in the world—one's future, one's very life——!

MRS. ALVING

No, no, my dear, darling boy; this is impossible!

[*Bends over him.*]

Things are not so desperate as you think.

OSWALD

Oh, you don't know——

[*Springs up.*]

And then, mother, to cause you all this sorrow! Many a time I have almost wished and hoped that at bottom you didn't care so very much about me.

MRS. ALVING

I, Oswald? My only boy! You are all I have in the world! The only thing I care about!

OSWALD [*Seizes both her hands and kisses them.*]

Yes, yes, I see it. When I'm at home, I see it, of course; and that's almost the hardest part for me.—But now you know the whole story; and now we won't talk any more about it to-day. I daren't think of it for long together.

[*Goes up the room.*]

Get me something to drink, mother.

MRS. ALVING

To drink? What do you want to drink now?

OSWALD

Oh, anything you like. You have some cold punch in the house.

MRS. ALVING

Yes, but my dear Oswald——

OSWALD

Don't refuse me, mother. Do be kind, now! I must have something to wash down all these gnawing thoughts.

[*Goes into the conservatory.*]

And then—it's so dark here!

[MRS. ALVING *pulls a bell-rope on the right.*]

And this ceaseless rain! It may go on week after week, for months together. Never to get a glimpse of the sun! I can't recollect ever having seen the sun shine all the times I've been at home.

MRS. ALVING

Oswald—you are thinking of going away from me.

OSWALD

H'm—

[*Drawing a heavy breath.*]

—I'm not thinking of anything. I cannot think of anything!

[*In a low voice.*]

I let thinking alone.

REGINA   [*From the dining-room.*]

Did you ring, ma'am?

MRS. ALVING

Yes; let us have the lamp in.

REGINA

Yes, ma am. It's ready lighted.

[*Goes out.*]

MRS. ALVING   [*Goes across to* OSWALD.]

Oswald, be frank with me.

OSWALD

Well, so I am, mother.

[*Goes to the table.*]

I think I have told you enough.

[REGINA *brings the lamp and sets it upon the table.*]

MRS. ALVING

Regina, you may bring us a small bottle of champagne.

REGINA

Very well, ma'am.

[*Goes out.*]

OSWALD   [*Puts his arm round* MRS. ALVING's *neck.*]

That's just what I wanted. I knew mother wouldn't let her boy go thirsty.

MRS. ALVING

My own, poor, darling Oswald; how could I deny you anything now?

OSWALD   [*Eagerly.*]

Is that true, mother? Do you mean it?

MRS. ALVING

How? What?

OSWALD

That you couldn't deny me anything.

MRS. ALVING

My dear Oswald——

OSWALD

Hush!

REGINA　[*Brings a tray with a half-bottle of champagne and two glasses, which she sets on the table.*]

Shall I open it?

OSWALD

No, thanks. I will do it myself.

[REGINA *goes out again.*]

MRS. ALVING　[*Sits down by the table.*]

What was it you meant——that I musn't deny you?

OSWALD　[*Busy opening the bottle.*]

First let us have a glass——or two.

[*The cork pops; he pours wine into one glass, and is about to pour it into the other.*]

MRS. ALVING　[*Holding her hand over it.*]

Thanks; not for me.

OSWALD

Oh! won't you? Then I will!

[*He empties the glass, fills, and empties it again; then he sits down by the table.*]

MRS. ALVING　[*In expectancy.*]

Well?

OSWALD　[*Without looking at her.*]

Tell me——I thought you and Pastor Manders seemed so odd——so quiet——at dinner to-day.

MRS. ALVING

Did you notice it?

OSWALD

Yes. H'm——

[*After a short silence.*]

Tell me: what do you think of Regina?

MRS. ALVING

What do I think?

OSWALD
Yes; isn't she splendid?

MRS. ALVING
My dear Oswald, you don't know her as I do——

OSWALD
Well?

MRS. ALVING
Regina, unfortunately, was allowed to stay at home too long. I ought to have taken her earlier into my house.

OSWALD
Yes, but isn't she splendid to look at, mother?
[*He fills his glass.*]

MRS. ALVING
Regina has many serious faults——

OSWALD
Oh, what does that matter?
[*He drinks again.*]

MRS. ALVING
But I am fond of her, nevertheless, and I am responsible for her. I wouldn't for all the world have any harm happen to her.

OSWALD   [*Springs up.*]
Mother, Regina is my only salvation!

MRS. ALVING   [*Rising.*]
What do you mean by that?

OSWALD
I cannot go on bearing all this anguish of soul alone.

MRS. ALVING
Have you not your mother to share it with you?

OSWALD
Yes; that's what I thought; and so I came home to you. But that will not do. I see it won't do. I cannot endure my life here.

MRS. ALVING
Oswald!

OSWALD
I must live differently, mother. That is why I must leave you. I will not have you looking on at it.

MRS. ALVING
My unhappy boy! But, Oswald, while you are so ill as this——

OSWALD

    If it were only the illness, I should stay with you, mother, you may be sure; for you are the best friend I have in the world.

MRS. ALVING

    Yes, indeed I am, Oswald; am I not?

OSWALD   [*Wanders restlessly about.*]

    But it's all the torment, the gnawing remorse—and then, the great, killing dread. Oh—that awful dread!

MRS. ALVING   [*Walking after him.*]

    Dread? What dread? What do you mean?

OSWALD

    Oh, you mustn't ask me any more. I don't know. I can't describe it.

MRS. ALVING   [*Goes over to the right and pulls the bell.*]

OSWALD

    What is it you want?

MRS. ALVING

    I want my boy to be happy—that is what I want. He sha'n't go on brooding over things.

    [*To* REGINA, *who appears at the door:*]

    More champagne—a large bottle.

    [REGINA *goes.*]

OSWALD

    Mother!

MRS. ALVING

    Do you think we don't know how to live here at home?

OSWALD

    Isn't she splendid to look at? How beautifully she's built! And so thoroughly healthy!

MRS. ALVING   [*Sits by the table.*]

    Sit down, Oswald; let us talk quietly together.

OSWALD   [*Sits.*]

    I daresay you don't know, mother, that I owe Regina some reparation.

MRS. ALVING

    You!

OSWALD

> For a bit of thoughtlessness, or whatever you like to call it—very innocent, at any rate. When I was home last time——

MRS. ALVING

> Well?

OSWALD

> She used often to ask me about Paris, and I used to tell her one thing and another. Then I recollect I happened to say to her one day, "Shouldn't you like to go there yourself?"

MRS. ALVING

> Well?

OSWALD

> I saw her face flush, and then she said, "Yes, I should like it of all things." "Ah, well," I replied, "it might perhaps be managed"—or something like that.

MRS. ALVING

> And then?

OSWALD

> Of course I had forgotten all about it; but the day before yesterday I happened to ask her whether she was glad I was to stay at home so long——

MRS. ALVING

> Yes?

OSWALD

> And then she gave me such a strange look, and asked, "But what's to become of my trip to Paris?"

MRS. ALVING

> Her trip!

OSWALD

> And so it came out that she had taken the thing seriously; that she had been thinking of me the whole time, and had set to work to learn French——

MRS. ALVING

> So that was why——!

OSWALD

> Mother—when I saw that fresh, lovely, splendid girl standing there before me—till then I had hardly noticed her—but when

she stood there as though with open arms ready to receive
me——

MRS. ALVING

Oswald!

OSWALD

—then it flashed upon me that in her lay my salvation; for I saw
that she was full of the joy of life.

MRS. ALVING   [*Starts.*]

The joy of life——? Can there be salvation in that?

REGINA   [*From the dining-room, with a bottle of champagne.*]

I'm sorry to have been so long, but I had to go to the cellar.
[*Places the bottle on the table.*]

OSWALD

And now bring another glass.

REGINA   [*Looks at him in surprise.*]

There is Mrs. Alving's glass, Mr. Alving.

OSWALD

Yes, but bring one for yourself, Regina.
[REGINA *starts and gives a lightning-like side glance at* MRS.
ALVING.]
Why do you wait?

REGINA   [*Softly and hesitatingly.*]

Is it Mrs. Alving's wish?

MRS. ALVING

Bring the glass, Regina.
[REGINA *goes out into the dining-room.*]

OSWALD   [*Follows her with his eyes.*]

Have you noticed how she walks?—so firmly and lightly!

MRS. ALVING

This can never be, Oswald!

OSWALD

It's a settled thing. Can't you see that? It's no use saying anything
against it.
[REGINA *enters with an empty glass, which she keeps in her hand.*]

OSWALD

Sit down, Regina.
[REGINA *looks inquiringly at* MRS. ALVING.]

MRS. ALVING

Sit down.

[REGINA *sits on a chair by the dining-room door, still holding the empty glass in her hand.*]

Oswald—what were you saying about the joy of life?

OSWALD

Ah, the joy of life, mother—that's a thing you don't know much about in these parts. I have never felt it here.

MRS. ALVING

Not when you are with me?

OSWALD

Not when I'm at home. But you don't understand that.

MRS. ALVING

Yes, yes; I think I almost understand it—now.

OSWALD

And then, too, the joy of work! At bottom, it's the same thing. But that, too, you know nothing about.

MRS. ALVING

Perhaps you are right. Tell me more about it, Oswald.

OSWALD

I only mean that here people are brought up to believe that work is a curse and a punishment for sin, and that life is something miserable, something it would be best to have done with, the sooner the better.

MRS. ALVING

"A vale of tears," yes; and we certainly do our best to make it one.

OSWALD

But in the great world people won't hear of such things. There, nobody really believes such doctrines any longer. There, you feel it a positive bliss and ecstasy merely to draw the breath of life. Mother, have you noticed that everything I have painted has turned upon the joy of life?—always, always upon the joy of life?—light and sunshine and glorious air—and faces radiant with happiness. That is why I'm afraid of remaining at home with you.

MRS. ALVING

Afraid? What are you afraid of here, with me?

OSWALD

I'm afraid lest all my instincts should be warped into ugliness.

MRS. ALVING   [*Looks steadily at him.*]

Do you think that is what would happen?

OSWALD

I know it. You may live the same life here as there, and yet it won't be the same life.

MRS. ALVING   [*Who has been listening eagerly, rises, her eyes big with thought, and says:*]

Now I see the sequence of things.

OSWALD

What is it you see?

MRS. ALVING

I see it now for the first time. And now I can speak.

OSWALD   [*Rising.*]

Mother, I don't understand you.

REGINA   [*Who has also risen.*]

Perhaps I ought to go?

MRS. ALVING

No. Stay here. Now I can speak. Now, my boy, you shall know the whole truth. And then you can choose. Oswald! Regina!

OSWALD

Hush! The Pastor——

MANDERS   [*Enters by the hall door.*]

There! We have had a most edifying time down there.

OSWALD

So have we.

MANDERS

We must stand by Engstrand and his Sailors' Home. Regina must go to him and help him——

REGINA

No thank you, sir.

MANDERS   [*Noticing her for the first time.*]

What——? You here? And with a glass in your hand!

REGINA   [*Hastily putting the glass down.*]

Pardon!

OSWALD

Regina is going with me, Mr. Manders.

MANDERS
Going! With you!

OSWALD
Yes; as my wife—if she wishes it.

MANDERS
But, merciful God——!

REGINA
I can't help it, sir.

OSWALD
Or she'll stay here, if I stay.

REGINA   [*Involuntarily.*]
Here!

MANDERS
I am thunderstruck at your conduct, Mrs. Alving.

MRS. ALVING
They will do neither one thing nor the other; for now I can
speak out plainly.

MANDERS
You surely will not do that! No, no, no!

MRS. ALVING
Yes, I can speak and I will. And no ideals shall suffer after all.

OSWALD
Mother—what is it you are hiding from me?

REGINA   [*Listening.*]
Oh, ma'am, listen! Don't you hear shouts outside.
[*She goes into the conservatory and looks out.*]

OSWALD   [*At the window on the left.*]
What's going on? Where does that light come from?

REGINA   [*Cries out.*]
The Orphanage is on fire!

MRS. ALVING   [*Rushing to the window.*]
On fire!

MANDERS
On fire! Impossible! I've just come from there.

OSWALD
Where's my hat? Oh, never mind it—Father's Orphanage——!
[*He rushes out through the garden door.*]

MRS. ALVING

My shawl, Regina! The whole place is in a blaze!

MANDERS

Terrible! Mrs. Alving, it is a judgment upon this abode of law-lessness.

MRS. ALVING

Yes, of course. Come, Regina.

[*She and* REGINA *hasten out through the hall.*]

MANDERS   [*Clasps his hands together.*]

And we left it uninsured!

[*He goes out the same way.*]

ACT THIRD

The room as before. All the doors stand open. The lamp is still burning on the table. It is dark out of doors, there is only a faint glow from the conflagration in the background to the left.

MRS. ALVING, *with a shawl over her head, stands in the conservatory, looking out.* REGINA, *also with a shawl on, stands a little behind her.*

MRS. ALVING

The whole thing burnt!——burnt to the ground!

REGINA

The basement is still burning.

MRS. ALVING

How is it Oswald doesn't come home? There's nothing to be saved.

REGINA

Should you like me to take down his hat to him?

MRS. ALVING

Has he not even got his hat on?

REGINA   [*Pointing to the hall.*]

No; there it hangs.

MRS. ALVING

Let it be. He must come up now. I shall go and look for him myself.

[*She goes out through the garden door.*]

MANDERS   [*Comes in from the hall.*]

Is not Mrs. Alving here?

REGINA

She has just gone down the garden.

MANDERS

This is the most terrible night I ever went through.

REGINA

Yes; isn't it a dreadful misfortune, sir?

MANDERS

Oh, don't talk about it! I can hardly bear to think of it.

REGINA

How can it have happened——?

MANDERS

Don't ask me, Miss Engstrand! How should *I* know? Do you, too——? Is it not enough that your father——?

REGINA

What about him?

MANDERS

Oh, he has driven me distracted——

ENGSTRAND   [*Enters through the hall.*]

Your Reverence——

MANDERS   [*Turns round in terror.*]

Are you after me here, too?

ENGSTRAND

Yes, strike me dead, but I must——! Oh, Lord! what am I saying? But this is a terrible ugly business, your Reverence.

MANDERS   [*Walks to and fro.*]

Alas! alas!

REGINA

What's the matter?

ENGSTRAND

Why, it all came of this here prayer-meeting, you see.
[*Softly.*]
The bird's limed, my girl.
[*Aloud.*]
And to think it should be my doing that such a thing should be his Reverence's doing!

MANDERS

But I assure you, Engstrand——

ENGSTRAND

There wasn't another soul except your Reverence as ever laid a finger on the candles down there.

MANDERS [*Stops.*]

So you declare. But I certainly cannot recollect that I ever had a candle in my hand.

ENGSTRAND

And I saw as clear as daylight how your Reverence took the candle and snuffed it with your fingers, and threw away the snuff among the shavings.

MANDERS

And you stood and looked on?

ENGSTRAND

Yes; I saw it as plain as a pike-staff, I did.

MANDERS

It's quite beyond my comprehension. Besides, it has never been my habit to snuff candles with my fingers.

ENGSTRAND

And terrible risky it looked, too, that it did! But is there such a deal of harm done after all, your Reverence?

MANDERS [*Walks restlessly to and fro.*]

Oh, don't ask me!

ENGSTRAND [*Walks with him.*]

And your Reverence hadn't insured it, neither?

MANDERS [*Continuing to walk up and down.*]

No, no, no; I have told you so.

ENGSTRAND [*Following him.*]

Not insured! And then to go straight away down and set light to the whole thing! Lord, Lord, what a misfortune!

MANDERS [*Wipes the sweat from his forehead.*]

Ay, you may well say that, Engstrand.

ENGSTRAND

And to think that such a thing should happen to a benevolent Institution, that was to have been a blessing both to town and country, as the saying goes! The newspapers won't be for handling your Reverence very gently, I expect.

MANDERS

No; that is just what I am thinking of. That is almost the worst of the whole matter. All the malignant attacks and imputations——! Oh, it makes me shudder to think of it!

MRS. ALVING [*Comes in from the garden.*]

He is not to be persuaded to leave the fire.

MANDERS

Ah, there you are, Mrs. Alving.

MRS. ALVING

So you have escaped your Inaugural Address, Pastor Manders.

MANDERS

Oh, I should so gladly——

MRS. ALVING [*In an undertone.*]

It is all for the best. That Orphanage would have done no one any good.

MANDERS

Do you think not?

MRS. ALVING

Do you think it would?

MANDERS

It is a terrible misfortune, all the same.

MRS. ALVING

Let us speak of it plainly, as a matter of business.——Are you waiting for Mr. Manders, Engstrand?

ENGSTRAND [*At the hall door.*]

That's just what I'm a-doing of, ma'am.

MRS. ALVING

Then sit down meanwhile.

ENGSTRAND

Thank you, ma'am; I'd as soon stand.

MRS. ALVING [*To* MANDERS.]

I suppose you are going by the steamer?

MANDERS

Yes; it starts in an hour.

MRS. ALVING

Then be so good as to take all the papers with you. I won't hear another word about this affair. I have other things to think of——

MANDERS

Mrs. Alving——

MRS. ALVING

Later on I shall send you a Power of Attorney to settle everything as you please.

MANDERS

That I will very readily undertake. The original destination of the endowment must now be completely changed, alas!

MRS. ALVING

Of course it must.

MANDERS

I think, first of all, I shall arrange that the Solvik property shall pass to the parish. The land is by no means without value. It can always be turned to account for some purpose or other. And the interest of the money in the Bank I could, perhaps, best apply for the benefit of some undertaking of acknowledged value to the town.

MRS. ALVING

Do just as you please. The whole matter is now completely indifferent to me.

ENGSTRAND

Give a thought to my Sailors' Home, your Reverence.

MANDERS

Upon my word, that is not a bad suggestion. That must be considered.

ENGSTRAND

Oh, devil take considering—Lord forgive me!

MANDERS   [*With a sigh.*]

And unfortunately I cannot tell how long I shall be able to retain control of these things—whether public opinion may not compel me to retire. It entirely depends upon the result of the official in-quiry into the fire——

MRS. ALVING

What are you talking about?

MANDERS

And the result can by no means be foretold.

ENGSTRAND   [*Comes close to him.*]

Ay, but it can though. For here stands old Jacob Engstrand.

MANDERS

Well well, but——?

ENGSTRAND   [*More softly.*]

And Jacob Engstrand isn't the man to desert a noble benefactor in the hour of need, as the saying goes.

MANDERS

Yes, but my good fellow—how———?

ENGSTRAND

Jacob Engstrand may be likened to a sort of a guardian angel, he may, your Reverence.

MANDERS

No, no; I really cannot accept that.

ENGSTRAND

Oh, that'll be the way of it, all the same. I know a man as has taken others' sins upon himself before now, I do.

MANDERS

Jacob!

[*Wrings his hand.*]

Yours is a rare nature. Well, you shall be helped with your Sailors' Home. That you may rely upon.

[ENGSTRAND *tries to thank him, but cannot for emotion.*]

MANDERS   [*Hangs his travelling-bag over his shoulder.*]

And now let us set out. We two will go together.

ENGSTRAND   [*At the dining-room door, softly to* REGINA.]

You come along too, my lass. You shall live as snug as the yolk in an egg.

REGINA   [*Tosses her head.*]

Merci!

[*She goes out into the hall and fetches* MANDER'S *overcoat.*]

MANDERS

Good-bye, Mrs. Alving! and may the spirit of Law and Order descend upon this house, and that quickly.

MRS. ALVING

Good-bye, Pastor Manders.

[*She goes up towards the conservatory, as she sees* OSWALD *coming in through the garden door.*]

ENGSTRAND   [*While he and* REGINA *help* MANDERS *to get his coat on.*]

Good-bye, my child. And if any trouble should come to you, you know where Jacob Engstrand is to be found.

[*Softly.*]

Little Harbour Street, h'm———!

[*To* MRS. ALVING *and* OSWALD]

And the refuge for wandering mariners shall be called
"Chamberlain Alving's Home," that it shall! And if so be as I'm
spared to carry on that house in my own way, I make so bold as
to promise that it shall be worthy of the Chamberlain's memory.

MANDERS   [*In the doorway.*]

H'm——h'm!——Come along, my dear Engstrand. Good-bye!
Good-bye!

[*He and* ENGSTRAND *go out through the hall.*]

OSWALD   [*Goes towards the table.*]

What house was he talking about?

MRS. ALVING

Oh, a kind of Home that he and Pastor Manders want to set up.

OSWALD

It will burn down like the other.

MRS. ALVING

What makes you think so?

OSWALD

Everything will burn. All that recalls father's memory is doomed.
Here am I, too, burning down.

[REGINA *starts and looks at him.*]

MRS. ALVING

Oswald! You oughtn't to have remained so long down there, my
poor boy.

OSWALD   [*Sits down by the table.*]

I almost think you are right.

MRS. ALVING

Let me dry your face, Oswald; you are quite wet.

[*She dries his face with her pocket-handkerchief.*]

OSWALD   [*Stares indifferently in front of him.*]

Thanks, mother.

MRS. ALVING

Are you not tired, Oswald? Should you like to sleep?

OSWALD   [*Nervously.*]

No, no——not to sleep. I never sleep. I only pretend to.

[*Sadly.*]

That will come soon enough.

MRS. ALVING   [*Looking sorrowfully at him.*]

Yes, you really are ill, my blessed boy.

REGINA   [*Eagerly.*]

    Is Mr. Alving ill?

OSWALD   [*Impatiently.*]

    Oh, do shut all the doors! This killing dread——

MRS. ALVING

    Close the doors, Regina.

    [REGINA *shuts them and remains standing by the hall door.* MRS. ALVING *takes her shawl off.* REGINA *does the same.* MRS. ALVING *draws a chair across to* OSWALD'S, *and sits by him.*]

MRS. ALVING

    There now! I am going to sit beside you——

OSWALD

    Yes, do. And Regina shall stay here too. Regina shall be with me always. You will come to the rescue, Regina, won't you?

REGINA

    I don't understand——

MRS. ALVING

    To the rescue?

OSWALD

    Yes—when the need comes.

MRS. ALVING

    Oswald, have you not your mother to come to the rescue?

OSWALD

    You?

    [*Smiles.*]

    No, mother; that rescue you will never bring me.

    [*Laughs sadly.*]

    You! ha ha!

    [*Looks earnestly at her.*]

    Though, after all, who ought to do it if not you?

    [*Impetuously.*]

    Why can't you say "thou"* to me, Regina? Why don't you call me "Oswald"?

REGINA   [*Softly.*]

    I don't think Mrs. Alving would like it.

---

*In the original *du,* the familiar "you," like *tu* in French; people use the familiar "you" when addressing those with whom they are closest.

MRS. ALVING

You shall have leave to, presently. And meanwhile sit over here beside us.

[REGINA *seats herself demurely and hesitatingly at the other side of the table.*]

MRS. ALVING

And now, my poor suffering boy, I am going to take the burden off your mind——

OSWALD

You, mother?

MRS. ALVING

——all the gnawing remorse and self-reproach you speak of.

OSWALD

And you think you can do that?

MRS. ALVING

Yes, now I can, Oswald. A little while ago you spoke of the joy of life; and at that word a new light burst for me over my life and everything connected with it.

OSWALD   [*Shakes his head.*]

I don't understand you.

MRS. ALVING

You ought to have known your father when he was a young lieutenant. He was brimming over with the joy of life!

OSWALD

Yes, I know he was.

MRS. ALVING

It was like a breezy day only to look at him. And what exuberant strength and vitality there was in him!

OSWALD

Well——?

MRS. ALVING

Well then, child of joy as he was—for he was like a child in those days—he had to live at home here in a half-grown town, which had no joys to offer him—only dissipations. He had no object in life—only an official position. He had no work into which he could throw himself heart and soul; he had only business. He had not a single comrade that could realise what the joy of life meant—only loungers and boon-companions——

OSWALD

Mother——!

MRS. ALVING

So the inevitable happened.

OSWALD

The inevitable?

MRS. ALVING

You told me yourself, this evening, what would become of you if
you stayed at home.

OSWALD

Do you mean to say that father——?

MRS. ALVING

Your poor father found no outlet for the overpowering joy of life
that was in him. And I brought no brightness into his home.

OSWALD

Not even you?

MRS. ALVING

They had taught me a great deal about duties and so forth, which
I went on obstinately believing in. Everything was marked out
into duties—into my duties, and his duties, and—I am afraid I
made his home intolerable for your poor father, Oswald.

OSWALD

Why have you never spoken of this in writing to me?

MRS. ALVING

I have never before seen it in such a light that I could speak of it
to you, his son.

OSWALD

In what light did you see it, then?

MRS. ALVING   [Slowly.]

I saw only this one thing: that your father was a broken-down
man before you were born.

OSWALD   [Softly.]

Ah——!

[He rises and walks away to the window.]

MRS. ALVING

And then, day after day, I dwelt on the one thought that by rights
Regina should be at home in this house—just like my own boy.

OSWALD   [*Turning round quickly.*]
  Regina——!
REGINA   [*Springs up and asks, with bated breath.*]
  I——?
MRS. ALVING
  Yes, now you know it, both of you.
OSWALD
  Regina!
REGINA   [*To herself.*]
  So mother was that kind of woman.
MRS. ALVING
  Your mother had many good qualities, Regina.
REGINA
  Yes, but she was one of that sort, all the same. Oh, I've often
  suspected it; but—— And now, if you please, ma'am, may I be
  allowed to go away at once?
MRS. ALVING
  Do you really wish it, Regina?
REGINA
  Yes, indeed I do.
MRS. ALVING
  Of course you can do as you like; but——
OSWALD   [*Goes towards* REGINA.]
  Go away now? Your place is here.
REGINA
  Merci, Mr. Alving!—or now, I suppose, I may say Oswald. But I
  can tell you this wasn't at all what I expected.
MRS. ALVING
  Regina, I have not been frank with you——
REGINA
  No, that you haven't indeed. If I'd known that Oswald was an in-
  valid, why—— And now, too, that it can never come to anything
  serious between us—— I really can't stop out here in the coun-
  try and wear myself out nursing sick people.
OSWALD
  Not even one who is so near to you?
REGINA
  No, that I can't. A poor girl must make the best of her young

days, or she'll be left out in the cold before she knows where she
is. And I, too, have the joy of life in me, Mrs. Alving!

MRS. ALVING

Unfortunately, you have. But don't throw yourself away, Regina.

REGINA

Oh, what must be, must be. If Oswald takes after his father, I
take after my mother, I daresay.—May I ask, ma'am, if Pastor
Manders knows all this about me?

MRS. ALVING

Pastor Manders knows all about it.

REGINA   [Busied in putting on her shawl.]

Well then, I'd better make haste and get away by this steamer.
The Pastor is such a nice man to deal with; and I certainly think
I've as much right to a little of that money as he has—that brute
of a carpenter.

MRS. ALVING

You are heartily welcome to it, Regina.

REGINA   [Looks hard at her.]

I think you might have brought me up as a gentleman's daughter,
ma'am; it would have suited me better.

[Tosses her head.]

But pooh—what does it matter!

[With a bitter side glance at the corked bottle.]

I may come to drink champagne with gentlefolks yet.

MRS. ALVING

And if you ever need a home, Regina, come to me.

REGINA

No, thank you, ma'am. Pastor Manders will look after me, I
know. And if the worst comes to the worst, I know of one house
where I've every right to a place.

MRS. ALVING

Where is that?

REGINA

"Chamberlain Alving's Home."

MRS. ALVING

Regina—now I see it—you are going to your ruin.

REGINA

Oh, stuff! Good-bye.

[*She nods and goes out through the hall.*]

OSWALD   [*Stands at the window and looks out.*]

Is she gone?

MRS. ALVING

Yes.

OSWALD   [*Murmuring aside to himself.*]

I think it was a mistake, this.

MRS. ALVING   [*Goes up behind him and lays her hands on his shoulders.*]

Oswald, my dear boy——has it shaken you very much?

OSWALD   [*Turns his face towards her.*]

All that about father, do you mean?

MRS. ALVING

Yes, about your unhappy father. I am so afraid it may have been
too much for you.

OSWALD

Why should you fancy that? Of course it came upon me as a
great surprise; but it can make no real difference to me.

MRS. ALVING   [*Draws her hands away.*]

No difference! That your father was so infinitely unhappy!

OSWALD

Of course I can pity him, as I would anybody else; but——

MRS. ALVING

Nothing more! Your own father!

OSWALD   [*Impatiently.*]

Oh, "father,"——"father"! I never knew anything of father. I
remember nothing about him, except that he once made me sick.

MRS. ALVING

This is terrible to think of! Ought not a son to love his father,
whatever happens?

OSWALD

When a son has nothing to thank his father for? has never known
him? Do you really cling to that old superstition?——you who are
so enlightened in other ways?

MRS. ALVING

Can it be only a superstition——?

OSWALD

Yes; surely you can see that, mother. It's one of those notions
that are current in the world, and so——

MRS. ALVING   [*Deeply moved.*]

Ghosts!

OSWALD   [*Crossing the room.*]

Yes; you may call them ghosts.

MRS. ALVING   [*Wildly.*]

Oswald—then you don't love me, either!

OSWALD

You I know, at any rate——

MRS. ALVING

Yes, you know me; but is that all!

OSWALD

And, of course, I know how fond you are of me, and I can't but be grateful to you. And then you can be so useful to me, now that I am ill.

MRS. ALVING

Yes, cannot I, Oswald? Oh, I could almost bless the illness that has driven you home to me. For I see very plainly that you are not mine: I have to win you.

OSWALD   [*Impatiently.*]

Yes yes yes; all these are just so many phrases. You must remember that I am a sick man, mother. I can't be much taken up with other people; I have enough to do thinking about myself.

MRS. ALVING   [*In a low voice.*]

I shall be patient and easily satisfied.

OSWALD

And cheerful too, mother!

MRS. ALVING

Yes, my dear boy, you are quite right.

[*Goes towards him.*]

Have I relieved you of all remorse and self-reproach now?

OSWALD

Yes, you have. But now who will relieve me of the dread?

MRS. ALVING

The dread?

OSWALD   [*Walks across the room.*]

Regina could have been got to do it.

MRS. ALVING

I don't understand you. What is this about dread—and Regina?

OSWALD

Is it very late, mother?

MRS. ALVING

It is early morning.

[*She looks out through the conservatory.*]

The day is dawning over the mountains. And the weather is clearing, Oswald. In a little while you shall see the sun.

OSWALD

I'm glad of that. Oh, I may still have much to rejoice in and live for——

MRS. ALVING

I should think so, indeed!

OSWALD

Even if I can't work——

MRS. ALVING

Oh, you'll soon be able to work again, my dear boy—now that you haven't got all those gnawing and depressing thoughts to brood over any longer.

OSWALD

Yes, I'm glad you were able to rid me of all those fancies. And when I've got over this one thing more——

[*Sits on the sofa.*]

Now we will have a little talk, mother——

MRS. ALVING

Yes, let us.

[*She pushes an arm-chair towards the sofa, and sits down close to him.*]

OSWALD

And meantime the sun will be rising. And then you will know all. And then I shall not feel this dread any longer.

MRS. ALVING

What is it that I am to know?

OSWALD   [*Not listening to her.*]

Mother, did you not say a little while ago, that there was nothing in the world you would not do for me, if I asked you?

MRS. ALVING

Yes, indeed I said so!

OSWALD

And you'll stick to it, mother?

MRS. ALVING

You may rely on that, my dear and only boy! I have nothing in the world to live for but you alone.

OSWALD

Very well, then; now you shall hear——Mother, you have a strong, steadfast mind, I know. Now you're to sit quite still when you hear it.

MRS. ALVING

What dreadful thing can it be——?

OSWALD

You're not to scream out. Do you hear? Do you promise me that? We will sit and talk about it quietly. Do you promise me, mother?

MRS. ALVING

Yes, yes; I promise. Only speak!

OSWALD

Well, you must know that all this fatigue—and my inability to think of work—all that is not the illness itself——

MRS. ALVING

Then what is the illness itself?

OSWALD

The disease I have as my birthright—

[*He points to his forehead and adds very softly:*]

—is seated here.

MRS. ALVING   [*Almost voiceless.*]

Oswald! No—no!

OSWALD

Don't scream. I can't bear it. Yes, mother, it is seated here— waiting. And it may break out any day—at any moment.

MRS. ALVING

Oh, what horror——!

OSWALD

Now, quiet, quiet. That is how it stands with me——

MRS. ALVING   [*Springs up.*]

It's not true, Oswald! It's impossible! It cannot be so!

OSWALD

I have had one attack down there already. It was soon over. But when I came to know the state I had been in, then the dread

descended upon me, raging and ravening; and so I set off home
to you as fast as I could.

MRS. ALVING

Then this is the dread——!

OSWALD

Yes—it's so indescribably loathsome, you know. Oh, if it had
only been an ordinary mortal disease——! For I'm not so afraid
of death—though I should like to live as long as I can.

MRS. ALVING

Yes, yes, Oswald, you must!

OSWALD

But this is so unutterably loathsome. To become a little baby
again! To have to be fed! To have to—— Oh, it's not to be
spoken of!

MRS. ALVING

The child has his mother to nurse him.

OSWALD   [*Springs up.*]

No, never that! That is just what I will not have. I can't endure to
think that perhaps I should lie in that state for many years—and
get old and grey. And in the meantime you might die and leave
me.

[*Sits in* MRS. ALVING's *chair.*]

For the doctor said it wouldn't necessarily prove fatal at once.
He called it a sort of softening of the brain—or something like
that.

[*Smiles sadly.*]

I think that expression sounds so nice. It always sets me thinking
of cherry-coloured velvet—something soft and delicate to
stroke.

MRS. ALVING   [*Shrieks.*]

Oswald!

OSWALD   [*Springs up and paces the room.*]

And now you have taken Regina from me. If I could only have
had her! She would have come to the rescue, I know.

MRS. ALVING   [*Goes to him.*]

What do you mean by that, my darling boy? Is there any help in
the world that I would not give you?

OSWALD

When I got over my attack in Paris, the doctor told me that
when it comes again—and it will come—there will be no more
hope.

MRS. ALVING

He was heartless enough to——

OSWALD

I demanded it of him. I told him I had preparations to make——
[*He smiles cunningly.*]
And so I had.
[*He takes a little box from his inner breast pocket and opens it.*]
Mother, do you see this?

MRS. ALVING

What is it?

OSWALD

Morphia.

MRS. ALVING   [*Looks at him horror-struck.*]

Oswald—my boy.

OSWALD

I've scraped together twelve pilules*——

MRS. ALVING   [*Snatches at it.*]

Give me the box, Oswald.

OSWALD

Not yet, mother.
[*He hides the box again in his pocket.*]

MRS. ALVING

I shall never survive this!

OSWALD

It must be survived. Now if I'd had Regina here, I should have
told her how things stood with me—and begged her to come to
the rescue at the last. She would have done it. I know she would.

MRS. ALVING

Never!

OSWALD

When the horror had come upon me, and she saw me lying there

*Pills (French).

helpless, like a little new-born baby, impotent, lost, hopeless—
past all saving——

MRS. ALVING

Never in all the world would Regina have done this!

OSWALD

Regina would have done it. Regina was so splendidly light-
hearted. And she would soon have wearied of nursing an invalid
like me.

MRS. ALVING

Then heaven be praised that Regina is not here.

OSWALD

Well then, it is you that must come to the rescue, mother.

MRS. ALVING   [*Shrieks aloud.*]

I!

OSWALD

Who should do it if not you?

MRS. ALVING

I! your mother!

OSWALD

For that very reason.

MRS. ALVING

I, who gave you life!

OSWALD

I never asked you for life. And what sort of a life have you given
me? I will not have it! You shall take it back again!

MRS. ALVING

Help! Help!
[*She runs out into the hall.*]

OSWALD   [*Going after her.*]

Do not leave me! Where are you going?

MRS. ALVING   [*In the hall.*]

To fetch the doctor, Oswald! Let me pass!

OSWALD   [*Also outside.*]

You shall not go out. And no one shall come in.
[*The locking of a door is heard.*]

MRS. ALVING   [*Comes in again.*]

Oswald! Oswald—my child!

OSWALD   [*Follows her.*]

Have you a mother's heart for me—and yet can see me suffer from this unutterable dread?

MRS. ALVING   [*After a moment's silence, commands herself, and says:*]

Here is my hand upon it.

OSWALD

Will you——?

MRS. ALVING

If it should ever be necessary. But it will never be necessary. No, no; it is impossible.

OSWALD

Well, let us hope so. And let us live together as long as we can. Thank you, mother.

[*He seats himself in the arm-chair which* MRS. ALVING *has moved to the sofa. Day is breaking. The lamp is still burning on the table.*]

MRS. ALVING   [*Drawing near cautiously.*]

Do you feel calm now?

OSWALD

Yes.

MRS. ALVING   [*Bending over him.*]

It has been a dreadful fancy of yours, Oswald—nothing but a fancy. All this excitement has been too much for you. But now you shall have a long rest; at home with your mother, my own blessed boy. Everything you point to you shall have, just as when you were a little child.——There now. The crisis is over. You see how easily it passed! Oh, I was sure it would.——And do you see, Oswald, what a lovely day we are going to have? Brilliant sunshine! Now you can really see your home.

[*She goes to the table and puts out the lamp. Sunrise. The glacier and the snow-peaks in the background glow in the morning light.*]

OSWALD   [*Sits in the arm-chair with his back towards the landscape, without moving. Suddenly he says:*]

Mother, give me the sun.

MRS. ALVING   [*By the table, starts and looks at him.*]

What do you say?

OSWALD   [*Repeats, in a dull, toneless voice.*]

The sun. The sun.

MRS. ALVING   [*Goes to him.*]
Oswald, what is the matter with you?

OSWALD   [*Seems to shrink together in the chair; all his muscles relax; his face is expressionless, his eyes have a glassy stare.*]

MRS. ALVING   [*Quivering with terror.*]
What is this?
[*Shrieks.*]
Oswald! what is the matter with you?
[*Falls on her knees beside him and shakes him.*]
Oswald! Oswald! look at me! Don't you know me?

OSWALD   [*Tonelessly as before.*]
The sun.—The sun.

MRS. ALVING   [*Springs up in despair, entwines her hands in her hair and shrieks.*]
I cannot bear it!
[*Whispers, as though petrified*];
I cannot bear it! Never!
[*Suddenly.*]
Where has he got them?
[*Fumbles hastily in his breast.*]
Here!
[*Shrinks back a few steps and screams:*]
No; no; no!—Yes!—No; no!
[*She stands a few steps away from him with her hands twisted in her hair, and stares at him in speechless horror.*]

OSWALD   [*Sits motionless as before and says:*]
The sun.—The sun.

THE WILD DUCK

(1884)

INTRODUCTION

Written after a series of quick successes—namely, *Enemy of the People, A Doll's House*, and *Ghosts*—*The Wild Duck* (1884; *Vildanden*) must be read as a moment of pause and reflection within Ibsen's career. It is a play that recycles most of Ibsen's earlier themes and topics: a harsh truth that is being covered up with lies; the dirty secret in the past of the now successful businessman; an isolated character who is willing to force out the truth. Gregers Werle returns to his father and his poor high school friend Hialmar Ekdal and slowly learns that this friend has been coaxed into marrying Gregers's father's mistress and to bring up their illegitimate child as his own. Financially relying on Gregers's father and his own competent wife, Hialmar has created for himself a fantasy world in which he is working on a great invention when in truth he does nothing of the sort. Hialmar is not the only self-deceiver. Hialmar's father and daughter have created, in an attic, a piece of wilderness in which they go a-hunting, trying to imagine the wilderness in which the grandfather used to live and which to the granddaughter is a fascinating escape from her impoverished life. Once more, an inherited disease provides for a tragic trajectory: The daughter is slowly growing blind, an inheritance from Gregers's father to his illegitimate child. Once more, an illegitimate affair is paid for by the next generation.

All of these elements can be reassembled into a play such as Ibsen's earlier ones—but this is not what happens. Rather than celebrating the difficult search for truth and the destruction of lies, here it is the very attempt to undo these lies that wreaks havoc among these characters. The term Ibsen employs is that of the "life lie" (*livslögnen*), implying that a certain amount of self-deception is necessary to bear life on this earth. A misguided idealist such as Gregers, who will have the truth no matter what the cost, only creates more misery for everyone. Indeed, Gregers seems like an Ibsenite character run amok, a preacher of truth who takes no prisoners and risks the happiness of everyone in the process.

Contemporary audiences were stunned. Had not Ibsen been propagating the virtues of ruthless criticism and violent revelations of unpleasant truths? Through *The Wild Duck* Ibsen responded to what he perceived to be a reductive image of himself as enemy of the home, what Shaw would later call "Ibsenism"—the simplistic understanding of his work as always out to shock the audience, always advocating destructive critique. Instead, *The Wild Duck* reminds us that from his early *Peer Gynt* to the late *The Master Builder*, Ibsen is more interested in analyzing the workings of self-deception than in undoing it. The whole Ekdal family is an exercise in living on imagination and fantasy. When the Ekdals go into the winter garden to play nature around the domesticated wild duck they keep there, their confined revels are the bourgeois counterpart to Gynt's excessive dances with the trolls. After many years of realist discipline, Ibsen here returns to his earlier interest in theatricality, masks, and deception. In this sense, *The Wild Duck* is not only a correction of a widespread misconception of Ibsen as the ruthless detector of bourgeois lies, but also of his strictly realist style. He did not allow himself to break with realism altogether, but he created a limited space in which wild fantasies may dwell.

The unusual setup whereby the stage has the poor drawing room open out onto the enclosed space of fantasy wilderness has inspired directors and set designers. For example, the first great naturalist director, André Antoine, staged *The Wild Duck* in 1891 with great attention to objects and set, turning it into a case study in naturalism. Set designers realized that everything in this play hinges on the contrast between inner and outer space, which Ibsen also detailed in his extensive stage directions. The entire play lives by these objects and how they are employed: the old uniform of Hialmar's grandfather; his rifles; the decoration of the winter garden; the old books and maps; the work tools in the front room that doubles as a photography studio. While the characters in *The Wild Duck* are somewhat less complex than those in other of Ibsen's plays, this perfect play for stage designers has inspired many realist productions throughout the twentieth century, including Halvdan Christensen's detailed production at the Nationaltheatret in Oslo in 1949. Even productions that are not realist address the centrality of space and stage props in this play, in response to the challenge posed by *The Wild Duck*, a play that calls for a theater of objects.

—Martin Puchner

CHARACTERS

WERLE, a merchant, manufacturer, etc.
GREGERS WERLE, his son.
OLD EKDAL.
HIALMAR EKDAL, his son, a photographer.
GINA EKDAL, Hialmar's wife.
HEDVIG, their daughter, a girl of fourteen.
MRS. SÖRBY, Werle's housekeeper.
RELLING, a doctor.
MOLVIK, a student of theology.
GRÅBERG, Werle's bookkeeper.
PETTERSEN, Werle's servant.
JENSEN, a hired waiter.
A FLABBY GENTLEMAN.
A THIN-HAIRED GENTLEMAN.
A SHORT-SIGHTED GENTLEMAN.
Six other gentlemen, guests at Werle's dinner-party.
Several hired waiters.

The first act passes in Werle's house, the remaining acts at Hialmar Ekdal's.

ACT FIRST

At WERLE'S house. A richly and comfortably furnished study; bookcases and upholstered furniture; a writing-table, with papers and documents, in the centre of the room; lighted lamps with green shades, giving a subdued light. At the back, open folding-doors with curtains drawn back. Within is seen a large and handsome room, brilliantly lighted with lamps and branching candlesticks. In front, on the right (in the study), a small baize door leads into WERLE'S office. On the left, in front, a fireplace with a glowing coal fire, and farther back a double door leading into the dining-room.

WERLE'S servant, PETTERSEN, in livery, and JENSEN, the hired waiter, in black, are putting the study in order. In the large room, two or three other hired waiters are moving about, arranging things and lighting more candles. From the dining-room, the hum of conversation and laughter of many voices are heard; a glass is tapped with a knife; silence follows, and a toast is proposed; shouts of "Bravo!" and then again a buzz of conversation.

PETTERSEN   [Lights a lamp on the chimney-place and places a shade over it.]
    Hark to them, Jensen! now the old man's on his legs holding a long palaver about Mrs. Sörby.
JENSEN   [Pushing forward an arm-chair.]
    Is it true, what folks say, that they're—very good friends, eh?
PETTERSON
    Lord knows.
JENSEN
    I've heard tell as he's been a lively customer in his day.
PETTERSON
    May be.
JENSEN
    And he's giving this spread in honour of his son, they say.

PETTERSEN

> Yes. His son came home yesterday.

JENSEN

> This is the first time I ever heard as Mr. Werle had a son.

PETTERSEN

> Oh yes, he has a son, right enough. But he's a fixture, as you might say, up at the Höidal works. He's never once come to town all the years I've been in service here.

A WAITER   [*In the doorway of the other room.*]

> Pettersen, here's an old fellow wanting——

PETTERSEN   [*Mutters.*]

> The devil—who's this now?

OLD EKDAL *appears from the right, in the inner room. He is dressed in a threadbare overcoat with a high collar; he wears woollen mittens, and carries in his hand a stick and a fur cap. Under his arm, a brown paper parcel. Dirty red-brown wig and small grey moustache.*

PETTERSEN   [*Goes towards him.*]

> Good Lord—what do you want here?

EKDAL   [*In the doorway.*]

> Must get into the office, Pettersen.

PETTERSEN

> The office was closed an hour ago, and——

EKDAL

> So they told me at the front door. But Gråberg's in there still. Let me slip in this way, Pettersen; there's a good fellow.
> [*Points towards the baize door.*]
> It's not the first time I've come this way.

PETTERSEN

> Well, you may pass.
> [*Opens the door.*]
> But mind you go out again the proper way, for we've got company.

EKDAL

> I know, I know—h'm! Thanks, Pettersen, good old friend! Thanks!
> [*Mutters softly.*]
> Ass!

[*He goes into the office;* PETTERSON *shuts the door after him.*]

JENSEN

Is he one of the office people?

PETTERSEN

No, he's only an outside hand that does odd jobs of copying. But he's been a tip-topper in his day, has old Ekdal.

JENSEN

You can see he's been through a lot.

PETTERSEN

Yes; he was an army officer, you know.

JENSEN

You don't say so?

PETTERSEN

No mistake about it. But then he went into the timber trade or something of the sort. They say he once played Mr. Werle a very nasty trick. They were partners in the Höidal works at the time. Oh, I know old Ekdal well, I do. Many a nip of bitters and bottle of ale we two have drunk at Madam Eriksen's.

JENSEN

He don't look as if he'd much to stand treat with.

PETTERSEN

Why, bless you, Jensen, it's me that stands treat. I always think there's no harm in being a bit civil to folks that have seen better days.

JENSEN

Did he go bankrupt then?

PETTERSEN

Worse than that. He went to prison.

JENSEN

To prison!

PETTERSEN

Or perhaps it was the Penitentiary.

[*Listens.*]

Sh! They're leaving the table.

The dining-room door is thrown open from within, by a couple of waiters. MRS. SÖRBY *comes out conversing with two gentlemen. Gradually the whole company follows, amongst them* WERLE. *Last come* HIALMAR EKDAL *and* GREGERS WERLE.

MRS. SÖRBY   [*In passing, to the servant.*]

Tell them to serve the coffee in the music-room, Pettersen.

PETTERSEN

Very well, Madam.

[*She goes with the two Gentlemen, into the inner room, and thence out to the right.* PETTERSEN *and* JENSEN *go out the same way.*]

A FLABBY GENTLEMAN   [*To a* THIN-HAIRED GENTLEMAN.]

Whew! What a dinner!—It was no joke to do it justice!

THE THIN-HAIRED GENTLEMAN

Oh, with a little good-will one can get through a lot in three hours.

THE FLABBY GENTLEMAN

Yes, but afterwards, afterwards, my dear Chamberlain!

A THIRD GENTLEMAN

I hear the coffee and maraschino* are to be served in the music-room.

THE FLABBY GENTLEMAN

Bravo! Then perhaps Mrs. Sörby will play us something.

THE THIN-HAIRED GENTLEMAN   [*In a low voice.*]

I hope Mrs. Sörby mayn't play us a tune we don't like, one of these days!

THE FLABBY GENTLEMAN

Oh no, not she! Bertha will never turn against her old friends.

[*They laugh and pass into the inner room.*]

WERLE   [*In a low voice, dejectedly.*]

I don't think anybody noticed it, Gregers.

GREGERS   [*Looks at him.*]

Noticed what?

WERLE

Did you not notice it either?

GREGERS

What do you mean?

WERLE

We were thirteen at table.

GREGERS

Indeed? Were there thirteen of us?

*An Italian cherry liqueur.

WERLE   [*Glances towards* HIALMAR EKDAL.]

> Our usual party is twelve.
>
> [*To the others.*]
>
> This way, gentlemen!
>
> [WERLE *and the others, all except* HIALMAR *and* GREGERS, *go out by the back, to the right.*]

HIALMAR   [*Who has overheard the conversation.*]

> You ought not to have invited me, Gregers.

GREGERS

> What! Not ask my best and only friend to a party supposed to be in my honour——?

HIALMAR

> But I don't think your father likes it. You see I am quite outside his circle.

GREGERS

> So I hear. But I wanted to see you and have a talk with you, and I certainly shan't be staying long.——Ah, we two old schoolfellows have drifted far apart from each other. It must be sixteen or seventeen years since we met.

HIALMAR

> Is it so long?

GREGERS

> It is indeed. Well, how goes it with you? You look well. You have put on flesh, and grown almost stout.

HIALMAR

> Well, "stout" is scarcely the word; but I daresay I look a little more of a man than I used to.

GREGERS

> Yes, you do; your outer man is in first-rate condition.

HIALMAR   [*In a tone of gloom.*]

> Ah, but the inner man! That is a very different matter, I can tell you! Of course you know of the terrible catastrophe that has befallen me and mine since last we met.

GREGERS   [*More softly.*]

> How are things going with your father now?

HIALMAR

> Don't let us talk of it, old fellow. Of course my poor unhappy father lives with me. He hasn't another soul in the world to care

for him. But you can understand that this is a miserable subject for me.—Tell me, rather, how you have been getting on up at the works.

GREGERS

I have had a delightfully lonely time of it—plenty of leisure to think and think about things. Come over here; we may as well make ourselves comfortable.

[*He seats himself in an arm-chair by the fire and draws* HIALMAR *down into another alongside of it.*]

HIALMAR   [*Sentimentally.*]

After all, Gregers, I thank you for inviting me to your father's table; for I take it as a sign that you have got over your feeling against me.

GREGERS   [*Surprised.*]

How could you imagine I had any feeling against you?

HIALMAR

You had at first, you know.

GREGERS

How at first?

HIALMAR

After the great misfortune. It was natural enough that you should. Your father was within an ace of being drawn into that— well, that terrible business.

GREGERS

Why should that give me any feeling against you? Who can have put that into your head?

HIALMAR

I know it did, Gregers; your father told me so himself.

GREGERS   [*Starts.*]

My father! Oh indeed. H'm.—Was that why you never let me hear from you?—not a single word.

HIALMAR

Yes.

GREGERS

Not even when you made up your mind to become a photographer?

HIALMAR

Your father said I had better not write to you at all, about anything.

GREGERS   [*Looking straight before him.*]

Well well, perhaps he was right.——But tell me now, Hialmar: are
you pretty well satisfied with your present position?

HIALMAR   [*With a little sigh.*]

Oh yes, I am; I have really no cause to complain. At first, as you
may guess, I felt it a little strange. It was such a totally new state
of things for me. But of course my whole circumstances were
totally changed. Father's utter, irretrievable ruin,——the shame
and disgrace of it, Gregers——

GREGERS   [*Affected.*]

Yes, yes; I understand.

HIALMAR

I couldn't think of remaining at college; there wasn't a shilling to
spare; on the contrary, there were debts—mainly to your father I
believe——

GREGERS

H'm——

HIALMAR

In short, I thought it best to break, once for all, with my old
surroundings and associations. It was your father that specially
urged me to it; and since he interested himself so much in me——

GREGERS

My father did?

HIALMAR

Yes, you surely knew that, didn't you? Where do you suppose I
found the money to learn photography, and to furnish a studio
and make a start? All that costs a pretty penny, I can tell you.

GREGERS

And my father provided the money?

HIALMAR

Yes, my dear fellow, didn't you know? I understood him to say he
had written to you about it.

GREGERS

Not a word about his part in the business. He must have

forgotten it. Our correspondence has always been purely a
business one. So it was my father that——!

HIALMAR

Yes, certainly. He didn't wish it to be generally known; but he it
was. And of course it was he, too, that put me in a position to
marry. Don't you—don't you know about that either?

GREGERS

No, I haven't heard a word of it.

[*Shakes him by the arm.*]

But, my dear Hialmar, I can't tell you what pleasure all this gives
me—pleasure, and self-reproach. I have perhaps done my father
injustice after all—in some things. This proves that he has a
heart. It shows a sort of compunction——

HIALMAR

Compunction——?

GREGERS

Yes, yes—whatever you like to call it. Oh, I can't tell you how
glad I am to hear this of father. —So you are a married man,
Hialmar! That is further than I shall ever get. Well, I hope you
are happy in your married life?

HIALMAR

Yes, thoroughly happy. She is as good and capable a wife as any
man could wish for. And she is by no means without culture.

GREGERS   [*Rather surprised.*]

No, of course not.

HIALMAR

You see, life is itself an education. Her daily intercourse with
me—— And then we know one or two rather remarkable men,
who come a good deal about us. I assure you, you would hardly
know Gina again.

GREGERS

Gina?

HIALMAR

Yes; had you forgotten that her name was Gina?

GREGERS

Whose name? I haven't the slightest idea——

HIALMAR

Don't you remember that she used to be in service here?

GREGERS [*Looks at him.*]

Is it Gina Hansen———?

HIALMAR

Yes, of course it is Gina Hansen.

GREGERS

———who kept house for us during the last year of my mother's illness?

HIALMAR

Yes, exactly. But, my dear friend, I'm quite sure your father told you that I was married.

GREGERS [*Who has risen.*]

Oh yes, he mentioned it; but not that———

[*Walking about the room.*]

Stay—perhaps he did—now that I think of it. My father always writes such short letters.

[*Half seats himself on the arm of the chair.*]

Now, tell me, Hialmar—this is interesting—how did you come to know Gina—your wife?

HIALMAR

The simplest thing in the world. You know Gina did not stay here long; everything was so much upset at that time, owing to your mother's illness and so forth, that Gina was not equal to it all; so she gave notice and left. That was the year before your mother died—or it may have been the same year.

GREGERS

It was the same year. I was up at the works then. But afterwards———?

HIALMAR

Well, Gina lived at home with her mother, Madam Hansen, an excellent hard-working woman, who kept a little eating-house. She had a room to let too; a very nice comfortable room.

GREGERS

And I suppose you were lucky enough to secure it?

HIALMAR

Yes; in fact, it was your father that recommended it to me. So it was there, you see, that I really came to know Gina.

GREGERS

And then you got engaged?

HIALMAR

Yes. It doesn't take young people long to fall in love——;
h'm——

GREGERS   [*Rises and moves about a little.*]

Tell me: was it after your engagement—was it then that my father—I mean was it then that you began to take up photography?

HIALMAR

Yes, precisely. I wanted to make a start, and to set up house as
soon as possible; and your father and I agreed that this
photography business was the readiest way. Gina thought so too.
Oh, and there was another thing in its favour, by-the-bye: it
happened, luckily, that Gina had learnt to retouch.

GREGERS

That chimed in marvellously.

HIALMAR   [*Pleased, rises.*]

Yes, didn't it? Don't you think it was a marvellous piece of luck?

GREGERS

Oh, unquestionably. My father seems to have been almost a kind
of providence for you.

HIALMAR   [*With emotion.*]

He did not forsake his old friend's son in the hour of his need.
For he has a heart, you see.

MRS. SÖRBY   [*Enters, arm-in-arm with* WERLE.]

Nonsense, my dear Mr. Werle; you mustn't stop there any longer
staring at all the lights. It's very bad for you.

WERLE   [*Lets go her arm and passes his hand over his eyes.*]

I daresay you are right.

[PETTERSEN *and* JENSEN *carry round refreshment trays.*]

MRS. SÖRBY   [*To the Guests in the other room.*]

This way, if you please, gentlemen. Whoever wants a glass of
punch must be so good as to come in here.

THE FLABBY GENTLEMAN   [*Comes up to* MRS. SÖRBY.]

Surely, it isn't possible that you have suspended our cherished
right to smoke?

MRS. SÖRBY

Yes. No smoking here, in Mr. Werle's sanctum, Chamberlain.

THE THIN-HAIRED GENTLEMAN
When did you enact these stringent amendments on the cigar law, Mrs. Sörby?

MRS. SÖRBY
After the last dinner, Chamberlain, when certain persons permitted themselves to overstep the mark.

THE THIN-HAIRED GENTLEMAN
And may one never overstep the mark a little bit, Madame Bertha? Not the least little bit?

MRS. SÖRBY
Not in any respect whatsoever, Mr. Balle.
[*Most of the Guests have assembled in the study; servants hand round glasses of punch.*]

WERLE   [*To* HIALMAR, *who is standing beside a table.*]
What are you studying so intently, Ekdal?

HIALMAR
Only an album, Mr. Werle.

THE THIN-HAIRED GENTLEMAN   [*Who is wandering about.*]
Ah, photographs! They are quite in your line of course.

THE FLABBY GENTLEMAN   [*In an arm-chair.*]
Haven't you brought any of your own with you?

HIALMAR
No, I haven't.

THE FLABBY GENTLEMAN
You ought to have; it's very good for the digestion to sit and look at pictures.

THE THIN-HAIRED GENTLEMAN
And it contributes to the entertainment, you know.

THE SHORT-SIGHTED GENTLEMAN
And all contributions are thankfully received.

MRS. SÖRBY
The Chamberlains think that when one is invited out to dinner, one ought to exert oneself a little in return, Mr. Ekdal.

THE FLABBY GENTLEMAN
Where one dines so well, that duty becomes a pleasure.

THE THIN-HAIRED GENTLEMAN
And when it's a case of the struggle for existence, you know——

MRS. SÖRBY
    I quite agree with you!
    [*They continue the conversation, with laughter and joking.*]
GREGERS   [*Softly.*]
    You must join in, Hialmar.
HIALMAR   [*Writhing.*]
    What am I to talk about?
THE FLABBY GENTLEMAN
    Don't you think, Mr. Werle, that Tokay may he considered one of
the more wholesome sorts of wine?
WERLE   [*By the fire.*]
    I can answer for the Tokay you had to-day, at any rate; it's of one
of the very finest seasons. Of course you would notice that.
THE FLABBY GENTLEMAN
    Yes, it had a remarkably delicate flavour.
HIALMAR   [*Shyly.*]
    Is there any difference between the seasons?
THE FLABBY GENTLEMAN   [*Laughs.*]
    Come! That's good!
WERLE   [*Smiles.*]
    It really doesn't pay to set fine wine before you.
THE THIN-HAIRED GENTLEMAN
    Tokay is like photographs, Mr. Ekdal: they both need sunshine.
Am I not right?
HIALMAR
    Yes, light is important no doubt.
MRS. SÖRBY
    And it's exactly the same with Chamberlains—they, too, depend
very much on sunshine,* as the saying is.
THE THIN-HAIRED GENTLEMAN
    Oh fie! That's a very threadbare sarcasm!
THE SHORT-SIGHTED GENTLEMAN
    Mrs. Sörby is coming out——
THE FLABBY GENTLEMAN
    ——and at our expense, too.
    [*Holds up his finger reprovingly.*]

*The "sunshine" of Court favour. (Translator's note)

Oh, Madame Bertha, Madame Bertha!

MRS. SÖRBY

Yes, and there's not the least doubt that the seasons differ greatly.
The old vintages are the finest.

THE SHORT-SIGHTED GENTLEMAN

Do you reckon me among the old vintages?

MRS. SÖRBY

Oh, far from it.

THE THIN-HAIRED GENTLEMAN

There now! But me, dear Mrs. Sörby——?

THE FLABBY GENTLEMAN

Yes, and me? What vintage should you say that we belong to?

MRS. SÖRBY

Why, to the sweet vintages, gentlemen.

[*She sips a glass of punch. The gentlemen laugh and flirt with her.*]

WERLE

Mrs. Sörby can always find a loop-hole—when she wants to. Fill
your glasses, gentlemen! Pettersen, will you see to it——!
Gregers, suppose we have a glass together.

[GREGERS *does not move.*]

Won't you join us, Ekdal? I found no opportunity of drinking
with you at table.

[GRÅBERG, *the Bookkeeper, looks in at the baize door.*]

GRÅBERG

Excuse me, sir, but I can't get out.

WERLE

Have you been locked in again?

GRÅBERG

Yes, and Flakstad has carried off the keys.

WERLE

Well, you can pass out this way.

GRÅBERG

But there's some one else——

WERLE

All right; come through, both of you. Don't be afraid.

[GRÅBERG *and* OLD EKDAL *come out of the office.*]

WERLE   [*Involuntarily.*]

Ugh!

[*The laughter and talk among the Guests cease.* HIALMAR *starts at the sight of his father, puts down his glass, and turns towards the fireplace.*]

EKDAL   [*Does not look up, but makes little bows to both sides as he passes, murmuring.*]

Beg pardon, come the wrong way. Door locked—door locked. Beg pardon.

[*He and* GRÅBERG *go out by the back, to the right.*]

WERLE   [*Between his teeth.*]

That idiot Gråberg!

GREGERS   [*Open-mouthed and staring, to* HIALMAR.]

Why surely that wasn't——!

THE FLABBY GENTLEMAN

What's the matter? Who was it?

GREGERS

Oh, nobody, only the bookkeeper and some one with him.

THE SHORT-SIGHTED GENTLEMAN   [*To* HIALMAR]

Did you know that man?

HIALMAR

I don't know—I didn't notice——

THE FLABBY GENTLEMAN

What the deuce has come over every one?

[*He joins another group who are talking softly.*]

MRS. SÖRBY   [*Whispers to the Servant.*]

Give him something to take with him;—something good, mind.

PETTERSEN   [*Nods.*]

I'll see to it.

[*Goes out.*]

GREGERS   [*Softly and with emotion, to* HIALMAR.]

So that was really he!

HIALMAR

Yes.

GREGERS

And you could stand there and deny that you knew him!

HIALMAR   [*Whispers vehemently.*]

But how could I——!

GREGERS

——acknowledge your own father?

HIALMAR   [*With pain.*]

 Oh, if you were in my place——

 [*The conversation amongst the Guests, which has been carried on in a low tone, now swells into constrained joviality.*]

THE THIN-HAIRED GENTLEMAN   [*Approaching* HIALMAR *and* GREGERS *in a friendly manner.*]

 Aha! Reviving old college memories, eh? Don't you smoke, Mr. Ekdal? May I give you a light? Oh, by-the-bye, we mustn't——

HIALMAR

 No, thank you, I won't——

THE FLABBY GENTLEMAN

 Haven't you a nice little poem you could recite to us, Mr. Ekdal? You used to recite so charmingly.

HIALMAR

 I am sorry I can't remember anything.

THE FLABBY GENTLEMAN

 Oh, that's a pity. Well, what shall we do, Balle?

 [*Both Gentlemen move away and pass into the other room.*]

HIALMAR   [*Gloomily.*]

 Gregers—I am going! When a man has felt the crushing hand of Fate, you see—— Say good-bye to your father for me.

GREGERS

 Yes, yes. Are you going straight home?

HIALMAR

 Yes. Why?

GREGERS

 Oh, because I may perhaps look in on you later.

HIALMAR

 No, you mustn't do that. You must not come to my home. Mine is a melancholy abode, Gregers; especially after a splendid banquet like this. We can always arrange to meet somewhere in the town.

MRS. SÖRBY   [*Who has quietly approached.*]

 Are you going, Ekdal?

HIALMAR

 Yes.

MRS. SÖRBY

 Remember me to Gina.

HIALMAR

Thanks.

MRS. SÖRBY

And say I am coming up to see her one of these days.

HIALMAR

Yes, thank you.

[*To* GREGERS.]

Stay here; I will slip out unobserved.

[*He saunters away, then into the other room, and so out to the right.*]

MRS. SÖRBY   [*Softly to the Servant, who has come back.*]

Well, did you give the old man something?

PETTERSEN

Yes; I sent him off with a bottle of cognac.

MRS. SÖRBY

Oh, you might have thought of something better than that.

PETTERSEN

Oh no, Mrs. Sörby; cognac is what he likes best in the world.

THE FLABBY GENTLEMAN   [*In the doorway with a sheet of music in his hand.*]

Shall we play a duet, Mrs. Sörby?

MRS. SÖRBY

Yes, suppose we do.

THE GUESTS

Bravo, bravo!

[*She goes with all the Guests through the back room, out to the right. GREGERS remains standing by the fire. WERLE is looking for something on the writing-table, and appears to wish that GREGERS would go; as GREGERS does not move, WERLE goes towards the door.*]

GREGERS

Father, won't you stay a moment?

WERLE   [*Stops.*]

What is it?

GREGERS

I must have a word with you.

WERLE

Can it not wait till we are alone?

GREGERS

No, it cannot; for perhaps we shall never be alone together.

WERLE   [*Drawing nearer.*]

What do you mean by that?

[*During what follows, the pianoforte is faintly heard from the distant music-room.*]

GREGERS

How has that family been allowed to go so miserably to the wall?

WERLE

You mean the Ekdals, I suppose.

GREGERS

Yes, I mean the Ekdals. Lieutenant Ekdal was once so closely associated with you.

WERLE

Much too closely; I have felt that to my cost for many a year. It is thanks to him that I—yes *I*—have had a kind of slur cast upon my reputation.

GREGERS   [*Softly.*]

Are you sure that he alone was to blame?

WERLE

Who else do you suppose——?

GREGERS

You and he acted together in that affair of the forests——

WERLE

But was it not Ekdal that drew the map of the tracts we had bought—that fraudulent map! It was he who felled all that timber illegally on Government ground. In fact, the whole management was in his hands. I was quite in the dark as to what Lieutenant Ekdal was doing.

GREGERS

Lieutenant Ekdal himself seems to have been very much in the dark as to what he was doing.

WERLE

That may be. But the fact remains that he was found guilty and I acquitted.

GREGERS

Yes, I know that nothing was proved against you.

WERLE

Acquittal is acquittal. Why do you rake up these old miseries that turned my hair grey before its time? Is that the sort of thing you have been brooding over up there, all these years? I can assure you, Gregers, here in the town the whole story has been forgotten long ago——so far as *I* am concerned.

GREGERS

But that unhappy Ekdal family.

WERLE

What would you have had me do for the people? When Ekdal came out of prison he was a broken-down being, past all help. There are people in the world who dive to the bottom the moment they get a couple of slugs in their body, and never come to the surface again. You may take my word for it, Gregers, I have done all I could without positively laying myself open to all sorts of suspicion and gossip——

GREGERS

Suspicion——? Oh, I see.

WERLE

I have given Ekdal copying to do for the office, and I pay him far, far more for it than his work is worth——

GREGERS   [*Without looking at him.*]

H'm; that I don't doubt.

WERLE

You laugh? Do you think I am not telling you the truth. Well, I certainly can't refer you to my books, for I never enter payments of that sort.

GREGERS   [*Smiles coldly.*]

No, there are certain payments it is best to keep no account of.

WERLE   [*Taken aback.*]

What do you mean by that?

GREGERS   [*Mustering up courage.*]

Have you entered what it cost you to have Hialmar Ekdal taught photography?

WERLE

I? How "entered" it?

GREGERS

I have learnt that it was you who paid for his training. And I have learnt, too, that it was you who enabled him to set up house so comfortably.

WERLE

Well, and yet you talk as though I had done nothing for the Ekdals! I can assure you these people have cost me enough in all conscience.

GREGERS

Have you entered any of these expenses in your books?

WERLE

Why do you ask?

GREGERS

Oh, I have my reasons. Now tell me: when you interested yourself so warmly in your old friend's son—it was just before his marriage, was it not?

WERLE

Why, deuce take it—after all these years, how can I——?

GREGERS

You wrote me a letter about that time—a business letter, of course; and in a postscript you mentioned—quite briefly—that Hialmar Ekdal had married a Miss Hansen.

WERLE

Yes, that was quite right. That was her name.

GREGERS

But you did not mention that this Miss Hansen was Gina Hansen—our former housekeeper.

WERLE   [*With a forced laugh of derision.*]

No; to tell the truth, it didn't occur to me that you were so particularly interested in our former housekeeper.

GREGERS

No more I was. But

[*lowers his voice*]

there were others in this house who were particularly interested in her.

WERLE

What do you mean by that?

[*Flaring up.*]

You are not alluding to me, I hope?

GREGERS   [*Softly but firmly.*]

Yes, I am alluding to you.

WERLE

And you dare——You presume to—— How can that ungrateful hound—that photographer fellow—how dare he go making such insinuations!

GREGERS

Hialmar has never breathed a word about this. I don't believe he has the faintest suspicion of such a thing.

WERLE

Then where have you got it from? Who can have put such notions in your head?

GREGERS

My poor unhappy mother told me; and that the very last time I saw her.

WERLE

Your mother! I might have known as much! You and she—you always held together. It was she who turned you against me, from the first.

GREGERS

No, it was all that she had to suffer and submit to, until she broke down and came to such a pitiful end.

WERLE

Oh, she had nothing to suffer or submit to; not more than most people, at all events. But there's no getting on with morbid, overstrained creatures—that I have learnt to my cost.—And you could go on nursing such a suspicion—burrowing into all sorts of old rumours and slanders against your own father! I must say, Gregers, I really think that at your age you might find something more useful to do.

GREGERS

Yes, it is high time.

WERLE

Then perhaps your mind would be easier than it seems to be now. What can be your object in remaining up at the works, year out and year in, drudging away like a common clerk, and not drawing a farthing more than the ordinary monthly wage? It is downright folly.

GREGERS

Ah, if I were only sure of that.

WERLE

> I understand you well enough. You want to be independent; you won't be beholden to me for anything. Well, now there happens to be an opportunity for you to become independent, your own master in everything.

GREGERS

> Indeed? In what way——?

WERLE

> When I wrote you insisting on your coming to town at once—h'm——

GREGERS

> Yes, what is it you really want of me? I have been waiting all day to know.

WERLE

> I want to propose that you should enter the firm, as partner.

GREGERS

> I Join your firm? As partner?

WERLE

> Yes. It would not involve our being constantly together. You could take over the business here in town, and I should move up to the works.

GREGERS

> You would?

WERLE

> The fact is, I am not so fit for work as I once was. I am obliged to spare my eyes, Gregers; they have begun to trouble me.

GREGERS

> They have always been weak.

WERLE

> Not as they are now. And besides, circumstances might possibly make it desirable for me to live up there—for a time, at any rate.

GREGERS

> That is certainly quite a new idea to me.

WERLE

> Listen, Gregers: there are many things that stand between us; but we are father and son after all. We ought surely to be able to come to some sort of understanding with each other.

GREGERS

Outwardly, you mean, of course?

WERLE

Well, even that would be something. Think it over, Gregers. Don't you think it ought to be possible? Eh?

GREGERS   [*Looking at him coldly.*]

There is something behind all this.

WERLE

How so?

GREGERS

You want to make use of me in some way.

WERLE

In such a close relationship as ours, the one can always be useful to the other.

GREGERS

Yes, so people say.

WERLE

I want very much to have you at home with me for a time. I am a lonely man Gregers; I have always felt lonely, all my life through; but most of all now that I am getting up in years. I feel the need of some one about me——

GREGERS

You have Mrs. Sörby.

WERLE

Yes, I have her; and she has become, I may say, almost indispensable to me. She is lively and even-tempered; she brightens up the house; and that is a very great thing for me.

GREGERS

Well then, you have everything just as you wish it.

WERLE

Yes, but I am afraid it can't last. A woman so situated may easily find herself in a false position, in the eyes of the world. For that matter it does a man no good, either.

GREGERS

Oh, when a man gives such dinners as you give, he can risk a great deal.

WERLE

Yes, but how about the woman, Gregers? I fear she won't accept

the situation much longer; and even if she did—even if, out of
attachment to me, she were to take her chance of gossip and
scandal and all that——? Do you think, Gregers—you with
your strong sense of justice——

GREGERS   [*Interrupts him.*]

Tell me in one word: are you thinking of marrying her?

WERLE

Suppose I were thinking of it? What then?

GREGERS

That's what I say: what then?

WERLE

Should you be inflexibly opposed to it!

GREGERS

Not at all. Not by any means.

WERLE

I was not sure whether your devotion to your mother's
memory——

GREGERS

I am not overstrained.

WERLE

Well, whatever you may or may not be, at all events you have
lifted a great weight from my mind. I am extremely pleased that
I can reckon on your concurrence in this matter.

GREGERS   [*Looking intently at him.*]

Now I see the use you want to put me to.

WERLE

Use to put you to? What an expression!

GREGERS

Oh, don't let us be nice in our choice of words—not when we
are alone together, at any rate.

[*With a short laugh.*]

Well well! So this is what made it absolutely essential that I
should come to town in person. For the sake of Mrs. Sörby, we
are to get up a pretence at family life in the house—a tableau* of
filial affection! That will be something new indeed.

---

*Image (French); here it means display, as in display of affection.

WERLE

How dare you speak in that tone!

GREGERS

Was there ever any family life here? Never since I can remember. But now, forsooth, your plans demand something of the sort. No doubt it will have an excellent effect when it is reported that the son has hastened home, on the wings of filial piety, to the grey-haired father's wedding-feast. What will then remain of all the rumours as to the wrongs the poor dead mother had to submit to? Not a vestige. Her son annihilates them at one stroke.

WERLE

Gregers—I believe there is no one in the world you detest as you do me.

GREGERS   [Softly.]

I have seen you at too close quarters.

WERLE

You have seen me with your mother's eyes.

[Lowers his voice a little.]

But you should remember that her eyes were—clouded now and then.

GREGERS   [Quivering.]

I see what you are hinting at. But who was to blame for mother's unfortunate weakness? Why you, and all those——! The last of them was this woman that you palmed off upon Hialmar Ekdal, when you were—— Ugh!

WERLE   [Shrugs his shoulders.]

Word for word as if it were your mother speaking!

GREGERS   [Without heeding.]

And there he is now, with his great, confiding, childlike mind, compassed about with all this treachery—living under the same roof with such a creature, and never dreaming that what he calls his home is built upon a lie!

[Comes a step nearer.]

When I look back upon your past, I seem to see a battle-field with shattered lives on every hand.

WERLE

I begin to think the chasm that divides us is too wide.

GREGERS [*Bowing, with self-command.*]

    So I have observed; and therefore I take my hat and go.

WERLE

    You are going! Out of the house?

GREGERS

    Yes. For at last I see my mission in life.

WERLE

    What mission?

GREGERS

    You would only laugh if I told you.

WERLE

    A lonely man doesn't laugh so easily, Gregers.

GREGERS [*Pointing towards the background.*]

    Look, father,—the Chamberlains are playing blind-man's-buff
with Mrs. Sörby.—Good-night and good-bye.

    [*He goes out by the back to the right. Sounds of laughter and merriment
from the company, who are now visible in the outer room.*]

WERLE [*Muttering contemptuously after* GREGERS.]

    Ha———! Poor wretch—and he says he is not overstrained!

ACT SECOND

HIALMAR EKDAL's *studio, a good-sized room, evidently in the top storey of the building. On the right, a sloping roof of large panes of glass, half-covered by a blue curtain. In the right-hand corner, at the back, the entrance door; farther forward, on the same side, a door leading to the sitting-room. Two doors on the opposite side, and between them an iron stove. At the back, a wide double sliding-door. The studio is plainly but comfortably fitted up and furnished. Between the doors on the right, standing out a little from the wall, a sofa with a table and some chairs; on the table a lighted lamp with a shade; beside the stove an old arm-chair. Photographic instruments and apparatus of different kinds lying about the room. Against the back wall, to the left of the double door, stands a bookcase containing a few books, boxes, and bottles of chemicals, instruments, tools, and other objects. Photographs and small articles, such as camel's-hair pencils, paper, and so forth, lie on the table.*

GINA EKDAL *sits on a chair by the table, sewing.* HEDVIG *is sitting on the sofa, with her hands shading her eyes and her thumbs in her ears, reading a book.*

GINA   [*Glances once or twice at* HEDVIG, *as if with secret anxiety; then says:*]
    Hedvig!
HEDVIG   [*Does not hear.*]
GINA   [*Repeats more loudly.*]
    Hedvig!
HEDVIG   [*Takes away her hands and looks up.*]
    Yes, mother?
GINA
    Hedvig dear, you mustn't sit reading any longer now.
HEDVIG
    Oh mother, mayn't I read a little more? Just a little bit?

GINA

No no, you must put away your book now. Father doesn't like it; he never reads hisself in the evening.

HEDVIG [*Shuts the book.*]

No, father doesn't care much about reading.

GINA [*Puts aside her sewing and takes up a lead pencil and a little account-book from the table.*]

Can you remember how much we paid for the butter to-day?

HEDVIG

It was one crown sixty-five.

GINA

That's right.

[*Puts it down.*]

It's terrible what a lot of butter we get through in this house. Then there was the smoked sausage, and the cheese—let me see—

[*Writes.*]

—and the ham—

[*Adds up.*]

Yes, that makes just———

HEDVIG

And then the beer.

GINA

Yes, to be sure.

[*Writes.*]

How it do mount up! But we can't manage with no less.

HEDVIG

And then you and I didn't need anything hot for dinner, as father was out.

GINA

No; that was so much to the good. And then I took eight crowns fifty for the photographs.

HEDVIG

Really! So much as that?

GINA

Exactly eight crowns fifty.

[*Silence. GINA takes up her sewing again, HEDVIG takes paper and pencil and begins to draw, shading her eyes with her left hand.*]

HEDVIG

Isn't it jolly to think that father is at Mr. Werle's big dinner-party?

GINA

You know he's not really Mr. Werle's guest. It was the son invited him.

[*After a pause.*]

We have nothing to do with that Mr. Werle.

HEDVIG

I'm longing for father to come home. He promised to ask Mrs. Sörby for something nice for me.

GINA

Yes, there's plenty of good things going in that house, I can tell you.

HEDVIG   [*Goes on drawing.*]

And I believe I'm a little hungry too.

[OLD EKDAL, *with the paper parcel under his arm and another parcel in his coat pocket, comes in by the entrance door.*]

GINA

How late you are to-day, grandfather!

EKDAL

They had locked the office door. Had to wait in Gråberg's room. And then they let me through—h'm.

HEDVIG

Did you get some more copying to do, grandfather?

EKDAL

This whole packet. Just look.

GINA

That's capital.

HEDVIG

And you have another parcel in your pocket.

EKDAL

Eh? Oh never mind, that's nothing.

[*Puts his stick away in a corner.*]

This work will keep me going a long time, Gina.

[*Opens one of the sliding-doors in the back wall a little.*]

Hush!

[*Peeps into the room for a moment, then pushes the door carefully to again.*]

Hee-hee! They're fast asleep, all the lot of them. And she's gone into the basket herself. Hee-hee!

HEDVIG

Are you sure she isn't cold in that basket, grandfather?

EKDAL

Not a bit of it! Cold? With all that straw?

[*Goes towards the farther door on the left.*]

There are matches in here, I suppose.

GINA

The matches is on the drawers.

[EKDAL *goes into his room.*]

HEDVIG

It's nice that grandfather has got all that copying.

GINA

Yes, poor old father; it means a bit of pocket-money for him.

HEDVIG

And he won't be able to sit the whole forenoon down at that horrid Madam Eriksen's.

GINA

No more he won't.

[*Short silence.*]

HEDVIG

Do you suppose they are still at the dinner-table?

GINA

Goodness knows; as like as not.

HEDVIG

Think of all the delicious things father is having to eat! I'm certain he'll be in splendid spirits when he comes. Don't you think so, mother?

GINA

Yes; and if only we could tell him that we'd got the room let——

HEDVIG

But we don't need that this evening.

GINA

Oh, we'd be none the worse of it, I can tell you. It's no use to us as it is.

HEDVIG

I mean we don't need it this evening, for father will be in a good humour at any rate. It is best to keep the letting of the room for another time.

GINA   [*Looks across at her.*]

You like having some good news to tell father when he comes home in the evening?

HEDVIG

Yes; for then things are pleasanter somehow.

GINA   [*Thinking to herself.*]

Yes, yes, there's something in that.

[OLD EKDAL *comes in again and is going out by the foremost door to the left.*]

GINA   [*Half turning in her chair.*]

Do you want something out of the kitchen, grandfather?

EKDAL

Yes, yes, I do. Don't you trouble.

[*Goes out.*]

GINA

He's not poking away at the fire, is he?

[*Waits a moment.*]

Hedvig, go and see what he's about.

[EKDAL *comes in again with a small jug of steaming hot water.*]

HEDVIG

Have you been getting some hot water, grandfather?

EKDAL

Yes, hot water. Want it for something. Want to write, and the ink has got as thick as porridge.—h'm.

GINA

But you'd best have your supper, first, grandfather. It's laid in there.

EKDAL

Can't be bothered with supper, Gina. Very busy, I tell you. No one's to come to my room. No one—h'm.

[*He goes into his room;* GINA *and* HEDVIG *look at each other.*]

GINA   [*Softly.*]

Can you imagine where he's got money from?

HEDVIG

From Gråberg, perhaps.

GINA

Not a bit of it. Gråberg always sends the money to me.

HEDVIG

Then he must have got a bottle on credit somewhere.

GINA

Poor grandfather, who'd give him credit?

HIALMAR EKDAL, *in an overcoat and grey felt hat, comes in from the right.*

GINA   [*Throws down her sewing and rises.*]

Why, Ekdal. Is that you already?

HEDVIG   [*At the same time jumping up.*]

Fancy your coming so soon, father!

HIALMAR   [*Taking off his hat.*]

Yes, most of the people were coming away.

HEDVIG

So early?

HIALMAR

Yes, it was a dinner-party, you know.

[*Is taking off his overcoat.*]

GINA

Let me help you.

HEDVIG

Me too.

[*They draw off his coat;* GINA *hangs it up on the back wall.*]

HEDVIG

Were there many people there, father?

HIALMAR

Oh no, not many. We were about twelve or fourteen at table.

GINA

And you had some talk with them all?

HIALMAR

Oh yes, a little; but Gregers took me up most of the time.

GINA

Is Gregers as ugly as ever?

HIALMAR

Well, he's not very much to look at. Hasn't the old man come home?

HEDVIG

Yes, grandfather is in his room, writing.

HIALMAR

Did he say anything?

GINA

No, what should he say?

HIALMAR

Didn't he say anything about——? I heard something about his having been with Gråberg. I'll go in and see him for a moment.

GINA

No, no, better not.

HIALMAR

Why not? Did he say he didn't want me to go in?

GINA

I don't think he wants to see nobody this evening——

HEDVIG   [Making signs.]

H'm——h'm!

GINA   [Not noticing.]

——he has been in to fetch hot water——

HIALMAR

Aha! Then he's——

GINA

Yes, I suppose so.

HIALMAR

Oh God! my poor old white-haired father!——Well, well; there let him sit and get all the enjoyment he can.

[OLD EKDAL, *in an indoor coat and with a lighted pipe, comes from his room.*]

EKDAL

Got home? Thought it was you I heard talking.

HIALMAR

Yes, I have just come.

EKDAL

You didn't see me, did you?

HIALMAR

No; but they told me you had passed through—so I thought I would follow you.

EKDAL

Hm, good of you, Hialmar.—Who were they, all those fellows?

HIALMAR

Oh, all sorts of people. There was Chamberlain Flor, and Chamberlain Balle, and Chamberlain Kasperseu, and Chamberlain—this, that, and the other—I don't know who all——

EKDAL   [*Nodding.*]

Hear that, Gina! Chamberlains every one of them!

GINA

Yes, I hear as they're terrible genteel in that house nowadays.

HEDVIG

Did the Chamberlains sing, father? Or did they read aloud?

HIALMAR

No, they only talked nonsense. They wanted me to recite something for them; but I knew better than that.

EKDAL

You weren't to be persuaded, eh?

GINA

Oh, you might have done it.

HIALMAR

No; one mustn't be at everybody's beck and call.
[*Walks about the room.*]
That's not my way, at any rate.

EKDAL

No no; Hialmar's not to be had for the asking, he isn't.

HIALMAR

I don't see why *I* should bother myself to entertain people on the rare occasions when I go into society. Let the others exert themselves. These fellows go from one great dinner-table to the next and gorge and guzzle day out and day in. It's for them to bestir themselves and do something in return for all the good feeding they get.

GINA

But you didn't say that?

HIALMAR   [*Humming.*]

    Ho-ho-ho———; faith, I gave them a bit of my mind.

EKDAL

    Not the Chamberlains?

HIALMAR

    Oh, why not?

    [*Lightly.*]

    After that, we had a little discussion about Tokay.

EKDAL

    Tokay! There's a fine wine for you!

HIALMAR   [*Comes to a standstill.*]

    It may be a fine wine. But of course you know the vintages
differ; it all depends on how much sunshine the grapes have had.

GINA

    Why, you know everything, Ekdal.

EKDAL

    And did they dispute that?

HIALMAR

    They tried to; but they were requested to observe that it was just
the same with Chamberlains——that with them, too, different
batches were of different qualities.

GINA

    What things you do think of!

EKDAL

    Hee-hee! So they got that in their pipes too?

HIALMAR

    Right in their teeth.

EKDAL

    Do you hear that, Gina? He said it right in the very teeth of all
the Chamberlains.

GINA

    Fancy——! Right in their teeth!

HIALMAR

    Yes, but I don't want it talked about. One doesn't speak of such
things. The whole affair passed off quite amicably of course. They
were nice, genial fellows; I didn't want to wound them——not I!

EKDAL

    Right in their teeth, though——!

HEDVIG [*Caressingly.*]

How nice it is to see you in a dress-coat! It suits you so well,
father.

HIALMAR

Yes, don't you think so? And this one really sits to perfection. It
fits almost as if it had been made for me;—a little tight in the
arm-holes perhaps;—help me, Hedvig.
[*Takes off the coat.*]
I think I'll put on my jacket. Where is my jacket, Gina?

GINA

Here it is.
[*Brings the jacket and helps him.*]

HIALMAR

That's it! Don't forget to send the coat back to Molvik first thing
to-morrow morning.

GINA [*Laying it away.*]
I'll be sure and see to it.

HIALMAR [*Stretching himself.*]

After all, there's a more homely feeling about this. A free-and-
easy indoor costume suits my whole personality better. Don't
you think so, Hedvig?

HEDVIG

Yes, father.

HIALMAR

When I loosen my necktie into a pair of flowing ends—like
this—eh?

HEDVIG

Yes, that goes so well with your moustache and the sweep of
your curls.

HIALMAR

I should not call them curls exactly; I should rather say locks.

HEDVIG

Yes, they are too big for curls.

HIALMAR

Locks describes them better.

HEDVIG [*After a pause, twitching his jacket.*]
Father.

HIALMAR

Well, what is it?

HEDVIG

Oh, you know very well.

HIALMAR

No, really I don't——

HEDVIG   [*Half laughing, half whimpering.*]

Oh yes, father; now don't tease me any longer!

HIALMAR

Why, what do you mean?

HEDVIG   [*Shaking him.*]

Oh what nonsense; come, where are they, father? All the good things you promised me, you know?

HIALMAR

Oh—if I haven't forgotten all about them!

HEDVIG

Now you're only teasing me, father! Oh, it's too bad of you! Where have you put them?

HIALMAR

No, I positively forgot to get anything. But wait a little! I have something else for you, Hedvig.

[*Goes and searches in the pockets of the coat.*]

HEDVIG   [*Skipping and clapping her hands.*]

Oh mother, mother!

GINA

There, you see; if you only give him time——

HIALMAR   [*With a paper.*]

Look, here it is.

HEDVIG

That? Why, that's only a paper.

HIALMAR

That is the bill of fare, my dear; the whole bill of fare. Here you see: "Menu"—that means bill of fare.

HEDVIG

Haven't you anything else?

HIALMAR

I forgot the other things, I tell you. But you may take my word for it, these dainties are very unsatisfying. Sit down at the table and read the bill of fare, and then I'll describe to you how the dishes taste. Here you are, Hedvig.

HEDVIG   [*Gulping down her tears.*]

Thank you.

[*She seats herself, but does not read; GINA makes signs to her; HIAL-MAR notices it.*]

HIALMAR   [*Pacing up and down the room.*]

It's monstrous what absurd things the father of a family is expected to think of; and if he forgets the smallest trifle, he is treated to sour faces at once. Well, well, one gets used to that too.

[*Stops near the stove, by the old man's chair.*]

Have you peeped in there this evening, father?

EKDAL

Yes, to be sure I have. She's gone into the basket.

HIALMAR

Ah, she has gone into the basket. Then she's beginning to get used to it.

EKDAL

Yes; just as I prophesied. But you know there are still a few little things——

HIALMAR

A few improvements, yes.

EKDAL

They've got to be made, you know.

HIALMAR

Yes, let us have a talk about the improvements, father. Come, let us sit on the sofa.

EKDAL

All right. H'm——think I'll just fill my pipe first. Must clean it out, too. H'm.

[*He goes into his room.*]

GINA   [*Smiling to HIALMAR.*]

His pipe!

HIALMAR

Oh yes yes, Gina; let him alone——the poor shipwrecked old man.——Yes, these improvements——we had better get them out of hand to-morrow.

GINA

You'll hardly have time to-morrow, Ekdal.

HEDVIG   [Interposing.]

Oh yes he will, mother!

GINA

——for remember them prints that has to be retouched; they've sent for them time after time.

HIALMAR

There now! those prints again! I shall get them finished all right! Have any new orders come in?

GINA

No, worse luck; to-morrow I have nothing but those two sittings, you know.

HIALMAR

Nothing else? Oh no, if people won't set about things with a will——

GINA

But what more can I do? Don't I advertise in the papers as much as we can afford?

HIALMAR

Yes, the papers, the papers; you see how much good they do. And I suppose no one has been to look at the room either?

GINA

No, not yet.

HIALMAR

That was only to be expected. If people won't keep their eyes open——. Nothing can be done without a real effort, Gina!

HEDVIG   [Going towards him.]

Shall I fetch you the flute, father?

HIALMAR

No; no flute for me; I want no pleasures in this world.

[Pacing about.]

Yes, indeed I will work to-morrow; you shall see if I don't. You may be sure I shall work as long as my strength holds out.

GINA

But my dear good Ekdal, I didn't mean it in that way.

HEDVIG

Father, mayn't I bring in a bottle of beer?

HIALMAR

No, certainly not. I require nothing, nothing——
[*Comes to a standstill.*]
Beer? Was it beer you were talking about?

HEDVIG   [*Cheerfully.*]

Yes, father; beautiful fresh beer.

HIALMAR

Well—since you insist upon it, you may bring in a bottle.

GINA

Yes, do; and we'll be nice and cosy.
[HEDVIG *runs towards the kitchen door.*]

HIALMAR   [*By the stove, stops her, looks at her, puts his arm round her neck and presses her to him.*]

Hedvig, Hedvig!

HEDVIG   [*With tears of joy.*]

My dear, kind father!

HIALMAR

No, don't call me that. Here have I been feasting at the rich man's table,—battening at the groaning board——! And I couldn't even——!

GINA   [*Sitting at the table.*]

Oh nonsense, nonsense, Ekdal.

HIALMAR

It's not nonsense! And yet you mustn't be too hard upon me. You know that I love you for all that.

HEDVIG   [*Throwing her arms round him.*]

And we love you, oh so dearly, father!

HIALMAR

And if I am unreasonable once in a while,—why then—you must remember that I am a man beset by a host of cares. There, there!
[*Dries his eyes.*]
No beer at such a moment as this. Give me the flute.
[HEDVIG *runs to the bookcase and fetches it.*]

HIALMAR

Thanks! That's right. With my flute in my hand and you two at my side—ah——!
[HEDVIG *seats herself at the table near* GINA; HIALMAR *paces back-*

wards and forwards, pipes up vigorously, and plays a Bohemian peasant dance, but in a slow plaintive tempo, and with sentimental expression.]

HIALMAR   [*Breaking off the melody, holds out his left hand to* GINA, *and says with emotion:*]

Our roof may be poor and humble, Gina; but it is home. And with all my heart I say here dwells my happiness.

[*He begins to play again; almost immediately after, a knocking is heard at the entrance door.*]

GINA   [*Rising.*]

Hush, Ekdal,——I think there's some one at the door.

HIALMAR   [*Laying the flute on the bookcase.*]

There! Again!

[GINA *goes and opens the door.*]

GREGERS WERLE   [*In the passage.*]

Excuse me——

GINA   [*Starting back slightly.*]

Oh!

GREGERS

——does not Mr. Ekdal, the photographer, live here?

GINA

Yes, he does.

HIALMAR   [*Going towards the door.*]

Gregers! You here after all? Well, come in then.

GREGERS   [*Coming in.*]

I told you I would come and look you up.

HIALMAR

But this evening——? Have you left the party?

GREGERS

I have left both the party and my father's house.——Good evening, Mrs. Ekdal. I don't know whether you recognise me?

GINA

Oh yes; it's not difficult to know young Mr. Werle again.

GREGERS

No, I am like my mother; and no doubt you remember her.

HIALMAR

Left your father's house, did you say?

GREGERS

Yes, I have gone to a hotel.

HIALMAR

Indeed. Well, since you're here, take off your coat and sit down.

GREGERS

Thanks.

[*He takes off his overcoat. He is now dressed in a plain grey suit of a coun-trified cut.*]

HIALMAR

Here, on the sofa. Make yourself comfortable.

[GREGERS *seats himself on the sofa;* HIALMAR *takes a chair at the table.*]

GREGERS   [*Looking around him.*]

So these are your quarters, Hialmar—this is your home.

HIALMAR

This is the studio, as you see——

GINA

But it's the largest of our rooms, so we generally sit here.

HIALMAR

We used to live in a better place; but this flat has one great advantage: there are such capital outer rooms——

GINA

And we have a room on the other side of the passage that we can let.

GREGERS   [*To* HIALMAR.]

Ah—so you have lodgers too?

HIALMAR

No, not yet. They're not so easy to find, you see; you have to keep your eyes open.

[*To* HEDVIG.]

What about that beer, eh?

[HEDVIG *nods and goes out into the kitchen.*]

GREGERS

So that is your daughter?

HIALMAR

Yes, that is Hedvig.

GREGERS

And she is your only child?

HIALMAR

Yes, the only one. She is the joy of our lives, and—

[*lowering his voice*]

—at the same time our deepest sorrow, Gregers.

GREGERS

What do you mean?

HIALMAR

She is in serious danger of losing her eyesight.

GREGERS

Becoming blind?

HIALMAR

Yes. Only the first symptoms have appeared as yet, and she may not feel it much for some time. But the doctor has warned us. It is coming, inexorably.

GREGERS

What a terrible misfortune! How do you account for it?

HIALMAR   [*Sighs.*]

Hereditary, no doubt.

GREGERS   [*Starting.*]

Hereditary?

GINA

Ekdal's mother had weak eyes.

HIALMAR

Yes, so my father says; I can't remember her.

GREGERS

Poor child! And how does she take it?

HIALMAR

Oh, you can imagine we haven't the heart to tell her of it. She dreams of no danger. Gay and careless and chirping like a little bird, she flutters onward into a life of endless night.

[*Overcome.*]

Oh, it is cruelly hard on me, Gregers.

[HEDVIG *brings a tray with beer and glasses, which she sets upon the table.*]

HIALMAR   [*Stroking her hair.*]

Thanks, thanks, Hedvig.

[HEDVIG *puts her arm round his neck and whispers in his ear.*]

HIALMAR

No, no bread and butter just now.

[*Looks up.*]

But perhaps you would like some, Gregers.

GREGERS   [*With a gesture of refusal.*]

No, no thank you.

HIALMAR   [*Still melancholy.*]

Well, you can bring in a little all the same. If you have a crust, that is all I want. And plenty of butter on it, mind.

[HEDVIG *nods gaily and goes out into the kitchen again.*]

GREGERS   [*Who has been following her with his eyes.*]

She seems quite strong and healthy otherwise.

GINA

Yes. In other ways there's nothing amiss with her, thank goodness.

GREGERS

She promises to be very like you, Mrs. Ekdal. How old is she now?

GINA

Hedvig is close on fourteen; her birthday is the day after to-morrow.

GREGERS

She is pretty tall for her age, then.

GINA

Yes, she's shot up wonderful this last year.

GREGERS

It makes one realise one's own age to see these young people growing up.——How long is it now since you were married?

GINA

We've been married—let me see—just on fifteen years.

GREGERS

Is it so long as that?

GINA   [*Becomes attentive; looks at him.*]

Yes, it is indeed.

HIALMAR

Yes, so it is. Fifteen years all but a few months.

[*Changing his tone.*]

They must have been long years for you, up at the works, Gregers.

GREGERS

They seemed long while I was living them; now they are over, I hardly know how the time has gone.

[OLD EKDAL *comes from his room without his pipe, but with his old-fashioned uniform cap on his head; his gait is somewhat unsteady.*]

EKDAL

Come now, Hialmar, let's sit down and have a good talk about this—h'm—what was it again?

HIALMAR   [*Going towards him.*]

Father, we have a visitor here—Gregers Werle.—I don't know if you remember him.

EKDAL   [*Looking at* GREGERS, *who has risen.*]

Werle? Is that the son? What does he want with me?

HIALMAR

Nothing; it's me he has come to see.

EKDAL

Oh! Then there's nothing wrong?

HIALMAR

No, no, of course not.

EKDAL   [*With a large gesture.*]

Not that I'm afraid, you know; but——

GREGERS   [*Goes over to him.*]

I bring you a greeting from your old hunting-grounds, Lieutenant Ekdal.

EKDAL

Hunting-grounds?

GREGERS

Yes, up in Höidal, about the works, you know.

EKDAL

Oh, up there. Yes, I knew all those places well in the old days.

GREGERS

You were a great sportsman then.

EKDAL

So I was, I don't deny it. You're looking at my uniform cap. I don't ask anybody's leave to wear it in the house. So long as I don't go out in the streets with it——

[HEDVIG *brings a plate of bread and butter, which she puts upon the table.*]

HIALMAR

Sit down, father, and have a glass of beer. Help yourself, Gregers. [EKDAL *mutters and stumbles over to the sofa.* GREGERS *seats himself on the chair nearest to him,* HIALMAR *on the other side of* GREGERS. GINA *sits a little way from the table, sewing;* HEDVIG *stands beside her father.*]

GREGERS

Can you remember, Lieutenant Ekdal, how Hialmar and I used to come up and visit you in the summer and at Christmas?

EKDAL

Did you? No, no, no; I don't remember it. But sure enough I've been a tidy bit of a sportsman in my day. I've shot bears too. I've shot nine of 'em, no less.

GREGERS　[*Looking sympathetically at him.*]

And now you never get any shooting?

EKDAL

Can't just say that, sir. Get a shot now and then perhaps. Of course not in the old way. For the woods you see—the woods, the woods——!
[*Drinks.*]
Are the woods fine up there now?

GREGERS

Not so fine as in your time. They have been thinned a good deal.

EKDAL

Thinned?
[*More softly, and as if afraid.*]
It's dangerous work that. Bad things come of it. The woods revenge themselves.

HIALMAR　[*Filling up his glass.*]

Come—a little more, father.

GREGERS

How can a man like you—such a man for the open air—live in the midst of a stuffy town, boxed within four walls?

EKDAL　[*Laughs quietly and glances at* HIALMAR.]

Oh, it's not so bad here. Not at all so bad.

GREGERS

But don't you miss all the things that used to be a part of your

very being—the cool sweeping breezes, the free life in the
woods and on the uplands, among beasts and birds——?

EKDAL   [Smiling.]

Hialmar, shall we let him see it?

HIALMAR   [Hastily and a little embarrassed.]

Oh no no, father; not this evening.

GREGERS

What does he want to show me?

HIALMAR

Oh, it's only something—you can see it another time.

GREGERS   [Continues, to the old man.]

You see I have been thinking, Lieutenant Ekdal, that you should
come up with me to the works; I am sure to be going back soon.
No doubt you could get some copying there too. And here, you
have nothing on earth to interest you—nothing to liven you up.

EKDAL   [Stares in astonishment at him.]

Have I nothing on earth to——!

GREGERS

Of course you have Hialmar; but then he has his own family. And
a man like you, who has always had such a passion for what is
free and wild——

EKDAL   [Thumps the table.]

Hialmar, he shall see it!

HIALMAR

Oh, do you think it's worth while, father? It's all dark.

EKDAL

Nonsense; it's moonlight.

[Rises.]

He shall see it, I tell you. Let me pass! Come and help me,
Hialmar.

HEDVIG

Oh yes, do, father!

HIALMAR   [Rising.]

Very well then.

GREGERS   [To GINA.]

What is it?

GINA

Oh, nothing so very wonderful, after all.

[EKDAL *and* HIALMAR *have gone to the back wall and are each push-ing back a side of the sliding door;* HEDVIG *helps the old man;* GREGERS *remains standing by the sofa;* GINA *sits still and sews. Through the open doorway a large, deep irregular garret is seen with odd nooks and corners; a couple of stove-pipes running through it, from rooms below. There are sky-lights through which clear moonbeams shine in on some parts of the great room; others lie in deep shadow.*]

EKDAL   [*To* GREGERS.]

You may come close up if you like.

GREGERS   [*Going over to them.*]

Why, what is it?

EKDAL

Look for yourself. H'm.

HIALMAR   [*Somewhat embarrassed.*]

This belongs to father, you understand.

GREGERS   [*At the door, looks into the garret.*]

Why, you keep poultry, Lieutenant Ekdal?

EKDAL

Should think we did keep poultry. They've gone to roost now. But you should just see our fowls by daylight, sir!

HEDVIG

And there's a――

EKDAL

Sh――sh! don't say anything about it yet.

GREGERS

And you have pigeons too, I see.

EKDAL

Oh yes, haven't we just got pigeons! They have their nest-boxes up there under the roof-tree; for pigeons like to roost high, you see.

HIALMAR

They aren't all common pigeons.

EKDAL

Common! Should think not indeed! We have tumblers, and a pair of pouters, too. But come here! Can you see that hutch down there by the wall?

GREGERS

Yes; what do you use it for?

EKDAL

> That's where the rabbits sleep, sir.

GREGERS

> Dear me; so you have rabbits too?

EKDAL

> Yes, you may take my word for it, we have rabbits! He wants to know if we have rabbits, Hialmar! H'm! But now comes the thing, let me tell you! Here we have it! Move away, Hedvig. Stand here; that's right,—and now look down there.—Don't you see a basket with straw in it?

GREGERS

> Yes. And I can see a fowl lying in the basket.

EKDAL

> H'm—"a fowl"——

GREGERS

> Isn't it a duck?

EKDAL   [*Hurt.*]

> Why, of course it's a duck.

HIALMAR

> But what kind of duck, do you think?

HEDVIG

> It's not just a common duck——

EKDAL

> Sh!

GREGERS

> And it's not a Muscovy duck either.

EKDAL

> No, Mr.—Werle; it's not a Muscovy duck; for it's a wild duck!

GREGERS

> Is it really? A wild duck?

EKDAL

> Yes, that's what it is. That "fowl" as you call it—is the wild duck. It's our wild duck, sir.

HEDVIG

> My wild duck. It belongs to me.

GREGERS

> And can it live up here in the garret? Does it thrive?

EKDAL

Of course it has a trough of water to splash about in, you know.

HIALMAR

Fresh water every other day.

GINA   [*Turning towards* HIALMAR.]

But my dear Ekdal, it's getting icy cold here.

EKDAL

H'm, we had better shut up then. It's as well not to disturb their night's rest, too. Close up, Hedvig.

[HIALMAR *and* HEDVIG *push the garret doors together.*]

EKDAL

Another time you shall see her properly.

[*Seats himself in the arm-chair by the stove.*]

Oh, they're curious things, these wild ducks, I can tell you.

GREGERS

How did you manage to catch it, Lieutenant Ekdal?

EKDAL

I didn't catch it. There's a certain man in this town whom we have to thank for it.

GREGERS   [*Starts slightly.*]

That man was not my father, was he?

EKDAL

You've hit it. Your father and no one else. H'm.

HIALMAR

Strange that you should guess that, Gregers.

GREGERS

You were telling me that you owed so many things to my father; and so I thought perhaps——

GINA

But we didn't get the duck from Mr. Werle himself——

EKDAL

It's Håkon Werle we have to thank for her, all the same, Gina.

[*To* GREGERS.]

He was shooting from a boat, you see, and he brought her down. But your father's sight is not very good now. H'm; she was only wounded.

GREGERS

Ah! She got a couple of slugs in her body, I suppose.

HIALMAR

Yes, two or three.

HEDVIG

She was hit under the wing, so that she couldn't fly.

GREGERS

And I suppose she dived to the bottom, eh?

EKDAL [*Sleepily, in a thick voice.*]

Of course. Always do that, wild ducks do. They shoot to the bottom as deep as they can get, sir——and bite themselves fast in the tangle and seaweed——and all the devil's own mess that grows down there. And they never come up again.

GREGERS

But your wild duck came up again, Lieutenant Ekdal.

EKDAL

He had such an amazingly clever dog, your father had. And that dog——he dived in after the duck and fetched her up again.

GREGERS [*Who has turned to* HIALMAR.]

And then she was sent to you here?

HIALMAR

Not at once; at first your father took her home. But she wouldn't thrive there; so Pettersen was told to put an end to her——

EKDAL [*Half asleep.*]

H'm——yes——Pettersen——that ass——

HIALMAR [*Speaking more softly.*]

That was how we got her, you see; for father knows Pettersen a little; and when he heard about the wild duck he got him to hand her over to us.

GREGERS

And now she thrives as well as possible in the garret there?

HIALMAR

Yes, wonderfully well. She has got fat. You see, she has lived in there so long now that she has forgotten her natural wild life; and it all depends on that.

GREGERS

You are right there, Hialmar. Be sure you never let her get a glimpse of the sky and the sea——. But I mustn't stay any longer; I think your father is asleep.

HIALMAR

Oh, as for that——

GREGERS

But, by-the-bye—you said you had a room to let—a spare room?

HIALMAR

Yes; what then? Do you know of anybody——?

GREGERS

Can *I* have that room?

HIALMAR

You?

GINA

Oh no, Mr. Werle, you——

GREGERS

May I have the room? If so, I'll take possession first thing
to-morrow morning.

HIALMAR

Yes, with the greatest pleasure——

GINA

But, Mr. Werle, I'm sure it's not at all the sort of room for you.

HIALMAR

Why, Gina! how can you say that?

GINA

Why, because the room's neither large enough nor light enough,
and——

GREGERS

That really doesn't matter, Mrs. Ekdal.

HIALMAR

I call it quite a nice room, and not at all badly furnished either.

GINA

But remember the pair of them underneath.

GREGERS

What pair?

GINA

Well, there's one as has been a tutor——

HIALMAR

That's Molvik—Mr. Molvik, B.A.

GINA

And then there's a doctor, by the name of Relling.

GREGERS

Relling? I know him a little; he practised for a time up in Höidal.

GINA

They're a regular rackety pair, they are. As often as not, they're out on the loose in the evenings; and then they come home at all hours, and they're not always just——

GREGERS

One soon gets used to that sort of thing. I daresay I shall be like the wild duck——

GINA

H'm; I think you ought to sleep upon it first, anyway.

GREGERS

You seem very unwilling to have me in the house, Mrs. Ekdal.

GINA

Oh no! What makes you think that?

HIALMAR

Well, you really behave strangely about it, Gina.

[*To* GREGERS.]

Then I suppose you intend to remain in the town for the present?

GREGERS   [*Pulling on his overcoat.*]

Yes, now I intend to remain here.

HIALMAR

And yet not at your father's? What do you propose to do, then?

GREGERS

Ah, if I only knew that, Hialmar, I shouldn't be so badly off! But when one has the misfortune to be called Gregers—! "Gregers"—and then "Werle" after it; did you ever hear anything so hideous?

HIALMAR

Oh, I don't think so at all.

GREGERS

Ugh! Bah! I feel I should like to spit upon the fellow that answers to such a name. But when a man is once for all doomed to be Gregers—Werle in this world, as I am——

HIALMAR   [*Laughs.*]

Ha ha! If you weren't Gregers Werle, what would you like to be?

GREGERS

If I could choose, I should like best to be a clever dog.

GINA

A dog!

HEDVIG   [*Involuntarily.*]

Oh no!

GREGERS

Yes, an amazingly clever dog; one that goes to the bottom after wild ducks when they dive and bite themselves fast in tangle and sea-weed, down among the ooze.

HIALMAR

Upon my word now, Gregers—I don't in the least know what you're driving at.

GREGERS

Oh well, you might not be much the wiser if you did. It's understood, then, that I move in early to-morrow morning.

[*To* GINA.]

I won't give you any trouble; I do everything for myself.

[*To* HIALMAR.]

We can talk about the rest to-morrow.—Good-night, Mrs. Ekdal.

[*Nods to* HEDVIG.]

Good-night.

GINA

Good-night, Mr. Werle.

HEDVIG

Good-night.

HIALMAR   [*Who has lighted a candle.*]

Wait a moment; I must show you a light; the stairs are sure to be dark.

[GREGERS *and* HIALMAR *go out by the passage door.*]

GINA   [*Looking straight before her, with her sewing in her lap.*]

Wasn't that queer-like talk about wanting to be a dog?

HEDVIG

Do you know, mother—I believe he meant something quite different by that.

GINA

Why, what should he mean?

HEDVIG

Oh, I don't know; but it seemed to me he meant something different from what he said—all the time.

GINA

Do you think so? Yes, it was sort of queer.

HIALMAR   [*Comes back.*]

The lamp was still burning.

[*Puts out the candle and sets it down.*]

Ah, now one can get a mouthful of food at last.

[*Begins to eat the bread and butter.*]

Well, you see, Gina—if only you keep your eyes open——

GINA

How, keep your eyes open——?

HIALMAR

Why, haven't we at last had the luck to get the room let? And just think—to a person like Gregers—a good old friend.

GINA

Well, I don't know what to say about it.

HEDVIG

Oh mother, you'll see; it'll be such fun!

HIALMAR

You're very strange—— You were so bent upon getting the room let before; and now you don't like it.

GINA

Yes I do, Ekdal; if it had only been to some one else—— But what do you suppose Mr. Werle will say?

HIALMAR

Old Werle? It doesn't concern him.

GINA

But surely you can see that there's something amiss between them again, or the young man wouldn't be leaving home. You know very well those two can't get on with each other.

HIALMAR

Very likely not, but——

GINA

And now Mr. Werle may fancy it's you that has egged him on——

HIALMAR

Let him fancy so, then! Mr. Werle has done a great deal for me;

far be it from me to deny it. But that doesn't make me everlastingly dependent upon him.

GINA

But, my dear Ekdal, maybe grandfather'll suffer for it. He may lose the little bit of work he gets from Gråberg.

HIALMAR

I could almost say: so much the better! Is it not humiliating for a man like me to see his grey-haired father treated as a pariah? But now I believe the fulness of time is at hand.

[*Takes a fresh piece of bread and butter.*]

As sure as I have a mission in life, I mean to fulfil it now!

HEDVIG

Oh yes, father, do!

GINA

Hush! Don't wake him!

HIALMAR   [*More softly.*]

I will fulfil it, I say. The day shall come when—— And that is why I say it's a good thing we have let the room; for that makes me more independent. The man who has a mission in life must be independent.

[*By the arm-chair, with emotion.*]

Poor old white-haired father! Rely on your Hialmar. He has broad shoulders—strong shoulders, at any rate. You shall yet wake up some fine day and——

[*To* GINA.]

Do you not believe it?

GINA   [*Rising.*]

Yes, of course I do; but in the meantime suppose we see about getting him to bed.

HIALMAR

Yes, come.

[*They take hold of the old man carefully.*]

ACT THIRD

HIALMAR EKDAL's *studio. It is morning: the daylight shines through the large window in the slanting roof; the curtain is drawn back.*

HIALMAR *is sitting at the table, busy retouching a photograph; several others lie before him. Presently* GINA, *wearing her hat and cloak, enters by the passage door; she has a covered basket on her arm.*

HIALMAR

Back already, Gina?

GINA

Oh yes, one can't let the grass grow under one's feet.

[*Sets her basket on a chair, and takes off her things.*]

HIALMAR

Did you look in at Gregers' room?

GINA

Yes, that I did. It's a rare sight, I can tell you; he's made a pretty mess to start off with.

HIALMAR

How so?

GINA

He was determined to do everything for himself he said; so he sets to work to light the stove, and what must he do but screw down the damper till the whole room is full of smoke. Ugh! There was a smell fit to——

HIALMAR

Well, really!

GINA

But that's not the worst of it; for then he thinks he'll put out the fire, and goes and empties his water-jug into the stove, and so makes the whole floor one filthy puddle.

HIALMAR

How annoying!

GINA

I've got the porter's wife to clear up after him, pig that he is! But the room won't be fit to live in till the afternoon.

HIALMAR

What's he doing with himself in the meantime?

GINA

He said he was going out for a little while.

HIALMAR

I looked in upon him too, for a moment—after you had gone.

GINA

So I heard. You've asked him to lunch.

HIALMAR

Just to a little bit of early lunch, you know. It's his first day—we can hardly do less. You've got something in the house, I suppose?

GINA

I shall have to find something or other.

HIALMAR

And don't cut it too fine, for I fancy Relling and Molvik are coming up too. I just happened to meet Relling on the stairs, you see; so I had to——

GINA

Oh, are we to have those two as well?

HIALMAR

Good Lord—a couple more or less can't make any difference.

OLD EKDAL   [*Opens his door and looks in.*]

I say, Hialmar——

[*Sees* GINA.]

Oh!

GINA

Do you want anything, grandfather?

EKDAL

Oh no, it doesn't matter. H'm!

[*Retires again.*]

GINA   [*Takes up the basket.*]

Be sure you see that he doesn't go out.

HIALMAR

All right, all right. And, Gina, a little herring-salad wouldn't be a bad idea; Relling and Molvik were out on the loose again last night.

GINA

If only they don't come before I'm ready for them——

HIALMAR

No, of course they won't; take your own time.

GINA

Very well; and meanwhile you can be working a bit.

HIALMAR

Well, I am working! I am working as hard as I can!

GINA

Then you'll have that job off your hands, you see.

[*She goes out to the kitchen with her basket.*]

[HIALMAR *sits for a time pencilling away at the photograph, in an indolent and listless manner.*]

EKDAL   [*Peeps in, looks round the studio, and says softly:*]

Are you busy?

HIALMAR

Yes I'm toiling at these wretched pictures——

EKDAL

Well well, never mind,—since you're so busy—h'm!

[*He goes out again; the door stands open.*]

HIALMAR   [*Continues for some time in silence; then he lays down his brush and goes over to the door.*]

Are you busy, father?

EKDAL   [*In a grumbling tone, within.*]

If you're busy, I'm busy too. H'm!

HIALMAR

Oh, very well, then.

[*Goes to his work again.*]

EKDAL   [*Presently, coming to the door again.*]

H'm; I say, Hialmar, I'm not so very busy, you know.

HIALMAR

I thought you were writing.

EKDAL

> Oh, devil take it! can't Gråberg wait a day or two? After all, it's not a matter of life and death.

HIALMAR

> No; and you're not his slave either.

EKDAL

> And about that other business in there——

HIALMAR

> Just what I was thinking of. Do you want to go in. Shall I open the door for you?

EKDAL

> Well, it wouldn't be a bad notion.

HIALMAR [*Rises.*]

> Then we'd have that off our hands.

EKDAL

> Yes, exactly. It's got to be ready first thing to-morrow. It is to-morrow, isn't it? H'm?

HIALMAR

> Yes, of course it's to-morrow.
>
> [HIALMAR *and* EKDAL *push aside each his half of the sliding door. The morning sun is shining in through the skylights; some doves are flying about; others sit cooing, upon the perches; the hens are heard clucking now and then, further back in the garret.*]

HIALMAR

> There; now you can get to work, father.

EKDAL [*Goes in.*]

> Aren't you coming too?

HIALMAR

> Well really, do you know——; I almost think——
>
> [*Sees* GINA *at the kitchen door.*]
>
> I? No; I haven't time; I must work.——But now for our new contrivance——
>
> [*He pulls a cord, a curtain slips down inside, the lower part consisting of a piece of old sailcloth, the upper part of a stretched fishing net. The floor of the garret is thus no longer visible.*]

HIALMAR [*Goes to the table.*]

> So! Now, perhaps I can sit in peace for a little while.

GINA

Is he rampaging in there again?

HIALMAR

Would you rather have had him slip down to Madam Eriksen's.
[*Seats himself.*]

Do you want anything? You know you said——

GINA

I only wanted to ask if you think we can lay the table for lunch
here?

HIALMAR

Yes; we have no early appointment, I suppose?

GINA

No, I expect no one to-day except those two sweethearts that are
to be taken together.

HIALMAR

Why the deuce couldn't they be taken together another day!

GINA

Don't you know, I told them to come in the afternoon, when
you are having your nap.

HIALMAR

Oh, that's capital. Very well, let us have lunch here then.

GINA

All right; but there's no hurry about laying the cloth; you can
have the table for a good while yet.

HIALMAR

Do you think I am not sticking at my work? I'm at it as hard as I
can!

GINA

Then you'll be free later on, you know.
[*Goes out into the kitchen again. Short pause.*]

EKDAL   [*In the garret doorway, behind the net.*]

Hialmar!

HIALMAR

Well?

EKDAL

Afraid we shall have to move the water-trough, after all.

HIALMAR

What else have I been saying all along?

EKDAL

    H'm—h'm—h'm.

    [*Goes away from the door again.*]

    [HIALMAR *goes on working a little; glances towards the garret and half rises.* HEDVIG *comes in from the kitchen.*]

HIALMAR   [*Sits down again hurriedly.*]

    What do you want?

HEDVIG

    I only wanted to come in beside you, father.

HIALMAR   [*After a pause.*]

    What makes you go prying around like that? Perhaps you are told off to watch me?

HEDVIG

    No, no.

HIALMAR

    What is your mother doing out there?

HEDVIG

    Oh, mother's in the middle of making the herring-salad.

    [*Goes to the table.*]

    Isn't there any little thing I could help you with, father?

HIALMAR

    Oh no. It is right that I should bear the whole burden—so long as my strength holds out. Set your mind at rest, Hedvig; if only your father keeps his health——

HEDVIG

    Oh no, father! You mustn't talk in that horrid way.

    [*She wanders about a little, stops by the doorway and looks into the garret.*]

HIALMAR

    Tell me, what is he doing?

HEDVIG

    I think he's making a new path to the water-trough.

HIALMAR

    He can never manage that by himself! And here am I doomed to sit——!

HEDVIG   [*Goes to him.*]

    Let me take the brush, father; I can do it, quite well.

HIALMAR

Oh nonsense; you will only hurt your eyes.

HEDVIG

Not a bit. Give me the brush.

HIALMAR   [*Rising.*]

Well, it won't take more than a minute or two.

HEDVIG

Pooh, what harm can it do then?

[*Takes the brush.*]

There!

[*Seats herself.*]

I can begin upon this one.

HIALMAR

But mind you don't hurt your eyes! Do you hear? *I* won't be
answerable; you do it on your own responsibility—understand
that.

HEDVIG   [*Retouching.*]

Yes yes, I understand.

HIALMAR

You are quite clever at it, Hedvig. Only a minute or two, you know.
[*He slips through by the edge of the curtain into the garret.* HEDVIG *sits
at her work.* HIALMAR *and* EKDAL *are heard disputing inside.*]

HIALMAR   [*Appears behind the net.*]

I say, Hedvig—give me those pincers that are lying on the shelf.
And the chisel.

[*Turns away inside.*]

Now you shall see, father. Just let me show you first what I
mean!

[HEDVIG *has fetched the required tools from the shelf, and hands them
to him through the net.*]

HIALMAR

Ah, thanks. I didn't come a moment too soon.

[*Goes back from the curtain again; they are heard carpentering and talking inside.* HEDVIG *stands looking in at them. A moment later there is a
knock at the passage door; she does not notice it.*]

GREGERS WERLE   [*Bareheaded, in indoor dress, enters and stops near
the door.*]

H'm——!

HEDVIG   [*Turns and goes towards him.*]

Good morning. Please come in.

GREGERS

Thank you.

[*Looking towards the garret.*]

You seem to have workpeople in the house.

HEDVIG

No, it is only father and grandfather. I'll tell them you are here.

GREGERS

No no, don't do that; I would rather wait a little.

[*Seats himself on the sofa.*]

HEDVIG

It looks so untidy here——

[*Begins to clear away the photographs.*]

GREGERS

Oh, don't take them away. Are those prints that have to be finished off?

HEDVIG

Yes, they are a few I was helping father with.

GREGERS

Please don't let me disturb you.

HEDVIG

Oh no.

[*She gathers the things to her and sits down to work; GREGERS looks at her, meanwhile, in silence.*]

GREGERS

Did the wild duck sleep well last night?

HEDVIG

Yes, I think so, thanks.

GREGERS   [*Turning towards the garret.*]

It looks quite different by day from what it did last night in the moonlight.

HEDVIG

Yes, it changes ever so much. It looks different in the morning and in the afternoon; and it's different on rainy days from what it is in fine weather.

GREGERS

Have you noticed that?

HEDVIG

Yes, how could I help it?

GREGERS

Are you, too, fond of being in there with the wild duck?

HEDVIG

Yes, when I can manage it——

GREGERS

But I suppose you haven't much spare time; you go to school, no doubt.

HEDVIG

No, not now; father is afraid of my hurting my eyes.

GREGERS

Oh; then he reads with you himself?

HEDVIG

Father has promised to read with me; but he has never had time yet.

GREGERS

Then is there nobody else to give you a little help?

HEDVIG

Yes, there is Mr. Molvik; but he is not always exactly—quite——

GREGERS

Sober?

HEDVIG

Yes, I suppose that's it!

GREGERS

Why, then you must have any amount of time on your hands. And in there I suppose it is a sort of world by itself?

HEDVIG

Oh yes, quite. And there are such lots of wonderful things.

GREGERS

Indeed?

HEDVIG

Yes, there are big cupboards full of books; and a great many of the books have pictures in them.

GREGERS

Aha!

HEDVIG

And there's an old bureau with drawers and flaps, and a big clock with figures that go out and in. But the clock isn't going now.

GREGERS

So time has come to a standstill in there—in the wild duck's domain.

HEDVIG

Yes. And then there's an old paint-box and things of that sort; and all the books.

GREGERS

And you read the books, I suppose?

HEDVIG

Oh yes, when I get the chance. Most of them are English though, and I don't understand English. But then I look at the pictures.—There is one great big book called "Harrison's History of London."* It must be a hundred years old; and there are such heaps of pictures in it. At the beginning there is Death with an hour-glass and a woman. I think that is horrid. But then there are all the other pictures of churches, and castles, and streets, and great ships sailing on the sea.

GREGERS

But tell me, where did all those wonderful things come from?

HEDVIG

Oh, an old sea captain once lived here, and he brought them home with him. They used to call him "The Flying Dutchman." That was curious, because he wasn't a Dutchman at all.

GREGERS

Was he not?

HEDVIG

No. But at last he was drowned at sea; and so he left all those things behind him.

GREGERS

Tell me now—when you are sitting in there looking at the pictures, don't you wish you could travel and see the real world for yourself?

HEDVIG

Oh no! I mean always to stay at home and help father and mother.

GREGERS

To retouch photographs?

A New and Universal History of the Cities of London and Westminster, by Walter Harrison. London, 1775, folio. (Translator's note)

HEDVIG

No, not only that. I should love above everything to learn to engrave pictures like those in the English books.

GREGERS

H'm. What does your father say to that?

HEDVIG

I don't think father likes it; father is strange about such things. Only think, he talks of my learning basket-making, and straw-plaiting! But I don't think that would be much good.

GREGERS

Oh no, I don't think so either.

HEDVIG

But father was right in saying that if I had learnt basket-making I could have made the new basket for the wild duck.

GREGERS

So you could; and it was you that ought to have done it, wasn't it?

HEDVIG

Yes, for it's my wild duck.

GREGERS

Of course it is.

HEDVIG

Yes, it belongs to me. But I lend it to father and grandfather as often as they please.

GREGERS

Indeed? What do they do with it?

HEDVIG

Oh, they look after it, and build places for it, and so on.

GREGERS

I see; for no doubt the wild duck is by far the most distinguished inhabitant of the garret?

HEDVIG

Yes, indeed she is; for she is a real wild fowl, you know. And then she is so much to be pitied; she has no one to care for, poor thing.

GREGERS

She has no family, as the rabbits have——

HEDVIG

No. The hens too, many of them, were chickens together; but she has been taken right away from all her friends. And then there is so much that is strange about the wild duck. Nobody knows her, and nobody knows where she came from either.

GREGERS

And she has been down in the depths of the sea.

HEDVIG   [*With a quick glance at him, represses a smile and asks:*]
Why do you say "the depths of the sea"?

GREGERS

What else should I say?

HEDVIG

You could say "the bottom of the sea."*

GREGERS

Oh, mayn't I just as well say the depths of the sea?

HEDVIG

Yes; but it sounds so strange to me when other people speak of the depths of the sea.

GREGERS

Why so? Tell me why?

HEDVIG

No, I won't; it's so stupid.

GREGERS

Oh no, I am sure it's not. Do tell me why you smiled.

HEDVIG

Well, this is the reason: whenever I come to realise suddenly—in a flash—what is in there, it always seems to me that the whole room and everything in it should be called "the depths of the sea."—But that is so stupid.

GREGERS

You mustn't say that.

HEDVIG

Oh yes, for you know it is only a garret.

GREGERS   [*Looks fixedly at her.*]
Are you so sure of that?

HEDVIG   [*Astonished.*]
That it's a garret?

*Gregers here uses the old-fashioned expression *havsens bund*, while Hedvig would have him use the more commonplace *havets bund* or *havbunden*.

GREGERS

Are you quite certain of it?

[HEDVIG *is silent, and looks at him openmouthed.* GINA *comes in from the kitchen with the table things.*]

GREGERS   [*Rising.*]

I have come in upon you too early.

GINA

Oh, you must be somewhere; and we're nearly ready now, any way. Clear the table, Hedvig.

[HEDVIG *clears away her things; she and* GINA *lay the cloth during what follows.* GREGERS *seats himself in the arm-chair and turns over an album.*]

GREGERS

I hear you can retouch, Mrs. Ekdal.

GINA   [*With a side glance.*]

Yes, I can.

GREGERS

That was exceedingly lucky.

GINA

How—lucky?

GREGERS

Since Ekdal took to photography, I mean.

HEDVIG

Mother can take photographs too.

GINA

Oh, yes; I was bound to learn that.

GREGERS

So it is really you that carry on the business, I suppose?

GINA

Yes, when Ekdal hasn't time himself——

GREGERS

He is a great deal taken up with his old father, I daresay.

GINA

Yes; and then you can't expect a man like Ekdal to do nothing but take car-de-visits of Dick, Tom and Harry.

GREGERS

I quite agree with you; but having once gone in for the thing——

GINA

> You can surely understand, Mr. Werle, that Ekdal's not like one
> of your common photographers.

GREGERS

> Of course not; but still——
>
> [*A shot is fired within the garret.*]

GREGERS   [*Starting up.*]

> What's that?

GINA

> Ugh! now they're firing again!

GREGERS

> Have they firearms in there?

HEDVIG

> They are out shooting.

GREGERS

> What!
>
> [*At the door of the garret.*]
>
> Are you shooting, Hialmar?

HIALMAR   [*Inside the net.*]

> Are you there? I didn't know; I was so taken up——
>
> [*To* HEDVIG.]
>
> Why did you not let us know?
>
> [*Comes into the studio.*]

GREGERS

> Do you go shooting in the garret?

HIALMAR   [*Showing a double-barrelled pistol.*]

> Oh, only with this thing.

GINA

> Yes, you and grandfather will do yourselves a mischief some day
> with that there pigstol.

HIALMAR   [*With irritation.*]

> I believe I have told you that this kind of firearm is called a
> pistol.

GINA

> Oh, that doesn't make it much better, that I can see.

GREGERS

> So you have become a sportsman too, Hialmar.

HIALMAR

Only a little rabbit-shooting now and then. Mostly to please father, you understand.

GINA

Men are strange beings; they must always have something to pervert theirselves with.

HIALMAR   [*Snappishly.*]

Just so; we must always have something to divert ourselves with.

GINA

Yes, that's just what I say.

HIALMAR

H'm.

[*To* GREGERS.]

You see the garret is fortunately so situated that no one can hear us shooting.

[*Lays the pistol on the top shelf of the bookcase.*]

Don't touch the pistol, Hedvig! One of the barrels is loaded; remember that.

GREGERS   [*Looking through the net.*]

You have a fowling-piece too, I see.

HIALMAR

That is father's old gun. It's of no use now; something has gone wrong with the lock. But it's fun to have it all the same; for we can take it to pieces now and then, and clean and grease it, and screw it together again.—Of course, it's mostly father that fiddle-faddles with all that sort of thing.

HEDVIG   [*Beside* GREGERS.]

Now you can see the wild duck properly.

GREGERS

I was just looking at her. One of her wings seems to me to droop a bit.

HEDVIG

Well, no wonder; her wing was broken, you know.

GREGERS

And she trails one foot a little. Isn't that so?

HIALMAR

Perhaps a very little bit.

HEDVIG
>Yes, it was by that foot the dog took hold of her.

HIALMAR
>But otherwise she hasn't the least thing the matter with her; and
>that is simply marvellous for a creature that has a charge of shot
>in her body, and has been between a dog's teeth——

GREGERS   [*With a glance at* HEDVIG.]
>——and that has lain in the depths of the sea—so long.

HEDVIG   [*Smiling.*]
>Yes.

GINA   [*Laying the table.*]
>That blessed wild duck! What a lot of fuss you do make over her.

HIALMAR
>H'm;—will lunch soon be ready?

GINA
>Yes, directly. Hedvig, you must come and help me now.
>[GINA *and* HEDVIG *go out into the kitchen.*]

HIALMAR   [*In a low voice.*]
>I think you had better not stand there looking in at father; he
>doesn't like it.
>[GREGERS *moves away from the garret door.*]
>Besides I may as well shut up before the others come.
>[*Claps his hands to drive the fowls back.*]
>Shh—shh, in with you!
>[*Draws up the curtain and pulls the doors together.*]
>All the contrivances are my own invention. It's really quite
>amusing to have things of this sort to potter with, and to put to
>rights when they get out of order. And it's absolutely necessary,
>too; for Gina objects to having rabbits and fowls in the studio.

GREGERS
>To be sure; and I suppose the studio is your wife's special
>department?

HIALMAR
>As a rule, I leave the everyday details of business to her; for then
>I can take refuge in the parlour and give my mind to more
>important things.

GREGERS
>What things may they be, Hialmar?

HIALMAR

> I wonder you have not asked that question sooner. But perhaps you haven't heard of the invention?

GREGERS

> The invention? No.

HIALMAR

> Really? Have you not? Oh no, out there in the wilds——

GREGERS

> So you have invented something, have you?

HIALMAR

> It is not quite completed yet; but I am working at it. You can easily imagine that when I resolved to devote myself to photography, it wasn't simply with the idea of taking likenesses of all sorts of commonplace people.

GREGERS

> No; your wife was saying the same thing just now.

HIALMAR

> I swore that if I consecrated my powers to this handicraft, I would so exalt it that it should become both an art and a science. And to that end I determined to make this great invention.

GREGERS

> And what is the nature of the invention? What purpose does it serve?

HIALMAR

> Oh, my dear fellow, you mustn't ask for details yet. It takes time, you see. And you must not think that my motive is vanity. It is not for my own sake that I am working. Oh no; it is my life's mission that stands before me night and day.

GREGERS

> What is your life's mission?

HIALMAR

> Do you forget the old man with the silver hair?

GREGERS

> Your poor father? Well, but what can you do for him?

HIALMAR

> I can raise up his self-respect from the dead, by restoring the name of Ekdal to honour and dignity.

GREGERS

Then that is your life's mission?

HIALMAR

Yes. I will rescue the shipwrecked man. For shipwrecked he was, by the very first blast of the storm. Even while those terrible investigations were going on, he was no longer himself. That pistol there—the one we use to shoot rabbits with—has played its part in the tragedy of the house of Ekdal.

GREGERS

The pistol? Indeed?

HIALMAR

When the sentence of imprisonment was passed—he had the pistol in his hand——

GREGERS

Had he——?

HIALMAR

Yes; but he dared not use it. His courage failed him. So broken, so demoralised was he even then! Oh, can you understand it? He, a soldier; he, who had shot nine bears, and who was descended from two lieutenant-colonels—one after the other of course. Can you understand it, Gregers?

GREGERS

Yes, I understand it well enough.

HIALMAR

I cannot. And once more the pistol played a part in the history of our house. When he had put on the grey clothes and was under lock and key—oh, that was a terrible time for me, I can tell you. I kept the blinds drawn down over both my windows. When I peeped out, I saw the sun shining as if nothing had happened. I could not understand it. I saw people going along the street, laughing and talking about indifferent things. I could not understand it. It seemed to me that the whole of existence must be at a standstill—as if under an eclipse.

GREGERS

I felt like that too, when my mother died.

HIALMAR

It was in such an hour that Hialmar Ekdal pointed the pistol at his own breast.

GREGERS

You too thought of——!

HIALMAR

Yes.

GREGERS

But you did not fire?

HIALMAR

No. At the decisive moment I won the victory over myself. I
remained in life. But I can assure you it takes some courage to
choose life under circumstances like those.

GREGERS

Well, that depends on how you look at it.

HIALMAR

Yes, indeed, it takes courage. But I am glad I was firm: for now I
shall soon perfect my invention; and Dr. Relling thinks, as I do
myself, that father may be allowed to wear his uniform again. I
will demand that as my sole reward.

GREGERS

So that is what he meant about his uniform——?

HIALMAR

Yes, that is what he most yearns for. You can't think how my
heart bleeds for him. Every time we celebrate any little family
festival—Gina's and my wedding-day, or whatever it may be—in
comes the old man in the lieutenant's uniform of happier days.
But if he only hears a knock at the door—for he daren't show
himself to strangers, you know—he hurries back to his room
again as fast as his old legs can carry him. Oh, it's heartrending
for a son to see such things!

GREGERS

How long do you think it will take you to finish your invention?

HIALMAR

Come now, you mustn't expect me to enter into particulars like
that. An invention is not a thing completely under one's own
control. It depends largely on inspiration—on intuition—and it
is almost impossible to predict when the inspiration may come.

GREGERS

But it's advancing?

HIALMAR

Yes, certainly, it is advancing. I turn it over in my mind every day; I am full of it. Every afternoon, when I have had my dinner, I shut myself up in the parlour, where I can ponder undisturbed. But I can't be goaded to it; it's not a bit of good; Relling says so too.

GREGERS

And you don't think that all that business in the garret draws you off and distracts you too much?

HIALMAR

No no no; quite the contrary. You mustn't say that. I cannot be everlastingly absorbed in the same laborious train of thought. I must have something alongside of it to fill up the time of waiting. The inspiration, the intuition, you see—when it comes, it comes, and there's an end of it.

GREGERS

My dear Hialmar, I almost think you have something of the wild duck in you.

HIALMAR

Something of the wild duck? How do you mean?

GREGERS

You have dived down and bitten yourself fast in the undergrowth.

HIALMAR

Are you alluding to the well-nigh fatal shot that has broken my father's wing—and mine too?

GREGERS

Not exactly to that. I don't say that your wing has been broken; but you have strayed into a poisonous marsh, Hialmar; an insidious disease has taken hold of you, and you have sunk down to die in the dark.

HIALMAR

I? To die in the dark? Look here, Gregers, you must really leave off talking such nonsense.

GREGERS

Don't be afraid; I shall find a way to help you up again. I too have a mission in life now; I found it yesterday.

HIALMAR

That's all very well; but you will please leave me out of it. I can

assure you that—apart from my very natural melancholy, of
course—I am as contented as any one can wish to be.

GREGERS

Your contentment is an effect of the marsh poison.

HIALMAR

Now, my dear Gregers, pray do not go on about disease and
poison; I am not used to that sort of talk. In my house nobody
ever speaks to me about unpleasant things.

GREGERS

Ah, that I can easily believe.

HIALMAR

It's not good for me you see. And there are no marsh poisons
here, as you express it. The poor photographer's roof is lowly, I
know—and my circumstances are narrow. But I am an inventor,
and I am the breadwinner of a family. That exalts me above my
mean surroundings.—Ah, here comes lunch!

GINA *and* HEDVIG *bring bottles of ale, a decanter of brandy, glasses, etc. At
the same time,* RELLING *and* MOLVIK *enter from the passage; they are both
without hat or overcoat.* MOLVIK *is dressed in black.*

GINA   [*Placing the things upon the table.*]

Ah, you two have come in the nick of time.

RELLING

Molvik got it into his head that he could smell herring-salad, and
then there was no holding him.—Good morning again, Ekdal.

HIALMAR

Gregers, let me introduce you to Mr. Molvik. Doctor—— Oh,
you know Relling, don't you?

GREGERS

Yes, slightly.

RELLING

Oh, Mr. Werle, junior! Yes, we two have had one or two little
skirmishes up at the Höidal works. You've just moved in?

GREGERS

I moved in this morning.

RELLING

Molvik and I live right under you; so you haven't far to go for the
doctor and the clergyman, if you should need anything in that line.

GREGERS

Thanks, it's not quite unlikely; for yesterday we were thirteen at table.

HIALMAR

Oh, come now, don't let us get upon unpleasant subjects again!

RELLING

You may make your mind easy, Ekdal; I'll be hanged if the finger of fate points to you.

HIALMAR

I should hope not, for the sake of my family. But let us sit down now, and eat and drink and be merry.

GREGERS

Shall we not wait for your father?

HIALMAR

No, his lunch will be taken in to him later. Come along!

[*The men seat themselves at table, and eat and drink.* GINA *and* HED-VIG *go in and out and wait upon them.*]

RELLING

Molvik was frightfully screwed yesterday, Mrs. Ekdal.

GINA

Really? Yesterday again?

RELLING

Didn't you hear him when I brought him home last night.

GINA

No, I can't say I did.

RELLING

That was a good thing, for Molvik was disgusting last night.

GINA

Is that true, Molvik?

MOLVIK

Let us draw a veil over last night's proceedings. That sort of thing is totally foreign to my better self.

RELLING   [*To* GREGERS.]

It comes over him like a sort of possession, and then I have to go out on the loose with him. Mr. Molvik is dæmonic, you see.

GREGERS

Dæmonic?

RELLING

Molvik is dæmonic, yes.

GREGERS

H'm.

RELLING

And dæmonic natures are not made to walk straight through the world; they must meander a little now and then.— Well, so you still stick up there at those horrible grimy works?

GREGERS

I have stuck there until now.

RELLING

And did you ever manage to collect that claim you went about presenting?

GREGERS

Claim?

[*Understands him.*]

Ah, I see.

HIALMAR

Have you been presenting claims, Gregers?

GREGERS

Oh, nonsense.

RELLING

Faith, but he has, though! He went round to all the cottars' cabins presenting something he called "the claim of the ideal."

GREGERS

I was young then.

RELLING

You're right; you were very young. And as for the claim of the ideal—you never got it honoured while *I* was up there.

GREGERS

Nor since either.

RELLING

Ah, then you've learnt to knock a little discount off, I expect.

GREGERS

Never, when I have a true man to deal with.

HIALMAR

No, I should think not, indeed. A little butter, Gina.

RELLING

And a slice of bacon for Molvik.

MOLVIK

Ugh! not bacon!

[*A knock at the garret door.*]

HIALMAR

Open the door, Hedvig; father wants to come out.

[HEDVIG *goes over and opens the door a little way;* EKDAL *enters with a fresh rabbit-skin; she closes the door after him.*]

EKDAL

Good morning, gentlemen! Good sport to-day. Shot a big one.

HIALMAR

And you've gone and skinned it without waiting for me———!

EKDAL

Salted it too. It's good tender meat, is rabbit; it's sweet; it tastes like sugar. Good appetite to you, gentlemen!

[*Goes into his room.*]

MOLVIK [*Rising.*]

Excuse me———; I can't———; I must get downstairs immediately ———

RELLING

Drink some soda water, man!

MOLVIK [*Hurrying away.*]

Ugh—ugh!

[*Goes out by the passage door.*]

RELLING [*To* HIALMAR.]

Let us drain a glass to the old hunter.

HIALMAR [*Clinks glasses with him.*]

To the undaunted sportsman who has looked death in the face!

RELLING

To the grey-haired———

[*Drinks.*]

By-the-bye, is his hair grey or white?

HIALMAR

Something between the two, I fancy; for that matter, he has very few hairs left of any colour.

RELLING

Well well, one can get through the world with a wig. After all, you are a happy man, Ekdal; you have your noble mission to labour for——

HIALMAR

And I do labour, I can tell you.

RELLING

And then you have your excellent wife, shuffling quietly in and out in her felt slippers, with that see-saw walk of hers, and making everything cosy and comfortable about you.

HIALMAR

Yes, Gina—

[*Nods to her.*]

—you are a good helpmate on the path of life.

GINA

Oh, don't sit there cricketizing me.

RELLING

And your Hedvig too, Ekdal!

HIALMAR   [*Affected.*]

The child, yes! The child before everything! Hedvig, come here to me.

[*Strokes her hair.*]

What day is it to-morrow, eh?

HEDVIG   [*Shaking him.*]

Oh no, you're not to say anything, father!

HIALMAR

It cuts me to the heart when I think what a poor affair it will be; only a little festivity in the garret——

HEDVIG

Oh, but that's just what I like!

RELLING

Just you wait till the wonderful invention sees the light, Hedvig!

HIALMAR

Yes indeed—then you shall see———! Hedvig, I have resolved to make your future secure. You shall live in comfort all your days. I will demand—something or other—on your behalf. That shall be the poor inventor's sole reward.

HEDVIG [*Whispering, with her arms round his neck.*]

Oh you dear, kind father!

RELLING [*To* GREGERS.]

Come now, don't you find it pleasant, for once in a way, to sit at a well-spread table in a happy family circle?

HIALMAR

Ah yes, I really prize these social hours.

GREGERS

For my part, I don't thrive in marsh vapours.

RELLING

Marsh vapours?

HIALMAR

Oh, don't begin with that stuff again!

GINA

Goodness knows there's no vapours in this house, Mr. Werle; I give the place a good airing every blessed day.

GREGERS [*Leaves the table.*]

No airing you can give will drive out the taint I mean.

HIALMAR

Taint!

GINA

Yes, what do you say to that, Ekdal!

RELLING

Excuse me—may it not be you yourself that have brought the taint from those mines up there?

GREGERS

It is like you to call what I bring into this house a taint.

RELLING [*Goes up to him.*]

Look here, Mr Werle, junior: I have a strong suspicion that you are still carrying about that "claim of the ideal" large as life, in your coat-tail pocket.

GREGERS

I carry it in my breast.

RELLING

Well, wherever you carry it, I advise you not to come dunning us
with it here, so long as *I* am on the premises.

GREGERS

And if I do so none the less?

RELLING

Then you'll go head-foremost down the stairs; now I've warned
you.

HIALMAR   [*Rising.*]

Oh, but Relling———!

GREGERS

Yes, you may turn me out———

GINA   [*Interposing between them.*]

We can't have that, Relling. But I must say, Mr. Werle, it ill
becomes you to talk about vapours and taints, after all the mess
you made with your stove.

[*A knock at the passage door.*]

HEDVIG

Mother, there's somebody knocking.

HIALMAR

There now, we're going to have a whole lot of people!

GINA

I'll go———

[*Goes over and opens the door, starts, and draws back.*]

Oh—oh dear!

WERLE, *in a fur coat, advances one step into the room.*

WERLE

Excuse me; but I think my son is staying here.

GINA   [*With a gulp.*]

Yes.

HIALMAR   [*Approaching him.*]

Won't you do us the honour to———?

WERLE

Thank you, I merely wish to speak to my son.

GREGERS

What is it? Here I am.

WERLE

I want a few words with you, in your room.

GREGERS

In my room? Very well——

[*About to go.*]

GINA

No, no, your room's not in a fit state——

WERLE

Well then, out in the passage here; I want to have a few words
with you alone.

HIALMAR

You can have them here, sir. Come into the parlour, Relling.

[HIALMAR *and* RELLING *go off to the right.* GINA *takes* HEDVIG
with her into the kitchen.]

GREGERS   [*After a short pause.*]

Well, now we are alone.

WERLE

From something you let fall last evening, and from your coming to lodge with the Ekdals, I can't help inferring that you
intend to make yourself unpleasant to me, in one way or
another.

GREGERS

I intend to open Hialmar Ekdal's eyes. He shall see his position as
it really is—that is all.

WERLE

Is that the mission in life you spoke of yesterday?

GREGERS

Yes. You have left me no other.

WERLE

Is it I, then, that have crippled your mind, Gregers?

GREGERS

You have crippled my whole life. I am not thinking of all that
about mother—— But it's thanks to you that I am continually
haunted and harassed by a guilty conscience.

WERLE

Indeed! It is your conscience that troubles you, is it?

GREGERS

I ought to have taken a stand against you when the trap was set

for Lieutenant Ekdal. I ought to have cautioned him; for I had a
misgiving as to what was in the wind.

WERLE

Yes, that was the time to have spoken.

GREGERS

I did not dare to, I was so cowed and spiritless. I was mortally
afraid of you—not only then, but long afterwards.

WERLE

You have got over that fear now, it appears.

GREGERS

Yes, fortunately. The wrong done to old Ekdal, both by me and
by—others, can never be undone; but Hialmar I can rescue
from all the falsehood and deception that are bringing him
to ruin.

WERLE

Do you think that will be doing him a kindness?

GREGERS

I have not the least doubt of it.

WERLE

You think our worthy photographer is the sort of man to
appreciate such friendly offices?

GREGERS

Yes, I do.

WERLE

H'm—we shall see.

GREGERS

Besides, if I am to go on living, I must try to find some cure for
my sick conscience.

WERLE

It will never be sound. Your conscience has been sickly from
childhood. That is a legacy from your mother, Gregers—the only
one she left you.

GREGERS   [With a scornful half-smile.]
Have you not yet forgiven her for the mistake you made in
supposing she would bring you a fortune?

WERLE

Don't let us wander from the point.——Then you hold to your

purpose of setting young Ekdal upon what you imagine to be the right scent?

GREGERS

Yes, that is my fixed resolve.

WERLE

Well, in that case I might have spared myself this visit; for of course it is useless to ask whether you will return home with me?

GREGERS

Quite useless.

WERLE

And I suppose you won't enter the firm either?

GREGERS

No.

WERLE

Very good. But as I am thinking of marrying again, your share in the property will fall to you at once.*

GREGERS   [*Quickly.*]

No, I do not want that.

WERLE

You don't want it?

GREGERS

No, I dare not take it, for conscience's sake.

WERLE   [*After a pause.*]

Are you going up to the works again?

GREGERS

No; I consider myself released from your service.

WERLE

But what are you going to do?

GREGERS

Only to fulfil my mission; nothing more.

WERLE

Well, but afterwards? What are you going to live upon?

---

*By Norwegian law [at this time], before a widower can marry again, a certain proportion of his property must be settled on his children by his former marriage. (Translator's note)

GREGERS

    I have laid by a little out of my salary.

WERLE

    How long will that last?

GREGERS

    I think it will last my time.

WERLE

    What do you mean?

GREGERS

    I shall answer no more questions.

WERLE

    Good-bye then, Gregers.

GREGERS

    Good-bye.

    [WERLE *goes.*]

HIALMAR   [*Peeping in.*]

    He's gone, isn't he?

GREGERS

    Yes.

HIALMAR *and* RELLING *enter; also* GINA *and* HEDVIG *from the kitchen.*

RELLING

    That luncheon-party was a failure.

GREGERS

    Put on your coat, Hialmar; I want you to come for a long walk with me.

HIALMAR

    With pleasure. What was it your father wanted? Had it anything to do with me?

GREGERS

    Come along. We must have a talk. I'll go and put on my overcoat.

    [*Goes out by the passage door.*]

GINA

    You shouldn't go out with him, Ekdal.

RELLING

No, don't you do it. Stay where you are.

HIALMAR   [*Gets his hat and overcoat.*]

Oh, nonsense! When a friend of my youth feels impelled to open his mind to me in private——

RELLING

But devil take it—don't you see that the fellow's mad, cracked, demented!

GINA

There, what did I tell you! His mother before him had crazy fits like that sometimes.

HIALMAR

The more need for a friend's watchful eye.

[*To* GINA.]

Be sure you have dinner ready in good time. Good-bye for the present.

[*Goes out by the passage door.*]

RELLING

It's a thousand pities the fellow didn't go to hell through one of the Höidal mines.

GINA

Good Lord! what makes you say that?

RELLING   [*Muttering.*]

Oh, I have my own reasons.

GINA

Do you think young Werle is really mad?

RELLING

No, worse luck; he's no madder than most other people. But one disease he has certainly got in his system.

GINA

What is it that's the matter with him?

RELLING

Well, I'll tell you, Mrs. Ekdal. He is suffering from an acute attack of integrity.

GINA

Integrity?

HEDVIG

Is that a kind of disease?

RELLING

Yes, it's a national disease; but it only appears sporadically.

[*Nods to* GINA.]

Thanks for your hospitality.

[*He goes out by the passage door.*]

GINA   [*Moving restlessly to and fro.*]

Ugh, that Gregers Werle—he was always a wretched creature.

HEDVIG   [*Standing by the table, and looking searchingly at her.*]

I think all this is very strange.

ACT FOURTH

HIALMAR EKDAL's *studio. A photograph has just been taken; a camera with the cloth over it, a pedestal, two chairs, a folding table, etc., are standing out in the room. Afternoon light; the sun is going down; a little later it begins to grow dusk.*

GINA *stands in the passage doorway, with a little box and a wet glass plate in her hand, and is speaking to somebody outside.*

GINA

Yes, certainly. When I make a promise I keep it. The first dozen shall be ready on Monday. Good afternoon.

[*Some one is heard going downstairs.* GINA *shuts the door, slips the plate into the box, and puts it into the covered camera.*]

HEDVIG [*Comes in from the kitchen.*]

Are they gone?

GINA [*Tidying up.*]

Yes, thank goodness, I've got rid of them at last.

HEDVIG

But can you imagine why father hasn't come home yet?

GINA

Are you sure he's not down in Relling's room?

HEDVIG

No, he's not; I ran down the kitchen stair just now and asked.

GINA

And his dinner standing and getting cold, too.

HEDVIG

Yes, I can't understand it. Father's always so careful to be home to dinner!

GINA

Oh, he'll be here directly, you'll see.

HEDVIG

I wish he would come; everything seems so queer to-day.

GINA   [*Calls out.*]

There he is!

HIALMAR EKDAL *comes in at the passage door.*

HEDVIG   [*Going to him.*]

Father! Oh what a time we've been waiting for you!

GINA   [*Glancing sidelong at him.*]

You've been out a long time, Ekdal.

HIALMAR   [*Without looking at her.*]

Rather long, yes.

[*He takes off his overcoat; GINA and HEDVIG go to help him; he motions them away.*]

GINA

Perhaps you've had dinner with Werle?

HIALMAR   [*Hanging up his coat.*]

No.

GINA   [*Going towards the kitchen door.*]

Then I'll bring some in for you.

HIALMAR

No; let the dinner alone. I want nothing to eat.

HEDVIG   [*Going nearer to him.*]

Are you not well, father?

HIALMAR

Well? Oh yes, well enough. We have had a tiring walk, Gregers and I.

GINA

You didn't ought to have gone so far, Ekdal; you're not used to it.

HIALMAR

H'm; there's many a thing a man must get used to in this world. [*Wanders about the room.*] Has any one been here whilst I was out?

GINA

Nobody but the two sweethearts.

HIALMAR

No new orders?

GINA

No, not to-day.

HEDVIG

There will be some to-morrow, father, you'll see.

HIALMAR

I hope there will; for to-morrow I am going to set to work in real earnest.

HEDVIG

To-morrow! Don't you remember what day it is to-morrow?

HIALMAR

Oh yes, by-the-bye———. Well, the day after, then. Henceforth I mean to do everything myself; I shall take all the work into my own hands.

GINA

Why, what can be the good of that, Ekdal? It'll only make your life a burden to you. I can manage the photography all right; and you can go on working at your invention.

HEDVIG

And think of the wild duck, father,—and all the hens and rabbits and———!

HIALMAR

Don't talk to me of all that trash! From to-morrow I will never set foot in the garret again.

HEDVIG

Oh but, father, you promised that we should have a little party———

HIALMAR

H'm, true. Well then, from the day after to-morrow. I should almost like to wring that cursed wild duck's neck!

HEDVIG   [*Shrieks.*]

The wild duck!

GINA

Well I never!

HEDVIG   [*Shaking him.*]

Oh no, father; you know it's my wild duck!

HIALMAR

That is why I don't do it. I haven't the heart to—for your sake, Hedvig. But in my inmost soul I feel that I ought to do it. I ought not to tolerate under my roof a creature that has been through those hands.

GINA

Why, good gracious, even if grandfather did get it from that poor creature, Pettersen——

HIALMAR   [*Wandering about.*]

There are certain claims—what shall I call them?—let me say claims of the ideal—certain obligations, which a man cannot disregard without injury to his soul.

HEDVIG   [*Going after him.*]

But think of the wild duck,—the poor wild duck!

HIALMAR   [*Stops.*]

I tell you I will spare it—for your sake. Not a hair of its head shall be—I mean, it shall be spared. There are greater problems than that to be dealt with. But you should go out a little now, Hedvig, as usual; it is getting dusk enough for you now.

HEDVIG

No, I don't care about going out now.

HIALMAR

Yes do; it seems to me your eyes are blinking a great deal; all these vapours in here are bad for you. The air is heavy under this roof.

HEDVIG

Very well then, I'll run down the kitchen stair and go for a little walk. My cloak and hat?—oh, they're in my own room. Father— be sure you don't do the wild duck any harm whilst I'm out.

HIALMAR

Not a feather of its head shall be touched.

[*Draws her to him.*]

You and I, Hedvig—we two——! Well, go along.

[HEDVIG *nods to her parents and goes out through the kitchen.*]

HIALMAR   [*Walks about without looking up.*]

Gina.

GINA

Yes?

HIALMAR

From to-morrow—or, say, from the day after to-morrow—I should like to keep the household account-book myself.

GINA

Do you want to keep the accounts too, now?

HIALMAR

Yes; or to check the receipts at any rate.

GINA

Lord help us! that's soon done.

HIALMAR

One would hardly think so; at any rate you seem to make the money go a very long way.

[*Stops and looks at her.*]

How do you manage it?

GINA

It's because me and Hedvig, we need so little.

HIALMAR

Is it the case that father is very liberally paid for the copying he does for Mr. Werle?

GINA

I don't know as he gets anything out of the way. I don't know the rates for that sort of work.

HIALMAR

Well, what does he get, about? Let me hear!

GINA

Oh, it varies; I daresay it'll come to about as much as he costs us, with a little pocket-money over.

HIALMAR

As much as he costs us! And you have never told me this before!

GINA

No, how could I tell you? It pleased you so much to think he got everything from you.

HIALMAR

And he gets it from Mr. Werle.

GINA

Oh well, he has plenty and to spare, he has.

HIALMAR

Light the lamp for me, please!

GINA   [*Lighting the lamp.*]

And of course we don't know as it's Mr. Werle himself; it may he Gråberg——

HIALMAR

Why attempt such an evasion?

GINA

I don't know; I only thought——

HIALMAR

H'm!

GINA

It wasn't me that got grandfather that copying. It was Bertha, when she used to come about us.

HIALMAR

It seems to me your voice is trembling.

GINA   [*Putting the lamp-shade on.*]

Is it?

HIALMAR

And your hands are shaking, are they not?

GINA   [*Firmly.*]

Come right out with it, Ekdal. What has he been saying about me?

HIALMAR

Is it true—can it be true that—that there was an—an understanding between you and Mr. Werle, while you were in service there?

GINA

That's not true. Not at that time. Mr. Werle did come after me, that's a fact. And his wife thought there was something in it, and then she made such a hocus-pocus and hurly-burly, and she hustled me and bustled me about so, that I left her service.

HIALMAR

But afterwards, then?

GINA

Well, then I went home. And mother—well, she wasn't the woman you took her for, Ekdal; she kept on worrying and worrying at me about one thing and another—for Mr. Werle was a widower by that time.

HIALMAR

Well, and then?

GINA

I suppose you've got to know it. He gave me no peace until he'd had his way.

HIALMAR   [*Striking his hands together.*]

And this is the mother of my child! How could you hide this from me?

GINA

Yes, it was wrong of me; I ought certainly to have told you long ago.

HIALMAR

You should have told me at the very first;—then I should have known the sort of woman you were.

GINA

But would you have married me all the same?

HIALMAR

How can you dream that I would?

GINA

That's just why I didn't dare tell you anything, then. For I'd come to care for you so much, you see; and I couldn't go and make myself utterly miserable——

HIALMAR   [*Walks about.*]

And this is my Hedvig's mother. And to know that all I see before me—

[*Kicks at a chair*]

—all that I call my home—I owe to a favoured predecessor! Oh that scoundrel Werle!

GINA

Do you repent of the fourteen—the fifteen years as we've lived together?

HIALMAR   [*Placing himself in front of her.*]

Have you not every day, every hour, repented of the spider's-web of deceit you have spun around me? Answer me that! How could you help writhing with penitence and remorse?

GINA

Oh, my dear Ekdal, I've had all I could do to look after the house and get through the day's work——

HIALMAR

Then you never think of reviewing your past?

GINA

No; Heaven knows I'd almost forgotten those old stories.

HIALMAR

Oh, this dull, callous contentment! To me there is something revolting about it. Think of it——never so much as a twinge of remorse!

GINA

But tell me, Ekdal——what would have become of you if you hadn't had a wife like me?

HIALMAR

Like you——!

GINA

Yes; for you know I've always been more practical and wide-awake than you. Of course I'm a year or two older.

HIALMAR

What would have become of me!

GINA

You'd got into all sorts of bad ways when first you met me; that you can't deny.

HIALMAR

"Bad ways" do you call them? Little do you know what a man goes through when he is in grief and despair——especially a man of my fiery temperament.

GINA

Well, well, that may be so. And I've no reason to crow over you, neither; for you turned a moral of a husband, that you did, as soon as ever you had a house and home of your own.——And now we'd got everything so nice and cosy about us; and me and Hedvig was just thinking we'd soon be able to let ourselves go a bit, in the way of both food and clothes.

HIALMAR

In the swamp of deceit, yes.

GINA

I wish to goodness that detestable being had never set his foot inside our doors!

HIALMAR

And I, too, thought my home such a pleasant one. That was a delusion. Where shall I now find the elasticity of spirit to bring

my invention into the world of reality? Perhaps it will die with
me; and then it will be your past, Gina, that will have killed it.

GINA [*Nearly crying.*]

You mustn't say such things, Ekdal. Me, that has only wanted to
do the best I could for you, all my days!

HIALMAR

I ask you, what becomes of the breadwinner's dream? When I
used to lie in there on the sofa and brood over my invention, I
had a clear enough presentiment that it would sap my vitality to
the last drop. I felt even then that the day when I held the patent
in my hand—that day—would bring my—release. And then it
was my dream that you should live on after me, the dead
inventor's well-to-do widow.

GINA [*Drying her tears.*]

No, you mustn't talk like that, Ekdal. May the Lord never let me
see the day I am left a widow!

HIALMAR

Oh, the whole dream has vanished. It is all over now. All over!

GREGERS WERLE *opens the passage door cautiously and looks in.*

GREGERS

May I come in?

HIALMAR

Yes, come in.

GREGERS [*Comes forward, his face beaming with satisfaction, and holds
out both his hands to them.*]

Well, dear friends——!

[*Looks from one to the other, and whispers to* HIALMAR.]

Have you not done it yet?

HIALMAR [*Aloud.*]

It is done.

GREGERS

It is?

HIALMAR

I have passed through the bitterest moments of my life.

GREGERS

But also, I trust, the most ennobling.

HIALMAR

Well, at any rate, we have got through it for the present.

GINA

God forgive you, Mr. Werle.

GREGERS   [*In great surprise.*]

But I don't understand this.

HIALMAR

What don't you understand?

GREGERS

After so great a crisis—a crisis that is to be the starting-point of an entirely new life—of a communion founded on truth, and free from all taint of deception——

HIALMAR

Yes yes, I know; I know that quite well.

GREGERS

I confidently expected, when I entered the room, to find the light of transfiguration shining upon me from both husband and wife. And now I see nothing but dulness, oppression, gloom——

GINA

Oh, is that it?

[*Takes off the lamp-shade.*]

GREGERS

You will not understand me, Mrs. Ekdal. Ah well, you, I suppose, need time to——. But you, Hialmar? Surely you feel a new consecration after the great crisis.

HIALMAR

Yes, of course I do. That is—in a sort of way.

GREGERS

For surely nothing in the world can compare with the joy of forgiving one who has erred, and raising her up to oneself in love.

HIALMAR

Do you think a man can so easily throw off the effects of the bitter cup I have drained?

GREGERS

No, not a common man, perhaps. But a man like you——!

HIALMAR

Good God! I know that well enough. But you must keep me up
to it, Gregers. It takes time, you know.

GREGERS

You have much of the wild duck in you, Hialmar.

RELLING *has come in at the passage door.*

RELLING

Oho! is the wild duck to the fore again?

HIALMAR

Yes; Mr. Werle's wing-broken victim.

RELLING

Mr. Werle's———? So it's him you are talking about?

HIALMAR

Him and—ourselves.

RELLING   [*In an undertone to* GREGERS.]

May the devil fly away with you!

HIALMAR

What is that you are saying?

RELLING

Only uttering a heartfelt wish that this quacksalver would take
himself off. If he stays here, he is quite equal to making an utter
mess of life, for both of you.

GREGERS

These two will not make a mess of life, Mr. Relling. Of course I
won't speak of Hialmar—him we know. But she, too, in her
innermost heart, has certainly something loyal and sincere———

GINA   [*Almost crying.*]

You might have let me alone for what I was, then.

RELLING   [*To* GREGERS.]

Is it rude to ask what you really want in this house?

GREGERS

To lay the foundations of a true marriage.

RELLING

So you don't think Ekdal's marriage is good enough as it is?

GREGERS

No doubt it is as good a marriage as most others, worse luck. But a true marriage it has yet to become.

HIALMAR

You have never had eyes for the claims of the ideal, Relling.

RELLING

Rubbish, my boy!——But excuse me, Mr. Werle: how many——in round numbers——how many true marriages have you seen in the course of your life?

GREGERS

Scarcely a single one.

RELLING

Nor I either.

GREGERS

But I have seen innumerable marriages of the opposite kind. And it has been my fate to see at close quarters what ruin such a marriage can work in two human souls.

HIALMAR

A man's whole moral basis may give away beneath his feet; that is the terrible part of it.

RELLING

Well, I can't say I've ever been exactly married, so I don't pretend to speak with authority. But this I know, that the child enters into the marriage problem. And you must leave the child in peace.

HIALMAR

Oh——Hedvig! my poor Hedvig!

RELLING

Yes, you must be good enough to keep Hedvig outside of all this. You two are grown-up people; you are free, in God's name, to make what mess and muddle you please of your life. But you must deal cautiously with Hedvig, I tell you; else you may do her a great injury.

HIALMAR

An injury!

RELLING

Yes, or she may do herself an injury——and perhaps others too.

GINA

    How can you know that, Relling?

HIALMAR

    Her sight is in no immediate danger, is it?

RELLING

    I am not talking about her sight. Hedvig is at a critical age. She
may be getting all sorts of mischief into her head.

GINA

    That's true——I've noticed it already! She's taken to carrying on
with the fire, out in the kitchen. She calls it playing at house-on-
fire. I'm often scared for fear she really sets fire to the house.

RELLING

    You see; I thought as much.

GREGERS   [*To* RELLING.]

    But how do you account for that?

RELLING   [*Sullenly.*]

    Her constitution's changing, sir.

HIALMAR

    So long as the child has me——! So long as *I* am above
ground——!

    [*A knock at the door.*]

GINA

    Hush, Ekdal; there's some one in the passage.

    [*Calls out.*]

    Come in!

    [MRS. SÖRBY, *in walking dress, comes in.*]

MRS. SÖRBY

    Good evening.

GINA   [*Going towards her.*]

    Is it really you, Bertha?

MRS. SÖRBY

    Yes, of course it is. But I'm disturbing you, I'm afraid?

HIALMAR

    No, not at all; an emissary from that house——

MRS. SÖRBY   [*To* GINA.]

    To tell the truth, I hoped your men-folk would be out at this
time. I just ran up to have a little chat with you, and to say good-
bye.

GINA

Good-bye? Are you going away, then?

MRS. SÖRBY

Yes, to-morrow morning,—up to Höidal. Mr. Werle started this afternoon.

[*Lightly to* GREGERS.]

He asked me to say good-bye for him.

GINA

Only fancy——!

HIALMAR

So Mr. Werle has gone? And now you are going after him?

MRS. SÖRBY

Yes, what do you say to that, Ekdal?

HIALMAR

I say: beware!

GREGERS

I must explain the situation. My father and Mrs. Sörby are going to be married.

HIALMAR

Going to be married!

GINA

Oh Bertha! So it's come to that at last!

RELLING   [*His voice quivering a little.*]

This is surely not true?

MRS. SÖRBY

Yes, my dear Relling, it's true enough.

RELLING

You are going to marry again?

MRS. SÖRBY

Yes, it looks like it. Werle has got a special licence, and we are going to be married quite quietly, up at the works.

GREGERS

Then I must wish you all happiness, like a dutiful stepson.

MRS. SÖRBY

Thank you very much—if you mean what you say. I certainly hope it will lead to happiness, both for Werle and for me.

RELLING

You have every reason to hope that. Mr. Werle never gets

drunk—so far as I know; and I don't suppose he's in the habit of thrashing his wives, like the late lamented horse-doctor.

MRS. SÖRBY

Come, now, let Sörby rest in peace. He had his good points too.

RELLING

Mr. Werle has better ones, I have no doubt.

MRS. SÖRBY

He hasn't frittered away all that was good in him, at any rate. The man who does that must take the consequences.

RELLING

I shall go out with Molvik this evening.

MRS. SÖRBY

You mustn't do that, Relling. Don't do it—for my sake.

RELLING

There's nothing else for it.

[*To* HIALMAR.]

If you're going with us, come along.

GINA

No, thank you. Ekdal doesn't go in for that sort of dissertation.

HIALMAR   [*Half aloud, in vexation.*]

Oh, do hold your tongue!

RELLING

Good-bye, Mrs.—Werle.

[*Goes out through the passage door.*]

GREGERS   [*To* MRS. SÖRBY.]

You seem to know Dr. Relling pretty intimately.

MRS. SÖRBY

Yes, we have known each other for many years. At one time it seemed as if things might have gone further between us.

GREGERS

It was surely lucky for you that they did not.

MRS. SÖRBY

You may well say that. But I have always been wary of acting on impulse. A woman can't afford absolutely to throw herself away.

GREGERS

Are you not in the least afraid that I may let my father know about this old friendship?

MRS. SÖRBY

Why, of course I have told him all about it myself.

GREGERS

Indeed?

MRS. SÖRBY

Your father knows every single thing that can, with any truth, be said about me. I have told him all; it was the first thing I did when I saw what was in his mind.

GREGERS

Then you have been franker than most people, I think.

MRS. SÖRBY

I have always been frank. We women find that the best policy.

HIALMAR

What do you say to that, Gina?

GINA

Oh, we're not all alike, us women aren't. Some are made one way, some another.

MRS. SÖRBY

Well, for my part, Gina, I believe it's wisest to do as I've done. And Werle has no secrets either, on his side. That's really the great bond between us, you see. Now he can talk to me as openly as a child. He has never had the chance to do that before. Fancy a man like him, full of health and vigour, passing his whole youth and the best years of his life in listening to nothing but penitential sermons! And very often the sermons had for their text the most imaginary offences—at least so I understand.

GINA

That's true enough.

GREGERS

If you ladies are going to follow up this topic, I had better withdraw.

MRS. SÖRBY

You can stay so far as that's concerned. I shan't say a word more. But I wanted you to know that I had done nothing secretly or in an underhand way. I may seem to have come in for a great piece of luck; and so I have, in a sense. But after all, I don't think I am getting any more than I am giving. I shall stand by him always,

and I can tend and care for him as no one else can, now that he is
getting helpless.

HIALMAR

Getting helpless?

GREGERS   [*To* MRS. SÖRBY.]

Hush, don't speak of that here.

MRS. SÖRBY

There is no disguising it any longer, however much he would like
to. He is going blind.

HIALMAR   [*Starts.*]

Going blind? That's strange. He too going blind!

GINA

Lots of people do.

MRS. SÖRBY

And you can imagine what that means to a business man. Well, I
shall try as well as I can to make my eyes take the place of his.
But I musn't stay any longer; I have such heaps of things to do.—
Oh, by-the-bye, Ekdal, I was to tell you that if there is anything
Werle can do for you, you must just apply to Gråberg.

GREGERS

That offer I am sure Hialmar Ekdal will decline with thanks.

MRS. SÖRBY

Indeed? I don't think he used to be so ——

GINA

No, Bertha, Ekdal doesn't need anything from Mr. Werle now.

HIALMAR   [*Slowly, and with emphasis.*]

Will you present my compliments to your future husband, and
say that I intend very shortly to call upon Mr. Gråberg——

GREGERS

What! You don't really mean that?

HIALMAR

To call upon Mr. Gråberg, I say, and obtain an account of the sum
I owe his principal. I will pay that debt of honour—ha ha ha! a
debt of honour, let us call it! In any case, I will pay the whole
with five per cent interest.

GINA

But, my dear Ekdal, God knows we haven't got the money to do it.

HIALMAR

Be good enough to tell your future husband that I am working assiduously at my invention. Please tell him that what sustains me in this laborious task is the wish to free myself from a torturing burden of debt. That is my reason for proceeding with the invention. The entire profits shall be devoted to releasing me from my pecuniary obligations to your future husband.

MRS. SÖRBY

Something has happened here.

HIALMAR

Yes, you are right.

MRS. SÖRBY

Well, good-bye. I had something else to speak to you about, Gina; but it must keep till another time. Good-bye.

[HIALMAR *and* GREGERS *bow silently.* GINA *follows* MRS. SÖRBY *to the door.*]

HIALMAR

Not beyond the threshold, Gina!

[MRS. SÖRBY *goes;* GINA *shuts the door after her.*]

HIALMAR

There now, Gregers; I have got that burden of debt off my mind.

GREGERS

You soon will, at all events.

HIALMAR

I think my attitude may be called correct.

GREGERS

You are the man I have always taken you for.

HIALMAR

In certain cases, it is impossible to disregard the claim of the ideal. Yet, as the breadwinner of a family, I cannot but writhe and groan under it. I can tell you it is no joke for a man without capital to attempt the repayment of a long-standing obligation, over which, so to speak, the dust of oblivion had gathered. But it cannot be helped: the Man in me demands his rights.

GREGERS   [*Laying his hand on* HIALMAR'*s shoulder.*]

My dear Hialmar—was it not a good thing I came?

HIALMAR

Yes.

GREGERS

Are you not glad to have had your true position made clear to you?

HIALMAR   [*Somewhat impatiently.*]

Yes, of course I am. But there is one thing that is revolting to my sense of justice.

GREGERS

And what is that?

HIALMAR

It is that—but I don't know whether I ought to express myself so unreservedly about your father.

GREGERS

Say what you please, so far as I am concerned.

HIALMAR

Well then, is it not exasperating to think that it is not I, but he, who will realise the true marriage?

GREGERS

How can you say such a thing?

HIALMAR

And yet, after all, I cannot but recognise the guiding finger of fate. He is going blind.

GINA

Oh, you can't be sure of that.

HIALMAR

There is no doubt about it. At all events there ought not to be; for in that very fact lies the righteous retribution. He has hoodwinked a confiding fellow creature in days gone by——

GREGERS

I fear he has hoodwinked many.

HIALMAR

And now comes inexorable, mysterious Fate, and demands Werle's own eyes.

GINA

Oh, how dare you say such dreadful things! You make me quite scared.

HIALMAR

It is profitable, now and then, to plunge deep into the night side of existence.

HEDVIG, *in her hat and cloak, comes in by the passage door. She is pleasur-ably excited, and out of breath.*

GINA

Are you back already?

HEDVIG

Yes, I didn't care to go any farther. It was a good thing, too; for I've just met some one at the door.

HIALMAR

It must have been that Mrs. Sörby.

HEDVIG

Yes.

HIALMAR   [*Walks up and down.*]

I hope you have seen her for the last time.

[*Silence.* HEDVIG, *discouraged, looks first at one and then at the other, trying to divine their frame of mind.*]

HEDVIG   [*Approaching, coaxingly.*]

Father.

HIALMAR

Well—what is it, Hedvig?

HEDVIG

Mrs. Sörby had something with her for me.

HIALMAR   [*Stops.*]

For you?

HEDVIG

Yes. Something for to-morrow.

GINA

Bertha has always given you some little thing on your birthday.

HIALMAR

What is it?

HEDVIG

Oh, you mustn't see it now. Mother is to give it to me to-morrow morning before I'm up.

HIALMAR

What is all this hocus-pocus that I am to be kept in the dark about!

HEDVIG   [*Quickly.*]

Oh no, you may see it if you like. It's a big letter.

[*Takes the letter out of her cloak pocket.*]

HIALMAR

A letter too?

HEDVIG

Yes, it is only a letter. The rest will come afterwards, I suppose. But fancy—a letter! I've never had a letter before. And there's "Miss" written upon it.

[*Reads.*]

"Miss Hedvig Ekdal." Only fancy—that's me!

HIALMAR

Let me see that letter.

HEDVIG   [*Hands it to him.*]

There it is.

HIALMAR

That is Mr. Werle's hand.

GINA

Are you sure of that, Ekdal?

HIALMAR

Look for yourself.

GINA

Oh, what do *I* know about such-like things?

HIALMAR

Hedvig, may I open the letter—and read it?

HEDVIG

Yes, of course you may, if you want to.

GINA

No, not to-night, Ekdal; it's to be kept till to-morrow.

HEDVIG   [*Softly.*]

Oh, can't you let him read it! It's sure to be something good; and then father will be glad, and everything will be nice again.

HIALMAR

I may open it then?

HEDVIG

Yes do, father. I'm so anxious to know what it is.

HIALMAR

Well and good.

[*Opens the letter, takes out a paper, reads it through, and appears bewildered.*]

What is this————!

GINA

Oh yes, father—tell us!

What does it say?

HEDVIG

Oh yes, father—tell us!

HIALMAR

Be quiet.

[*Reads it through again; he has turned pale, but says with self-control:*]
It is a deed of gift, Hedvig.

HEDVIG

Is it? What sort of gift am I to have?

HIALMAR

Read for yourself.

[HEDVIG *goes over and reads for a time by the lamp.*]

HIALMAR   [*Half-aloud, clenching his hands.*]

The eyes! The eyes—and then that letter!

HEDVIG   [*Leaves off reading.*]

Yes, but it seems to me that it's grandfather that's to have it.

HIALMAR   [*Takes the letter from her.*]

Gina—can you understand this?

GINA

I know nothing whatever about it; tell me what's the matter.

HIALMAR

Mr. Werle writes to Hedvig that her old grandfather need not
trouble himself any longer with the copying, but that he can
henceforth draw on the office for a hundred crowns a month————

GREGERS

Aha!

HEDVIG

A hundred crowns, mother! I read that.

GINA

What a good thing for grandfather!

HIALMAR

————a hundred crowns a month so long as he needs it—that
means, of course, so long as he lives.

GINA

Well, so he's provided for, poor dear.

HIALMAR

But there is more to come. You didn't read that, Hedvig.
Afterwards this gift is to pass on to you.

HEDVIG

To me! The whole of it?

HIALMAR

He says that the same amount is assured to you for the whole of
your life. Do you hear that, Gina?

GINA

Yes, I hear.

HEDVIG

Fancy—all that money for me!
[*Shakes him.*]
Father, father, aren't you glad——?

HIALMAR   [*Eluding her.*]

Glad!
[*Walks about.*]
Oh what vistas—what perspectives open up before me! It is
Hedvig, Hedvig that he showers these benefactions upon!

GINA

Yes, because it's Hedvig's birthday——

HEDVIG

And you'll get it all the same, father! You know quite well I shall
give all the money to you and mother.

HIALMAR

To mother, yes! There we have it.

GREGERS

Hialmar, this is a trap he is setting for you.

HIALMAR

Do you think it's another trap?

GREGERS

When he was here this morning he said: Hialmar Ekdal is not the
man you imagine him to be.

HIALMAR

Not the man——!

GREGERS

That you shall see, he said.

HIALMAR

He meant you should see that I would let myself be bought
off——!

HEDVIG

Oh mother, what does all this mean?

GINA

Go and take off your things.

[HEDVIG *goes out by the kitchen door, half-crying.*]

GREGERS

Yes, Hialmar—now is the time to show who was right, he or I.

HIALMAR　[*Slowly tears the paper across, lays both pieces on the table, and
says:*]

Here is my answer.

GREGERS

Just what I expected.

HIALMAR　[*Goes over to* GINA, *who stands by the stove, and says in a low
voice:*]

Now please make a clean breast of it. If the connection between
you and him was quite over when you—came to care for me, as
you call it—why did he place us in a position to marry?

GINA

I suppose he thought as he could come and go in our house.

HIALMAR

Only that? Was not he afraid of a possible contingency?

GINA

I don't know what you mean.

HIALMAR

I want to know whether—your child has the right to live under
my roof.

GINA　[*Draws herself up; her eyes flash.*]

You ask that!

HIALMAR

You shall answer me this one question: Does Hedvig belong to
me—or——? Well!

GINA　[*Looking at him with cold defiance.*]

I don't know.

HIALMAR　[*Quivering a little.*]

You don't know!

GINA

How should *I* know? A creature like me——

HIALMAR   [*Quietly turning away from her.*]

Then I have nothing more to do in this house.

GREGERS

Take care, Hialmar! Think what you are doing!

HIALMAR   [*Puts on his overcoat.*]

In this case, there is nothing for a man like me to think twice about.

GREGERS

Yes indeed, there are endless things to be considered. You three must be together if you are to attain the true frame of mind for self-sacrifice and forgiveness.

HIALMAR

I don't want to attain it. Never, never! My hat!

[*Takes his hat.*]

My home has fallen in ruins about me.

[*Bursts into tears.*]

Gregers, I have no child!

HEDVIG   [*Who has opened the kitchen door.*]

What is that you're saying?

[*Coming to him.*]

Father, father!

GINA

There, you see!

HIALMAR

Don't come near me, Hedvig! Keep far away. I cannot bear to see you. Oh! those eyes——! Good-bye.

[*Makes for the door.*]

HEDVIG   [*Clinging close to him and screaming loudly.*]

No! no! Don't leave me!

GINA   [*Cries out.*]

Look at the child, Ekdal! Look at the child!

HIALMAR

I will not! I cannot! I must get out—away from all this!

[*He tears himself away from* HEDVIG, *and goes out by the passage door.*]

HEDVIG [*With despairing eyes.*]

He is going away from us, mother! He is going away from us! He will never come back again!

GINA

Don't cry, Hedvig. Father's sure to come back again.

HEDVIG [*Throws herself sobbing on the sofa.*]

No, no, he'll never come home to us any more.

GREGERS

Do you believe I meant all for the best, Mrs. Ekdal?

GINA

Yes, I daresay you did; but God forgive you, all the same.

HEDVIG [*Lying on the sofa.*]

Oh, this will kill me! What have I done to him? Mother, you must fetch him home again!

GINA

Yes yes yes; only be quiet, and I'll go out and look for him. [*Puts on her outdoor things.*]

Perhaps he's gone in to Relling's. But you mustn't lie there and cry. Promise me!

HEDVIG [*Weeping convulsively.*]

Yes, I'll stop, I'll stop; if only father comes back!

GREGERS [*To* GINA, *who is going.*]

After all, had you not better leave him to fight out his bitter fight to the end?

GINA

Oh, he can do that afterwards. First of all, we must get the child quieted.

[*Goes out by the passage door.*]

HEDVIG [*Sits up and dries her tears.*]

Now you must tell me what all this means. Why doesn't father want me any more?

GREGERS

You mustn't ask that till you are a big girl—quite grown-up.

HEDVIG [*Sobs.*]

But I can't go on being as miserable as this till I'm grown-up.—I think I know what it is.—Perhaps I'm not really father's child.

GREGERS [*Uneasily.*]

How could that be?

HEDVIG

Mother might have found me. And perhaps father has just got to know it; I've read of such things.

GREGERS

Well, but if it were so——

HEDVIG

I think he might be just as fond of me for all that. Yes, fonder almost. We got the wild duck in a present, you know, and I love it so dearly all the same.

GREGERS [*Turning the conversation.*]

Ah, the wild duck, by-the-bye! Let us talk about the wild duck a little, Hedvig.

HEDVIG

The poor wild duck! He doesn't want to see it any more either. Only think, he wanted to wring its neck!

GREGERS

Oh, he won't do that.

HEDVIG

No; but he said he would like to. And I think it was horrid of father to say it; for I pray for the wild duck every night, and ask that it may be preserved from death and all that is evil.

GREGERS [*Looking at her.*]

Do you say your prayers every night?

HEDVIG

Yes.

GREGERS

Who taught you to do that?

HEDVIG

I myself; one time when father was very ill, and had leeches on his neck, and said that death was staring him in the face.

GREGERS

Well?

HEDVIG

Then I prayed for him as I lay in bed; and since then I have always kept it up.

GREGERS

And now you pray for the wild duck too?

HEDVIG

> I thought it was best to bring in the wild duck; for she was so weakly at first.

GREGERS

> Do you pray in the morning, too?

HEDVIG

> No, of course not.

GREGERS

> Why not in the morning as well?

HEDVIG

> In the morning it's light, you know, and there's nothing in particular to be afraid of.

GREGERS

> And your father was going to wring the neck of the wild duck that you love so dearly?

HEDVIG

> No; he said he ought to wring its neck, but he would spare it for my sake; and that was kind of father.

GREGERS   [Coming a little nearer.]

> But suppose you were to sacrifice the wild duck of your own free will for his sake.

HEDVIG   [Rising.]

> The wild duck!

GREGERS

> Suppose you were to make a free-will offering, for his sake, of the dearest treasure you have in the world!

HEDVIG

> Do you think that would do any good?

GREGERS

> Try it, Hedvig.

HEDVIG   [Softly, with flashing eyes.]

> Yes, I will try it.

GREGERS

> Have you really the courage for it, do you think?

HEDVIG

> I'll ask grandfather to shoot the wild duck for me.

GREGERS

> Yes, do. But not a word to your mother about it.

HEDVIG

Why not?

GREGERS

She doesn't understand us.

HEDVIG

The wild duck! I'll try it to-morrow morning.

[GINA *comes in by the passage door.*]

HEDVIG   [*Going towards her.*]

Did you find him, mother?

GINA

No, but I heard as he had called and taken Relling with him.

GREGERS

Are you sure of that?

GINA

Yes, the porter's wife said so. Molvik went with them too, she said.

GREGERS

This evening, when his mind so sorely needs to wrestle in solitude——!

GINA   [*Takes off her things.*]

Yes, men are strange creatures, so they are. The Lord only knows where Relling has dragged him to! I ran over to Madam Eriksen's, but they weren't there.

HEDVIG   [*Struggling to keep back her tears.*]

Oh, if he should never come home any more!

GREGERS

He will come home again. I shall have news to give him to-morrow; and then you shall see how he comes home. You may rely upon that, Hedvig, and sleep in peace. Good-night.

[*He goes out by the passage door.*]

HEDVIG   [*Throws herself sobbing on* GINA's *neck.*]

Mother, mother!

GINA   [*Pats her shoulder and sighs.*]

Ah yes; Relling was right, he was. That's what comes of it when crazy creatures go about presenting the claims of the—what-you-may-call-it.

ACT FIFTH

HIALMAR EKDAL's *studio. Cold, grey, morning light. Wet snow lies upon the large panes of the sloping roof-window.*

GINA *comes from the kitchen with an apron and bib on, and carrying a dusting-brush and a duster; she goes towards the sitting-room door. At the same moment* HEDVIG *comes hurriedly in from the passage.*

GINA   [*Stops.*]
    Well?
HEDVIG
    Oh, mother, I almost think he's down at Relling's——
GINA
    There, you see!
HEDVIG
    ——because the porter's wife says she could hear that Relling had two people with him when he came home last night.
GINA
    That's just what I thought.
HEDVIG
    But it's no use his being there, if he won't come up to us.
GINA
    I'll go down and speak to him at all events.

OLD EKDAL, *in dressing-gown and slippers, and with a lighted pipe, appears at the door of his room.*

EKDAL
    Hialmar—— Isn't Hialmar at home?
GINA
    No, he's gone out.

EKDAL

So early? And in such a tearing snowstorm? Well well; just as he pleases; I can take my morning walk alone.

[*He slides the garret door aside;* HEDVIG *helps him; he goes in; she closes it after him.*]

HEDVIG   [*In an undertone.*]

Only think, mother, when poor grandfather hears that father is going to leave us.

GINA

Oh, nonsense; grandfather mustn't hear anything about it. It was a heaven's mercy he wasn't at home yesterday in all that burly-burly.

HEDVIG

Yes, but——

[GREGERS *comes in by the passage door.*]

GREGERS

Well, have you any news of him?

GINA

They say he's down at Relling's.

GREGERS

At Relling's! Has he really been out with those creatures?

GINA

Yes, like enough.

GREGERS

When he ought to have been yearning for solitude, to collect and clear his thoughts——

GINA

Yes, you may well say so.

RELLING *enters from the passage.*

HEDVIG   [*Going to him.*]

Is father in your room?

GINA   [*At the same time.*]

Is he there?

RELLING

Yes, to be sure he is.

HEDVIG

And you never let us know!

RELLING

Yes; I'm a brute. But in the first place I had to look after the
other brute; I mean our dæmonic friend, of course; and then I
fell so dead asleep that——

GINA

What does Ekdal say to-day?

RELLING

He says nothing whatever.

HEDVIG

Doesn't he speak?

RELLING

Not a blessed word.

GREGERS

No no; I can understand that very well.

GINA

But what's he doing then?

RELLING

He's lying on the sofa, snoring.

GINA

Oh is he? Yes, Ekdal's a rare one to snore.

HEDVIG

Asleep? Can he sleep?

RELLING

Well, it certainly looks like it.

GREGERS

No wonder, after the spiritual conflict that has rent him——

GINA

And then he's never been used to gadding about out of doors at
night.

HEDVIG

Perhaps it's a good thing that he's getting sleep, mother.

GINA

Of course it is; and we must take care we don't wake him up too
early. Thank you, Relling. I must get the house cleaned up a bit
now, and then—— Come and help me, Hedvig.

[GINA *and* HEDVIG *go into the sitting-room.*]

GREGERS   [*Turning to* RELLING.]
What is your explanation of the spiritual tumult that is now
going on in Hialmar Ekdal?
RELLING
Devil a bit of a spiritual tumult have *I* noticed in him.
GREGERS
What! Not at such a crisis, when his whole life has been placed
on a new foundation——? How can you think that such an
individuality as Hialmar's——?
RELLING
Oh, individuality—he! If he ever had any tendency to the
abnormal developments you call individuality, I can assure you it
was rooted out of him while he was still in his teens.
GREGERS
That would be strange indeed,—considering the loving care with
which he was brought up.
RELLING
By those two high-flown, hysterical maiden aunts, you mean?
GREGERS
Let me tell you that they were women who never forgot the
claim of the ideal—but of course you will only jeer at me again.
RELLING
No, I'm in no humour for that. I know all about those ladies; for
he has ladled out no end of rhetoric on the subject of his "two
soul-mothers." But I don't think he has much to thank them for.
Ekdal's misfortune is that in his own circle he has always been
looked upon as a shining light——
GREGERS
Not without reason, surely. Look at the depth of his mind!
RELLING
I have never discovered it. That his father believed in it I don't so
much wonder; the old lieutenant has been an ass all his days.
GREGERS
He has had a child-like mind all his days; that is what you cannot
understand.
RELLING
Well, so be it. But then, when our dear, sweet Hialmar went to
college, he at once passed for the great light of the future

amongst his comrades too! He was handsome, the rascal—red and white—a shop-girl's dream of manly beauty; and with his superficially emotional temperament, and his sympathetic voice, and his talent for declaiming other people's verses and other people's thoughts——

GREGERS   [Indignantly.]

Is it Hialmar Ekdal you are talking about in this strain?

RELLING

Yes, with your permission; I am simply giving you an inside view of the idol you are grovelling before.

GREGERS

I should hardly have thought I was quite stone blind.

RELLING

Yes you are—or not far from it. You are a sick man, too, you see.

GREGERS

You are right there.

RELLING

Yes. Yours is a complicated case. First of all there is that plaguy integrity-fever; and then—what's worse—you are always in a delirium of hero-worship; you must always have something to adore, outside yourself.

GREGERS

Yes, I must certainly seek it outside myself.

RELLING

But you make such shocking mistakes about every new phœnix you think you have discovered. Here again you have come to a cotter's cabin with your claim of the ideal; and the people of the house are insolvent.

GREGERS

If you don't think better than that of Hialmar Ekdal, what pleasure can you find in being everlastingly with him?

RELLING

Well, you see, I'm supposed to be a sort of a doctor—save the mark! I can't but give a hand to the poor sick folk who live under the same roof with me.

GREGERS

Oh, indeed! Hialmar Ekdal is sick too, is he!

RELLING

Most people are, worse luck.

GREGERS

And what remedy are you applying in Hialmar's case?

RELLING

My usual one. I am cultivating the life-illusion* in him.

GREGERS

Life—illusion? I didn't catch what you said.

RELLING

Yes, I said illusion. For illusion, you know, is the stimulating principle.

GREGERS

May I ask with what illusion Hialmar is inoculated?

RELLING

No, thank you; I don't betray professional secrets to quacksalvers. You would probably go and muddle his case still more than you have already. But my method is infallible. I have applied it to Molvik as well. I have made him "dæmonic." That's the blister I have to put on his neck.

GREGERS

Is he not really dæmonic then?

RELLING

What the devil do you mean by dæmonic! It's only a piece of gibberish I've invented to keep up a spark of life in him. But for that, the poor harmless creature would have succumbed to self-contempt and despair many a long year ago. And then the old lieutenant! But he has hit upon his own cure, you see.

GREGERS

Lieutenant Ekdal? What of him?

RELLING

Just think of the old bear-hunter shutting himself up in that dark garret to shoot rabbits! I tell you there is not a happier sportsman in the world than that old man pottering about in there among all that rubbish. The four or five withered Christmas-trees he has saved up are the same to him as the whole great fresh Höidal forest; the cock and the hens are big

*Livslögnen,—literally, "the life-lie." (Translator's note)

game-birds in the fir-tops; and the rabbits that flop about the
garret floor are the bears he has to battle with—the mighty
hunter of the mountains!

GREGERS

Poor unfortunate old man! Yes; he has indeed had to narrow the
ideals of his youth.

RELLING

While I think of it, Mr. Werle, junior—don't use that foreign
word: ideals. We have the excellent native word: lies.

GREGERS

Do you think the two things are related?

RELLING

Yes, just about as closely as typhus and putrid fever.

GREGERS

Dr. Relling, I shall not give up the struggle until I have rescued
Hialmar from your clutches!

RELLING

So much the worse for him. Rob the average man of his life-
illusion, and you rob him of his happiness at the same stroke.
[*To* HEDVIG, *who comes in from the sitting-room.*]
Well, little wild-duck-mother, I'm just going down to see
whether papa is still lying meditating upon that wonderful
invention of his.
[*Goes out by the passage door.*]

GREGERS   [*Approaches* HEDVIG.]

I can see by your face that you have not yet done it.

HEDVIG

What? Oh, that about the wild duck! No.

GREGERS

I suppose your courage failed when the time came.

HEDVIG

No, that wasn't it. But when I awoke this morning and
remembered what we had been talking about, it seemed so strange.

GREGERS

Strange?

HEDVIG

Yes, I don't know——. Yesterday evening, at the moment, I
thought there was something so delightful about it; but since I

have slept and thought of it again, it somehow doesn't seem
worth while.

GREGERS

Ah, I thought you could not have grown up quite unharmed in
this house.

HEDVIG

I don't care about that, if only father would come up——

GREGERS

Oh, if only your eyes had been opened to that which gives life its
value—if you possessed the true, joyous, fearless spirit of
sacrifice, you would soon see how he would come up to you.——
But I believe in you still, Hedvig.

[*He goes out by the passage door.*]

[HEDVIG *wanders about the room for a time; she is on the point of going
into the kitchen when a knock is heard at the garret door.* HEDVIG *goes
over and opens it a little; old* EKDAL *comes out; she pushes the door to
again.*]

EKDAL

H'm, it's not much fun to take one's morning walk alone.

HEDVIG

Wouldn't you like to go shooting, grandfather?

EKDAL

It's not the weather for it to-day. It's so dark there, you can
scarcely see where you're going.

HEDVIG

Do you never want to shoot anything besides the rabbits?

EKDAL

Do you think the rabbits aren't good enough?

HEDVIG

Yes, but what about the wild duck?

EKDAL

Ho-ho! are you afraid I shall shoot your wild duck? Never in the
world. Never.

HEDVIG

No, I suppose you couldn't; they say it's very difficult to shoot
wild ducks.

EKDAL

Couldn't! Should rather think I could.

HEDVIG

How would you set about it, grandfather?—I don't mean with my wild duck, but with others?

EKDAL

I should take care to shoot them in the breast, you know; that's the surest place. And then you must shoot against the feathers, you see—not the way of the feathers.

HEDVIG

Do they die then, grandfather?

EKDAL

Yes, they die right enough—when you shoot properly. Well, I must go and brush up a bit. H'm—understand—h'm.

[*Goes into his room.*]

[HEDVIG *waits a little, glances towards the sitting-room door, goes over to the bookcase, stands on tip-toe, takes the double-barrelled pistol down from the shelf, and looks at it.* GINA, *with brush and duster, comes from the sitting-room.* HEDVIG *hastily lays down the pistol, unobserved.*]

GINA

Don't stand raking amongst father's things, Hedvig.

HEDVIG   [*Goes away from the bookcase.*]

I was only going to tidy up a little.

GINA

You'd better go into the kitchen, and see if the coffee's keeping hot; I'll take his breakfast on a tray, when I go down to him.

[HEDVIG *goes out.* GINA *begins to sweep and clean up the studio. Presently the passage door is opened with hesitation, and* HIALMAR EKDAL *looks in. He has on his overcoat, but not his hat; he is unwashed, and his hair is dishevelled and unkempt. His eyes are dull and heavy.*]

GINA   [*Standing with the brush in her hand, and looking at him.*]

Oh, there now, Ekdal—so you've come after all?

HIALMAR   [*Comes in and answers in a toneless voice.*]

I come—only to depart again immediately.

GINA

Yes, yes, I suppose so. But, Lord help us! what a sight you are!

HIALMAR

A sight?

GINA

And your nice winter coat too! Well, that's done for.

HEDVIG   [*At the kitchen door.*]

Mother, hadn't I better———?

[*Sees* HIALMAR, *gives a loud scream of joy, and runs to him.*]

Oh, father, father!

HIALMAR   [*Turns away and makes a gesture of repulsion.*]

Away, away, away!

[*To* GINA.]

Keep her away from me, I say!

GINA   [*In a low tone.*]

Go into the sitting-room, Hedvig.

[HEDVIG *does so without a word.*]

HIALMAR   [*Fussily pulls out the table-drawer.*]

I must have my books with me. Where are my books?

GINA

Which books?

HIALMAR

My scientific books, of course; the technical magazines I require for my invention.

GINA   [*Searches in the bookcase.*]

Is it these here paper-covered ones?

HIALMAR

Yes, of course.

GINA   [*Lays a heap of magazines on the table.*]

Shan't I get Hedvig to cut them for you?

HIALMAR

I don't require to have them cut for me.

[*Short silence.*]

GINA

Then you're still set on leaving us, Ekdal?

HIALMAR   [*Rummaging amongst the books.*]

Yes, that is a matter of course, I should think.

GINA

Well, well.

HIALMAR   [*Vehemently.*]

How can I live here, to be stabbed to the heart every hour of the day?

GINA

God forgive you for thinking such vile things of me.

HIALMAR

Prove——!

GINA

I think it's you as has got to prove.

HIALMAR

After a past like yours? There are certain claims——I may almost call them claims of the ideal——

GINA

But what about grandfather? What's to become of him, poor dear?

HIALMAR

I know my duty; my helpless father will come with me. I am going out into the town to make arrangements——. H'm— [*hesitatingly*] has any one found my hat on the stairs?

GINA

No. Have you lost your hat?

HIALMAR

Of course I had it on when I came in last night; there's no doubt about that; but I couldn't find it this morning.

GINA

Lord help us! where have you been to with those two ne'er-do-weels?

HIALMAR

Oh, don't bother me about trifles. Do you suppose I am in the mood to remember details?

GINA

If only you haven't caught cold, Ekdal.

[*Goes out into the kitchen.*]

HIALMAR [*Talks to himself in a low tone of irritation, whilst he empties the table-drawer.*]

You're a scoundrel, Relling!—You're a low fellow!—Ah, you shameless tempter!—I wish I could get some one to stick a knife into you!

[*He lays some old letters on one side, finds the torn document of yesterday, takes it up and looks at the pieces; puts it down hurriedly as* GINA *enters.*]

GINA   [*Sets a tray with coffee, etc., on the table.*]

Here's a drop of something hot, if you'd fancy it. And there's
some bread and butter and a snack of salt meat.

HIALMAR   [*Glancing at the tray.*]

Salt meat? Never under this roof! It's true I have not had a
mouthful of solid food for nearly twenty-four hours; but no
matter.——My memoranda! The commencement of my
autobiography! What has become of my diary, and all my
important papers?

[*Opens the sitting-room door but draws back.*]

She is there too!

GINA

Good Lord! the child must be somewhere!

HIALMAR

Come out.

[*He makes room, HEDVIG comes, scared, into the studio.*]

HIALMAR   [*With his hand upon the door-handle, says to* GINA:]

In these, the last moments I spend in my former home, I wish to
be spared from interlopers——

[*Goes into the room.*]

HEDVIG   [*With a bound towards her mother, asks softly, trembling.*]

Does that mean me?

GINA

Stay out in the kitchen, Hedvig; or, no—you'd best go into your
own room.

[*Speaks to* HIALMAR *as she goes in to him.*]

Wait a bit, Ekdal; don't rummage so in the drawers; *I* know
where everything is.

HEDVIG   [*Stands a moment immovable, in terror and perplexity, biting her
lips to keep back the tears; then she clenches her hands convulsively, and
says softly:*]

The wild duck.

[*She steals over and takes the pistol from the shelf, opens the garret door a
little way, creeps in, and draws the door to after her.*]

[HIALMAR *and* GINA *can be heard disputing in the sitting-room.*]

HIALMAR   *[Comes in with some manuscript books and old loose papers, which he lays upon the table.]*

That portmanteau is of no use! There are a thousand and one things I must drag with me.

GINA   *[Following with the portmanteau.]*

Why not leave all the rest for the present, and only take a shirt and a pair of woollen drawers with you?

HIALMAR

Whew!—all these exhausting preparations———!

[Pulls off his overcoat and throws it upon the sofa.]

GINA

And there's the coffee getting cold.

HIALMAR

H'm.

[Drinks a mouthful without thinking of it, and then another.]

GINA   *[Dusting the backs of the chairs.]*

A nice job you'll have to find such another big garret for the rabbits.

HIALMAR

What! Am I to drag all those rabbits with me too?

GINA

You don't suppose grandfather can get on without his rabbits.

HIALMAR

He must just get used to doing without them. Have not *I* to sacrifice very much greater things than rabbits!

GINA   *[Dusting the bookcase.]*

Shall I put the flute in the portmanteau for you?

HIALMAR

No. No flute for me. But give me the pistol!

GINA

Do you want to take the pistol with you?

HIALMAR

Yes. My loaded pistol.

GINA   *[Searching for it.]*

It's gone. He must have taken it in with him.

HIALMAR

Is he in the garret?

GINA

Yes, of course he's in the garret.

HIALMAR

H'm—poor lonely old man.

[*He takes a piece of bread and butter, eats it, and finishes his cup of coffee.*]

GINA

If we hadn't have let that room, you could have moved in there.

HIALMAR

And continued to live under the same roof with——! Never,—never!

GINA

But couldn't you put up with the sitting-room for a day or two? You could have it all to yourself.

HIALMAR

Never within these walls!

GINA

Well then, down with Relling and Molvik.

HIALMAR

Don't mention those wretches' names to me! The very thought of them almost takes away my appetite.—Oh no, I must go out into the storm and the snow-drift,—go from house to house and seek shelter for my father and myself.

GINA

But you've got no hat, Ekdal! You've been and lost your hat, you know.

HIALMAR

Oh those two brutes, those slaves of all the vices! A hat must be procured.

[*Takes another piece of bread and butter.*]

Some arrangement must be made. For I have no mind to throw away my life, either.

[*Looks for something on the tray.*]

GINA

What are you looking for?

HIALMAR

Butter.

GINA

> I'll get some at once.
>
> [*Goes out into the kitchen.*]

HIALMAR   [*Calls after her.*]

> Oh it doesn't matter; dry bread is good enough for me.

GINA   [*Brings a dish of butter.*]

> Look here; this is fresh churned.
>
> [*She pours out another cup of coffee for him; he seats himself on the sofa, spreads more butter on the already buttered bread, and eats and drinks awhile in silence.*]

HIALMAR

> Could I, without being subject to intrusion—intrusion of any sort—could I live in the sitting-room there for a day or two?

GINA

> Yes, to be sure you could, if you only would.

HIALMAR

> For I see no possibility of getting all father's things out in such a hurry.

GINA

> And besides, you've surely got to tell him first as you don't mean to live with us others no more.

HIALMAR   [*Pushes away his coffee cup.*]

> Yes, there is that too; I shall have to lay bare the whole tangled story to him——. I must turn matters over; I must have breathing-time; I cannot take all these burdens on my shoulders in a single day.

GINA

> No, especially in such horrible weather as it is outside.

HIALMAR   [*Touching* WERLE's *letter.*]

> I see that paper is still lying about here.

GINA

> Yes, *I* haven't touched it.

HIALMAR

> So far as I am concerned it is mere waste paper——

GINA

> Well, *I* have certainly no notion of making any use of it.

HIALMAR

————but we had better not let it get lost all the same;——in all the upset when I move, it might easily————

GINA

I'll take good care of it, Ekdal.

HIALMAR

The donation is in the first instance made to father, and it rests with him to accept or decline it.

GINA [*Sighs.*]

Yes, poor old father————

HIALMAR

To make quite safe————Where shall I find some gum?

GINA [*Goes to the bookcase.*]

Here's the gum-pot.

HIALMAR

And a brush?

GINA

The brush is here too.

[*Brings him the things.*]

HIALMAR [*Takes a pair of scissors.*]

Just a strip of paper at the back————

[*Clips and gums.*]

Far be it from me to lay hands upon what is not my own——and least of all upon what belongs to a destitute old man——and to—— the other as well.—— There now. Let it lie there for a time; and when it is dry, take it away. I wish never to see that document again. Never!

GREGERS WERLE *enters from the passage.*

GREGERS [*Somewhat surprised.*]

What,——are you sitting here, Hialmar?

HIALMAR [*Rises hurriedly.*]

I had sunk down from fatigue.

GREGERS

You have been having breakfast, I see.

HIALMAR

The body sometimes makes its claims felt too.

GREGERS

>What have you decided to do?

HIALMAR

>For a man like me, there is only one course possible. I am just putting my most important things together. But it takes time, you know.

GINA   [*With a touch of impatience.*]

>Am I to get the room ready for you, or am I to pack your portmanteau?

HIALMAR   [*After a glance of annoyance at* GREGERS.]

>Pack—and get the room ready!

GINA   [*Takes the portmanteau.*]

>Very well; then I'll put in the shirt and the other things.

>[*Goes into the sitting-room and draws the door to after her.*]

GREGERS   [*After a short silence.*]

>I never dreamed that this would be the end of it. Do you really feel it a necessity to leave house and home?

HIALMAR   [*Wanders about restlessly.*]

>What would you have me do?—I am not fitted to bear unhappiness, Gregers. I must feel secure and at peace in my surroundings.

GREGERS

>But can you not feel that here? Just try it. I should have thought you had firm ground to build upon now—if only you start afresh. And remember, you have your invention to live for.

HIALMAR

>Oh don't talk about my invention. It's perhaps still in the dim distance.

GREGERS

>Indeed.

HIALMAR

>Why, great heavens, what would you have me invent? Other people have invented almost everything already. It becomes more and more difficult every day——

GREGERS

>And you have devoted so much labour to it.

HIALMAR

>It was that blackguard Relling that urged me to it.

GREGERS

Relling?

HIALMAR

Yes, it was he that first made me realise my aptitude for making some notable discovery in photography.

GREGERS

Aha—it was Relling!

HIALMAR

Oh, I have been so truly happy over it! Not so much for the sake of the invention itself, as because Hedvig believed in it—believed in it with a child's whole eagerness of faith.—At least, I have been fool enough to go and imagine that she believed in it.

GREGERS

Can you really think that Hedvig has been false towards you?

HIALMAR

I can think anything now. It is Hedvig that stands in my way. She will blot out the sunlight from my whole life.

GREGERS

Hedvig! Is it Hedvig you are talking of? How should she blot out your sunlight?

HIALMAR   [*Without answering.*]

How unutterably I have loved that child! How unutterably happy I have felt every time I came home to my humble room, and she flew to meet me, with her sweet little blinking eyes. Oh, confiding fool that I have been! I loved her unutterably;—and I yielded myself up to the dream, the delusion, that she loved me unutterably in return.

GREGERS

Do you call that a delusion?

HIALMAR

How should I know? I can get nothing out of Gina; and besides, she is totally blind to the ideal side of these complications. But to you I feel impelled to open my mind, Gregers. I cannot shake off this frightful doubt—perhaps Hedvig has never really and honestly loved me.

GREGERS

What would you say if she were to give you a proof of her love? [*Listens.*]

What's that? I thought I heard the wild duck——?

HIALMAR

It's the wild duck quacking. Father's in the garret.

GREGERS

Is he?

[*His face lights up with joy.*]

I say you may yet have proof that your poor misunderstood Hedvig loves you!

HIALMAR

Oh, what proof can she give me? I dare not believe in any assurances from that quarter.

GREGERS

Hedvig does not know what deceit means.

HIALMAR

Oh Gregers, that is just what I cannot be sure of. Who knows what Gina and that Mrs. Sörby may many a time have sat here whispering and tattling about? And Hedvig usually has her ears open, I can tell you. Perhaps the deed of gift was not such a surprise to her, after all. In fact, I'm not sure but that I noticed something of the sort.

GREGERS

What spirit is this that has taken possession of you?

HIALMAR

I have had my eyes opened. Just you notice;——you'll see, the deed of gift is only a beginning. Mrs. Sörby has always been a good deal taken up with Hedvig; and now she has the power to do whatever she likes for the child. They can take her from me whenever they please.

GREGERS

Hedvig will never, never leave you.

HIALMAR

Don't be so sure of that. If only they beckon to her and throw out a golden bait——! And oh! I have loved her so unspeakably! I would have counted it my highest happiness to take her tenderly by the hand and lead her, as one leads a timid child through a great dark empty room!——I am cruelly certain now that the poor photographer in his humble attic has never really

and truly been anything to her. She has only cunningly contrived
to keep on a good footing with him until the time came.

GREGERS

You don't believe that yourself, Hialmar.

HIALMAR

That is just the terrible part of it—I don't know what to
believe,—I never can know it. But can you really doubt that it
must be as I say? Ho-ho, you have far too much faith in the claim
of the ideal, my good Gregers! If those others came, with the
glamour of wealth about them, and called to the child:—"Leave
him: come to us: here life awaits you——"

GREGERS   [*Quickly.*]

Well, what then?

HIALMAR

If I then asked her: Hedvig, are you willing to renounce that life
for me?
[*Laughs scornfully.*]
No thank you! You would soon hear what answer I should get.
[*A pistol shot is heard from within the garret.*]

GREGERS   [*Loudly and joyfully.*]

Hialmar!

HIALMAR

There now; he must needs go shooting too.

GINA   [*Comes in.*]

Oh Ekdal, I can hear grandfather blazing away in the garret by
hisself.

HIALMAR

I'll look in——

GREGERS   [*Eagerly, with emotion.*]

Wait a moment! Do you know what that was?

HIALMAR

Yes, of course I know.

GREGERS

No you don't know. But *I* do. That was the proof!

HIALMAR

What proof?

GREGERS

> It was a child's free-will offering. She has got your father to shoot the wild duck.

HIALMAR

> To shoot the wild duck!

GINA

> Oh, think of that——!

HIALMAR

> What was that for?

GREGERS

> She wanted to sacrifice to you her most cherished possession; for then she thought you would surely come to love her again.

HIALMAR   [*Tenderly, with emotion.*]

> Oh, poor child!

GINA

> What things she does think of!

GREGERS

> She only wanted your love again, Hialmar. She could not live without it.

GINA   [*Struggling with her tears.*]

> There, you can see for yourself, Ekdal.

HIALMAR

> Gina, where is she?

GINA   [*Sniffs.*]

> Poor dear, she's sitting out in the kitchen, I dare say.

HIALMAR   [*Goes over, tears open the kitchen door, and says:*]

> Hedvig, come, come in to me!
>
> [*Looks round.*]
>
> No, she's not here.

GINA

> Then she must be in her own little room.

HIALMAR   [*Without.*]

> No, she's not here either.
>
> [*Comes in.*]
>
> She must have gone out.

GINA

> Yes, you wouldn't have her anywheres in the house.

HIALMAR

>Oh, if she would only come home quickly, so that I can tell her—— Everything will come right now, Gregers; now I believe we can begin life afresh.

GREGERS   [*Quietly.*]

>I knew it; I knew the child would make amends.

OLD EKDAL *appears at the door of his room; he is in full uniform, and is busy buckling on his sword.*

HIALMAR   [*Astonished.*]

>Father! Are you there?

GINA

>Have you been firing in your room?

EKDAL   [*Resentfully, approaching.*]

>So you go shooting alone, do you, Hialmar?

HIALMAR   [*Excited and confused.*]

>Then it wasn't you that fired that shot in the garret?

EKDAL

>Me that fired? H'm.

GREGERS   [*Calls out to* HIALMAR.]

>She has shot the wild duck herself!

HIALMAR

>What can it mean?

>[*Hastens to the garret door, tears it aside, looks in and calls loudly:*]

>Hedvig!

GINA   [*Runs to the door.*]

>Good God, what's that!

HIALMAR   [*Goes in.*]

>She's lying on the floor!

GREGERS

>Hedvig! lying on the floor!

>[*Goes in to* HIALMAR.]

GINA   [*At the same time.*]

>Hedvig!

>[*Inside the garret.*]

>No, no, no!

EKDAL

Ho-ho! does she go shooting too, now?

[HIALMAR, GINA, *and* GREGERS *carry* HEDVIG *into the studio; in her dangling right hand she holds the pistol fast clasped in her fingers.*]

HIALMAR   [*Distracted.*]

The pistol has gone off. She has wounded herself. Call for help! Help!

GINA   [*Runs into the passage and calls down.*]

Relling! Relling! Doctor Relling; come up as quick as you can!

[HIALMAR *and* GREGERS *lay* HEDVIG *down on the sofa.*]

EKDAL   [*Quietly.*]

The woods avenge themselves.

HIALMAR   [*On his knees beside* HEDVIG.]

She'll soon come to now. She's coming to———; yes, yes, yes.

GINA   [*Who has come in again.*]

Where has she hurt herself? I can't see anything———

[RELLING *comes hurriedly, and immediately after him* MOLVIK; *the latter without his waistcoat and necktie, and with his coat open.*]

RELLING

What's the matter here?

GINA

They say Hedvig has shot herself.

HIALMAR

Come and help us!

RELLING

Shot herself!

[*He pushes the table aside and begins to examine her.*]

HIALMAR   [*Kneeling and looking anxiously up at him.*]

It can't be dangerous? Speak, Relling! She is scarcely bleeding at all. It can't be dangerous?

RELLING

How did it happen?

HIALMAR

Oh, we don't know———!

GINA

She wanted to shoot the wild duck.

RELLING

The wild duck?

HIALMAR

The pistol must have gone off.

RELLING

H'm. Indeed.

EKDAL

The woods avenge themselves. But I'm not afraid, all the same.

[*Goes into the garret and closes the door after him.*]

HIALMAR

Well, Relling,——why don't you say something?

RELLING

The ball has entered the breast.

HIALMAR

Yes, but she's coming to!

RELLING

Surely you can see that Hedvig is dead.

GINA   [*Bursts into tears.*]

Oh my child, my child!

GREGERS   [*Huskily.*]

In the depths of the sea——

HIALMAR   [*Jumps up.*]

No, no, she must live! Oh, for God's sake, Relling—only a moment—only just till I can tell her how unspeakably I loved her all the time!

RELLING

The bullet has gone through her heart. Internal hemorrhage. Death must have been instantaneous.

HIALMAR

And I! I hunted her from me like an animal! And she crept terrified into the garret and died for love of me!

[*Sobbing.*]

I can never atone to her! I can never tell her——!

[*Clenches his hands and cries, upwards.*]

O thou above——! If thou be indeed! Why hast thou done this thing to me?

GINA

Hush, hush, you mustn't go on that awful way. We had no right to keep her, I suppose.

MOLVIK

    The child is not dead, but sleepeth.

RELLING

    Bosh!

HIALMAR   [*Becomes calm, goes over to the sofa, folds his arms, and looks at* HEDVIG.]

    There she lies so stiff and still.

RELLING   [*Tries to loosen the pistol.*]

    She's holding it so tight, so tight.

GINA

    No, no, Relling, don't break her fingers; let the pistol be.

HIALMAR

    She shall take it with her.

GINA

    Yes, let her. But the child mustn't lie here for a show. She shall go to her own room, so she shall. Help me, Ekdal.

    [HIALMAR *and* GINA *take* HEDVIG *between them.*]

HIALMAR   [*As they are carrying her.*]

    Oh Gina, Gina, can you survive this!

GINA

    We must help each other to bear it. For now at least she belongs to both of us.

MOLVIK   [*Stretches out his arms and mumbles.*]

    Blessed be the Lord; to earth thou shalt return; to earth thou shalt return——

RELLING   [*Whispers.*]

    Hold your tongue, you fool; you're drunk.

    [HIALMAR *and* GINA *carry the body out through the kitchen door.* RELLING *shuts it after them.* MOLVIK *slinks out into the passage.*]

RELLING   [*Goes over to* GREGERS *and says:*]

    No one shall ever convince me that the pistol went off by accident.

GREGERS   [*Who has stood terrified, with convulsive twitchings.*]

    Who can say how the dreadful thing happened?

RELLING

    The powder has burnt the body of her dress. She must have pressed the pistol right against her breast and fired.

GREGERS

Hedvig has not died in vain. Did you not see how sorrow set free what is noble in him?

RELLING

Most people are ennobled by the actual presence of death. But how long do you suppose this nobility will last in him?

GREGERS

Why should it not endure and increase throughout his life?

RELLING

Before a year is over, little Hedvig will be nothing to him but a pretty theme for declamation.

GREGERS

How dare you say that of Hialmar Ekdal?

RELLING

We will talk of this again, when the grass has first withered on her grave. Then you'll hear him spouting about "the child too early torn from her father's heart;" then you'll see him steep himself in a syrup of sentiment and self-admiration and self-pity. Just you wait!

GREGERS

If you are right and I am wrong, then life is not worth living.

RELLING

Oh, life would be quite tolerable, after all, if only we could be rid of the confounded duns that keep on pestering us, in our poverty, with the claim of the ideal.

GREGERS [*Looking straight before him.*]

In that case, I am glad that my destiny is what it is.

RELLING

May I inquire,——what is your destiny?

GREGERS [*Going.*]

To be the thirteenth at table.

RELLING

The devil it is.

HEDDA GABLER

(1890)

INTRODUCTION

WHILE IN *THE WILD DUCK* THE burden of discussing ideas is placed on the shoulders of the misguided and discredited idealist Gregers, in *Hedda Gabler* (1890) ideas are banished from the play entirely. It is as if Ibsen wanted to continue the project of correcting the distorted image of himself as a playwright of radical ideas by turning ideas into objects that can be touched, lost, and burned—in short, by turning them into a manuscript. What the manuscript says we will never know, except for the fact that it deals with the future. But this is precisely its point. In a play, it is not ideas that matter but things, and as an object the manuscript serves excellently well—at least as well as pistols, the other prominent prop Ibsen employs here.

The primary manipulator of all of these props is not Ibsen but Hedda Gabler, a true master plotter. She is Ibsen's alter ego, someone who spends all day scheming and constructing traps, manipulating people and objects like an author. Ibsen competes not with Lövborg, the author of ideas, but with Hedda Gabler, the author of intrigue. After having been known as a radical in both ideas and dramatic forms, Ibsen here returns to the craft of dramaturgy, asserting his mastery over the plot.

This is not to say that *Hedda Gabler* is only a mannered exercise in how to construct a good play. It is also a renewed effort to create a modern tragedy. If *Ghosts* is Ibsen's *King Oedipus, Hedda Gabler* is his *Medea*—a *Medea* frighteningly rationalized. Instead of hot witchcraft, Hedda possesses the powers of cold calculation; her every action is precisely calibrated to effect, whether in the service of a larger purpose or out of pure habit. She simply cannot not manipulate, cannot not use her powers of plotting; her whole character is consumed by these features. It is in the same manner and, in fact, for the same reason that she finally commits suicide, out of calculation that she would be in the power of another plot, of the plot of another character, who now has power over her and will use it to make her his mistress. This is the one thing Hedda Gabler cannot tolerate because it goes against her nature to be manipulated by someone else. And so she kills herself, this most rational of all turn-of-the-century *femme fatales.*

In her isolated hostility toward the world surrounding her, *Hedda Gabler* can be seen as Ibsen's return to the one-protagonist play with which he had begun his European triumph: for example, *Brand* and *Peer Gynt.* Hedda Gabler is perhaps less successful in battling the world, but she is ready to pursue this goal to the bitter end. Given this focus on the one, single protagonist, this is a play that has always attracted actors. Henry James wrote a notable review of *Hedda Gabler,* at the beginning of his fascination with Ibsen, noting how much this play catered to the profession of actors. The first London *Hedda Gabler* (1891) was directed by William Archer, with Elizabeth Robins in the title role; she claimed she had become interested in Ibsen through André Antoine's production of *Ghosts* in 1890. Since then, *Hedda Gabler* has remained a challenge for famous actors, the crowning achievement of many an acting career, including Charles Ludlam's drag performance at the American Ibsen Theatre in 1984.

It was through the challenge to acting that directors interested in acting technique took on this play as well, most notably so Vsevolod Meyerhold, the inventor of a system called biomechanics, in 1906. The entire production, including the shape of the stage and the set design was stylized and centered around the one dominating figure of Hedda Gabler, whom the audience encountered sitting in a white fur before a background of blue. Meyerhold's lead was much later followed by Ingmar Bergman's 1964 production at the Royal Dramatic Theatre in Stockholm, which stripped away all unnecessary clutter, creating a bare stage laid with a dark red velvet carpet. In both productions, the entire stage becomes an extension of Hedda Gabler's persona, a costume that she wears and that dissolves only with her final suicide. If in *The Wild Duck* the stage and its objects assert their primacy over the actor, here they become entirely subsumed under the overbearing personality of the protagonist.

—Martin Puchner

CHARACTERS

GEORGE TESMAN.*
HEDDA TESMAN, *his wife.*
MISS JULIANA TESMAN, *his aunt.*
MRS. ELVSTED.
JUDGE† BRACK.
EILERT LÖVBORG.
BERTA, *servant at the Tesmans'.*

The scene of the action is Tesman's villa, in the west end of Christiania.

---

*Tesman, whose Christian name in the original is "Jörgen," is described as *stipendiat i kulturhistorie*—that is to say, the holder of a scholarship for purposes of research into the History of Civilisation. (Translator's note)

†In the original "Assessor." (Translator's note)

ACT FIRST

A spacious, handsome, and tastefully furnished drawing-room, decorated in dark colours. In the back, a wide doorway with curtains drawn back, leading into a smaller room decorated in the same style as the drawing-room. In the right-hand wall of the front room, a folding door leading out to the hall. In the opposite wall, on the left, a glass door, also with curtains drawn back. Through the panes can be seen part of a veranda outside, and trees covered with autumn foliage. An oval table, with a cover on it, and surrounded by chairs, stands well forward. In front, by the wall on the right, a wide stove of dark porcelain, a high-backed arm-chair, a cushioned foot-rest, and two foot-stools. A settee, with a small round table in front of it, fills the upper right-hand corner. In front, on the left, a little way from the wall, a sofa. Further back than the glass door, a piano. On either side of the doorway at the back a whatnot with terra-cotta and majolica ornaments.——Against the back wall of the inner room a sofa, with a table, and one or two chairs. Over the sofa hangs the portrait of a handsome elderly man in a General's uniform. Over the table a hanging lamp, with an opal glass shade.——A number of bouquets are arranged about the drawing-room, in vases and glasses. Others lie upon the tables. The floors in both rooms are covered with thick carpets.——Morning light. The sun shines in through the glass door.

MISS JULIANA TESMAN, *with her bonnet on and carrying a parasol, comes in from the hall, followed by* BERTA, *who carries a bouquet wrapped in paper.* MISS TESMAN *is a comely and pleasant-looking lady of about sixty-five. She is nicely but simply dressed in a grey walking-costume.* BERTA *is a middle-aged woman of plain and rather countrified appearance.*

MISS TESMAN   [*Stops close to the door, listens, and says softly:*]
  Upon my word, I don't believe they are stirring yet!
BERTA   [*Also softly.*]
  I told you so, Miss. Remember how late the steamboat got in last

night. And then, when they got home! —good Lord, what a lot the young mistress had to unpack before she could get to bed.

MISS TESMAN

Well well—let them have their sleep out. But let us see that they get a good breath of the fresh morning air when they do appear. [*She goes to the glass door and throws it open.*]

BERTA [*Beside the table, at a loss what to do with the bouquet in her hand.*]

I declare there isn't a bit of room left. I think I'll put it down here, Miss.

[*She places it on the piano.*]

MISS TESMAN

So you've got a new mistress now, my dear Berta. Heaven knows it was a wrench to me to part with you.

BERTA [*On the point of weeping.*]

And do you think it wasn't hard for me too, Miss? After all the blessed years I've been with you and Miss Rina.

MISS TESMAN

We must make the best of it, Berta. There was nothing else to be done. George can't do without you, you see—he absolutely can't. He has had you to look after him ever since he was a little boy.

BERTA

Ah but, Miss Julia, I can't help thinking of Miss Rina lying helpless at home there, poor thing. And with only that new girl too! She'll never learn to take proper care of an invalid.

MISS TESMAN

Oh, I shall manage to train her. And of course, you know, I shall take most of it upon myself. You needn't be uneasy about my poor sister, my dear Berta.

BERTA

Well, but there's another thing, Miss. I'm so mortally afraid I shan't be able to suit the young mistress.

MISS TESMAN

Oh well—just at first there may be one or two things——

BERTA

Most like she'll be terrible grand in her ways.

MISS TESMAN

Well, you can't wonder at that—General Gabler's daughter!
Think of the sort of life she was accustomed to in her father's
time. Don't you remember how we used to see her riding down
the road along with the General? In that long black habit—and
with feathers in her hat?

BERTA

Yes indeed—I remember well enough!—But, good Lord, I
should never have dreamt in those days that she and Master
George would make a match of it.

MISS TESMAN

Nor I.—But by-the-bye, Berta—while I think of it: in future you
mustn't say Master George. You must say Dr. Tesman.

BERTA

Yes, the young mistress spoke of that too—last night—the
moment they set foot in the house. Is it true then, Miss?

MISS TESMAN

Yes, indeed it is. Only think, Berta—some foreign university has
made him a doctor—while he has been abroad, you understand.
I hadn't heard a word about it, until he told me himself upon the
pier.

BERTA

Well well, he's clever enough for anything, he is. But I didn't
think he'd have gone in for doctoring people too.

MISS TESMAN

No no, it's not that sort of doctor he is.

[*Nods significantly.*]

But let me tell you, we may have to call him something still
grander before long.

BERTA

You don't say so! What can that be, Miss?

MISS TESMAN   [*Smiling.*]

H'm—wouldn't you like to know!

[*With emotion.*]

Ah, dear dear—if my poor brother could only look up from his
grave now, and see what his little boy has grown into!

[*Looks around.*]

But bless me, Berta—why have you done this? Taken the chintz covers off all the furniture?

BERTA

The mistress told me to. She can't abide covers on the chairs, she says.

MISS TESMAN

Are they going to make this their everyday sitting-room then?

BERTA

Yes, that's what I understood—from the mistress. Master George—the doctor—he said nothing.

GEORGE TESMAN *comes from the right into the inner room, humming to himself, and carrying an unstrapped empty portmanteau. He is a middle-sized, young-looking man of thirty-three, rather stout, with a round, open, cheerful face, fair hair and beard. He wears spectacles, and is somewhat carelessly dressed in comfortable indoor clothes.*

MISS TESMAN

Good morning, good morning, George.

TESMAN   [*In the doorway between the rooms.*]

Aunt Julia! Dear Aunt Julia!

[*Goes up to her and shakes hands warmly.*]

Come all this way—so early! Eh?

MISS TESMAN

Why, of course I had to come and see how you were getting on.

TESMAN

In spite of your having had no proper night's rest?

MISS TESMAN

Oh, that makes no difference to me.

TESMAN

Well, I suppose you got home all right from the pier? Eh?

MISS TESMAN

Yes, quite safely, thank goodness. Judge Brack was good enough to see me right to my door.

TESMAN

We were so sorry we couldn't give you a seat in the carriage. But you saw what a pile of boxes Hedda had to bring with her.

MISS TESMAN

    Yes, she had certainly plenty of boxes.

BERTA   [*To* TESMAN.]

    Shall I go in and see if there's anything I can do for the mistress?

TESMAN

    No thank you, Berta—you needn't. She said she would ring if she wanted anything.

BERTA   [*Going towards the right.*]

    Very well.

TESMAN

    But look here—take this portmanteau with you.

BERTA   [*Taking it.*]

    I'll put it in the attic.

    [*She goes out by the hall door.*]

TESMAN

    Fancy, Auntie—I had the whole of that portmanteau chock full of copies of documents. You wouldn't believe how much I have picked up from all the archives I have been examining—curious old details that no one has had any idea of——

MISS TESMAN

    Yes, you don't seem to have wasted your time on your wedding trip, George.

TESMAN

    No, that I haven't. But do take off your bonnet, Auntie. Look here! Let me untie the strings—eh?

MISS TESMAN   [*While he does so.*]

    Well well—this is just as if you were still at home with us.

TESMAN   [*With the bonnet in his hand, looks at it from all sides.*]

    Why, what a gorgeous bonnet you've been investing in!

MISS TESMAN

    I bought it on Hedda's account.

TESMAN

    On Hedda's account? Eh?

MISS TESMAN

    Yes, so that Hedda needn't be ashamed of me if we happened to go out together.

TESMAN   [*Patting her cheek.*]

    You always think of everything, Aunt Julia.

[*Lays the bonnet on a chair beside the table.*]

And now, look here—suppose we sit comfortably on the sofa and have a little chat, till Hedda comes.

[*They seat themselves. She places her parasol in the corner of the sofa.*]

MISS TESMAN   [*Takes both his hands and looks at him.*]

What a delight it is to have you again, as large as life, before my very eyes, George! My George—my poor brother's own boy!

TESMAN

And it's a delight for me, too, to see you again, Aunt Julia! You, who have been father and mother in one to me.

MISS TESMAN

Oh yes, I know you will always keep a place in your heart for your old aunts.

TESMAN

And what about Aunt Rina? No improvement—eh?

MISS TESMAN

Oh no—we can scarcely look for any improvement in her case, poor thing. There she lies, helpless, as she has lain for all these years. But heaven grant I may not lose her yet awhile! For if I did, I don't know what I should make of my life, George— especially now that I haven't you to look after any more.

TESMAN   [*Patting her back.*]

There, there, there——!

MISS TESMAN   [*Suddenly changing her tone.*]

And to think that here are you a married man, George!—And that you should be the one to carry off Hedda Gabler—the beautiful Hedda Gabler! Only think of it—she, that was so beset with admirers!

TESMAN   [*Hums a little and smiles complacently.*]

Yes, I fancy I have several good friends about town who would like to stand in my shoes—eh?

MISS TESMAN

And then this fine long wedding-tour you have had! More than five—nearly six months——

TESMAN

Well, for me it has been a sort of tour of research as well. I have had to do so much grubbing among old records—and to read no end of books too, Auntie.

MISS TESMAN

Oh yes, I suppose so.

[*More confidentially, and lowering her voice a little.*]

But listen now, George,—have you nothing—nothing special to tell me?

TESMAN

As to our journey?

MISS TESMAN

Yes.

TESMAN

No, I don't know of anything except what I have told you in my letters. I had a doctor's degree conferred on me—but that I told you yesterday.

MISS TESMAN

Yes, yes, you did. But what I mean is—haven't you any—any—expectations——?

TESMAN

Expectations?

MISS TESMAN

Why you know, George—I'm your old auntie!

TESMAN

Why, of course I have expectations.

MISS TESMAN

Ah!

TESMAN

I have every expectation of being a professor one of these days.

MISS TESMAN

Oh yes, a professor——

TESMAN

Indeed, I may say I am certain of it. But my dear Auntie—you know all about that already!

MISS TESMAN [*Laughing to herself.*]

Yes, of course I do. You are quite right there.

[*Changing the subject.*]

But we were talking about your journey. It must have cost a great deal of money, George?

TESMAN

Well, you see—my handsome travelling-scholarship went a good way.

MISS TESMAN

But I can't understand how you can have made it go far enough for two.

TESMAN

No, that's not so easy to understand—eh?

MISS TESMAN

And especially travelling with a lady—they tell me that makes it ever so much more expensive.

TESMAN

Yes, of course—it makes it a little more expensive. But Hedda *had* to have this trip, Auntie! She really *had* to. Nothing else would have done.

MISS TESMAN

No no, I suppose not. A wedding-tour seems to be quite indispensable nowadays.—But tell me now—have you gone thoroughly over the house yet?

TESMAN

Yes, you may be sure I have. I have been afoot ever since daylight.

MISS TESMAN

And what do you think of it all?

TESMAN

I'm delighted! Quite delighted! Only I can't think what we are to do with the two empty rooms between this inner parlour and Hedda's bedroom.

MISS TESMAN   [*Laughing.*]

Oh my dear George, I daresay you may find some use for them—in the course of time.

TESMAN

Why of course you are quite right, Aunt Julia! You mean as my library increases—eh?

MISS TESMAN

Yes, quite so, my dear boy. It was your library I was thinking of.

TESMAN

I am specially pleased on Hedda's account. Often and often,

before we were engaged, she said that she would never care to
live anywhere but in Secretary Falk's villa.*

MISS TESMAN

Yes, it was lucky that this very house should come into the
market, just after you had started.

TESMAN

Yes, Aunt Julia, the luck was on our side, wasn't it—eh?

MISS TESMAN

But the expense, my dear George! You will find it very
expensive, all this.

TESMAN   [*Looks at her, a little cast down.*]

Yes, I suppose I shall, Aunt!

MISS TESMAN

Oh, frightfully!

TESMAN

How much do you think? In round numbers?—Eh?

MISS TESMAN

Oh, I can't even guess until all the accounts come in.

TESMAN

Well, fortunately, Judge Brack has secured the most favourable
terms for me,—so he said in a letter to Hedda.

MISS TESMAN

Yes, don't be uneasy, my dear boy.—Besides, I have given
security for the furniture and all the carpets.

TESMAN

Security? You? My dear Aunt Julia— what sort of security could
you give?

MISS TESMAN

I have given a mortgage on our annuity.

TESMAN   [*Jumps up.*]

What! On your—and Aunt Rina's annuity!

MISS TESMAN

Yes, I knew of no other plan, you see.

---

*In the original *Statsrådinde Falks villa*—showing that it had belonged to the
widow of a cabinet minister. (Translator's note)

TESMAN   [*Placing himself before her.*]

Have you gone out of your senses, Auntie! Your annuity—it's all that you and Aunt Rina have to live upon.

MISS TESMAN

Well well—don't get so excited about it. It's only a matter of form you know—Judge Brack assured me of that. It was he that was kind enough to arrange the whole affair for me. A mere matter of form, he said.

TESMAN

Yes, that may be all very well. But nevertheless——

MISS TESMAN

You will have your own salary to depend upon now. And, good heavens, even if we did have to pay up a little——! To eke things out a bit at the start——! Why, it would be nothing but a pleasure to us.

TESMAN

Oh Auntie—will you never be tired of making sacrifices for me!

MISS TESMAN   [*Rises and lays her hand on his shoulders.*]

Have I any other happiness in this world except to smooth your way for you, my dear boy? You, who have had neither father nor mother to depend on. And now we have reached the goal, George! Things have looked black enough for us, sometimes; but, thank heaven, now you have nothing to fear.

TESMAN

Yes, it is really marvellous how everything has turned out for the best.

MISS TESMAN

And the people who opposed you—who wanted to bar the way for you—now you have them at your feet. They have fallen, George. Your most dangerous rival—his fall was the worst.— And now he has to lie on the bed he has made for himself—poor misguided creature.

TESMAN

Have you heard anything of Eilert? Since I went away, I mean.

MISS TESMAN

Only that he is said to have published a new book.

TESMAN

What! Eilert Lövborg! Recently—eh?

MISS TESMAN

>Yes, so they say. Heaven knows whether it can be worth anything! Ah, when *your* new book appears—that will be another story, George! What is it to be about?

TESMAN

>It will deal with the domestic industries of Brabant* during the Middle Ages.

MISS TESMAN

>Fancy—to be able to write on such a subject as that!

TESMAN

>However, it may be some time before the book is ready. I have all these collections to arrange first, you see.

MISS TESMAN

>Yes, collecting and arranging—no one can beat you at that. There you are my poor brother's own son.

TESMAN

>I am looking forward eagerly to setting to work at it; especially now that I have my own delightful home to work in.

MISS TESMAN

>And, most of all, now that you have got the wife of your heart, my dear George.

TESMAN   [*Embracing her.*]

>Oh yes, yes, Aunt Julia, Hedda—she is the best part of it all! [*Looks towards the doorway.*] I believe I hear her coming—eh?

HEDDA *enters from the left through the inner room. She is a woman of nine-and-twenty. Her face and figure show refinement and distinction. Her complexion is pale and opaque. Her steel-grey eyes express a cold, unruffled repose. Her hair is of an agreeable medium brown, but not particularly abundant. She is dressed in a tasteful, somewhat loose-fitting morning gown.*

MISS TESMAN   [*Going to meet* HEDDA.]

>Good morning, my dear Hedda! Good morning, and a hearty welcome!

*Area in Belgium.

HEDDA   [*Holds out her hand.*]

Good morning, dear Miss Tesman! So early a call! That is kind of
you.

MISS TESMAN   [*With some embarrassment.*]

Well—has the bride slept well in her new home?

HEDDA

Oh yes, thanks. Passably.

TESMAN   [*Laughing.*]

Passably! Come, that's good, Hedda! You were sleeping like a
stone when I got up.

HEDDA

Fortunately. Of course one has always to accustom one's self to
new surroundings, Miss Tesman—little by little.

[*Looking towards the left.*]

Oh—there the servant has gone and opened the veranda door,
and let in a whole flood of sunshine!

MISS TESMAN   [*Going towards the door.*]

Well, then we will shut it.

HEDDA

No no, not that! Tesman, please draw the curtains. That will give
a softer light.

TESMAN   [*At the door.*]

All right—all right.—There now, Hedda, now you have both
shade and fresh air.

HEDDA

Yes, fresh air we certainly must have, with all these stacks of
flowers———. But—won't you sit down, Miss Tesman?

MISS TESMAN

No, thank you. Now that I have seen that everything is all right
here—thank heaven!—I must be getting home again. My sister is
lying longing for me, poor thing.

TESMAN

Give her my very best love, Auntie; and say I shall look in and see
her later in the day.

MISS TESMAN

Yes, yes, I'll be sure to tell her. But by-the-bye, George—

[*Feeling in her dress pocket*]

—I had almost forgotten—I have something for you here.

TESMAN
What is it, Auntie? Eh?

MISS TESMAN   [*Produces a flat parcel wrapped in newspaper and hands it to him.*]
Look here, my dear boy.

TESMAN   [*Opening the parcel.*]
Well, I declare!——Have you really saved them for me, Aunt Julia! Hedda! isn't this touching——eh?

HEDDA   [*Beside the whatnot on the right.*]
Well, what is it?

TESMAN
My old morning-shoes! My slippers.

HEDDA
Indeed. I remember you often spoke of them while we were abroad.

TESMAN
Yes, I missed them terribly.
[*Goes up to her.*]
Now you shall see them, Hedda!

HEDDA   [*Going towards the stove.*]
Thanks, I really don't care about it.

TESMAN   [*Following her.*]
Only think——ill as she was, Aunt Rina embroidered these for me. Oh you can't think how many associations cling to them.

HEDDA   [*At the table.*]
Scarcely for me.

MISS TESMAN
Of course not for Hedda, George.

TESMAN
Well, but now that she belongs to the family, I thought——

HEDDA   [*Interrupting.*]
We shall never get on with this servant, Tesman.

MISS TESMAN
Not get on with Berta?

TESMAN
Why, dear, what puts *that* in your head? Eh?

HEDDA   [*Pointing.*]
Look there! She has left her old bonnet lying about on a chair.

TESMAN   [*In consternation, drops the slippers on the floor.*]
> Why, Hedda——

HEDDA
> Just fancy, if any one should come in and see it!

TESMAN
> But Hedda—that's Aunt Julia's bonnet.

HEDDA
> Is it!

MISS TESMAN   [*Taking up the bonnet.*]
> Yes, indeed it's mine. And, what's more, it's not old, Madam
> Hedda.

HEDDA
> I really did not look closely at it, Miss Tesman.

MISS TESMAN   [*Trying on the bonnet.*]
> Let me tell you it's the first time I have worn it—the very first
> time.

TESMAN
> And a very nice bonnet it is too—quite a beauty!

MISS TESMAN
> Oh, it's no such great things, George.
> [*Looks around her.*]
> My parasol——? Ah, here.
> [*Takes it.*]
> For this is mine too—
> [*mutters*]
> —not Berta's.

TESMAN
> A new bonnet and a new parasol! Only think, Hedda!

HEDDA
> Very handsome indeed.

TESMAN
> Yes, isn't it? Eh? But Auntie, take a good look at Hedda before
> you go! See how handsome *she* is!

MISS TESMAN
> Oh, my dear boy, there's nothing new in *that*. Hedda was always
> lovely.
> [*She nods and goes towards the right.*]

TESMAN   [*Following.*]

Yes, but have you noticed what splendid condition she is in? How she has filled out on the journey?

HEDDA   [*Crossing the room.*]

Oh, do be quiet——!

MISS TESMAN   [*Who has stopped and turned.*]

Filled out?

TESMAN

Of course you don't notice it so much now that she has that dress on. But I, who can see——

HEDDA   [*At the glass door, impatiently.*]

Oh, you can't see anything.

TESMAN

It must be the mountain air in the Tyrol——

HEDDA   [*Curtly, interrupting.*]

I am exactly as I was when I started.

TESMAN

So you insist; but I'm quite certain you are not. Don't you agree with me, Auntie?

MISS TESMAN   [*Who has been gazing at her with folded hands.*]

Hedda is lovely—lovely—lovely.

[*Goes up to her, takes her head between both hands, draws it downwards, and kisses her hair.*]

God bless and preserve Hedda Tesman—for George's sake.

HEDDA   [*Gently freeing herself.*]

Oh——! Let me go.

MISS TESMAN   [*In quiet emotion.*]

I shall not let a day pass without coming to see you.

TESMAN

No you won't, will you, Auntie? Eh?

MISS TESMAN

Good-bye—good-bye!

[*She goes out by the hall door. TESMAN accompanies her. The door remains half open. TESMAN can be heard repeating his message to Aunt Rina and his thanks for the slippers.*]

[*In the meantime, HEDDA walks about the room, raising her arms and clenching her hands as if in desperation. Then she flings back the curtains from the glass door, and stands there looking out.*]

[*Presently* TESMAN *returns and closes the door behind him.*]

TESMAN   [*Picks up the slippers from the floor.*]

What are you looking at, Hedda?

HEDDA   [*Once more calm and mistress of herself.*]

I am only looking at the leaves. They are so yellow—so withered.

TESMAN   [*Wraps up the slippers and lays them on the table.*]

Well you see, we are well into September now.

HEDDA   [*Again restless.*]

Yes, to think of it!—Already in—in September.

TESMAN

Don't you think Aunt Julia's manner was strange, dear? Almost solemn? Can you imagine what was the matter with her? Eh?

HEDDA

I scarcely know her, you see. Is she not often like that?

TESMAN

No, not as she was to-day.

HEDDA   [*Leaving the glass door.*]

Do you think she was annoyed about the bonnet?

TESMAN

Oh, scarcely at all. Perhaps a little, just at the moment——

HEDDA

But what an idea, to pitch her bonnet about in the drawing-room! No one does that sort of thing.

TESMAN

Well you may be sure Aunt Julia won't do it again.

HEDDA

In any case, I shall manage to make my peace with her.

TESMAN

Yes, my dear, good Hedda, if you only would.

HEDDA

When you call this afternoon, you might invite her to spend the evening here.

TESMAN

Yes, that I will. And there's one thing more you could do that would delight her heart.

HEDDA

What is it?

TESMAN

> If you could only prevail on yourself to say *du** to her. For my sake, Hedda? Eh?

HEDDA

> No no, Tesman—you really mustn't ask that of me. I have told you so already. I shall try to call her "Aunt"; and you must be satisfied with that.

TESMAN

> Well well. Only I think now that you belong to the family, you——

HEDDA

> H'm—I can't in the least see why——
> [*She goes up towards the middle doorway.*]

TESMAN   [*After a pause.*]

> Is there anything the matter with you, Hedda? Eh?

HEDDA

> I'm only looking at my old piano. It doesn't go at all well with all the other things.

TESMAN

> The first time I draw my salary, we'll see about exchanging it.

HEDDA

> No, no—no exchanging. I don't want to part with it. Suppose we put it there in the inner room, and then get another here in its place. When it's convenient, I mean.

TESMAN   [*A little taken aback.*]

> Yes—of course we could do that.

HEDDA   [*Takes up the bouquet from the piano.*]

> These flowers were not here last night when we arrived.

TESMAN

> Aunt Julia must have brought them for you.

HEDDA   [*Examining the bouquet.*]

> A visiting-card.
> [*Takes it out and reads:*]
> "Shall return later in the day." Can you guess whose card it is?

*Du is the familiar "you," like *tu* in French; people use the familiar "you" when addressing those with whom they are closest.

TESMAN

No. Whose? Eh?

HEDDA

The name is "Mrs. Elvsted."

TESMAN

Is it really? Sheriff Elvsted's wife? Miss Rysing that was.

HEDDA

Exactly. The girl with the irritating hair, that she was always showing off. An old flame of yours I've been told.

TESMAN   [*Laughing.*]

Oh, that didn't last long; and it was before I knew you, Hedda. But fancy her being in town!

HEDDA

It's odd that she should call upon us. I have scarcely seen her since we left school.

TESMAN

I haven't seen her either for——heaven knows how long. I wonder how she can endure to live in such an out-of-the-way hole——eh?

HEDDA   [*After a moment's thought, says suddenly:*]

Tell me, Tesman——isn't it somewhere near there that he——that——Eilert Lövborg is living?

TESMAN

Yes, he is somewhere in that part of the country.

BERTA *enters by the hall door.*

BERTA

That lady, ma'am, that brought some flowers a little while ago, is here again.

[*Pointing.*]

The flowers you have in your hand, ma'am.

HEDDA

Ah, is she? Well, please show her in.

BERTA *opens the door for* MRS. ELVSTED, *and goes out herself.*——MRS. ELVSTED *is a woman of fragile figure, with pretty, soft features. Her eyes are light blue, large, round, and somewhat prominent, with a startled, inquiring expression. Her hair is remarkably light, almost flaxen, and unusually abundant*

and wavy. She is a couple of years younger than HEDDA. *She wears a dark visiting dress, tasteful, but not quite in the latest fashion.*

HEDDA   [*Receives her warmly.*]
    How do you do, my dear Mrs. Elvsted? It's delightful to see you
    again.
MRS. ELVSTED   [*Nervously, struggling for self-control.*]
    Yes, it's a very long time since we met.
TESMAN   [*Gives her his hand.*]
    And we too——eh?
HEDDA
    Thanks for your lovely flowers——
MRS. ELVSTED
    Oh, not at all——. I would have come straight here yesterday
    afternoon; but I heard that you were away——
TESMAN
    Have you just come to town? Eh?
MRS. ELVSTED
    I arrived yesterday, about midday. Oh, I was quite in despair
    when I heard that you were not at home.
HEDDA
    In despair! How so?
TESMAN
    Why, my dear Mrs. Rysing—I mean Mrs. Elvsted   ——
HEDDA
    I hope that you are not in any trouble?
MRS. ELVSTED
    Yes, I am. And I don't know another living creature here that I
    can turn to.
HEDDA   [*Laying the bouquet on the table.*]
    Come—let us sit here on the sofa——
MRS. ELVSTED
    Oh, I am too restless to sit down.
HEDDA
    Oh no, you're not. Come here.
    [*She draws* MRS. ELVSTED *down upon the sofa and sits at her side.*
TESMAN
    Well? What is it, Mrs. Elvsted?

HEDDA

Has anything particular happened to you at home?

MRS. ELVSTED

Yes—and no. Oh—I am so anxious you should not
misunderstand me——

HEDDA

Then your best plan is to tell us the whole story, Mrs. Elvsted.

TESMAN

I suppose that's what you have come for—eh?

MRS. ELVSTED

Yes, yes—of course it is. Well then, I must tell you—if you
don't already know—that Eilert Lövborg is in town, too.

HEDDA

Lövborg——!

TESMAN

What! Has Eilert Lövborg come back? Fancy that, Hedda!

HEDDA

Well well—I hear it.

MRS. ELVSTED

He has been here a week already. Just fancy—a whole week! In
this terrible town, alone! With so many temptations on all sides.

HEDDA

But, my dear Mrs. Elvsted—how does *he* concern you so much?

MRS. ELVSTED   [*Looks at her with a startled air, and says rapidly.*]
He was the children's tutor.

HEDDA

Your children's?

MRS. ELVSTED

My husband's. I have none.

HEDDA

Your step-children's, then?

MRS. ELVSTED

Yes.

TESMAN   [*Somewhat hesitatingly.*]
Then was he—I don't know how to express it—was he—regular
enough in his habits to be fit for the post? Eh?

MRS. ELVSTED

For the last two years his conduct has been irreproachable.

TESMAN

Has it indeed? Fancy that, Hedda!

HEDDA

I hear it.

MRS. ELVSTED

Perfectly irreproachable, I assure you! In every respect. But all the same—now that I know he is here—in this great town—and with a large sum of money in his hands—I can't help being in mortal fear for him.

TESMAN

Why did he not remain where he was? With you and your husband? Eh?

MRS. ELVSTED

After his book was published he was too restless and unsettled to remain with us.

TESMAN

Yes, by-the-bye, Aunt Julia told me he had published a new book.

MRS. ELVSTED

Yes, a big book, dealing with the march of civilisation—in broad outline, as it were. It came out about a fortnight ago. And since it has sold so well, and been so much read—and made such a sensation——

TESMAN

Has it indeed? It must be something he has had lying by since his better days.

MRS. ELVSTED

Long ago, you mean?

TESMAN

Yes.

MRS. ELVSTED

No, he has written it all since he has been with us—within the last year.

TESMAN

Isn't that good news, Hedda? Think of that.

MRS. ELVSTED

Ah yes, if only it would last!

HEDDA

Have you seen him here in town?

MRS. ELVSTED

> No, not yet. I have had the greatest difficulty in finding out his address. But this morning I discovered it at last.

HEDDA   [*Looks searchingly at her.*]

> Do you know, it seems to me a little odd of your husband—h'm——

MRS. ELVSTED   [*Starting nervously.*]

> Of my husband! What?

HEDDA

> That he should send *you* to town on such an errand—that he does not come himself and look after his friend.

MRS. ELVSTED

> Oh no, no—my husband has no time. And besides, I—I had some shopping to do.

HEDDA   [*With a slight smile.*]

> Ah, that is a different matter.

MRS. ELVSTED   [*Rising quickly and uneasily.*]

> And now I beg and implore you, Mr. Tesman—receive Eilert Lövborg kindly if he comes to you! And that he is sure to do. You see you were such great friends in the old days. And then you are interested in the same studies—the same branch of science—so far as I can understand.

TESMAN

> We used to be, at any rate.

MRS. ELVSTED

> That is why I beg so earnestly that you—you too—will keep a sharp eye upon him. Oh, you will promise me that, Mr. Tesman—won't you?

TESMAN

> With the greatest of pleasure, Mrs. Rysing——

HEDDA

> Elvsted.

TESMAN

> I assure you I shall do all I possibly can for Eilert. You may rely upon me.

MRS. ELVSTED

> Oh, how very, very kind of you!
>
> [*Presses his hands.*]

Thanks, thanks, thanks!

[*Frightened.*]

You see, my husband is so very fond of him!

HEDDA   [*Rising.*]

You ought to write to him, Tesman. Perhaps he may not care to come to you of his own accord.

TESMAN

Well, perhaps it would be the right thing to do, Hedda? Eh?

HEDDA

And the sooner the better. Why not at once?

MRS. ELVSTED   [*Imploringly.*]

Oh, if you only would!

TESMAN

I'll write this moment. Have you his address, Mrs.——Mrs. Elvsted.

MRS. ELVSTED

Yes.

[*Takes a slip of paper from her pocket, and hands it to him.*]

Here it is.

TESMAN

Good, good. Then I'll go in——

[*Looks about him.*]

By the-bye,——my slippers? Oh, here.

[*Takes the packet, and is about to go.*]

HEDDA

Be sure you write him a cordial, friendly letter. And a good long one too.

TESMAN

Yes, I will.

MRS. ELVSTED

But please, please don't say a word to show that I have suggested it.

TESMAN

No, how could you think I would? Eh?

[*He goes out to the right, through the inner room.*]

HEDDA   [*Goes up to* MRS. ELVSTED, *smiles, and says in a low voice.*]

There! We have killed two birds with one stone.

MRS. ELVSTED

What do you mean?

HEDDA

Could you not see that I wanted him to go?

MRS. ELVSTED

Yes, to write the letter——

HEDDA

And that I might speak to you alone.

MRS. ELVSTED [Confused.]

About the same thing?

HEDDA

Precisely.

MRS. ELVSTED [Apprehensively.]

But there is nothing more, Mrs. Tesman! Absolutely nothing!

HEDDA

Oh yes, but there is. There is a great deal more——I can see that.
Sit here——and we'll have a cosy, confidential chat.

[She forces MRS. ELVSTED to sit in the easy-chair beside the stove, and
seats herself on one of the footstools.]

MRS. ELVSTED [Anxiously, looking at her watch.]

But, my dear Mrs. Tesman——I was really on the point of going.

HEDDA

Oh, you can't be in such a hurry.——Well? Now tell me
something about your life at home.

MRS. ELVSTED

Oh, that is just what I care least to speak about.

HEDDA

But to me, dear——? Why, weren't we schoolfellows?

MRS. ELVSTED

Yes, but you were in the class above me. Oh, how dreadfully
afraid of you I was then!

HEDDA

Afraid of me?

MRS. ELVSTED

Yes, dreadfully. For when we met on the stairs you used always
to pull my hair.

HEDDA

Did I, really?

MRS. ELVSTED

Yes, and once you said you would burn it off my head.

HEDDA

Oh that was all nonsense, of course.

MRS. ELVSTED

Yes, but I was so silly in those days.——And since then, too——we have drifted so far——far apart from each other. Our circles have been so entirely different.

HEDDA

Well then, we must try to drift together again. Now listen! At school we said *du** to each other; and we called each other by our Christian names——

MRS. ELVSTED

No, I am sure you must be mistaken.

HEDDA

No, not at all! I can remember quite distinctly. So now we are going to renew our old friendship.

[*Draws the footstool closer to* MRS. ELVSTED.]

There now!

[*Kisses her cheek.*]

You must say *du* to me and call me Hedda.

MRS. ELVSTED [*Presses and pats her hands.*]

Oh, how good and kind you are! I am not used to such kindness.

HEDDA

There, there, there! And I shall say *du* to you, as in the old days, and call you my dear Thora.

MRS. ELVSTED

My name is Thea.

HEDDA

Why, of course! I meant Thea.

[*Looks at her compassionately.*]

So you are not accustomed to goodness and kindness, Thea? Not in your own home?

*See the note on pg. 593.

MRS. ELVSTED

Oh, if I only had a home! But I haven't any; I have never had a home.

HEDDA   [Looks at her for a moment.]

I almost suspected as much.

MRS. ELVSTED   [Gazing helplessly before her.]

Yes—yes—yes.

HEDDA

I don't quite remember—was it not as housekeeper that you first went to Mr. Elvsted's?

MRS. ELVSTED

I really went as governess. But his wife—his late wife—was an invalid,—and rarely left her room. So I had to look after the housekeeping as well.

HEDDA

And then—at last—you became mistress of the house.

MRS. ELVSTED   [Sadly.]

Yes, I did.

HEDDA

Let me see—about how long ago was that?

MRS. ELVSTED

My marriage?

HEDDA

Yes.

MRS. ELVSTED

Five years ago.

HEDDA

To be sure; it must be that.

MRS. ELVSTED

Oh those five years——! Or at all events the last two or three of them! Oh, if you* could only imagine——

HEDDA   [Giving her a little slap on the hand.]

De? Fie, Thea!

---

*Mrs. Elvsted here uses the formal pronoun De, whereupon Hedda rebukes her. In her next speech Mrs. Elvsted says du. (Translator's note)

MRS. ELVSTED

Yes, yes, I will try—— Well, if—you could only imagine and understand——

HEDDA   [*Lightly.*]

Eilert Lövborg has been in your neighbourhood about three years, hasn't he?

MRS. ELVSTED   [*Looks at her doubtfully.*]

Eilert Lövborg? Yes—he has.

HEDDA

Had you known him before, in town here?

MRS. ELVSTED

Scarcely at all. I mean——I knew him by name of course.

HEDDA

But you saw a good deal of him in the country?

MRS. ELVSTED

Yes, he came to us every day. You see, he gave the children lessons; for in the long run I couldn't manage it all myself.

HEDDA

No, that's clear.——And your husband——? I suppose he is often away from home?

MRS. ELVSTED

Yes. Being sheriff, you know, he has to travel about a good deal in his district.

HEDDA   [*Leaning against the arm of the chair.*]

Thea—my poor, sweet Thea—now you must tell me everything—exactly as it stands.

MRS. ELVSTED

Well then, you must question me.

HEDDA

What sort of a man *is* your husband, Thea? I mean—you know—in everyday life. Is he kind to you?

MRS. ELVSTED   [*Evasively.*]

I am sure he means well in everything.

HEDDA

I should think he must be altogether too old for you. There is at least twenty years' difference between you, is there not?

MRS. ELVSTED   [*Irritably.*]

Yes, that is true, too. Everything about him is repellent to me!

We have not a thought in common. We have no single point of
sympathy——he and I.

HEDDA

But is he not fond of you all the same? In his own way?

MRS. ELVSTED

Oh I really don't know. I think he regards me simply as a useful
property. And then it doesn't cost much to keep me. I am not
expensive.

HEDDA

That is stupid of you.

MRS. ELVSTED   [Shakes her head.]

It cannot be otherwise——not with him. I don't think he really
cares for any one but himself——and perhaps a little for the
children.

HEDDA

And for Eilert Lövborg, Thea.

MRS. ELVSTED   [Looking at her.]

For Eilert Lövborg? What puts that into your head?

HEDDA

Well, my dear——I should say, when he sends you after him all the
way to town——

[Smiling almost imperceptibly.]

And besides, you said so yourself, to Tesman.

MRS. ELVSTED   [With a little nervous twitch.]

Did I? Yes, I suppose I did.

[Vehemently, but not loudly.]

No——I may just as well make a clean breast of it at once! For it
must all come out in any case.

HEDDA

Why, my dear Thea——?

MRS. ELVSTED

Well, to make a long story short: My husband did not know that
I was coming.

HEDDA

What! Your husband didn't know it!

MRS. ELVSTED

No, of course not. For that matter, he was away from home
himself——he was travelling. Oh, I could bear it no longer, Hedda!

I couldn't indeed—so utterly alone as I should have been in future.

HEDDA

Well? And then?

MRS. ELVSTED

So I put together some of my things—what I needed most—as quietly as possible. And then I left the house.

HEDDA

Without a word?

MRS. ELVSTED

Yes—and took the train straight to town.

HEDDA

Why, my dear, good Thea—to think of you daring to do it!

MRS. ELVSTED   [*Rises and moves about the room.*]

What else could I possibly do?

HEDDA

But what do you think your husband will say when you go home again?

MRS. ELVSTED   [*At the table, looks at her.*]

Back to *him*?

HEDDA

Of course.

MRS. ELVSTED

I shall never go back to him again.

HEDDA   [*Rising and going towards her.*]

Then you have left your home—for good and all?

MRS. ELVSTED

Yes. There was nothing else to be done.

HEDDA

But then—to take flight so openly!

MRS. ELVSTED

Oh, it's impossible to keep things of that sort secret.

HEDDA

But what do you think people will say of you, Thea?

MRS. ELVSTED

They may say what they like, for aught *I* care.

[*Seats herself wearily and sadly on the sofa.*]

I have done nothing but what I *had* to do.

HEDDA   [*After a short silence.*]

And what are your plans now? What do you think of doing?

MRS. ELVSTED

I don't know yet. I only know this, that I *must* live here, where Eilert Lövborg is—if I am to live at all.

HEDDA   [*Takes a chair from the table, seats herself beside her, and strokes her hands.*]

My dear Thea—how did this—this friendship—between you and Eilert Lövborg come about?

MRS. ELVSTED

Oh it grew up gradually. I gained a sort of influence over him.

HEDDA

Indeed?

MRS. ELVSTED

He gave up his old habits. Not because I asked him to, for I never dared do that. But of course he saw how repulsive they were to me; and so he dropped them.

HEDDA   [*Concealing an involuntary smile of scorn.*]

Then you have reclaimed him—as the saying goes—my little Thea.

MRS. ELVSTED

So he says himself, at any rate. And he, on his side, has made a real human being of me—taught me to think, and to understand so many things.

HEDDA

Did he give *you* lessons too, then?

MRS. ELVSTED

No, not exactly lessons. But he talked to me—talked about such an infinity of things. And then came the lovely, happy time when I began to share in his work—when he allowed me to help him!

HEDDA

Oh he did, did he?

MRS. ELVSTED

Yes! He never wrote anything without my assistance.

HEDDA

You were two good comrades, in fact?

MRS. ELVSTED   [*Eagerly.*]

Comrades! Yes, fancy, Hedda—that is the very word he used!—

Oh, I ought to feel perfectly happy; and yet I cannot; for I don't know how long it will last.

HEDDA

Are you no surer of him than that?

MRS. ELVSTED [*Gloomily.*]

A woman's shadow stands between Eilert Lövborg and me.

HEDDA [*Looks at her anxiously.*]

Who can *that* be?

MRS. ELVSTED

I don't know. Some one he knew in his—in his past. Some one he has never been able wholly to forget.

HEDDA

What has he told you—about this?

MRS. ELVSTED

He has only once—quite vaguely—alluded to it.

HEDDA

Well! And what did he say?

MRS. ELVSTED

He said that when they parted, she threatened to shoot him with a pistol.

HEDDA [*With cold composure.*]

Oh nonsense! No one does that sort of thing here.

MRS. ELVSTED

No. And that is why I think it must have been that red-haired singing-woman whom he once——

HEDDA

Yes, very likely.

MRS. ELVSTED

For I remember they used to say of her that she carried loaded firearms.

HEDDA

Oh—then of course it must have been she.

MRS. ELVSTED [*Wringing her hands.*]

And now just fancy, Hedda—I hear that this singing-woman—that she is in town again! Oh, I don't know what to do——

HEDDA [*Glancing towards the inner room.*]

Hush! Here comes Tesman.

[*Rises and whispers.*]

Thea—all this must remain between you and me.

MRS. ELVSTED [*Springing up.*]

Oh yes—yes! For heaven's sake———!

GEORGE TESMAN, *with a letter in his hand, comes from the right through the inner room.*

TESMAN

There now—the epistle is finished.

HEDDA

That's right. And now Mrs. Elvsted is just going. Wait a moment—I'll go with you to the garden gate.

TESMAN

Do you think Berta could post the letter, Hedda dear?

HEDDA [*Takes it.*]

I will tell her to.

BERTA *enters from the hall.*

BERTA

Judge Brack wishes to know if Mrs. Tesman will receive him.

HEDDA

Yes, ask Judge Brack to come in. And look here—put this letter in the post.

BERTA [*Taking the letter.*]

Yes, ma'am.

[*She opens the door for* JUDGE BRACK *and goes out herself.* BRACK *is a man of forty-five; thick set, but well-built and elastic in his movements. His face is roundish with an aristocratic profile. His hair is short, still almost black, and carefully dressed. His eyes are lively and sparkling. His eyebrows thick. His moustaches are also thick, with short-cut ends. He wears a well-cut walking-suit, a little too youthful for his age. He uses an eyeglass, which he now and then lets drop.*]

JUDGE BRACK [*With his hat in his hand, bowing.*]

May one venture to call so early in the day?

HEDDA

Of course one may.

TESMAN [*Presses his hand.*]

You are welcome at any time.

[*Introducing him.*]
Judge Brack——Miss Rysing——
HEDDA
Oh——!
BRACK   [*Bowing.*]
Ah——delighted——
HEDDA   [*Looks at him and laughs.*]
It's nice to have a look at you by daylight, Judge!
BRACK
Do you find me——altered?
HEDDA
A little younger, I think.
BRACK
Thank you so much.
TESMAN
But what do you think of Hedda——eh? Doesn't she look
flourishing? She has actually——
HEDDA
Oh, do leave me alone. You haven't thanked Judge Brack for all
the trouble he has taken——
BRACK
Oh, nonsense——it was a pleasure to me——
HEDDA
Yes, you are a friend indeed. But here stands Thea all impatience
to be off——so *au revoir*,* Judge. I shall be back again presently.
[*Mutual salutations.* MRS. ELVSTED *and* HEDDA *go out by the hall
door.*]
BRACK
Well,——is your wife tolerably satisfied——
TESMAN
Yes, we can't thank you sufficiently. Of course she talks of a little
re-arrangement here and there; and one or two things are still
wanting. We shall have to buy some additional trifles.
BRACK
Indeed!

*Good-bye (French). All foreign words used in the translation appear in the
original.

TESMAN

But we won't trouble you about these things. Hedda says she herself will look after what is wanting.——Shan't we sit down? Eh?

BRACK

Thanks, for a moment.

[*Seats himself beside the table.*]

There is something I wanted to speak to you about, my dear Tesman.

TESMAN

Indeed? Ah, I understand!

[*Seating himself.*]

I suppose it's the serious part of the frolic that is coming now. Eh?

BRACK

Oh, the money question is not so very pressing; though, for that matter, I wish we had gone a little more economically to work.

TESMAN

But that would never have done, you know! Think of Hedda, my dear fellow! You, who know her so well——. I couldn't possibly ask her to put up with a shabby style of living!

BRACK

No, no——that is just the difficulty.

TESMAN

And then——fortunately——it can't be long before I receive my appointment.

BRACK

Well, you see——such things are often apt to hang fire for a time.

TESMAN

Have you heard anything definite? Eh?

BRACK

Nothing exactly definite——.

[*Interrupting himself.*]

But by-the-bye——I have one piece of news for you.

TESMAN

Well?

BRACK

Your old friend, Eilert Lövborg, has returned to town.

TESMAN

    I know that already.

BRACK

    Indeed! How did you learn it?

TESMAN

    From that lady who went out with Hedda.

BRACK

    Really? What was her name? I didn't quite catch it.

TESMAN

    Mrs. Elvsted.

BRACK

    Aha—Sheriff Elvsted's wife? Of course—he has been living up in their regions.

TESMAN

    And fancy—I'm delighted to hear that he is quite a reformed character!

BRACK

    So they say.

TESMAN

    And then he has published a new book—eh?

BRACK

    Yes, indeed he has.

TESMAN

    And I hear it has made some sensation!

BRACK

    Quite an unusual sensation.

TESMAN

    Fancy—isn't that good news! A man of such extraordinary talents———. I felt so grieved to think that he had gone irretrievably to ruin.

BRACK

    That was what everybody thought.

TESMAN

    But I cannot imagine what he will take to now! How in the world will he be able to make his living? Eh?

    [*During the last words,* HEDDA *has entered by the hall door.*]

HEDDA   [*To* BRACK, *laughing with a touch of scorn.*]
Tesman is for ever worrying about how people are to make their
living.

TESMAN
Well you see, dear—we were talking about poor Eilert Lövborg.

HEDDA   [*Glancing at him rapidly.*]
Oh, indeed?
[*Seats herself in the arm-chair beside the stove and asks indifferently:*]
What is the matter with *him*?

TESMAN
Well—no doubt he has run through all his property long ago;
and he can scarcely write a new book every year—eh? So I really
can't see what is to become of him.

BRACK
Perhaps I can give you some information on that point.

TESMAN
Indeed!

BRACK
You must remember that his relations have a good deal of
influence.

TESMAN
Oh, his relations, unfortunately, have entirely washed their hands
of him.

BRACK
At one time they called him the hope of the family.

TESMAN
At one time, yes! But he has put an end to all that.

HEDDA
Who knows?
[*With a slight smile.*]
I hear they have reclaimed him up at Sheriff Elvsted's——

BRACK
And then this book that he has published——

TESMAN
Well well, I hope to goodness they may find something for him
to do. I have just written to him. I asked him to come and see us
this evening, Hedda dear.

BRACK

But my dear fellow, you are booked for my bachelors' party this evening. You promised on the pier last night.

HEDDA

Had you forgotten, Tesman?

TESMAN

Yes, I had utterly forgotten.

BRACK

But it doesn't matter, for you may be sure he won't come.

TESMAN

What makes you think that? Eh?

BRACK   [*With a little hesitation, rising and resting his hands on the back of his chair.*]

My dear Tesman—and you too, Mrs. Tesman—I think I ought not to keep you in the dark about something that—that——

TESMAN

That concerns Eilert——?

BRACK

Both you and him.

TESMAN

Well, my dear Judge, out with it.

BRACK

You must be prepared to find your appointment deferred longer than you desired or expected.

TESMAN   [*Jumping up uneasily.*]

Is there some hitch about it? Eh?

BRACK

The nomination may perhaps be made conditional on the result of a competition——

TESMAN

Competition! Think of that, Hedda!

HEDDA   [*Leans further back in the chair.*]

Aha—aha!

TESMAN

But who can my competitor be? Surely not——?

BRACK

Yes, precisely—Eilert Lövborg.

TESMAN   [*Clasping his hands.*]

No, no——it's quite inconceivable! Quite impossible! Eh?

BRACK

H'm——that is what it may come to, all the same.

TESMAN

Well but, Judge Brack——it would show the most incredible lack of consideration for me.

[*Gesticulates with his arms.*]

For——just think——I'm a married man! We have married on the strength of these prospects, Hedda and I; and run deep into debt; and borrowed money from Aunt Julia too. Good heavens, they had as good as promised me the appointment. Eh?

BRACK

Well, well, well——no doubt you will get it in the end; only after a contest.

HEDDA   [*Immovable in her arm-chair.*]

Fancy, Tesman, there will be a sort of sporting interest in that.

TESMAN

Why, my dearest Hedda, how can you be so indifferent about it.

HEDDA   [*As before.*]

I am not at all indifferent. I am most eager to see who wins.

BRACK

In any case, Mrs. Tesman, it is best that you should know how matters stand. I mean——before you set about the little purchases I hear you are threatening.

HEDDA

This can make no difference.

BRACK

Indeed! Then I have no more to say. Good-bye!

[*To* TESMAN.]

I shall look in on my way back from my afternoon walk, and take you home with me.

TESMAN

Oh yes, yes——your news has quite upset me.

HEDDA   [*Reclining, holds out her hand.*]

Good-bye, Judge; and be sure you call in the afternoon.

BRACK

Many thanks. Good-bye, good-bye!

TESMAN   [*Accompanying him to the door.*]

Good-bye, my dear Judge! You must really excuse me——

[JUDGE BRACK *goes out by the hall door.*]

TESMAN   [*Crosses the room.*]

Oh Hedda—one should never rush into adventures. Eh?

HEDDA   [*Looks at him, smiling.*]

Do *you* do *that*?

TESMAN

Yes, dear—there is no denying—it *was* adventurous to go and marry and set up house upon mere expectations.

HEDDA

Perhaps you are right there.

TESMAN

Well—at all events, we have our delightful home, Hedda! Fancy, the home we both dreamed of—the home we were in love with, I may almost say. Eh?

HEDDA   [*Rising slowly and wearily.*]

It was part of our compact that we were to go into society—to keep open house.

TESMAN

Yes, if you only knew how I had been looking forward to it! Fancy—to see you as hostess—in a select circle! Eh? Well, well, well—for the present we shall have to get on without society, Hedda—only to invite Aunt Julia now and then.—Oh, I intended you to lead such an utterly different life, dear——!

HEDDA

Of course I cannot have my man in livery just yet.

TESMAN

Oh no, unfortunately. It would be out of the question for us to keep a footman, you know.

HEDDA

And the saddle-horse I was to have had——

TESMAN   [*Aghast.*]

The saddle-horse!

HEDDA

——I suppose I must not think of that now.

TESMAN

Good heavens, no!—that's as clear as daylight!

HEDDA   [*Goes up the room.*]

Well, I shall have one thing at least to kill time with in the meanwhile.

TESMAN   [*Beaming.*]

Oh thank heaven for that! What is it, Hedda? Eh?

HEDDA   [*In the middle doorway, looks at him with covert scorn.*]

My pistols, George.

TESMAN   [*In alarm.*]

Your pistols!

HEDDA   [*With cold eyes.*]

General Gabler's pistols.

[*She goes out through the inner room, to the left.*]

TESMAN   [*Rushes up to the middle doorway and calls after her:*]

No, for heaven's sake, Hedda darling—don't touch those dangerous things! For my sake, Hedda! Eh?

ACT SECOND

The room at the TESMANS' *as in the first Act, except that the piano has been removed, and an elegant little writing-table with book-shelves put in its place. A smaller table stands near the sofa on the left. Most of the bouquets have been taken away.* MRS. ELVSTED's *bouquet is upon the large table in front.——It is afternoon.*

HEDDA, *dressed to receive callers, is alone in the room. She stands by the open glass door, loading a revolver. The fellow to it lies in an open pistol-case on the writing-table.*

HEDDA   [*Looks down the garden, and calls:*]
    So you are here again, Judge!
BRACK   [*Is heard calling from a distance.*]
    As you see, Mrs. Tesman!
HEDDA   [*Raises the pistol and points.*]
    Now I'll shoot you, Judge Brack!
BRACK   [*Calling unseen.*]
    No, no, no! Don't stand aiming at me!
HEDDA
    This is what comes of sneaking in by the back way.*
    [*She fires.*]
BRACK   [*Nearer.*]
    Are you out of your senses——!
HEDDA
    Dear me—did I happen to hit you?
BRACK   [*Still outside.*]
    I wish you would let these pranks alone!
HEDDA
    Come in then, Judge.

*Bagveje means both "back ways" and "underhand courses."

JUDGE BRACK, *dressed as though for a men's party, enters by the glass door. He carries a light overcoat over his arm.*

BRACK

What the deuce—haven't you tired of that sport, yet? What are you shooting at?

HEDDA

Oh, I am only firing in the air.

BRACK [*Gently takes the pistol out of her hand.*]

Allow me, madam!

[*Looks at it.*]

Ah—I know this pistol well!

[*Looks around.*]

Where is the case? Ah, here it is.

[*Lays the pistol in it, and shuts it.*]

Now we won't play at that game any more to-day.

HEDDA

Then what in heaven's name would you have me do with myself?

BRACK

Have you had no visitors?

HEDDA [*Closing the glass door.*]

Not one. I suppose all our set are still out of town.

BRACK

And is Tesman not at home either?

HEDDA [*At the writing-table, putting the pistol-case in a drawer which she shuts.*]

No. He rushed off to his aunt's directly after lunch; he didn't expect you so early.

BRACK

H'm—how stupid of me not to have thought of that!

HEDDA [*Turning her head to look at him.*]

Why stupid?

BRACK

Because if I had thought of it I should have come a little—earlier.

HEDDA [*Crossing the room.*]

Then you would have found no one to receive you; for I have been in my room changing my dress ever since lunch.

BRACK

And is there no sort of little chink that we could hold a parley through?

HEDDA

You have forgotten to arrange one.

BRACK

That was another piece of stupidity.

HEDDA

Well, we must just settle down here—and wait. Tesman is not likely to be back for some time yet.

BRACK

Never mind; I shall not be impatient.

HEDDA *seats herself in the corner of the sofa.* BRACK *lays his overcoat over the back of the nearest chair, and sits down, but keeps his hat in his hand. A short silence. They look at each other.*

HEDDA

Well?

BRACK   [*In the same tone.*]

Well?

HEDDA

I spoke first.

BRACK   [*Bending a little forward.*]

Come, let us have a cosy little chat, Mrs. Hedda.*

HEDDA   [*Leaning further back in the sofa.*]

Does it not seem like a whole eternity since our last talk? Of course I don't count those few words yesterday evening and this morning.

BRACK

You mean since our last confidential talk? Our last *tête-à-tête*?†

*As this form of address is contrary to English usage, and as the note of familiarity would be lacking in "Mrs. Tesman," Brack may, in stage representation, say "Miss Hedda," thus ignoring her marriage and reverting to the form of address no doubt customary between them of old. (Translator's note)

†A *tête-à-tête* (French) is an intimate, face-to-face encounter.

HEDDA

Well yes——since you put it so.

BRACK

Not a day has passed but I have wished that you were home again.

HEDDA

And I have done nothing but wish the same thing.

BRACK

You? Really, Mrs. Hedda? And I thought you had been enjoying your tour so much!

HEDDA

Oh yes, you may be sure of that!

BRACK

But Tesman's letters spoke of nothing but happiness.

HEDDA

Oh, *Tesman!* You see, he thinks nothing so delightful as grubbing in libraries and making copies of old parchments, or whatever you call them.

BRACK [*With a spice of malice.*]

Well, that is his vocation in life——or part of it at any rate.

HEDDA

Yes, of course; and no doubt when it's your vocation——. But *I!* Oh, my dear Mr. Brack, how mortally bored I have been.

BRACK [*Sympathetically.*]

Do you really say so? In downright earnest?

HEDDA

Yes, you can surely understand it——! To go for six whole months without meeting a soul that knew anything of *our* circle, or could talk about the things we are interested in.

BRACK

Yes, yes——I too should feel that a deprivation.

HEDDA

And then, what I found most intolerable of all——

BRACK

Well?

HEDDA

——was being everlastingly in the company of——one and the same person——

BRACK   [*With a nod of assent.*]

 Morning, noon, and night, yes—at all possible times and
 seasons.

HEDDA

 I said "everlastingly."

BRACK

 Just so. But I should have thought, with our excellent Tesman,
 one could——

HEDDA

 Tesman is—a specialist, my dear Judge.

BRACK

 Undeniably.

HEDDA

 And specialists are not at all amusing to travel with. Not in the
 long run at any rate.

BRACK

 Not even—the specialist one happens to *love*?

HEDDA

 Faugh—don't use that sickening word!

BRACK   [*Taken aback.*]

 What do you say, Mrs. Hedda?

HEDDA   [*Half laughing, half irritated.*]

 You should just try it! To hear of nothing but the history of
 civilisation, morning, noon, and night——

BRACK

 Everlastingly.

HEDDA

 Yes, yes, yes! And then all this about the domestic industry of the
 middle ages——! That's the most disgusting part of it!

BRACK   [*Looks searchingly at her.*]

 But tell me—in that case, how am I to understand your——?
 H'm——

HEDDA

 My accepting George Tesman, you mean?

BRACK

 Well, let us put it so.

HEDDA

 Good heavens, do you see anything so wonderful in that?

BRACK

Yes and no——Mrs. Hedda.

HEDDA

I had positively danced myself tired, my dear Judge. My day was done——

[*With a slight shudder.*]

Oh no——I won't say that; nor think it either!

BRACK

You have assuredly no reason to.

HEDDA

Oh, reasons——

[*Watching him closely.*]

And George Tesman——after all, you must admit that he is correctness itself.

BRACK

His correctness and respectability are beyond all question.

HEDDA

And I don't see anything absolutely ridiculous about him. ——Do you?

BRACK

Ridiculous? N——no——I shouldn't exactly say so——

HEDDA

Well——and his powers of research, at all events, are untiring.——I see no reason why he should not one day come to the front, after all.

BRACK   [*Looks at her hesitatingly.*]

I thought that you, like every one else, expected him to attain the highest distinction.

HEDDA   [*With an expression of fatigue.*]

Yes, so I did.——And then, since he was bent, at all hazards, on being allowed to provide for me——I really don't know why I should not have accepted his offer?

BRACK

No——if you look at it in *that* light——

HEDDA

It was more than my other adorers were prepared to do for me, my dear Judge.

BRACK   [*Laughing.*]

Well, I can't answer for all the rest; but as for myself, you know quite well that I have always entertained a—a certain respect for the marriage tie—for marriage as an institution, Mrs. Hedda.

HEDDA   [*Jestingly.*]

Oh, I assure you I have never cherished any hopes with respect to *you*.

BRACK

All I require is a pleasant and intimate interior, where I can make myself useful in every way, and am free to come and go as—as a trusted friend——

HEDDA

Of the master of the house, do you mean?

BRACK   [*Bowing.*]

Frankly—of the mistress first of all; but of course of the master too, in the second place. Such a triangular friendship—if I may call it so—is really a great convenience for all parties, let me tell you.

HEDDA

Yes, I have many a time longed for some one to make a third on our travels. Oh—those railway-carriage *tête-à-têtes*——!

BRACK

Fortunately your wedding journey is over now.

HEDDA   [*Shaking her head.*]

Not by a long—long way. I have only arrived at a station on the line.

BRACK

Well, then the passengers jump out and move about a little, Mrs. Hedda.

HEDDA

I never jump out.

BRACK

Really?

HEDDA

No—because there is always some one standing by to——

BRACK   [*Laughing.*]

To look at your ankles, do you mean?

HEDDA

Precisely.

BRACK

Well but, dear me——

HEDDA   [*With a gesture of repulsion.*]

I won't have it. I would rather keep my seat where I happen to be—and continue the *tête-à-tête.*

BRACK

But suppose a third person were to jump in and join the couple.

HEDDA

Ah—*that* is quite another matter!

BRACK

A trusted, sympathetic friend——

HEDDA

——with a fund of conversation on all sorts of lively topics——

BRACK

——and not the least bit of a specialist!

HEDDA   [*With an audible sigh.*]

Yes, that would be a relief indeed.

BRACK   [*Hears the front door open, and glances in that direction.*]

The triangle is completed.

HEDDA   [*Half aloud.*]

And on goes the train.

GEORGE TESMAN, *in a grey walking-suit, with a soft felt hat, enters from the hall. He has a number of unbound books under his arm and in his pockets.*

TESMAN   [*Goes up to the table beside the corner settee.*]

Ouf—what a load for a warm day—all these books.

[*Lays them on the table.*]

I'm positively perspiring, Hedda. Hallo—are you there already, my dear Judge? Eh? Berta didn't tell me.

BRACK   [*Rising.*]

I came in through the garden.

HEDDA

What books have you got there?

TESMAN   [*Stands looking them through.*]

Some new books on my special subjects—quite indispensable to me.

HEDDA

Your special subjects?

BRACK

Yes, books on his special subjects, Mrs. Tesman.

[BRACK *and* HEDDA *exchange a confidential smile.*]

HEDDA

Do you need still more books on your special subjects?

TESMAN

Yes, my dear Hedda, one can never have too many of them. Of course one must keep up with all that is written and published.

HEDDA

Yes, I suppose one must.

TESMAN

[*Searching among his books.*]

And look here—I have got hold of Eilert Lövborg's new book too.

[*Offering it to her.*]

Perhaps you would like to glance through it, Hedda? Eh?

HEDDA

No, thank you. Or rather—afterwards perhaps.

TESMAN

I looked into it a little on the way home.

BRACK

Well, what do you think of it—as a specialist?

TESMAN

I think it shows quite remarkable soundness of judgment. He never wrote like that before.

[*Putting the books together.*]

Now I shall take all these into my study. I'm longing to cut the leaves——! And then I must change my clothes.

[*To* BRACK.]

I suppose we needn't start just yet? Eh?

BRACK

Oh, no—dear there is not the slightest hurry.

TESMAN

Well then, I will take my time.

[*Is going with his books, but stops in the doorway and turns.*]

By-the-bye, Hedda—Aunt Julia is not coming this evening.

HEDDA

Not coming? Is it that affair of the bonnet that keeps her away?

TESMAN

Oh, not at all. How could you think such a thing of Aunt Julia?

Just fancy——! The fact is, Aunt Rina is very ill.

HEDDA

She always is.

TESMAN

Yes, but to-day she is much worse than usual, poor dear.

HEDDA

Oh, then it's only natural that her sister should remain with her. I

must bear my disappointment.

TESMAN

And you can't imagine, dear, how delighted Aunt Julia seemed to

be—because you had come home looking so flourishing!

HEDDA   [*Half aloud, rising.*]

Oh, those everlasting Aunts!

TESMAN

What?

HEDDA   [*Going to the glass door.*]

Nothing.

TESMAN

Oh, all right.

[*He goes through the inner room, out to the right.*]

BRACK

What bonnet were you talking about?

HEDDA

Oh, it was a little episode with Miss Tesman this morning. She

had laid down her bonnet on the chair there—

[*Looks at him and smiles.*]

—and I pretended to think it was the servant's.

BRACK   [*Shaking his head.*]

Now my dear Mrs. Hedda, how could you do such a thing? To

that excellent old lady, too!

HEDDA   [*Nervously crossing the room.*]

Well, you see—these impulses come over me all of a sudden; and I *cannot* resist them.

[*Throws herself down in the easy-chair by the stove.*]

Oh, I don't know how to explain it.

BRACK   [*Behind the easy-chair.*]

You are not really happy—that is at the bottom of it.

HEDDA   [*Looking straight before her.*]

I know of no reason why I should be—happy. Perhaps you can give me one?

BRACK

Well—amongst other things, because you have got exactly the home you had set your heart on.

HEDDA   [*Looks up at him and laughs.*]

Do you too believe in that legend?

BRACK

Is there nothing in it, then?

HEDDA

Oh yes, there is *something* in it.

BRACK

Well?

HEDDA

There is this in it, that I made use of Tesman to see me home from evening parties last summer——

BRACK

I, unfortunately, had to go quite a different way.

HEDDA

That's true. I know you were going a different way last summer.

BRACK   [*Laughing.*]

Oh fie, Mrs. Hedda! Well, then—you and Tesman——?

HEDDA

Well, we happened to pass here one evening; Tesman, poor fellow, was writhing in the agony of having to find conversation; so I took pity on the learned man——

BRACK   [*Smiles doubtfully.*]

You took pity? H'm——

HEDDA

Yes, I really did. And so—to help him out of his torment—I

happened to say, in pure thoughtlessness, that I should like to live
in this villa.

BRACK

No more than that?

HEDDA

Not *that* evening.

BRACK

But afterwards?

HEDDA

Yes, my thoughtlessness had consequences, my dear Judge.

BRACK

Unfortunately that too often happens, Mrs. Hedda.

HEDDA

Thanks! So you see it was this enthusiasm for Secretary Falk's
villa that first constituted a bond of sympathy between George
Tesman and me. From *that* came our engagement and our
marriage, and our wedding journey, and all the rest of it. Well,
well, my dear Judge—as you make your bed so you must lie, I
could almost say.

BRACK

This is exquisite! And you really cared not a rap about it all the
time?

HEDDA

No, heaven knows I didn't.

BRACK

But now? Now that we have made it so homelike for you?

HEDDA

Uh—the rooms all seem to smell of lavender and dried rose-
leaves.—But perhaps it's Aunt Julia that has brought that scent
with her.

BRACK   [*Laughing.*]

No, I think it must be a legacy from the late Mrs. Secretary Falk.

HEDDA

Yes, there is an odour of mortality about it. It reminds me of a
bouquet—the day after the ball.

[*Clasps her hands behind her head, leans back in her chair and looks at
him.*]

Oh, my dear Judge—you cannot imagine how horribly I shall bore myself here.

BRACK

Why should not you, too, find some sort of vocation in life, Mrs. Hedda?

HEDDA

A vocation—that should attract me?

BRACK

If possible, of course.

HEDDA

Heaven knows what sort of a vocation that could be. I often wonder whether——

[*Breaking off.*]

But that would never do either.

BRACK

Who can tell? Let me hear what it is.

HEDDA

Whether I might not get Tesman to go into politics, I mean.

BRACK   [*Laughing.*]

Tesman? No really now, political life is not the thing for him— not at all in his line.

HEDDA

No, I daresay not.—But if I could get him into it all the same?

BRACK

Why—what satisfaction could you find in that? If he is not fitted for that sort of thing, why should you want to drive him into it?

HEDDA

Because I am bored, I tell you!

[*After a pause.*]

So you think it quite out of the question that Tesman should ever get into the ministry?

BRACK

H'm—you see, my dear Mrs. Hedda—to get into the ministry, he would have to be a tolerably rich man.

HEDDA   [*Rising impatiently.*]

Yes, there we have it! It is this genteel poverty I have managed to drop into——!

[*Crosses the room.*]

That is what makes life so pitiable! So utterly ludicrous!—For that's what it is.

BRACK

Now *I* should say the fault lay elsewhere.

HEDDA

Where, then?

BRACK

You have never gone through any really stimulating experience.

HEDDA

Anything serious, you mean?

BRACK

Yes, you may call it so. But now you may perhaps have one in store.

HEDDA   [*Tossing her head.*]

Oh, you're thinking of the annoyances about this wretched professorship! But that must be Tesman's own affair. I assure you I shall not waste a thought upon it.

BRACK

No, no, I daresay not. But suppose now that what people call—in elegant language—a solemn responsibility were to come upon you?

[*Smiling.*]

A new responsibility, Mrs. Hedda?

HEDDA   [*Angrily.*]

Be quiet! Nothing of that sort will ever happen!

BRACK   [*Warily.*]

We will speak of this again a year hence—at the very outside.

HEDDA   [*Curtly.*]

I have no turn for anything of the sort, Judge Brack. No responsibilities for me!

BRACK

Are you so unlike the generality of women as to have no turn for duties which——?

HEDDA   [*Beside the glass door.*]

Oh, be quiet, I tell you!—I often think there is only one thing in the world I have any turn for.

BRACK   [*Drawing near to her.*]

And what is that, if I may ask?

HEDDA   [*Stands looking out.*]
> Boring myself to death. Now you know it.
> [*Turns, looks towards the inner room, and laughs.*]
> Yes, as I thought! Here comes the Professor.

BRACK   [*Softly, in a tone of warning.*]
> Come, come, come, Mrs. Hedda!

GEORGE TESMAN, *dressed for the party, with his gloves and hat in his hand, enters from the right through the inner room.*

TESMAN
> Hedda, has no message come from Eilert Lövborg? Eh?

HEDDA
> No.

TESMAN
> Then you'll see he'll be here presently.

BRACK
> Do you really think he will come?

TESMAN
> Yes, I am almost sure of it. For what you were telling us this morning must have been a mere floating rumour.

BRACK
> You think so?

TESMAN
> At any rate, Aunt Julia said she did not believe for a moment that he would ever stand in my way again. Fancy that!

BRACK
> Well then, that's all right.

TESMAN   [*Placing his hat and gloves on a chair on the right.*]
> Yes, but you must really let me wait for him as long as possible.

BRACK
> We have plenty of time yet. None of my guests will arrive before seven or half-past.

TESMAN
> Then meanwhile we can keep Hedda company, and see what happens. Eh?

HEDDA   [*Placing* BRACK's *hat and overcoat upon the corner settee.*]
And at the worst Mr. Lövborg can remain here with me.

BRACK   [*Offering to take his things.*]
Oh, allow me, Mrs. Tesman!—What do you mean by "At the worst"?

HEDDA
If he won't go with you and Tesman.

TESMAN.   [*Looks dubiously at her.*]
But, Hedda dear—do you think it would quite do for him to remain with you? Eh? Remember, Aunt Julia can't come.

HEDDA
No, but Mrs. Elvsted is coming. We three can have a cup of tea together.

TESMAN
Oh, yes *that* will be all right.

BRACK   [*Smiling.*]
And that would perhaps be the safest plan for him.

HEDDA
Why so?

BRACK
Well, you know, Mrs. Tesman, how you used to gird at my little bachelor parties. You declared they were adapted only for men of the strictest principles.

HEDDA
But no doubt Mr. Lövborg's principles are strict enough now. A converted sinner——
[BERTA *appears at the hall door.*]

BERTA
There's a gentleman asking if you are at home, ma'am——

HEDDA
Well, show him in.

TESMAN   [*Softly.*]
I'm sure it is he! Fancy that!

EILERT LÖVBORG *enters from the hall. He is slim and lean; of the same age as* TESMAN, *but looks older and somewhat worn-out. His hair and beard are of a blackish brown, his face long and pale, but with patches of colour on the cheek-bones. He is dressed in a well-cut black visiting suit, quite new. He has dark gloves and a silk hat. He stops near the door, and makes a rapid bow, seeming somewhat embarrassed.*

TESMAN   [*Goes up to him and shakes him warmly by the hand.*]
　　Well, my dear Eilert—so at last we meet again!
EILERT LÖVBORG   [*Speaks in a subdued voice.*]
　　Thanks for your letter, Tesman.
　　[*Approaching HEDDA*]
　　Will you too shake hands with me, Mrs. Tesman?
HEDDA   [*Taking his hand.*]
　　I am glad to see you, Mr. Lövborg.
　　[*With a motion of her hand.*]
　　I don't know whether you two gentlemen——?
LÖVBORG   [*Bowing slightly.*]
　　Judge Brack, I think.
BRACK   [*Doing likewise.*]
　　Oh yes,—in the old days——
TESMAN   [*To* LÖVBORG, *with his hands on his shoulders.*]
　　And now you must make yourself entirely at home, Eilert!
　　Mustn't he, Hedda?—For I hear you are going to settle in town
　　again? Eh?
LÖVBORG
　　Yes, I am.
TESMAN
　　Quite right, quite right. Let me tell you, I have got hold of your
　　new book; but I haven't had time to read it yet.
LÖVBORG
　　You may spare yourself the trouble.
TESMAN
　　Why so?
LÖVBORG
　　Because there is very little in it.
TESMAN
　　Just fancy—how can you say so?
BRACK
　　But it has been very much praised, I hear.

LÖVBORG

That was what I wanted; so I put nothing into the book but what every one would agree with.

BRACK

Very wise of you.

TESMAN

Well but, my dear Eilert——!

LÖVBORG

For now I mean to win myself a position again—to make a fresh start.

TESMAN   [A little embarrassed.]

Ah, that is what you wish to do? Eh?

LÖVBORG   [Smiling, lays down his hat, and draws a packet, wrapped in paper, from his coat pocket.]

But when this one appears, George Tesman, you will have to read it. For this is the real book—the book I have put my true self into.

TESMAN

Indeed? And what is it?

LÖVBORG

It is the continuation.

TESMAN

The continuation? Of what?

LÖVBORG

Of the book.

TESMAN

Of the new book?

LÖVBORG

Of course.

TESMAN

Why, my dear Eilert—does it not come down to our own days?

LÖVBORG

Yes, it does; and this one deals with the future.

TESMAN

With the future! But, good heavens, we know nothing of the future!

LÖVBORG

> No; but there is a thing or two to be said about it all the same.
>
> [*Opens the packet.*]
>
> Look here——

TESMAN

> Why, that's not your handwriting.

LÖVBORG

> I dictated it.
>
> [*Turning over the pages.*]
>
> It falls into two sections. The first deals with the civilising forces of the future. And here is the second—
>
> [*running through the pages towards the end*]
>
> —forecasting the probable line of development.

TESMAN

> How odd now! I should never have thought of writing anything of that sort.

HEDDA   [*At the glass door, drumming on the pane.*]

> H'm——. I daresay not.

LÖVBORG   [*Replacing the manuscript in its paper and laying the packet on the table.*]

> I brought it, thinking I might read you a little of it this evening.

TESMAN

> That was very good of you, Eilert. But this evening——?
>
> [*Looking at BRACK.*]
>
> I don't quite see how we can manage it——

LÖVBORG

> Well then, some other time. There is no hurry.

BRACK

> I must tell you, Mr. Lövborg—there is a little gathering at my house this evening—mainly in honour of Tesman, you know——

LÖVBORG   [*Looking for his hat.*]

> Oh—then I won't detain you——

BRACK

> No, but listen—will you not do me the favour of joining us?

LÖVBORG   [*Curtly and decidedly.*]

> No, I can't—thank you very much.

BRACK

Oh, nonsense—do! We shall be quite a select little circle. And I assure you we shall have a "lively time," as Mrs. Hed—as Mrs. Tesman says.

LÖVBORG

I have no doubt of it. But nevertheless——

BRACK

And then you might bring your manuscript with you, and read it to Tesman at my house. I could give you a room to yourselves.

TESMAN

Yes, think of that, Eilert,—why shouldn't you? Eh?

HEDDA [Interposing.]

But, Tesman, if Mr. Lövborg would really rather not! I am sure Mr. Lövborg is much more inclined to remain here and have supper with me.

LÖVBORG [Looking at her.]

With you, Mrs. Tesman?

HEDDA

And with Mrs. Elvsted.

LÖVBORG

Ah——

[Lightly.]

I saw her for a moment this morning.

HEDDA

Did you? Well, she is coming this evening. So you see you are almost bound to remain, Mr. Lövborg, or she will have no one to see her home.

LÖVBORG

That's true. Many thanks, Mrs. Tesman—in that case I will remain.

HEDDA

Then I have one or two orders to give the servant——

[She goes to the hall door and rings. BERTA enters. HEDDA talks to her in a whisper, and points towards the inner room. BERTA nods and goes out again.]

TESMAN [At the same time, to LÖVBORG.]

Tell me, Eilert—is it this new subject—the future—that you are going to lecture about?

LÖVBORG

Yes.

TESMAN

They told me at the bookseller's that you are going to deliver a course of lectures this autumn.

LÖVBORG

That is my intention. I hope you won't take it ill, Tesman.

TESMAN

Oh no, not in the least! But——?

LÖVBORG

I can quite understand that it must be disagreeable to you.

TESMAN [*Cast down.*]

Oh, I can't expect you, out of consideration for me, to——

LÖVBORG

But I shall wait till you have received your appointment.

TESMAN

Will you wait? Yes but—yes but—are you not going to compete with me? Eh?

LÖVBORG

No; it is only the moral victory I care for.

TESMAN

Why, bless me—then Aunt Julia was right after all! Oh yes—I knew it! Hedda! Just fancy—Eilert Lövborg is not going to stand in our way!

HEDDA [*Curtly.*]

Our way? Pray leave me out of the question.

[*She goes up towards the inner room, where* BERTA *is placing a tray with decanters and glasses on the table.* HEDDA *nods approval, and comes forward again.* BERTA *goes out.*]

TESMAN [*At the same time.*]

And you, Judge Brack—what do you say to this? Eh?

BRACK

Well, I say that a moral victory—h'm—may be all very fine——

TESMAN

Yes, certainly. But all the same——

HEDDA [*Looking at* TESMAN *with a cold smile.*]

You stand there looking as if you were thunder-struck——

TESMAN

Yes—so I am—I almost think——

BRACK

Don't you see, Mrs. Tesman, a thunderstorm has just passed over?

HEDDA [*Pointing towards the inner room.*]

Will you not take a glass of cold punch, gentlemen?

BRACK [*Looking at his watch.*]

A stirrup-cup? Yes, it wouldn't come amiss.

TESMAN

A capital idea, Hedda! Just the thing! Now that the weight has been taken off my mind——

HEDDA

Will you not join them, Mr. Lövborg?

LÖVBORG [*With a gesture of refusal.*]

No, thank you. Nothing for me.

BRACK

Why bless me—cold punch is surely not poison.

LÖVBORG

Perhaps not for every one.

HEDDA

I will keep Mr. Lövborg company in the meantime.

TESMAN

Yes, yes, Hedda dear, do.

[*He and* BRACK *go into the inner room, seat themselves, drink punch, smoke cigarettes, and carry on a lively conversation during what follows.* EILERT LÖVBORG *remains standing beside the stove.* HEDDA *goes to the writing-table.*]

HEDDA [*Raising her voice a little.*]

Do you care to look at some photographs, Mr. Lövborg? You know Tesman and I made a tour in the Tyrol on our way home?

[*She takes up an album, and places it on the table beside the sofa, in the further corner of which she seats herself.* EILERT LÖVBORG *approaches, stops, and looks at her. Then he takes a chair and seats himself to her left, with his back towards the inner room.*]

HEDDA [*Opening the album.*]

Do you see this range of mountains, Mr. Lövborg? It's the Ortler group. Tesman has written the name underneath. Here it is: "The Ortler group near Meran."

LÖVBORG   [*Who has never taken his eyes off her, says softly and slowly:*]

Hedda—Gabler!

HEDDA   [*Glancing hastily at him.*]

Ah! Hush!

LÖVBORG   [*Repeats softly.*]

Hedda Gabler!

HEDDA   [*Looking at the album.*]

That was my name in the old days—when we two knew each other.

LÖVBORG

And I must teach myself never to say Hedda Gabler again— never, as long as I live.

HEDDA   [*Still turning over the pages.*]

Yes, you must. And I think you ought to practise in time. The sooner the better, I should say.

LÖVBORG   [*In a tone of indignation.*]

Hedda Gabler married? And married to—George Tesman!

HEDDA

Yes—so the world goes.

LÖVBORG

Oh, Hedda, Hedda—how could you* throw yourself away!

HEDDA   [*Looks sharply at him.*]

What? I can't allow this!

LÖVBORG

What do you mean?

[TESMAN *comes into the room and goes towards the sofa.*]

HEDDA   [*Hears him coming and says in an indifferent tone.*]

And this is a view from the Val d'Ampezzo, Mr. Lövborg. Just look at these peaks!

[*Looks affectionately up at* TESMAN.]

What's the name of these curious peaks, dear?

TESMAN

Let me see. Oh, those are the Dolomites.

*He uses the familiar *du*. (Translator's note)

HEDDA

Yes, that's it!—Those are the Dolomites, Mr. Lövborg.

TESMAN

Hedda dear,—I only wanted to ask whether I shouldn't bring you a little punch after all? For yourself at any rate—eh?

HEDDA

Yes, do, please; and perhaps a few biscuits.

TESMAN

No cigarettes?

HEDDA

No.

TESMAN

Very well.

[*He goes into the inner room and out to the right.* BRACK *sits in the inner room, and keeps an eye from time to time on* HEDDA *and* LÖVBORG.]

LÖVBORG   [*Softly, as before.*]

Answer me, Hedda—how could you go and do this?

HEDDA   [*Apparently absorbed in the album.*]

If you continue to say *du* to me I won't talk to you.

LÖVBORG

May I not say *du* even when we are alone?

HEDDA

No. You may think it; but you mustn't say it.

LÖVBORG

Ah, I understand. It is an offence against George Tesman, whom you*—love.

HEDDA   [*Glances at him and smiles.*]

Love? What an idea!

LÖVBORG

You don't love him then!

HEDDA

But I won't hear of any sort of unfaithfulness! Remember that.

---

*From this point onward Lövborg uses the formal *De*. (Translator's note)

LÖVBORG

    Hedda——answer me one thing——

HEDDA

    Hush!

    [TESMAN *enters with a small tray from the inner room.*]

TESMAN

    Here you are! Isn't this tempting?

    [*He puts the tray on the table.*]

HEDDA

    Why do you bring it yourself?

TESMAN   [*Filling the glasses.*]

    Because I think it's such fun to wait upon you, Hedda.

HEDDA

    But you have poured out two glasses. Mr. Lövborg said he
    wouldn't have any——

TESMAN

    No, but Mrs. Elvsted will soon be here, won't she?

HEDDA

    Yes, by-the-bye——Mrs. Elvsted——

TESMAN

    Had you forgotten her? Eh?

HEDDA

    We were so absorbed in these photographs.

    [*Shows him a picture.*]

    Do you remember this little village?

TESMAN

    Oh, it's that one just below the Brenner Pass. It was there we
    passed the night——

HEDDA

    ——and met that lively party of tourists.

TESMAN

    Yes, that was the place. Fancy——if we could only have had *you*
    with us, Eilert! Eh?

    [*He returns to the inner room and sits beside* BRACK.

LÖVBORG

    Answer me this one thing, Hedda——

HEDDA

    Well?

LÖVBORG

Was there no love in your friendship for *me* either? Not a
spark—not a tinge of love in it?

HEDDA

I wonder if there was? To me it seems as though we were two
good comrades—two thoroughly intimate friends.
[*Smilingly.*]
You especially were frankness itself.

LÖVBORG

It was you that made me so.

HEDDA

As I look back upon it all, I think there was really something
beautiful, something fascinating—something daring—in—in that
secret intimacy—that comradeship which no living creature so
much as dreamed of.

LÖVBORG

Yes, yes, Hedda! Was there not?—When I used to come to your
father's in the afternoon—and the General sat over at the
window reading his papers—with his back towards us——

HEDDA

And we two on the corner sofa——

LÖVBORG

Always with the same illustrated paper before us——

HEDDA

For want of an album, yes.

LÖVBORG

Yes, Hedda, and when I made my confessions to you—told you
about myself, things that at that time no one else knew! There I
would sit and tell you of my escapades—my days and nights of
devilment. Oh, Hedda—what was the power in you that forced
me to confess these things?

HEDDA

Do you think it was any power in me?

LÖVBORG

How else can I explain it? And all those—those roundabout
questions you used to put to me——

HEDDA

Which you understood so particularly well——

LÖVBORG

How could you sit and question me like that? Question me quite frankly——

HEDDA

In roundabout terms, please observe.

LÖVBORG

Yes, but frankly nevertheless. Cross-question me about——all that sort of thing?

HEDDA

And how could you answer, Mr. Lövborg?

LÖVBORG

Yes, that is just what I can't understand——in looking back upon it. But tell me now, Hedda——was there not love at the bottom of our friendship? On your side, did you not feel as though you might purge my stains away——if I made you my confessor? Was it not so?

HEDDA

No, not quite.

LÖVBORG

What was your motive, then?

HEDDA

Do you think it quite incomprehensible that a young girl——when it can be done——without any one knowing——

LÖVBORG

Well?

HEDDA

——should be glad to have a peep, now and then, into a world which——

LÖVBORG

Which——?

HEDDA

——which she is forbidden to know anything about?

LÖVBORG

So that was it?

HEDDA

Partly. Partly——I almost think.

LÖVBORG
    Comradeship in the thirst for life. But why should not *that*, at
    any rate, have continued?
HEDDA
    The fault was yours.
LÖVBORG
    It was you that broke with me.
HEDDA
    Yes, when our friendship threatened to develop into something
    more serious. Shame upon you, Eilert Lövborg! How could you
    think of wronging your—your frank comrade?
LÖVBORG   [*Clenching his hands.*]
    Oh, why did you not carry out your threat? Why did you not
    shoot me down?
HEDDA
    Because I have such a dread of scandal.
LÖVBORG
    Yes, Hedda, you are a coward at heart.
HEDDA
    A terrible coward.
    [*Changing her tone.*]
    But it was a lucky thing for you. And now you have found ample
    consolation at the Elvsteds'.
LÖVBORG
    I know what Thea has confided to you.
HEDDA
    And perhaps you have confided to her something about us?
LÖVBORG
    Not a word. She is too stupid to understand anything of that
    sort.
HEDDA
    Stupid?
LÖVBORG
    She is stupid about matters of that sort.
HEDDA
    And I am cowardly.
    [*Bends over towards him, without looking him in the face, and says more
    softly:*]

But now I will confide something to *you*.

LÖVBORG   [*Eagerly.*]

Well?

HEDDA

The fact that I dared not shoot you down——

LÖVBORG

Yes!

HEDDA

——*that* was not my most arrant cowardice—that evening.

LÖVBORG   [*Looks at her a moment, understands, and whispers passionately.*]

Oh, Hedda! Hedda Gabler! Now I begin to see a hidden reason beneath our comradeship! You* and I——! After all, then, it was your craving for life——

HEDDA   [*Softly, with a sharp glance.*]

Take care! Believe nothing of the sort!

[*Twilight has begun to fall. The hall door is opened from without by* BERTA.]

HEDDA   [*Closes the album with a bang and calls smilingly:*]

Ah, at last! My darling Thea,—come along!

MRS. ELVSTED *enters from the hall. She is in evening dress. The door is closed behind her.*

HEDDA   [*On the sofa, stretches out her arms towards her.*]

My sweet Thea—you can't think how I have been longing for you!

[MRS. ELVSTED, *in passing, exchanges slight salutations with the gentlemen in the inner room, then goes up to the table and gives* HEDDA *her hand.* EILERT LÖVBORG *has risen. He and* MRS. ELVSTED *greet each other with a silent nod.*]

MRS. ELVSTED

Ought I to go in and talk to your husband for a moment?

---

*In this speech he once more says *du*. Hedda addresses him throughout as *De*. (Translator's note)

HEDDA

Oh, not at all. Leave those two alone. They will soon be going.

MRS. ELVSTED

Are they going out?

HEDDA

Yes, to a supper-party.

MRS. ELVSTED [*Quickly, to* LÖVBORG.]

Not *you*?

LÖVBORG

No.

HEDDA

Mr. Lövborg remains with us.

MRS. ELVSTED [*Takes a chair and is about to seat herself at his side.*]

Oh, how nice it is here!

HEDDA

No, thank you, my little Thea! Not *there*! You'll be good enough to come over here to me. I will sit between you.

MRS. ELVSTED

Yes, just as you please.

[*She goes round the table and seats herself on the sofa on* HEDDA's *right.* LÖVBORG *re-seats himself on his chair.*]

LÖVBORG [*After a short pause, to* HEDDA.]

Is not she lovely to look at?

HEDDA [*Lightly stroking her hair.*]

Only to look at?

LÖVBORG

Yes. For *we* two—she and I—*we* are two real comrades. We have absolute faith in each other; so we can sit and talk with perfect frankness——

HEDDA

Not round about, Mr. Lövborg?

LÖVBORG

Well——

MRS. ELVSTED [*Softly clinging close to* HEDDA.]

Oh, how happy I am, Hedda! For, only think, he says I have inspired him too!

HEDDA [*Looks at her with a smile.*]

Ah! Does he say that, dear?

LÖVBORG

> And then she is so brave, Mrs. Tesman!

MRS. ELVSTED

> Good heavens—am I brave?

LÖVBORG

> Exceedingly—where your comrade is concerned.

HEDDA

> Ah yes—courage! If one only had *that!*

LÖVBORG

> What then? What do you mean?

HEDDA

> Then life would perhaps be liveable, after all.
> [*With a sudden change of tone.*]
> But now, my dearest Thea, you really must have a glass of cold
> punch.

MRS. ELVSTED

> No, thanks—I never take anything of that kind.

HEDDA

> Well then, *you*, Mr. Lövborg.

LÖVBORG

> Nor I, thank you.

MRS. ELVSTED

> No, he doesn't either.

HEDDA   [*Looks fixedly at him.*]

> But if I say you *shall?*

LÖVBORG

> It would be no use.

HEDDA   [*Laughing.*]

> Then I, poor creature, have no sort of power over you?

LÖVBORG

> Not in *that* respect.

HEDDA

> But seriously, I think you ought to—for your own sake.

MRS. ELVSTED

> Why, Hedda——!

LÖVBORG

> How so?

HEDDA

Or rather on account of other people.

LÖVBORG

Indeed?

HEDDA

Otherwise people might be apt to suspect that—in your heart of hearts—you did not feel quite secure—quite confident in yourself.

MRS. ELVSTED [*Softly.*]

Oh please, Hedda——!

LÖVBORG

People may suspect what they like—for the present.

MRS. ELVSTED [*Joyfully.*]

Yes, let them!

HEDDA

I saw it plainly in Judge Brack's face a moment ago.

LÖVBORG

What did you see?

HEDDA

His contemptuous smile, when you dared not go with them into the inner room.

LÖVBORG

Dared not? Of course I preferred to stop here and talk to *you.*

MRS. ELVSTED

What could be more natural, Hedda?

HEDDA

But the Judge could not guess that. And I saw, too, the way he smiled and glanced at Tesman when you dared not accept his invitation to this wretched little supper-party of his.

LÖVBORG

Dared not! Do you say I dared not?

HEDDA

I don't say so. But that was how Judge Brack understood it.

LÖVBORG

Well, let him.

HEDDA

Then you are not going with them?

LÖVBORG
> I will stay here with you and Thea.

MRS. ELVSTED
> Yes, Hedda—how can you doubt that?

HEDDA   [*Smiles and nods approvingly to* LÖVBORG.]
> Firm as a rock! Faithful to your principles, now and for ever! Ah, that is how a man should be!
> [*Turns to* MRS. ELVSTED *and caresses her.*]
> Well now, what did I tell you, when you came to us this morning in such a state of distraction——

LÖVBORG   [*Surprised.*]
> Distraction!

MRS. ELVSTED   [*Terrified.*]
> Hedda—oh Hedda——!

HEDDA
> You can see for yourself! You haven't the slightest reason to be in such mortal terror——
> [*Interrupting herself.*]
> There! Now we can all three enjoy ourselves.

LÖVBORG   [*Who has given a start.*]
> Ah—what is all this, Mrs. Tesman?

MRS. ELVSTED
> Oh my God, Hedda! What are you saying? What are you doing?

HEDDA
> Don't get excited! That horrid Judge Brack is sitting watching you.

LÖVBORG
> So she was in mortal terror! On my account!

MRS. ELVSTED   [*Softly and piteously.*]
> Oh, Hedda—now you have ruined everything!

LÖVBORG   [*Looks fixedly at her for a moment. His face is distorted.*]
> So *that* was my comrade's frank confidence in me?

MRS. ELVSTED   [*Imploringly.*]
> Oh, my dearest friend—only let me tell you——

LÖVBORG   [*Takes one of the glasses of punch, raises it to his lips, and says in a low, husky voice.*]
> Your health, Thea!
> [*He empties the glass, puts it down, and takes the second.*]

MRS. ELVSTED   [*Softly.*]

 Oh, Hedda, Hedda—how *could* you do this?

HEDDA

 I do it? *I*? Are you crazy?

LÖVBORG

 Here's to your health too, Mrs. Tesman. Thanks for the truth. Hurrah for the truth!

 [*He empties the glass and is about to re-fill it.*]

HEDDA   [*Lays her hand on his arm.*]

 Come, come—no more for the present. Remember you are going out to supper.

MRS. ELVSTED

 No, no, no!

HEDDA

 Hush! They are sitting watching you.

LÖVBORG   [*Putting down the glass.*]

 Now, Thea—tell me the truth——

MRS. ELVSTED

 Yes.

LÖVBORG

 Did your husband know that you had come after me?

MRS. ELVSTED   [*Wringing her hands.*]

 Oh, Hedda—do you hear what he is asking?

LÖVBORG

 Was it arranged between you and him that you were to come to town and look after me? Perhaps it was the Sheriff himself that urged you to come? Aha, my dear—no doubt he wanted my help in his office! Or was it at the card-table that he missed me?

MRS. ELVSTED   [*Softly, in agony.*]

 Oh, Lövborg, Lövborg——!

LÖVBORG   [*Seizes a glass and is on the point of filling it.*]

 Here's a glass for the old Sheriff too! .

HEDDA

 [*Preventing him.*]

 No more just now. Remember, you have to read your manuscript to Tesman.

LÖVBORG   [*Calmly, putting down the glass.*]

 It was stupid of me all this, Thea—to take it in this way, I mean.

Don't be angry with me, my dear, dear comrade. You shall see—
both you and the others—that if I was fallen once—now I have
risen again! Thanks to *you*, Thea.

MRS. ELVSTED   [*Radiant with joy.*]
Oh, heaven be praised——!
[BRACK *has in the meantime looked at his watch. He and* TESMAN *rise
and come into the drawing-room.*]

BRACK   [*Takes his hat and overcoat.*]
Well, Mrs. Tesman, our time has come.

HEDDA
I suppose it has.

LÖVBORG   [*Rising.*]
Mine too, Judge Brack.

MRS. ELVSTED   [*Softly and imploringly.*]
Oh, Lövborg, don't do it!

HEDDA   [*Pinching her arm.*]
They can hear you!

MRS. ELVSTED   [*With a suppressed shriek.*]
Ow!

LÖVBORG   [*To* BRACK.]
You were good enough to invite me.

BRACK
Well, are you coming after all?

LÖVBORG
Yes, many thanks.

BRACK
I'm delighted——

LÖVBORG   [*To* TESMAN, *putting the parcel of MS. in his pocket.*]
I should like to show you one or two things before I send it to
the printers.

TESMAN
Fancy—that will be delightful. But, Hedda dear, how is Mrs.
Elvsted to get home? Eh?

HEDDA
Oh, that can be managed somehow.

LÖVBORG   [*Looking towards the ladies.*]
Mrs. Elvsted? Of course, I'll come again and fetch her.
[*Approaching.*]

At ten or thereabouts, Mrs. Tesman? Will that do?

HEDDA

Certainly. That will do capitally.

TESMAN

Well, then, that's all right. But you must not expect me so early, Hedda.

HEDDA

Oh, you may stop as long—as long as ever you please.

MRS. ELVSTED   [*Trying to conceal her anxiety.*]

Well then, Mr. Lövborg—I shall remain here until you come.

LÖVBORG   [*With his hat in his hand.*]

Pray do, Mrs. Elvsted.

BRACK

And now off goes the excursion train, gentlemen! I hope we shall have a lively time, as a certain fair lady puts it.

HEDDA

Ah, if only the fair lady could be present unseen——!

BRACK

Why unseen?

HEDDA

In order to hear a little of your liveliness at first hand, Judge Brack.

BRACK   [*Laughing.*]

I should not advise the fair lady to try it.

TESMAN   [*Also laughing.*]

Come, you're a nice one, Hedda! Fancy that!

BRACK

Well, good-bye, good-bye, ladies.

LÖVBORG   [*Bowing.*]

About ten o'clock, then.

[BRACK, LÖVBORG, and TESMAN *go out by the hall door. At the same time*, BERTA *enters from the inner room with a lighted lamp, which she places on the drawing-room table; she goes out by the way she came.*]

MRS. ELVSTED   [*Who has risen and is wandering restlessly about the room.*]

Hedda—Hedda—what will come of all this?

HEDDA

At ten o'clock—he will be here. I can see him already—with vine-leaves in his hair—flushed and fearless——

MRS. ELVSTED

Oh, I hope he may.

HEDDA

And then, you see—then he will have regained control over himself. Then he will be a free man for all his days.

MRS. ELVSTED

Oh God !—if he would only come as you see him now!

HEDDA

He will come as I see him—so, and not otherwise!

[*Rises and approaches* THEA.]

You may doubt him as long as you please; *I* believe in him. And now we will try——

MRS. ELVSTED

You have some hidden motive in this, Hedda!

HEDDA

Yes, I have. I want for once in my life to have power to mould a human destiny.

MRS. ELVSTED

Have you not the power?

HEDDA

I have not—and have never had it.

MRS. ELVSTED

Not your husband's?

HEDDA

Do you think *that* is worth the trouble? Oh, if you could only understand how poor I am. And fate has made *you* so rich!

[*Clasps her passionately in her arms.*]

I think I must burn your hair off, after all.

MRS. ELVSTED

Let me go! Let me go! I am afraid of you, Hedda!

BERTA   [*In the middle doorway.*]

Tea is laid in the dining-room, ma'am.

HEDDA

Very well. We are coming.

MRS. ELVSTED

No, no, no! I would rather go home alone! At once!

HEDDA

Nonsense! First you shall have a cup of tea, you little stupid. And then—at ten o'clock—Eilert Lövborg will be here—with vine-leaves in his hair.

[*She drags* MRS. ELVSTED *almost by force towards the middle doorway*.]

ACT THIRD

The room at the TESMANS. The curtaIns are drawn over the middle doorway, and also over the glass door. The lamp, half turned down, and with a shade over it, is burning on the table. In the stove, the door of which stands open, there has been a fire, which is now nearly burnt out.

MRS. ELVSTED, *wrapped in a large shawl, and with her feet upon a foot-rest, sits close to the stove, sunk back in the arm-chair.* HEDDA, *fully dressed, lies sleeping upon the sofa, with a sofa-blanket over her.*

MRS. ELVSTED   [*After a pause, suddenly sits up in her chair, and listens eagerly. Then she sinks back again wearily, moaning to herself.*]
   Not yet!—Oh God—oh God—not yet!

BERTA *slips cautiously in by the hall door. She has a letter in her hand.*

MRS. ELVSTED   [*Turns and whispers eagerly.*]
   Well—has any one come?
BERTA   [*Softly.*]
   Yes, a girl has just brought this letter.
MRS. ELVSTED   [*Quickly, holding out her hand.*]
   A letter! Give it to me!
BERTA
   No, it's for Dr. Tesman, ma'am.
MRS. ELVSTED
   Oh, indeed.
BERTA
   It was Miss Tesman's servant that brought it. I'll lay it here on the table.
MRS. ELVSTED
   Yes, do.

BERTA   [*Laying down the letter.*]

I think I had better put out the lamp. It's smoking.

MRS. ELVSTED

Yes, put it out. It must soon be daylight now.

BERTA   [*Putting out the lamp.*]

It is daylight already, ma'am.

MRS. ELVSTED

Yes, broad day! And no one come back yet——!

BERTA

Lord bless you, ma'am—I guessed how it would be.

MRS. ELVSTED

You guessed?

BERTA

Yes, when I saw that a certain person had come back to town—
and that he went off with them. For we've heard enough about
that gentleman before now.

MRS. ELVSTED

Don't speak so loud. You will waken Mrs. Tesman.

BERTA   [*Looks towards the sofa and sighs.*]

No, no—let her sleep, poor thing. Shan't I put some wood on
the fire?

MRS. ELVSTED

Thanks, not for me.

BERTA

Oh, very well.

[*She goes softly out by the hall door.*]

HEDDA   [*Is wakened by the shutting of the door, and looks up.*]

What's that——?

MRS. ELVSTED

It was only the servant——

HEDDA   [*Looking about her.*]

Oh, we're here——! Yes, now I remember.

[*Sits erect upon the sofa, stretches herself, and rubs her eyes.*]

What o'clock is it, Thea?

MRS. ELVSTED   [*Looks at her watch.*]

It's past seven.

HEDDA

When did Tesman come home?

MRS. ELVSTED

He has not come.

HEDDA

Not come home yet?

MRS. ELVSTED   [*Rising.*]

No one has come.

HEDDA

Think of our watching and waiting here till four in the
morning——

MRS. ELVSTED   [*Wringing her hands.*]

And *how* I watched and waited for him!

HEDDA   [*Yawns, and says with her hand before her mouth.*]

Well well—we might have spared ourselves the trouble.

MRS. ELVSTED

Did you get a little sleep?

HEDDA

Oh yes; I believe I have slept pretty well. Have you not?

MRS. ELVSTED

Not for a moment. I couldn't, Hedda!—not to save my life.

HEDDA   [*Rises and goes towards her.*]

There, there, there! There's nothing to be so alarmed about. I
understand quite well what has happened.

MRS. ELVSTED

Well, what do you think? Won't you tell me?

HEDDA

Why, of course it has been a very late affair at Judge Brack's——

MRS. ELVSTED

Yes, yes—that is clear enough. But all the same——

HEDDA

And then, you see, Tesman hasn't cared to come home and ring
us up in the middle of the night.

[*Laughing.*]

Perhaps he wasn't inclined to show himself either—immediately
after a jollification.

MRS. ELVSTED

But in that case—where can he have gone?

HEDDA

Of course he has gone to his Aunts' and slept there. They have his old room ready for him.

MRS. ELVSTED

No, he can't be with *them*; for a letter has just come for him from Miss Tesman. There it lies.

HEDDA

Indeed?

[*Looks at the address.*]

Why yes, it's addressed in Aunt Julia's own hand. Well then, he has remained at Judge Brack's. And as for Eilert Lövborg—he is sitting, with vine-leaves in his hair, reading his manuscript.

MRS. ELVSTED

Oh Hedda, you are just saying things you don't believe a bit.

HEDDA

You really are a little blockhead, Thea.

MRS. ELVSTED

Oh yes, I suppose I am.

HEDDA

And how mortally tired you look.

MRS. ELVSTED

Yes, I *am* mortally tired.

HEDDA

Well then, you must do as I tell you. You must go into my room and lie down for a little while.

MRS. ELVSTED

Oh no, no—I shouldn't be able to sleep.

HEDDA

I am sure you would.

MRS. ELVSTED

Well, but your husband is certain to come soon now; and then I want to know at once——

HEDDA

I shall take care to let you know when he comes.

MRS. ELVSTED

Do you promise me, Hedda?

HEDDA

Yes, rely upon me. Just you go in and have a sleep in the meantime.

MRS. ELVSTED

Thanks; then I'll try to.

[*She goes off through the inner room.*]

[HEDDA *goes up to the glass door and draws back the curtains. The broad daylight streams into the room. Then she takes a little hand-glass from the writing-table, looks at herself in it, and arranges her hair. Next she goes to the hall door and presses the bell-button.*]

BERTA *presently appears at the hall door.*

BERTA

Did you want anything, ma'am?

HEDDA

Yes; you must put some more wood in the stove. I am shivering.

BERTA

Bless me—I'll make up the fire at once.

[*She rakes the embers together and lays a piece of wood upon them; then stops and listens.*]

That was a ring at the front door, ma'am.

HEDDA

Then go to the door. I will look after the fire.

BERTA

It'll soon burn up.

[*She goes out by the hall door.*]

[HEDDA *kneels on the foot-rest and lays some more pieces of wood in the stove.*]

After a short pause, GEORGE TESMAN *enters from the hall. He looks tired and rather serious. He steals on tiptoe towards the middle doorway and is about to slip through the curtains.*

HEDDA [*At the stove, without looking up.*]

Good morning.

TESMAN [*Turns.*]

Hedda!

[*Approaching her.*]

Good heavens—are you up so early? Eh?

HEDDA

Yes, I am up very early this morning.

TESMAN

And I never doubted you were still sound asleep! Fancy that,
Hedda!

HEDDA

Don't speak so loud. Mrs. Elvsted is resting in my room.

TESMAN

Has Mrs. Elvsted been here all night?

HEDDA

Yes, since no one came to fetch her.

TESMAN

Ah, to be sure.

HEDDA   [*Closes the door of the stove and rises.*]

Well, did you enjoy yourselves at Judge Brack's?

TESMAN

Have you been anxious about me? Eh?

HEDDA

No, I should never think of being anxious. But I asked if you had
enjoyed yourself.

TESMAN

Oh yes,—for once in a way. Especially the beginning of the
evening; for then Eilert read me part of his book. We arrived
more than an hour too early—fancy that! And Brack had all sorts
of arrangements to make—so Eilert read to me.

HEDDA   [*Seating herself by the table on the right.*]

Well? Tell me, then——

TESMAN   [*Sitting on a footstool near the stove.*]

Oh Hedda, you can't conceive what a book that is going to be! I
believe it is one of the most remarkable things that have ever
been written. Fancy that!

HEDDA

Yes yes; I don't care about that——

TESMAN

I must make a confession to you, Hedda. When he had finished
reading—a horrid feeling came over me.

HEDDA

A horrid feeling?

TESMAN

I felt jealous of Eilert for having had it in him to write such a book. Only think, Hedda!

HEDDA

Yes, yes, I am thinking!

TESMAN

And then how pitiful to think that he—with all his gifts—should be irreclaimable, after all.

HEDDA

I suppose you mean that he has more courage than the rest?

TESMAN

No, not at all—I mean that he is incapable of taking his pleasures in moderation.

HEDDA

And what came of it all—in the end?

TESMAN

Well, to tell the truth, I think it might best be described as an orgy, Hedda.

HEDDA

Had he vine-leaves in his hair?

TESMAN

Vine-leaves? No, I saw nothing of the sort. But he made a long, rambling speech in honour of the woman who had inspired him in his work—that was the phrase he used.

HEDDA

Did he name her?

TESMAN

No, he didn't; but I can't help thinking he meant Mrs. Elvsted. You may be sure he did.

HEDDA

Well—where did you part from him?

TESMAN

On the way to town. We broke up—the last of us at any rate—all together; and Brack came with us to get a breath of fresh air. And then, you see, we agreed to take Eilert home; for he had had far more than was good for him.

HEDDA

I daresay.

TESMAN

But now comes the strange part of it, Hedda; or, I should rather say, the melancholy part of it. I declare I am almost ashamed— on Eilert's account—to tell you——

HEDDA

Oh, go on——!

TESMAN

Well, as we were getting near town, you see, I happened to drop a little behind the others. Only for a minute or two—fancy that!

HEDDA

Yes, yes, yes, but——?

TESMAN

And then, as I hurried after them—what do you think I found by the wayside? Eh?

HEDDA

Oh, how should I know!

TESMAN

You mustn't speak of it to a soul, Hedda! Do you hear! Promise me, for Eilert's sake.

[*Draws a parcel, wrapped in paper, from his coat pocket.*]

Fancy, dear—I found this.

HEDDA

Is not that the parcel he had with him yesterday?

TESMAN

Yes, it is the whole of his precious, irreplaceable manuscript! And he had gone and lost it, and knew nothing about it. Only fancy, Hedda! So deplorably——

HEDDA

But why did you not give him back the parcel at once?

TESMAN

I didn't dare to—in the state he was then in——

HEDDA

Did you not tell any of the others that you had found it?

TESMAN

Oh, far from it! You can surely understand that, for Eilert's sake, I wouldn't do that.

HEDDA

So no one knows that Eilert Lövborg's manuscript is in your possession?

TESMAN

No. And no one *must* know it.

HEDDA

Then what did you say to him afterwards?

TESMAN

I didn't talk to him again at all; for when we got in among the streets, he and two or three of the others gave us the slip and disappeared. Fancy that!

HEDDA

Indeed! They must have taken him home then.

TESMAN

Yes, so it would appear. And Brack, too, left us.

HEDDA

And what have you been doing with yourself since?

TESMAN

Well, I and some of the others went home with one of the party, a jolly fellow, and took our morning coffee with him; or perhaps I should rather call it our night coffee—eh? But now, when I have rested a little, and given Eilert, poor fellow, time to have his sleep out, I must take this back to him.

HEDDA   [*Holds out her hand for the packet.*]

No—don't give it to him! Not in such a hurry, I mean. Let me read it first.

TESMAN

No, my dearest Hedda, I mustn't, I really mustn't.

HEDDA

You must not?

TESMAN

No—for you can imagine what a state of despair he will be in when he wakens and misses the manuscript. He has no copy of it, you must know! He told me so.

HEDDA   [*Looking searchingly at him.*]

Can such a thing not be reproduced? Written over again?

TESMAN

No, I don't think that would be possible. For the inspiration, you see——

HEDDA

Yes, yes—I suppose it depends on that——

[*Lightly.*]

But, by-the-bye—here is a letter for you.

TESMAN

Fancy——!

HEDDA   [*Handing it to him.*]

It came early this morning.

TESMAN

It's from Aunt Julia! What can it be?

[*He lays the packet on the other footstool, opens the letter, runs his eye through it, and jumps up.*]

Oh, Hedda—she says that poor Aunt Rina is dying!

HEDDA

Well, we were prepared for that.

TESMAN

And that if I want to see her again, I must make haste. I'll run in to them at once.

HEDDA   [*Suppressing a smile.*]

Will you run?

TESMAN

Oh, my dearest Hedda—if you could only make up your mind to come with me! Just think!

HEDDA   [*Rises and says wearily, repelling the idea.*]

No, no, don't ask me. I will not look upon sickness and death. I loathe all sorts of ugliness.

TESMAN

Well, well, then——!

[*Bustling around.*]

My hat——? My overcoat——? Oh, in the hall——. I do hope I mayn't come too late, Hedda! Eh?

HEDDA

Oh, if you run——

[BERTA *appears at the hall door.*]

BERTA

Judge Brack is at the door, and wishes to know if he may come in.

TESMAN

At this time! No, I can't possibly see him.

HEDDA

But I can.

[*To* BERTA.]

Ask Judge Brack to come in.

[BERTA *goes out.*]

HEDDA.   [*Quickly, whispering.*]

The parcel, Tesman!

[*She snatches it up from the stool.*]

TESMAN

Yes, give it to me!

HEDDA

No, no, I will keep it till you come back.

[*She goes to the writing-table and places it in the bookcase.* TESMAN *stands in a flurry of haste, and cannot get his gloves on.*]

JUDGE BRACK *enters from the hall.*

HEDDA   [*Nodding to him.*]

You are an early bird, I must say.

BRACK

Yes, don't you think so?

[*To* TESMAN.]

Are you on the move, too?

TESMAN

Yes, I *must* rush off to my aunts'. Fancy—the invalid one is lying at death's door, poor creature.

BRACK

Dear me, is she indeed? Then on no account let me detain you. At such a critical moment——

TESMAN

Yes, I must really rush——Good-bye! Good-bye!

[*He hastens out by the hall door.*]

HEDDA   [*Approaching.*]

You seem to have made a particularly lively night of it at your rooms, Judge Brack.

BRACK

I assure you I have not had my clothes off, Mrs. Hedda.

HEDDA

Not you, either?

BRACK

No, as you may see. But what has Tesman been telling you of the night's adventures?

HEDDA

Oh, some tiresome story. Only that they went and had coffee somewhere or other.

BRACK

I have heard about that coffee-party already. Eilert Lövborg was not with them, I fancy?

HEDDA

No, they had taken him home before that.

BRACK

Tesman too?

HEDDA

No, but some of the others, he said.

BRACK   [*Smiling.*]

George Tesman is really an ingenuous creature, Mrs. Hedda.

HEDDA

Yes, heaven knows he is. Then is there something behind all this?

BRACK

Yes, perhaps there may be.

HEDDA

Well then, sit down, my dear Judge, and tell your story in comfort.

[*She seats herself to the left of the table. BRACK sits near her, at the long side of the table.*]

HEDDA

Now then?

BRACK

I had special reasons for keeping track of my guests—or rather of some of my guests—last night.

HEDDA

Of Eilert Lövborg among the rest, perhaps?

BRACK

Frankly—yes.

HEDDA

Now you make me really curious——

BRACK

Do you know where he and one or two of the others finished the
night, Mrs. Hedda?

HEDDA

If it is not quite unmentionable, tell me.

BRACK

Oh no, it's not at all unmentionable. Well, they put in an
appearance at a particularly animated soirée.*

HEDDA

Of the lively kind?

BRACK

Of the very liveliest——

HEDDA

Tell me more of this, Judge Brack——

BRACK

Lövborg, as well as the others, had been invited in advance. I
knew all about it. But he had declined the invitation; for now, as
you know, he has become a new man.

HEDDA

Up at the Elvsteds', yes. But he went after all, then?

BRACK

Well, you see, Mrs. Hedda—unhappily the spirit moved him at
my rooms last evening——

HEDDA

Yes, I hear he found inspiration.

BRACK

Pretty violent inspiration. Well, I fancy that altered his purpose;
for we menfolk are unfortunately not always so firm in our
principles as we ought to be.

*Evening gathering (French).

HEDDA

Oh, I am sure *you* are an exception, Judge Brack. But as to
Lövborg——?

BRACK

To make a long story short—he landed at last in Mademoiselle
Diana's rooms.

HEDDA

Mademoiselle Diana's?

BRACK

It was Mademoiselle Diana that was giving the soirée to a select
circle of her admirers and her lady friends.

HEDDA

Is she a red-haired woman?

BRACK

Precisely.

HEDDA

A sort of a—singer?

BRACK

Oh yes—in her leisure moments. And moreover a mighty
huntress—of men—Mrs. Hedda. You have no doubt heard of
her. Eilert Lövborg was one of her most enthusiastic
protectors—in the days of his glory.

HEDDA

And how did all this end?

BRACK

Far from amicably, it appears. After a most tender meeting, they
seem to have come to blows——

HEDDA

Lövborg and she?

BRACK

Yes. He accused her or her friends of having robbed him. He
declared that his pocket-book had disappeared—and other things
as well. In short, he seems to have made a furious disturbance.

HEDDA

And what came of it all?

BRACK

It came to a general scrimmage,* in which the ladies as well as the gentlemen took part. Fortunately the police at last appeared on the scene.

HEDDA

The police too?

BRACK

Yes. I fancy it will prove a costly frolic for Eilert Lövborg, crazy being that he is.

HEDDA

How so?

BRACK

He seems to have made a violent resistance—to have hit one of the constables on the head and torn the coat off his back. So they had to march him off to the police-station with the rest.

HEDDA

How have you learnt all this?

BRACK

From the police themselves.

HEDDA   [*Gazing straight before her.*]

So that is what happened. Then he had no vine-leaves in his hair.

BRACK

Vine-leaves, Mrs. Hedda?

HEDDA   [*Changing her tone.*]

But tell me now, Judge—what is your real reason for tracking out Eilert Lövborg's movements so carefully?

BRACK

In the first place, it could not be entirely indifferent to me if it should appear in the police-court that he came straight from my house.

HEDDA

Will the matter come into court then?

BRACK

Of course. However, I should scarcely have troubled so much about that. But I thought that, as a friend of the family, it was my

*Quarrel.

duty to supply you and Tesman with a full account of his nocturnal exploits.

HEDDA

Why so, Judge Brack?

BRACK

Why, because I have a shrewd suspicion that he intends to use you as a sort of blind.

HEDDA

Oh, how can you think such a thing!

BRACK

Good heavens, Mrs. Hedda—we have eyes in our head. Mark my words! This Mrs. Elvsted will be in no hurry to leave town again.

HEDDA

Well, even if there should be anything between them, I suppose there are plenty of other places where they could meet.

BRACK

Not a single *home*. Henceforth, as before, every respectable house will be closed against Eilert Lövborg.

HEDDA

And so ought mine to be, you mean?

BRACK

Yes. I confess it would be more than painful to me if this personage were to be made free of your house. How superfluous, how intrusive, he would be, if he were to force his way into——

HEDDA

——into the triangle?

BRACK

Precisely. It would simply mean that I should find myself homeless.

HEDDA   [Looks at him with a smile.]

So you want to be the one cock in the basket*—that is your aim.

BRACK   [Nods slowly and lowers his voice.]

Yes, that is my aim. And for that I will fight—with every weapon I can command.

HEDDA   [Her smile vanishing.]

I see you are a dangerous person—when it comes to the point.

*Eneste hane i kurven—a proverbial saying.

BRACK
Do you think so?

HEDDA
I am beginning to think so. And I am exceedingly glad to think—
that you have no sort of hold over me.

BRACK   [*Laughing equivocally.*]
Well, well, Mrs. Hedda—perhaps you are right there. If I had,
who knows what I might be capable of?

HEDDA
Come come now, Judge Brack! That sounds almost like a threat.

BRACK   [*Rising.*]
Oh, not at all! The triangle, you know, ought, if possible, to be
spontaneously constructed.

HEDDA
There I agree with you.

BRACK
Well, now I have said all I had to say; and I had better be getting
back to town. Good-bye, Mrs. Hedda.
[*He goes towards the glass door.*]

HEDDA   [*Rising.*]
Are you going through the garden?

BRACK
Yes, it's a short cut for me.

HEDDA
And then it is a back way, too.

BRACK
Quite so. I have no objection to back ways. They may be piquant
enough at times.

HEDDA
When there is ball practice going on, you mean?

BRACK   [*In the doorway, laughing to her.*]
Oh, people don't shoot their tame poultry, I fancy.

HEDDA   [*Also laughing.*]
Oh no, when there is only one cock in the basket——
[*They exchange laughing nods of farewell. He goes. She closes the door be-
hind him.*]
[HEDDA, *who has become quite serious, stands for a moment looking out.
Presently she goes and peeps through the curtain over the middle doorway.*

Then she goes to the writing-table, takes LÖVBORG's *packet out of the bookcase, and is on the point of looking through its contents.* BERTA *is heard speaking loudly in the hall.* HEDDA *turns and listens. Then she hastily locks up the packet in the drawer, and lays the key on the inkstand.*]

EILERT LÖVBORG, *with his greatcoat on and his hat in his hand, tears open the hall door. He looks somewhat confused and irritated.*

LÖVBORG   [*Looking towards the hall.*]
    And I tell you I must and will come in! There!
    [*He closes the door, turns, sees* HEDDA, *at once regains his self-control, and bows.*]
HEDDA   [*At the writing-table.*]
    Well, Mr. Lövborg, this is rather a late hour to call for Thea.
LÖVBORG
    You mean rather an early hour to call on you. Pray pardon me.
HEDDA
    How do you know that she is still here?
LÖVBORG
    They told me at her lodgings that she had been out all night.
HEDDA   [*Going to the oval table.*]
    Did you notice anything about the people of the house when they said that?
LÖVBORG   [*Looks inquiringly at her.*]
    Notice anything about them?
HEDDA
    I mean, did they seem to think it odd?
LÖVBORG   [*Suddenly understanding.*]
    Oh yes, of course! I am dragging her down with me! However, I didn't notice anything.—I suppose Tesman is not up yet?
HEDDA
    No—I think not——
LÖVBORG
    When did he come home?
HEDDA
    Very late.
LÖVBORG
    Did he tell you anything?

HEDDA

Yes, I gathered that you had had an exceedingly jolly evening at Judge Brack's.

LÖVBORG

Nothing more?

HEDDA

I don't think so. However, I was so dreadfully sleepy——

MRS. ELVSTED *enters through the curtains of the middle doorway.*

MRS. ELVSTED   [*Going towards him.*]

Ah, Lövborg! At last——!

LÖVBORG

Yes, at last. And too late!

MRS. ELVSTED   [*Looks anxiously at him.*]

What is too late?

LÖVBORG

Everything is too late now. It is all over with me.

MRS. ELVSTED

Oh no, no—don't say that!

LÖVBORG

You will say the same when you hear——

MRS. ELVSTED

I won't hear anything!

HEDDA

Perhaps you would prefer to talk to her alone? If so, I will leave you.

LÖVBORG

No, stay—you too. I beg you to stay.

MRS. ELVSTED

Yes, but I won't hear anything, I tell you.

LÖVBORG

It is not last night's adventures that I want to talk about.

MRS. ELVSTED

What is it then——?

LÖVBORG

I want to say that now our ways must part.

MRS. ELVSTED

Part!

HEDDA   [*Involuntarily.*]

   I knew it!

LÖVBORG

   You can be of no more service to me, Thea.

MRS. ELVSTED

   How can you stand there and say that! No more service to you!
Am I not to help you now, as before? Are we not to go on
working together?

LÖVBORG

   Henceforward I shall do no work.

MRS. ELVSTED   [*Despairingly.*]

   Then what am I to do with my life?

LÖVBORG

   You must try to live your life as if you had never known me.

MRS. ELVSTED

   But you know I cannot do that!

LÖVBORG

   Try if you cannot, Thea. You must go home again——

MRS. ELVSTED   [*In vehement protest.*]

   Never in this world! Where you are, there will I be also! I will
not let myself be driven away like this! I will remain here! I will
be with you when the book appears.

HEDDA   [*Half aloud, in suspense.*]

   Ah yes—the book!

LÖVBORG   [*Looks at her.*]

   My book and Thea's; for *that* is what it is.

MRS. ELVSTED

   Yes, I feel that it is. And that is why I have a right to be with you
when it appears! I will see with my own eyes how respect and
honour pour in upon you afresh. And the happiness—the
happiness—oh, I must share it with you!

LÖVBORG

   Thea—our book will never appear.

HEDDA

   Ah!

MRS. ELVSTED

   Never appear!

LÖVBORG
Can never appear.

MRS. ELVSTED [*In agonised foreboding.*]
Lövborg—what have you done with the manuscript?

HEDDA [*Looks anxiously at him.*]
Yes, the manuscript——?

MRS. ELVSTED
Where is it?

LÖVBORG
Oh Thea—don't ask me about it!

MRS. ELVSTED
Yes, yes, I *will* know. I demand to be told at once.

LÖVBORG
The manuscript——. Well then—I have torn the manuscript
into a thousand pieces.

MRS. ELVSTED [*Shrieks.*]
Oh no, no——!

HEDDA [*Involuntarily.*]
But that's not——

LÖVBORG [*Looks at her.*]
Not true, you think?

HEDDA [*Collecting herself*]
Oh well, of course—since you say so. But it sounded so
improbable——

LÖVBORG
It is true, all the same.

MRS. ELVSTED [*Wringing her hands.*]
Oh God—oh God, Hedda—torn his own work to pieces!

LÖVBORG
I have torn my own life to pieces. So why should I not tear my
life-work too——?

MRS. ELVSTED
And you did this last night?

LÖVBORG
Yes, I tell you! Tore it into a thousand pieces—and scattered
them on the fiord—far out. There there is cool sea-water at any
rate—let them drift upon it—drift with the current and the

wind. And then presently they will sink——deeper and deeper——as I shall, Thea.

MRS. ELVSTED

Do you know, Lövborg, that what you have done with the book——I shall think of it to my dying day as though you had killed a little child.

LÖVBORG

Yes, you are right. It is a sort of child-murder.

MRS. ELVSTED

How could you, then——! Did not the child belong to me too?

HEDDA   [Almost inaudibly.]

Ah, the child——

MRS. ELVSTED   [Breathing heavily.]

It is all over then. Well well, now I will go, Hedda.

HEDDA

But you are not going away from town?

MRS. ELVSTED

Oh, I don't know what I shall do. I see nothing but darkness before me.

[She goes out by the hall door.]

HEDDA   [Stands waiting for a moment.]

So you are not going to see her home, Mr. Lövborg?

LÖVBORG

I? Through the streets? Would you have people see her walking with me?

HEDDA

Of course I don't know what else may have happened last night. But is it so utterly irretrievable?

LÖVBORG

It will not end with last night——I know that perfectly well. And the thing is that now I have no taste for that sort of life either. I won't begin it anew. She has broken my courage and my power of braving life out.

HEDDA   [Looking straight before her.]

So that pretty little fool has had her fingers in a man's destiny.

[Looks at him.]

But all the same, how could you treat her so heartlessly.

LÖVBORG

Oh, don't say that it was heartless!

HEDDA

To go and destroy what has filled her whole soul for months and years! You do not call that heartless!

LÖVBORG

To you I can tell the truth, Hedda.

HEDDA

The truth?

LÖVBORG

First promise me——give me your word——that what I now confide to you Thea shall never know.

HEDDA

I give you my word.

LÖVBORG

Good. Then let me tell you that what I said just now was untrue.

HEDDA

About the manuscript?

LÖVBORG

Yes. I have not torn it to pieces——nor thrown it into the fiord.

HEDDA

No, no——. But——where is it then?

LÖVBORG

I have destroyed it none the less——utterly destroyed it, Hedda!

HEDDA

I don't understand.

LÖVBORG

Thea said that what I had done seemed to her like a child-murder.

HEDDA

Yes, so she said.

LÖVBORG

But to kill his child——that is not the worst thing a father can do to it.

HEDDA

Not the worst?

LÖVBORG

No. I wanted to spare Thea from hearing the worst.

HEDDA

Then what is the worst?

LÖVBORG

Suppose now, Hedda, that a man—in the small hours of the morning—came home to his child's mother after a night of riot and debauchery, and said: "Listen—I have been here and there—in this place and in that. And I have taken our child with me—to this place and to that. And I have lost the child—utterly lost it. The devil knows into what hands it may have fallen—who may have had their clutches on it."

HEDDA

Well—but when all is said and done, you know—this was only a book——

LÖVBORG

Thea's pure soul was in that book.

HEDDA

Yes, so I understand.

LÖVBORG

And you can understand, too, that for her and me together no future is possible.

HEDDA

What path do you mean to take then?

LÖVBORG

None. I will only try to make an end of it all—the sooner the better.

HEDDA [*A step nearer him.*]

Eilert Lövborg—listen to me.—Will you not try to—to do it beautifully?

LÖVBORG

Beautifully?

[*Smiling.*]

With vine-leaves in my hair, as you used to dream in the old days——?

HEDDA

No, no. I have lost my faith in the vine-leaves. But beautifully nevertheless! For once in a way!—Good-bye! You must go now—and do not come here any more.

LÖVBORG

Good-bye, Mrs. Tesman. And give George Tesman my love.

[*He is on the point of going.*]

HEDDA

No, wait! I must give you a memento to take with you.

[*She goes to the writing-table and opens the drawer and the pistol-case;
then returns to* LÖVBORG *with one of the pistols.*]

LÖVBORG   [*Looks at her.*]

This? Is *this* the memento?

HEDDA   [*Nodding slowly.*]

Do you recognise it? It was aimed at you once.

LÖVBORG

You should have used it then.

HEDDA

Take it—and do *you* use it now.

LÖVBORG   [*Puts the pistol in his breast pocket.*]

Thanks!

HEDDA

And beautifully, Eilert Lövborg. Promise me that!

LÖVBORG

Good-bye, Hedda Gabler.

[*He goes out by the hall door.*]

[HEDDA *listens for a moment at the door. Then she goes up to the
writing-table, takes out the packet of manuscript, peeps under the cover,
draws a few of the sheets half out, and looks at them. Next she goes over
and seats herself in the arm-chair beside the stove, with the packet in her
lap. Presently she opens the stove door, and then the packet.*]

HEDDA   [*Throws one of the quires into the fire and whispers to herself.*]

Now I am burning your child, Thea!—Burning it, curly-locks!

[*Throwing one or two more quires into the stove.*]

Your child and Eilert Lövborg's.

[*Throws the rest in.*]

I am burning—I am burning your child.

ACT FOURTH

The same rooms at the TESMANS'. It is evening. The drawing-room is in darkness. The back room is lighted by the hanging lamp over the table. The curtains over the glass door are drawn close.

HEDDA, dressed in black, walks to and fro in the dark room. Then she goes into the back room and disappears for a moment to the left. She is heard to strike a few chords on the piano. Presently she comes in sight again, and returns to the drawing-room.

BERTA enters from the right, through the inner room, with a lighted lamp, which she places on the table in front of the corner settee in the drawing-room. Her eyes are red with weeping, and she has black ribbons in her cap. She goes quietly and circumspectly out to the right. HEDDA goes up to the glass door, lifts the curtain a little aside, and looks out into the darkness.

Shortly afterwards, MISS TESMAN, in mourning, with a bonnet and veil on, comes in from the hall. HEDDA goes towards her and holds out her hand.

MISS TESMAN

Yes, Hedda, here I am, in mourning and forlorn; for now my poor sister has at last found peace.

HEDDA

I have heard the news already, as you see. Tesman sent me a card.

MISS TESMAN

Yes, he promised me he would. But nevertheless I thought that to Hedda—here in the house of life—I ought myself to bring the tidings of death.

HEDDA

That was very kind of you.

MISS TESMAN

Ah, Rina ought not to have left us just *now*. This is not the time for Hedda's house to be a house of mourning.

HEDDA [*Changing the subject.*]

She died quite peacefully, did she not, Miss Tesman?

MISS TESMAN

Oh, her end was so calm, so beautiful. And then she had the unspeakable happiness of seeing George once more—and bidding him good-bye.—Has he not come home yet?

HEDDA

No. He wrote that he might be detained. But won't you sit down?

MISS TESMAN

No, thank you, my dear, dear Hedda. I should like to, but I have so much to do. I must prepare my dear one for her rest as well as I can. She shall go to her grave looking her best.

HEDDA

Can I not help you in any way?

MISS TESMAN

Oh, you must not think of it! Hedda Tesman must have no hand in such mournful work. Nor let her thoughts dwell on it either—not at this time.

HEDDA

One is not always mistress of one's thoughts——

MISS TESMAN [*Continuing.*]

Ah yes, it is the way of the world. At home we shall be sewing a shroud; and here there will soon be sewing too, I suppose—but of another sort, thank God!

GEORGE TESMAN *enters by the hall door.*

HEDDA

Ah, you have come at last!

TESMAN

You here, Aunt Julia? With Hedda? Fancy that!

MISS TESMAN

I was just going, my dear boy. Well, have you done all you promised?

TESMAN

> No; I'm really afraid I have forgotten half of it. I must come to you again to-morrow. To-day my brain is all in a whirl. I can't keep my thoughts together.

MISS TESMAN

> Why, my dear George, you mustn't take it in this way.

TESMAN

> Mustn't——? How do you mean?

MISS TESMAN

> Even in your sorrow you must rejoice, as I do—rejoice that she is at rest.

TESMAN

> Oh yes, yes—you are thinking of Aunt Rina.

HEDDA

> You will feel lonely now, Miss Tesman.

MISS TESMAN

> Just at first, yes. But that will not last very long, I hope. I daresay I shall soon find an occupant for poor Rina's little room.

TESMAN

> Indeed? Who do you think will take it? Eh?

MISS TESMAN

> Oh, there's always some poor invalid or other in want of nursing, unfortunately.

HEDDA

> Would you really take such a burden upon you again?

MISS TESMAN

> A burden! Heaven forgive you, child—it has been no burden to me.

HEDDA

> But suppose you had a total stranger on your hands——

MISS TESMAN

> Oh, one soon makes friends with sick folk; and it's such an absolute necessity for me to have some one to live for. Well, heaven be praised, there may soon be something in this house, too, to keep an old aunt busy.

HEDDA

> Oh, don't trouble about anything here.

TESMAN

Yes, just fancy what a nice time we three might have together,
if——?

HEDDA

If——?

TESMAN   [*Uneasily.*]

Oh, nothing. It will all come right. Let us hope so—eh?

MISS TESMAN

Well well, I daresay you two want to talk to each other.
[*Smiling.*]
And perhaps Hedda may have something to tell you too, George.
Good-bye! I must go home to Rina.
[*Turning at the door.*]
How strange it is to think that now Rina is with me and with my
poor brother as well!

TESMAN

Yes, fancy that, Aunt Julia! Eh?

[MISS TESMAN *goes out by the hall door.*]

HEDDA   [*Follows* TESMAN *coldly and searchingly with her eyes.*]

I almost believe your Aunt Rina's death affects *you* more than it
does your Aunt Julia.

TESMAN

Oh, it's not that alone. It's Eilert I am so terribly uneasy about.

HEDDA   [*Quickly.*]

Is there anything new about him?

TESMAN

I looked in at his rooms this afternoon, intending to tell him the
manuscript was in safe keeping.

HEDDA

Well, did you not find him?

TESMAN

No. He wasn't at home. But afterwards I met Mrs. Elvsted, and
she told me that he had been here early this morning.

HEDDA

Yes, directly after you had gone.

TESMAN

And he said that he had torn his manuscript to pieces—eh?

HEDDA

Yes, so he declared.

TESMAN

Why, good heavens, he must have been completely out of his mind! And I suppose you thought it best not to give it back to him, Hedda?

HEDDA

No, he did not get it.

TESMAN

But of course you told him that we had it?

HEDDA

No.

[*Quickly.*]

Did you tell Mrs. Elvsted?

TESMAN

No; I thought I had better not. But you ought to have told *him*. Fancy, if, in desperation, he should go and do himself some injury! Let me have the manuscript, Hedda! I will take it to him at once. Where is it?

HEDDA   [*Cold and immovable, leaning on the arm-chair.*]

I have not got it.

TESMAN

Have not got it? What in the world do you mean?

HEDDA

I have burnt it—every line of it.

TESMAN   [*With a violent movement of terror.*]

Burnt! Burnt Eilert's manuscript!

HEDDA

Don't scream so. The servant might hear you.

TESMAN

Burnt! Why, good God——! No, no, no! It's impossible!

HEDDA

It is so, nevertheless.

TESMAN

Do you know what you have done, Hedda? It's unlawful appropriation of lost property. Fancy that! Just ask Judge Brack, and he'll tell you what it is.

HEDDA

I advise you not to speak of it—either to Judge Brack, or to any one else.

TESMAN

But how could you do anything so unheard-of? What put it into your head? What possessed you? Answer me that—eh?

HEDDA   [*Suppressing an almost imperceptible smile.*]

I did it for your sake, George.

TESMAN

For my sake!

HEDDA

This morning, when you told me about what he had read to you——

TESMAN

Yes, yes—what then?

HEDDA

You acknowledged that you envied him his work.

TESMAN

Oh, of course I didn't mean that literally.

HEDDA

No matter—I could not bear the idea that any one should throw you into the shade.

TESMAN   [*In an outburst of mingled doubt and joy.*]

Hedda! Oh, is this true? But—but—I never knew you to show your love like that before. Fancy that!

HEDDA

Well, I may as well tell you that—just at this time——
[*Impatiently, breaking off.*]

No, no; you can ask Aunt Julia. *She* will tell you, fast enough.

TESMAN

Oh, I almost think I understand you, Hedda!
[*Clasps his hands together.*]

Great heavens! do you really mean it! Eh?

HEDDA

Don't shout so. The servant might hear.

TESMAN   [*Laughing in irrepressible glee.*]

The servant! Why, how absurd you are, Hedda. It's only my old Berta! Why, I'll tell Berta myself.

HEDDA   [*Clenching her hands together in desperation.*]
Oh, it is killing me,——it is killing me, all this!

TESMAN
What is, Hedda? Eh?

HEDDA   [*Coldly, controlling herself.*]
All this——absurdity!——George.

TESMAN
Absurdity! Do you see anything absurd in my being overjoyed at
the news! But after all——perhaps I had better not say anything to
Berta.

HEDDA
Oh——why not that too?

TESMAN
No, no, not yet! But I must certainly tell Aunt Julia. And then
that you have begun to call me George too! Fancy that! Oh, Aunt
Julia will be so happy——so happy!

HEDDA
When she hears that I have burnt Eilert Lövborg's manuscript——
for your sake?

TESMAN
No, by-the-bye——that affair of the manuscript——of course nobody must know about that. But that you love me so much,*
Hedda——Aunt Julia must really share my joy in that! I wonder,
now, whether this sort of thing is usual in young wives? Eh?

HEDDA
I think you had better ask Aunt Julia that question too.

TESMAN
I will indeed, some time or other.
[*Looks uneasy and downcast again.*]
And yet the manuscript——the manuscript! Good God! it is
terrible to think what will become of poor Eilert now.

MRS. ELVSTED, *dressed as in the first Act, with hat and cloak, enters by the
hall door.*

*Literally, "That you burn for me." (Translator's note)

MRS. ELVSTED   [*Greets them hurriedly, and says in evident agitation.*]

Oh, dear Hedda, forgive my coming again.

HEDDA

What is the matter with you, Thea?

TESMAN

Something about Eilert Lövborg again——eh?

MRS. ELVSTED

Yes! I am dreadfully afraid some misfortune has happened to him.

HEDDA   [*Seizes her arm.*]

Ah,——do you think so!

TESMAN

Why, good Lord——what makes you think that, Mrs. Elvsted?

MRS. ELVSTED

I heard them talking of him at my boarding-house——just as I came in. Oh, the most incredible rumours are afloat about him to-day.

TESMAN

Yes, fancy, so I heard too! And I can bear witness that he went straight home to bed last night. Fancy that!

HEDDA

Well, what did they say at the boarding-house?

MRS. ELVSTED

Oh, I couldn't make out anything clearly. Either they knew nothing definite, or else———. They stopped talking when they saw me; and I did not dare to ask.

TESMAN   [*Moving about uneasily.*]

We must hope——we must hope that you misunderstood them, Mrs. Elvsted.

MRS. ELVSTED

No, no; I am sure it was of him they were talking. And I heard something about the hospital or——

TESMAN

The hospital?

HEDDA

No——surely that cannot be!

MRS. ELVSTED

Oh, I was in such mortal terror! I went to his lodgings and asked for him there.

HEDDA

You could make up your mind to that, Thea!

MRS. ELVSTED

What else could I do? I really could bear the suspense no longer.

TESMAN

But you didn't find him either—eh?

MRS. ELVSTED

No. And the people knew nothing about him. He hadn't been home since yesterday afternoon, they said.

TESMAN

Yesterday! Fancy, how could they say that?

MRS. ELVSTED

Oh, I am sure something terrible must have happened to him.

TESMAN

Hedda dear—how would it be if I were to go and make inquiries——?

HEDDA

No, no—don't you mix yourself up in this affair.

JUDGE BRACK, *with his hat in his hand, enters by the hall door, which* BERTA *opens, and closes behind him. He looks grave and bows in silence.*

TESMAN

Oh, is that you, my dear Judge? Eh?

BRACK

Yes. It was imperative I should see you this evening.

TESMAN

I can see you have heard the news about Aunt Rina?

BRACK

Yes, that among other things.

TESMAN

Isn't it sad—eh?

BRACK

Well, my dear Tesman, that depends on how you look at it.

TESMAN   [*Looks doubtfully at him.*]

Has anything else happened?

BRACK

Yes.

HEDDA   [*In suspense.*]

Anything sad, Judge Brack?

BRACK

That, too, depends on how you look at it, Mrs. Tesman.

MRS. ELVSTED   [*Unable to restrain her anxiety.*]

Oh! it is something about Eilert Lövborg!

BRACK   [*With a glance at her.*]

What makes you think that, Madam? Perhaps you have already
heard something——?

MRS. ELVSTED   [*In confusion.*]

No, nothing at all, but——

TESMAN

Oh, for heaven's sake, tell us!

BRACK   [*Shrugging his shoulders.*]

Well, I regret to say Eilert Lövborg has been taken to the
hospital. He is lying at the point of death.

MRS. ELVSTED   [*Shrieks.*]

Oh God! oh God——!

TESMAN

To the hospital! And at the point of death!

HEDDA   [*Involuntarily.*]

So soon then——

MRS. ELVSTED   [*Wailing.*]

And we parted in anger, Hedda!

HEDDA   [*Whispers.*]

Thea—Thea—be careful!

MRS. ELVSTED   [*Not heeding her.*]

I must go to him! I must see him alive!

BRACK

It is useless, Madam. No one will be admitted.

MRS. ELVSTED

Oh, at least tell me what has happened to him? What is it?

TESMAN

You don't mean to say that he has himself—— Eh?

HEDDA

    Yes, I am sure he has.

TESMAN

    Hedda, how can you———?

BRACK   [*Keeping his eyes fixed upon her.*]

    Unfortunately you have guessed quite correctly, Mrs. Tesman.

MRS. ELVSTED

    Oh, how horrible!

TESMAN

    Himself, then! Fancy that!

HEDDA

    Shot himself!

BRACK

    Rightly guessed again, Mrs. Tesman.

MRS. ELVSTED   [*With an effort at self-control.*]

    When did it happen, Mr. Brack?

BRACK

    This afternoon—between three and four.

TESMAN

    But, good Lord, where did he do it? Eh?

BRACK   [*With some hesitation.*]

    Where? Well—I suppose at his lodgings.

MRS. ELVSTED

    No, that cannot be; for I was there between six and seven.

BRACK

    Well then, somewhere else. I don't know exactly. I only know
that he was found———. He had shot himself—in the breast.

MRS. ELVSTED

    Oh, how terrible! That he should die like that!

HEDDA   [*To* BRACK.]

    Was it in the breast?

BRACK

    Yes—as I told you.

HEDDA

    Not in the temple?

BRACK

    In the breast, Mrs. Tesman.

HEDDA

Well, well—the breast is a good place, too.

BRACK

How do you mean, Mrs. Tesman?

HEDDA   [*Evasively.*]

Oh, nothing—nothing.

TESMAN

And the wound is dangerous, you say—eh?

BRACK

Absolutely mortal. The end has probably come by this time.

MRS. ELVSTED

Yes, yes, I feel it. The end! The end! Oh, Hedda——!

TESMAN

But tell me, how have you learnt all this?

BRACK   [*Curtly.*]

Through one of the police. A man I had some business with.

HEDDA   [*In a clear voice.*]

At last a deed worth doing!

TESMAN   [*Terrified.*]

Good heavens, Hedda! what are you saying?

HEDDA

I say there is beauty in this.

BRACK

H'm, Mrs. Tesman——

TESMAN

Beauty! Fancy that!

MRS. ELVSTED

Oh, Hedda, how can you talk of beauty in such an act!

HEDDA

Eilert Lövborg has himself made up his account with life. He has
had the courage to do—the one right thing.

MRS. ELVSTED

No, you must never think *that* was how it happened! It must have
been in delirium that he did it.

TESMAN

In despair!

HEDDA

That he did not. I am certain of that.

MRS. ELVSTED

Yes, yes! In delirium! Just as when he tore up our manuscript.

BRACK [*Starting.*]

The manuscript? Has he torn that up?

MRS. ELVSTED

Yes, last night.

TESMAN [*Whispers softly.*]

Oh, Hedda, we shall never get over this.

BRACK

H'm, very extraordinary.

TESMAN [*Moving about the room.*]

To think of Eilert going out of the world in this way! And not leaving behind him the book that would have immortalised his name——

MRS. ELVSTED

Oh, if only it could be put together again!

TESMAN

Yes, if it only could! I don't know what I would not give——

MRS. ELVSTED

Perhaps it can, Mr. Tesman.

TESMAN

What do you mean?

MRS. ELVSTED [*Searches in the pocket of her dress.*]

Look here. I have kept all the loose notes he used to dictate from.

HEDDA [*A step forward.*]

Ah——!

TESMAN

You have kept them, Mrs. Elvsted! Eh?

MRS. ELVSTED

Yes, I have them here. I put them in my pocket when I left home. Here they still are——

TESMAN

Oh, do let me see them!

MRS. ELVSTED [*Hands him a bundle of papers.*]

But they are in such disorder—all mixed up.

TESMAN

Fancy, if we could make something out of them, after all!

Perhaps if we two put our heads together——

MRS. ELVSTED

Oh yes, at least let us try——

TESMAN

We *will* manage it! We *must*! I will dedicate my life to this task.

HEDDA

You, George? Your life?

TESMAN

Yes, or rather all the time I can spare. My own collections must wait in the meantime. Hedda—you understand, eh? I owe this to Eilert's memory.

HEDDA

Perhaps.

TESMAN

And so, my dear Mrs. Elvsted, we will give our whole minds to it. There is no use in brooding over what can't be undone—eh? We must try to control our grief as much as possible, and——

MRS. ELVSTED

Yes, yes, Mr. Tesman, I will do the best I can.

TESMAN

Well then, come here. I can't rest until we have looked through the notes. Where shall we sit? Here? No, in there, in the back room. Excuse me, my dear Judge. Come with me, Mrs. Elvsted.

MRS. ELVSTED

Oh, if only it were possible!

[TESMAN *and* MRS. ELVSTED *go into the back room. She takes off her hat and cloak. They both sit at the table under the hanging lamp, and are soon deep in an eager examination of the papers.* HEDDA *crosses to the stove and sits in the arm-chair. Presently* BRACK *goes up to her.*]

HEDDA [*In a low voice.*]

Oh, what a sense of freedom it gives one, this act of Eilert Lövborg's.

BRACK

Freedom, Mrs. Hedda? Well, of course, it is a release for him——

HEDDA

I mean for me. It gives me a sense of freedom to know that a deed of deliberate courage is still possible in this world,—a deed of spontaneous beauty.

BRACK   [*Smiling.*]

H'm—my dear Mrs. Hedda——

HEDDA

Oh, I know what you are going to say. For you are a kind of specialist too, like—you know!

BRACK   [*Looking hard at her.*]

Eilert Lövborg was more to you than perhaps you are willing to admit to yourself. Am I wrong?

HEDDA

I don't answer such questions. I only know that Eilert Lövborg has had the courage to live his life after his own fashion. And then—the last great act, with its beauty! Ah! that he should have the will and the strength to turn away from the banquet of life—so early.

BRACK

I am sorry, Mrs. Hedda,—but I fear I must dispel an amiable illusion.

HEDDA

Illusion?

BRACK

Which could not have lasted long in any case.

HEDDA

What do you mean?

BRACK

Eilert Lövborg did not shoot himself—voluntarily.

HEDDA

Not voluntarily?

BRACK

No. The thing did not happen exactly as I told it.

HEDDA   [*In suspense.*]

Have you concealed something? What is it?

BRACK

For poor Mrs. Elvsted's sake I idealised the facts a little.

HEDDA

What *are* the facts?

BRACK

First, that he is already dead.

HEDDA

At the hospital?

BRACK

Yes—without regaining consciousness.

HEDDA

What more have you concealed?

BRACK

This—the event did not happen at his lodgings.

HEDDA

Oh, that can make no difference.

BRACK

Perhaps it may. For I must tell you—Eilert Lövborg was found shot in—in Mademoiselle Diana's boudoir.

HEDDA   [*Makes a motion as if to rise, but sinks back again.*]

That is impossible, Judge Brack! He cannot have been *there* again to-day.

BRACK

He was there this afternoon. He went there, he said, to demand the return of something which they had taken from him. Talked wildly about a lost child——

HEDDA

Ah—so that was why——

BRACK

I thought probably he meant his manuscript; but now I hear he destroyed that himself. So I suppose it must have been his pocket-book.

HEDDA

Yes, no doubt. And there—there he was found?

BRACK

Yes, there. With a pistol in his breast-pocket, discharged. The ball had lodged in a vital part.

HEDDA

In the breast—yes.

BRACK

> No—in the bowels.

HEDDA [*Looks up at him with an expression of loathing.*]

> That too! Oh, what curse is it that makes everything I touch turn ludicrous and mean?

BRACK

> There is one point more, Mrs. Hedda—another disagreeable feature in the affair.

HEDDA

> And what is that?

BRACK

> The pistol he carried——

HEDDA [*Breathless.*]

> Well? What of it?

BRACK

> He must have stolen it.

HEDDA [*Leaps up.*]

> Stolen it! That is not true! He did not steal it!

BRACK

> No other explanation is possible. He *must* have stolen it——. Hush!

TESMAN *and* MRS. ELVSTED *have risen from the table in the back room, and come into the drawing-room.*

TESMAN [*With the papers in both his hands.*]

> Hedda dear, it is almost impossible to see under that lamp! Think of that!

HEDDA

> Yes, I am thinking.

TESMAN

> Would you mind our sitting at your writing-table—eh?

HEDDA

> If you like.
>
> [*Quickly.*]
>
> No, wait! Let me clear it first!

TESMAN

> Oh, you needn't trouble, Hedda. There is plenty of room.

HEDDA

No, no, let me clear it, I say! I will take these things in and put them on the piano. There!

[*She has drawn out an object, covered with sheet music, from under the bookcase, places several other pieces of music upon it, and carries the whole into the inner room, to the left.* TESMAN *lays the scraps of paper on the writing-table, and moves the lamp there from the corner table. He and* MRS. ELVSTED *sit down and proceed with their work.* HEDDA *returns.*]

HEDDA   [*Behind* MRS. ELVSTED's *chair, gently ruffling her hair.*]

Well, my sweet Thea,—how goes it with Eilert Lövborg's monument?

MRS. ELVSTED   [*Looks dispiritedly up at her.*]

Oh, it will be terribly hard to put in order.

TESMAN

We *must* manage it. I am determined. And arranging other people's papers is just the work for me.

[HEDDA *goes over to the stove, and seats herself on one of the footstools.* BRACK *stands over her, leaning on the arm-chair.*]

HEDDA   [*Whispers.*]

What did you say about the pistol?

BRACK   [*Softly.*]

That he must have stolen it.

HEDDA

Why stolen it?

BRACK

Because every other explanation *ought* to be impossible, Mrs. Hedda.

HEDDA

Indeed?

BRACK   [*Glances at her.*]

Of course Eilert Lövborg was here this morning. Was he not?

HEDDA

Yes.

BRACK

Were you alone with him?

HEDDA

Part of the time.

BRACK

Did you not leave the room whilst he was here?

HEDDA

No.

BRACK

Try to recollect. Were you not out of the room a moment?

HEDDA

Yes, perhaps just a moment—out in the hall.

BRACK

And where was your pistol-case during that time?

HEDDA

I had it locked up in——

BRACK

Well, Mrs. Hedda?

HEDDA

The case stood there on the writing-table.

BRACK

Have you looked since, to see whether both the pistols are there?

HEDDA

No.

BRACK

Well, you need not. I saw the pistol found in Lövborg's pocket, and I knew it at once as the one I had seen yesterday—and before, too.

HEDDA

Have you it with you?

BRACK

No; the police have it.

HEDDA

What will the police do with it?

BRACK

Search till they find the owner.

HEDDA

Do you think they will succeed?

BRACK [Bends over her and whispers.]

No, Hedda Gabler—not so long as I say nothing.

HEDDA [Looks frightened at him.]

And if you do not say nothing,—what then?

BRACK   [*Shrugs his shoulders.*]

   There is always the possibility that the pistol was stolen.

HEDDA   [*Firmly.*]

   Death rather than that.

BRACK   [*Smiling.*]

   People say such things—but they don't *do* them.

HEDDA   [*Without replying.*]

   And supposing the pistol was not stolen, and the owner is
   discovered? What then?

BRACK

   Well, Hedda—then comes the scandal.

HEDDA

   The scandal!

BRACK

   Yes, the scandal—of which you are so mortally afraid. You will,
   of course, be brought before the court—both you and
   Mademoiselle Diana. She will have to explain how the thing
   happened—whether it was an accidental shot or murder. Did the
   pistol go off as he was trying to take it out of his pocket, to
   threaten her with? Or did she tear the pistol out of his hand,
   shoot him, and push it back into his pocket? That would be quite
   like her; for she is an able-bodied young person, this same
   Mademoiselle Diana.

HEDDA

   But *I* have nothing to do with all this repulsive business.

BRACK

   No. But you will have to answer the question: Why did you give
   Eilert Lövborg the pistol? And what conclusions will people
   draw from the fact that you did give it to him?

HEDDA   [*Lets her head sink.*]

   That is true. I did not think of that.

BRACK

   Well, fortunately, there is no danger, so long as I say nothing.

HEDDA   [*Looks up at him.*]

   So I am in your power, Judge Brack. You have me at your beck
   and call, from this time forward.

BRACK   [*Whispers softly.*]

   Dearest Hedda—believe me—I shall not abuse my advantage.

HEDDA

I am in your power none the less. Subject to your will and your demands. A slave, a slave then!

[*Rises impetuously.*]

No, I cannot endure the thought of that! Never!

BRACK [*Looks half-mockingly at her.*]

People generally get used to the inevitable.

HEDDA [*Returns his look.*]

Yes, perhaps.

[*She crosses to the writing-table. Suppressing an involuntary smile, she imitates* TESMAN's *intonations.*]

Well? Are you getting on, George? Eh?

TESMAN

Heaven knows, dear. In any case it will be the work of months.

HEDDA [*As before.*]

Fancy that!

[*Passes her hands softly through* MRS. ELVSTED's *hair.*]

Doesn't it seem strange to you, Thea? Here are you sitting with Tesman—just as you used to sit with Eilert Lövborg?

MRS. ELVSTED

Ah, if I could only inspire your husband in the same way!

HEDDA

Oh, that will come too—in time.

TESMAN

Yes, do you know, Hedda—I really think I begin to feel something of the sort. But won't you go and sit with Brack again?

HEDDA

Is there nothing I can do to help you two?

TESMAN

No, nothing in the world.

[*Turning his head.*]

I trust to you to keep Hedda company, my dear Brack.

BRACK [*With a glance at* HEDDA.]

With the very greatest of pleasure.

HEDDA

Thanks. But I am tired this evening. I will go in and lie down a little on the sofa.

TESMAN

Yes, do dear—eh?

[HEDDA *goes into the back room and draws the curtains. A short pause. Suddenly she is heard playing a wild dance on the piano.*]

MRS. ELVSTED   [*Starts from her chair.*]

Oh—what is that?

TESMAN   [*Runs to the doorway.*]

Why, my dearest Hedda—don't play dance-music to-night! Just think of Aunt Rina! And of Eilert too!

HEDDA   [*Puts her head out between the curtains.*]

And of Aunt Julia. And of all the rest of them.—After this, I will be quiet.

[*Closes the curtains again.*]

TESMAN   [*At the writing-table.*]

It's not good for her to see us at this distressing work. I'll tell you what, Mrs. Elvsted,—you shall take the empty room at Aunt Julia's and then I will come over in the evenings, and we can sit and work *there*—eh?

HEDDA   [*In the inner room.*]

I hear what you are saying, Tesman. But how am *I* to get through the evenings out here?

TESMAN   [*Turning over the papers.*]

Oh, I daresay Judge Brack will be so kind as to look in now and then, even though I am out.

BRACK   [*In the arm-chair, calls out gaily.*]

Every blessëd evening, with all the pleasure in life, Mrs. Tesman! We shall get on capitally together, we two!

HEDDA   [*Speaking loud and clear.*]

Yes, don't you flatter yourself we will, Judge Brack? Now that you are the one cock in the basket——

[*A shot is heard within. TESMAN, MRS. ELVSTED, and BRACK leap to their feet.*]

TESMAN

Oh, now she is playing with those pistols again.

[*He throws back the curtains and runs in, followed by MRS. ELVSTED. HEDDA lies stretched on the sofa lifeless. Confusion and cries. BERTA enters in alarm from the right.*]

TESMAN   [*Shrieks to* BRACK.]

Shot herself! Shot herself in the temple! Fancy that!

BRACK   [*Half-fainting in the arm-chair.*]

Good God!—people don't *do* such things!

THE MASTER BUILDER

(1892)

INTRODUCTION

IN *GHOSTS*, THE LACK OF fire insurance exposed the destructive hypocrisy of a pastor, but in *The Master Builder* (1892; *Bygmester Solness*) Ibsen realized that the theme of insurance provides a much more powerful tool for the genre most dear to his heart: the tragic double bind. Master Builder Solness owes his fame as a builder of homes to the fire that destroyed his own house and, indirectly, his children's and their mother's happiness. His whole life has been spent attempting to rebuild a home that would somehow compensate for this original loss. But no matter how much he tries, no matter how great his powers as a Master Builder, everything he does will be nothing but a shallow substitute. The fire made him Master Builder and at the same time marks the limits of his skill; it makes and unmakes him at the same time.

It is difficult not to read Ibsen's own biography into this obsession with the home, which appears in almost all of his plays and which receives here its culminating treatment. Ibsen had spent almost his entire career away from his native Norway and away from the village in which he was born and to which he returned only once. While he was constantly on the move across the continent, his plays incessantly reveal the bourgeois home to be built on deception and lies. It is as if his own lack of a real home made him perceptive of the cracks in those of others.

The Master Builder was the first play he wrote after returning to Norway when he was in his early sixties—but this return did not prompt him to make peace with the idea of the home. On the contrary, it led to a play that traps the attempt to create a home in an impossible double bind of loss and compensation. Ibsen infuses this tragic plot with a Christian language of innocence and guilt. Even though the Master Builder did not cause the fire and therefore is, strictly speaking, innocent of its consequences, the fact that he owes everything he is to this fire means that he is also complicit and guilty. One might say that Ibsen sought to rethink Greek tragedy in the terms of original sin: The fire is Solness's original sin, from which there is no escape.

This tragic impossibility of (re)building a home, of undoing something like an original sin, collides with a second plot. On one of his first assignments, the Master Builder had met a child and promised to build her a castle in the air. Now a young woman, this independent and spontaneous siren turns up on the Solness doorstep to bring into the open the intractable rift in this bourgeois family. In particular, she makes Solness realize that he will never be able to rebuild his original home. Suddenly, harking back to the past is no longer the only task the Master Builder sees for himself. While he knows he must fail in rebuilding a home, he might succeed in erecting a castle in the air instead. And so he gives up on the home, substituting the tragic plot with a second one, for as he climbs up onto the newly erected tower he knows exactly what will happen: His one flaw, as the play calls it, will cause him to fall. To everyone this seems like a perfectly tragic ending, a heroic master builder undone by vertigo. But the young temptress and he know that what looks like failure to the others is really his flight into an entirely different place: the castle in the air.

By the time of *The Master Builder*, Ibsen's reputation was so unquestionable that this play was quickly performed all over Europe and the United States, including Berlin, Christiania, Copenhagen, Chicago, and London shortly after its publication in 1893. The play puzzled audiences because many of its elements seemed familiar from earlier Ibsen plays, such as the insurance, the dirty secret at the source of success, and the young and independent woman threatening a defunct marriage, but they were arranged in a more intangible play. The castle in the air, the nine puppets that were burned, and other elements seemed incomprehensible symbols, at odds with the putative realism of Ibsen's earlier plays. They should be seen as powerful attempts by the playwright to rethink the treatment of his most elemental themes, the question of the home and of modern tragedy. Both are placed in a startling new form that continues to exert its mysterious influence on directors and playwrights today.

—Martin Puchner

CHARACTERS

HALVARD SOLNESS, Master Builder.
ALINE SOLNESS, his wife.
DOCTOR HERDAL, physician.
KNUT BROVIK, formerly an architect, now in SOLNESS's employment.
RAGNAR BROVIK, his son, draughtsman.
KAIA FOSLI, his niece, book-keeper.
MISS HILDA WANGEL.
Some Ladies.
A Crowd in the street.

The action passes in and about SOLNESS's *house.*

ACT FIRST

A plainly-furnished work-room in the house of HALVARD SOLNESS.
*Folding doors on the left lead out to the hall. On the right is the door
leading to the inner rooms of the house. At the back is an open door into
the draughtsmen's office. In front, on the left, a desk with books, papers
and writing materials. Further back than the folding door, a stove. In the
right-hand corner, a sofa, a table, and one or two chairs. On the table a
water-bottle and glass. A smaller table, with a rocking-chair and arm-
chair, in front on the right. Lighted lamps, with shades, on the table in
the draughtsmen's office, on the table in the corner, and on the desk.*

In the draughtsmen's office sit KNUT BROVIK *and his son* RAGNAR, *occupied with plans and calculations. At the desk in the outer office stands* KAIA
FOSLI, *writing in the ledger.* KNUT BROVIK *is a spare old man with white
hair and beard. He wears a rather threadbare but well-brushed black coat, spectacles, and a somewhat discoloured white neckcloth.* RAGNAR BROVIK *is a
well-dressed, light-haired man in his thirties, with a slight stoop.* KAIA FOSLI
*is a slightly built girl, a little over twenty, carefully dressed, and delicate-
looking. She has a green shade over her eyes.——All three go on working for some
time in silence.*

KNUT BROVIK   [*Rises suddenly, as if in distress, from the table; breathes
    heavily and laboriously as he comes forward into the doorway.*]
    No, I can't bear it much longer!
KAIA   [*Going up to him.*]
    You are feeling very ill this evening, are you not, uncle?
BROVIK
    Oh, I seem to get worse every day.
RAGNAR   [*Has risen and advances.*]
    You ought to go home, father. Try to get a little sleep——
BROVIK   [*Impatiently.*]
    Go to bed, I suppose? Would you have me stifled outright?

KAIA
>Then take a little walk.

RAGNAR
>Yes, do. I will come with you.

BROVIK [*With warmth.*]
>I will not go till he comes! I am determined to have it out this
>evening with—
>[*in a tone of suppressed bitterness*]
>—with him—with the chief.

KAIA [*Anxiously.*]
>Oh no, uncle,—do wait awhile before doing that!

RAGNAR
>Yes, better wait, father!

BROVIK [*Draws his breath laboriously.*]
>Ha—ha—! *I* haven't much time for waiting.

KAIA [*Listening.*]
>Hush! I hear him on the stairs.
>[*All three go back to their work. A short silence.*]

HALVARD SOLNESS *comes in through the hall door. He is a man no longer
young, but healthy and vigorous, with close-cut curly hair, dark moustache and
dark thick eyebrows. He wears a greyish-green buttoned jacket with an up-
standing collar and broad lapels. On his head he wears a soft grey felt hat, and
he has one or two light portfolios under his arm.*

SOLNESS [*Near the door, points towards the draughtsmen's office, and asks
>in a whisper:*]
>Are they gone?

KAIA [*Softly, shaking her head.*]
>No.
>[*She takes the shade off her eyes. SOLNESS crosses the room, throws his
>hat on a chair, places the portfolios on the table by the sofa, and ap-
>proaches the desk again. KAIA goes on writing without intermission, but
>seems nervous and uneasy.*]

SOLNESS [*Aloud*]
>What is that you are entering, Miss Fosli?

KAIA [*Starts*]
>Oh, it is only something that——

SOLNESS

    Let me look at it, Miss Fosli.

    [*Bends over her, pretends to be looking into the ledger, and whispers:*]
Kaia!

KAIA   [*Softly, still writing.*]

    Well?

SOLNESS

    Why do you always take that shade off when I come?

KAIA   [*As before.*]

    I look so ugly with it on.

SOLNESS   [*Smiling.*]

    Then you don't like to look ugly, Kaia?

KAIA   [*Half glancing up at him.*]

    Not for all the world. Not in *your* eyes.

SOLNESS   [*Strokes her hair gently.*]

    Poor, poor little Kaia——

KAIA   [*Bending her head.*]

    Hush——they can hear you!

    [SOLNESS *strolls across the room to the right, turns and pauses at the
door of the draughtsmen's office.*

SOLNESS

    Has any one been here for me?

RAGNAR   [*Rising.*]

    Yes, the young couple who want a villa built, out at Lövstrand.

SOLNESS   [*Growling.*]

    Oh, those two! They must wait. I am not quite clear about the
plans yet.

RAGNAR   [*Advancing, with some hesitation.*]

    They were very anxious to have the drawings at once.

SOLNESS   [*As before.*]

    Yes, of course——so they all are.

BROVIK   [*Looks up.*]

    They say they are longing so to get into a house of their own.

SOLNESS

    Yes, yes——we know all that! And so they are content to take
whatever is offered them. They get a——a roof over their heads——
an address——but nothing to call a home. No thank you! In that

case, let them apply to somebody else. Tell them that, the next
time they call.

BROVIK   [*Pushes his glasses up on to his forehead and looks in astonishment at him.*]

To somebody else? Are you prepared to give up the commission?

SOLNESS   [*Impatiently.*]

Yes, yes, yes, devil take it! If that is to be the way of it———.
Rather that, than build away at random.

[*Vehemently.*]

Besides, I know very little about these people as yet.

BROVIK

The people are safe enough. Ragnar knows them. He is a friend
of the family. Perfectly safe people.

SOLNESS

Oh, safe—safe enough! That is not at all what I mean. Good
lord—don't you understand me either?

[*Angrily.*]

I won't have anything to do with these strangers. They may apply
to whom they please, so far as I am concerned.

BROVIK   [*Rising.*]

Do you really mean *that*?

SOLNESS   [*Sulkily.*]

Yes, I do.—For once in a way.

[*He comes forward.*]

[BROVIK *exchanges a glance with* RAGNAR, *who makes a warning
gesture. Then* BROVIK *comes into the front room.*]

BROVIK

May I have a few words with you?

SOLNESS

Certainly.

BROVIK   [*To* KAIA.]

Just go in there for a moment, Kaia.

KAIA   [*Uneasily.*]

Oh, but uncle———

BROVIK

Do as I say, child. And shut the door after you.

[KAIA *goes reluctantly into the draughtsmen's office, glances anxiously
and imploringly at* SOLNESS, *and shuts the door.*]

BROVIK   [*Lowering his voice a little.*]
>   I don't want the poor children to know how ill I am.

SOLNESS
>   Yes, you have been looking very poorly of late.

BROVIK
>   It will soon be all over with me. My strength is ebbing—from
>   day to day.

SOLNESS
>   Won't you sit down?

BROVIK
>   Thanks—may I?

SOLNESS   [*Placing the arm-chair more conveniently.*]
>   Here—take this chair.—And now?

BROVIK   [*Has seated himself with difficulty.*]
>   Well, you see, it's about Ragnar. That is what weighs most upon
>   me. What is to become of him?

SOLNESS
>   Of course your son will stay with me as long as ever he likes.

BROVIK
>   But that is just what he does not like. He feels that he cannot stay
>   here any longer.

SOLNESS
>   Why, I should say he was very well off here. But if he wants
>   more money, I should not mind——

BROVIK
>   No, no! It is not that.
>   [*Impatiently.*]
>   But sooner or later he, too, must have a chance of doing some-
>   thing on his own account.

SOLNESS   [*Without looking at him.*]
>   Do you think that Ragnar has quite talent enough to stand alone?

BROVIK
>   No, that is just the heartbreaking part of it—I have begun to
>   have my doubts about the boy. For you have never said so much
>   as—as one encouraging word about him. And yet I cannot but
>   think there must be something in him—he can't be without
>   talent.

SOLNESS

Well, but he has learnt nothing—nothing thoroughly, I mean. Except, of course, to draw.

BROVIK   [*Looks at him with covert hatred, and says hoarsely.*]

You had learned little enough of the business when you were in my employment. But that did not prevent you from setting to work—

[*breathing with difficulty*]

—and pushing your way up, and taking the wind out of my sails—mine, and so many other people's.

SOLNESS

Yes, you see—circumstances favoured me.

BROVIK

You are right there. Everything favoured you. But then how can you have the heart to let me go to my grave—without having seen what Ragnar is fit for? And of course I am anxious to see them married, too—before I go.

SOLNESS   [*Sharply.*]

Is it she who wishes it?

BROVIK

Not Kaia so much as Ragnar—he talks about it every day.

[*Appealingly.*]

You must—you *must* help him to get some independent work now! I *must* see something that the lad has done. Do you hear?

SOLNESS   [*Peevishly.*]

Hang it, man, you can't expect me to drag commissions down from the moon for him!

BROVIK

He has the chance of a capital commission at this very moment. A big bit of work.

SOLNESS   [*Uneasily, startled.*]

Has he?

BROVIK

If you would give your consent.

SOLNESS

What sort of work do you mean?

BROVIK   [*With some hesitation.*]

He can have the building of that villa out at Lövstrand.

SOLNESS

That! Why I am going to build that myself.

BROVIK

Oh you don't much care about doing it.

SOLNESS   [*Flaring up.*]

Don't care! I! Who dares to say that?

BROVIK

You said so yourself just now.

SOLNESS

Oh, never mind what I *say*.——Would they give Ragnar the building of that villa?

BROVIK

Yes. You see, he knows the family. And then—just for the fun of
the thing—he has made drawings and estimates and so forth——

SOLNESS

Are they pleased with the drawings? The people who will have to
live in the house?

BROVIK

Yes. If you would only look through them and approve of
them——

SOLNESS

Then they would let Ragnar build their home for them?

BROVIK

They were immensely pleased with his idea. They thought it
exceedingly original, they said.

SOLNESS

Oho! Original! Not the old-fashioned stuff that *I* am in the habit
of turning out!

BROVIK

It seemed to them *different*.

SOLNESS   [*With suppressed irritation.*]

So it was to see Ragnar that they came here—whilst I was out!

BROVIK

They came to call upon you—and at the same time to ask
whether you would mind retiring——

SOLNESS   [*Angrily.*]

Retire? I?

BROVIK

In case you thought that Ragnar's drawings——

SOLNESS

I! Retire in favour of your son!

BROVIK

Retire from the agreement, they meant.

SOLNESS

Oh, it comes to the same thing.

[*Laughs angrily.*]

So that is it, is it? Halvard Solness is to see about retiring now!
To make room for younger men! For the very youngest, perhaps!
He must make room! Room! Room!

BROVIK

Why, good heavens! there is surely room for more than one
single man——

SOLNESS

Oh, there's not so very much room to spare either. But, be that
as it may—I will never retire! I will never give way to anybody!
Never of my own free will. Never in this world will I do *that*!

BROVIK [*Rises with difficulty.*]

Then I am to pass out of life without any certainty? Without a
gleam of happiness? Without any faith or trust in Ragnar?
Without having seen a single piece of work of his doing? Is that
to be the way of it?

SOLNESS [*Turns half aside, and mutters.*]

H'm—don't ask more just now.

BROVIK

I must have an answer to this one question. Am I to pass out of
life in such utter poverty?

SOLNESS [*Seems to struggle with himself; finally he says, in a low but
firm voice:*]

You must pass out of life as best you can.

BROVIK

Then be it so.

[*He goes up the room.*]

SOLNESS [*Following him, half in desperation.*]

Don't you understand that I cannot help it? I am what I am, and I
cannot change my nature!

BROVIK

    No, no; I suppose you can't.

    [*Reels and supports himself against the sofa-table.*]

    May I have a glass of water?

SOLNESS

    By all means.

    [*Fills a glass and hands it to him.*]

BROVIK

    Thanks.

    [*Drinks and puts the glass down again.*]

    [SOLNESS *goes up and opens the door of the draughtsmen's office.*]

SOLNESS

    Ragnar—you must come and take your father home.

RAGNAR *rises quickly. He and* KAIA *come into the work-room.*

RAGNAR

    What is the matter, father?

BROVIK

    Give me your arm. Now let us go.

RAGNAR

    Very well. You had better put your things on, too, Kaia.

SOLNESS

    Miss Fosli must stay—just for a moment. There is a letter I want
    written.

BROVIK   [*Looks at* SOLNESS.]

    Good night. Sleep well—if you can.

SOLNESS

    Good night.

    [BROVIK *and* RAGNAR *go out by the hall-door.* KAIA *goes to the
    desk.* SOLNESS *stands with bent head, to the right, by the arm-chair.*

KAIA   [*Dubiously.*]

    Is there any letter———?

SOLNESS   [*Curtly.*]

    No, of course not.

    [*Looks sternly at her.*]

    Kaia!

KAIA   [*Anxiously, in a low voice.*]

    Yes!

SOLNESS [*Points imperatively to a spot on the floor.*]
Come here! At once!
KAIA [*Hesitatingly.*]
Yes.
SOLNESS [*As before.*]
Nearer!
KAIA [*Obeying.*]
What do you want with me?
SOLNESS [*Looks at her for a while.*]
Is it you I have to thank for all this?
KAIA
No, no, don't think that!
SOLNESS
But confess now—you want to get married!
KAIA [*Softly.*]
RAGNAR and I have been engaged for four or five years, and
so——
SOLNESS
And so you think it time there were an end of it. Is not that so?
KAIA
RAGNAR and Uncle say I *must*. So I suppose I shall have to give
in.
SOLNESS [*More gently.*]
Kaia, don't you really care a little bit for Ragnar, too?
KAIA
I cared very much for Ragnar once—before I came here to you.
SOLNESS
But you don't now? Not in the least?
KAIA [*Passionately, clasping her hands and holding them out towards him.*]
Oh, you know very well there is only one person I care for now!
One, and one only, in all the world! I shall never care for any one
else.
SOLNESS
Yes, you say that. And yet you go away from me—leave me alone
here with everything on my hands.
KAIA
But could I not stay with you, even if Ragnar——?

SOLNESS   [*Repudiating the idea.*]

   No, no, that is quite impossible. If Ragnar leaves me and starts work on his own account, then of course he will need you himself.

KAIA   [*Wringing her hands.*]

   Oh, I feel as if I *could* not be separated from you! It's quite, quite impossible!

SOLNESS

   Then be sure you get those foolish notions out of Ragnar's head. Marry him as much as you please—

   [*Alters his tone.*]

   I mean—don't let him throw up his good situation with me. For then I can keep you too, my dear Kaia.

KAIA

   Oh yes, how lovely that would be, if it could only be managed!

SOLNESS   [*Clasps her head with his two hands and whispers.*]

   For I cannot get on without you, you see. I must have you with me every single day.

KAIA   [*In nervous exaltation.*]

   My God! My God!

SOLNESS   [*Kisses her hair.*]

   Kaia—Kaia!

KAIA   [*Sinks down before him.*]

   Oh, how good you are to me! How unspeakably good you are!

SOLNESS   [*Vehemently.*]

   Get up! For goodness' sake get up! I think I hear some one!

   [*He helps her to rise. She staggers over to the desk.*]

MRS. SOLNESS *enters by the door on the right. She looks thin and wasted with grief, but shows traces of bygone beauty. Blonde ringlets. Dressed with good taste, wholly in black. Speaks somewhat slowly and in a plaintive voice.*

MRS. SOLNESS   [*In the doorway.*]

   Halvard!

SOLNESS   [*Turns.*]

   Oh, are you there, my dear——?

MRS. SOLNESS   [*With a glance at* KAIA.]

   I am afraid I am disturbing you.

SOLNESS

Not in the least. Miss Fosli has only a short letter to write.

MRS. SOLNESS

Yes, so I see.

SOLNESS

What do you want with me, Aline?

MRS. SOLNESS

I merely wanted to tell you that Dr. Herdal is in the drawing-room. Won't you come and see him, Halvard?

SOLNESS   [Looks suspiciously at her.]

H'm——is the doctor so very anxious to talk to me?

MRS. SOLNESS

Well, not exactly anxious. He really came to see me; but he would like to say how-do-you-do to you at the same time.

SOLNESS   [Laughs to himself.]

Yes, I daresay. Well, you must ask him to wait a little.

MRS. SOLNESS

Then you will come in presently?

SOLNESS

Perhaps I will. Presently, presently, dear. In a little while.

MRS. SOLNESS   [Glancing again at KAIA.]

Well now, don't forget, Halvard.

[Withdraws and closes the door behind her.]

KAIA   [Softly.]

Oh dear, oh dear——I am sure Mrs. Solness thinks ill of me in some way!

SOLNESS

Oh, not in the least. Not more than usual at any rate. But all the same, you had better go now, Kaia.

KAIA

Yes, yes, now I must go.

SOLNESS   [Severely.]

And mind you get that matter settled for me. Do you hear?

KAIA

Oh, if it only depended on me——

SOLNESS

I will have it settled, I say! And to-morrow too——not a day later!

KAIA   [*Terrified.*]

If there's nothing else for it, I am quite willing to break off the engagement.

SOLNESS   [*Angrily.*]

Break it off. Are you mad? Would you think of breaking it off?

KAIA   [*Distracted.*]

Yes, if necessary. For I must—I must stay here with you! I *can't* leave you! That is utterly—utterly impossible!

SOLNESS   [*With a sudden outburst.*]

But deuce take it—how about Ragnar then! It's Ragnar that I——

KAIA   [*Looks at him with terrified eyes.*]

It is chiefly on Ragnar's account, that—that you——?

SOLNESS   [*Collecting himself.*]

No, no, of course not! You don't understand me either.

[*Gently and softly.*]

Of course it is you I want to keep—you above everything, Kaia. But for that very reason, you must prevent Ragnar, too, from throwing up his situation. There, there,—now go home.

KAIA

Yes, yes—good-night, then.

SOLNESS

Good-night.

[*As she is going.*]

Oh, stop a moment! Are Ragnar's drawings in there?

KAIA

I did not see him take them with him.

SOLNESS

Then just go and find them for me. I might perhaps glance over them, after all.

KAIA   [*Happy.*]

Oh yes, please do!

SOLNESS

For your sake, Kaia dear. Now, let me have them at once, please.

[KAIA *hurries into the draughtstmen's office, searches anxiously in the table-drawer, finds a portfolio and brings it with her.*

KAIA

Here are all the drawings.

SOLNESS

Good. Put them down there on the table.

KAIA   [*Putting down the portfolio.*]

Good-night, then.

[*Beseechingly.*]

And please, please think kindly of me.

SOLNESS

Oh, that I always do. Good-night, my dear little Kaia.

[*Glances to the right.*]

Go, go now!

MRS. SOLNESS *and* DR. HERDAL *enter by the door on the right. He is a stoutish, elderly man, with a round, good-humoured face, clean shaven, with thin, light hair, and gold spectacles.*

MRS. SOLNESS   [*Still in the doorway.*]

Halvard, I cannot keep the doctor any longer.

SOLNESS

Well then, come in here.

MRS. SOLNESS   [*To KAIA, who is turning down the desk-lamp.*]

Have you finished the letter already, Miss Fosli?

KAIA   [*In confusion.*]

The letter——?

SOLNESS

Yes, it was quite a short one.

MRS. SOLNESS

It must have been very short.

SOLNESS

You may go now, Miss Fosli. And please come in good time
to-morrow morning.

KAIA

I will be sure to. Good-night, Mrs. Solness.

[*She goes out by the hall-door.*]

MRS. SOLNESS

She must be quite an acquisition to you, Halvard, this Miss Fosli.

SOLNESS

Yes, indeed. She is useful in all sorts of ways.

MRS. SOLNESS
So it seems.

DR. HERDAL
Is she good at book-keeping too?

SOLNESS
Well—of course she has had a good deal of practice during these two years. And then she is so nice and willing to do whatever one asks of her.

MRS. SOLNESS
Yes, that must be very delightful——

SOLNESS
It is. Especially when one is not too much accustomed to that sort of thing.

MRS. SOLNESS   [*In a tone of gentle remonstrance.*]
Can *you* say that, Halvard?

SOLNESS
Oh, no, no, my dear Aline; I beg your pardon.

MRS. SOLNESS
There's no occasion.—Well then, doctor, you will come back later on, and have a cup of tea with us?

DR. HERDAL
I have only that one patient to see, and then I'll come back.

MRS. SOLNESS
Thank you.
[*She goes out by the door on the right.*]

SOLNESS
Are you in a hurry, doctor?

DR. HERDAL
No, not at all.

SOLNESS
May I have a little chat with you?

DR. HERDAL
With the greatest of pleasure.

SOLNESS
Then let us sit down.
[*He motions the doctor to take the rocking-chair, and sits down himself in the arm-chair. Looks searchingly at him.*]
Tell me—did you notice anything odd about Aline?

DR. HERDAL

Do you mean just now, when she was here?

SOLNESS

Yes, in her manner to me. Did you notice anything?

DR. HERDAL   [*Smiling.*]

Well, I admit——one couldn't well avoid noticing that your wife——h'm——

SOLNESS

Well?

DR. HERDAL

——that your wife is not particularly fond of this Miss Fosli.

SOLNESS

Is that all? I have noticed that myself.

DR. HERDAL

And I must say I am scarcely surprised at it.

SOLNESS

At what?

DR. HERDAL

That she should not exactly approve of your seeing so much of another woman, all day and every day.

SOLNESS

No, no, I suppose you are right there——and Aline too. But it's impossible to make any change.

DR. HERDAL

Could you not engage a clerk?

SOLNESS

The first man that came to hand? No, thank you——that would never do for me.

DR. HERDAL

But now, if your wife——? Suppose, with her delicate health, all this tries her too much?

SOLNESS

Even then——I might almost say——it can make no difference. I *must* keep Kaia Fosli. No one else could fill her place.

DR. HERDAL

No one else?

SOLNESS   [*Curtly.*]

No, no one.

DR. HERDAL   [*Drawing his chair closer.*]
>   Now listen to me, my dear Mr. Solness. May I ask you a
>   question, quite between ourselves?

SOLNESS
>   By all means.

DR. HERDAL
>   Women, you see—in certain matters, they have a deucedly keen
>   intuition——

SOLNESS
>   They have, indeed. There is not the least doubt of that. But——?

DR. HERDAL
>   Well, tell me now—if your wife can't endure this Kaia Fosli——?

SOLNESS
>   Well, what then?

DR. HERDAL
>   —may she not have just—just the least little bit of reason for
>   this instinctive dislike?

SOLNESS   [*Looks at him and rises.*]
>   Oho!

DR. HERDAL
>   Now don't be offended—but *hasn't* she?

SOLNESS   [*With curt decision.*]
>   No.

DR. HERDAL
>   No reason of any sort?

SOLNESS
>   No other reason than her own suspicious nature.

DR. HERDAL
>   I know you have known a good many women in your time.

SOLNESS
>   Yes, I have.

DR. HERDAL
>   And have been a good deal taken with some of them, too.

SOLNESS
>   Oh yes, I don't deny it.

DR. HERDAL
>   But as regards Miss Fosli, then? There is nothing of that sort in
>   the case?

SOLNESS

No; nothing at all——on my side.

DR. HERDAL

But on her side?

SOLNESS

I don't think you have any right to ask that question, doctor.

DR. HERDAL

Well, you know, we were discussing your wife's intuition.

SOLNESS

So we were. And for that matter—

[*lowers his voice*]

—Aline's intuition, as you call it——in a certain sense, it has not been so far astray.

DR. HERDAL

Aha! there we have it!

SOLNESS [*Sits down.*]

Doctor Herdal——I am going to tell you a strange story——if you care to listen to it.

DR. HERDAL

I like listening to strange stories.

SOLNESS

Very well then. I daresay you recollect that I took Knut Brovik and his son into my employment——after the old man's business had gone to the dogs.

DR. HERDAL

Yes, so I have understood.

SOLNESS

You see, they really are clever fellows, these two. Each of them has talent in his own way. But then the son took it into his head to get engaged; and the next thing, of course, was that he wanted to get married——and begin to build on his own account. That is the way with all these young people.

DR. HERDAL [*Laughing.*]

Yes, they have a bad habit of wanting to marry.

SOLNESS

Just so. But of course that did not suit my plans; for I needed Ragnar myself——and the old man too. He is exceedingly good at calculating bearing-strains and cubic contents—and all that sort of deviltry, you know.

DR. HERDAL

Oh yes, no doubt that's indispensable.

SOLNESS

Yes, it is. But Ragnar was absolutely bent on setting to work for himself. He would hear of nothing else.

DR. HERDAL

But he has stayed with you all the same.

SOLNESS

Yes, I'll tell you how that came about. One day this girl, Kaia Fosli, came to see them on some errand or other. She had never been here before. And when I saw how utterly infatuated they were with each other, the thought occurred to me: if I could only get her into the office here, then perhaps Ragnar too would stay where he is.

DR. HERDAL

That was not at all a bad idea.

SOLNESS

Yes, but at the time I did not breathe a word of what was in my mind. I merely stood and looked at her—and kept on wishing intently that I could have her here. Then I talked to her a little, in a friendly way—about one thing and another. And then she went away.

DR. HERDAL

Well?

SOLNESS

Well then, next day, pretty late in the evening, when old Brovik and Ragnar had gone home, she came here again, and behaved as if I had made an arrangement with her.

DR. HERDAL

An arrangement? What about?

SOLNESS

About the very thing my mind had been fixed on. But I hadn't said one single word about it.

DR. HERDAL

That was most extraordinary.

SOLNESS

Yes, was it not? And now she wanted to know what she was to do here—whether she could begin the very next morning, and so forth.

DR. HERDAL

Don't you think she did it in order to be with her sweetheart?

SOLNESS

That was what occurred to me at first. But no, that was not it. She seemed to drift quite away from *him*—when once she had come here to me.

DR. HERDAL

She drifted over to you, then?

SOLNESS

Yes, entirely. If I happen to look at her when her back is turned, I can tell that she feels it. She quivers and trembles the moment I come near her. What do you think of *that*?

DR. HERDAL

H'm—that's not very hard to explain.

SOLNESS

Well, but what about the other thing? That she believed I had said to her what I had only wished and willed—silently—inwardly—to myself? What do you say to *that*? Can you explain that, Dr. Herdal?

DR. HERDAL

No, I won't undertake to do that.

SOLNESS

I felt sure you would not; and so I have never cared to talk about it till now.—But it's a cursed nuisance to me in the long run, you understand. Here have I got to go on day after day pretending——. And it's a shame to treat her so, too, poor girl. [*Vehemently.*]

But I cannot do anything else. For if she runs away from me— then Ragnar will be off too.

DR. HERDAL

And you have not told your wife the rights of the story?

SOLNESS

No.

DR. HERDAL

Then why on earth don't you?

SOLNESS   [*Looks fixedly at him, and says in a low voice:*]

Because I seem to find a sort of—of salutary self-torture in allowing Aline to do me an injustice.

DR. HERDAL   [*Shakes his head.*]

I don't in the least understand what you mean.

SOLNESS

Well, you see—it is like paying off a little bit of a huge, immeasurable debt——

DR. HERDAL

To your wife?

SOLNESS

Yes; and that always helps to relieve one's mind a little. One can breathe more freely for a while, you understand.

DR. HERDAL

No, goodness knows, I don't understand at all——

SOLNESS   [*Breaking off, rises again.*]

Well, well, well—then we won't talk any more about it.

[*He saunters across the room, returns, and stops beside the table. Looks at the doctor with a sly smile.*]

I suppose you think you have drawn me out nicely now, doctor?

DR. HERDAL   [*With some irritation.*]

Drawn you out? Again I have not the faintest notion what you mean, Mr. Solness.

SOLNESS

Oh come, out with it; I have seen it quite clearly, you know.

DR. HERDAL

What have you seen?

SOLNESS   [*In a low voice, slowly.*]

That you have been quietly keeping an eye upon me.

DR. HERDAL

That *I* have! And why in all the world should I do *that*?

SOLNESS

Because you think that I——.

[*Passionately.*]

Well, devil take it—you think the same of me as Aline does.

DR. HERDAL

And what does *she* think about you?

SOLNESS   [*Having recovered his self-control.*]

She has begun to think that I am—that I am—ill.

DR. HERDAL

Ill! You! She has never hinted such a thing to me. Why, what can she think is the matter with you?

SOLNESS   [*Leans over the back of the chair and whispers.*]

Aline has made up her mind that I am mad. *That* is what she thinks.

DR. HERDAL   [*Rising.*]

Why, my dear good fellow——!

SOLNESS

Yes, on my soul she does! I tell you it is so. And she has got you to think the same! Oh, I can assure you, doctor, I see it in your face as clearly as possible. You don't take me in so easily, I can tell you.

DR. HERDAL   [*Looks at him in amazement.*]

Never, Mr. Solness—never has such a thought entered my mind.

SOLNESS   [*With an incredulous smile.*]

Really? Has it not?

DR. HERDAL

No, never! Nor your wife's mind either, I am convinced. I could almost swear to that.

SOLNESS

Well, I wouldn't advise you to. For, in a certain sense, you see, perhaps—perhaps she is not so far wrong in thinking something of the kind.

DR. HERDAL

Come now, I really must say——

SOLNESS   [*Interrupting, with a sweep of his hand.*]

Well, well, my dear doctor—don't let us discuss this any further. We had better agree to differ.

[*Changes to a tone of quiet amusement.*]

But look here now, doctor—h'm——

DR. HERDAL

Well?

SOLNESS

Since you don't believe that I am——ill——and crazy——and mad, and so forth——

DR. HERDAL

What then?

SOLNESS

Then I daresay you fancy that I am an extremely happy man.

DR. HERDAL

Is *that* mere fancy?

SOLNESS   [*Laughs.*]

No, no——of course not! Heaven forbid! Only think——to be Solness the master builder! Halvard Solness! What could be more delightful?

DR. HERDAL

Yes, I must say it seems to me you have had the luck on your side to an astounding degree.

SOLNESS   [*Suppresses a gloomy smile.*]

So I have. I can't complain on that score.

DR. HERDAL

First of all that grim old robbers' castle was burnt down for you. And *that* was certainly a great piece of luck.

SOLNESS   [*Seriously.*]

It was the home of Aline's family. Remember that.

DR. HERDAL

Yes, it must have been a great grief to *her*.

SOLNESS

She has not got over it to this day——not in all these twelve or thirteen years.

DR. HERDAL

Ah, but what followed must have been the worst blow for her.

SOLNESS

The one thing with the other.

DR. HERDAL

But you——yourself——you rose upon the ruins. You began as a poor boy from a country village——and now you are at the head of your profession. Ah, yes, Mr. Solness, you have undoubtedly had the luck on your side.

SOLNESS   [*Looking at him with embarrassment.*]

Yes, but that is just what makes me so horribly afraid.

DR. HERDAL

Afraid? Because you have the luck on your side!

SOLNESS

It terrifies me—terrifies me every hour of the day. For sooner or later the luck must turn, you see.

DR. HERDAL

Oh nonsense! What should make the luck turn?

SOLNESS   [*With firm assurance.*]

The younger generation.

DR. HERDAL

Pooh! The younger generation! You are not laid on the shelf yet, I should hope. Oh no—your position here is probably firmer now than it has ever been.

SOLNESS

The luck will turn. I know it—I feel the day approaching. Some one or other will take it into his head to say: Give me a chance! And then all the rest will come clamouring after him, and shake their fists at me and shout: Make room—make room—make room! Yes, just you see, doctor—presently the younger generation will come knocking at my door——

DR. HERDAL   [*Laughing.*]

Well, and what if they do?

SOLNESS

What if they do? Then there's an end of Halvard Solness.

[*There is a knock at the door on the left.*]

SOLNESS   [*Starts.*]

What's that? Did you not hear something?

DR. HERDAL

Some one is knocking at the door.

SOLNESS   [*Loudly.*]

Come in.

HILDA WANGEL *enters by the hall door. She is of middle height, supple, and delicately built. Somewhat sunburnt. Dressed in a tourist costume, with skirt caught up for walking, a sailor's collar open at the throat, and a small sailor hat on her head. Knapsack on back, plaid in strap, and alpenstock.*

HILDA   [*Goes straight up to* SOLNESS, *her eyes sparkling with happiness.*]

Good evening!

SOLNESS   [*Looks doubtfully at her.*]

Good evening——

HILDA   [*Laughs.*]

I almost believe you don't recognise me!

SOLNESS

No—I must admit that—just for the moment——

DR. HERDAL   [*Approaching.*]

But *I* recognise you, my dear young lady——

HILDA   [*Pleased.*]

Oh, is it you that——

DR. HERDAL

Of course it is.

[*To* SOLNESS.]

We met at one of the mountain stations this summer.

[*To* HILDA.]

What became of the other ladies?

HILDA

Oh, *they* went westward.

DR. HERDAL

They didn't much like all the fun we used to have in the evenings.

HILDA

No, I believe they didn't.

DR. HERDAL   [*Holds up his finger at her.*]

And I am afraid it can't be denied that you flirted a little with us.

HILDA

Well, that was better fun than to sit there knitting stockings with all those old women.

DR. HERDAL   [*Laughs.*]

There I entirely agree with you!

SOLNESS

Have you come to town this evening?

HILDA

Yes, I have just arrived.

DR. HERDAL

Quite alone, Miss Wangel?

HILDA

Oh yes!

SOLNESS

Wangel? Is your name Wangel?

HILDA   [*Looks in amused surprise at him.*]

Yes, of course it is.

SOLNESS

Then you must be a daughter of the district doctor up at
Lysanger?

HILDA   [*As before.*]

Yes, who else's daughter should I be?

SOLNESS

Oh, then I suppose we met up there, that summer when I was
building a tower on the old church.

HILDA   [*More seriously.*]

Yes, of course it was then we met.

SOLNESS

Well, that is a long time ago.

HILDA   [*Looks hard at him.*]

It is exactly the ten years.

SOLNESS

You must have been a mere child then, I should think.

HILDA   [*Carelessly.*]

Well, I was twelve or thirteen.

DR. HERDAL

Is this the first time you have ever been up to town, Miss
Wangel?

HILDA

Yes, it is indeed.

SOLNESS

And don't you know any one here?

HILDA

Nobody but you. And of course, your wife.

SOLNESS

So you know her, too?

HILDA

Only a little. We spent a few days together at the sanatorium.

SOLNESS

Ah, up there?

HILDA

She said I might come and pay her a visit if ever I came up to town.

[*Smiles.*]

Not that that was necessary.

SOLNESS

Odd that she should never have mentioned it.

[HILDA *puts her stick down by the stove, takes off the knapsack and lays it and the plaid on the sofa.* DR. HERDAL *offers to help her.* SOLNESS *stands and gazes at her.*

HILDA   [*Going towards him.*]

Well, now I must ask you to let me stay the night here.

SOLNESS

I am sure there will be no difficulty about that.

HILDA

For I have no other clothes than those I stand in, except a change of linen in my knapsack. And that has to go to the wash, for it's very dirty.

SOLNESS

Oh yes, that can be managed. Now I'll just let my wife know——

DR. HERDAL

Meanwhile I will go and see my patient.

SOLNESS

Yes, do; and come again later on.

DR. HERDAL   [*Playfully, with a glance at* HILDA.]

Oh that I will, you may be very certain!

[*Laughs.*]

So your prediction has come true, Mr. Solness!

SOLNESS

How so?

DR. HERDAL

The younger generation did come knocking at your door.

SOLNESS   [*Cheerfully.*]

Yes, but in a very different way from what I meant.

DR. HERDAL

Very different, yes. That's undeniable.

[*He goes out by the hall-door.* SOLNESS *opens the door on the right and speaks into the side room.*]

SOLNESS

Aline! Will you come in here, please. Here is a friend of yours— Miss Wangel.

MRS. SOLNESS   [*Appears in the doorway.*]

Who do you say it is?

[*Sees* HILDA.]

Oh, is it *you*, Miss Wangel?

[*Goes up to her and offers her hand.*]

So you have come to town after all.

SOLNESS

Miss Wangel has this moment arrived; and she would like to stay the night here.

MRS. SOLNESS

Here with us? Oh yes, certainly.

SOLNESS

Till she can get her things a little in order, you know.

MRS. SOLNESS

I will do the best I can for you. It's no more than my duty. I suppose your trunk is coming on later?

HILDA

I *have* no trunk.

MRS. SOLNESS

Well, it will be all right, I daresay. In the meantime, you must excuse my leaving you here with my husband, until I can get a room made a little comfortable for you.

SOLNESS

Can we not give her one of the nurseries? *They* are all ready as it is.

MRS. SOLNESS

Oh yes. There we have room and to spare.

[*To* HILDA.]

Sit down now, and rest a little.

[*She goes out to the right.*]

[HILDA, *with her hands behind her back, strolls about the room and looks at various objects.* SOLNESS *stands in front, beside the table, also with his hands behind his back, and follows her with his eyes.*]

HILDA   [*Stops and looks at him.*]

Have you several nurseries?

SOLNESS

There are three nurseries in the house.

HILDA

That's a lot. Then I suppose you have a great many children?

SOLNESS

No. We have no child. But now you can be the child here, for the time being.

HILDA

For to-night, yes. I shall not cry. I mean to sleep as sound as a stone.

SOLNESS

Yes, you must be very tired, I should think.

HILDA

Oh no! But all the same———. It's so delicious to lie and dream.

SOLNESS

Do you dream much of nights?

HILDA

Oh yes! Almost always.

SOLNESS

What do you dream about most?

HILDA

I sha'n't tell you to-night. Another time, perhaps.

[*She again strolls about the room, stops at the desk and turns over the books and papers a little.*]

SOLNESS   [*Approaching.*]

Are you searching for anything?

HILDA

No, I am merely looking at all these things.

[*Turns.*]

Perhaps I mustn't?

SOLNESS

Oh, by all means.

HILDA

Is it *you* that writes in this great ledger?

SOLNESS

No, it's my book-keeper.

HILDA

Is it a woman?

SOLNESS

[*Smiles.*]

Yes.

HILDA

One you employ here, in your office?

SOLNESS

Yes.

HILDA

Is she married?

SOLNESS

No, she is single.

HILDA

Oh, indeed!

SOLNESS

But I believe she is soon going to be married.

HILDA

That's a good thing for *her*.

SOLNESS

But not such a good thing for *me*. For then I shall have nobody to help me.

HILDA

Can't you get hold of some one else who will do just as well?

SOLNESS

Perhaps *you* would stay here and—and write in the ledger?

HILDA   [*Measures him with a glance.*]

Yes, I daresay! No, thank you—nothing of that sort for me.

[*She again strolls across the room, and sits down in the rocking-chair.* SOLNESS *too goes to the table.*]

HILDA   [*Continuing.*]

For there must surely be plenty of other things to be done here.

[*Looks smilingly at him.*]

Don't you think so, too?

SOLNESS

Of course. First of all, I suppose, you want to make a round of
the shops, and get yourself up in the height of fashion.

HILDA   [*Amused.*]

No, I think I shall let *that* alone!

SOLNESS

Indeed?

HILDA

For you must know I have run through all my money.

SOLNESS   [*Laughs.*]

Neither trunk nor money, then!

HILDA

Neither one nor the other. But never mind—it doesn't matter
now.

SOLNESS

Come now, I like you for *that*.

HILDA

Only for *that?*

SOLNESS

For that among other things.

[*Sits in the arm-chair.*]

Is your father alive still?

HILDA

Yes, father's alive.

SOLNESS

Perhaps you are thinking of studying here?

HILDA

No, that hadn't occurred to me.

SOLNESS

But I suppose you will be staying for some time?

HILDA

That must depend upon circumstances.

[*She sits awhile rocking herself and looking at him, half seriously, half with
a suppressed smile. Then she takes off her hat and puts it on the table in
front of her.*]

Mr. Solness!

SOLNESS

Well?

HILDA

Have you a very bad memory?

SOLNESS

A bad memory? No, not that I am aware of.

HILDA

Then have you nothing to say to me about what happened up there?

SOLNESS   [*In momentary surprise.*]

Up at Lysanger?

[*Indifferently.*]

Why, it was nothing much to talk about, it seems to me.

HILDA   [*Looks reproachfully at him.*]

How can you sit there and say such things?

SOLNESS

Well, then, *you* talk to *me* about it.

HILDA

When the tower was finished, we had grand doings in the town.

SOLNESS

Yes, I shall not easily forget that day.

HILDA   [*Smiles.*]

Will you not? That comes well from *you*.

SOLNESS

Comes well?

HILDA

There was music in the churchyard—and many, many hundreds of people. We school-girls were dressed in white; and we all carried flags.

SOLNESS

Ah, yes, those flags—I can tell you I remember *them*!

HILDA

Then you climbed right up the scaffolding, straight to the very top; and you had a great wreath with you; and you hung that wreath right away up on the weather-vane.

SOLNESS   [*Curtly interrupting.*]

I always did that in those days. It is an old custom.

HILDA

It was so wonderfully thrilling to stand below and look up at you. Fancy, if he should fall over! He——the master builder himself!

SOLNESS   [*As if to divert her from the subject.*]

Yes, yes, yes, that might very well have happened, too. For one of those white-frocked little devils,——she went on in such a way, and screamed up at me so——

HILDA   [*Sparkling with pleasure.*]

"Hurra for Master Builder Solness!" Yes!

SOLNESS

——and waved and flourished with her flag, so that I——so that it almost made me giddy to look at it.

HILDA   [*In a lower voice, seriously.*]

That little devil——that was *I*.

SOLNESS   [*Fixes his eyes steadily upon her.*]

I am sure of that now. It must have been you.

HILDA   [*Lively again.*]

Oh, it was so gloriously thrilling! I could not have believed there was a builder in the whole world that could build such a tremendously high tower. And then, that you yourself should stand at the very top of it, as large as life! And that you should not be the least bit dizzy! It was *that* above everything that made one——made one dizzy to think of.

SOLNESS

How could you be so certain that I was not——?

HILDA   [*Scouting the idea.*]

No indeed! Oh no! I knew that instinctively. For if you had been, you could never have stood up there and sung.

SOLNESS   [*Looks at her in astonishment.*]

Sung? Did *I* sing?

HILDA

Yes, I should think you did.

SOLNESS   [*Shakes his head.*]

I have never sung a note in my life.

HILDA

Yes, indeed, you sang then. It sounded like harps in the air.

SOLNESS   [*Thoughtfully.*]

This is very strange——all this.

HILDA [*Is silent awhile, looks at him and says in a low voice:*]

But then,—it was after that—that the *real* thing happened.

SOLNESS

The real thing?

HILDA [*Sparkling with vivacity.*]

Yes, I surely don't need to remind you of *that*?

SOLNESS

Oh yes, do remind me a little of *that*, too.

HILDA

Don't you remember that a great dinner was given in your honour at the Club?

SOLNESS

Yes, to be sure. It must have been the same afternoon, for I left the place next morning.

HILDA

And from the Club you were invited to come round to our house to supper.

SOLNESS

Quite right, Miss Wangel. It is wonderful how all these trifles have impressed themselves on your mind.

HILDA

Trifles! I like that! Perhaps it was a trifle, too, that I was *alone* in the room when you came in?

SOLNESS

Were you alone?

HILDA [*Without answering him.*]

You didn't call me a little devil *then*?

SOLNESS

No, I suppose I did not.

HILDA

You said I was lovely in my white dress, and that I looked like a little princess.

SOLNESS

I have no doubt you did, Miss Wangel.—And besides—I was feeling so buoyant and free that day——

HILDA

And then you said that when I grew up I should be *your* princess.

SOLNESS   [*Laughing a little.*]

> Dear, dear——did I say *that* too?

HILDA

> Yes, you did. And when I asked how long I should have to wait, you said that you would come again in ten years——like a troll—— and carry me off——to Spain or some such place. And you promised you would buy me a kingdom there.

SOLNESS   [*As before.*]

> Yes, after a good dinner one doesn't haggle about the halfpence. But did I really *say* all that?

HILDA   [*Laughs to herself.*]

> Yes. And you told me, too, what the kingdom was to be called.

SOLNESS

> Well, what was it?

HILDA

> It was to be called the kingdom of Orangia,* you said.

SOLNESS

> Well, that was an appetising name.

HILDA

> No, I didn't like it a bit; for it seemed as though you wanted to make game of me.

SOLNESS

> I am sure *that* cannot have been my intention.

HILDA

> No, I should hope not——considering what you did next——

SOLNESS

> What in the world did I do next?

HILDA

> Well, that's the finishing touch, if you have forgotten *that* too. I should have thought no one could help remembering such a thing as that.

SOLNESS

> Yes, yes, just give me a hint, and then perhaps——Well?

HILDA   [*Looks fixedly at him.*]

> You came and kissed me, Mr. Solness.

*In the original *Appelsinia*, *appelsin* meaning "orange." (Translator's note)

SOLNESS   [*Open-mouthed, rising from his chair.*]

I did!

HILDA

Yes, indeed you did. You took me in both your arms, and bent my head back, and kissed me——many times.

SOLNESS

Now really, my dear Miss Wangel——!

HILDA   [*Rises.*]

You surely cannot mean to deny it?

SOLNESS

Yes, I do. I deny it altogether!

HILDA   [*Looks scornfully at him.*]

Oh, indeed!

[*She turns and goes slowly close up to the stove, where she remains standing motionless, her face averted from him, her hands behind her back. Short pause.*]

SOLNESS   [*Goes cautiously up behind her.*]

Miss Wangel——!

HILDA   [*Is silent and does not move.*]

SOLNESS

Don't stand there like a statue. You must have dreamt all this.

[*Lays his hand on her arm.*]

Now just listen——

HILDA   [*Makes an impatient movement with her arm.*]

SOLNESS   [*As a thought flashes upon him.*]

Or——! Wait a moment! There is something under all this, you may depend!

HILDA   [*Does not move.*]

SOLNESS   [*In a low voice, but with emphasis.*]

I must have thought all that. I must have wished it——have *willed* it——have longed to do it. And then——. May not that be the explanation?

HILDA   [*Is still silent.*]

SOLNESS   [*Impatiently.*]

Oh very well, deuce take it all——then I *did* do it, I suppose.

HILDA   [*Turns her head a little, but without looking at him.*]

Then you admit it now?

SOLNESS

Yes—whatever you like.

HILDA

You came and put your arms around me?

SOLNESS

Oh, yes!

HILDA

And bent my head back?

SOLNESS

Very far back.

HILDA

And kissed me?

SOLNESS

Yes, I did.

HILDA

Many times?

SOLNESS

As many as ever you like.

HILDA   [*Turns quickly towards him and has once more the sparkling expression of gladness in her eyes.*]

Well, you see, I got it out of you at last!

SOLNESS   [*With a slight smile.*]

Yes—just think of my forgetting such a thing as that.

HILDA   [*Again a little sulky, retreats from him.*]

Oh, you have kissed so many people in your time, I suppose.

SOLNESS

No, you mustn't think *that* of me.

[HILDA *seats herself in the arm-chair.* SOLNESS *stands and leans against the rocking-chair. Looks observantly at her.*]

Miss Wangel!

HILDA

Yes!

SOLNESS

How *was* it now? What came of all this—between us two?

HILDA

Why, nothing more came of it. You know that quite well. For then the other guests came in, and then—bah!

SOLNESS

Quite so! The others came in. To think of my forgetting *that* too!

HILDA

Oh, you haven't really forgotten anything: you are only a little ashamed of it all. I am sure one doesn't forget things of that kind.

SOLNESS

No, one would suppose not.

HILDA   [*Lively again, looks at him.*]

Perhaps you have even forgotten what day it was?

SOLNESS

What day——?

HILDA

Yes, on what day did you hang the wreath on the tower? Well? Tell me at once!

SOLNESS

H'm—I confess I have forgotten the particular day. I only know it was ten years ago. Some time in the autumn.

HILDA   [*Nods her head slowly several times.*]

It was ten years ago—on the 19th of September.

SOLNESS

Yes, it must have been about that time. Fancy your remembering that too!

[*Stops.*]

But wait a moment——! Yes—it's the 19th of September to-day.

HILDA

Yes, it is; and the ten years are gone. And you didn't come—as you had promised me.

SOLNESS

Promised you? Threatened, I suppose you mean?

HILDA

I don't think there was any sort of threat in *that*.

SOLNESS

Well then, a little bit of fun.

HILDA

Was *that* all you wanted? To make fun of me?

SOLNESS

Well, or to have a little joke with you. Upon my soul, I don't recollect. But it must have been something of that kind; for you were a mere child then.

HILDA

Oh, perhaps I wasn't quite such a child either. Not such a mere chit as you imagine.

SOLNESS [*Looks searchingly at her.*]

Did you really and seriously expect me to come again?

HILDA [*Conceals a half-teasing smile.*]

Yes, indeed! I did expect *that* of you.

SOLNESS

That I should come back to your home, and take you away with me?

HILDA

Just like a troll—yes.

SOLNESS

And make a princess of you?

HILDA

That's what you promised.

SOLNESS

And give you a kingdom as well?

HILDA [*Looks up at the ceiling.*]

Why not? Of course it need not have been an actual, every-day sort of a kingdom.

SOLNESS

But something else just as good?

HILDA

Yes, at least as good.

[*Looks at him a moment.*]

I thought, if you could build the highest church-towers in the world, you could surely manage to raise a kingdom of one sort or another as well.

SOLNESS [*Shakes his head.*]

I can't quite make you out, Miss Wangel.

HILDA

Can you not? To me it seems all so simple.

SOLNESS

No, I can't make up my mind whether you mean all you say, or are simply having a joke with me.

HILDA   [Smiles.]

Making fun of you, perhaps? I, too?

SOLNESS

Yes, exactly. Making fun—of both of us.

[Looks at her.]

Is it long since you found out that I was married?

HILDA

I have known it all along. Why do you ask me that?

SOLNESS   [Lightly.]

Oh, well, it just occurred to me.

[Looks earnestly at her, and says in a low voice.]

What have you come for?

HILDA

I want my kingdom. The time is up.

SOLNESS   [Laughs involuntarily.]

What a girl you are!

HILDA   [Gaily.]

Out with my kingdom, Mr. Solness!

[Raps with her fingers.]

The kingdom on the table!

SOLNESS   [Pushing the rocking-chair nearer and sitting down.]

Now, seriously speaking—what have you come for? What do you really want to do here?

HILDA

Oh, first of all, I want to go round and look at all the things that you have built.

SOLNESS

That will give you plenty of exercise.

HILDA

Yes, I know you have built a tremendous lot.

SOLNESS

I have indeed—especially of late years.

HILDA

Many church-towers among the rest? Immensely high ones?

SOLNESS

No. I build no more church-towers now. Nor churches either.

HILDA

What do you build then?

SOLNESS

Homes for human beings.

HILDA   [*Reflectively.*]

Couldn't you build a little—a little bit of a church-tower over these homes as well?

SOLNESS   [*Starting.*]

What do you mean by *that?*

HILDA

I mean—something that points—points up into the free air. With the vane at a dizzy height.

SOLNESS   [*Pondering a little.*]

Strange that you should say *that*—for that is just what I am most anxious to do.

HILDA   [*Impatiently.*]

Why don't you do it, then?

SOLNESS   [*Shakes his head.*]

No, the people will not have it.

HILDA

Fancy their not wanting it!

SOLNESS   [*More lightly.*]

But now I am building a new home for myself—just opposite here.

HILDA

For yourself?

SOLNESS

Yes. It is almost finished. And on that there is a tower.

HILDA

A high tower?

SOLNESS

Yes.

HILDA

Very high?

SOLNESS

No doubt people will say it is *too* high—too high for a dwelling-house.

HILDA

I'll go out and look at that tower the first thing tomorrow morning.

SOLNESS [*Sits resting his cheek on his hand, and gazes at her.*]

Tell me, Miss Wangel—what is your name? Your Christian name, I mean?

HILDA

Why, Hilda, of course.

SOLNESS [*As before.*]

Hilda? Indeed?

HILDA

Don't you remember *that*? You called me Hilda yourself—that day when you misbehaved.

SOLNESS

Did I really?

HILDA

But then you said "*little* Hilda"; and I didn't like that.

SOLNESS

Oh, you didn't like that, Miss Hilda?

HILDA

No, not at such a time as that. But—"Princess Hilda"—that will sound very well, I think.

SOLNESS

Very well indeed. Princess Hilda of—of—what was to be the name of the kingdom?

HILDA

Pooh! I won't have anything to do with *that* stupid kingdom. I have set my heart upon quite a different one!

SOLNESS [*Has leaned back in the chair, still gazing at her.*]

Isn't it strange——? The more I think of it now, the more it seems to me as though I had gone about all these years torturing myself with—h'm——

HILDA

With what?

SOLNESS

With the effort to recover something—some experience, which I seemed to have forgotten. But I never had the least inkling of what it could be.

HILDA

You should have tied a knot in your pocket-handkerchief, Mr. Solness.

SOLNESS

In that case, I should simply have had to go racking my brains to discover what the knot could mean.

HILDA

Oh, yes, I suppose there are trolls of *that* kind in the world, too.

SOLNESS   [*Rises slowly.*]

What a good thing it is that *you* have come to me now.

HILDA   [*Looks deeply into his eyes.*]

Is it a good thing?

SOLNESS

For I have been so lonely here. I have been gazing so helplessly at it all.

[*In a lower voice.*]

I must tell you—I have begun to be so afraid—so terribly afraid of the younger generation.

HILDA   [*With a little snort of contempt.*]

Pooh—is the younger generation a thing to be afraid of?

SOLNESS

It is indeed. And that is why I have locked and barred myself in.

[*Mysteriously.*]

I tell you the younger generation will one day come and thunder at my door! They will break in upon me!

HILDA

Then I should say you ought to go out and open the door to the younger generation.

SOLNESS

Open the door?

HILDA

Yes. Let them come in to you on friendly terms, as it were.

SOLNESS

No, no, no! The younger generation—it means retribution, you see. It comes, as if under a new banner, heralding the turn of fortune.

HILDA [*Rises, looks at him, and says with a quivering twitch of her lips.*]

Can *I* be of any use to you, Mr. Solness?

SOLNESS

Yes, you can indeed! For you, too, come—under a new banner, it seems to me. Youth marshalled against youth——!

DR. HERDAL *comes in by the hall-door.*

DR. HERDAL

What—you and Miss Wangel here still?

SOLNESS

Yes. We have had no end of things to talk about.

HILDA

Both old and new.

DR. HERDAL

Have you really?

HILDA

Oh, it has been the greatest fun. For Mr. Solness—he has such a miraculous memory. All the least little details he remembers instantly.

MRS. SOLNESS *enters by the door on the right.*

MRS. SOLNESS

Well, Miss Wangel, your room is quite ready for you now.

HILDA

Oh, how kind you are to me!

SOLNESS [*To* MRS. SOLNESS.]

The nursery?

MRS. SOLNESS

Yes, the middle one. But first let us go in to supper.

SOLNESS [*Nods to* HILDA.]

Hilda shall sleep in the nursery, she shall.

MRS. SOLNESS [*Looks at him.*]

Hilda?

SOLNESS

Yes, Miss Wangel's name is Hilda. I knew her when she was a child.

MRS. SOLNESS

Did you really, Halvard? Well, shall we go? Supper is on the table.

[*She takes* DR. HERDAL's *arm and goes out with him to the right.* HILDA *has meanwhile been collecting her travelling things.*]

HILDA   [*Softly and rapidly to* SOLNESS.]

Is it true, what you said? *Can* I be of use to you?

SOLNESS   [*Takes the things from her.*]

You are the very being I have needed most.

HILDA   [*Looks at him with happy, wondering eyes and clasps her hands.*]

But then, great heavens———!

SOLNESS   [*Eagerly.*]

What———?

HILDA

Then I *have* my kingdom!

SOLNESS   [*Involuntarily.*]

Hilda———!

HILDA   [*Again with the quivering twitch of her lips.*]

Almost—I was going to say.

[*She goes out to the right,* SOLNESS *follows her.*]

ACT SECOND

A prettily furnished small drawing-room in SOLNESS's *house. In the back, a glass-door leading out to the veranda and garden. The right-hand corner is cut off transversely by a large bay-window, in which are flower-stands. The left-hand corner is similarly cut off by a transverse wall, in which is a small door papered like the wall. On each side, an ordinary door. In front, on the right, a console table with a large mirror over it. Well-filled stands of plants and flowers. in front, on the left, a sofa with a table and chairs. Further back, a bookcase. Well forward in the room, before the bay-window, a small table and some chairs. It is early in the day.*

SOLNESS *sits by the little table with* RAGNAR BROVIK's *portfolio open in front of him. He is turning the drawings over and closely examining some of them.* MRS. SOLNESS *moves about noiselessly with a small watering-pot, attending to her flowers. She is dressed in black as before. Her hat, cloak and parasol lie on a chair near the mirror. Unobserved by her,* SOLNESS *now and again follows her with his eyes. Neither of them speaks.*

KAIA FOSLI *enters quietly by the door on the left.*

SOLNESS   [*Turns his head, and says in an off-hand tone of indifference.*]
　　Well, is that you?
KAIA
　　I merely wished to let you know that I have come.
SOLNESS
　　Yes, yes, that's all right. Hasn't Ragnar come too?
KAIA
　　No, not yet. He had to wait a little while to see the doctor. But he is coming presently to hear——
SOLNESS
　　How is the old man to-day?

KAIA

Not well. He begs you to excuse him; he is obliged to keep his bed to-day.

SOLNESS

Why, of course; by all means let him rest. But now, get to your work.

KAIA

Yes.

[*Pauses at the door.*]

Do you wish to speak to Ragnar when he comes?

SOLNESS

No——I don't know that I have anything particular to say to him.

[KAIA *goes out again to the left.* SOLNESS *remains seated, turning over the drawings.*]

MRS. SOLNESS   [*Over beside the plants.*]

I wonder if *he* isn't going to die now, as well?

SOLNESS   [*Looks up at her.*]

As well as who?

MRS. SOLNESS   [*Without answering.*]

Yes, yes——depend upon it, Halvard, old Brovik is going to die too. You'll see that he will.

SOLNESS

My dear Aline, ought you not to go out for a little walk?

MRS. SOLNESS

Yes, I suppose I ought to.

[*She continues to attend to the flowers.*]

SOLNESS   [*Bending over the drawings.*]

Is she still asleep?

MRS. SOLNESS   [*Looking at him.*]

Is it Miss Wangel you are sitting there thinking about?

SOLNESS   [*Indifferently.*]

I just happened to recollect her.

MRS. SOLNESS

Miss Wangel was up long ago.

SOLNESS

Oh, was she?

MRS. SOLNESS

When I went in to see her, she was busy putting her things in order.

[*She goes in front of the mirror and slowly begins to put on her hat.*]

SOLNESS [*After a short pause.*]

So we have found a use for one of our nurseries after all, Aline.

MRS. SOLNESS

Yes, we have.

SOLNESS

That seems to me better than to have them all standing empty.

MRS. SOLNESS

That emptiness is dreadful; you are right there.

SOLNESS [*Closes the portfolio, rises and approaches her.*]

You will find that we shall get on far better after this, Aline. Things will be more comfortable. Life will be easier—especially for *you*.

MRS. SOLNESS [*Looks at him.*]

After this?

SOLNESS

Yes, believe me, Aline——

MRS. SOLNESS

Do you mean—because *she* has come here?

SOLNESS [*Checking himself.*]

I mean, of course—when once we have moved into the new house.

MRS. SOLNESS [*Takes her cloak.*]

Ah, do you think so, Halvard? Will it be better then?

SOLNESS

I can't think otherwise. And surely you think so too?

MRS. SOLNESS

I think nothing at all about the new house.

SOLNESS [*Cast down.*]

It's hard for me to hear you say that; for you know it is mainly for your sake that I have built it.

[*He offers to help her on with her cloak.*]

MRS. SOLNESS [*Evades him.*]

The fact is, you do far too much for my sake.

SOLNESS   [*With a certain vehemence.*]

 No, no, you really mustn't say that, Aline! I cannot bear to hear
 you say such things!

MRS. SOLNESS

 Very well, then I won't say it, Halvard.

SOLNESS

 But I stick to what *I* said. You'll see that things will be easier for
 you in the new place.

MRS. SOLNESS

 Oh Heavens——easier for me——!

SOLNESS   [*Eagerly.*]

 Yes, indeed they will! You may be quite sure of that! For you
 see——there will be so very, very much *there* that will remind you
 of your own home——

MRS. SOLNESS

 The home that used to be father's and mother's——and that was
 burnt to the ground——

SOLNESS   [*In a low voice.*]

 Yes, yes, my poor Aline. That was a terrible blow for you.

MRS. SOLNESS   [*Breaking out in lamentation.*]

 You may build as much as ever you like, Halvard——you can never
 build up again a real home for *me*!

SOLNESS   [*Crosses the room.*]

 Well, in Heaven's name, let us talk no more about it then.

MRS. SOLNESS

 We are not in the habit of talking about it. For you always put
 the thought away from you——

SOLNESS   [*Stops suddenly and looks at her.*]

 Do I? And why should I do *that*? Put the thought away from me?

MRS. SOLNESS

 Oh yes, Halvard, I understand you very well. You are so anxious
 to spare me——and to find excuses for me too——as much as ever
 you can.

SOLNESS   [*With astonishment in his eyes.*]

 You! Is it *you*——yourself, that you are talking about, Aline?

MRS. SOLNESS

 Yes, who else should it be but myself?

SOLNESS [*Involuntarily to himself.*]

That too!

MRS. SOLNESS

As for the old house, I wouldn't mind so much about that. When once misfortune was in the air—why——

SOLNESS

Ah, you are right there. Misfortune will have its way—as the saying goes.

MRS. SOLNESS

But it's what came of the fire—the dreadful thing that followed——! *That* is the thing! That, that, that!

SOLNESS [*Vehemently.*]

Don't think about *that*, Aline!

MRS. SOLNESS

Ah, that is exactly what I cannot help thinking about. And now, at last, I must speak about it, too; for I don't seem able to bear it any longer. And then never to be able to forgive myself——

SOLNESS [*Exclaiming.*]

Yourself——!

MRS. SOLNESS

Yes, for I had duties on both sides—both towards you and towards the little ones. I ought to have hardened myself—not to have let the horror take such hold upon me—nor the grief for the burning of my home.

[*Wrings her hands.*]

Oh, Halvard, if I had only had the strength!

SOLNESS [*Softly, much moved, comes closer.*]

Aline—you must promise me never to think these thoughts any more.—Promise me that, dear!

MRS. SOLNESS

Oh, promise, promise! One can promise anything.

SOLNESS [*Clenches his hands and crosses the room.*]

Oh, but this is hopeless, hopeless! Never a ray of sunlight! Not so much as a gleam of brightness to light up our home!

MRS. SOLNESS

This is no home, Halvard.

SOLNESS

Oh no, you may well say that.

[*Gloomily.*]

And God knows whether you are not right in saying that it will be no better for us in the new house, either.

MRS. SOLNESS

It will never be any better. Just as empty—just as desolate—there as here.

SOLNESS   [*Vehemently.*]

Why in all the world have we built it then? Can you tell me that?

MRS. SOLNESS

No; you must answer that question for yourself.

SOLNESS   [*Glances suspiciously at her.*]

What do you mean by *that*, Aline?

MRS. SOLNESS

What do I mean?

SOLNESS

Yes, in the devil's name! You said it so strangely—as if you had some hidden meaning in it.

MRS. SOLNESS

No, indeed, I assure you——

SOLNESS   [*Comes closer.*]

Oh, come now—I know what I know. I have both my eyes and my ears about me, Aline—you may depend upon that!

MRS. SOLNESS

Why, what are you talking about? What is it?

SOLNESS   [*Places himself in front of her.*]

Do you mean to say you don't find a kind of lurking, hidden meaning in the most innocent word I happen to say?

MRS. SOLNESS

I, do you say? *I* do that?

SOLNESS   [*Laughs.*]

Ho-ho-ho! It's natural enough, Aline! When you have a sick man on your hands——

MRS. SOLNESS   [*Anxiously.*]

Sick? Are you ill, Halvard?

SOLNESS   [*Violently.*]

A half-mad man then! A crazy man! Call me what you will.

MRS. SOLNESS   [*Feels blindly for a chair and sits down.*]

Halvard—for God's sake——

SOLNESS

> But you are wrong, both you and the doctor. I am not in the
> state you imagine.
>
> [*He walks up and down the room.* MRS. SOLNESS *follows him anxiously with her eyes. Finally he goes up to her.*]

SOLNESS [*Calmly.*]

> In reality there is nothing whatever the matter with me.

MRS. SOLNESS

> No, there isn't, is there? But then what is it that troubles you so?

SOLNESS

> Why *this*, that I often feel ready to sink under this terrible
> burden of debt——

MRS. SOLNESS

> Debt, do you say? But you owe no one anything, Halvard!

SOLNESS [*Softly, with emotion.*]

> I owe a boundless debt to you—to you—to you, Aline.

MRS. SOLNESS [*Rises slowly.*]

> What is behind all this? You may just as well tell me at once.

SOLNESS

> But there *is* nothing behind it! I have never done you any
> wrong—not wittingly and wilfully, at any rate. And yet—and yet
> it seems as though a crushing debt rested upon me and weighed
> me down.

MRS. SOLNESS

> A debt to me?

SOLNESS

> Chiefly to you.

MRS. SOLNESS

> Then you are—ill after all, Halvard.

SOLNESS [*Gloomily.*]

> I suppose I must be—or not far from it.
>
> [*Looks towards the door to the right, which is opened at this moment.*]
> Ah! now it grows lighter.

HILDA WANGEL *comes in. She has made some alteration in her dress, and
let down her skirt.*

HILDA

Good morning, Mr. Solness!

SOLNESS   [*Nods.*]

Slept well?

HILDA

Quite deliciously! Like a child in a cradle. Oh—I lay and stretched myself like—like a princess!

SOLNESS   [*Smiles a little.*]

You were thoroughly comfortable then?

HILDA

I should think so.

SOLNESS

And no doubt you dreamed, too.

HILDA

Yes, I did. But *that* was horrid.

SOLNESS

Was it?

HILDA

Yes, for I dreamed I was falling over a frightfully high, sheer precipice. Do you never have that kind of dream?

SOLNESS

Oh yes—now and then——

HILDA

It's tremendously thrilling—when you fall and fall——

SOLNESS

It seems to make one's blood run cold.

HILDA

Do you draw your legs up under you while you are falling?

SOLNESS

Yes, as high as ever I can.

HILDA

So do I.

MRS. SOLNESS   [*Takes her parasol.*]

I must go into town now, Halvard.

[*To* HILDA.]

And I'll try to get one or two things that you may require.

HILDA   [*Making a motion to throw her arms round her neck.*]

Oh, you dear, sweet Mrs. Solness! You are really much too kind to me! Frightfully kind——

MRS. SOLNESS   [*Deprecatingly, freeing herself.*]

Oh, not at all. It's only my duty, so I am very glad to do it.

HILDA   [*Offended, pouts.*]

But really, I think I am quite fit to be seen in the streets——now that I've put my dress to rights. Or do you think I am not?

MRS. SOLNESS

To tell you the truth, I think people would stare at you a little.

HILDA   [*Contemptuously.*]

Pooh! Is that all? That only amuses me.

SOLNESS   [*With suppressed ill-humour.*]

Yes, but people might take it into their heads that *you* were mad too, you see.

HILDA

Mad? Are there so many mad people here in town, then?

SOLNESS   [*Points to his own forehead.*]

Here you see *one* at all events.

HILDA

You——Mr. Solness!

MRS. SOLNESS

Oh, don't talk like that, my dear Halvard!

SOLNESS

Have you not noticed *that* yet?

HILDA

No, I certainly have not.

[*Reflects and laughs a little.*]

And yet——perhaps in one single thing.

SOLNESS

Ah, do you hear *that*, Aline?

MRS. SOLNESS

What is that one single thing, Miss Wangel?

HILDA

No, I won't say.

SOLNESS

Oh yes, do!

HILDA

No thank you——I am not *so* mad as that.

MRS. SOLNESS

When you and Miss Wangel are alone, I daresay she will tell you, Halvard.

SOLNESS

Ah——you think she will?

MRS. SOLNESS

Oh yes, certainly. For you have known her so well in the past. Ever since she was a child——you tell me.

[*She goes out by the door on the left.*]

HILDA   [*After a little while.*]

Does your wife dislike me very much?

SOLNESS

Did you think you noticed anything of the kind?

HILDA

Did you not notice it yourself?

SOLNESS   [*Evasively.*]

Aline has become exceedingly shy with strangers of late years.

HILDA

Has she really?

SOLNESS

But if only you could get to know her thoroughly——! Ah, she is so good——so kind——so excellent a creature——

HILDA   [*Impatiently.*]

But if she is all that——what made her say that about her duty?

SOLNESS

Her duty?

HILDA

She said that she would go out and buy something for me, because it was her *duty*. Oh I can't bear that ugly, horrid word!

SOLNESS

Why not?

HILDA

It sounds so cold, and sharp, and stinging. Duty——duty——duty. Don't *you* think so, too? Doesn't it seem to sting you?

SOLNESS

H'm——haven't thought much about it.

HILDA

Yes, it does. And if she is so good—as you say she is—why should she talk in that way?

SOLNESS

But, good Lord, what would you have had her say, then?

HILDA

She might have said she would do it because she had taken a tremendous fancy to me. She might have said something like that—something really warm and cordial, you understand.

SOLNESS   [Looks at her.]

Is that how you would like to have it?

HILDA

Yes, precisely.

[She wanders about the room, stops at the bookcase and looks at the books.]

What a lot of books you have.

SOLNESS

Yes, I have got together a good many.

HILDA

Do you read them all, too?

SOLNESS

I used to try to. Do you read much?

HILDA

No, never! I have given it up. For it all seems so irrelevant.

SOLNESS

That is just my feeling.

[HILDA wanders about a little, stops at the small table, opens the portfolio and turns over the contents.

HILDA

Are all these drawings yours?

SOLNESS

No, they are drawn by a young man whom I employ to help me.

HILDA

Some one you have taught?

SOLNESS

Oh yes, no doubt he has learnt something from me, too.

HILDA   [Sits down.]

Then I suppose he is very clever.

[Looks at a drawing.]

Isn't he?

SOLNESS

Oh, he might be worse. For *my* purpose——

HILDA

Oh yes—I'm sure he is frightfully clever.

SOLNESS

Do you think you can see that in the drawings?

HILDA

Pooh—these scrawlings! But if he has been learning from
you——

SOLNESS

Oh, so far as that goes——there are plenty of people here that
have learnt from *me*, and have come to little enough for all that.

HILDA   [*Looks at him and shakes her head.*]

No, I can't for the life of me understand how you can be so
stupid.

SOLNESS

Stupid? Do you think I am so very stupid?

HILDA

Yes, I do indeed. If you are content to go about here teaching all
these people——

SOLNESS   [*With a slight start.*]

Well, and why not?

HILDA   [*Rises, half serious, half laughing.*]

No indeed, Mr. Solness! What can be the good of that? No one
but *you* should be allowed to build. You should stand quite
alone—do it all yourself. Now you know it.

SOLNESS   [*Involuntarily.*]

Hilda——!

HILDA

Well!

SOLNESS

How in the world did *that* come into your head?

HILDA

Do you think I am so very far wrong then?

SOLNESS

No, that's not what I mean. But now I'll tell you something.

HILDA

    Well?

SOLNESS

    I keep on——incessantly——in silence and alone——brooding on that very thought.

HILDA

    Yes, that seems to me perfectly natural.

SOLNESS   [*Looks somewhat searchingly at her.*]

    Perhaps you have noticed it already?

HILDA

    No, indeed I haven't.

SOLNESS

    But just now——when you said you thought I was——off my balance? In one thing, you said——

HILDA

    Oh, I was thinking of something quite different.

SOLNESS

    What was it?

HILDA

    I am not going to tell you.

SOLNESS   [*Crosses the room.*]

    Well, well——as you please.

    [*Stops at the bow-window.*]

    Come here, and I will show you something.

HILDA   [*Approaching.*]

    What is it?

SOLNESS

    Do you see——over there in the garden——?

HILDA

    Yes?

SOLNESS   [*Points.*]

    Right above the great quarry——?

HILDA

    That new house, you mean?

SOLNESS

    The one that is being built, yes. Almost finished.

HILDA

    It seems to have a very high tower.

SOLNESS

The scaffolding is still up.

HILDA

Is that your new house?

SOLNESS

Yes.

HILDA

The house you are soon going to move into?

SOLNESS

Yes.

HILDA   [*Looks at him.*]

Are there nurseries in *that* house, too?

SOLNESS

Three, as there are here.

HILDA

And no child.

SOLNESS

And there never will be one.

HILDA   [*With a half-smile.*]

Well, isn't it just as I said——?

SOLNESS

That——?

HILDA

That you *are* a little—a little mad after all.

SOLNESS

Was that what you were thinking of?

HILDA

Yes, of all the empty nurseries I slept in.

SOLNESS   [*Lowers his voice.*]

We *have* had children—Aline and I.

HILDA   [*Looks eagerly at him.*]

Have you——?

SOLNESS

Two little boys. They were of the same age.

HILDA

Twins, then.

SOLNESS

Yes, twins. It's eleven or twelve years ago now.

HILDA   [*Cautiously.*]

And so both of them———? You have lost both the twins, then?

SOLNESS   [*With quiet emotion.*]

We kept them only about three weeks. Or scarcely so much.

[*Bursts forth.*]

Oh, Hilda, I can't tell you what a good thing it is for me that you have come! For now at last I have some one I can talk to!

HILDA

Can you not talk to——*her*, too?

SOLNESS

Not about this. Not as I want to talk and must talk.

[*Gloomily.*]

And not about so many other things, either.

HILDA   [*In a subdued voice.*]

Was that all you meant when you said you needed me?

SOLNESS

That was mainly what I meant—at all events, yesterday. For to-day I am not so sure—

[*Breaking off.*]

Come here and let us sit down, Hilda. Sit there on the sofa—so that you can look into the garden.

[HILDA *seats herself in the corner of the sofa.* SOLNESS *brings a chair closer.*]

Should you like to hear about it?

HILDA

Yes, I shall love to sit and listen to you.

SOLNESS   [*Sits down.*]

Then I will tell you all about it.

HILDA

Now I can see both the garden and you, Mr. Solness. So now, tell away! Begin!

SOLNESS   [*Points towards the bow-window.*]

Out there on the rising ground—where you see the new house———

HILDA

Yes?

SOLNESS

Aline and I lived there in the first years of our married life.

There was an old house up there that had belonged to her
mother; and we inherited it, and the whole of the great garden
with it.

HILDA

Was there a tower on *that* house, too?

SOLNESS

No, nothing of the kind. From the outside it looked like a great,
dark, ugly wooden box; but all the same, it was snug and comfortable enough inside.

HILDA

Then did you pull down the ramshackle old place?

SOLNESS

No, it was burnt down.

HILDA

The whole of it?

SOLNESS

Yes.

HILDA

Was that a great misfortune for you?

SOLNESS

That depends on how you look at it. As a builder, the fire was the
making of me——

HILDA

Well, but——?

SOLNESS

It was just after the birth of the two little boys——

HILDA

The poor little twins, yes.

SOLNESS

They came healthy and bonny into the world. And they were
growing too—you could see the difference from day to day.

HILDA

Little children do grow quickly at first.

SOLNESS

It was the prettiest sight in the world to see Aline lying with the
two of them in her arms.—But then came the night of the
fire——

HILDA   [*Excitedly.*]

What happened? Do tell me! Was any one burnt?

SOLNESS

No, not that. Every one got safe and sound out of the house———

HILDA

Well, and what then———?

SOLNESS

The fright had shaken Aline terribly. The alarm—the escape—the break-neck hurry—and then the ice-cold night air—for they had to be carried out just as they lay—both she and the little ones.

HILDA

Was it too much for them?

SOLNESS

Oh no, *they* stood it well enough. But Aline fell into a fever, and it affected her milk. She would insist on nursing them herself; because it was her duty, she said. And both our little boys, they—

[*Clenching his hands.*]

—they—oh!

HILDA

They did not get over *that*?

SOLNESS

No, *that* they did not get over. *That* was how we lost them.

HILDA

It must have been terribly hard for you.

SOLNESS

Hard enough for me: but ten times harder for Aline.

[*Clenching his hands in suppressed fury.*]

Oh, that such things should be allowed to happen here in the world!

[*Shortly and firmly.*]

From the day I lost them, I had no heart for building churches.

HILDA

Did you not like building the church-tower in our town?

SOLNESS

I didn't like it. I know how free and happy I felt when that tower was finished.

HILDA

I know that, too.

SOLNESS

And now I shall never—never build anything of that sort again!
Neither churches nor church-towers.

HILDA   [*Nods slowly.*]

Nothing but houses for people to live in.

SOLNESS

Homes for human beings, Hilda.

HILDA

But homes with high towers and pinnacles upon them.

SOLNESS

If possible.

[*Adopts a lighter tone.*]

But, as I said before, that fire was the making of me—as a
builder, I mean.

HILDA

Why don't you call yourself an architect, like the others?

SOLNESS

I have not been systematically enough taught for that. Most of
what I know I have found out for myself.

HILDA

But you succeeded all the same.

SOLNESS

Yes, thanks to the fire. I laid out almost the whole of the garden
in villa lots; and *there* I was able to build after my own heart. So I
came to the front with a rush.

HILDA   [*Looks keenly at him.*]

You must surely be a very happy man, as matters stand with you.

SOLNESS   [*Gloomily.*]

Happy? Do *you* say that, too—like all the rest of them?

HILDA

Yes, I should say you must be. If you could only cease thinking
about the two little children——

SOLNESS   [*Slowly.*]

The two little children—they are not so easy to forget, Hilda.

HILDA   [*Somewhat uncertainly.*]

Do you still feel their loss so much—after all these years?

SOLNESS [*Looks fixedly at her, without replying.*]

A happy man you said——

HILDA

Well, now, *are* you not happy—in other respects?

SOLNESS [*Continues to look at her.*]

When I told you all this about the fire—h'm——

HILDA

Well?

SOLNESS

Was there not one special thought that you—that you seized upon?

HILDA [*Reflects in vain.*]

No. What thought should *that* be?

SOLNESS [*With subdued emphasis.*]

It was simply and solely by that fire that I was enabled to build homes for human beings. Cosy, comfortable, bright homes, where father and mother and the whole troop of children can live in safety and gladness, feeling what a happy thing it is to be alive in the world—and most of all to belong to each other—in great things and in small.

HILDA [*Ardently.*]

Well, and is it not a great happiness for you to be able to build such beautiful homes?

SOLNESS

The price, Hilda! The terrible price I had to pay for the opportunity!

HILDA

But can you *never* get over that?

SOLNESS

No. That I might build homes for others, I had to forego—to forego for all time—the home that might have been my own. I mean a home for a troop of children—and for father and mother, too.

HILDA [*Cautiously.*]

But *need* you have done that? For all time, you say?

SOLNESS [*Nods slowly.*]

That was the price of this happiness that people talk about. [*Breathes heavily.*]

This happiness—h'm—this happiness was not to be bought any cheaper, Hilda.

HILDA   [*As before.*]

But may it not come right even yet?

SOLNESS

Never in this world—never. That is another consequence of the fire—and of Aline's illness afterwards.

HILDA   [*Looks at him with an indefinable expression.*]

And yet you build all these nurseries?

SOLNESS   [*Seriously.*]

Have you never noticed, Hilda, how the impossible—how it seems to beckon and cry aloud to one?

HILDA   [*Reflecting.*]

The impossible?

[*With animation.*]

Yes, indeed! Is that how *you* feel too?

SOLNESS

Yes, I do.

HILDA

Then there must be—a little of the troll in you too.

SOLNESS

Why of the troll?

HILDA

What would *you* call it, then?

SOLNESS   [*Rises.*]

Well, well, perhaps you are right.

[*Vehemently.*]

But how can I help turning into a troll, when this is how it always goes with me in everything—in everything!

HILDA

How do you mean?

SOLNESS   [*Speaking low, with inward emotion.*]

Mark what I say to you, Hilda. All that I have succeeded in doing, building, creating—all the beauty, security, cheerful comfort— ay, and magnificence too—

[*Clenches his hands.*]

Oh, is it not terrible even to think of——!

HILDA

What is so terrible?

SOLNESS

That all this I have to make up for, to pay for—not in money, but in human happiness. And not with my own happiness only, but with other people's too. Yes, yes, do you see *that*, Hilda? That is the price which my position as an artist has cost me—and others. And every single day I have to look on while the price is paid for me anew. Over again, and over again—and over again for ever!

HILDA   [*Rises and looks steadily at him.*]

Now I can see that you are thinking of—of *her*.

SOLNESS

Yes, mainly of Aline. For Aline—*she*, too, had her vocation in life, just as much as I had mine.

[*His voice quivers.*]

But her vocation has had to be stunted, and crushed, and shattered—in order that mine might force its way to—to a sort of great victory. For you must know that Aline—she, too, had a talent for building.

HILDA

She! For building?

SOLNESS   [*Shakes his head.*]

Not houses and towers, and spires—not such things as I work away at——

HILDA

Well, but *what* then?

SOLNESS   [*Softly, with emotion.*]

For building up the souls of little children, Hilda. For building up children's souls in perfect balance, and in noble and beautiful forms. For enabling them to soar up into erect and full-grown human souls. *That* was Aline's talent. And there it all lies now—unused and unusable for ever—of no earthly service to any one—just like the ruins left by a fire.

HILDA

Yes, but even if this were so——?

SOLNESS

It is so! It is so! I know it!

HILDA

Well, but in any case it is not *your* fault.

SOLNESS   [*Fixes his eyes on her, and nods slowly.*]

Ah, *that* is the great, the terrible question. *That* is the doubt that is gnawing me—night and day.

HILDA

That?

SOLNESS

Yes. Suppose the fault *was* mine—in a certain sense.

HILDA

Your fault! The fire!

SOLNESS

All of it; the whole thing. And yet, perhaps—I may not have had anything to do with it.

HILDA   [*Looks at him with a troubled expression.*]

Oh, Mr. Solness—if you can talk like that, I am afraid you must be—ill, after all.

SOLNESS

H'm—I don't think I shall ever be of quite sound mind on that point.

RAGNAR BROVIK *cautiously opens the little door in the left-hand corner.* HILDA *comes forward.*

RAGNAR   [*When he sees* HILDA.]

Oh. I beg pardon, Mr. Solness——

[*He makes a movement to withdraw.*]

SOLNESS

No, no, don't go. Let us get it over.

RAGNAR

Oh, yes—if only we could.

SOLNESS

I hear your father is no better?

RAGNAR

Father is fast growing weaker—and therefore I beg and implore you to write a few kind words for me on one of the plans! Something for father to read before he——

SOLNESS   [*Vehemently.*]

    I won't hear anything more about those drawings of yours!

RAGNAR

    Have you looked at them?

SOLNESS

    Yes—I have.

RAGNAR

    And they are good for nothing? And *I* am good for nothing, too?

SOLNESS   [*Evasively.*]

    Stay here with me, Ragnar. You shall have everything your own way. And then you can marry Kaia, and live at your ease—and happily too, who knows? Only don't think of building on your own account.

RAGNAR

    Well, well, then I must go home and tell father what you say—I promised I would.—*Is* this what I am to tell father—before he dies?

SOLNESS   [*With a groan.*]

    Oh tell him—tell him what you will, for me. Best to say nothing at all to him!

    [*With a sudden outburst.*]

    I *cannot* do anything else, Ragnar!

RAGNAR

    May I have the drawings to take with me?

SOLNESS

    Yes, take them—take them by all means! They are lying there on the table.

RAGNAR   [*Goes to the table.*]

    Thanks.

HILDA   [*Puts her hand on the portfolio.*]

    No, no; leave them here.

SOLNESS

    Why?

HILDA

    Because I want to look at them, too.

SOLNESS

    But you *have* been——

    [*To* RAGNAR.]

Well, leave them here, then.

RAGNAR

Very well.

SOLNESS

And go home at once to your father.

RAGNAR

Yes, I suppose I must.

SOLNESS   [*As if in desperation.*]

Ragnar—you *must* not ask me to do what is beyond my power! Do you hear, Ragnar? You *must* not!

RAGNAR

No, no. I beg your pardon——

[*He bows, and goes out by the corner door.* HILDA *goes over and sits down on a chair near the mirror.*]

HILDA   [*Looks angrily at* SOLNESS.]

That was a very ugly thing to do.

SOLNESS

Do *you* think so, too?

HILDA

Yes, it was horribly ugly—and hard and bad and cruel as well.

SOLNESS

Oh, you don't understand my position.

HILDA

No matter——. I say you ought not to be like that.

SOLNESS

You said yourself, only just now, that no one but *I* ought to be allowed to build.

HILDA

I may say such things—but *you* must not.

SOLNESS

I most of all, surely, who have paid so dear for my position.

HILDA

Oh yes—with what you call domestic comfort—and that sort of thing.

SOLNESS

And with my peace of soul into the bargain.

HILDA   [*Rising.*]

Peace of soul!

[*With feeling.*]

Yes, yes, you are right in that! Poor Mr. Solness—you fancy
that——

SOLNESS   [*With a quiet, chuckling laugh.*]

Just sit down again, Hilda, and I'll tell you something funny.

HILDA   [*Sits down; with intent interest.*]

Well?

SOLNESS

It sounds such a ludicrous little thing; for, you see, the whole
story turns upon nothing but a crack in a chimney.

HILDA

No more than that?

SOLNESS

No, not to begin with.

[*He moves a chair nearer to* HILDA *and sits down.*]

HILDA   [*Impatiently, taps on her knee.*]

Well, now for the crack in the chimney!

SOLNESS

I had noticed the split in the flue long, long before the fire. Every
time I went up into the attic, I looked to see if it was still there.

HILDA

And it *was*?

SOLNESS

Yes; for no one else knew about it.

HILDA

And you said nothing?

SOLNESS

Nothing.

HILDA

And did not think of repairing the flue either?

SOLNESS

Oh yes, I thought about it—but never got any further. Every
time I intended to set to work, it seemed just as if a hand held
me back. Not to-day, I thought—tomorrow; and nothing ever
came of it.

HILDA

But why did you keep putting it off like that?

SOLNESS

Because I was revolving something in my mind.

[*Slowly, and in a low voice.*]

Through that little black crack in the chimney, I might, perhaps, force my way upwards—as a builder.

HILDA   [*Looking straight in front of her.*]

That must have been thrilling.

SOLNESS

Almost irresistible—quite irresistible. For at that time it appeared to me a perfectly simple and straight-forward matter. I would have had it happen in the winter-time—a little before midday. I was to be out driving Aline in the sleigh. The servants at home would have made huge fires in the stoves.

HILDA

For, of course, it was to be bitterly cold that day?

SOLNESS

Rather biting, yes—and they would want Aline to find it thoroughly snug and warm when she came home.

HILDA

I suppose she is very chilly by nature?

SOLNESS

She *is*. And as we drove home, we were to see the smoke.

HILDA

Only the smoke?

SOLNESS

The smoke first. But when we came up to the garden gate, the whole of the old timber-box was to be a rolling mass of flames.—That is how I wanted it to be, you see.

HILDA

Oh why, *why* could it not have happened so!

SOLNESS

You may well say that, Hilda.

HILDA

Well, but now listen, Mr. Solness. Are you perfectly certain that the fire was caused by that little crack in the chimney!

SOLNESS

No, on the contrary—I am perfectly certain that the crack in the chimney had nothing whatever to do with the fire.

HILDA

 What!

SOLNESS

 It has been clearly ascertained that the fire broke out in a
clothes-cupboard—in a totally different part of the house.

HILDA

 Then what is all this nonsense you are talking about the crack in
the chimney!

SOLNESS

 May I go on talking to you a little, Hilda?

HILDA

 Yes, if you'll only talk sensibly——

SOLNESS

 I will try to.

 [*He moves his chair nearer.*]

HILDA

 Out with it, then, Mr. Solness.

SOLNESS [*Confidentially.*]

 Don't you agree with me, Hilda, that there exist special, chosen
people who have been endowed with the power and faculty of
desiring a thing, *craving* for a thing, *willing* a thing—so persistently
and so—so inexorably—that at last it *has* to happen? Don't you
believe that?

HILDA [*With an indefinable expression in her eyes.*]

 If that is so, we shall see, one of these days, whether *I* am one of
the chosen.

SOLNESS

 It is not one's self *alone* that can do such great things. Oh, no—
the helpers and the servers—they must do their part too, if it is
to be of any good. But they never come of themselves. One has
to call upon them very persistently—inwardly, you understand.

HILDA

 What are these helpers and servers?

SOLNESS

 Oh, we can talk about that some other time. For the present, let
us keep to this business of the fire.

HILDA

Don't you think that fire would have happened all the same—
even without your wishing for it?

SOLNESS

If the house had been old Knut Brovik's it would never have
burnt down so conveniently for *him*. I am sure of that; for he
does not know how to call for the helpers—no, nor for the
servers, either.

[*Rises in unrest.*]

So you see, Hilda—it is my fault, after all, that the lives of the
two little boys had to be sacrificed. And do you think it is not my
fault, too, that Aline has never been the woman she should and
might have been—and that she most longed to be?

HILDA

Yes, but if it is all the work of those helpers and servers——?

SOLNESS

Who called for the helpers and servers? It was I! And they came
and obeyed my will.

[*In increasing excitement.*]

That is what people call having the luck on your side; but I must
tell you what this sort of luck feels like! It feels like a great raw
place here on my breast. And the helpers and servers keep on
flaying pieces of skin off other people in order to close *my*
sore!—But still the sore is not healed—never, never! Oh, if you
knew how it can sometimes gnaw and burn!

HILDA   [*Looks attentively at him.*]

You *are* ill, Mr. Solness. Very ill, I almost think.

SOLNESS

Say *mad*; for that is what you mean.

HILDA

No, I don't think there is much amiss with your intellect.

SOLNESS

With *what* then? Out with it!

HILDA

I wonder whether you were not sent into the world with a sickly
conscience.

SOLNESS

A sickly conscience? What deviltry is that?

HILDA

> I mean that your conscience is feeble—too delicately built, as it were—hasn't strength to take a grip of things—to lift and bear what is heavy.

SOLNESS [*Growls.*]

> H'm! May I ask, then, what sort of a conscience one ought to have?

HILDA

> I should like *your* conscience to be—to be thoroughly robust.

SOLNESS

> Indeed? Robust, eh? Is your own conscience robust, may I ask?

HILDA

> Yes, I think it is. I have never noticed that it wasn't.

SOLNESS

> It has not been put very severely to the test, I should think.

HILDA [*With a quivering of the lips.*]

> Oh, it was no such simple matter to leave father—I am so awfully fond of him.

SOLNESS

> Dear me! for a month or two——

HILDA

> I think I shall never go home again.

SOLNESS

> Never? Then why did you leave him?

HILDA [*Half-seriously, half-banteringly.*]

> Have you forgotten again that the ten years are up?

SOLNESS

> Oh nonsense. Was anything wrong at home? Eh?

HILDA [*Quite seriously.*]

> It was this impulse within me that urged and goaded me to come—and lured and drew me on, as well.

SOLNESS [*Eagerly.*]

> There we have it! There we have it, Hilda! There is a troll in you too, as in me. For it's the troll in one, you see—it is *that* that calls to the powers outside us. And then you *must* give in—whether you will or no.

HILDA

> I almost think you are right, Mr. Solness.

SOLNESS   [*Walks about the room.*]

Oh, there are devils innumerable abroad in the world, Hilda, that one never *sees!*

HILDA

Devils, too?

SOLNESS   [*Stops.*]

Good devils and bad devils; light-haired devils and black-haired devils. If only you could always tell whether it is the light or dark ones that have got hold of you!

[*Paces about.*]

Ho-ho! Then it would be simple enough!

HILDA   [*Follows him with her eyes.*]

Or if one had a really vigorous, radiantly healthy conscience——so that one *dared* to do what one *would.*

SOLNESS   [*Stops beside the console table.*]

I believe, now, that most people are just as puny creatures as I am in that respect.

HILDA

I shouldn't wonder.

SOLNESS   [*Leaning against the table.*]

In the sagas——. Have you read any of the old sagas?

HILDA

Oh yes! When I used to read books, I——

SOLNESS

In the sagas you read about vikings, who sailed to foreign lands, and plundered and burned and killed men——

HILDA

And carried off women——

SOLNESS

——and kept them in captivity——

HILDA

——took them home in their ships——

SOLNESS

——and behaved to them like—like the very worst of trolls.

HILDA   [*Looks straight before her, with a half-veiled look.*]

I think *that* must have been thrilling.

SOLNESS   [*With a short, deep laugh.*]

To carry off women, eh?

HILDA

> To *be* carried off.

SOLNESS   [*Looks at her a moment.*]

> Oh, indeed.

HILDA   [*As if breaking the thread of the conversation.*]

> But what made you speak of these vikings, Mr. Solness?

SOLNESS

> Why, *those* fellows must have had robust consciences, if you like!
> When they got home again, they could eat and drink, and be as
> happy as children. And the women, too! They often would not
> leave them on any account. Can you understand that, Hilda?

HILDA

> Those women I can understand exceedingly well.

SOLNESS

> Oho! Perhaps you could do the same yourself?

HILDA

> Why not?

SOLNESS

> Live—of your own free will—with a ruffian like that?

HILDA

> If it was a ruffian I had come to love——

SOLNESS

> *Could* you come to love a man like that?

HILDA

> Good heavens, you know very well one can't choose whom one
> is going to love.

SOLNESS   [*Looks meditatively at her.*]

> Oh no, I suppose it is the troll within one that's responsible for
> that.

HILDA   [*Half-laughing.*]

> And all those blessëd devils, that *you* know so well—both the
> light-haired and the dark-haired ones.

SOLNESS   [*Quietly and warmly.*]

> Then I hope with all my heart that the devils will choose care-
> fully for you, Hilda.

HILDA

> For me they *have* chosen already—once and for all.

SOLNESS   [*Looks earnestly at her.*]

Hilda—you are like a wild bird of the woods.

HILDA

Far from it. I don't hide myself away under the bushes.

SOLNESS

No, no. There is rather something of the bird of prey in you.

HILDA

That is nearer it—perhaps.

[*Very vehemently.*]

And why not a bird of prey? Why should not *I* go a-hunting—I, as well as the rest? Carry off the prey I want—if only I can get my claws into it, and do with it as I will.

SOLNESS

Hilda—do you know what you are?

HILDA

Yes, I suppose I am a strange sort of bird.

SOLNESS

No. You are like a dawning day. When I look at you—I seem to be looking towards the sunrise.

HILDA

Tell me, Mr. Solness—are you certain that you have never called me to you? Inwardly, you know?

SOLNESS   [*Softly and slowly.*]

I almost think I must have.

HILDA

What did you want with me?

SOLNESS

You are the younger generation, Hilda.

HILDA   [*Smiles.*]

That younger generation that you are so afraid of?

SOLNESS   [*Nods slowly.*]

And which, in my heart, I yearn towards so deeply.

[HILDA *rises, goes to the little table, and fetches* RAGNAR BROVIK's *portfolio.*]

HILDA   [*Holds out the portfolio to him.*]

We were talking of these drawings——

SOLNESS   [*Shortly, waving them away.*]

Put those things away! I have seen enough of them.

HILDA

Yes, but you have to write your approval on them.

SOLNESS

Write my approval on them? Never!

HILDA

But the poor old man is lying at death's door! Can't you give him and his son this pleasure before they are parted? And perhaps he might get the commission to carry them out, too.

SOLNESS

Yes, that is just what he would get. He has made sure of that—has my fine gentleman!

HILDA

Then, good heavens—if that is so—can't you tell the least little bit of a lie for once in a way?

SOLNESS

A lie?

[*Raging.*]

Hilda—take those devil's drawings out of my sight!

HILDA   [*Draws the portfolio a little nearer to herself*.]

Well, well, well—don't bite me.—You talk of trolls—but I think you go on like a troll yourself.

[*Looks round.*]

Where do you keep your pen and ink?

SOLNESS

There is nothing of the sort in here.

HILDA   [*Goes towards the door.*]

But in the office where that young lady is——

SOLNESS

Stay where you are, Hilda!—I ought to tell a lie, you say. Oh yes, for the sake of his old father I might well do that—for in my time I have crushed him, trodden him under foot——

HILDA

Him, too?

SOLNESS

I needed room for myself. But this Ragnar—he must on no account be allowed to come to the front.

HILDA

Poor fellow, there is surely no fear of that. If he has nothing in him——

SOLNESS   [*Comes closer, looks at her, and whispers.*]

If Ragnar Brovik gets his chance, he will strike *me* to the earth. Crush me—as I crushed his father.

HILDA

Crush you? Has he the ability for that?

SOLNESS

Yes, you may depend upon it *he* has the ability! He is the younger generation that stands ready to knock at my door—to make an end of Halvard Solness.

HILDA   [*Looks at him with quiet reproach.*]

And yet you would bar him out. Fie, Mr. Solness!

SOLNESS

The fight I have been fighting has cost heart's blood enough.—— And I am afraid, too, that the helpers and servers will not obey me any longer.

HILDA

Then you must go ahead without them. There is nothing else for it.

SOLNESS

It is hopeless, Hilda. The luck is bound to turn. A little sooner or a little later. Retribution is inexorable.

HILDA   [*In distress, putting her hands over her ears.*]

Don't talk like that! Do you want to kill me? To take from me what is more than my life?

SOLNESS

And what is that?

HILDA

The longing to see you great. To see you, with a wreath in your hand, high, high up upon a church-tower.

[*Calm again.*]

Come, out with your pencil now. You must have a pencil about you?

SOLNESS   [*Takes out his pocket-book.*]

I have one here.

HILDA   [*Lays the portfolio on the sofa-table.*]

Very well. Now let us two sit down here, Mr. Solness.

[SOLNESS *seats himself at the table.* HILDA *stands behind him, leaning over the back of the chair.*]

And now we will write on the drawings. We must write very, very nicely and cordially—for this horrid Ruar—or whatever his name is.

SOLNESS   [*Writes a few words, turns his head and looks at her.*]

Tell me one thing, Hilda.

HILDA

Yes!

SOLNESS

If you have been waiting for me all these ten years——

HILDA

What then?

SOLNESS

Why have you never written to me? Then I could have answered you.

HILDA   [*Hastily.*]

No, no, no! That was just what I did not want.

SOLNESS

Why not?

HILDA

I was afraid the whole thing might fall to pieces.—But we were going to write on the drawings, Mr. Solness.

SOLNESS

So we were.

HILDA   [*Bends forward and looks over his shoulder while he writes.*]

Mind now, kindly and cordially! Oh how I hate—how I hate this Ruald——

SOLNESS   [*Writing.*]

Have you never really cared for any one, Hilda?

HILDA   [*Harshly.*]

What do you say?

SOLNESS

Have you never cared for any one?

HILDA

For any one else, I suppose you mean?

SOLNESS   [*Looks up at her.*]

    ' For any one else, yes. Have you never? In all these ten years? Never?

HILDA

    Oh yes, now and then. When I was perfectly furious with you for not coming.

SOLNESS

    Then you did take an interest in other people, too?

HILDA

    A little bit—for a week or so. Good heavens, Mr. Solness, you surely know how such things come about.

SOLNESS

    Hilda—what is it you have come for?

HILDA

    Don't waste time talking. The poor old man might go and die in the meantime.

SOLNESS

    Answer me, Hilda. What do you want of me?

HILDA

    I want my kingdom.

SOLNESS

    H'm——

He gives a rapid glance towards the door on the left, and then goes on writing on the drawings. At the same moment MRS. SOLNESS *enters; she has some packages in her hand.*

MRS. SOLNESS

    Here are a few things I have got for you, Miss Wangel. The large parcels will be sent later on.

HILDA

    Oh, how very, very kind of you!

MRS. SOLNESS

    Only my simple duty. Nothing more than that.

SOLNESS   [*Reading over what he has written.*]

    Aline!

MRS. SOLNESS

    Yes?

SOLNESS

Did you notice whether the——the book-keeper was out there?

MRS. SOLNESS

Yes, of course, she was there.

SOLNESS   [*Puts the drawings in the portfolio.*]

H'm——

MRS. SOLNESS

She was standing at the desk, as she always is——when *I* go through the room.

SOLNESS   [*Rises.*]

Then I'll give this to her, and tell her that——

HILDA   [*Takes the portfolio from him.*]

Oh, no, let me have the pleasure of doing that!

[*Goes to the door, but turns.*]

What is her name?

SOLNESS

Her name is Miss Fosli.

HILDA

Pooh, that sounds so cold! Her Christian name, I mean?

SOLNESS

Kaia——I believe.

HILDA   [*Opens the door and calls out.*]

Kaia, come in here! Make haste! Mr. Solness wants to speak to you.

KAIA FOSLI *appears at the door.*

KAIA   [*Looking at him in alarm.*]

Here I am——?

HILDA   [*Handing her the portfolio.*]

See here, Kaia! You can take this home; Mr. Solness has written on them now.

KAIA

Oh, at last!

SOLNESS

Give them to the old man as soon as you can.

KAIA

I will go straight home with them.

SOLNESS

Yes, do. Now Ragnar will have a chance of building for himself.

KAIA

Oh, may he come and thank you for all———?

SOLNESS   [*Harshly.*]

I won't have any thanks! Tell him *that* from me.

KAIA

Yes, I will———

SOLNESS

And tell him at the same time that henceforward I do not require his services—nor yours either.

KAIA   [*Softly and quiveringly.*]

Not mine either?

SOLNESS

You will have other things to think of now, and to attend to; and that is a very good thing for you. Well, go home with the drawings now, Miss Fosli. At once! Do you hear?

KAIA   [*As before.*]

Yes, Mr. Solness.

[*She goes out.*]

MRS. SOLNESS

Heavens! what deceitful eyes she has.

SOLNESS

She? That poor little creature?

MRS. SOLNESS

Oh—I can see what I can see, Halvard——— Are you really dismissing them?

SOLNESS

Yes.

MRS. SOLNESS

Her as well?

SOLNESS

Was not that what you wished?

MRS. SOLNESS

But how can you get on without *her*———? Oh well, no doubt you have some one else in reserve, Halvard.

HILDA   [*Playfully.*]

Well, *I* for one am not the person to stand at that desk.

SOLNESS

Never mind, never mind—it will be all right, Aline. Now all you
have to do is to think about moving into our new home—as
quickly as you can. This evening we will hang up the wreath—
[*Turns to* HILDA]

—right on the very pinnacle of the tower. What do you say to
that, Miss Hilda?

HILDA [*Looks at him with sparkling eyes.*]

It will be splendid to see you so high up once more.

SOLNESS

Me!

MRS. SOLNESS

For Heaven's sake, Miss Wangel, don't imagine such a thing! My
husband!—when he always gets so dizzy!

HILDA

He get dizzy! No, I know quite well he does not!

MRS. SOLNESS

Oh yes, indeed he does.

HILDA

But I have seen him with my own eyes right up at the top of a
high church-tower!

MRS. SOLNESS

Yes, I hear people talk of that; but it is utterly impossible——

SOLNESS [*Vehemently.*]

Impossible—impossible, yes! But there I stood all the same!

MRS. SOLNESS

Oh, how can you say so, Halvard? Why, you can't even bear to
go out on the second-storey balcony here. You have always been
like that.

SOLNESS

You may perhaps see something different this evening.

MRS. SOLNESS [*In alarm.*]

No, no, no! Please God I shall never see that. I will write at once
to the doctor—and I am sure he won't let you do it.

SOLNESS

Why, Aline——!

MRS. SOLNESS

Oh, you know you're ill, Halvard. This *proves* it! Oh God—Oh God!

[*She goes hastily out to the right.*]

HILDA   [*Looks intently at him.*]

Is it so, or is it not?

SOLNESS

That I turn dizzy?

HILDA

That my master builder *dares* not—*cannot*—climb as high as he builds?

SOLNESS

Is that the way you look at it?

HILDA

Yes.

SOLNESS

I believe there is scarcely a corner in me that is safe from you.

HILDA   [*Looks towards the bow-window.*]

Up there, then. Right up there——

SOLNESS   [*Approaches her.*]

You might have the topmost room in the tower, Hilda—there you might live like a princess.

HILDA   [*Indefinably, between earnest and jest.*]

Yes, that is what you promised me.

SOLNESS

Did I really?

HILDA

Fie, Mr. Solness! You said I should be a princess, and that you would give me a kingdom. And then you went and——Well!

SOLNESS   [*Cautiously.*]

Are you quite certain that this is not a dream—a fancy, that has fixed itself in your mind?

HILDA   [*Sharply.*]

Do you mean that you did not do it?

SOLNESS

I scarcely know myself.

[*More softly.*]

But now I know *so much* for certain, that I——

HILDA

That you———? Say it at once!

SOLNESS

———that I *ought* to have done it.

HILDA   [*Exclaims with animation.*]

Don't tell me *you* can ever be dizzy!

SOLNESS

This evening, then, we will hang up the wreath——Princess Hilda.

HILDA   [*With a bitter curve of the lips.*]

Over your new home, yes.

SOLNESS

Over the new house, which will never be a *home* for me.

[*He goes out through the garden door.*]

HILDA   [*Looks straight in front of her with a far-away expression and whispers to herself. The only words audible are:*]

——— frightfully thrilling———

ACT THIRD

The large, broad veranda of SOLNESS's *dwelling-house. Part of the house, with outer door leading to the veranda, is seen to the left. A railing along the veranda to the right. At the back, from the end of the veranda, a flight of steps leads down to the garden below. Tall old trees in the garden spread their branches over the veranda and towards the house. Far to the right, in among the trees, a glimpse is caught of the lower part of the new villa, with scaffolding round so much as is seen of the tower. In the background the garden is bounded by an old wooden fence. Outside the fence, a street with low, tumble-down cottages.*

Evening sky with sun-lit clouds.

On the veranda, a garden bench stands along the wall of the house, and in front of the bench a long table. On the other side of the table, an arm-chair and some stools. All the furniture is of wicker-work.

MRS. SOLNESS, *wrapped in a large white crape shawl, sits resting in the arm-chair and gazes over to the right. Shortly after,* HILDA WANGEL *comes up the flight of steps from the garden. She is dressed as in the last act, and wears her hat. She has in her bodice a little nosegay of small common flowers.*

MRS. SOLNESS   [*Turning her head a little.*]

Have you been round the garden, Miss Wangel?

HILDA

Yes, I have been taking a look at it.

MRS. SOLNESS

And found some flowers too, I see.

HILDA

Yes, indeed! There are such heaps of them in among the bushes.

MRS. SOLNESS

Are there really? Still? You see I scarcely ever go there.

HILDA   [*Closer.*]

What! Don't you take a run down into the garden every day,
then?

MRS. SOLNESS   [*With a faint smile.*]

I don't "run" anywhere, nowadays.

HILDA

Well, but do you not go down now and then to look at all the
lovely things there?

MRS. SOLNESS

It has all become so strange to me. I am almost afraid to see it
again.

HILDA

Your own garden!

MRS. SOLNESS

I don't feel that it is *mine* any longer.

HILDA

What do you mean——?

MRS. SOLNESS

No, no, it is not—not as it was in my mother's and father's time.
They have taken away so much—so much of the garden, Miss
Wangel. Fancy—they have parcelled it out—and built houses for
strangers—people that I don't know. And *they* can sit and look in
upon me from their windows.

HILDA   [*With a bright expression.*]

Mrs. Solness!

MRS. SOLNESS

Yes!

HILDA

May I stay here with you a little?

MRS. SOLNESS

Yes, by all means, if you care to.

[HILDA *moves a stool close to the arm-chair and sits down.*]

HILDA

Ah—here one can sit and sun oneself like a cat.

MRS. SOLNESS   [*Lays her hand softly on* HILDA's *neck.*]

It is nice of you to be willing to sit with *me.* I thought you
wanted to go in to my husband.

HILDA

>What should I want with him?

MRS. SOLNESS

>To help him, I thought.

HILDA

>No, thank you. And besides, he is not in. He is over there with his workmen. But he looked so fierce that I did not dare to talk to him.

MRS. SOLNESS

>He is so kind and gentle in reality.

HILDA

>*He*!

MRS. SOLNESS

>You do not really know him yet, Miss Wangel.

HILDA   [*Looks affectionately at her.*]

>Are you pleased at the thought of moving over to the new house?

MRS. SOLNESS

>I *ought* to be pleased; for it is what Halvard wants——

HILDA

>Oh, not just on that account, surely.

MRS. SOLNESS

>Yes, yes, Miss Wangel; for it is only my duty to submit myself to *him*. But very often it is dreadfully difficult to force one's mind to obedience.

HILDA

>Yes, that must be difficult indeed.

MRS. SOLNESS

>I can tell you it is—when one has so many faults as I have——

HILDA

>When one has gone through so much trouble as you have——

MRS. SOLNESS

>How do you know about that?

HILDA

>Your husband told me.

MRS. SOLNESS

>To me he very seldom mentions these things.—Yes, I can tell you I have gone through more than enough trouble in my life, Miss Wangel.

HILDA   [*Looks sympathetically at her and nods slowly.*]

Poor Mrs. Solness. First of all there was the fire——

MRS. SOLNESS   [*With a sigh.*]

Yes, everything that was *mine* was burnt.

HILDA

And then came what was worse.

MRS. SOLNESS   [*Looking inquiringly at her.*]

Worse?

HILDA

The worst of all.

MRS. SOLNESS

What do you mean?

HILDA   [*Softly.*]

You lost the two little boys.

MRS. SOLNESS

Oh yes, the boys. But, you see, *that* was a thing apart. That was a dispensation of Providence; and in such things one can only bow in submission——yes, and be thankful, too.

HILDA

Then you are so?

MRS. SOLNESS

Not always, I am sorry to say. I know well enough that it is my duty——but all the same I *cannot*.

HILDA

No, no, I think that is only natural.

MRS. SOLNESS

And often and often I have to remind myself that it was a righteous punishment for me——

HILDA

Why?

MRS. SOLNESS

Because I had not fortitude enough in misfortune.

HILDA

But I don't see that——

MRS. SOLNESS

Oh, no, no, Miss Wangel——do not talk to me any more about the two little boys. We ought to feel nothing but joy in thinking of *them*; for they are so happy——so happy now. No, it is the *small* losses in life that cut one to the heart——the loss of all that other people look upon as almost nothing.

HILDA   [*Lays her arms on* MRS. SOLNESS's *knees, and looks up at her affectionately*.]

Dear Mrs. Solness—tell me what things you mean!

MRS. SOLNESS

As I say, only little things. All the old portraits were burnt on the walls. And all the old silk dresses were burnt, that had belonged to the family for generations and generations. And all mother's and grandmother's lace—that was burnt, too. And only think—the jewels, too!

[*Sadly*.]

And then all the dolls.

HILDA

The dolls?

MRS. SOLNESS   [*Choking with tears*.]

I had nine lovely dolls.

HILDA

And *they* were burnt too?

MRS. SOLNESS

All of them. Oh, it was hard—so hard for me.

HILDA

Had you put by all these dolls, then? Ever since you were little?

MRS. SOLNESS

I had not put them by. The dolls and I had gone on living together.

HILDA

After you were grown up?

MRS. SOLNESS

Yes, long after that.

HILDA

After you were married, too?

MRS. SOLNESS

Oh yes, indeed. So long as he did not see it——. But they were all burnt up, poor things. No one thought of saving *them*. Oh, it is so miserable to think of. You mustn't laugh at me, Miss Wangel.

HILDA

I am not laughing in the least.

MRS. SOLNESS

For you see, in a certain sense, there was life in them, too. I carried them under my heart—like little unborn children.

DR. HERDAL, *with his hat in his hand, comes out through the door, and observes* MRS. SOLNESS *and* HILDA.

DR. HERDAL

Well, Mrs. Solness, so you are sitting out here catching cold?

MRS. SOLNESS

I find it so pleasant and warm here to-day.

DR. HERDAL

Yes, yes. But is there anything going on here? I got a note from you.

MRS. SOLNESS   [*Rises.*]

Yes, there is something I must talk to you about.

DR. HERDAL

Very well; then perhaps we had better go in.

[*To* HILDA.]

Still in your mountaineering dress, Miss Wangel?

HILDA   [*Gaily, rising.*]

Yes—in full uniform! But to-day I am not going climbing and breaking my neck. We two will stop quietly below and look on, doctor.

DR. HERDAL

What are we to look on at?

MRS. SOLNESS   [*Softly, in alarm, to* HILDA.]

Hush, hush—for God's sake! He is coming! Try to get that idea out of his head. And let us be friends, Miss Wangel. Don't you think we can?

HILDA   [*Throws her arms impetuously round* MRS. SOLNESS's *neck.*]

Oh, if we only could!

MRS. SOLNESS   [*Gently disengages herself.*]

There, there, there! There he comes, doctor. Let me have a word with you.

DR. HERDAL

Is it about *him*!

MRS. SOLNESS

Yes, to be sure it's about him. Do come in.

She and the doctor enter the house. Next moment SOLNESS *comes up from the garden by the flight of steps. A serious look comes over* HILDA's *face.*

SOLNESS   [*Glances at the house-door, which is closed cautiously from within.*]

Have you noticed, Hilda, that as soon as I come, she goes?

HILDA

I have noticed that as soon as you come, you *make* her go.

SOLNESS

Perhaps so. But I cannot help it.

[*Looks observantly at her.*]

Are you cold, Hilda? I think you look cold.

HILDA

I have just come up out of a tomb.

SOLNESS

What do you mean by *that*?

HILDA

That I have got chilled through and through, Mr. Solness.

SOLNESS   [*Slowly.*]

I believe I understand——

HILDA

What brings you up here just now?

SOLNESS

I caught sight of you from over there.

HILDA

But then you must have seen her too?

SOLNESS

I knew she would go at once if I came.

HILDA

Is it very painful for you that she should avoid you in this way?

SOLNESS

In one sense, it's a relief as well.

HILDA

Not to have her before your eyes?

SOLNESS

Yes.

HILDA

Not to be always seeing how heavily the loss of the little boys
weighs upon her?

SOLNESS

Yes. Chiefly that.

[HILDA *drifts across the veranda with her hands behind her back, stops at
the railing and looks out over the garden.*]

SOLNESS   [*After a short pause.*]

Did you have a long talk with her?

[HILDA *stands motionless and does not answer.*]

SOLNESS

Had you a long talk, I asked?

[HILDA *is silent as before.*]

SOLNESS

What was she talking about, Hilda?

[HILDA *continues silent.*]

SOLNESS

Poor Aline! I suppose it was about the little boys.

HILDA   [*A nervous shudder runs through her; then she nods hurriedly once
or twice.*]

SOLNESS

She will never get over it—never in this world.

[*Approaches her.*]

Now you are standing there again like a statue; just as you stood
last night.

HILDA   [*Turns and looks at him, with great serious eyes.*]

I am going away.

SOLNESS   [*Sharply.*]

Going away!

HILDA

Yes.

SOLNESS

But I won't allow you to!

HILDA

What am I to do *here* now?

SOLNESS

Simply to *be* here, Hilda!

HILDA   [*Measures him with a look.*]

Oh, thank you. You know it wouldn't end *there*.

SOLNESS   [*Heedlessly.*]

So much the better!

HILDA   [*Vehemently.*]

I *cannot* do any harm to one whom I *know*! I can't take away
anything that belongs to her.

SOLNESS

Who wants you to do that?

HILDA   [*Continuing.*]

A stranger, yes! for that is quite a different thing! A person I have
never set eyes on. But one that I have come into close contact
with——! Oh no! Oh no! Ugh!

SOLNESS

Yes, but I never proposed you should.

HILDA

Oh, Mr. Solness, you know quite well what the end of it would
be. And that is why I am going away.

SOLNESS

And what is to become of *me* when you are gone? What shall I
have to live for *then*?——After that?

HILDA   [*With the indefinable look in her eyes.*]

It is surely not so hard for *you*. You have your duties to her. Live
for those duties.

SOLNESS

Too late. These powers—these—these——

HILDA

——devils——

SOLNESS

Yes, these devils! And the troll within me as well—they have
drawn all the life-blood out of her.

[*Laughs in desperation.*]

They did it for my *happiness*! Yes, yes!

[*Sadly.*]

And now she is dead——for my sake. And I am chained alive to a dead woman.

[*In wild anguish.*]

I——I who cannot live without joy in life!

[HILDA *moves round the table and seats herself on the bench, with her elbows on the table, and her head supported by her hands.*]

HILDA   [*Sits and looks at him awhile.*]

What will you build next?

SOLNESS   [*Shakes his head.*]

I don't believe I shall build much more.

HILDA

Not those cosy, happy homes for mother and father, and for the troop of children?

SOLNESS

I wonder whether there will be any use for such homes in the coming time.

HILDA

Poor Mr. Solness! And you have gone all these ten years——and staked your whole life——on that alone.

SOLNESS

Yes, you may well say so, Hilda.

HILDA   [*With an outburst.*]

Oh, it all seems to me so foolish——so foolish!

SOLNESS

All what?

HILDA

Not to be able to grasp at your own happiness——at your own life! Merely because some one you know happens to stand in the way!

SOLNESS

One whom you have no right to set aside.

HILDA

I wonder whether one really *has not* the right! And yet, and yet——. Oh! if one could only sleep the whole thing away!

[*She lays her arms flat down on the table, rests the left side of her head on her hands, and shuts her eyes.*

SOLNESS   [*Turns the arm-chair and sits down at the table.*]

Had *you* a cosy, happy home——up there with your father, Hilda?

HILDA   [*Without stirring, answers as if half asleep.*]
>   I had only a cage.

SOLNESS
>   And you are determined not to go back to it?

HILDA   [*As before.*]
>   The wild bird never wants to go into the cage.

SOLNESS
>   Rather range through the free air——

HILDA   [*Still as before.*]
>   The bird of prey loves to range——

SOLNESS   [*Lets his eyes rest on her.*]
>   If only one had the viking-spirit in life——

HILDA   [*In her usual voice; opens her eyes but does not move.*]
>   And the other thing? Say what *that* was!

SOLNESS
>   A robust conscience.

HILDA *sits erect on the bench, with animation. Her eyes have once more the sparkling expression of gladness.*

HILDA   [*Nods to him.*]
>   *I* know what you are going to build next!

SOLNESS
>   Then you know more than I do, Hilda.

HILDA
>   Yes, builders are such stupid people.

SOLNESS
>   What is it to be then?

HILDA   [*Nods again.*]
>   The castle.

SOLNESS
>   What castle?

HILDA
>   *My* castle, of course.

SOLNESS
>   Do you want a castle now?

HILDA
>   Don't you owe me a kingdom, I should like to know?

SOLNESS

You say I do.

HILDA

Well—you admit you owe me this kingdom. And you can't have a kingdom without a royal castle, I should think!

SOLNESS   [*More and more animated.*]

Yes, they usually go together.

HILDA

Good! Then build it for me! This moment!

SOLNESS   [*Laughing.*]

Must you have that on the instant, too?

HILDA

Yes, to be sure! For the ten years are up now, and I am not going to wait any longer. So—out with the castle, Mr. Solness!

SOLNESS

It's no light matter to owe *you* anything, Hilda.

HILDA

You should have thought of that before. It is too late now. So—
[*tapping the table*]
—the castle on the table! It is *my* castle! I will have it *at once!*

SOLNESS   [*More seriously, leans over towards her, with his arms on the table.*]

What sort of castle have you imagined, Hilda?

[*Her expression becomes more and more veiled. She seems gazing inwards at herself.*]

HILDA   [*Slowly.*]

My castle shall stand on a height—on a very great height—with a clear outlook on all sides, so that I can see far—far around.

SOLNESS

And no doubt it is to have a high tower!

HILDA.

A tremendously high tower. And at the very top of the tower there shall be a balcony. And I will stand out upon it——

SOLNESS   [*Involuntarily clutches at his forehead.*]

How can you like to stand at such a dizzy height——?

HILDA

Yes, I will! Right up there will I stand and look down on the other people—on those that are building churches, and homes for mother and father and the troop of children. And *you* may come up and look on at it, too.

SOLNESS   [*In a low tone.*]

Is the builder to be allowed to come up beside the princess?

HILDA

If the builder *will*.

SOLNESS   [*More softly.*]

Then I think the builder will come.

HILDA   [*Nods.*]

The builder—he will come.

SOLNESS

But he will never be able to build any more. Poor builder!

HILDA   [*Animated.*]

Oh yes, he will! We two will set to work together. And then we will build the loveliest—the very loveliest—thing in all the world.

SOLNESS   [*Intently.*]

Hilda—tell me what that is!

HILDA   [*Looks smilingly at him, shakes her head a little, pouts, and speaks as if to a child.*]

Builders—they are such very—very stupid people.

SOLNESS

Yes, no doubt they are stupid. But now tell me what it is—the loveliest thing in the world—that we two are to build together?

HILDA   [*Is silent a little while, then says with an indefinable expression in her eyes.*]

Castles in the air.

SOLNESS

Castles in the air?

HILDA   [*Nods.*]

Castles in the air, yes! Do you know what sort of thing a castle in the air is?

SOLNESS

It is the loveliest thing in the world, you say.

HILDA   [*Rises with vehemence, and makes a gesture of repulsion with her hand.*]

Yes, to be sure it is! Castles in the air—they are so easy to take refuge in. And so easy to build, too—

[*looks scornfully at him*]

—especially for the builders who have a—a dizzy conscience.

SOLNESS   [*Rises.*]

After this day we two will build together, Hilda.

HILDA   [*With a half-dubious smile.*]

A *real* castle in the air?

SOLNESS

Yes. One with a firm foundation under it.

RAGNAR BROVIK *comes out from the house. He is carrying a large, green wreath with flowers and silk ribbons.*

HILDA   [*With an outburst of pleasure.*]

The wreath! Oh, that will be glorious!

SOLNESS   [*In surprise.*]

Have *you* brought the wreath, Ragnar?

RAGNAR

I promised the foreman I would.

SOLNESS   [*Relieved.*]

Ah, then I suppose your father is better?

RAGNAR

No.

SOLNESS

Was he not cheered by what I wrote?

RAGNAR

It came too late.

SOLNESS

Too late!

RAGNAR

When she came with it he was unconscious. He had had a stroke.

SOLNESS

Why, then, you must go home to him! You must attend to your father!

RAGNAR

He does not need me any more.

SOLNESS

But surely you ought to be with him.

RAGNAR

She is sitting by his bed.

SOLNESS   [*Rather uncertainly.*]

Kaia?

RAGNAR   [*Looking darkly at him.*]

Yes——Kaia.

SOLNESS

Go home, Ragnar—both to him and to her. Give *me* the wreath.

RAGNAR   [*Suppresses a mocking smile.*]

You don't mean that you yourself——?

SOLNESS

I will take it down to them myself.

[*Takes the wreath from him.*]

And now you go home; we don't require you to-day.

RAGNAR

I know you do not require me any more; but to-day I shall remain.

SOLNESS

Well, remain then, since you are bent upon it.

HILDA   [*At the railing.*]

Mr. Solness, I will stand here and look on at you.

SOLNESS

At me!

HILDA

It will be fearfully thrilling.

SOLNESS   [*In a low tone.*]

We will talk about that presently, Hilda.

[*He goes down the flight of steps with the wreath, and away through the garden.*]

HILDA   [*Looks after him, then turns to* RAGNAR.]

I think you might at least have thanked him.

RAGNAR

Thanked him? Ought I to have thanked *him*?

HILDA

Yes, of course you ought!

RAGNAR

I think it is rather *you* I ought to thank.

HILDA

How can you say such a thing?

RAGNAR [*Without answering her.*]

But I advise you to take care, Miss Wangel! For you don't know *him* rightly yet.

HILDA [*Ardently.*]

Oh, no one knows him as I do!

RAGNAR [*Laughs in exasperation.*]

Thank him, when he has held me down year after year! When he made father disbelieve in me—made me disbelieve in myself! And all merely that he might——!

HILDA [*As if divining something.*]

That he might——? Tell me at once!

RAGNAR

That he might keep her with him.

HILDA [*With a start towards him.*]

The girl at the desk.

RAGNAR

Yes.

HILDA [*Threateningly, clenching her hands.*]

That is not true! You are telling falsehoods about him!

RAGNAR

I would not believe it either until to-day—when she said so herself.

HILDA [*As if beside herself.*]

What did she say? I *will* know! At once! at once!

RAGNAR

She said that he had taken possession of her mind—her whole mind—centred all her thoughts upon himself alone. She says that she can never leave him—that she will remain here, where *he* is——

HILDA [*With flashing eyes.*]

She will not be allowed to!

RAGNAR [*As if feeling his way.*]

Who will not allow her?

HILDA [*Rapidly.*]

He will not either!

RAGNAR

Oh no—I understand the whole thing now. After this, she would merely be—in the way.

HILDA

You understand nothing—since you can talk like that! No, *I* will tell you why he kept hold of her.

RAGNAR

Well then, why?

HILDA

In order to keep hold of *you*.

RAGNAR

Has he told you so?

HILDA

No, but it *is* so. It *must* be so!

[*Wildly.*]

I will—I *will* have it so!

RAGNAR

And at the very moment when *you* came—he let her go.

HILDA

It was *you*—*you* that he let go! What do you suppose he cares about strange women like her?

RAGNAR   [*Reflects.*]

Is it possible that all this time he has been afraid of me?

HILDA

He afraid! I would not be so conceited if I were you.

RAGNAR

Oh, he must have seen long ago that I had something in me, too. Besides—cowardly—that is just what he is, you see.

HILDA

He! Oh yes, I am likely to believe *that*!

RAGNAR

In a certain sense he *is* cowardly—he, the great master builder. He is not afraid of robbing others of their life's happiness—as he has done both for my father and for me. But when it comes to climbing up a paltry bit of scaffolding—he will do anything rather than *that*.

HILDA

Oh, you should just have seen him high, high up—at the dizzy
height where I once saw him.

RAGNAR

Did you see that?

HILDA

Yes, indeed I did. How free and great he looked as he stood and
fastened the wreath to the church vane!

RAGNAR

I know that he ventured that, *once* in his life—one solitary time.
It is a legend among us younger men. But no power on earth
would induce him to do it again.

HILDA

To-day he will do it again!

RAGNAR   [*Scornfully.*]

Yes, I daresay!

HILDA

We shall see it!

RAGNAR

That neither you nor I will see.

HILDA   [*With uncontrollable vehemence.*]

I *will* see it! I *will* and I *must* see it!

RAGNAR

But he will not do it. He simply dare not do it. For you see he
cannot get over this infirmity—master builder though he be.

MRS. SOLNESS *comes from the house on to the veranda.*

MRS. SOLNESS   [*Looks around.*]

Is he not here? Where has he gone to?

RAGNAR

Mr. Solness is down with the men.

HILDA

He took the wreath with him.

MRS. SOLNESS   [*Terrified.*]

Took the wreath with him! Oh God! oh God! Brovik—you must
go down to him! Get him to come back here!

RAGNAR

Shall I say you want to speak to him, Mrs. Solness?

MRS. SOLNESS

Oh yes, do!——No, no——don't say that *I* want anything! You can say that somebody is here, and that he must come at once.

RAGNAR

Good. I will do so, Mrs. Solness.

[*He goes down the flight of steps and away through the garden.*]

MRS. SOLNESS

Oh, Miss Wangel, you can't think how anxious I feel about him.

HILDA

Is there anything in this to be so terribly frightened about?

MRS. SOLNESS

Oh yes; surely you can understand. Just think, if he were really to do it! If he should take it into his head to climb up the scaffolding!

HILDA   [*Eagerly.*]

Do you think he will?

MRS. SOLNESS

Oh, one can never tell what he might take into his head. I am afraid there is nothing he mightn't think of doing.

HILDA

Aha! Perhaps you too think that he is—well——?

MRS. SOLNESS

Oh, I don't know what to think about him now. The Doctor has been telling me all sorts of things; and putting it all together with several things I have heard him say——

DR. HERDAL *looks out, at the door.*

DR. HERDAL

Is he not coming soon?

MRS. SOLNESS

Yes, I think so. I have sent for him at any rate.

DR. HERDAL   [*Advancing.*]

I am afraid you will have to go in, my dear lady——

MRS. SOLNESS

Oh no! Oh no! I shall stay out here and wait for Halvard.

DR. HERDAL

But some ladies have just come to call on you——

MRS. SOLNESS

Good heavens, *that* too! And just at this moment!

DR. HERDAL

They say they positively must see the ceremony.

MRS. SOLNESS

Well, well; I suppose I must go to them after all. It is my duty.

HILDA

Can't you ask the ladies to go away?

MRS. SOLNESS

No, that would never do. Now that they are here, it is my duty to see them. But do you stay out here in the meantime—and receive him when he comes.

DR. HERDAL

And try to occupy his attention as long as possible——

MRS. SOLNESS

Yes, do, dear Miss Wangel. Keep as firm hold of him as ever you can.

HILDA

Would it not be best for you to do that?

MRS. SOLNESS

Yes; God knows that is *my* duty. But when one has duties in so many directions——

DR. HERDAL [*Looks towards the garden.*]

There he is coming.

MRS. SOLNESS

And I have to go in!

DR. HERDAL [*To* HILDA]

Don't say anything about *my* being here.

HILDA

Oh no! I daresay I shall find something else to talk to Mr. Solness about.

MRS. SOLNESS

And be sure you keep firm hold of him. I believe *you* can do it best.

[MRS. SOLNESS *and* DR. HERDAL *go into the house.* HILDA *re-*

mains standing on the veranda. SOLNESS *comes from the garden, up the flight of steps.*]

SOLNESS

Somebody wants me, I hear.

HILDA

Yes; it is I, Mr. Solness.

SOLNESS

Oh, is it you, Hilda? I was afraid it might be Aline or the Doctor.

HILDA

You are very easily frightened, it seems!

SOLNESS

Do you think so?

HILDA

Yes; people say that you are afraid to climb about——on the scaffoldings, you know.

SOLNESS

Well, that is quite a special thing.

HILDA

Then it is true that you are afraid to do it?

SOLNESS

Yes, I am.

HILDA

Afraid of falling down and killing yourself?

SOLNESS

No, not of that.

HILDA

Of what, then?

SOLNESS

I am afraid of retribution, Hilda.

HILDA

Of retribution?

[*Shakes her head.*]

I don't understand that.

SOLNESS

Sit down, and I will tell you something.

HILDA

Yes, do! At once!

[*She sits on a stool by the railing, and looks expectantly at him.*]

SOLNESS   [*Throws his hat on the table.*]

    You know that I began by building churches.

HILDA   [*Nods.*]

    I know that well.

SOLNESS

    For, you see, I came as a boy from a pious home in the country; and so it seemed to me that this church-building was the noblest task I could set myself.

HILDA

    Yes, yes.

SOLNESS

    And I venture to say that I built those poor little churches with such honest and warm and heartfelt devotion that—that——

HILDA

    That——? Well?

SOLNESS

    Well, that I think that he ought to have been pleased with me.

HILDA

    He? What *he*?

SOLNESS

    He who was to have the churches, of course! He to whose honour and glory they were dedicated.

HILDA

    Oh, indeed! But are you certain, then, that—that he was not— pleased with you?

SOLNESS   [*Scornfully.*]

    He pleased with *me*! How can you talk so, Hilda? He who gave the troll in me leave to lord it just as it pleased. He who bade them be at hand to serve me, both day and night—all these—all these——

HILDA

    Devils——

SOLNESS

    Yes, of both kinds. Oh no, he made me feel clearly enough that he was not pleased with me.

    [*Mysteriously.*]

    You see, that was really the reason why he made the old house burn down.

HILDA

Was that why?

SOLNESS

Yes, don't you understand? He wanted to give me the chance of becoming an accomplished master in my own sphere—so that I might build all the more glorious churches for him. At first I did not understand what he was driving at; but all of a sudden it flashed upon me.

HILDA

When was that?

SOLNESS

It was when I was building the church-tower up at Lysanger.

HILDA

I thought so.

SOLNESS

For you see, Hilda—up there, amidst those new surroundings, I used to go about musing and pondering within myself. Then I saw plainly why he had taken my little children from me. It was that I should have nothing else to attach myself to. No such thing as love and happiness, you understand. I was to be only a master builder—nothing else. And all my life long I was to go on building for him. [*Laughs.*]

But I can tell you nothing came of *that*!

HILDA

What did you do, then?

SOLNESS

First of all, I searched and tried my own heart——

HILDA

And then?

SOLNESS

Then I did the *impossible*—I no less than *he*.

HILDA

The impossible?

SOLNESS

I had never before been able to climb up to a great, free height. But that day I did it.

HILDA   [*Leaping up.*]

Yes, yes, you did!

SOLNESS

> And when I stood there, high over everything, and was hanging the wreath over the vane, I said to him: Hear me now, thou Mighty One! From this day forward I will be a free builder—I too, in my sphere—just as thou in thine. I will never more build churches for thee—only homes for human beings.

HILDA   [*With great sparkling eyes.*]

> *That* was the song that I heard through the air!

SOLNESS

> But afterwards his turn came.

HILDA

> What do you mean by *that*?

SOLNESS   [*Looks despondently at her.*]

> Building homes for human beings—is not worth a rap, Hilda.

HILDA

> Do you say *that* now?

SOLNESS

> Yes, for now I see it. Men have no use for these homes of theirs—to be happy in. And I should not have had any use for such a home, if I had had one.
>
> [*With a quiet, bitter laugh.*]
>
> See, that is the upshot of the whole affair, however far back I look. Nothing really built; nor anything sacrificed for the chance of building. Nothing, nothing! the whole is nothing!

HILDA

> Then you will never build anything more?

SOLNESS   [*With animation.*]

> On the contrary, I am just going to begin!

HILDA

> What, then? What will you build? Tell me at once!

SOLNESS

> I believe there is only one possible dwelling-place for human happiness—and that is what I am going to build now.

HILDA   [*Looks fixedly at him.*]

> Mr. Solness—you mean our castles in the air.

SOLNESS

> The castles in the air—yes.

HILDA
I am afraid you would turn dizzy before we got half-way up.

SOLNESS
Not if I can mount hand in hand with you, Hilda.

HILDA   [*With an expression of suppressed resentment.*]
Only with me? Will there be no others of the party?

SOLNESS
Who else should there be?

HILDA
Oh—that girl—that Kaia at the desk. Poor thing—don't you
want to take her with you too?

SOLNESS
Oho! Was it about her that Aline was talking to you?

HILDA
Is it so—or is it not?

SOLNESS   [*Vehemently.*]
I will not answer such a question. You must believe in me,
wholly and entirely!

HILDA
All these ten years I have believed in you so utterly—so utterly.

SOLNESS
You must go on believing in me!

HILDA
Then let me see you stand free and high up!

SOLNESS   [*Sadly.*]
Oh Hilda—it is not every day that I can do that.

HILDA   [*Passionately.*]
I will have you do it! I will have it!
[*Imploringly.*]
Just once more, Mr. Solness! Do the *impossible* once again!

SOLNESS   [*Stands and looks deep into her eyes.*]
If I try it, Hilda, I will stand up there and talk to him as I did that
time before.

HILDA   [*In rising excitement.*]
What will you say to him?

SOLNESS
I will say to him: Hear me, Mighty Lord—thou may'st judge me

as seems best to thee. But hereafter I will build nothing but the loveliest thing in the world——

HILDA   [*Carried away.*]

Yes—yes—yes!

SOLNESS

—build it together with a princess, whom I love——

HILDA

Yes, tell him that! Tell him that!

SOLNESS

Yes. And then I will say to him: Now I shall go down and throw my arms round her and kiss her——

HILDA

—many times! Say that!

SOLNESS

—many, many times, I will say!

HILDA

And then——?

SOLNESS

Then I will wave my hat—and come down to the earth—and do as I said to him.

HILDA   [*With outstretched arms.*]

Now I see you again as I did when there was song in the air!

SOLNESS   [*Looks at her with his head bowed.*]

How have you become what you are, Hilda?

HILDA

How have you made me what I am?

SOLNESS   [*Shortly and firmly.*]

The princess shall have her castle.

HILDA   [*Jubilant, clapping her hands.*]

Oh, Mr. Solness——! My lovely, lovely castle. Our castle in the air!

SOLNESS

On a firm foundation.

[*In the street a crowd of people has assembled, vaguely seen through the trees. Music of wind-instruments is heard far away behind the new house.*]

MRS. SOLNESS, *with a fur collar round her neck,* DOCTOR HERDAL *with her white shawl on his arm, and some ladies, come out on the veranda.* RAGNAR BROVIK *comes at the same time up from the garden.*

MRS. SOLNESS   [*To* RAGNAR.]

Are we to have music, too?

RAGNAR

Yes. It's the band of the Mason's Union.

[*To* SOLNESS.]

The foreman asked me to tell you that he is ready now to go up with the wreath.

SOLNESS   [*Takes his hat.*]

Good. I will go down to him myself.

MRS. SOLNESS   [*Anxiously.*]

What have you to do down there, Halvard?

SOLNESS   [*Curtly.*]

I must be down below with the men.

MRS. SOLNESS

Yes, down below—only down below.

SOLNESS

That is where I always stand—on everyday occasions.

[*He goes down the flight of steps and away through the garden.*]

MRS. SOLNESS   [*Calls after him over the railing.*]

But do beg the man to be careful when he goes up! Promise me that, Halvard!

DR. HERDAL   [*To* MRS. SOLNESS.]

Don't you see that I was right? He has given up all thought of that folly.

MRS. SOLNESS

Oh, what a relief! Twice workmen have fallen, and each time they were killed on the spot.

[*Turns to* HILDA.]

Thank you, Miss Wangel, for having kept such a firm hold upon him. I should never have been able to manage him.

DR. HERDAL   [*Playfully.*]

Yes, yes, Miss Wangel, you know how to keep firm hold on a man, when you give your mind to it.

[MRS. SOLNESS *and* DR. HERDAL *go up to the ladies, who are standing nearer to the steps and looking over the garden.* HILDA *remains standing beside the railing in the foreground.* RAGNAR *goes up to her.*]

RAGNAR   [*With suppressed laughter, half whispering.*]

Miss Wangel—do you see all those young fellows down in the street?

HILDA

Yes.

RAGNAR

They are my fellow students, come to look at the master.

HILDA

What do they want to look at *him* for?

RAGNAR

They want to see how he daren't climb to the top of his own house.

HILDA

Oh, *that* is what those boys want, is it?

RAGNAR   [*Spitefully and scornfully.*]

He has kept us down so long—now we are going to see *him* keep quietly down below himself.

HILDA

You will not see that—not this time.

RAGNAR   [*Smiles.*]

Indeed! Then where shall we see him?

HILDA

High—high up by the vane! That is where you will see him!

RAGNAR   [*Laughs.*]

Him! Oh yes, I daresay!

HILDA

His *will* is to reach the top—so at the top you shall see him.

RAGNAR

His *will*, yes; that I can easily believe. But he simply *cannot* do it. His head would swim round, long, long before he got half-way. He would have to crawl down again on his hands and knees.

DR. HERDAL   [*Points across.*]

Look! There goes the foreman up the ladders.

MRS. SOLNESS

And of course he has the wreath to carry too. Oh, I do hope he will be careful!

RAGNAR   [*Stares incredulously and shouts.*]

Why, but it's——

HILDA   [*Breaking out in jubilation.*]

It is the master builder himself?

MRS. SOLNESS   [*Screams with terror.*]

Yes, it is Halvard! Oh my great God——! Halvard! Halvard!

DR. HERDAL

Hush! Don't shout to him!

MRS. SOLNESS   [*Half beside herself.*]

I must go to him! I must get him to come down again!

DR. HERDAL   [*Holds her.*]

Don't move, any of you! Not a sound!

HILDA   [*Immovable, follows* SOLNESS *with her eyes.*]

He climbs and climbs. Higher and higher! Higher and higher!
Look! Just look!

RAGNAR   [*Breathless.*]

He *must* turn now. He can't possibly help it.

HILDA

He climbs and climbs. He will soon be at the top now.

MRS. SOLNESS

Oh, I shall die of terror. I cannot bear to see it.

DR. HERDAL

Then don't look up at him.

HILDA

There he is standing on the topmost planks. Right at the top!

DR. HERDAL

Nobody must move! Do you hear?

HILDA   [*Exulting, with quiet intensity.*]

At last! At last! Now I see him great and free again!

RAGNAR   [*Almost voiceless.*]

But this is im——

HILDA

So I have seen him all through these ten years. How secure he
stands! Frightfully thrilling all the same. Look at him! Now he is
hanging the wreath round the vane!

RAGNAR

I feel as if I were looking at something utterly impossible.

HILDA

Yes, it *is* the *impossible* that he is doing now!

[*With the indefinable expression in her eyes.*]

Can you see any one else up there with him?

RAGNAR

There is no one else.

HILDA

Yes, there is one he is striving with.

RAGNAR

You are mistaken.

HILDA

Then do you hear no song in the air, either?

RAGNAR

It must be the wind in the tree-tops.

HILDA

I hear a song—a mighty song!

[*Shouts in wild jubilation and glee.*]

Look, look! Now he is waving his hat! He is waving it to us down here! Oh, wave, wave back to him! For now it is finished!

[*Snatches the white shawl from the* DOCTOR, *waves it, and shouts up to* SOLNESS.]

Hurrah for Master Builder Solness!

DR. HERDAL

Stop! Stop! For God's sake———!

[*The ladies on the veranda wave their pocket-handkerchiefs, and the shouts of "Hurrah" are taken up in the street below. Then they are suddenly silenced, and the crowd bursts out into a shriek of horror. A human body, with planks and fragments of wood, is vaguely perceived crashing down behind the trees.*]

MRS. SOLNESS AND THE LADIES   [*At the same time.*]

He is falling! He is falling!

[MRS. SOLNESS *totters, falls backwards, swooning, and is caught, amid cries and confusion, by the ladies. The crowd in the street breaks down the fence and storms into the garden. At the same time* DR. HERDAL, *too, rushes down thither. A short pause.*]

HILDA   [*Stares fixedly upwards and says, as if petrified.*]

My Master Builder!

RAGNAR   [*Supports himself, trembling, against the railing.*]

    He must be dashed to pieces—killed on the spot.

ONE OF THE LADIES   [*Whilst* MRS. SOLNESS *is carried into the house.*]

    Run down for the Doctor——

RAGNAR

    I can't stir a foot——

ANOTHER LADY

    Then call to some one!

RAGNAR   [*Tries to call out.*]

    How is it? Is he alive?

A VOICE   [*Below, in the garden.*]

    Mr. Solness is dead!

INSPIRED BY HENRIK IBSEN

A New Drama

Henrik Ibsen founded modern drama. For this he is not only remembered, he is worshiped; his home in Oslo, Norway, the site of the Ibsen Museum, has become a shrine, a veritable holy place in the world of theater. Among Ibsen's disciples are some of the greatest dramatists of the nineteenth and twentieth centuries: Anton Chekhov, George Bernard Shaw, Bertolt Brecht, and Samuel Beckett. Shaw, who found the London theater scene of his day vacuous and stale, poured tremendous energy into popularizing Ibsen in the English-speaking world.

Ibsen's plays are continually revived in theaters around the world, have been adapted by August Strindberg and Arthur Miller, and have been made into dozens of films. Many of his memorable characters are women, and numerous renowned Shakespearean and film actresses—including Dame Peggy Ashcroft, Claire Bloom, Joan Collins, Jane Fonda, Vanessa Redgrave, and Liv Ullmann—have played Anitra, Hedda, and Nora.

James Joyce

Though Ibsen is generally remembered for his use of plain, everyday language, he was a great influence on the preeminent stylist of twentieth-century literature, James Joyce. So fervent was Joyce's early loyalty to Ibsen that he taught himself Norwegian so that he could read Ibsen's dramas in the original. Joyce's first publication was "Ibsen's New Drama," an article on Ibsen's last play, *When We Dead Awaken*, that appeared in the *Fortnightly Review* in 1900 and in which Joyce declared that Ibsen was the pinnacle of Western Civilization. Ibsen sent a letter of thanks to Joyce, who was still an undergraduate. Joyce went on to write a poem entitled "Epilogue to Ibsen's Ghosts."

Joyce most consciously imitated Ibsen in his play *Exiles* (1918), which has been compared to Ibsen's *An Enemy of the People* for its political subject matter; yet Joyce's play also deals with the domestic issues found in all of Ibsen's plays. Indeed, the play reads more like Ibsen than Joyce, although it lacks the confident voice of either writer. The main character of *Exiles* is Richard Rowan, a writer living in Dublin; in the finale of the third act he speaks to his lover, Bertha:

> I have wounded my soul for you—a deep wound of doubt which can never be healed. I can never know, never in this world. I do not wish to know or to believe. I do not care. It is not in the darkness of belief that I desire you. But in restless living wounding doubt. To hold you by no bonds, even of love, to be united with you in body and soul in utter nakedness—for this I longed. And now I am tired for a while, Bertha. My wound tires me.

Exiles opened in Munich in 1919 but was not a success.

Music

Onstage an Ibsen production is a symphony of awkward silences, dissonance, and the thunderous cacophony of the characters' inner lives, and it follows that composers would attempt to harness that vitality in their music. Among those who have taken Ibsen's work as an inspiration for their own are Norma Beecroft, Antonio Bibalo, Mark Brunswick, Werner Egk, Edward Harper, and Harald Saeverud.

In 1874 Ibsen commissioned Edvard Grieg to write the incidental music for a staging of *Peer Gynt*; the production set to music premiered on February 24, 1876, and was an immediate and resounding success. Much of Grieg's international reputation rests on the *Peer Gynt Suites*, which are some of the most frequently played pieces in today's symphonic repertoire. In these pieces, which combine dramatic orchestral music with catchy, memorable tunes, Grieg captures the landscape of the Peer Gynt legend—for example, the rising of the sun in the first movement—along with the passion of Ibsen's drama and its characteristic moments of suspense, celebration, and devastating lament. The fourth movement of the first *Peer Gynt Suite*, "In the Hall of the Mountain King," is a tumultuous, epic chase scene that has become a classical music standard and been featured as incidental music in several films. The suites as Grieg published them are:

PEER GYNT SUITE I (Op. 46, published in 1888)

1. Morning
2. The Death of Åse
3. Anitra's Dance
4. In the Hall of the Mountain King

PEER GYNT SUITE II (Op. 55, published in 1893)

1. The Abduction of the Bride. Ingrid's Lament
2. Arabian Dance
3. Peer Gynt's Homecoming (Stormy Evening on the Sea)
4. Salvejg's Song

Grieg also set six of Ibsen's poems to music (Op. 25). Today Edvard Grieg is widely regarded as Norway's greatest composer. His work had an enormous influence on Bela Bartok, Claude Debussy, and Maurice Ravel.

COMMENTS & QUESTIONS

In this section, we aim to provide the reader with an array of perspectives on the text, as well as questions that challenge those perspectives. The commentary has been culled from sources as diverse as reviews contemporaneous with the work, letters written by the author, literary criticism of later generations, and appreciations written throughout the history of the plays. Following the commentary, a series of questions seeks to filter Six Plays by Henrik Ibsen *through a variety of points of view and bring about a richer understanding of this enduring work.*

COMMENTS

Robert Bridges, writing under the pseudonym "Droch"

Since we live a very little while and have so many beautiful things to choose to see and so many pleasant people to know, why should an intelligent man deliberately select what is unlovely and disagreeable? And yet a considerable number of intelligent people are of choice reading Ibsen's "Hedda Gabler," and they believe that they find in it an unusual amount of mental sustenance. We do not live for pleasant sensations, they say, but for truth, and *here* is truth that is valuable. It is probable that this point-of-view appeals most vigorously to that class of mind which believes that it is "literary," which looks on the spectacle of life as a conglomerate of strange things to be classified by their eccentricities. After a decade of this attitude toward his fellow-beings the literary man is apt to consider valuable only what is unusual. He has got entirely out of a normal perspective, and the impressive pageant of an army of people leading sane, wholesome, and, in the main, happy lives, is to him the least interesting part of the picture.

It is easy to see why "Hedda Gabler" appeals to this constituency—for it is a powerful presentation of the unusual and disagreeable. If we put aside our predilection for what is beautiful and pleasant, it is impossible not to come under the force and fascination of this drama.

While firmly believing that there are inadequate reasons why people should write or read books of this kind, we can have no sympathy with the howl against this book that it is immoral. Stern, uncompromising morality is the lesson of it, with a most acute consciousness on every page of what Henry James has so pertinently called "the immitigability of our moral predicament."

We have heretofore pointed out that we cannot see in Ibsen's works the pessimism with which he is usually credited—and this last (and most offensive of his dramas) confirms that opinion. Here, as in his other works, there is a character which points the way to a sane and wholesome way of living. In *Miss Tesman* the author shows good-will and good works, charity and simplicity weaving from day to day a happy life. And at the close of the play when trouble comes to *Miss Tesman* (as to all the rest of the characters), the author shows her clearly seeing her way out of it through her sympathies with the unfortunate.

The "literary" people who are making so much ado over "Hedda Gabler," must, if they really have their eyes open to its intention, receive some very acute thrusts. For it is difficult to recall a more telling exposure of the supreme selfishness of the literary point-of-view. There are two authors among the *dramatis personæ*. One of them says of the woman who has sacrificed everything for him and has been the inspiration of his best work, "It is the courage of life and the defiance of life that she has snapped in me,"—and then protests that he is not "heartless." The other man of letters is perfectly joyous when he hears that his wife has burned the manuscript of his rival and friend—because she tells him that she "could not bear the idea that anyone else should put you into the shade." This he considers a final proof of her love, and is elated accordingly.

Was there ever a better exhibition of the egotism of men who spend their lives seeking for a new emotion at any cost?

—from *Life Magazine* (June 18, 1891)

George Bernard Shaw

A Doll's House will be as flat as ditchwater when *A Midsummer Night's Dream* will still be as fresh as paint; but it will have done more work in the world; and that is enough for the highest genius, which is always intensely utilitarian.

—from *The Humanitarian* (May 1895)

William S. Bishop

In *Peer Gynt* we have a drama of the human soul in its relation to its moral environment, to the great forces which play upon it from without, or work upon and through it from within. In its development through the changes and chances of a typical earthly career, through weakness and failure and consequent loss, we discern in *Peer Gynt* a parable of life. Peer himself is representative of a class of humanity, and of a large class. Not, indeed, of humanity in its highest and heroic development, for Peer is himself the antithesis of a hero; but although, or rather just because Peer does represent a distinctly unheroic type, in his very weaknesses, in his hedging, in his cowardice, he reminds us of what we are ourselves, or at least are inclined to be. The question on which Peer's life hinges is the old question which the Danish prince Hamlet, as depicted by Shakespeare, had put to himself long ago—the question, "To be, or not to be?" But in the case of Peer it was not the mere bald question of existence or non-existence, whether now or after death. The question in Peer's case is a subtler one. Existence— that is, some kind of existence after death, is certain. But the great problem before us here is: Existence *of what kind?* For all souls (such is Ibsen's thought) will have a continuance after death. But of what sort the future existence will be will depend upon what sort of a life shall have been led by the individual in this earthly stage of being. As regarded from the standpoint of our poet-philosopher, there are upon earth two and only two classes of people. But Ibsen's canon of classification is not—at least, is not primarily and directly—the moral one. Rather, it is a psychological or metaphysical one. In accordance with this standard, people are not classified as good or bad, like the sheep and the goats in the familiar parable of judgment. No! they are classified as those, on the one hand, who have been or who are content merely to *live*, to exist from day to day, satisfying the whims, or gratifying the passions, or allowing themselves to be molded by the environment of the moment; and, on the other hand, those who accentuate their individuality as superior to their environment; those to whom existence as mere existence is not sufficient, is not satisfying; those whose desire and aim and effort it is, not simply to be, but to be something, to be somebody; to achieve self-hood, personality. These two classes of persons include all humankind. And for these two classes two diverse sorts of fate are reserved. Those who have been satisfied with the mere fact of existing; those who have followed the egoist Troll-maxim, "To thyself be sufficient," shall at last be turned into the casting-ladle, there to be melted up into the indistinguishable mass from which future souls are to be fashioned. Such souls will, it is true, continue to exist after death, but not as distinct individuals. Why? Simply because they have not achieved individuality during their earthly career. Neither by good deeds, nor yet by evil, have they given proof of a strong or robust self-hood. They have indeed been egoists in a sense, but only in a false sense. They have indulged the passions or the whims of the moment; but this is not true and genuine egoism. True and genuine egoism means individualism; that is, it means the development of individuality. It is this individuality, the transcendent value of it, the all-surpassing need of it that is Ibsen's message in *Peer Gynt*. "Better to be a sinner than a non-entity."

—from *The Sewanee Review* (October 1909)

Alma L. La Victoire

The majority of critics and students of drama speak of Ibsen, the dramatist, as an individualist. He is, to them, a man who believes, and who writes plays to support the belief, that an individual, be it man or woman, has the right to overturn existing social order for his own freedom and development, no matter how universally accepted or of what value to mankind this same order may be. . . .

[In *The Master Builder*] Ibsen's effort is toward construction rather than destruction, that instead of advocating individual freedom, he strives to point the way to adjustment of the universal order. This means, of course, the greatest freedom for the greatest number. Not individual freedom, but individual responsibility.

In writing a play Ibsen is confronted by two problems. First, he has to utter a protest against certain wrongs that exist, for Ibsen is ever and always a reformer. Then, he must make his play enlist the interest and sympathy of his hearers, for, as he makes Rosmer say, "men are only ennobled from within." Reformation endures only when it comes from the heart. There are few who would choose the wrong if right were clearly seen, and wrong and all that it means fully comprehended. Eliza

Allen Starr described heaven as a place where right is so plainly seen that wrong is impossible. . . .

[*The Master Builder*] is Ibsen's protest against the motive of expediency, which is so great a factor in the world to-day, a protest against work not done for work's sake. Anatole France says that a man who strives for the approval of posterity can never be great. It is not his name nor what he creates that is known to future generations. Other men have voiced the same idea in a different way. It is the Bible story of the five talents, the two talents, the one talent, in a new form. It is, too, the story of the house built on shifting sands.

"The Master Builder" was written in the latter part of Ibsen's life, when, after years of accomplishment and strife always for the fine and true, he could see that the greatest blessing and not the greatest hardship of life is work. That there is no satisfaction so deep, no pleasure so lasting, as good work well done.

—from *The North American Review* (August 1912)

Edward Garnett

"What is really wanted is a revolution of the spirit of man," wrote Ibsen to Brandes in 1870, and this saying actually reveals the source of Ibsen's power over us better than any lengthy criticism could do. It is because Ibsen is so dissatisfied with average human nature, because he pierces through its self-regarding egoism and realizes its shallow pretentiousness that he has had the power to treat public opinion in ordinary as the Voice of mediocrity, without himself being either a superior person, or pessimist, or idealistic preacher. As a poet of insight Ibsen sympathizes with humanity, as a moralist he sets his face against the average man's pettiness and self-complacency; it is this two-sidedness that makes him formidable to our middle-class communities so naïvely in love with their own special limitations, so bold in developing their life on material lines, so fearful of applying to themselves unwelcome truths.

—from *Friday Nights* (1922)

William Butler Yeats

Two or three years after our return to Bedford Park *A Doll's House* had been played at the Royalty Theatre in Dean Street, the first Ibsen play to be played in England, and somebody had given me a seat for the gallery. In the middle of the first act, while the heroine was asking for macaroons, a middle-aged washerwoman who sat in front of me, stood up and said to the little boy at her side, "Tommy, if you promise to go home straight, we will go now"; and at the end of the play, as I wandered through the entrance hall, I heard an elderly critic murmur, "A series of conversations terminated by an accident." I was divided in mind, I hated the play; what was it but Carolus Duran, Bastien-Lepage, Huxley and Tyndall all over again; I resented being invited to admire dialogue so close to modern educated speech that music and style were impossible.

"Art is art because it is not nature," I kept repeating to myself, but how could I take the same side with critic and washerwoman? As time passed Ibsen became in my eyes the chosen author of very clever young journalists, who, condemned to their treadmill of abstraction, hated music and style; and yet neither I nor my generation could escape him because, though we had not the same friends, we had the same enemies. I bought his collected works in Mr. Archer's translation out of my thirty shillings a week and carried them to and fro upon my journeys to Ireland and Sligo, and Florence Farr, who had but one great gift, the most perfect poetical elocution, became prominent as an Ibsen actress and had almost a success in *Rosmersholm*, where there is symbolism and a stale odour of spilt poetry. She and I and half our friends found ourselves involved in a quarrel with the supporters of old-fashioned melodrama, and conventional romance, in the support of the new dramatists who wrote in what the *Daily Press* chose to consider the manner of Ibsen.

—from *The Trembling of the Veil* (1922)

QUESTIONS

1. Are any of Ibsen's plays still shocking? If so, which ones? What is shocking about them?

2. Is Nora in *The Doll's House* a sympathetic character? Is she believable?

3. From plays in this volume, is it possible to draw general conclusions about Ibsen's attitude toward women?

4. If you were directing *Hedda Gabler*, what directions would you give the actress playing the title role? Be cool, superior, disdainful? Make large, theatrical gestures? Act as though you were just barely able to contain the explosive forces within you? Be seductive or manly or bitchy? Or hurt and therefore vengeful? Or cold, heartless, calculating? Something different?

5. In some ways Ibsen can seem like a puritan—sin is always punished. Yet sometimes he seems to be a radical individualist who believes that each person should make his or her own rules. Which attitude most often prevails? Or does Ibsen strike you as an impersonal artist, one who keeps his own ideas, attitudes, and values out of sight?

FOR FURTHER READING

BIOGRAPHY

Meyer, Michael. *Ibsen: A Biography.* Garden City, NY: Doubleday, 1971.

EARLY REACTIONS

Brandes, Georg. *Henrik Ibsen.* Translated by Jesse Muir and William Archer. New York: Benjamin Blom, 1964.

Gosse, Edmund. *Henrik Ibsen.* New York: Charles Scribner's Sons, 1907.

Shaw, George Bernard. 1891. *The Quintessence of Ibsenism.* New York: Dover Publications, 1994.

Weigand, Hermann J. 1925. *The Modern Ibsen: A Reconsideration.* Salem, NH: Ayer Company, 1984.

William Archer on Ibsen: The Major Essays, 1889–1919. Edited by Thomas Postlewait. Westport, CT: Greenwood Press, 1984.

CRITICAL STUDIES, CHRONOLOGICALLY ARRANGED

Northam, John. *Ibsen's Dramatic Method: A Study of the Prose Dramas.* London: Faber and Faber, 1953.

Lucas, F. L. *The Drama of Ibsen and Strindberg.* New York: MacMillan, 1962.

Szondi, Peter. 1963. *The Theory of Modern Drama.* Edited and translated by Michael Hays. Minneapolis: University of Minnesota Press, 1987.

Brustein, Robert. 1964. *The Theatre of Revolt: An Approach to the Modern Drama.* Chicago: Elephant Paperbacks, 1991.

Williams, Raymond. *Drama from Ibsen to Brecht.* Oxford: Oxford University Press, 1968.

Ibsen: The Critical Heritage. Edited by Michael Egan. London and Boston: Routledge and Kegan Paul, 1972.

Gilman, Richard. *The Making of Modern Drama: A Study of Büchner, Ibsen, Strindberg, Chekhov, Pirandello, Brecht, Beckett, Handke.* New York: Farrar, Straus and Giroux, 1974.

Haugen, Einar. *Ibsen's Drama: Author to Audience.* Minneapolis: University of Minnesota Press, 1979.

Quigley, Austin E. *The Modern Stage and Other Worlds.* New York: Methuen, 1985.

Postlewait, Thomas. *Prophet of the New Drama: William Archer and the Ibsen Campaign.* Westport, CT: Greenwood Press, 1986.

The Cambridge Companion to Ibsen. Edited by James McFarlane. Cambridge and New York: Cambridge University Press, 1994.

Shepherd-Barr, Kirsten. *Ibsen and Early Modernist Theatre, 1890–1900.* Westport, CT: Greenwood Press, 1997.

Goldman, Michael. *Ibsen: The Dramaturgy of Fear.* New York: Columbia University Press, 1999.